SHADOW OF IRELAND

SHADOW OF IRELAND

G.M. COLLINS

Rowe Publishing

ISBN 13: 978-1-939054-31-9
ISBN 10: 1-939054-31-1

Cover Art by Chris Rallis.

3 5 7 9 8 6 4 2

Printed in the United States of America
Published by

Rowe Publishing

www.rowepub.com
Stockton, Kansas

Dedication

To Kris Toft

A great friend that never knew

the meaning of 'give up'

~

Thank you

We will meet again

Chapter 1

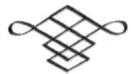

Over time, societies in Ireland were no longer simply farm-based communities—though tradition still existed, it was more for nostalgia than necessity. Well into the twenty second century, the world abounded with technological wonders that had once been considered fanciful imaginings of dreamers of old or the works of science fiction. No longer were people afflicted with incurable illnesses, and most lived to be at least 200 years old. The mind, however, could not be made to work past that lengthy timeframe. Since no one could find a physical cause why people would simply not wake up after reaching two centuries of age, scientists attributed this to what people called essence or the soul simply not wishing to continue with life.

Worldly climatic pollution had been addressed and Ireland had been lucky enough to remain overall untouched, except for isolated city areas of its green rolling hills. Weather could be controlled, but people of the Irish governing body insisted their land's climate remain as it had always been historically; people preferred maintaining their heritage and traditions.

Covert factions developed, with global ties still struggling for age old bids to gain power and wealth, Ireland became a haven for those who would fade into the trapping of traditions of the people. One such place near Thurles had been an ancient barony, and a very disreputable man named Liam Kendall had resurrected a crumbling manor with funds he acquired through his shady business ventures. Long ago, though few remembered it, ancestors of the O'Keefes had once resided about the ruin and knew its history well.

The Kendall operation was on a watch list of one faction identified as the Agency, that was known secretly as Maoirseacht, and headed by a council that included Aiden Keane though few knew that fact, but Liam Kendall suspected. Because of his suspicions, Liam Kendall wooed Aiden Keane's only daughter, Fiona—a headstrong, free-willed girl, as well as planted several spies in the Keane household, but so far he had not acquired the information that he sought.

"Where is my wife?" roared Liam Kendall, a self-styled businessman who was really a criminal with connections from arms sales to illegal drugs.

"In her room, sir, since yeh ordered she was t'remain in d'e mansion," said one of the underlings.

"Bring her here now! Drag her if necessary," snarled Liam unconsciously crumpling a report in his hand.

Unseen in the shadows, a man named Rory O'Keefe heard the demand, and worried that Fiona Kendall was about to be confronted about their secret relationship; she was pregnant by him. If Liam Kendall found out, he would probably have them both killed and though Rory did not care if that was his fate, he could not accept Fiona suffering. He waited apprehensively to hear what had Liam so enraged.

When a man came to her bedroom door, Fiona Kendall did not bother to refuse accompanying him, knowing her husband would have told the man to drag her, if necessary, into his presence. How she hated the man legally considered her husband! It had taken only a few short months to realize Liam Kendall only married her for family money she would inherit, particularly if he fathered a child. Unknown to him, Fiona made certain no seed of his would ever take in her womb using drugs every time he forced his conjugal rights on her. Could he have found out? No, thought Fiona, this had to be something else, and she was now carrying Rory O'Keefe's child, a secret Liam would never know if she could help it. *Ah,* she thought with a grim smile, *Da must have withheld money after our last conversation.* Fiona had wasted no time informing her father of Liam Kendall's goal to seize the Keane family wealth, but her father was too important to be threatened, and even someone like Liam Kendall knew better than to try such tactics.

Fiona walked as slowly as she dared to see her husband, twisting her lustrous reddish-golden hair into a bun and carefully adjusting thick-rimmed glasses on her nose to look as unattractive as possible to the man. With careful attention to her clothing and outward appearance, Fiona had been able to disgust her husband enough to leave her alone for intimacy, knowing that he would seek only women dressed more sensually.

Since the double doors of Liam's office were thrown wide open, Fiona was able to catch sight of her beloved Rory off to the right as she entered, but did not acknowledge his presence and kept her eyes riveted on Liam. Pointedly, Fiona stopped ten feet away watching her husband waving a piece of paper in his hands.

"What is your father up to?" snarled Liam bending his gaze on his wife.

It took resolve for Fiona to remain where she stood as Liam leaned toward her, his face suffced with blood, "The money. Your dowry or whatever you wish to call it," snapped Liam.

"Oh, I told him I didn't need it because you could provide everything I needed," said Fiona sweetly, reveling in the satisfaction of seeing Liam swell in apoplectic rage.

That minor victory cost Fiona as Liam launched across the intervening space and backhanded her across the face with enough force to knock her several feet away into a crumpled heap on the floor. She gasped in concern for the unborn child. Standing back up was not an option or Liam would hit her again so Fiona lay as if barely conscious and heard the order to take her back to the bedroom, she did not dare protest when the henchman literally dragged her across the floor.

Once the man tossed her in the bedroom, Fiona struggled to her feet, stifling a groan as her body protested the bruises and stiffness, so that she could sit on the chair at the vanity. The noise of the bedroom door opening made Fiona turn in apprehension, which turned to relief when she saw Rory's worried face.

"You mustn't be found here, pet," said Fiona lovingly, which Rory ignored as he wet a cloth to apply to her bruised cheek.

"You can't stay here any longer, love. He means t' use dh'e threat of torture t' get yer father t' release dhat money t' him. Even if Ireland is better t'an the old days for a woman, t'many men still get away wit beating dh'eir wives," said Rory quietly.

"Where can I go that he won't find me pet?" Fiona sighed knowing enough of her husband that he would hunt her down like an animal.

"We'll leave the country. I'll disguise us. Yer Da suggested it and t' change our names. He has tickets waiting for Nort' America," said Rory very softly.

"But how do we get out?" gasped Fiona nervously, "He'll kill you if we're caught."

"Dh'is mansion is old. It has a few secret passages dh'at even Liam doesn't know about. One of me ancestors worked as a steward in this place in dh'e sixteen hundreds he kept a diary dh'at has been passed down through dh'e family. We'll get out tonight," said Rory soothingly.

The fact that her father was involved eased some of Fiona's fears, but once they left Ireland, she would not be able to speak to her father again, lest she give away where they finally settled. Bitterly she lamented her foolishness marrying Liam Kendall especially when a friend warned her all his charm hid the kind of person he really was. There had been rumors, even her father tried to warn her, but Fiona had not listened and rebelled against his order to stay away from the man, even worse, she abandoned someone she had truly loved before meeting Rory.

"What do I need to do?" said Fiona fatalistically.

Rory squeezed her hands, "We can't take much or we'll be noticed. Be ready in t'ree hours. I will make certain dh'e surveillance is fooled so we'll be invisible. With luck, t'will be late tomorrow before anyone knows yer missing and by dh'en t'will be t'late," he said.

Checking the sack for the fifth time, Fiona nervously waited for Rory hoping he would not be caught before they could implement their escape. The sack was not large, but held items dear to her heart: gifts from her father and mother, as well as a few practical items like under garments and toiletries.

Her father's words mocked Fiona, *"He's a bad man my dear. He might seem exciting, but Liam Kendall is a criminal cloaked by glamour. You won't mean anything to him,"* said Aiden Keane, and he had been so right.

Time seemed to crawl by and she resisted the urge to check the table clock again until a soft knock sounded which made her jump, in spite of expecting it, heralding Rory's appearance. He did not enter the room; instead, Rory gestured her to follow him, and Fiona scurried quietly in his wake until they entered a little used room relegated to storage. Once the door closed behind them,

Rory carefully ran his hand across the wall to the right
of the door and pressed a corroded looking ornamen-
tation that sounded with a soft click. A door perfectly
disguised by the wall brick shifted slightly with a crunch
that sounded far too loud to Fiona, and she winced; but
Rory pushed it wider, gesturing her forward before slipping in behind her. A grating clunk sounded as he pushed
it closed leaving them both in pitch black darkness, until
Rory turned on an electric torch and shined about to reveal old clothing accompanied by grey-haired wigs. They
changed quickly, but Fiona found her hands trembling
so much it was difficult buttoning the shirt Rory waited
patiently; unlike Liam, who would have been kicking her
for lagging behind.

Even with light they stumbled down the dark passage, until they came to a dank mossy wall that opened
up near a river, invisible from the outside with the
overgrown foliage forming a tunnel of trees. To Fiona's
surprise the huge manor house seemed far and distant,
but she knew they were not safe; maybe they never
would be safe from Liam.

Since it was summer, the sun still lit the sky at six
o'clock in the evening and Rory had timed their arrival perfectly so that they managed to catch the last bus
running to Dublin. Ireland had resisted the cutting-edge
technology of mass transportation, even though some,
like Liam, had some of the high priced vehicles capable
of hovering over the ground at high speeds. People were
proud of their heritage, even if transportation no longer
ran on fossil fuels.

No one gave them a second glance assuming they
were an elderly couple; and once at the airport, officials
did not bother to check their DNA, since their passports
indicated a chronological age before DNA of births were
recorded. Now Fiona appreciated Rory's deception because with no DNA record of them leaving Ireland, Liam
would assume they were hiding within the country somewhere and would not bother to search abroad for them.

To preserve their image, they took an impossibly long flight to North America making them more difficult to locate if Liam thought of checking international departures, Rory confided to Fiona. A first class flight would be the first thing that Liam would check because of her father's background so she endured the tedious journey with stoicism.

Their economy flight to New York had taken many hours compared to those paying for premium flights. Exhausted and stiff, Fiona followed Rory departing from the airplane in their guise as an elderly couple that ended in a short journey to a hotel.

With a sigh, Fiona sank gratefully into the bed, not even bothering to pull back the bedspread, and was asleep before Rory could say a word. Rory glanced at Fiona lovingly before carefully pulling out a small notebook to review, and then he quickly scrawled a note in case she woke before he returned to the room.

The creak of the door opening jolted Fiona out of her sleep in terror, and she looked about her in alarm at the unfamiliar surroundings before she remembered where she was and scuttled to the bathroom to hide. It was then she realized Rory was not in the room, yet she was too terrified to check to see if the door heralded his return—she so dreaded Liam finding her.

"Fiona?" called Rory's voice tentatively sounding worried.

A sigh of relief escaped Fiona's lips and she exited the bathroom only to see Rory was not alone. She gasped in terror before she had a chance to recognize the visitor nearly stumbling in hasty retreat.

"Tis ok, love," said Rory hurriedly.

That was when Fiona saw it was her brother, Jimmy, to her amazement and concern. "We can't drag my brother into this! Liam will kill him!" Fiona all but wailed.

"Now, now, Fiona, you know Da would never let that happen. He's been coordinating with Rory for a bit and assigned me to work at one of his subsidiaries here in

North America. Liam Kendall doesn't care about me or anything I do, and he's too confident in his own superiority to believe you could ever get out of Ireland," said Jimmy.

Fiona only groaned in dismay, thinking they underestimated Liam not to check all possibilities, and she was not mollified or comforted by Rory's embrace at all.

"Da and I have it all worked out Fiona, never fear. I've brought identities for you both to say you are legal-born citizens. Liam could never find you, and there is no record of you leaving Ireland. I have a work history for you both, birth certificates, credit cards; everything you can think of, even a house. You both won't live close to me, and Rory already has a job and bank account with a modest amount of money that won't look suspicious. You will already be considered married as Mr. and Mrs. Samuel Smith. Your name will be Elizabeth, all common, hard-to-trace names," said Jimmy in a business-like tone, laying everything out on the hotel room table.

Rory deposited a suitcase on the valet and hung up a garment bag obviously containing a small wardrobe for them both until they could acquire additional clothing. It certainly sounded as if her father, Jimmy, and Rory thought of everything, as Fiona glanced at all the documentation on the table. She had to agree the names would be generic.

"But we don't sound like we are from North America…," said Fiona uncertainly.

"At the house, I have set up a computer with audio lessons to acquire a North American accent. It will take time, but you can acquire the necessary speech patterns, and the more you practice, the easier it will be," said Jimmy.

"Jimmy…if Liam ever finds out you helped us…he'll kill you and Irene," said Fiona unable to quell her terror in the face of his confidence.

"Fiona, I came here before you left Liam, so he has no reason to suspect I am connected to you. Da set rumors circulating that he disowned me for leaving Ireland, and not even Liam will think we are in contact for any reason," said Jimmy pointedly.

Fiona let the matter drop, but she promised herself that they would not contact Jimmy, unless it was absolutely necessary, in case Liam decided to check on the rumor of an estranged brother.

Aiden Keane sat in his office reviewing a coded letter sent to him by his son Jimmy about Fiona hiding safely under an assumed identity. He sighed at the necessity of the subterfuge, since most people assumed he recently buried his daughter after a horrific accident. He had not had a DNA test done because it would have revealed the body did not belong to his daughter, but some unfortunate that had died in another accident. Men loyal to him had stolen a corpse and rigged a stolen car, making it appear as if Rory O'Keefe might be responsible, before arranging an accident that mangled the corpse so badly that no visual identification could be made.

Aiden's organization had been investigating Liam Kendall's activities though he had kept this information from his youngest child, Fiona, but the man was too clever and wooed his daughter. The more Aiden attempted to warn Fiona, the more rebellious and stubborn she became, which literally drove her into the criminal's arms. Unfortunately, Fiona found out the hard way about Liam Kendall, and the only reason the disgusting man had married Aiden's daughter was to have leverage against the investigations into his dealings. Liam Kendall knew Aiden Keane would never risk anything happening to his daughter.

A buzzer sounded announcing someone outside his office, so Aiden put the letter away, as he saw one of his assistants via the door camera waiting outside. He pressed the release for the door to allow the man to enter; it was the only way into the office, and Aiden had seen to that carefully for several reasons, one of which was at least one suspected spy of Liam Kendall's in the midst of his employees.

The man who entered was named Quade, actually a grandnephew. He had not worked with Aiden as long as most of his other employees, but was very efficient and business-like. He noticed the man's eyes dart about the room and wondered what he expected to see.

"Sir, a Liam Kendall is demanding a meeting with you. He said it's in regards to your daughter, and he will not wait until the traditional grieving is over to see you," said Quade distastefully.

"Bring him in and see that he is escorted by two men," said Aiden neutrally.

Quade knew an escort meant guards Aiden did not trust Liam Kendall a millimeter and suspected what the man really wanted, though he would not come out and say it initially, as he was not stupid—just twisted.

When the buzzer sounded again, Aiden glanced at the camera to see Liam Kendall flanked by two burly men, and he pressed the door release to admit them. Liam Kendall entered with a look of rage on his face, no doubt because the escort put his plans awry, and sat without greeting or invitation across from Aiden.

"You had no right to bury Fiona without notifying me," snapped Liam immediately.

"I had every right. She was my daughter," said Aiden smoothly.

"I had the right to attend the funeral," snarled Liam without a pause.

"You have never been welcome on my estate and Fiona knew that before she married you. You are not part of this family, nor did marrying my daughter give you any status here," said Aiden silkily.

Blood rushed to Liam's face, so that he appeared to have a severe sunburn, but he did not dare retaliate because Aiden knew what the man really wanted and he was not about to antagonize him before he got to the point.

"You never paid her dowry," spat Liam coming to the real point.

"My daughter indicated she did not need such a bestowment from me," said Aiden smoothly, inwardly enjoying the other man's fury.

"She made that claim without clearing it with me," said Liam hotly.

"My daughter's dowry was of her choice to receive. She declined. So there is nothing more to discuss on this subject," said Aiden firmly and stared the other man in the eye.

Liam Kendall leaned forward so menacingly that the two guards shifted defensively, "This is not over. You will regret interfering in my affairs, and just because that bitch of a daughter is gone doesn't mean I can't make you suffer," hissed Liam dangerously, before he stood abruptly to storm out of the office, his guards in tow.

Finally, the fury Aiden felt bubbled to the surface. He suspected the man had planted surveillance devices during his contemptible visit, but anything he left in the office would be useless. Unless electronic equipment had a specialized shield that he developed it would short out or not work and it was the primary reason for the lack of technology in the room. Off the office was a stocked panic room, not convenient for everyday business, though it was shielded from the emission used to disable other electronic equipment. Even cellular telephones would not work in the office, which was the reason he used a landline for his computer and telephone, both heavily encrypted.

Chapter 2

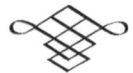

It had been nearly eleven years since Liam Kendall's wife did a runner, thought Mahoney, one of Kendall's men, as he shifted nervously before the door to his boss' office, clutching an improbable report from some North American contacts. His boss did not believe his wife to be dead though he never told his underlings the reason for his belief. In his rage to locate his wife, Liam Kendall had disseminated his wife's photograph along with one of his missing men, Rory O'Keefe, whom he believed had assisted her escape, to every contact he had on almost every continent.

Mahoney was uncertain about this information, since it came from a source organization that was in Liam Kendall's bad books and was likely to say anything to gain his favor again, even sending him on a wild goose chase or fingering a look-a-like to salve Liam's temper. Depending on his boss' attitude about the information, Mahoney could find himself on the receiving end of a painful punishment; no one but no one ever mentioned O'Keefe or his wife to Kendall.

Squaring his shoulders, Mahoney gave one brief knock, in case Liam was busy, but a voice barked,

"Enter!" so there would not be a reprieve, and Mahoney took a deep breath and opened the door.

"What?" snapped Liam Kendall at his man Mahoney, even though he had seen the report in the man's hand.

Clearing his throat Mahoney said, "Sir, a report came in from Nort' America on an old matter."

Liam scowled, "What matter?"

"Perhaps tis better dh'at yeh reat'it," countered Mahoney quickly, in hopes of being at a distance when his boss read the contents of the report.

At that response Liam's expression darkened, "What the hell is your problem? Just tell me what it's about," he snarled at the evasive man.

The demand from Liam made Mahoney keep his distance, knowing the kind of response his boss was going to have to the report which was not verified by any trusted source.

"Sir, t' Cade organization reports a possible sighting of Rory O'Keefe..." was all Mahoney managed to say before Liam Kendall launched across the room in rage, practically spitting in fury at the mention of the name.

With a backhanded swing that Mahoney knew better than to avoid, Liam knocked him to the floor, and he remained laying there as his boss literally ripped the report from his fingers while swearing vociferously.

"Those fools! If they are making up this tale to avoid paying me back for that blunder of theirs at the docks, I'll be sure to ruin them!" raged Liam, his hands shaking with anger as he read the report.

As expected, the report had no details other than a man, which matched Rory O'Keefe's appearance after almost eleven years, and no mention of his lamented wife whose father claimed died in an accident the night she went missing from the manor house. Rumor said O'Keefe was attempting to return Fiona to her father's home under the cover of night and had run a vehicle off a bridge completely crushing the passenger side of the car. The driver, assumed to be O'Keefe, had fled the scene leaving

Fiona dead, and her body, retrieved by the Garda was so mangled that even her own father, Aiden Keane, could not identify her features. He buried his daughter in a small, private ceremony on his estate, to which Liam had not been invited, and had been reclusive ever since, apparently grieving for Fiona. In addition, it was rumored that he and his son were estranged. Word spread that James Keane had left Ireland before his sister's death, and Liam did not know if Aiden Keane ever notified him of Fiona's passing, though word was he did not attend the burial.

Ever since Liam had turned the countryside upside down looking for the traitor Rory O'Keefe, resolving to torture the truth out of him and to find out how he managed to sneak Fiona out of the manor house without any guards seeing them. No one left his employ—absolutely no one!

Still breathing heavily in fury, reason began to reassert itself, and Liam knew it was possible Rory had found a way out of Ireland without a DNA scan, but it would not be easy; illegally retrieved records indicated O'Keefe had not left Ireland through normal channels over ten years ago, since there was no registration of the man's DNA. It would not have been cheap either, and Liam was bitterly aware that Aiden Keane may have given the man money to sneak his daughter away from the manor, even if it ended in her accidental death.

"I want a small group of men who knew O'Keefe well to meet with the Cades and see if it truly is our traitor or some sham of theirs. If it is, I want him brought back here alive by any means possible, and he will tell me what I want to know," said Liam dangerously.

Mahoney leapt up from the floor and raced to the door without question, thankful to still be alive after delivering that report, to send a selection of men to see Liam Kendall.

Though originally Fiona had thought Jimmy and Rory too complacent, they had not been and remained vigilant over the years in case Liam Kendall had word of their whereabouts. Rory had always coached Fiona to stay out of the city and shop rurally for anything she needed or order in anonymously by computer so few people as possible ever saw her face. He knew Liam would have disseminated photographs of them both to his worldwide contacts, even though Aiden Keane had set up events to indicate his daughter had died in a vehicle accident.

As Samuel Smith, Rory had kept a low profile with mundane employment carefully dressing to blend in so people would find him unremarkable and invisible, he even wore non-prescription glasses. Liam Kendall's rage at his defection would be bad enough, but Rory also knew a great deal about the man's organization and could provide enough information to put Liam in prison the rest of his natural life—if he survived long enough to get it to the right authorities in Ireland. Kendall had informants everywhere and Rory would have been dead before he could tell his story.

Over the years he painstakingly notated everything and saved it to a chip that could be easily hidden before giving it to Fiona's brother for safe-keeping. Of course, he never told his wife about any of this, as she would only worry.

They had a beautiful daughter now, Bryn—an almost perfect copy of her beautiful mother, with reddish, golden hair. She was truly his daughter; Fiona had a paternity test to prove it to him though Rory had never doubted it. Fiona loved Bryn fiercely, as did he, and the first thing she asked him to do once. Bryn began to walk was to teach their daughter to protect herself. She did not want Bryn to ever be at the mercy of any man. Rory knew without words that Fiona was referring to men like Liam Kendall.

Making discreet inquiries, Rory finally found an old sensei and during the interview the man, Master Nyoga, had sensed there was more to their family story than he put into words. Though Rory was careful, he did confide some of their past to the trustworthy man and, in turn, the sensei arranged a very unique program for Bryn. As soon as Bryn was five years old, Master Nyoga rotated Bryn through various senseis and other combat training experts, taking into consideration her young body was still growing.

Unusual though this activity was for a girl, Fiona encouraged Bryn and Rory and supported them both—even when Rory added other techniques from his less glamorous years involving breaching locks, hacking computer programs, and rappelling. One thing Rory could not in conscience do was to teach his daughter to use standard weapons like guns, and he hoped she would never be in a situation that required such tools.

His reverie broke at the sound of the front door opening, Fiona returning with Bryn from her gymnastics class, and both were speaking so happily that Rory smiled. Before he could do more than hug them, the telephone rang, much to Rory's disgust, since it was nearly dinner time, and he noted it was a number from his employment.

"Hey Sam, sorry to bother you," said a male voice on the line, after Fiona handed him the receiver.

"Is this important Tim? We are about to sit down to dinner," said Rory impatiently.

"Well…I don't know Sam…it's kinda weird ya know? This guy came in earlier asking all kinds of questions about ya like when ya started working here, where did ya come from, ya know…personal stuff like he was looking for someone special. He had a funny accent too," said Tim uncertainly.

Rory felt a stab of coldness in his gut, "Did you tell them where I live?" he asked with trepidation.

"No way. Told him it was against company policy to give out personal information. He got pretty pissed off and stormed out. He didn't look like police, but someone is investigating ya, man," said Tim in a tone begging for information.

"I suspect it's nothing Tim. Somebody probably has the wrong person. It's not like I have an uncommon name," said Rory offhandedly, trying to sound unconcerned.

"Ya true. Guess he may come back while you're here tomorrow. Told them ya would be in so he could ask ya questions directly," said Tim.

"Thanks Tim. Talk to you tomorrow," Rory said, and hung up.

Turning slowly, Rory noted by her tense posture that Fiona had been listening to the conversation and thankfully their daughter was not in the room, "Love, get some things together for us quickly. I'll toss food into a cooler. We need to get out of here. I don't know what is going on yet, but someone is looking for me at work. It could be nothing, but…" he left the comment hanging.

Fiona asked no questions and immediately grabbed suitcases while Rory grimly added a selection of food to a cooler. Rory called Jimmy on the disposable cellular phone he always used to explain the situation. They never used a landline or regular cellular phone to call just in case of a situation like this. It protected Jimmy.

"I don't know yet Jimmy. I'm going t'toss dh'is phone down into t'sewer until we stop somewhere. I can't take dh'e risk and if you don't hear from me wit'in twenty four hours, toss yer phone, too. If anything happens t'me or Fiona…please take care of Bryn, she has a chip implanted t'indicate next of kin or guardians. Fiona's Da set up a trust for Bryn, but be careful using it or yeh could end up in danger," said Rory, his Irish brogue pronounced as he spoke.

"I hope it won't come to that. Be careful…and I mean it. You needn't worry about Bryn, we love like she's our own," said Jimmy.

With that, Rory hung up and Fiona appeared with a very confused Bryn, but the girl did not ask questions and followed him out, he surreptitiously tossed the cell phone down the street drain.

As he entered the car, Fiona handed him a laptop computer, "Pet, can you do me a favor and start a reformat just to be certain," said Rory and she set the computer on her lap to begin the process.

"Bryn, pet, put on your seat belt please," said Rory looking in the rearview mirror as he started the car.

Soon as he pulled away from the house, Rory saw a black SUV turn onto their street in the rearview mirror and sweat beaded on his forehead, if they were lucky that vehicle would have nothing to do with them. Maintaining an unhurried pace, Rory turned onto another street as if they had been on that road already and not from any particular house, but he caught sight of the SUV screeching to halt in front of their house just as their car passed another house making it impossible to see anymore.

Rory looked at Fiona and she read the concern on his face, which reflected terror in her own expression so stealth was no longer an option if they knew enough about their residence, they would know the car. No choice left. Rory took off at a dangerous speed heading into the city to lose them in the traffic knowing that it was their only hope and then they would have to switch vehicles.

"Jimmy?" said Fiona in breathless fear.

"They will never know. All contact was on the burner phones and I tossed mine into the sewer. Jimmy will toss his if he doesn't hear from us tomorrow," said Rory shortly because he was concentrating on the road, but he heard Fiona breathe a sigh.

"How did they find us?" said Fiona so softly Rory almost did not hear her.

"Tim," he sighed, "They must have bugged his line and traced the call. There was no way he could have known not to call me."

Rory thought they just might lose these men until another SUV appeared out of nowhere in front of them to block their car, but he was ready for something like that and veered over the sidewalk to circumvent the other vehicle. He spared a glance at his daughter in the rear-view mirror, but the brave little soul neither cried nor screamed even if she did look terrified.

When gunfire pinged off the chrome bumper, Rory was glad he thought to get solid rubber tires as a failsafe and their car was able to continue unhindered by the attempt to deflate their tires.

When Fiona gasped in fright, he said, "It's alright pet. They are trying to hit the tires. Apparently they want me alive so we have that in our favor."

"But Rory, at the speed we are driving there could be a horrible accident," said Fiona urgently, "What about Bryn?"

"I can stop, but if they recognize you love…" said Rory worriedly though he would willingly sacrifice himself for his wife and daughter, "and take Bryn as leverage…"

Fiona moaned in horror, "No, no that beast will never touch my daughter. Do what you must," she said.

In the following vehicles Liam Kendall shouted on the car telephone at the men all the way from Ireland, "You fools! Stop that damn car!"

"Sir, we tried t'take out dh'e tires, but he must'ave solid rubber. I guess he was expectin' dh'is could happen," said one of the men.

Watching the live video feed in his office, Liam Kendall roared back, "Force them off the road idiots! Do I have to think of everything?"

"At dh'is speed he might not survive sir and dh'ere's someone else in dh'e car. A passenger we haven't seen," said the man.

"Take the risk damn it. That bastard is going to pay. If you lose him…" snarled Liam so that the men all knew the fate they would suffer.

Kendall's men followed, boxing in the car and then slamming it to sideswipe it off the road, but the driver was not running scared or erratic, he knew how to drive in such situations using the momentum in his favor. If the driver was Rory O'Keefe then he would know exactly how to avoid them.

The car agilely avoided every trap the SUVs attempted to force it into either circumventing parked cars or obstacles like lampposts expertly all the way to an on-ramp to a major highway. Liam Kendall shrieked at the men not to lose their quarry when a tractor trailer began to merge from a blind spot catching all of them off guard.

The fleeing car was going too fast to avoid the sudden appearance of the truck, but attempted to maneuver away using the concrete guides lining the onramp, which forced the car into an uncontrolled roll into the tractor trailer. Men in the SUVs began swearing as the car literally soared airborne across the hoods of their vehicles, part of the bumper catching the second SUV and smashing in its window as men inside cried out.

Breaks screeched behind them as other cars attempted to avoid the accident, several rear-ending the first SUV and one hitting the second SUV broadside so that the pursuing men lost track of the rolling car. Sounds of shattering glass and screaming of twisting metal filled the air, but suddenly stopped leaving only the sound of the unaffected traffic as smoke and steam billowed about the piled up vehicles.

"What the hell happened?" yelled Liam Kendall's voice.

Groans answered him initially as stunned men in the two SUVs attempted to reorient their wits and one finally got out of the first SUV scanning about for the car they had pursued to finally locate it overturned in the V between the onramp and highway. The man stumbled over to look inside to see the man identified as Rory O'Keefe, but to his utter shock, he knew the woman as Fiona Kendall and no mistake.

"Sir, look at dh'is," said the man holding out a video communication unit so that Liam Kendall could see the features of each adult.

"Son of a bitch. Aiden Keane lied to me!" roared Liam Kendall when he saw the woman's face.

In the interim, the man knelt to check for signs of life, but both man and woman were dead, "Dhey're done sir," he said and then noticed the girl lying through the windshield with grimness, "Dh'ere was a kid in dh'e car too."

Inventive swearing filled the COM unit, "She ran because she was pregnant, damn her," roared Liam.

"Sir, dh'ere is no way of knowing dh'at. She doesn't look dh'at old so it probably happened here. Too bad dh'ey brought her wit' dh'em," said the man with a shrug, "Anyway, dh'ere's no point worrying about it now dh'ey're gone."

Liam Kendall was not in the mood to hear a logical or practical statement no matter how true it was, but then there was nothing he could do and ordered the men to get out of there before the authorities reached the scene to investigate.

An insistent buzzing at the office door disrupted Aiden Keane train of thought and he irritably glanced at the camera to see one of his men, which had been located in North America to watch over his daughter covertly. Immediately his irritation vanished and Aiden pressed the door release.

At the pale expression on Devin's face, Aiden felt coldness settle into his chest and knew before the man open his mouth something terrible had happened involving his daughter's family.

"Sir...someone from North America recognized Rory O'Keefe after all this time and had connections with Liam Kendall...Rory got wind of it, but he didn't have enough to time to hide your daughter and granddaughter. They left, but Liam's men started a high speed chase and there was a terrible accident, which killed Rory and your daughter," said Devin with sympathy in his eyes.

Aiden closed his eyes against the grief he felt, "My granddaughter?" he said quietly.

"She is alive, barely. They flew her to the best trauma hospital in the country. I don't know any more than that for now. I wanted to tell you in person about your daughter though….Jimmy is watching over young Bryn. He said he will take care of her," Devin said just as quietly.

Aiden nodded silently and the other man stood slowly nodding in sympathy for Fiona's death, he turned and left the room leaving Aiden to privately grieve. Reaching out, the older man picked up a picture of his granddaughter, his hands holding it so tightly it threatened to bend the frame and tears dropped onto the glass surface.

Chapter 3

Pain! That was all Bryn could remember, that and darkness when there had once been light as she opened her eyes and she lay on something soft, heard sounds of movement around her, but her sight was blank as a dark windowless room. Pressing her awareness further, she could hear the murmur of voices, not too close, with a quality that made her think of hallways or a tunnel and occasionally a metal rumble, like a cart on wheels, seemed to grow louder as if passing by a doorway before fading into the distance.

Where are mom and dad? She thought in fright. Soon as she attempted to push upright, Bryn cried out in unexpected pain in her side, left arm, and her head, throbbing horribly which summoned a rustling visitor. An unfamiliar hand touched her arm and Bryn flinched away from it gasping at the pain that followed the abrupt movement until a kind voice spoke to reassure her.

"You're safe my dear," said a kind female voice. "I'm the duty nurse. You've been in a bad accident. You must move slowly until the injuries heal sufficiently. The doctor will be in to speak with you later."

"My mom and dad, where are they?" said Bryn fearfully.

"Later dear. You still need rest," said the nurse's evasive voice.

A sudden, but irresistible urge to sleep overcame Bryn and she lost the battle to remain awake long enough to get the answers she sought.

Voices penetrated an unexpected grogginess when Bryn woke again. Though the murmurs were soft, she could begin to understand the conversation.

"Her left arm is broken along with several ribs. She's lucky to be alive especially when the emergency personnel reported her safety belt ripped loose and the momentum sent her through the windshield," said a male voice.

Another male voice, vaguely familiar said, "What happened to her eyes?"

"Apparently the car that hit them forced the entire vehicle into a tractor trailer carrying glass panes. The glass splinters have damaged her corneas and lenses beyond repair," said the male voice regretfully.

A sob sounded, "But she's only ten years old. Surely you can do something for her?" said another vaguely familiar voice, female this time.

"Not yet. There are experimental treatments close to approval, but until those pass medical association and government approval, she would not be eligible. It is illegal to experiment on a child and unfortunately, her optic nerves will atrophy in the interim," the unknown male sighed voice.

"Has anyone explained about her parents?" said the first male voice that she thought she recognized.

"Not to my knowledge. They usually will not divulge information like that to a child in the absence of relations or a social worker," said the strange male voice.

That last comment jolted Bryn to complete wakefulness, "Where are my mom and dad?" she wailed in terror.

A gasp of horror indicated the people had no idea Bryn could hear them and then one said, "It's Aunt Irene, darling," her voice sound choked with sadness, "Uncle Jimmy is here too."

With a sigh, Uncle Jimmy said, "Pet, your mom and dad died in the accident. You're lucky to be alive."

At those words the pain in Bryn's body was nothing compared to pain of loss in her heart and sobs wracked her body, she knew now the dream about the car accident was no nightmare. Hands clutched her own small hands and she barely heard the sounds of weeping coming from her aunt, Bryn would never hear her parents again or have a chance to say goodbye.

Four months later, Bryn sat in a room designated for her at her aunt and uncle's house, her aunt had stubbornly refused to accept there was no help for her niece to regain use of her eyes and sought specialist after specialist. They all echoed the doctor in the hospital because she was a child.

That was when Aunt Irene began bringing tutors to the house to educate Bryn to use Braille and navigate with a walking cane. She rebelled against this form of instruction at first until she had an unexpected visitor. Her ears had sharpened to know even when someone who walked quietly entered her room, but she ignored the presence thinking the tutor had returned or her aunt had sought someone else to speak with her.

"Child, why do you sit as if you have nothing left?" said the quiet voice of Sensei Nyoga.

Bryn jumped violently, her relatives would not know of her sensei to contact him, which meant that he sought her, she stood suddenly and knocked over her chair and would have fallen except for the old man's hand catching her arm.

"I don't understand why you are here. There isn't anything you can do for me now," said Bryn bitterly.

"It was always your father's wish that I continue to train you whatever might occur," he paused for a few seconds before adding, "There are other ways to see the world and nothing prevents you continuing instruction with me. I've spent five years as your teacher, and I will continue to introduce you to others that will prove you do not have limits others may see in you," said the old man.

That was the turning point of her life and Bryn began to apply herself to her studies and instruction, not allowed to feel self-pity for her circumstances. Each year, her sensei would continue to introduce her to a new sensei and each new master imparted different skills to teach her awareness to face life until she forgot about her sight.

When she was twelve, Aunt Irene and Uncle Jimmy legally adopted Bryn and changed her name from Bryn Smith to Bryn Keane though she continued to call them aunt and uncle which they did not mind.

It was not until she was fourteen that Bryn's aunt delivered the news that one of the experimental treatments for her blindness had been approved and an appointment scheduled to meet a specialist. His diagnosis was not heartening as Bryn hoped and she might have foregone the treatment if her aunt had not been so excited at the change her niece might have some of her sight returned.

The surgery attempted to restore the atrophied optic nerves and repair her corneas with special grafts, which were a revolution from the old days where nothing could be done to replace or repair any nerve tissue. The procedure was marginally successful allowing Bryn to see light, albeit out of focus. It was enough to allow her to determine large objects, but she still would need her cane for warning of smaller, less obvious obstacles.

Her life continued unremarkably, Bryn applied for and was accepted into a good university in another state though her aunt fussed about her niece alone with strangers, but Bryn reassured her that they had advocates as needed. Unable to take notes like most students, Bryn recorded her lectures and professors set up special verbal quizzes or exams for her to complete so that no other students could complain of exceptions from the rules.

People began to speak to her and Bryn made acquaintances, some even asked her to parties or to restaurants until 'he' began to talk to her. His names was Vander, and at first he seemed funny, sensitive, even attentive until he began to turn possessive of her company, driving acquaintances Bryn made away, isolating her. It all happened so subtly that Bryn was unaware of it happening, until one day she was speaking with a friend named Greg. While walking in a meadow area with him and Vander, Vander bent down suddenly to pick up something off the ground and hit her over the head with a pipe. Greg yelled at Vander, asking him what possessed him to hit Bryn, but he never gave any verbal response and ran off.

Knowing that she couldn't return to her trailer that Vander and she rented, Greg offered her to stay in his small dormitory room, sleeping on the floor until she could find another place to stay. Greg and a few of his friends retrieved Bryn's belongings while Vander was away.

Then Bryn nearly made a fatal error, she answered a knock on Greg's door to hear Vander's voice when she opened it, he spoke with contrition about his behavior, pain he caused her, and wished to start over with her. Even though he sounded sincere, Bryn distrusted him and said, "It will have to wait until I find my own place first," as politely as possible.

When he mentioned a couple of items belonging to her were left at the trailer, he offered to take her to retrieve them. Bryn should have been more suspicious, but he seemed to take her polite refusal equitably. In hindsight, she realized waiting for Greg would have been the wisest course of action.

Vander drove unhurriedly, talked cheerfully as if nothing was wrong and even helped her from his car, but the entire charade ended at the slamming of the main door into the trailer leaving Bryn inside with the sound of a hammer at the door as if he was nailing it shut. Her heart beat in a frenzy of terror, but Bryn did not scream even though instinctively it was all she wanted to do so she could be free. Unable to see more than shadows in what light there was, Bryn felt about the window hoping to find a way out, only to find them secured shut—Vander had prepared to hold her prisoner.

Why? Her mind reeled in confusion; Bryn knew she had nothing, not even much money. It was not until all the light faded from the trailer that Bryn knew Vander intended to terrorize her. She frantically felt every window for an opening and the back door. Her hands found a towel which Bryn wrapped about her hand before breaking the glass on a window so her voice could carry outside for someone in the park to hear her cries.

The glass crunched under her towel covered hand and Bryn began to yell for help which abruptly became a gasp as some liquid splashed through the window burning her skin where it hit, it smelled like drain cleaner. Frantically, she stumbled to the sink to wash away the burning fluid and heard Vander laughing manically, "You're mine and you will see that in time. As long as you keep me happy, things will go well, but try to leave me again and I'll kill you," he snarled from outside.

Panting in terror, Bryn knew he would find ways to make her capitulate no matter how much training her senseis' gave her and he was not above starving her into submission if necessary. If she had even a moments warning to disable him, but then where would she run? Who would have helped her?

Think Bryn, stop panicking, you were trained better than that! She berated herself after several deep breaths and it dawned on her that she let panic rule her action, no matter how briefly. She never considered carrying a cell phone as keeping track of it would be difficult blind and her father always warned her people could track her via GPS. Her thoughts stopped: The telephone! So she carefully searched the counter where he kept it and found it gone, but decided he might have moved it to another room so she kept searching, but found nothing knowing that Vander must have hidden the phone. Bryn began to check the walls for a jack hoping he had not thought through the fact she was used to living blind or nearly blind. When she found a jack with a cord still connected, Bryn had to cut off a shout of triumph and followed it to the opposite end, which led to a dresser drawer which she pulled open to find the telephone.

Picking up the handset indicated a dial tone so it was no problem for Bryn to dial by feel after so many years unable to read like a normal person and in her panic, the first person she thought of calling was Greg instead of the police. In her recital to Greg, Bryn was never certain what she said exactly, but she did catch his words about police before he hung up and she knew he would drive out to get her.

It did not take long for sirens to blare in the distance and Bryn waited listening hard for Vander to do something before they arrived, but in the minutes it took for the police to pull up to the trailer nothing else happened. Pounding sounded on the door and Bryn yelled back the situation that was followed by two crashing thuds before the door broke inwards. Feet rushed in and the police began to ask questions, she could see the shine of their flashlights in the darkness as one examined her before he said, "You need to see a doctor for those chemical burns, miss."

Within minutes, Bryn heard Greg's worried voice calling out and the police met him with questions after which they had an ambulance take her to the emergency room for the chemical burns. As Greg climbed into the ambulance with her, Bryn heard one officer radioing about Vander missing as his partner searched the surrounding area to find him. No doubt Vander fled as soon as he heard the sirens.

All the way to the emergency room, Greg berated Bryn for going anywhere with Vander and she could offer no defense of his diatribe because he was absolutely correct.

Aunt Irene and Uncle Jimmy came for graduation; Bryn received her master of business diploma before most students finished a regular bachelor's degree. She decided to return and live with her relatives so she could be near the only family she had left. Master Nyoga renewed training with selected senseis some of which surprised Bryn involving secrecy, stealth, and hitherto unknown skills like subtle manipulations of locks. Long ago Bryn learned not to question the reasons for any training particularly after her father impressed upon her it would all be useful someday.

A local business hired her at a good salary even though she was only twenty one. After two years, her life settled down to something approaching normal for any person, she rented her own place, visited her relatives often, and celebrated holidays with family and friends until the second Thanksgiving following her graduation.

It was the day after Thanksgiving; her aunt suggested they celebrate a day late since Bryn was doing a favor for a co-worker on the actual holiday, so Bryn cheerfully made her way over to Aunt Irene's house to spend the day.

Without bothering to knock, because Aunt Irene would scold her for acting like a visitor, Bryn reached to feel for the door handle only to find the door ajar to her surprise, especially at eight o'clock in the morning. Aunt Irene would just have risen, preparing breakfast, drinking coffee, and reading the newspaper, but disturbingly, Bryn smelled no coffee or other sign of cooking. Carefully, she moved forward with the cane even though Aunt Irene always kept the house free of clutter only to find the floor littered with oddments. Bryn bent to feel what the items could be and found a lamp, what felt like a newspaper, letters, and knickknacks strewn uncharacteristically about the floor, she felt a coldness creep into her stomach.

"Aunt Irene? Uncle Jimmy?" she called out, but only silence greeted Bryn's ears.

Using her cane and the wall, Bryn navigated the debris worried for her aunt and uncle and wondering if they had a burglary or could be hurt. Her slow progress down the hall to the kitchen introduced a new scent, sort of metallic, almost sweet and rusty in combination, nothing Bryn could recall ever experiencing before in the past. The scent grew stronger and so did her fear, Bryn felt the doorway into the kitchen feeling forward with the cane which encountered a chair out of place, she reached out only to jerk her hand back with a gasp when it met the cold form of a body.

"No!" Anguish tore through Bryn, she reached out again to be certain and it was her uncle from the size of the arm. With a sob, Bryn stumbled backwards into the hall afraid to go into the kitchen any further only to find her aunt as well and tripped over the telephone from the dull bell sound since her aunt refused to get the newer technology available so it was an antique.

Of their own volition, her fingers dialed nine-one-one and she sobbed into the receiver about her relatives' house left open and they were unresponsive adding that she was legally blind. Soon as the dispatcher understood Bryn's disability, she asked for what information Bryn could logically give and to stay on the line until police arrived.

Though the dispatch spoke to Bryn attempting to reassure her, the voice in her mind screamed in despair that they were all gone, anyone she ever cared about, who cared about her and now there was no one. Detectives came, they asked question after question that Bryn could not answer since she had not been present when the break in occurred. They wanted to know the last time she saw her relatives, the last time they spoke, and on and on.

All this continued for days, but the detectives could not find a motive, as far as anyone could determine there were no items missing from the house and her aunt or uncle had willingly opened the door to their attacker since there were no signs of forced entry. The person or persons were either someone they knew or they did not think presented a threat at the time though the detective sided with the theory multiple people were involved to restrain two people in their own home.

For the second time in twelve years, Aiden stared at Devin, his most trusted employee, faced with terrible news of his son and daughter-in-law's deaths and felt the crushing weight of grief that now both of his children were gone. According to the data retrieved by Devin, local authorities deemed his son's death as a house invasion gone bad or at least on the surface and what the newspapers had printed, but there were rumors that someone had been looking for his granddaughter. Could it be Liam Kendall after all this time? How could he possibly know anything about Bryn when public record indicated she was an adopted child? Adoption records were legally sealed so there would be no way anyone could access his granddaughter's background.

Aiden Keane faced the terrible conclusion that someone in his household could have leaked information to Liam Kendall and correlated via the girl's birth date to trace her back to Fiona in some fashion. However, it could be that a man like Kendall had grown so vindictive about Aiden's assistance in the investigation of the man's criminal actions that he made the strike against Jimmy to punish the father for interference. Whichever reason, his granddaughter was in serious danger.

"Please contact the detective in charge of the case. We need help to hide my granddaughter in case Liam

Kendall is involved in the murders and it must be kept quiet from now on. I fear we have a leak within the estate," said Aiden grimly to Devin.

"I'll take care of it," said Devin immediately and asked no questions, he knew what was expected.

It was not until after the autopsies and the funeral that the detectives had something else to add calling Bryn into the precinct again. "Please sit, Miss Keane," said a detective.

Sitting quietly, Bryn waited, refusing refreshment and wishing all of this was over until the woman spoke again, "We uncovered new information, which your uncle had the forethought to provide us with though not much of it is usable unfortunately. We found the motive and it is important that you hear it."

The sound of something being set on the table came to Bryn's ears and then the click of a button that was followed by a recording, a bad one from the sound quality, her uncle's voice was barely recognizable. There was another voice, but distorted in some way, making it completely foreign and impossible to understand all the words, but her uncle's response gave more than enough information.

A person was demanding to know where Bryn could be found and her uncle refused to divulge the information, apparently the person stopped by on the holiday expecting to find Bryn unaware of previous arrangements. Instead of fear, Bryn felt silent tears coursing down her cheeks knowing her aunt and uncle died to protect her from whoever tried to locate her, which explained why they let someone in initially.

"Why do you think someone wants to locate you so badly Miss Keane?" said Detective Medina interrogatively.

"I don't know. I have nothing. I'm not wealthy, far from it. My job offers no special access and no one attempted to find me there. It cannot be anyone I know or they would have called or located me easily," said Bryn honestly.

Medina looked at information in front of her regarding the young woman and saw that there was a blind trust fund involved, but the assets were frozen due to her guardians' manner of death. Actually the girl's aunt and uncle had adopted her so she had assumed their last name. Of her birth parents there was very little information other than their names; it was as if they blossomed into existence twenty three years ago under the names of Samuel and Elizabeth Smith. Apparently her adoptive father had connections overseas and someone had been attempting access his information, but for what purpose Medina could not fathom. What connections her adoptive father had, the report did not elaborate and that omission alerted the detective.

Oddly enough the young woman sincerely seemed ignorant of the trust fund's existence and her guardians raised her on their own modest income. They were named as executors of the trust, but where did it come from? *Why hide the knowledge from their niece?* Medina thought she knew the answer and did not like it: They were trying to protect the young woman. But from what or maybe the better question in light of their deaths would be, from whom?

"We concluded that as well, Miss Keane, but someone wants to locate you badly enough to torture your guardians for information. That can only mean unpleasantness for you given the way they attempted to retrieve your location. What concerns us is we have no reason to place you under protection, for example, you are not a witness to a crime so it would not get sanctioned. We do recommend you disappear in some fashion on your own for protection, but we cannot help you unfortunately, at least with more than advice. I'll offer suggestions about changing your appearance and giving you general advice about living off the grid until we catch this murderer or murderers. Keep in touch with us using disposable cell phones, change your residence, and follow the advice as closely as possible," said Medina carefully, though her tone told Bryn the detective wished they could help her further.

After a very thorough briefing from Detective Medina, who worked undercover regularly, Bryn knew she could not return to her job, apartment, or her relatives' home and had to literally drop off the face of the earth. Though not sanctioned, the detective arranged for Bryn's possessions to be placed in storage when she was off duty while Bryn closed bank accounts knowing she could not pick up any future pay checks. Another thing the detective did for Bryn was obtain an alternate social security number for her so she could seek employment under another name in a different city, advising her to seek a larger population to blend into the background.

"I will be your only contact from now on. Never use a public line for any reason and get rid of the cellular phone immediately after you call in. Do you understand?" said Medina and Bryn nodded.

To hide her long reddish golden hair, Bryn acquired a black wig with a short cut style and started wearing sunglass to hide her eyes, but she had no choice about her blindness so she continued as normal. As a job, Bryn applied for a position beneath her degree and away from executive type work so no one would know where to search for her, she did not maintain a bank account to further the charade of invisibility. She became *Jean Easley*.

A routine developed and Bryn settled into life as Jean Easley. No one paid much attention to her—people tended to ignore the disabled, that way they did not have to acknowledge their existence. In another time, Bryn might have resented such a disparaging attitude in people around her, but now it was a saving grace, she was no one and not worth a second glance to whoever might be searching for Bryn Keane.

Life became lonely, Bryn would not trust anyone
again after her relatives' brutal murders and she often
sat in solitude in a park near her work listening to the
tinkling of water in the fountain, birds singing, or smelling the sun on the grass. Then one day, someone began to
sit near her, but Bryn remained aloof and it turned out to
be an older man from the tone of his voice, he was very
kind often speaking about humorous things. Gradually
Bryn thawed toward him when she realized he wanted
nothing from her and they would enjoy companionable
chats often during her lunch time or even after work.

He introduced himself as Donal and said he was
retired though he did not immediately discuss his past
work as he fed the pigeons while they spoke carefully
probing about her blindness, how it happened or what
treatments they eventually gave her. The questions were
so subtle and offhanded that Bryn never suspected Donal
had any reason for asking for the information until a year
later.

"I used to be a scientist of sorts girl. Developed new
things to help people until they said I was too old," snorted Donal derisively.

Bryn laughed with a 'ha' and could not imagine Donal
too old for anything after listening to him speak on many
subjects and hearing him often subjecting his observations to his wit.

"I think I can help you girl," he said suddenly out of
the blue.

A shaft of wariness pierced Bryn at his sudden interest in helping her and she sensed he was aware of
her change in mood by the silence, which followed his
announcement.

"You don't deserve to stay blind just because you
have no money. Society sweeps people under the carpet
they prefer to ignore when they can't pay the premium. I
like to change the rules, help those who never get a fair
shake in life, but I will tell you that most of what I do is

experimental, or they would call it that, because I don't give it to people to make money," he growled.

His explanation rang true, Bryn could tell Donal meant every word and he would have no way of knowing why she hid from the world, he did not even know her real name besides he was not the type to murder people after listening to him for a year.

After a great deal of consideration, Bryn decided to accept Donal's offer, especially since her aunt and uncle would have wanted this for her.

Donal explained, "You will need to stay with me girl. It will take some time to do it right and keep you from infections. I don't want to attract attention either or those corporate fools will hound me for my work which they don't deserve. That means you will need to take a sabbatical from work for a while," he said apologetically.

All that suited Bryn, it kept her off the grid and hidden so she readily agreed to his terms before allowing Donal to lead her to his 'special place' as he called it. Everything smelled clean and well aired and he gave her a private room which soothed any remaining apprehension Bryn had about Donal's intentions that briefly crossed her mind.

Examinations that followed were an experience beyond Bryn's previous medical encounters even if she could not see much and Donal even sedated her frequently, frightening at first, to explore what would obviously hurt if she had been awake. Then procedures began, Donal would explain actions afterwards when he first addressed her atrophied optic nerves, he removed the implants previously given to her as a child. There was some pain when nanites were introduced, microscopic machines he developed that initiated the restore of the optic nerves, actually enhancing them. From that point forward, he kept her eyes bandage.

Once he was satisfied with the restoration of her optic nerves, Donal explained he would give Bryn special corneas and lenses he developed, cybernetic implants using her own tissue instead of a transplant from a donor.

"The implants," he said, "will help your brain decoded visual information that normal humans can't process or even see."

This procedure involved several surgeries that ended with special transmitters implanted under the skin behind Bryn's ears. Instead of instantly removing the bandages, Donal kept them intact, but lightened the density of material over time to avoid overloading her brain, he said, with new information because he had no way of knowing how her brain would interpret the new signals. The gradual reduction of material density led to the removal of bandages in a completely dark room, which at first made Bryn wonder if there had been any change at all. He introduced light carefully and slowly to give her brain time to accommodate to the concept of sight again until one day there was sufficient light that Bryn could see the old man clearly.

Tears ran down her cheeks seeing the world again. Bryn could not find the words to express the gratitude she felt for the freedom from a dimness she thought to haunt her life the rest of days. It did not stop there though, Bryn would happily have rejoiced in normal vision.

Gradually, her brain began to decipher new information; Bryn saw unusual spectrums of light and eventually even in the absence of almost all light, to thermal images in complete darkness. In time, she could control what she focused on within her new abilities as the old man continued to test each new improvement and her trust in him continued until she admitted her real name. She told him the reasons for hiding, what had happened to her aunt and uncle, and she knew he would never betray her confidence.

Then he began to send Bryn on tasks to acquire equipment he needed for his work, special supplies could not be bought by the average person not associated with a hospital or related corporation. Bryn was only too glad

to help after receiving the gift of sight she never expected to have again.

Donal encouraged her to develop new skills and continue with her old training, but cautioned her to maintain
an image of blindness to the public to avoid questions
when she was among people. So Bryn returned to her
wig, sunglasses and cane to create the illusion of previous life quite competently from her past experience.

It was not until Bryn developed an ability to view in
an x-ray type spectrum that she decided to take more
risks and develop an alter ego that would subsidize a
more lucrative lifestyle.

Chapter 4

Detective Medina was plowing through a pile of paperwork when she noticed two men standing by the information desk, she was about to discount them when they looked straight at her and moved in her general direction. Something about these men reminded her of military, maybe the haircuts, she thought and decided to ignore the fact they were approaching by continue to update paperwork she had to turn in that day.

Cognizant the men stopped at her desk, Medina did not look up and continued her paperwork as if she was unaware of the men's presence until one of them cleared their throat.

"Ms. Medina..." he began.

"Detective," she said flatly finally looking up at the men coldly for the subtle insult.

"Detective," he said, his face neutral, but the tone made it an insult and flashed a badge of Federal Authority, "We understand you were the last person to speak to one Bryn Keane."

Though Medina recognized the name instantly, even after two years, she kept her expression blank. From the glimpse of that badge, she did not believe it was legitimate and she had no time to prove it, so instead of challenging the man, she said, "I don't recall that name from my cases, but then we handle a lot of situations."

The man who spoke also kept a blank expression, but Medina noted an angry shine in his eyes when she did not offer to look up information or inquire why he needed to know.

"A colleague indicated you had a lengthy conversation with Bryn Keane, long enough to be remarkable, about hiding until you solved her guardian's murders," said the man coldly.

Medina snarled inwardly at the indiscreet colleague revealing information, particularly in conjunction with an unsolved murder case and potentially unnatural death of the girl's parents. It had been a wise choice to keep Bryn Keane's location a secret.

Without comment, Medina looked in her file drawer as if she needed to jog her memory, along with precinct computer database she kept hard copies of unsolved cases to peruse and make special personal notes. She pulled out Bryn Keane's before looking up at the men.

"Ah yes, I remember her now. Blind woman whose aunt and uncle were murdered. I did ask her a lot of questions hoping she could recall anything that might explain such senseless murders with no apparent motive, not even robbery. I did recommend the she consider hiding since we had no idea why her guardians were targeted, but what she chose to do, I have no idea. Her situation did not qualify for police protection or relocation," drawled Medina in false consideration of the file.

The second man swore under his breath and said nothing, but the man, who originally spoke, said, "Bullshit! That's not what your colleague said," his eyes blazing with anger.

"You need to understand, *sir*," she said making the title an insult, "I can't help every person needing protection that comes through here, man or woman. What you are suggesting my colleague inferred is against regulations and if I had taken such liberties, my supervisor would have put a reprimand in my file. If you don't believe me, you are welcome to ask him."

The man leaned across her desk, but Medina did not flinch or look away, "You have no idea what you're dealing with," he snarled.

"Am I to construe that as a threat?" said Medina with deceptive mildness.

His face flushed deep red and she thought he might shout at her, but he the man grated out, "Give me that file."

"I'm sorry I don't *see* any authorization for any of our case files. Any request like that goes straight through the Chief, even if you had the right," said Medina coldly.

By now most of other detectives and officers were aware of the confrontation from the silence that fell in the room and it was enough to bring the Chief out of his office.

"What the hell is going on here?" demanded the Chief.

"Apparently these men claiming to be Federal Authorities have decided they have rights to one of my case files sir. I have seen no authorization and certainly have no word from you to hand over any case," said Medina without taking her eyes off the men.

Then all hell broke loose. The first man who spoke to her made a lunge for the Bryn Keane's case file, but Medina had expected such a ploy and shoved her wheeled chair smoothly out of his reach leaving him grasping at empty air. In the same motion the two men whirled about and ran for the exit which was so unexpected, the other officers failed to react for a few heartbeats. There were cries of halt as guns were drawn, but the men seemed to know as long as they drew no weapons, the police would not fire and certainly not when bullets might hit other officers.

In seconds almost every single officer was in pursuit except the Chief and Medina, but to no avail as the two men leapt into a waiting unmarked van, the driver gunned the accelerator in a haze of burning rubber. Some of the officers attempted to follow in vehicles while others returned to inform the Chief what happened and resume their interrupted activities to await the report of the pursuit.

"Medina, in my office," snapped the Chief.

The door shut behind her with a firm snap and Medina's supervisor gestured at the chair in front of the desk as he sat, "Explain," he said, so explain she did.

After she finished her narrative, the Chief said, "I remember the case. What do they want with the girl?"

"They never said, but obviously they can't find her and are desperate," said Medina.

"No indications the guardians were in trouble with anyone?" said the Chief bemused.

"None at all sir. Average people, not even a parking ticket between them," said Medina.

"Check further back. I know it says the parents died in an accident, but…this lack of information on her birth parents…who knows what the hell they were into or who they really were," said the Chief and Medina nodded.

Medina was not pleased with what she found either which happened to be a dead end regarding Samuel and Elizabeth Smith, no past, no one who knew them except for Jimmy Keane and his wife. That told her the Smiths were probably in hiding for some reason or had something to do with a government agency and any further attempts to glean information about Bryn Keane's parents would probably get the Chief a visit from whichever agency restricted the information. When Medina apprised her supervisor of the facts, he gave her a speculative look before picking up the telephone.

Since he did not indicate the need for privacy nor dismiss her, Medina waited and saw a change come over the Chief as he began to sit straighter uttering short answers to unheard questions his expression scowling.

His jaw muscles flexing with anger, the Chief set the telephone receiver down firmly, "You're not to investigate the case any further. This involves something to do with Interpol," he said flatly.

Medina stared at him incredulously, but he gave her a blank look and pointed to the door so she knew that was the end of the conversation. Suspicious of what the Chief heard, Medina made a copy of Bryn Keane's case file and altered the one she planned to file in her desk on the off chance it was directly or indirectly removed by whoever spoke to her supervisor.

A few days later Medina was glad she took the initiative on Bryn Keane's case file after some hooded men literally held the precinct hostage until the case file was located and removed which fortunately she altered to protect the young woman. The real file was taped beneath her desk.

A group of men sat around a conference table observing a state of the art holographic display with an air of surprised confusion, their leader Kolski, usually referred to as the Commander, found the stats very disturbing and the fact none of his team could account for the thefts of certain sensitive equipment or information.

"A rogue agent?" said one of the men pensively.

"Not possible. Not this clean and the safeguards breached would require gear impossible to bring into these settings without triggering alarms or being seen by guards," said the Commander dismissively.

Other men began to offer suggestions except one, as usual the Commander noticed the one called Nighthawk remained aloof and kept his summations to himself, but he was the best of them all. None of the other men could match his abilities mental or physical and the Commander knew if this thief could be caught, Nighthawk would find a way, he usually worked alone unless a mission required a team.

This thief, an extraordinary operator, would provide an asset to upcoming missions facing their facility. What puzzled the Commander most was this thief was a new operator, not just in their area, but worldwide from the unique lack of signature of any other comparable peers and some had attempted to lay claim to these jobs. Those claims were easily dismissed by the knowledgeable like this group of men, many thieves arrogant and jealous of their abilities left calling cards, but not this one or did anyone come forward to correct attempts to take the credit.

Smooth, thought the Commander, *this person does not care if anyone takes credit for those jobs, almost as if the person welcomed people looking away, confident in their own abilities without need for fanfare.* Such a lack of reaction spoke of long experience except the Commander knew these high profile thefts were recent occurrences in the past two years or word would have spread long ago about such skill. The person was selective, not greedy and must have insurmountable patience to pull off these jobs which left no evidence, not even a trace of a clue to follow which was completely improbable with the technology available to their facility.

The corporations, private parties, or military targets breached found this idea of a ghost-like entity very unnerving, not at all consoled there appeared to be no malice associated with this thief; agendas could always change.

"This guy is good," said an abrasive man called Stanton.

"If it's a man," said a quiet voice from Nighthawk's direction.

Stanton sneered at the other man, but the Commander considered the possibility of a woman even though female thieves of this caliber were somewhat rare and usually not involved with such risk factors. However, the lack of arrogance claiming the jobs and the understatement hinted at a female touch, but he would not believe it until they caught the person.

Over six months later the conference room hosted a bawling lecture from the Commander, "Don't tell me you can't find anything! You people are the best in the world, you have the best equipment so it's impossible none of you can find a hint of the person involved!" he snarled furiously.

Not even Nighthawk managed a scrap of information and that was shocking to them all that anyone could operate so completely invisible leaving absolutely no clues other than a missing item in question.

"No technology exists small enough for one person to carry that can breach all the barriers at these locations. Is it possible that there is more than one person gaining access to these targets?" demanded the Commander.

"It must be," said the man called Stanton, but the Commander ignored him and looked straight at Nighthawk.

With a slight shake of his head, Nighthawk said, "Highly doubtful. More people, more opportunity for error or for others to see and one person can exit easily, change strategy quickly if something goes wrong."

Stanton glared at the quiet man, "Ok know-it-all then how do they get in? There are too many safe guards for one person to enter these buildings from all angles," he sneered.

The Commander jumped in, "If we knew that we could catch the person fool and we wouldn't be having this discussion!" he shouted.

They were all out of ideas and they needed this person's expertise to succeed in several future missions, thought the Commander fuming at the list of items, which mysteriously disappeared from their original locations. Standing to pace, looking for some obvious information that was not present in the holographic display, it dawned on him, why those items at those specific times and not within a short period of time from each other? None of them had bothered to consider the problem from this angle.

"Have any of you noticed that these acquisitions follow no set pattern of time, change in company statistics or public investment reports?" said the Commander musingly.

Most of the men either pursed their lips or looked blatantly confused with the exception of Nighthawk, his head rose to consider the holographic display at the center of the table.

"None of the items is related to the other in any particular way, no company advertising or attempting to bid for any of the missing items or information through normal channels," drawled Nighthawk slowly.

"Exactly! So there must be some hidden avenue in which people make these requests known to our sly culprit since obvious channels are eschewed," said the Commander with satisfaction though he was daunted at the prospect of finding this point of contact.

"You mean the thief could have stolen any of these things whenever he wanted, but chose not to?" A man nicknamed Tank mused.

"My point exactly. No one can stop this person, no measures are effective, but yet there is no particular pattern to these missing items, at least that we know of right now," stressed the Commander, pleased by his own stroke of brilliance.

"So the thief already has a buyer for the item before the actual theft," murmured Foss and the Commander nodded sharply, "That's why they never appeared on any black market."

"Get going, all of you. More eyes on this will increase our chances of finding this client to thief contact," said the Commander only vaguely aware of the men leaving the conference room.

As it happened Stanton was the person that stumbled across the online dummy notice board because one of the potential client bidders had used weaker encryption than any of the other potential clients and they were able to access the offer. Once they knew the item in question, the Commander was able to apply their facilities considerable high tech resources to decrypting other ads or offers from potential clients. Actually the Commander realized they should not be surprised the weakness would be on the client-side as careful as this thief operated and this would be where they would find the mistakes or holes to capture the thief.

Thinking all they would need to do was backtrack any of the thief's posted replies became a ludicrous lesson in overconfidence on their part because any connections via internet bounced off so many nodes only to terminate at a point of disposable WiFi, they achieved nothing. The thief was far too careful in case of a potential sting operation.

An attempt to pose as a client only left them in more confusion and less answers, accounts which could not be traced, delivery they could not corroborate which had them all pulling out hair until Nighthawk finally made a suggestion.

"We can find out where an item is located prior to acquisition and observe, but not capture. It is the only way we can see what we are up against so we have an idea how to proceed," he said quietly.

His suggestion had merit and really was the only alternative so they watched the bulletin board and waited for months until another tempting request, though in the meantime another "unscheduled" removal had occurred, not connected with any posting, from a pharmaceutical company. They had to focus on the client posting on the board since the Riticon Corporation refused to give details on the actual form of loss they experienced.

Though the Commander brushed aside the information, Nighthawk discovered that Riticon's experimental area had been breached and rumor said involved some form of robotics, which the corporation refused to corroborate.

Now they had an area to observe, but no idea when a breach would occur, even though their target had responded to the request after a fashion in very brief, encrypted term which of course was untraceable. It took time to locate the firm that held an unusual ancient piece of artwork a client sought on private display in a massive skyscraper in which the current owner occupied the entire twenty-second floor of the thirty-story edifice. What the Commander had not anticipated was the lengthy wait for the thief to act though he realized it should not have surprised him, he thought in hindsight after previous meticulous breaches in the past. By logical deduction the thief would operate at night since there would be less people hence less chance of observation and that complicated matters somewhat when they had to spread their forces to keep constant surveillance on the building.

Most of the men wore special hi-tech visors developed for the Facility that could decode various visual inputs from light to data, but the Commander was taking no chances. Every man covered some portion of the building with powerful scopes imbued with night vision, thermal imaging, x-ray, various motion sensors, and quite a few other spectrum enhancements so that nothing inside or outside the building would go unnoticed. Communication came via special ear buds enhanced with microphones and the scopes transmitted all data back to the Commander for recording as well as review later.

Sighing in frustration of the prospect of another fruitless night of waiting, the Commander considered calling off this recon mission until a hiss of surprise filled the speaker on the conference room desk.

"What?" snarled the Commander immediately.

"Look at the side of the building," murmured the voice and the Commander was about to make a sharp reply until the lighting shifted to combination of night vision and ultra violet.

Even with the sophisticated resolution it was difficult to make out, but he could see it finally, a figure climbing the walls and glass like a gecko, each move was so sure and confident the Commander could hardly credit it.

"How the hell is he doing that?" snarled the Commander, but not expecting a response.

It was hard to tell anything about the figure at the distance the men kept for observation and even with serious magnification, there was little in the way of detail, but the Commander decided the figure was on the small side. Then he thought carefully, *he would have to be or risk falling from those heights as fast as the unknown figure propelled upward.*

There were mutters of surprise when the figure stopped a floor above the object of art in question so that the men's view were on an angle, but it was apparent the figure used something to access a window without cutting the glass or leaving sign of passage.

The Commander breathed a sigh of wonder, so fast, no noise or sign anyone entered that window from the scope trained on it and no alarms, but now what?

With the special ranges on the scopes all the men could easily see the laser beams of security on the floor of the building in question which held the target art and they knew the room contained heat and motion sensors. They waited, watching in fascination as the figure materialized from one of the ventilation covers and the Commander noted the figure had no thermal image, he swore, the person wore some suit that protected against body heat radiation. Nothing they had worked as efficiently as this one, who the hell was this person?

They were all left gaping as beam after beam disappeared, even though some were on different wave lengths yet they could see no visible equipment which allowed the thief to acquire such knowledge of placement of each light source. One of the men tightened focus onto the artifact, sitting on a special display and no doubt pressure sensitive to the items weight, but they could not clearly see what the figure did to offset this security. However, they all seemed to blink and the artifact was gone from the display with a smooth movement which did not agitate motion sensors.

Graceful controlled movements returned the figure to wall with the open vent and beam after beam returned as if their light had never been interrupted and the figure seemed to ooze back through the vent like smoke until everything returned to its original state. In only moments, the figure slipped out of the breached window from the floor above, replaced the glass and began to shimmy down the side of the building back the way he came.

"I can get him," said Stanton suddenly, "Soon as he comes down."

"Move an inch off recon and I want the rest of you men to push him off the building," snapped the Commander, "You spook this guy and we will never get another chance. You saw enough to know this person is ready for anything."

So the men waited though the Commander could partially understand the desire to seize this elusive figure it took nearly a year just to find, but he was cagey, experienced, and had some significant technology they did not possess.

"Nighthawk will follow. The rest of you stay where you are until the target is well away from the building. We can't risk the thief knowing we observed him and we need to find his hideout or who he reports to if we can't." said the Commander.

The Commander heard Stanton grumble bitterly, but he did as ordered and the visual switched to Nighthawk's visor as they watched the figure finally appear on the street out of a nearby alleyway. The Commander could safely say the figure was small as he initially assumed, slightly built yet moved with the expected strength required to climb rough terrain.

More lighting appeared as the figure made its way into a hotel district with astonishing speed slipping from shadow to shadow like a breath of air until the figure circled a rather high priced hotel and then paused, as if uncertain.

"Damn," muttered the Commander, it appeared the figure sensed he was not alone or someone might be watching.

Predictably Nighthawk froze as well, carefully concealed from a chance glance if the figure turned his head and waited while the man hesitated, as if checking the area carefully with some unseen equipment. Apparently he seemed satisfied and continued behind the hotel, but then to their surprise, he promptly began to climb the hotel outer wall like someone might take a walk in a park and moved so quickly, even Nighthawk barely caught him disappearing into an open window on the sixteenth floor.

"Did he see you?" said the Commander worriedly, but Nighthawk's answer was a hand gesture indicating he did not know.

"Tomorrow we visit that room. If we are lucky we might meet our elusive thief," said the Commander, "One of you dress in street clothes and relieve Nighthawk. That building stays under surveillance until we know if this temporary halfway point or a likely residence and if anyone leaves before morning, I want a record of it."

The following day, all the men except Foss and Tank gathered in the conference room to watch the two men acting a segment of law enforcement insisted on seeing the room their quarry entered by window. They listened as Tank officiously demanded to know about the occupant, length of stay, and other pertinent information only to find the room completely empty of items or people to their astonishment.

"Officers, I tried to tell you. This room has been unoccupied for weeks. Even housekeeping has no reason to enter," said the manager nervously.

In keeping with their role, Foss said, "We will need to test for fingerprints and fibers, sir. I'm sorry for the inconvenience."

The manager paled obviously expecting a mess, which would make the room unusable until thoroughly cleaned and nodded with no choice believing the two men represented an establishment of no appeals. Men from the Facility arrived to perform evidence gathering tasks only to report there was no evidence to find to the Commander's disgust which meant the figure probably did sense observation. It would be the first time anyone managed to catch Nighthawk when the man could vanish like smoke and it meant this person was going to a be force to be reckoned with, *if* they caught him.

"Has anyone left the building at all during the night or this morning?" demanded the Commander.

"No sir," said the man outside.

"Hmm, so our quarry could still be inside and we might have spooked him, damn it" snarled the Commander. "Check other rooms for evidence, even though we don't need them. Make it look random so this guy doesn't think he's the target."

They set up a discreet watch noting people leaving, each less likely than the first to leave that day ranging from families, businessmen, vacationers, and even a blind woman to the Commander's irritation. Unnoticed by any of them in the conference room, Nighthawk left quietly as if something on the holographic display caught his eye and it was not until the Commander wanted to speak to him that they realized he vanished.

It was not until two days later than the Commander laid eyes on Nighthawk as he walked into the conference room and he was blistering with questions about the man's unannounced absence.

"Where the hell have you been?" demanded the Commander in front of all the men in the conference room. "You disappear without a word or orders and then silence. Now you walk in here like you've been on vacation!"

The other man looked at the Commander levelly to his discomfort obviously not the least bit cowed or ruffled by the harangue, "I investigated a hunch on one of the people that left that hotel," he said quietly.

"Oh?" said the Commander sarcastically.

"I found it odd that a blind woman would stay at such a prestigious establishment when most people from wealthy backgrounds are able to afford procedures to reverse their disability," he said.

"Bah! They might not be able to fix the injury or it's a birth defect that can't be corrected," said Stanton scornfully and for once the Commander tended to agree with him.

"And?" snapped the Commander.

"Strangely, she reports to a modest job and lives in a modest apartment. So why would she stay in a pricey hotel, especially if she lives in this city?" said Nighthawk to the stunned silence.

"Well? You obviously have a reason for telling us this...," said the Commander impatiently.

"I checked her background and until a few years ago, Jean Easley did not exist. She has no bank account, no public record at all other than she has a social security number and files her taxes. No one seems to know much about her and she keeps to herself. She seems to have a routine and often goes to a park where an older man sits nearby and speaks with her, but he stays silent if anyone is within earshot," said Nighthawk.

"So what are you saying?" sneered Stanton condescendingly, "She's some rest home widow?"

Several coughed laughs sounded about the room, but Nighthawk stared at the Commander, he knew what the man was pointing out and there were unusual inconsistencies. How could a blind woman be important? He could not see a connection worth mentioning, but he would humor the man, he was never wrong when he picked up on these odd occurrences.

"The old man, do you want someone to speak with him about the blind woman?" asked the Commander with forced calm.

"He knows more than he appears or why avoid speaking when others are nearby," stated Nighthawk with certainty.

After a week of observation and though the Commander could see nothing out of the ordinary about the woman or the old man. He had Foss and Tank unobtrusively follow the man until they were certain he always returned to the same building. It was almost derelict from the outside and seemed deserted after careful investigation and research indicated the entire building belonged to a Donal Meany, a retired scientist whose previous employment involved classified experiments.

That information suddenly drew the Commander's attention when he reviewed some of the theft items, which mysteriously disappeared, associated with their elusive quarry; it seemed Nighthawk's suspicions might have merit after all. Now was the woman a go between or an acquaintance of chance?

Under the guise of agents, Foss and Tank approached Donal Meany in direct fashion prepared to question, frighten if necessary, to get answers which would lead them to the elusive thief.

Their knock was answered by the old man himself, "Yes, can I help you?" he said, somewhat warily the Commander noted from his visual.

"We need to ask you some questions about a few thefts in the area," said Tank smoothly. "May we come in please?"

"Do you have a warrant?" said the old man quickly, he was no fool.

"Sir, our agency doesn't concern itself with warrants. This can be a pleasant conversation or we can take you with us until you satisfy our curiosity. The choice is yours," said Tank flatly, even the Commander knew his

man could make a stalwart figure blench from presence
alone as big as he was.

Donal visibly paled, sweat beaded his brow so the
Commander knew the man had something to hide as he
stepped back to allow the two fictitious agents to enter
his door.

Both men began to ask a variety of questions from
Donal's occupation, his acquaintances, hobbies, and income as they wandered about the room opening doors
until one led down a hallway to another door with a security keypad. The old man seemed to shrink in on himself
when Tank demanded entry into the secure room, but he
did what he was told and even the Commander gasped
in wonder at some of the technological marvels contained within an area that occupied several floors of the
building.

"What do you do here? If you're retired, how do you
afford all this state of the art equipment?" said Tank flatly.

Though the man was obviously terrified, he maintained some of his composure, "Most of this has been
donated to me," he said firmly.

"I see," said Tank looming over the man. "By who?"

Straightening up, Donal barely came to Tank's shoulder, "Anonymous donations. I try helping people the
system has forgotten because they don't have money to
pay for fancy cures," he said.

The voice stress monitors indicated the old man told
the truth to an extent, but there was more, someone
would have to know what the old man needed to acquire
in order to donate or it would be useless junk to him.

So the Commander pointed this out through the two
men's ear buds and Tank said, "How do they know what
you need? This is not random equipment I see here."

The old man began to sweat in earnest now and nervously angled his watch with his right hand to check the
time, as if he expected someone to arrive soon before he
answered.

"A nice young woman helps me list items on the Internet and the donations come," said Donal neutrally as he straightened his watch nervously.

"Who is this young woman?" pressed Tank.

"Her name is Jean Easley. I've been helping her to regain some of her sight and she tries to help me in small ways in return," said Donal, but the voice stress went through the roof, he was lying.

They knew of the woman's name so that was not the lie, it had something to do with the help she provided to the old man or maybe it was her disability, but the Commander could not decide which point was the fabrication.

"When will this woman come to see you? We would like to speak to her?" demanded Tank and the old man's heart rate jumped so severely they all thought he might have a coronary in front of them.

"Back off Tank, don't scare the man to death. Take some fingerprints inside that lab of his and then go to the woman's apartment. Get her prints too and we'll run them all through the system and see what we get. Something is damn strange here. This man is too frightened just for helping people," said the Commander urgently.

"I...I don't know when I will see her next. She occasionally meets me in the park, but we have no set meetings," stammered Donal.

"It's no problem. We just wanted to ask her some questions about unusual people approaching her. We can wait until another time," said Tank smoothly and the old man visibly calmed down.

It was not until they arrived at the residence of Jean Easley that the men knew the old man had alerted the woman from the signs of a hurried departure, "Did he make a phone call or send a signal from a computer?" demanded Tank.

"We didn't trace any activity once you left," snarled the Commander, so the woman did know more than Donal Meany revealed.

The two men's visual inputs showed Foss bending down to pick up something off the floor, it looked almost like a shirt button made into a ring and then he began to swear, "Boss, when the old man adjusted his watch, what do you want to bet he sent a scram signal to this ring. Damn, right in front of us and we had no clue. She left it behind to be certain the signal couldn't be traced. Clever bitch," he snarled.

"Surely a blind woman couldn't get far," shouted the Commander in frustration.

"*If* she is blind," said a quiet voice which stunned all of them to silence.

The Commander turned to Nighthawk slowly, "Check those fingerprints. Find out if she's who that man said or she's undercover. Since she ran, there was no time for her to wipe down the apartment," he said furiously.

Once the men returned, they checked every single fingerprint against records worldwide and the old man was who he claimed, one Donal Meany a retired physician immigrant from Ireland. The woman's prints however, presented a dilemma because they possessed no whorls and had been intentionally blurred or burned. This forced them to acquire a DNA sample from a hair found in the apartment, which led to an open murder case listed as unsolved, two people husband and wife, had been killed by unknown intruders on Thanksgiving day four years previously. They were found the following day by their blind niece, Bryn Keane, and after further digging into sealed reports, the Commander saw that evidence recorded suggested the killer had been after the girl.

Sitting back, he pursed his lips uncertain about this new information. It would explain the woman running, living off the grid, and changing her location from the city and state of the murder. He read it had been the uncle who managed to record some of his torture in effort to warn his niece. Grunting in approval of the effort it must have taken the man to think under duress to protect the girl.

They needed more information about the girl, she and Jean Easley obviously had to be the same person, but the police report was carefully blank about pictures or a description of her in their attempt to protect her. It seemed improbable if she had not witnessed the crime or any crime, protective custody or subsidized relocation would be out of the question and that would explain why she was alone now.

"Foss, Tank, I want you to investigate this suburb where this murder took place. Find out everything you can about the niece, where she came from, why she was living with relatives and not her parents, even her shoe size if you have to," snapped the Commander.

Both men were very thorough, but even with their efficiency it took effort to get the data they sought because the police turned obstructive to protect the girl with the unsolved murder still indicating she was sought by the killer. Gradually they pieced together most of the relevant data which led them back to Donal Meany, he finally admitted to some repair to the woman's sight, but could not measure the extent of improvement since he did not formally test her limitations.

Though the Commander could see the voice stress indicate the man told the truth, he had no doubt Donal Meany withheld a great deal he suspected about the woman's eyesight that the rest of them could only guess in their imaginations.

Returning to the background of the woman, they could find nothing out of the ordinary or special talents other than she had been home schooled, had graduated young both in high school and college. Other than the situation surrounding a murderer seeking her years ago, there appeared nothing remarkable about her, but she

was their only connection to their quarry. Some early
martial arts training was insignificant, her education benign in relation to high tech equipment, but she seemed
to be the go between the thief and his acquired wares.

Slamming his hand onto the conference table to express his frustration, "Now she is gone and we have no
way to track her unless she contacts the old man. She'll
wait for him to give the all clear before that ever happens
and he's far too scared to even think about that, damn it,"
The Commander said.

One of the newer men just recently assigned to the
Facility named Crease said, "The old man never told
Tank anything about the virtual notice board, if the old
man even knows about it, and Tank never mentioned
we already knew about the board. They won't know it's
compromised so there is no reason she will stop communicating with the thief or stop him using it as a place to
seek clients."

The Commander stared at the man startled, he had
forgotten about that and there was no reason for the
thief to avoid his cliental even if the woman had been a
go between besides she probably only handled items for
the old man anyway.

"Very good point. This time we will stake out this
guy to capture, but we need to be thorough and careful,
all of you saw what he was like and how quick he was.
There can be no mistakes and he is not to be injured," he
said staring straight at Stanton. "I repeat, he is not to be
injured. Nighthawk will make the capture once we are
set up."

At those orders, Stanton began to sputter, but the
Commander slapped his hand on the desk, "You heard
me and it's not open for discussion. If this guy ends up
with a mark on him, you will find privileges removed, pay
cut, and possibly a stay in the brig. Have I made myself
plain?" he said glaring at the dissenter.

Stanton's face colored to red of fury, but he nodded
tightly and stormed from the room.

Chapter 5

She called herself Shadow. It was a good name and fitting for a thief, she thought pausing to listen for noise in the distance and she had an edge that no one knew about, it kept her under the radar from law enforcement, at least her true identity.

A mask revealed only a pair of light blue eyes while her special bodysuit hid her from infrared sensors and kept sensitive cool rooms from changing temperature that would send alarms screeching, but even that was not her secret. Carefully she ran her sensitive fingers along the wall, a seemingly normal wall until she encountered an almost imperceptible raised area. Smiling, she pressed and searched for another pressing it as she continued in the same vein until there was a barely audible click. Blinking once suddenly displayed a scan of the area behind the wall so Shadow could see traps waiting for her, this was her secret: Her eyes.

Many years ago, her eyes had been like everyone else's until that day when she lost both her parents in the car accident. The tragedy cost her sight in addition to several broken bones.

Her relatives continued martial arts training once she recovered and it had been the only reason she managed not to despair her disability. With continued study she managed to find confidence even unable to see the world through her eyes, using other senses and became unmatched in skill by other students in the dojos.

At fourteen, relatives sought newly developed implants to enable her to see, but the surgery had been only marginally successful by allowing her to see the difference between light and dark, occasionally the shadow of people within a lighted area.

It was not until after college that her life took a disastrous turn and someone murdered her guardians, which still remained an unsolved case. Evidence uncovered led authorities to believe the killer had actually been seeking her and attempted to torture her relatives to reveal her whereabouts. Worried police had no legal grounds to place her into protective custody so they advised her to go into hiding until they caught the murderer, but unfortunately that precaution turned into years, not the months projected.

At twenty four, living under a new name, was when her situation changed beyond what modern medicine could offer someone in her condition. A man approached her one day, she could tell he was older by his voice and began to speak with her about blindness since she still carried a cane to find her way around in the city. His interest worried her at first after a man, who claimed interest in dating her, turned vindictive and tormented her.

But the man, who called himself Donal, explained he developed experimental solutions to disabilities, he offered to examine her situation to see if he could help her achieve a higher quality of life. Wariness warred with hope, Donal introduced her to previous patients he helped and they all spoke highly of him yet it took her over a year to finally summon enough trust to allow him to just examine her.

Tempering her hope with reality, she knew chances were small normal sight would return to her eyes, but continued to allow the extensive tests and she continued to work a basic low paying job. That was when Donal offered her a place to stay even though she told him no payment would be forth coming since she had to refrain from using her education or potentially reveal her location. It took a year of tests and then development before Donal declared he had a resolution for her sight, she greeted his announcement with interested apprehension. Surgery was never an option for pleasure and after explaining the implants, which would send signals to her optic nerve that would be repaired with revolutionary nanites, cybernetic lenses, and special cornea replacements, sounded extensive.

Recovery took a long time because Donal had to constantly fine tune the cybernetic implants behind her ears, but once satisfied, he left her with a remarkable gift of vision, which superseded anything a normal human possessed. After that, she reinvented herself and went disguised by day, her eyes allowing her to seek a profession obtaining items for a price by night. By day, she wore a dark wig with sunglasses and carried her cane to continue the impression that she was blind, blending into the background beneath the notice of other people. Now she was an unsurpassed thief.

With extreme caution, Shadow disabled each supposed failsafe to prevent exactly what she was doing until encountering the final obstacle: A coded fingerprint scanner. Her vision easily displayed the oily fingerprint residue revealing the code pattern of numbers and a careful application of special latex, Shadow lifted a fingerprint. Blinking again revealed the order of the inner mechanism attached to the keypad and she softly typed in the code before rolling her gloved finger onto the latex print, she placed it on the scanner until the flash of light passed that was followed by a click.

Smiling, Shadow opened the door, but disregarded the hard currency, assorted paperwork and even gems as she reached in to retrieve a small object, which resembled a microchip. Quickly she placed it in a protective pouch and began to hide evidence of her presence, it was time to go.

The sound of a lock turning made her freeze, no one should be up here at this hour, Shadow always researched well and the guard was not due for ten minutes so she had no choice, but to flee without hiding her entry into the room. She ran for the window swearing under her breath as the motion sensor detected her movement, *such a rookie error*, she thought repressively, but the room was square and furnishings too austere to offer hiding.

Though not her big secret, Shadow's bodysuit was another marvel with special pads on hands, back, stomach, and feet that would allow her to scale almost anything. She quickly leapt out onto the smooth building surface, but instead of climbing up or down initially, she went sideways. Quickly as she dared, Shadow crawled to a balcony, nearly losing her hold when one foot was not placed securely before moving her other leg and crawled under the balcony. She froze just as a head looked out of the window Shadow vacated, the silhouette turned looking for the intruder and she heard swearing words as a voice announced, "Nothing," that prompted her to action.

The building would be alive with security from basement to roof now cutting off her first line of escape, but no matter, she never had only one way out and always planned for the unexpected.

Crawling around the corner of the building, Shadow grabbed at a round device on her belt with a pointed end and set it against the building, she pressed a button. The pointed end detached with a crunching thunk as it embedded in the crack of the wall and Shadow quickly attached a tough thin cord to it before slamming the

device to her belt to pick up a twin of the pointed instrument with cord already hooked to it. Stretching her arm
out, Shadow pointed the device to the building across
from her and pressed the button again, but this time
noise was much fainter so that ears less sensitive than
hers would never hear it.

To aid her escape, Shadow had secured the remaining end lower than its partner in the nearer wall and she
clipped on the wheel of a special handlebar on the cord
before sliding across to the other building. Climbing
down would not be an option, people would be looking
for individuals and questioning them as suspects or potential witnesses so ascending was her only choice. As if
she were a lizard, Shadow crawled upward which took
some time since the newer building was taller than the
original one she left, inter-dispersed with ledges, until
she finally climbed over the lip of the roof.

She had prepared for such potential problems,
Shadow always did and that is what made her a good
thief, she always had a way out no matter what, and
there was always an alternate plan. Sounds below and
across were faint from this roof and with barely a pause
Shadow strode across for gear she had stowed there
weeks before she breached the first building.

The sound of a rolling stone brought her up short.
No bird had taken flight or she would have heard it, a
startled pigeon made a great deal of noise and this building was too tall to invite such birds to roost. Besides,
Shadow always checked for such potentially revealing
noises long before she began a breach.

Blinking, Shadow scanned the area about her and realized to her discomfort that there were enough obstacles
to hide more people than just her, if they possessed a similar suit, but someone would have to know all her plans
because she could have chosen any number of escape
routes. Her gear was always well hidden and looked as if
it belonged wherever she stowed it. No matter how good
she was at her job Shadow never taunted authorities by

leaving signature items and kept a low profile, let others brag foolishly, anonymity kept her safe. Clients knew her worth and her discretion.

No other sound came to her ears, but all the same, Shadow advanced with more care so that she truly appeared as her namesake just a shadow and with studied speed, she donned a special suit over her current gear. It was then she felt, rather than saw, a figure materialize near her and Shadow instinctively avoided the hand that appeared from nowhere like a striking snake, she knew how to take care of herself.

The figure was a good deal larger than she was, but size did not help the person, Shadow trained with many senseis and combat experts, she could kill if necessary though abhorred such brutality. A flurry of blows exchanged between them until the opponent audibly swore identifying him as a man, not that it would help him as Shadow's open palm connected with his chest and sent him flying backward onto his back.

With the man stunned, Shadow bent to grab her pack to assemble a hang glider until she heard hurried footsteps of more people and knew she would never secure it in time to get off the roof as planned, she ran for the edge of the roof. An arm appeared out of the darkness as a barrier for her to run into so it would knock Shadow down, but she ducked and delivered a crippling blow to the figure's knee, again a man cried out in pain.

Diving and rolling, Shadow came up facing several more shadowy figures, apparently men from the muted swearing, but this time she caught the flash of metal in the dim light, most likely a knife. The man with the knife lunged and found his body sailing over her in a judo move, while the other men closed ranks to overwhelm her. Instead of running, Shadow used her body as if it were a log and launched at the men's legs literally knocking them off their feet, she sprang to her feet, sprinting in the opposite direction to the lip of the roof ripping off the second suit as she ran so she could use the special pads.

The muted sound of rotors close by told Shadow that these people were not the authorities, no one shouted for her to stop nor were there sirens.

In a graceful dive, Shadow prepared to find a hold on a one of the ledges surrounding each floor, possibly one of the flag poles at each corner on the levels if her trajectory was not far off.

"Stop him," screamed a male voice up and behind her and barely registered they assumed she was male.

One hand luckily caught one pole and the other the cord to extend the flags so she used her momentum to swing up like a world class gymnast to make her way to the windows and walls to descend. The rotors sounded like they were on top of the roof briefly and unfortunately she found out that these men were tenacious.

Keeping her descent erratic so that what turned out to be a stealth helicopter could not stay level with her, Shadow continued to search for an alternative way to escape the building. There was a very tall flag pole lower down, so once Shadow reached a low enough ledge, she ran about the narrow edge of the building as if it were a road with the helicopter following and took another dive, this time toward the flagpole. The extra suit would have protected her from snags and abrasions on the metal pole even if it were never intended for such use, but Shadow could not have descended the walls with it so she prepared to feel her suit tear.

As she dropped through the air Shadow felt a sharp pain in her thigh and her body literally jerked back by the same thigh so that she was dangling below the helicopter. Pain lanced through her leg as tension abruptly snapped and stars sparkled in her vision from the jolt, she was able to see she was rising due the building flashing by. She hit the wall then roof hard enough to wind her as the helicopter hovered over the edge of the building roof to set down, and then Shadow saw several figures leap out of the vehicle. Men were advancing menacingly until another figure descended over her waving an arm in warning for the others to back away.

In her daze, Shadow felt down her thigh and found an object that reminded her of the special darts she used to secure the cord between buildings, it expanded after leaving her flesh so it would not pull out. A similar cord she used attached to the end protruding from the back of her thigh and her captors held the cord, she would not escape this particular situation.

The figure that stood over her, as if guarding her, stooped and tossed Shadow over a shoulder as if she was no inconvenience. She felt him pause, sensing vibrations in one of his arms, as if he was manipulating something. Shortly afterwards, the man carried her aboard the helicopter followed by the other shadowy figures. She was able to see enough about the men to confirm her original assessment that these people were not the authorities.

Bending over, the man that carried Shadow set her down gently to her surprise because such consideration seemed peculiar to him rather than the other men as she heard soft snarling comments about her.

"The bastard broke my arm!" and "He blew my knee!" Well, they did not expect her to go quietly, did they? And he? They did think she was a man for some reason.

A soft light appeared as a man reached up to secure it and then angled it to illuminate Shadow in such way she could not see any of the people other than the hands nearest her that contained a white cloth that he was wetting with water.

When the hand with the cloth rose to her face, Shadow swiftly reacted to strike it away, but the man's unoccupied hand was faster and caught her arm in a vise-like grip, though he avoided crushing strength. The men in the shadows laughed and one commented, "He still has some fight in him," she fumed silently at the male reference again.

Her reaction did not deter the man with the cloth however, he retained the hold on Shadow's arm and began to dab at her face leaving bloody marks on the white material, which was when Shadow realized she must have lost her mask in the confrontation. Attempting to retreat from the cloth was unsuccessful since she was against the wall that separated the cabin from the cockpit so she wrenched her arm from the man's grasp and to Shadow's surprise, he released it.

Since there was no luxury left to her other than thinking that is what Shadow did: Think. Somehow these people knew enough about her to find her and they were not authorities, her method of capture told Shadow that much as well as the stealth they used to accomplish it.

Was it one of them and not a guard that sent her fleeing out the window recklessly? The guard had no reason to come to that room early, she made certain of it so it seemed likely that these people forced her to flee so she would take the quickest escape route. That would explain how they managed to be waiting for her, so that meant they knew she was going to be there and she never even revealed a date or time to a client.

These people could not possibly know of her persona in the real world, she had been very careful and to the world at large she was beneath notice since they considered her disabled. No fingerprint could identify her as the thief anywhere, she left none and made certain she had none, *so how did they find me? The client?* More disturbingly she thought, *did they find the notice board and break the encryption, but how could they locate it with myriads of information roaming the Internet.* More likely they pirated the contact information from a careless would be client, but even they would not know exactly how to get to her or find her. All these thoughts disturbed Shadow, it meant these people were more careful, possibly even more resourceful than she was, but then why would they care about her?

A cup held out to Shadow distracted her thoughts, it appeared to contain water and she would need it after this encounter, besides if they wanted her dead she would be already.

Though it was still dark outside, it felt like a long time when Shadow noticed a change in the engine noise, but even with her sight, she could not determine anything of consequence. A slight bump followed by the rotors slowing, indicated the helicopter had landed and the man hovering over her reached out to slide back a door. Men shifted and began to jump out of the open door and she found her guard, for lack of a better term, tossing her over his shoulder before exiting the vehicle as he followed the others.

Eventually her captor negotiated several doorways and dark halls until he entered an elevator surrounded by the other men, a jolt of motion told Shadow they were descending. What she did not expect was how long it took to descend. As she suspected, they ended up significantly below the surface of the building's foundations. When the elevator doors finally did open, the light nearly blinded Shadow, even shielded by the man's body that carried her. She quickly closed her eyes so they could adjust less painfully.

Soon as she could comfortably open her eyes, Shadow could determine little around her from the awkward position the man carried her, but she could see some of his clothing, which appeared to be some sort of bodysuit though the material was different from what she wore. That was about all she managed to notice when doors to the man's left slide open with a hiss and he entered alone, but the smell told her it was some sort of infirmary.

As his arms adjusted, Shadow realized he was preparing to lower her and he did so gently again surprising her as if to avoid jarring her injured leg so that she ended up on a sort of gurney. That was when she caught sight of her captors face or maybe it would have been more accurate to say what covered his face. His suit covered his hair completely just as hers did, but he had partial mask over his mouth and nose that might have been a communications device and over his eyes rested a dark tinted visor that might provide him with some unique input from the surroundings. He seemed to hesitate as he looked at her and then his head swiveled to look at a woman in a white coat, he nodded briefly before leaving the room.

Before Shadow could decide whether she wanted to ask questions or not, she felt a sharp pain in her arm and heard a soft noise followed by the light about her fading into blackness.

With a gasp the woman yelled, "Doc!" and a man in a white coat entered the room at the urgency in his assistant's voice to see an ugly projection sticking from, what he thought was a man's thigh.

"Of all the stupidity," snarled Doc as he stabbed at the COM unit. "Whose brilliant idea was it to use a climbing instrument as a weapon?" he said sarcastically. "You're bloody lucky it missed the femoral artery or you might have delivered a dead person. I thought you intended to work with this person, not introduce him to physical therapy techniques. Even with a repair laser it will take time for the muscle to recover from this abuse."

Without waiting for a response or justification, both Doc and his assistant removed the dart the only way they could by pulling it through the leg to prevent more damage than the leg muscle had already suffered.

After the projectile was out of the way, both of them painstakingly removed the suit to check for additional injuries hoping that grim wound was the only one and there were no more grisly surprises. When the assistant removed the hood, she gasped again and Doc looked at long golden red hair spilling onto the gurney in amazement, which prompted him to check other areas of the prone body to discover that his patient was indeed female. Once all injuries of their patient had been treated, Doc returned to the COM pointedly announcing they had a female guest and would need to plan accordingly. Given the woman's lack of cooperation arriving at the Facility, Doc had his assistant attach restraints to their patient and at the Commander's request began a thorough physical until he decided what to do with her.

Men filed into a high tech conference room where several men waited in plain navy blue uniforms, one of the men glanced up at the newcomers as if counting and his eyebrows rose indicating the number did not match his expectation until he saw an individual coming down the hall through the open door. The other men sat down sharply giving full attention to the men in uniform, but silence continued until the last figure entered the room and the doors closed with a hiss. In spite of his late entry, the last man sat with no apparent haste, removing his mouthpiece to place in a pouch on his suit before giving attention to the men in uniform.

At a glance from the uniformed man in the center, the man on his right began to type and a holographic display appeared in the center of the table showing a side of a building that the helicopter had obviously recorded.

They all watched as a figure left a window and crawled like a lizard to a slightly lower balcony, remain stationary until unobserved, and continue to crawl around the building as well as setup the corded escaped route. The night vision camera following the figure up the next building, rising as it rose in height until it crawled over the lip of the roof and then the ensuing conflict that ultimately ended in capture of the elusive figure.

"I warned you he was not to be injured. Would someone like to explain why that happened?" said the Commander flatly gesturing at the dart protruding from the leg.

One of the men cleared his throat, "Commander, you could easily see that he attempted to dive off the building, so it was the only way to stop him. He…injured several men, so my immediate force effectiveness was reduced."

"I told you to let Nighthawk make the capture. All of you were a backup team for him, not the other way around which is what happened. I doubt he would have made it off the roof if you held your positions," said the Commander sardonically as he gestured at the figure warding the men away from the injured man on the roof.

Stanton glanced sourly at the latecomer, but he remained aloof and silent. "He did not seem to take the opportunity when it arrived, sir. The man reached for his gear and if he managed to assemble it, only the chopper would have been able to catch him. If he managed to get to that flagpole we would have lost him after all the trouble it took to set up," he said stiffly.

"I did not give you enough information to think! You have done this before Stanton and I warned you to back off unless given specific orders. I gave you no leeway to alter your orders and now the man's injuries have set us back. That kind of muscle damage will take time to heal even with our medical care. In case you think I forgot, your privileges are revoked and pay cut in force. I haven't decided if time in the brig is sufficient yet," said the Commander, his eyes narrowing dangerously.

Faced flushed with anger and embarrassment. The man called Stanton knew better than to say another word, he knew he underestimated the man because of his lack of size and the bruises on his body offered in testament to that fact.

"Make certain your men get treatment," the Commander said finally without looking up from the display on the table.

All the men rose with the exception of Nighthawk and Stanton gave him a glare, but he seemed oblivious to the regard before following the others from the conference room.

When the door slid shut again, the Commander looked up at Nighthawk, "I gather you allowed the man to fight since Stanton exceeded his orders," he said.

"I did," said the soft voice of Nighthawk, "Some lessons need reinforcement though Stanton must have hidden the scale dart before boarding the helicopter. I managed to defect it or we might have had to remove it from our guest's back."

"What a fool! They were all warned not to use lethal force for any reason if you somehow failed. I am beginning to question Stanton's mental stability for these missions. The man's injury will make it more difficult to gain his cooperation even if you managed to salvage the situation. At least the wound does not present any life threatening issues from the report the doctor sent," glancing down at his digital pad. "We will continue to finalize the training area for now and maybe begin with some of the men while we wait," said the Commander with a sigh.

Abruptly the COM blared with Nighthawk still in the room, but since it was from the infirmary, the Commander indicated for the man to stay and hear what Doc had to say about the man's injuries.

"You led me to believe I would be treating a man, Commander or were you not aware that our guest is a woman?" said Doc's voice heavy with sarcasm.

All the Commander could do was stare at the COM looking at Doc's face before glancing at Nighthawk with incredulity, but the other man's expression went through various subtle changes though surprise was not one of them.

"We didn't know, Doc," said the Commander lamely.

"I suggest you prepare for the fact and arrange suitable accommodation. I will forward her statistics for clothing," said Doc dryly.

Clearing his throat, the Commander said, "Please run a comprehensive physical on her. Anything you can think of, so there are no more surprises, implant a GPS tag and make certain she is restrained," and he broke the connection.

Looking at Nighthawk, "You suspected," said the Commander.

"Yes, but I couldn't confirm it," said Nighthawk.

"It won't take long to see if it's the one we've been looking for," said the Commander.

After nodding, Nighthawk stood and returned to the infirmary. The woman's surgery completed, she now wore a medical gown instead of the bodysuit, her reddish golden hair spilling over the side of the gurney, as she lay unconscious. His eyes noted the restraints on her wrists and ankles; the medical personnel did not have extensive facilities to restrain the woman while they tested her so they performed the physical under anesthesia. Those procedures would take time so he returned to his quarters to await further developments.

Dreams plagued Shadow ranging from her aunt and uncle's murders, to running from some unknown beast, and vague recalls of an old nemesis named Vander. The final subject of her restless recalls brought her to a semi-conscious state though still confused about her location and the unusual scents assailing her nose.

Sounds came next; she could hear soft movements nearby and the murmur of voices discussing medical jargon so next she opened her eyes to careful slits to avoid alerting anyone to her return to consciousness. Blurriness clouded Shadow's vision and she had to blink several times until her sight cleared though the sounds nearby remained consistent which told her no one noticed her alertness yet. With careful judicious movement, Shadow found that her arms and legs had restraints while she focused on the odors, once identified told her that she was still in the medical area of this unknown place. Pressing her awareness further, she found pain in her body minimal and no unusual soreness in her leg telling her that the dart no longer remained in her body, but she moved her head slightly so she could glance down to be certain. That was when she noticed her restraints and would have laughed had she dared: Buckled leather? After all the effort to capture her and they use a simplistic form a restraint, they underestimated her if that was the case.

Bending her knees ever so slightly, Shadow inched her torso down to allow wrist restraints to slide up away from the wrist joints so that she could maneuver her hand toward the buckles. Only her fingertips touched, but it was enough to tease the buckle loose on one arm and then swiftly undid the remaining arm and ankles while the medical personnel had their backs to her.

Just as she managed to slip off the gurney, the woman in the lab coat turned and gasped which incited the man with her to turn in surprise.

"Wait!" said the woman holding out a protesting arm, "Your leg wound may be mended, but the muscle damage will take time to heal before you use it extensively."

Shadow did not deign to comment and moved back toward the doors until the man attempted to advance so she grabbed a sharp looking instrument to add a threat so he would keep his distance. The doors behind her opened, but before Shadow could back out a hand grabbed her wrist from behind and pressed the tendon painfully against bone forcing her to drop the instrument so she sent her free elbow back only to find empty air. The man had side stepped the blow, but with barely a pause, shadow kicked her injured leg high until it connected against the man behind her eliciting a grunt when it impacted. Then she spun under his arm and freed her arm with a twist, immediately followed by blows that rarely connected; he was incredibly fast, but at last she found an opening and flung her entire weight in a flat-handed blow to his chest that sent him stumbling backward.

With a bound, Shadow leapt for the doors only to feel a powerful arm circle her waist and pulled her off her feet. She used elbows and the heels of her feet to attempt damage on her captor until she saw the man in the lab coat rush forward. One powerful kick sent the man in the lab shooting back into equipment with a crash knowing he planned to sedate her.

Since blows did not loosen the hold of her captor, Shadow swung her legs up to clasp the man's head and neck in crushing grip between her knees giving him no option, but to release her waist or choke to death. Soon as her waist was free, Shadow flipped her torso forward so she could secure a handhold and flipped the man to the floor on his side, again giving him no choice or she would have broken his neck.

She sprang to her feet only to feel a vise-like grip seize the ankle of her injured leg so Shadow spun around, planted the captured leg preparing to break the man's arm, if necessary, to free the leg, but the woman's words about the muscle damage came home. The leg began to tremble soon as she placed her entire weight on it, her leg instantly gave out sending her to the floor which gave the quick man more than enough time toss her over his shoulder.

Instead of returning her to the gurney, the man carried her from the medical facility and Shadow sought pressure points on his back, which quickly resulted in a stinging smack on her backside. It was then she realized that except for the hospital gown, she was absolutely naked to her supreme disgust and the prolonged stinging on her bottom brought Shadow to her senses.

Something told her this was the same man that carried her from the helicopter, who knew how long ago now, and that he was more than capable of preventing her escape. It did not improve her temper to know she was probably entertaining quite a few people bare assed to the world either.

A few minutes later the man slowed and Shadow heard the sound of another door sliding open that led into a room where her captor lowered her to the ground. She glared up at the man tensing for another confrontation when he raised a hand holding up a finger wagging back and forth as if she were a naughty child. Her expression changed to indignant and a small smile appeared on his well-shaped lips, which was when she realized he had removed the device covering the lower portion of his face, before backing out the room.

In the conference room the Commander and his two assistants watched the confrontation with some amusement as Nighthawk delivered the woman to a room with her dignity barely intact. She was a quick one and more skilled than anyone expected. Strong enough to send Nighthawk reeling several times even dazed from sedation partially recovered from her injuries.

The Commander sat to review her medical data Doc forwarded attempting to correlate past information about a woman known as Bryn Keane to this woman that was now their guest. The fingerprints were inconclusive and DNA from a childhood surgery matched, but nothing in her records indicated anything relating to special skills witnessed or her methods of defense from generic martial arts. Too many of her early years she had been legitimately blind.

Soon as he finished his review of the data, the Commander called the men together directing Nighthawk to bring their guest to the conference room once she had suitable attire.

Back in the room, Shadow fumed silently suspecting she was under constant surveillance and left with nothing to do for entertainment, but sit, stand, or pace in the small area. A brief investigation of the spartan room yielded bare necessities like a hygiene unit, bed, and several empty recesses that could serve as storage had she possessed anything, but a hospital gown. The door she ignored since it was secured and probably guarded without checking.

She was beginning to wonder how long they intended to leave her in this room with no explanation why they brought her to this place when the door slid open admitting the same man that brought her here. Uttering no comment, he set folded clothing beside her and set a pair of soft shoes on top before turning his back to allow her to change though it annoyed her that he did not step out of the room, not that it probably made any difference if the place was monitored. In that case, she did not know why he bothered to turn his back at all, she thought caustically.

The gown was the only thing that offered any guaranteed privacy so Shadow used that to her advantage to don undergarments and pants leaving her with only a shirt she quickly slid over her head to prevent any extended display of her body. Everything fit perfectly so someone obviously took the time to arrange for her clothing even if the notion left her feeling violated.

At the cessation of her movements, another man outside the room handed her guard something and he in turn gave her a pouch containing an assortment of toiletries. At this semi-civilized treatment, Shadow moved to the hygiene unit to wash her face, brush her hair and teeth and then surprisingly the man stepped out into the hall to offer more privacy. She took that opportunity to empty her very full bladder wondering at the unexpected courtesy and noted he did not step back inside until she began to wash her hands.

Once she appeared ready, he stepped into the hall and offered a polite gesture for Shadow to leave the room; he blocked a portion of the hall so she knew he intended her to turn right out of the room. It was uncomfortable with the man following her and Shadow did not know how he expected her to have an idea where to go. As she proceed down the hall, men stood at various points leaving only one route open to her which ended at a door a short while later.

When the door opened, Shadow hesitated because the room seemed quite full of people, but instead of a rude prod from behind, her guard gently laid fingers on her shoulder, almost in reassurance. Two strides took her into the room and her guard actually pulled out a chair for her, Shadow nearly made a tart comment, but clamped her mouth shut before she sat, very aware her guard stood directly behind her chair.

Most of the men about the table wore a similar black bodysuit as her guard except for three men in plain navy blue uniforms, every set of eyes seemed to assess her and Shadow felt very exposed, even vulnerable. She crossed her arms defensively and gentle fingers touched her shoulder again as if in reassurance.

The men all glanced at the fierce blue eyed woman of medium height noting her lustrous reddish gold colored hair though unlike so many other people with such coloring, she did not have an abundance of freckles, but rather smoothly tanned skin.

"Welcome," said one of the men in uniform. "Please forgive the unorthodox retrieval, but you are a difficult woman to find."

She nearly laughed out-loud at the term 'retrieval' since the entire experience could be more accurately described as seizure, but Shadow remained silent.

"We have a proposition for you," said the center most man in uniform. "We would like you to join our team."

Before the man said anymore, a scowling man to her right burst out, "That is what gave us so much trouble? Are you even certain this is the same person? She doesn't look intelligent enough to find her way out of a paper bag," was his scathing diatribe.

Shadow stiffened at the insult and this time a gentle hand clasped her shoulder.

"It must be the paper bag you remain lost in Stanton because if I recall she flattened your entire team with little effort," said the man in the middle dangerously.

At that comment, Shadow relaxed and the hand on her shoulder disappeared, but from her peripheral vision she saw the rude man's face suffice with blood. Suddenly a holographic display materialized in front of her nose and it took great effort to suppress her embarrassment when the scene in the infirmary played out the confrontation with her guard.

"I think that explains a few things," drawled the Commander, as if he was enjoying the effect the recording had on the men in the room.

With a complete change of tack, "You see Commander? We had no option, but to injure her," snarled Stanton watching the monitors along with several other men who chuckled at the scene not Stanton's comment.

"It may have escaped your notice Stanton, but Nighthawk never once injured the woman and was able to contain her. You will not air this subject again to justify disregarding your orders," snapped the Commander and the other men wisely sobered.

The Commander turned toward Bryn after a last repressive glance at Stanton, "I apologize for the injury you received. I assure you that was unintentional and due to a disregard in orders," he said again and she glanced at the rude man to see his knuckles whiten as he clenched his fist.

When she did not comment, he continued, "Your skills would increase the efficiency of our specialized team and provide quite a challenge for you. Our resources are essentially unlimited and additional training superb."

"We have found in our research that you are the best at your work to surface in recorded history and unusually discreet unlike most of your, shall we say, peers. General authorities can only guess at your existence so you may wonder how we discovered you," he said shrewdly.

Still Shadow said nothing, but she suspected what was coming.

"As you may have already surmised, it was via your cliental we discovered you." At her raised eyebrow indicating her disbelief he added, "Oh not that they divulged who you were or how to find you. You are far too careful for that, but by the items that people purchased after, shall we say, making known the supreme difficulty obtaining these certain items."

Damn, she thought, *they found the board and penetrated the encryption which means one of the would-be clients did get careless.*

"We only had to wait for some similar item to circulate before we could attempt contact even if we did not know the date or time you might move to obtain it. Of course we had to force you into an error so we could follow you and I must say that you are amazingly resourceful."

Silence lengthened and Shadow knew they expected her input at this point, "I work alone," she said quietly and felt a single finger touch her neck as if in reprimand.

"Think of what you could accomplish with our resources and support," said the man smoothly.

"I don't need to prove myself to anyone," she said flatly and the hand gripped her shoulder firmly this time.

"We know that or it wouldn't have taken so long to locate you. What we offer you is more than stealing, you would serve a greater good and have all the challenges you could desire," he said, but his nostrils flared with impatience.

"And how often will this result in my body pierced with darts?"

At that comment she felt a pinch on the softer area in back of her arm and realized she did sound petulant.

"As I said earlier, that was not intentional," said the man narrowly.

Expressionlessly Shadow asked, "How long do I live if I refuse?"

That comment resulted in a very painful grip on her shoulder and she felt some shame that she lowered her standard to the offensiveness of the man to her right. Twisting her neck and rolling her shoulder incited her guard to release his painful hold though she gave no other sign of discomfort, did they really think it was that easy to cow her?

"Work with us for one mission and see if it measures up to your standards and then we can speak again of alternatives," said the man smoothly.

Though it was left unsaid, she knew they had the microchip and all they would need to do is deliver her to the authorities with the item on her person; it would be an instant admission of guilt. No one hinted the term, but blackmail hung in the air like smoke so Shadow had little choice.

"Let me think about it," she said just as smoothly.

"Why not tour the Facility while you think?" countered the man, which meant think all you want as long as we get an answer within the next hour.

Her guard extended his hand politely and Shadow nearly knocked it away in bad temper before reminding herself not to act like a cretin, she nodded acknowledgement of the aid, but ignored the offer as she stood.

Leaving the other men behind, this time her guard walked to the side as they followed the man in uniform listening to him explaining areas they encountered, which Shadow found interesting in spite of her irritation with captivity. Actually she began to wonder how she could offer anything to such a facility as more technological wonders appeared in each new area.

"My skills are pale compared to all of this equipment you possess. I cannot supersede anything here," she said candidly.

"You think so?" said the man unexpectedly. "Jean Easley aka Bryn Keane, you should be blind, but are not and can scale a building like a human fly. You say you have no comparable skills?"

She stiffened at the use of her given name, no one, not ever had known to associate that name with her away from the regular streets of the city, especially since she began living off the grid. A large hand on her upper arm swiftly followed her reaction, but the vise-like hold was surprisingly gentle and she felt the thumb move in a soothing manner.

"No one knows that name! How did you find out?" she said in a taught voice.

"When we could find no viable fingerprints, we resorted to a DNA search and of course, your sight that gave us the clue," said the man to Bryn's dismay. "You should be completely blind, but are not. The cybernetic implants behind your ears can only be the work of a gifted scientist, beyond any scientist I've ever seen."

The attempt to wrench her arm free met with instant resistance, "Did you harm him? He has done nothing, but good for people," she said fiercely.

There was no way Donal told them her true name, he knew what she was hiding from and the old man would protect her, but then how? There were no fingerprints, Bryn made certain of that and then the man's words sunk in: DNA! Her original implants when Bryn was fourteen, the hospital had checked for genetic predisposition for rejection of the surgical procedure and materials. That meant they searched her apartment and Bryn had no time to clean it before Donal sent the scram signal.

"Of course we didn't harm him," waving a hand impatiently, "I cannot deny he might have been frightened when questioned, but no one injured him or caused damage to his work. Those implants are quite a marvel, but we believe they provide more than just normal vision in spite of his modest claims. As matter of fact, I suspect from the data of your physical, your eyes give you unparalleled input which place your vision in a category all its own. Coupled with what we believe is also extraordinary hearing, sense of smell and touch which make you quite a unique individual," said the man, albeit somewhat warily after the way she reacted.

She knew he was fishing for information now, Donal would never reveal the extent of her sight he tested so far and he kept no physical or digital records, he stored that information in his head, but it was too close to the truth for comfort.

Twisting of her arm to shake the hold of her guard was unsuccessful and he only released it once he felt she sufficiently calmed as they proceeded on the tour. Her anger had to be monitored or her guard would only restrict her movements and if she were to believe the man in charge, Donal was never harmed; she would never forgive anyone for injuring the kind man.

During the rest of the tour, Bryn felt her injured leg stiffening and her guard adjusted to support her, but she waved him away. "Just give me something as a support, I will managed on my own," she said impatiently.

"We can't do that in case you plan to use it to dent a few heads," said the Commander acidly.

"I don't plan to dent any heads. It would achieve nothing at this point," she said tightly.

The Commander glanced at her guard before nodding to another man and he returned offering her an old fashioned wooden cane, she nodded her thanks before accepting it then continued to follow the uniformed man on the tour.

Once the tour reached its conclusion, the man turned to her and said, "What do you think?"

"I don't need money and I already serve a greater good," said Bryn coldly.

"If by that you are referring to Donal Meany, you can hardly aid him if we have you here," said the Commander in a brittle voice.

She did not respond and held her chin up implacably, Bryn was not about to let anyone bully her into a life not of her own choosing even if they basically were giving her no choice. There was only so much they could force out of her and some things they could never force her to do, they would see that very quickly.

"We would prefer you choose to agree, but if that is the only response you will give us then you will have a

GPS device implanted until we deem you trustworthy," said the man with no patience at all.

She bristled at those words feeling as if the man ordered her to be a slave and for the first time she sensed her guard reacted in a similar fashion, which Bryn did not understand. If they wanted a fight, she would give it to them and Bryn would make certain she won.

A different man from her guard gestured for Bryn to follow him and she turned stiffly, ignoring the Commander fuming at her back, her shoulders squared with determination.

"Stubborn woman," snarled the Commander. "What?" he said when he caught Nighthawk watching him.

"Threatening her is not the way to gain her cooperation. The way she arrived did not incite trust," said Nighthawk.

"What would you have done then?" snapped the Commander.

"Expose her to training. Give her things to do, not use our knowledge of her secrets to make her feel vulnerable," said Nighthawk.

"Fine! Since you seem to have so much insight then she is your responsibility. I have no time to coddle difficult women," said the Commander as he stalked away in the opposite direction.

Once in her room, Bryn sat to relieve her leg that ached so badly now she knew she would never be able to sleep and monitors or not, she decided to shower hoping the water might help soothe the muscle enough for rest. On the heels of that thought, she hesitated knowing she had no towels to dry with which meant she would have to dress wet until the increasing discomfort of her leg outweighed the thought of wet clothing.

Soothing sounds of the water falling on her body hid the noise of the door opening again so that when Bryn left the shower, she started in surprise to see towels resting in the recess outside the hygiene unit. Gratefully she toweled dry before donning the clothing again, relieved the shower had helped the pain in her leg somewhat.

Again the door opened and her original guard stood there, still wearing the visor or goggles he had when she first saw him so she decided they must provide a variety of virtual input that made them more than they seemed. He gestured for Bryn to follow him, but she sat down and crossed her arms in silent refusal, he hesitated a few moments before backing out of the room letting the door shut.

Moments later the man returned again, but this time with a tray that wafted scents of food into the room which he set to one side without comment and left. Her stomach grumbled loudly, but this one thing they could not force her to do and Bryn ignored the food as if it were poison.

Since her room had no time device and anything she owned had been removed, Bryn could only gauge time by the arrival of meals, which she left uneaten until she estimated about a week had passed. Apparently the Commander did not accept this form of rebellion and arrived at her room demanding a different man from her normal guard to pull her physically from the room to which Bryn was more than happy to retaliate.

What she did not expect was the side effects of forgoing sustenance and immediately collapsed unconscious to the floor while the men watched thinking it some form of a ruse initially until she failed to react to applied pain.

A man carried Bryn to the infirmary and Doc soon had choice words for the Commander about the woman's condition, unimpressed by protestations of ignorance and wanting to know why this was the first time he has seen her since it happened.

Snarling, the Commander demanded to see Nighthawk. "Why in hell didn't you tell me she refused to eat?" he said as Nighthawk walked through the door.

"You said she was my responsibility. Trust isn't gained overnight and she has had no reason to trust us or our motives. You never told me you intended to force her out of that room," he said flatly.

"Why didn't you make her eat?" snapped the Commander unreasonably.

One eyebrow rose on Nighthawk's otherwise impassive face, "How do you propose I do that?"

"Then we find another way to force her," growled the Commander.

"That would not be wise," said Nighthawk.

While Doc nourished the woman intravenously in the infirmary, the Commander sought some means of coercing the woman; she had no ties or family to use as leverage until he recalled her quick concern over Donal Meany. It was Nighthawk who spoke harshly against this course of action, but instead he recommended offering to aid the older man in return for the woman's aid as a show of good faith.

"She is far too intelligent to threaten like that and you might find she decides to die rather than cause that man any harm," warned Nighthawk.

They had not considered that aspect of her personality, Doc said she had the traits psychologically and with no family, she could well make such a dire choice to get free of them as well as protect the older man. As much as he hated to give away any control, the Commander suspected Nighthawk had a better measure of this woman than anyone else in the Facility and if she turned rogue on them during a mission, it could be fatal.

When Doc said the woman recovered sufficiently, the Commander had Nighthawk bring Bryn to the conference room for a private meeting because he was not about to lose face in front of the men or be seen negotiating terms.

As soon as she entered the room, the Commander was taken aback slightly at the gauntness reflected in her face in just over a week and glanced at Nighthawk following her to see he was not particularly happy about her condition either. When he gestured the woman to take a seat, she did so stiffly, her entire posture oozing wariness and fierceness of a caged animal.

"I have a revised proposal for you," said the Commander smoothly, "After considering your previous arguments."

Her face paled and the Commander wondered if the woman felt she had revealed more information inadvertently than she cared to admit.

"Since you apparently provided some manner of aid to one Donal Meany, I offer this: While you aid us, we will provide support up to, but not exceeding, what you usually granted him. This is to include monetary as well as equipment needs per his specifications, no interference in his day-to-day affairs and autonomy from this Facility," said the Commander, ticking off the points on his fingers.

Some subtle change must have occurred in the woman because he saw Nighthawk tense behind her, but she remained seated giving no obvious sign the Commander could see as he watched the woman's reactions. He waited as she considered the angles of the proposal.

Bryn was quite prepared to continue any form of resistance prior to entering this room, even if it meant starving to death until the Commander made his proposal to an oddly empty room. That was when she knew they had her and she hated him for it. Donal was her weak point, which she had revealed during her supposed tour of the Facility. They had to know they had her so why this farce of a proposal? Unsaid threat hung in the air regarding the kind old man, he had become like family to her and had tried to protect her from discovery, but these men still managed to corner her. Well she was not going to make it easy on them by quickly capitulating, admitting her weak spot or that she made Donal vulnerable and on the heels of those thoughts, for the barest instant,

Bryn considered physically retaliating. Pointless effort, she decided, especially with the man behind her.

"Do you have that in writing?" she finally said to avoid showing any weakness.

At the flash of annoyance on the Commander's face, Bryn accorded herself a point in the standoff, albeit a minor point, when the man thrust his digital tablet across the table for her to read. Continuing the charade, Bryn read everything carefully and made a show of considering it, but knowing she truly had no choice, she felt every fiber of her being struggling to rebel against any stricture yet knew she could not push these men any further.

Passing the digital tablet back to the Commander, Bryn nodded tightly and omitted the fact she basically had no choice with the bitter realization these men owned her until they said otherwise.

"Until your leg heals sufficiently you might as well return to your quarters. Any future training will be physically intense and your body must work at one hundred percent," he said in dismissal.

Her guard stepped into her line of sight and gestured courteously for Bryn to follow him so she complied while struggling to hide a sense of defeat regarding her future tenure in this place. The previously injured leg began to stiffen before Bryn realized her guard was leading her down several different halls she did not associate with her previous quarter's and then he stopped at a new door. At their approach, the door opened revealing a set of quarter's, which bore signs of established residency and her guard courteously gestured her to precede him inside.

Instantly it became apparent this set of quarters contained more square footage than the room originally assigned to her and the fact her guard followed her inside, Bryn surmised quickly that these rooms belonged to him. With silent gestures he indicated another room with a bed and an extensive hygiene unit opening off the sleeping area.

Though she watched him warily, he seemed oblivious to Bryn's regard as he made one final stop to indicate a panel that provided catering. Unhurriedly, he demonstrated use of the panel before moving in direction of the second room and the hygiene facilities so she deduced he meant for her to obtain her own sustenance.

Starving had not achieved its desired effect and Bryn was ravenous as she scrolled through the database selecting various dishes while her stomach rumbled at the thought of finally eating. Pressing the interface for several items, Bryn stood back wondering where the actual meal was available when the portion of the wall under the electronic pad slid upward silently to reveal a variety of steaming dishes. The odors made Bryn' mouth water in anticipation so that she had to exercise a great deal of self-control to eat slowly so she would not get sick.

As the last morsel entered her mouth, Bryn nearly choked in surprise when the man re-entered the room, but instead of a bodysuit, he wore similar comfortable clothing to her own, while his uncovered head sported slightly wavy medium length dark blond hair. For some reason Bryn had not expected such an attractive appearance in this man with his prominent cheekbones and square jaw, he no longer wore the visor, which revealed piercing grey eyes filled with intelligence that immediately made her feel uncomfortable.

His body was as well muscled as the bodysuit had reflected and his skin surprisingly tanned so that she wondered if it was a natural hue or artificially induced by exposure to certain lights. When he walked toward the catering unit, Bryn was uncertain where to place the empty dishes until he retrieved them to deposit in a different area, which opened when he pressed the interface. She quickly vacated the table to make room for him.

Unwilling to sleep until she knew what this man was going to do, Bryn carefully propped up her leg to relieve as much pain and swelling as possible which she aggravated by her recent activity. The man must have noticed because suddenly he was standing next to her, which made Bryn jump in surprise, holding a small cup and pointing to her leg. Warily she took the cup and sniffed the contents before gulping it quickly, he held out his hand for the cup before returning to the table. It was not long before the pain mercifully faded.

Soon as the man finished eating, he gestured for Bryn to take the room with the bed and she shook her head violently retreating to the sofa type sectional since it was obviously his quarters, he was also bigger which made the smaller area more practical for her. Well that at least was one reason Bryn admitted to herself and the other was she did not quite trust this man or the fact these were his personal quarters.

A sigh escaped his lips, but he was not looking at her and he strode from the room only to return with a pillow and blanket, which he set on the sofa obviously unwilling to argue with her before he left her alone.

Sleep was in short supply, Bryn kept starting awake plagued with dreams of someone sneaking up on her in the dark and expected to see a dark figure looming over her each time she opened her eyes so that by morning, she was thoroughly exhausted.

Matters did not improve when she woke to find the man squatting next to the sofa fully dressed in his bodysuit with visor in place, it smacked of Bryn's dreams so closely that she lurched backward on the sofa. Her sudden momentum only stopped when Bryn's head collided against the nearest wall and the man held up a placating hand, wisely not changing his position to give her time to assimilate the situation. She froze breathing heavily and her heart hammering a hundred miles an hour realizing there was nowhere to run, Bryn managed to get control of her reaction even though she continued to watch the man warily.

Once she relaxed sufficiently, the man stood slowly and gestured in the direction of the table which Bryn took as encouragement to get something to eat, she noted with some annoyance, a selection of food waiting for her. Arrogant of him to assume what she might choose to eat, she sniffed.

Rather than waste the food she moved to the table slightly limping due to her stiff thigh even though Bryn did not want to admit it was a sensible selection of items or offer a charitable thought toward the man's initiative. It was unnerving knowing the man watched her, though her surreptitious observation said he was not staring at her, but she knew he was monitoring her, *probably every morsel I place in my mouth*, Bryn thought sourly. He must have deemed her finished eating because he approached her with a stack of fresh clothing and politely gestured toward the hygiene facilities, she nodded briefly before accepting the garments.

After attending to her appearance and changing her clothing, Bryn found the man waiting patiently for her in the outer room, he held out his hand as if to assist her which told her that he intended to take her somewhere. Instead, Bryn waved away his assistance wondering if the Commander had some protocol for her to follow or if her guard would determine her activities. She did not have to think hard to know this man had been assigned as her caretaker, Bryn found that unusual, but then she had only seen one other woman since she arrived.

Upon sour reflection, she decided they did not trust her to be alone and no doubt her guard would never be far away, Bryn wondered for whose benefit this surveillance would serve. She considered the possibility of sneaking out of this facility, but that would not help Donal and Bryn knew these men could get to him before she could warn the older man, besides he was not up to a life on the run. They were counting on her possessing an innate sense of responsibility to the scientist and she hated they were correct in that assessment, Bryn wondered if any of these men ever cared about anyone the way they easily used Donal for leverage.

Her thoughts came to an abrupt halt when Bryn near-ly walked into the back of her guard as he paused before a door with a keypad on it, she did not bother to check the code because she did not feel there was anything to gain accessing this room on her own. The door opened and her guard stepped to one side to allow Bryn to en-ter first, she twisted her lips sardonically at the courtesy since she suspected there would be no choice regarding her activities.

An amazing amount of technology filled the room, a good deal of it Bryn had never seen before and most of the machines defied her ability to recognize any pertinent application even if she had shrewd basic idea. This room became the bane of her first days spent in the Facility while her guard painstakingly demonstrated uses of each machine, provided additional documentation for her to read and ultimately tested her competence. How he managed to accomplish all that without uttering a word to her over the months and using gestures, Bryn had no idea, but it relieved her of the obligation of polite conver-sation within his quarters.

It was not until at least a month following this rou-tine that Bryn suspected her lack of physical activity might be prescribed by medical when a day began with a visit to the infirmary to check the healing progress of her leg muscle. Medical staff seemed unwilling to approach her and Bryn sniffed irritably at their expressions, they acted like she was some wild animal though the fairer portion of her mind knew they had reason after their first encounter with her.

The same woman was on duty that Bryn remembered from her first visit, she approached hesitantly, "Please remove your pants. We need to use an ultrasound to de-termine if deeper healing has occurred in the muscle," she said.

Bryn complied passively for the painless process observing the infirmary noting the man in the lab coat stayed well away from the examination until the mixture of warm and cold of the ultrasound wand on the gel refocused her attention on the procedure. A monitor displayed the woman's search though Bryn could not determine what she was looking for while watching mass of rolling grey on the monitor, but evidently in meant something to the woman.

"It looks like everything is completely healed. Carefully begin to exercise and stretch the muscle, but go slowly to prevent tears in the area. Sometimes massaging the area can aid loosening the tissue and increase the blood flow without the significant stress of exercise. It won't take long to regain normal use of your leg. In a few days we'll send a schedule of physical therapy," said the woman calmly.

Bryn nodded in gratitude before sliding off the table to pull her outer pants back on and noted her guard kept his back turned for the entire procedure, why he continued this respectful behavior eluded her. His manners did not seem to be a charade even if Bryn did not trust his motives, but there had been no wavering in his respect for her privacy.

In his private office, Kolski, the Commander of the Drury Facility reviewed personnel files on his dedicated server when his secure encrypted COM line bleeped an incoming transmission and he glanced up at it frowning at the originating code. A feeling of uneasiness jarred him, that code never meant a good thing and Kolski wondered what had incited this contact as he pressed the button to receive the call.

"Yes?" he said neutrally since there was no reason to stand on ceremony.

"You finally secured the thief?" said a toneless voice that sounded neither male nor female.

"We think so…" said Kolski temporizing.

"You think? You have doubts?" demanded the toneless voice.

"We didn't know we retrieved a woman until return to the Facility. There is speculation she may not have been working alone," said Kolski even though he knew the woman was alone.

What the Commander would like to know is how these people knew of the retrieval when he had not submitted a report and suspected he had a mole planted in his personnel, but if so, they were well camouflaged in the personnel records. That was to be expected.

"A woman? Did she have any special technology to perform the security breaches?" inquired the voice.

"None that we found. So far she has not divulged any information other than to demand we allow her to leave. She only had assorted generic items on her person, like small mirrors and a disassembled hang glider at the retrieval spot," said Kolski carefully, skirting the truth as close as he dared.

"Medical tests?" insisted the voice.

"Almost normal except for corneal implants since the woman had previously been blind and medical cannot find any special enhancements," said Kolski shrewdly, again all true.

"So it is possible the target remains at large?" said the voice, this time a hint of disapproval tinged the tone.

"Yes, it's possible," said Kolski hoping to divert the voice.

"We will see on a mission then and test her. If she is not the one we seek, her loss will not be a burden," said the voice and then there was silence.

That statement sent a chill through Kolski: Just what did they have in mind? Would they intentionally set up a mission for the woman to fail if she did not have the required skills? It meant they intended the wrong asset to be terminated during the mission and now he regretted finding this woman if she was unable to meet their high standards.

Chapter 6

After she was pronounced fit, her guard took Bryn to an exercise area to demonstrate a variety of stretches which not only benefited her leg, but Bryn's entire body after a month of relative inactivity.

When her guard bent to massage the previously wounded area though, Bryn stumbled backwards in surprise, shaking her head vigorously and felt her face burn when the visor failed to hide his one eyebrow rose at her reaction. It had nothing to do with trusting him it was pure discomfort of any man touching her thigh in such a familiar way after Vander's mistreatment years ago.

Soon her guard began to physically challenge Bryn as she was able to resume her combat exercises, but he made her wear protective gear as the sessions became more brutal and it piqued her that she seemed to make little impression on him even if she landed blows. At times he did allow her to practice on her own though she was rarely truly by herself as other men use the gym area regularly.

Other men frequented the area, but none of them seemed interested in joining any of her sessions though they occasionally had an audience during the more intense encounters. One day when her guard left her briefly to work alone on a body length punching bag and the rude man she recalled from the meeting, named Stanton, happened to arrive.

His stride turned mocking when he saw Bryn in the exercise area and she took no notice of the man knowing her guard would not be far away, he had a way of silently enforcing his displeasure when she made trouble.

Her tactic did not work and Stanton marched over pointing at the mat in front of him as if ordering a dog to heel, she looked at him coldly daring him to force obedience to his rude behavior. What she failed to take in account is he was fully garbed for his duties compared to her basic comfortable clothing, not that Bryn ever chose to carry weapons of any sort.

"Hey now, Stanton, don't start trouble," said one of the men using the equipment.

Since she was not sparring with her guard, Bryn had not donned any protective gear and decided to turn her back on the man, which was a mistake. A change in pressure at her back was the only warning Bryn had before she instinctively evaded a blow near her ear as she felt the wind of its passing.

Stanton had a sneer on his face as he advanced again with a baton type item similar to a night stick police might use and a full blow from it could easily break a bone. Avoiding retaliation against him did not discourage the man and Bryn knew she had to fight back or risk a serious injury so she used several kicks that eventually sent the stick spinning from his grasp.

Quite a few men now watched the faceoff between Bryn and Stanton, some of them muttered wagers to each other on the outcome and did nothing to stop the scenario. Whistles of appreciation sounded as men watched Bryn throw some kicks and punches that had Stanton stumbling for balance, they even laughed as she skid between his legs to avoid a backhanded blow.

Loss of his first weapon only prompted Stanton to grab a knife at his side, "Now wait a minute Stanton, we don't use knives in sparring," shouted another man.

Finally, one of the men came forward to pull Stanton away, but he viciously elbowed the man in the face with the crunch that told Bryn the man's nose broke even without the copious amount of blood spurting from his face.

Shouting back and forth made no sense to Bryn as she ducked or twisted away from the flashing blade until a tear sounded followed a stinging sensation at her side. He grazed her and she knew then that she had to get the knife out of his hand.

With a feint to one side, Bryn lured Stanton in so that he overreached his goal and gave him a numbing blow to the wrist forcing him to release the knife, but that same move left her vulnerable to the man's free hand which landed on her cheekbone with enough force to send her to floor. Light about her began to dim and the voices grew distant, Bryn wondered if she would ever wake again.

Commander Kolski reviewed the data on their woman guest and had to grudgingly admit Nighthawk knew how to handle her from the results he was perusing. Though it grated to admit he was wrong, but he did to the man standing before him. Unfortunately, the woman was still not forthcoming about any of her skills to her guard though he had been testing her limitations, but they could easily see that she was very intelligent.

"It's a miracle what you achieved with her so far. None of the men learned the systems so quickly. How is the physical training progressing?" he said looking up curiously.

"Very well. She has an encompassing background in many forms. We will soon be ready for the rigors to train for missions," said Nighthawk in his soft tone.

Shouting in the halls distracted them and men running past the office window, the Commander slammed on a button yelling, "What the hell is going on?"

"Stanton lost it. He's going after the woman with a knife and he's in full gear. She has nothing to protect her," said a voice on the COM.

Before the voice finished reporting Nighthawk was gone from the office, even before the Commander noticed and he jumped up to head to the area before the fool set them back even further for the mission than he already had.

By the time the Commander arrived, he only managed to see Stanton sailing through the air, hit the wall, and slide to the floor in a crumpled heap. The woman lay motionless on the mat and the Commander felt a sick sensation in the pit of his stomach hoping that Stanton had not killed her after everything they went through to get her here. With barely a pause Nighthawk scooped up Bryn and disappeared in the direction of the infirmary so the Commander felt a brief moment of relief, it meant she was still alive.

The man with a broken nose was in the infirmary already as Nighthawk raced through the doors and laid Bryn on a gurney, he quickly checked her wounds before the doctor arrived to see the bloody graze at her side.

"That will require sealing, but doesn't seem to be more than a graze. Here," she handed Nighthawk a cloth, "put pressure on it while I prepare to clean and seal it."

Soon as the doctor began to attend to the cut, Nighthawk carefully pushed Bryn's hair away from her face to view the abraded cheekbone already coloring with a bruise attesting to force of the blow from Stanton's fist.

Once the doctor sealed the cut, she said, "Bring her to that CAT scan so we can check for fractures and then we'll do an MRI to check for subdural hematomas," watching Nighthawk lift the limp body to place on the machine.

After a few moments she said, "No fractures or hematomas thankfully, but she probably has a concussion, which will leave her with a headache for several days. She will need to rest until the headache fades. We'll check again in ten days. A cold pack will help with the swelling on her cheek."

With a nod, Nighthawk gathered Bryn again and returned to his quarters placing her gently on the sofa before retrieving a cold pack to hold against her cheek. He was half tempted to change the torn bloody clothing, but decided against it, especially if she woke during the process, which could destroy any trust he managed to build with her.

It was a wise decision because a few minutes later, Bryn's eyes flitted and opened, she turned her head groaning at the movement until she noticed her guard sitting above her. She reached up and felt the cold pack covered by his hand before saying, "I can hold it," so he relinquished it to her.

A hesitation as she sat up told Nighthawk she felt the stressed muscle under the wound at her side yet she gave no other sign of pain though she did carefully part the slash in the bloody cloth to examine the area revealing closed skin. He left the sofa briefly to retrieve something for the headache prescribed by the doctor and touched her head gently to indicate what he was offering her.

Then he brought Bryn clean clothing, but suspected the pain at her side might inhibit the process from the expression on her face so he draped a blanket over her gesturing for Bryn to slide her pants down far enough so he could reach around to remove them. He placed her feet in the clean pair of pants and inched them up far enough that she would not need to bend to pull them the rest of the way on.

She finally accepted he was trying to help and pulled the blanket under her shirt so he could remove the top to prevent her stretching the painful side. Holding the clean shirt, he waited until she pushed her arms through the sleeves before pulling it over her head and then removed the bloody clothing from the floor.

"Do you have the occasion to dress women often?" she said to his back.

Turning quickly wondering if he offended her, Nighthawk saw the first humorous glint in her eyes since meeting her and he snorted in amusement before shaking his head with a slight smile on his face. She did not often speak to him even after all the time they spent together thus far.

"There will be some offsite training upcoming. We have a couple of new people that need testing or instruction in various activities," said the Commander blandly as he examined a digital note pad. He flipped through virtual pages before continuing, "I want to check survival skills so, Foss you're going to take Janski, Tank, you take Crease, and Stanton takes Keane" (referring to Bryn).

With an oath, Stanton hit the conference table with a flat hand to emphasize his denial. "No way!" he snarled and Bryn privately agreed with that assessment after various encounters with the man.

"We don't have time to deal with personality conflicts. All of you need to work as a team or I'll sit people out of missions and that will only lessen our effectiveness," snapped the Commander bristling at Stanton. He waited for further protest from the disagreeable man, but wordless muted swearing was all he managed to utter.

At a glance about the room, the Commander caught a brittle smile on Crease's face as the man looked at Stanton and said, "This is no joke. If I get wind of any of you winding each other up for any reason, you will find yourselves on janitor duty for a month," effectively wiping any humor from faces in the room.

"You're dismissed to get gear prepped," said the Commander glaring about the room until the men rose and filed out of the room.

One of his assistants muttered about a notice on his own pad gesturing for the Commander to examine it, but paused in surprise looking in the direction of the door, distracted all three of them glanced over to see Nighthawk sitting stiffly forward.

"Did you have something to add?" said the Commander flatly.

"You're sending her into a survival situation with Stanton?" said Nighthawk quietly though there was bite in his tone.

"They need to work with each other. He needs to swallow his pride and get with the program," said the Commander.

His assistants began to shuffle nervously as Nighthawk stood slowly, planted his fists on the table and leaned toward all of them, "Has it occurred to you he could invent any accident and she will be missing in the wilderness?" said Nighthawk dangerously.

"He wouldn't dare. Stanton knows he would be held responsible. I don't like the man, but he's professional and he's good. I think you're overreacting and you know she has a GPS tag so we can find her. Besides, I thought you would be pleased not to be saddled with the woman constantly," sneered the Commander disdainfully and then he regretted his tone.

Nighthawk's quiet demeanor at this point gave an impression that reminded the Commander of a poisonous snake someone prodded once too often and he felt his assistants freeze beside him. After a moment or two, Nighthawk turned on his heel and left the conference room. The Commander heard relieved sighs from his assistants and realized his armpits were damp from tension of a near escape, but why Nighthawk cared about who trained the woman he had no idea.

Turning his head, the Commander said to one assistant, "The woman has her own quarter's now, correct?"

The man glanced at his digital note pad, prodded it a few times and said, "She has assigned quarters, but no activity registered."

The Commander mused over that information and wondered why Nighthawk continued to keep the woman in his quarters, surely if he considered her untrustworthy he would have alerted them.

Since Bryn had not received any sky diving training to date, a helicopter would drop her and Stanton into the middle of a vast unoccupied forest. As she watched the treetops stream by the open door, Bryn reviewed items in her backpack, which Stanton had irritably ordered her to pack, none of which was food. They wore bodysuits though the packs contained minimal clothing accoutrements in case weather changed drastically, a thermal blanket each, compass, and various other peripheral accessories she would learn how to use. They would be totally incommunicado with no prospect of outside aid and pickup to occur a huge distance from the drop point, hence the Commander permitted Stanton a map yet no GPS handheld. If Stanton had not protested so volubly about the lack of the GPS locator, Bryn would have, but all the Commander said was, "She already knows how to use electronics. You need to teach her how to survive without technology."

Her pack was heavy and would only get heavier, Bryn knew better than to say a word about it especially to Stanton, he already considered her a liability from the day she arrived at the Facility. Suddenly she felt extremely vulnerable. Bryn knew she was completely out of her element and that all her skills learned prior to coming to the Facility would be almost useless. There were no safes, alarms, heat sensors or any variety of technology she knew how to overcome, it would be raw nature, physical and unforgiving and she had to learn to survive without running to a corner store. She had never foraged or hunted for food in her life and until recent years, Bryn had never been able to see enough to even consider such skills. Certainly no reason to read about them, she thought.

Soon as they had ascended to the roof, Stanton had stalked out toward the helicopter without glancing at Bryn to see if she followed him, not that she expected any courtesy and certainly not from this man.

Her thoughts jerked back to the trees below, waving in the downdraft of the rotors as the helicopter began to hover. Stanton stood and secured his pack and clipped onto a rope preparing to drop into the trees below. Feeling far from confident, Bryn followed him down at least secure in the knowledge this was something she practiced earlier in life and at the Facility, she released the cord once she touched down. One of the men in the helicopter pulled up the line and then the sound of rotors faded beyond even her hearing, leaving them in a small clearing surrounded by a canopy of trees.

With irritable movements, Stanton spread a map on the ground so she could see the drop point in relation to the pickup point and then he gruffly told her to slip the compass over her wrist with its securing band. That way she was able to get a bearing, but Bryn did not need the man to tell her walking a straight line to the pickup point would probably be impossible especially after glancing at the topography.

Every time Stanton explained reasons for a task, he would bite off the words as if someone prodded the instruction from him indicating to Bryn if the man had any other choice he would not help her in any way. Given such reluctance, she wisely forbore to ask questions, which seemed to make Stanton more irritable. Fortunately Bryn had a logical mind and after thinking through tasks, she could eventually deduce the purposes of seemly useless actions. She was very careful to pay close attention to anything her unwilling companion performed knowing it could mean her life or death in the future.

Two days later, a storm moved into the area and they both worked on a suspended platform to keep them off the wet ground overnight. Actually, Bryn found these solutions quite ingenious even if she had the company of bad tempered Stanton and she had to admit that the man knew how to survive in the wilderness. Though not as palatable as food Bryn was accustomed to, she was never truly hungry between hunting game animals or foraging for wild edibles, however she decided she had a new appreciation for seasoning.

When they had been roughing it for a full week, Bryn noticed Stanton's humor eventually improved; well at least from what she knew of the man, and he actually spoke to her in short sentences, even asking if she had any questions. He estimated they would have another five days to reach the pickup point and warned Bryn they would cover some rough terrain once they were closer to the area.

Since they did not have the benefit of a GPS unit, Stanton indicated how to mark a path when foraging so she could find her way back to the camp set up though initially Bryn thought he intended to leave her lost in the forest. She had finally dismissed that thought after the first week, but it re-emerged when she returned to camp after foraging to find Stanton missing. Her first reaction was terror that he left her alone in this wilderness with no map so she could not find her way to the pickup zone until her panicked gaze settled on Stanton's backpack. Once that fact registered, Bryn knew the man would never have left his pack if he intended to leave her, he would need everything he carried and then she began to worry if the man had an accident while hunting.

The ground had become rough terrain as he warned and Bryn knew if some of the loose rock could shift to create a slide down the slope, Stanton had told her accidents like that happened to even the most experienced survivalists. After investigation, Bryn found the markers Stanton left as he exited the camp to hunt, her eyes scanning the area, particularly the rocky depths to check for unstable rock or for sign of a recent slide. With the sun sinking behind the mountains, night would come early and even if that would not inhibit Bryn, but it could make Stanton's situation critical no matter what kind of illumination he used. Of course no one at the Facility could possibly know exactly how Bryn's eyes worked even if they guessed to some degree, she was certain Donal never revealed any details and unless she chose to reveal the information, they would largely remain ignorant. If Stanton had been threatened about her safety, Bryn suspected the man might be uneasy leaving her alone too long unless he was injured.

Stop that! She told herself, inventing problems would not help matters.

As dusk began to settle, Bryn's tension increased twofold because she knew the silence about her indicated Stanton was nowhere nearby and she had to now assume the worst. Her eyes began to pick up residual thermal images of his footsteps as darkness began to settle, something she never attempted to do before until she found an area muddled with many footprints. The various sizes indicated more than one person and the ground disturbed in such a way it was obvious there had been some sort of struggle which puzzled Bryn completely. From the Commander's briefing the areas the teams would be dropped should have no human population or even be close enough for them to hike to within a month.

It was full dark now, but Bryn continued to follow the trail wearily for another hour until she thought she heard the sounds of voices filtering through the trees. Reverting to her previous specialty of stealth, Bryn practically floated forward like a breeze scanning the area constantly looking for body heat and paused when she caught sight of someone in a tree. Flicking through various aspects of her vision, she saw it was a man sitting in what looked like a mounted hunting blind in the tree like deer hunters tended to use and he had a gun. Refining her vision, Bryn took note that this man's gun was in no way like a hunting rifle, it was military issue like those she learned to identify in some of the data Nighthawk had given her to learn. He was dressed in dirty camouflaged fatigues, his face unshaven, and similar colored cap on his head.

Carefully, she slipped onward following the tracks and saw a glow in the distance that turned out to be a large bonfire with a lot more men dressed in camouflaged fatigues moving about, some cleaning guns, some moving gear or boxes. Beyond them, she could see vehicles like various trucks or ATVs and wondered if these people had a connection with the Facility.

Stanton mulled over his thoughts, still tinged with some bitterness about the survival training for the woman particularly after the Commander said it was supposed to be for his own good. No matter how he argued the woman would slow him down or that he was unsuitable to be her trainer, the flaming Commander would not listen. Fortunately the woman had not been a burden thus far to his surprise and she learned quickly, did not babble inanely, and paid attention. He grudgingly had to admit, at least to himself, that she was no slouch or idiot, but he would never admit that to anyone even under torture. *Just six more days and this damn trip will be over,* he thought in disgust and next time he would stop acting out where the Commander could see him to avoid this duty again. *Let Nighthawk deal with her since he seemed to stick up for the bit...,* he paused in thoughts and changed it to, *...woman.* He felt a fool changing his label for the woman, but no one would ever know.

A rustling brought him up short and Stanton began swinging the makeshift sling he made to prepare to stun or kill the animal he expected to see leave the brush. He moved forward silently, but he stopped in shock when he saw a man kneeling about ten yards away. A quick assessment told Stanton this man had no connection with the Facility which meant he should not be out here, this area was supposed to be completely devoid of people hence the reason they were dropped in the area.

His observation quickly told Stanton that this man was no hunter either, not with an old style AK-47 and those dirty fatigues had no military insignia so it was no training mission which the military often did similar to his reason for being in the wilderness. Besides, they would never allow them to take anything, but a knife into a survival training exercise he knew that from past experience and definitely not an antique projectile weapon.

That left an option Stanton did not like to contemplate, that this man could be part of some militia group with who knew what kind of agenda and they were usually dangerous to outsiders since often they were hiding from law enforcement. All these thoughts only took him less than a minute and he carefully began to back away from the man before he could turn in that direction only to hear the click on the hammer of a gun next to his ear.

"So what do we have here?" sneered a male voice behind Stanton.

Swearing inwardly, Stanton cursed his inattentiveness that allowed the fool behind him to sneak up from behind even if he never expected to find people out in this area.

"Hey Jones, you got a peeping Tom," yelled the man behind Stanton as he pressed the barrel to his temple.

Stanton knew he could disarm the fool, but he had no idea how many others might have a bead on him that he could not see and he could not leave the woman out here without aid, she also would not be able to carry him if he sustained a serious injury.

The man he had seen first, obviously Jones, since he responded to the name walked toward them and growled out, "So what you been staring at? You the law?"

"No, my company dropped me out here for survival testing," said Stanton, which was truthful enough.

"So you say," Jones sneered. "And that's just what some spy would say before he sneaked back to tell the cops something now wouldn't it?"

"I have no gun or badge, you can check," said Stanton controlling his temper as the man checked him over finding neither item.

"So if you're out here like you say, where's your gear?" said the man behind Stanton shoving the gun barrel into his head and pushing his head at an angle.

"It's over in the trees somewhere. I was just trying to catch a meal and thought I heard something in the brush," said Stanton gesturing vaguely in another direction rather than the real one.

"Take us to it. You could have a badge and gun hidden there just so you could be cute," snapped Jones.

With the man behind him pushing the gun into the back of his head, they shoved Stanton in the general direction he had indicated his gear, but when they could not find any after forty-five minutes, the men grew impatient.

"This fool could be lost and some toe rag from the city, but we can't take the chance," snarled Jones at his companion.

Stanton had to decide whether to take a chance or not that these two men were alone. He could easily disable them both, but if they had people undercover watching, he could find himself wounded or worse, he decided to chance it.

Whirling about with blinding speed, Stanton grabbed the gun from the man behind him and sent him to the ground within seconds and just as fast turned about to level the man called Jones, both were down so he turned to run. He stopped dead in his tracks when a bullet splintered the bark off a tree inches from him, Stanton knew he would not get far and his gamble had failed. More men came out of the brush dressed like the other two men, but the ones holding the guns did not approach after watching him deck their friends.

One of the men that approached him used the butt of his old AK-47 to hit Stanton in the stomach so he decided to fold like a weakling in hopes of staving off more serious injury and making a point of moaning as if in pain. Another man used plastic cuffs to secure Stanton's arms behind his back and he found this a grim surprise, it would be nearly impossible to slip out of such restraint without removing his hands first.

The two men he assaulted got to their feet and began kicking him with venom for their humiliation so Stanton made another show of being cowed and weaker than he was, not that it helped much from the deep bruising he felt. Finally, several of the men yanked him to his feet, shoving Stanton at a stumbling pace in another direction away from the camp where the woman would be waiting for him to return. At least he would not be responsible for her among these fools, he thought grimly.

They marched him a about an hour Stanton estimated until they arrived at a fortified camp with at least forty men all similarly garbed, his eyes darted about to take measure of their defenses, supplies, and armament and confirmed that this was some extreme militia group. Since the Facility's intelligence did not indicate any population in this area, Stanton knew these men must have recently moved into this location or satellite would have confirmed heat images. Those thoughts were rudely interrupted by a brutal shove from behind that sent Stanton sprawling to the ground, cutting his lip and then he was dragged from behind, set at the base of a tree and tied against it.

He acted barely conscious though he listened carefully about him as the first two men explained where they found him, his story and the fact they could not find his gear. Footsteps approached him and someone through a bucket of water in his face, Stanton muttered deliriously about being lost when another voice demanded to know why he was in the forest.

"Idiots, how hard did you hit him? We won't get any sense out of him right now," snapped the man who had been asking the questions.

Daylight faded and the smell of food came to Stanton's nose, he opened his eyes to slits glancing about to see what was going on in the camp. Tied as he was, he knew there was no chance of escaping even if they had not taken the knife from his calf sheath. Manipulating his numb hands, Stanton also realized these men took his compass and he swore under his breath at the loss making his return to his own camp very slim. It would be easy to walk fifty yards beyond it and never see his pack or the woman if he managed to get free.

On the positive side, he left the map with his pack so if she proceeded to the pickup point and made contact with the chopper, they would send people to look for him, provided he lived that long. All he could do was wait and hope he could talk his way out of this mess. The fire burned low as the night wore on and the men quieted down bundling up in sleeping bags. Stanton was aware of motion nearby which told him he had a guard.

He had decided he might as well try to sleep, uncomfortable as he was, when he heard a soft grunt behind him and he carefully twisted his head noting that his guard was gone. *Probably asleep on duty*, he thought until he felt the plastic cuffs give way followed by the rope about his chest and the prickling in his hands said circulation was returning.

A knife handle was placed in his hands and then quiet words came to his ear, "The guard is unconscious when you're ready to move," he knew the woman had found him.

Irritation mixed with consternation that she found him instead of making her way to the pickup point and then the fact that he owed her for his escape, he had no idea how they would manage in the dark even if it provided cover.

Assured that no other men were watching him, Stanton crept away from the tree and soon found the woman tugging at his arm, which he jerked away, "Where are the packs?" he breathed noting she did not have hers.

"I left them at camp when you didn't return, I followed your trail," she said quietly.

"We won't find our way without light and anything we might use will attract attention when they notice I'm gone," he snarled quietly.

"I can get us there if you let me lead you," she said quietly with a note of impatience.

Incredulously Stanton hesitated, he could not see how this woman could possibly negotiate in the darkness, but she was tugging at his arm again and weaving about as if she saw exactly where she was going. Then he remembered a few comments the Commander made about this woman's vision, but he found it hard to believe that she could see in the dark. Eventually he had to concede she was able to see where she was going from the pace she set, avoiding obstacles even though he occasionally stumbled on loose rocks.

Suddenly a huge clamor rose back the way they had come. "Shit, shit, they know I'm missing," snarled Stanton and he wondered if they had night vision goggles, but they would still need to know the direction.

"Can you manage if I go faster?" she said in front of him.

"Yes, just do it. We need to get our gear before they get enough light to track us," he snapped back at her thinking it was a stupid question even if he risked breaking his legs or ankles.

Her speed increased to the point that Stanton found himself swearing under his breath as he seemed to stumble every other step and switched so he was holding her arm instead of her pulling him along so he could find more balance. Noise behind them faded as they obtained distance from the militia camp, but Stanton knew they were not safe when those men had enough light to track and he suspected they left a notable trail. However that was unavoidable under the circumstances.

Since he did not have his wrist unit any longer, he could not tell how long they had been moving, but his knees and ankles screaming from abuse said it had been long enough when he suddenly ran into the back of the woman.

"We're here. Your pack is right in front of me," she said and Stanton waved his hands blindly as he bent over until they connected with the pack, "Here," and she shoved her wrist unit at him, which also contained a compass.

Both of them shuffled about securing their packs and Stanton was thinking quickly which way they should take until he finally decided to go up the slope into the rocks so they would not leave such a significant trail. The men would know they headed up, but once there was more stone, they could change direction and no one would know for certain where they were heading. That would force the men to split up and lessen the odds against them.

Stanton quickly viewed the map shielding the glow of the penlight and then checked the illuminated wrist unit for bearings; he folded the map, pushing it out of sight.

"Ok, take us this way," he gestured to Bryn before grabbing her arm as a guide in the darkness.

It had already been a long night for Bryn, especially with no food and now the prospect of traveling until sun up was not a welcome thought, but she understood the urgency. Stanton might be an annoying person, but he knew what he was doing and he did not need to tell her the searching men would probably kill them both. She refused to allow her mind to consider other alternatives those men may apply to her.

When Stanton said, "Stop, we need to rest," it was only pride that kept Bryn from collapsing in front of the man noticing the sky had lightened considerably and knew it had been hours they stumbled up the slope of the mountain. At least they were on bare rock now even if loose rock was still a stumbling hazard.

Bryn did not even have the energy to remove her pack and was quite prepared to sleep with it on until she felt it jostle as Stanton removed it from her body. "You need to rest as much as possible and this will cause stiffness that will slow us down," he said as if concerned she might label it a courtesy.

He held out a canteen for her and Bryn waved it away, but he pushed it roughly into her hands. "You need to hydrate or you won't recover your energy," he snapped with impatience, "No one can do without water for long."

Stanton accepted the canteen back wordlessly once he was certain the woman had something to drink and with another sideways glance, he saw her curl up on the stone to sleep. He knew she was exhausted, but the woman said nothing, not once, about pausing or stopping to rest to which Stanton inwardly accorded her grudging approval. For someone used to the city and its comforts she was doing quite well in the wilderness; not that he would elaborate on that fact back at the Facility because he was not about to get saddled with her again.

The woman was still sleeping when he woke so Stanton decided to forage for food while there was still some daylight, but he knew he could not go far and there was still a risk those idiots might have split up to hunt for them once they lost their trail. Consequently, he was unable to hunt game and returned with a variety of plants and grubs. He was looking forward to the woman's reaction to the grubs, not his favorite meal item either, but they needed the energy and this was all that was available denied the ability to hunt to avoid observation.

When Bryn woke, every part of her body seemed to hurt and the sun was already behind the mountain, which meant they would move out soon. It was then she saw Stanton had set out a variety of items he foraged for them and Bryn's eyes settled on the grubs, she took one look at his face only to see a challenging gleam in his eye. He was expecting her to protest and Bryn just barely managed to keep a blank expression on her face, even when he pointedly began to eat some of the grubs obviously deciding she would demur if he did not eat first.

Masking her revulsion, Bryn popped the grubs in her mouth refusing to chew them and swallowed each one whole, she knew arguing or abstaining from eating would only fuel Stanton for a lecture. He would love nothing better than to make her squirm over the available food.

After a drink from the canteen, Bryn settled the pack onto her shoulders, sore from carrying it so long the previous day and would have moved off to their left until Stanton stopped her with a firm grip on her arm.

"Not that way. I set up some surprises if anyone gets up this far and we'll trip them if we get too close to them," he said gesturing her up and to the right more.

Soon as night advanced on them, Bryn felt Stanton's strong grip on her arm so that she could guide him though occasionally he had to alter her direction since he must have glanced at the wrist unit she gave him.

"This is going to delay us to the pickup point?" she said quietly over her shoulder.

"Yes, but can't be helped now. They'll make certain someone is waiting for us, but they won't have any way of locating us since we have veered off course so much," he said quietly though his tone had a bite to it.

Though Bryn did not contradict him, she recalled the Commander's threat about the GPS tag and suspected any searchers from the Facility would not have the difficulty that Stanton assumed which told her that he was probably unaware of that addition to her person.

The night grew colder than the previous week and in part Bryn knew that was the altitude, she could see ice crystal forming from frost on the stone, even Stanton could not. Their trek was the only thing keeping them both warm. Another sound began to take shape for Bryn, which reminded her of running water, a lot of it and eventually Stanton could hear it as they came closer to what turned out to be a fast flowing river.

It was deep enough Bryn knew that they would both be soaked with cold water and Stanton finally pulled her to a halt swearing under his breath.

"Damn it, we can't risk getting wet in these temperatures when we can't light a fire. Take us down into the trees, I have an idea," he said.

The sky began to lighten as they reached the tree line and Stanton dropped her arm to examine some of the young trees for some reason, she could hardly believe they had traveled so long already. After giving her an appraising glance, Stanton picked up a stone that fit in his hand well and began to use the knife she gave him to chop one of the trees. He made surprisingly short work of it.

He picked a second young tree, but stouter than the first he cut and repeated the process before he explained the reasons for his actions.

"The water is too cold and since we can't light a fire to dry any clothing, we can't risk getting wet. These poles will help us get across the water without getting wet. Fire has hardened these tree trunks so they will hold our weight. Watch what I do and follow exactly where I place my pole," he ordered.

With trepidation, Bryn watched as Stanton probed the riverbed looking for placement for his pole and apparently found a spot that satisfied him before he looked back at her to be ready to follow him. To her surprise, with the pole planted firmly, Stanton essentially pole-vaulted over to the other side of the river quite easily, in spite of the strong current and soon he found his footing, he gestured her to do the same thing.

Bryn tried to hide her nervousness as she planted her pole in approximately the same spot as Stanton, testing it for instability because she was certain she would fall in before reaching the other side. Then took a few backward steps so she could get a small run at it and leapt, clinging to the pole, as it propelled her to the other side so forcefully that she stumbled and would have fallen if Stanton had not caught her arm. She heard him snort, but Bryn was too embarrassed to look up to see if he was amused or disgusted by her over compensation.

"Keep it for now," he said when she made a move to throw the pole aside.

Without further comment, Stanton trekked back up the slope out of the trees again until he found some rocks large enough to conceal their presence where they could rest. He removed her canteen and walked back to refill their water since this was the first water they had encountered in days. That was the last thing Bryn remembered before she woke with a start to see Stanton carrying several fish back from the river along with a primitive spear he had made from smaller branches.

"We'll need to eat these raw. The smoke scent will carry and give us away. I have no idea how far those fools are searching, but they will still be looking for me. If they had half a brain they will know I had help," he said sourly.

It was all Bryn could do to mask her revulsion when Stanton handed her a fish, which he fortunately gutted already, and bit into the raw flesh. She found it was not quite as bad as she expected having eaten sushi before even though never presented with a whole fish to consume and hunger helped her forget the blandness. When they finished, Bryn moved to the river to wash her face and hands so she would be prepared to move again.

They continued to travel several more days like this and Bryn wondered if she would have the stamina to go any farther, especially on such little food and rationed water. Sleep was always restless and uncomfortable, barely restoring the energy she needed to keep going, glancing at Stanton told her even he was feeling the strain.

The Commander was reviewing brief from the two teams, which reported in from their survival training grunting with approval at the success of the ventures and wondering, partly with grim humor, just how Stanton's travels were fairing. A chopper was on the way to pick up both him and the woman though he did expect bitter complaints from Stanton whether real or imagined reasons Keane was an unsuitable team member. It was not until a message chimed for him and he saw the chopper pilot that the Commander had a very bad feeling about sending the woman with Stanton.

"Commander, there is no one here or any sign they have been at the pickup," said the pilot.

"Wait for them. It's possible they hit a snag on the way," said the Commander with lack of concern he did not feel.

"Sir, we aren't equipped to stay here overnight let alone for days if they are delayed," the pilot pointed out.

"I copy. I'll send an equipped chopper, but until it gets close I want you to stay in place. If they show, radio in," said the Commander after mentally reviewing options.

Damn it, he thought furiously, *if Stanton caused this I just might have him flogged.*

Pressing one of the COM buttons, he arranged for another chopper, this time loaded to stay in place and to include a medic since it was possible injury could be the reason for the delay with that rough terrain. As much as he did not want to do it, he contacted Nighthawk and told him to be on the chopper or the man might consider causing bodily harm to even a commander, something he truly did not want to experience. Only he, Doc, and Nighthawk knew about the woman's GPS tag so he could check to be certain it was on the move or stationary. He pulled up the display overlaying satellite images and found that the tag was indeed moving, albeit slowly, from the telemetry transmitted which could indicate injury.

Pressing the COM again, "Be advised that our missing team members could be injured. Bring the necessary equipment," ordered the Commander as he watched the display pensively.

Bryn could hear Stanton swearing under his breath as they negotiated a huge rock butte they encountered which he said they would have missed had they taken the original track he planned. Rocks slithered underfoot making unavoidable noise, one of the reasons for Stanton's irritation so Bryn strained her sharp hearing for sounds of pursuit. They had to take the gamble to move during daylight confronted with such a hazardous climb, as Stanton needed to see for foot or handholds that Bryn could not lead him through.

"Finally," said Stanton as they reached lowest point of the butte so they could circumvent it.

At the precise moment, a crack sounded and flecks of rocks split near them causing Stanton to swear vociferously, the hunters finally caught up with them. Tired and panicked, they scrambled up the opposite side of the butte for protection or as much as it could offer with the sound of bullets ricocheting off the stone and rock far too close for comfort.

"Damn it, they are going to force us up beyond the pickup point," snarled Stanton.

"Does that mean they will cut us off?" Bryn found herself asking.

"A good possibility," fumed Stanton as he stumbled on another loose stone.

Stanton had pushed hard to get to the pickup point and avoided doing any foraging, they had not even rested yet since they needed to circumvent the butte so this encounter came a bad time for them. Soon it became much worse.

Bryn's ears suddenly began to ring from an unexpected explosion and then she felt the ground tremble beneath her feet, struggling to keep her footing, uncertain what had just happened.

"Morons!" roared Stanton mingled with inventive swearing not bothering to adjust his language, not that he ever did around her, Bryn mused.

Pin prick sore spots dotted her side, but Bryn barely noticed and followed Stanton's urgent scramble up the rock until another explosion sounded nearby, this time the rock under her feet began to slide away. Crying out in fear, Bryn grabbed desperately at the rock for some hold only to find it came away in her hands when a strong hand caught her wrist in a vise-like hold, steadying her so she could get her footing.

Large chunks of rock separated and eventually they could hear cries below them as if people had been caught in the rockslide, she could hear Stanton laugh mirthlessly.

"Bastards got a wakeup call," he sneered nastily. "Move, now, while they have to regroup."

Apparently the men hunting them had not learned a valuable lesson and eventually began throwing whatever it was, but Bryn chose not to ask Stanton to clarify since it would probably make little difference to their circumstance.

"Get down," he shouted suddenly and Bryn found herself face first into the rock. She heard a skittering noise and then another explosion so close it deafened her painfully. Inventive swearing next to her ear said Stanton had thrown himself on top of her and then his weight was gone as his hand grabbed her arm literally dragging her with him behind a huge boulder.

As her dazed sight cleared, Bryn could see blood staining the rock under Stanton's left calf and she flicked through her various vision capabilities to see he had shrapnel in the wound.

"I can get some of that out, but not all of it," she said to him.

"What? You can see it?" he asked incredulously forgetting his pain momentarily.

"Yes, but most of it is too deep to reach with fingers," said Bryn examining the area critically.

"Grab what you can while I look for something to bind this with," he said begin to sort through his pack.

When Bryn yanked a large piece of shrapnel out quickly, Stanton began to swear quite colorfully before he resumed looking for something to bind the wound.

"You should try to clean it," began Bryn, but he just snapped back, "No time. We have to keep them from pinning us down here."

The men below were too wary to run up at them and Stanton used their indecision to move upward using boulders to block their movement from line of sight from the hunters below. As the sun began to descend behind the mountain, the balance shifted back into their favor except for the fact Stanton's injured leg began to seize up from the muscle damage. Though he never said anything, Bryn could tell he was still bleeding from the scent and knew his pain had increased when Stanton's pace slowed; she paused at the sound of rolling rocks from behind.

"I think they are following," she said suddenly and Stanton began to swear softly.

"They probably have night vision equipment which means they will hunt us right to the pickup point," snarled Stanton.

"You keep going. You have the map and compass. I'll catch up later," said Bryn firmly.

"And what are you going to do? Shout at them?" he said disdainfully.

"They're plenty of rocks here. It will force them to stop and I can avoid them," she said dryly.

"You said you never use weapons so what did you plan to do with rocks?" he said scathingly.

"I never said I *couldn't* use weapons. I just don't carry them or prefer to use them," she retorted in the same vein, "Go on. I'll delay them and they won't know when I leave here."

As much as Stanton wanted to argue, he knew Bryn was right and if those men had the suspected night vision equipment, they would catch up to them before they managed to get to the pickup point. What he could not understand was how she would catch up, but he vividly remembered her finding him in the blackness of the forest and leading him away in the same darkness, straight back to their camp. Whatever it was with her eyes, she could see far better than equipment he ever heard of or came across in his career.

At the cries of pain and surprise from behind, Stanton spared himself a snort of humor as he stumbled over stone using the backlit compass to keep his bearings. He wondered just how much the Commander knew about her abilities, how could they test such a subjective sense? No one except the Commander really knew everyone's backgrounds and all Stanton could remember that was disclosed in the initial meeting to catch this woman was that she had been incredibly elusive. Actually they had thought her a man at the time.

His thoughts reoriented to listen and Stanton noted the sounds behind finally faded so he either managed to get some distance or the hunters retreated out of range of the rocks that were being hurled at them. *Unless they caught her*, he thought belatedly, and knew the Commander might do something dire if that happened.

A glimpse of light through one of the trees made Stanton pause, he was close to the pickup point, but if those men following had another camp in the area, he certainly did not want to run into them. Difficult as it was, he carefully moved down the slope and nearly yelled in surprise when Bryn appeared at his side like a ghost, he did not even hear her get close.

Then Stanton had to halt when his injured leg finally would no longer hold his weight, "Damn leg won't hold me any longer," he snarled.

"Let me carry your pack. It might help," said Bryn which only increased Stanton's swearing, she suspected he did not want to appear weak, but she could not carry him and if she dragged him, he would definitely have a lot to complain about later.

With impatient movements, Stanton removed his pack furious that he had to have her help, but again, her solution made sense even if he did not have to like it.

"Can you see what's down there where that light is?" said Stanton suddenly.

Bryn could tell he was wary and she squatted down to get a better look in case it might be another camp of unknown men, but she saw a helicopter, which she relayed to Stanton. His answer was only a grunt as he continued to limp forward as Bryn's ears strained for sounds of pursuit and hoped this was their pickup. She knew she was operating on adrenalin right now and soon as it wore off, she would be close to collapse with no food for days and little water.

The sound of Stanton stumbling and swearing made Bryn pause, "I can lead you around a lot of the rough spots," she said cautiously.

His response was more swearing and a firm hold on her upper arm so Bryn proceeded at a measured pace to reduce the strain on Stanton's injured leg; she did not dare indicate her speed was for his benefit. Once they were closer, Stanton began to wave his penlight so people in the helicopter would see their approach instead of unwisely startling them since their delay would indicate trouble which no doubt had the pickup team on edge.

Soon as they left the bracken onto a plateau where the helicopter sat, several men ran to meet them while Stanton practically swearing every other word explained his injury and the following men hunting them. Bryn nearly fell on her face when someone literally ripped Stanton's backpack out of her hands and then someone steadied her before removing the pack from her own shoulders, but she was too tired to care at that point. The adrenalin rush was now wearing off and her legs felt like rubber.

Relieved to finally sit, Bryn crawled to the rear of the helicopter cargo area on hands and knees noting Stanton gave no particular details about the men, which hunted them other than to say they followed so she suspected he would wait until they returned to the Facility. Because of their late arrival and Stanton's injury the Commander would probably insist on debriefing them.

As the helicopter's rotors began to engage, Bryn had a more difficult time hearing much of anything until Stanton yelled for some water and then moments later someone shoved a plastic bottle into her hand beaded with condensation. She only took a few sips and would have set it down when Stanton barked at her to drink the whole thing, Bryn was about to argue, but someone snatched the bottle from her hand holding it to her lips. At that point she was too tired to argue and drank it as it was held to her lips.

Stanton glanced over at the woman in the dim light of the cargo area and suddenly realized Nighthawk was with them, he snorted at that observation wondering why the man was present. You would think he was concerned for the woman the way the man watched her as she leaned her head back limply, probably grateful to rest as he was. Originally, Stanton thought the Commander made the woman Nighthawk's responsibility to teach the man a lesson, but he certainly did not act like a person glad to have a reprieve from an unpalatable assignment. Well, it was nothing to him and Stanton could care less how the other man's life was impacted as long as no one saddled him with that woman again and how he would be glad to stay away from her, as far away as he could get.

Once the chopper landed on the roof of the Facility, Stanton spared a moment of inward humor when Bryn irritably waved away any assistance out of the helicopter and the medic. Two other men made a human armchair to take him down to the infirmary, but allowed Stanton to stand in the elevator car until it reached the end destination. Since men helped him exit first, Stanton saw

Nighthawk snag the woman's arm when she attempted to circumvent the infirmary and he snorted again at the glare she gave the man for halting her progress.

"I'm fine," snapped Bryn wrenching her arm from Nighthawk's grasp just as one of the infirmary staff approached her.

"Everyone has to clear medical after a demanding mission whether actual or training," said the medic sternly.

Actually Stanton found the woman's intractability, in this case, entertaining since it seemed to annoy Nighthawk and it was about time that man's cool exterior had a few barbs thrown at it. He nearly laughed out loud at the woman's expression as Nighthawk hovered to be certain medical examined her, not that she mentioned any injuries and suddenly Stanton wondered if she might withhold that information, if so the Commander could come down on him hard. He glanced back at her again and suddenly caught the pallor in her face and he barely had time to yell, "She's crashing," before the woman began to wilt in front of them.

The speed of Nighthawk's reflexes were all that kept the woman from hitting the floor as he scooped her up and laid her on one of the gurneys.

"What happened to her?" said Doc turning to Stanton accusingly.

"We've both been running on adrenalin for at least eight hours. I suspect it just wore off and I'm next. She never announced any injuries," said Stanton defensively.

"Did either of you bother to eat and drink?" said Doc flatly.

"Circumstances prevented us from foraging for the past three days and we had to go sparingly on the water until we got to the chopper. It certainly wasn't intentional," growled Stanton.

Doc sighed looking at the ceiling for patience before telling one of the assistants, "Put her on an IV. We need to get nutrients and fluid into her before she goes into shock. When you're done, this one needs the same," he said glaring at Stanton.

Stanton gave Doc a sardonic look, but did not comment, he felt a wave of weariness hit him moments later and it took supreme effort to hide it. If he had not already been on one of the table's he knew he probably would have shamed himself imitating the woman's collapse, but unfortunately, Doc noticed the change in him.

"Bloody fools. You should have carried emergency rations. I've told the Commander about this before after some of you have come back from these missions," said Doc irritably, then to one of the assistants, "Give me a scanner to check for this shrapnel. I should put him in the MRI so the magnet can pull at what's left."

That final statement kept Stanton from snarling back at Doc because he could see the physician actually doing that to teach him a lesson and he remembered a very painful experience awhile back on some old tattoos he had made with metal dyes. He had to get those removed.

The COM blared with the Commander's voice, "Are you done with those two, Doc? We need to debrief them," he said.

Doc marched over to the COM and slammed his hand down on the button, "They won't be leaving here until *I am* satisfied their health has improved. In a couple of days you will probably have to make do with Stanton since he weathered the situation better due to his background. I warned you to give these people emergency rations," he said, all but snarling.

All the Commander replied was, "Understood," and signed off, he obviously did not want to get into a war of words which he would probably lose.

A few days later Stanton was sitting in the conference room staring at the Commander and his two assistants though he was annoyed Nighthawk had been included in the debrief, apparently the man still had some responsibility for the woman. Thankfully that was the limit of the audience so Stanton knew anything he said would not make it to any of the other men's ears.

"Ok, what went wrong with a simple training mission?" said the Commander neutrally telling Stanton the man was attempting to appear non-combative.

"Everything was going fine until I ran into some wannabe soldiers," said Stanton irritably.

"Excuse me?" said the Commander in disbelief.

"It seems some militia group moved into that area since the last satellite reconnaissance. The idiots thought I was some type of law enforcement so they dragged me into their camp to question me," snarled Stanton, just remembering the incident made him furious.

"And the woman?" said the Commander with a too calm voice.

"Oh she wasn't there when I stumbled on them. We split foraging and hunting duties so they never knew I had a companion," snorted Stanton dryly.

"Since I am well aware of your training, why did you let them take you?" said the Commander with narrow eyes.

Stanton snorted derisively this time, "If it had just been the two I saw it would have been no problem. As a matter of fact, I did make the attempt to get free, but they had backup nearby. So rather than die and leave the woman stranded in the woods, I deemed it necessary to let them take me," he said.

"I see. Then how did you manage to escape? No doubt they restrained you after your first attempt to part their company," said the Commander narrowly.

Stanton stared at the Commander for a long moment trying to decide what to say, he owed the woman and suspected the Commander did not know the extent of the uses the woman could apply to her vision.

"She managed to track me down. It's possible she saw them take me, but I didn't ask. She cut me loose and we snuck out of their camp in the dark," said Stanton carefully neutral.

Not one word of that was a lie, but he left out quite a bit and hopefully the Commander would not think to ask specific questions regarding how they managed to maneuver in the darkness.

"So how did you manage to get your gear back?" said the Commander.

"They never found our gear so we returned to get it. I used the compass so we could move through the night since it would be more difficult to track us. We stayed out of their way for several days, at least until they split up their search parties. Once they stumbled onto our trail, they started tossing grenades which is where the shrapnel came from. After that we couldn't halt for long so we were unable to gather food and had to ration the water we had until we managed to get to the chopper," said Stanton flatly, "I did not ignore her welfare and she knew there was nothing we could do. You can ask her yourself."

The Commander sighed, he did not like Stanton, but he could see the man was telling the truth and knew better than to abandon the woman so there really was nothing he could do to reprimand him.

"It seems you did the best you could under the circumstances. If those fools are still in that area I'll slip word to the authorities so we get them cleared out. That area is too good for training to abandon it. If that's all, you're dismissed," said the Commander as he made some notes on his digital pad.

Soon as he was certain Stanton left the conference room, the Commander glanced up at Nighthawk, "I want the woman returned to her own quarters," he said.

"And how do you propose to monitor her eating habits?" said Nighthawk dryly.

"The cater unit will let us know what she is eating and how often," said the Commander waving away the consideration.

"It won't work. She doesn't feel safe here and she has no reason to trust us. She needs to be monitored," said Nighthawk sternly even though he kept his voice soft.

"The men are already talking about those arrangements. If they continue it's possible they might try to take advantage of her or proposition her," said the Commander.

"And you think her being in isolation will prevent that?" said Nighthawk with a mocking smile.

That comment annoyed the Commander because he knew Nighthawk was correct and he wondered if there was more to it than just taking responsibility for the woman.

"What is this really about?" demanded the Commander.

"This woman sees herself as a prisoner here. She is not going to be cooperative left on her own and needs to feel safe before she will work willingly with us," said Nighthawk succinctly.

"So she is untrustworthy?" snapped the Commander.

"Would you be trustworthy under the same circumstances? What if someone took you against your will to work for them? Wouldn't you do anything you could to be free of what she sees as indentured slavery? You are judging her against the men. She has no military background, she did not volunteer for any assignments, and she has no one she can trust," said Nighthawk pointedly.

The Commander opened his mouth to argue and stopped, he was correct and they had handled this all wrong. It would have been so much simpler if she had been a man as they previously assumed, a man would have probably seen the benefits of working for the Facility and even been flattered to be considered an asset to them. Women were too temperamental.

"What do you suggest?" growled the Commander.

"Let her decide where she wants to stay. For now it is best if she doesn't feel alone and she does need monitoring on her eating habits. She forgets to eat as it is and

I've had to remind her on many occasions. She's not an idiot. She knows she can stay somewhere else because we gave her a room initially," said Nighthawk quirking an eyebrow.

"Fine. Just keep her cooperating. The sooner she works with us, the quicker we can deal with the missions we need her for and then send her on her way," snapped the Commander.

Diagnostics took longer than usual as Foss tapped his foot impatiently during his rotation in the communications room and irritated he punched a few keys to get a read out when an unexpected blip indicated an unknown internal transmission. Out of habit Foss hit record and it was a good thing he did because the transmission lasted only seconds. It was highly unusual for any transmission to be broadcast within the Facility unless they were testing new equipment and so he checked to see if that was the case. To his astonishment, the short message was heavily encrypted and then Foss knew something was off, they never encrypted test transmissions on any new equipment.

It took him the better part of three hours to realize the encryption was nothing recorded within the Facility databases and that spelled trouble to Foss, nothing transmitted in or out of the Facility should have encryption foreign to their records. Since other men were in the communications room, Foss sent a private digital message to the Commander about the irregularity and received almost an instant reply to secure the message before working on the encryption, his eyes only.

Deciphering encryption was one of Foss' specialties, but this message had him fuming at his unsuccessful attempts to find a key, at least until he began to try other languages besides English. Partial success came when he began to try Scandinavian languages when someone might expect Russian, Chinese, or Arabic and even as he puzzled over the source, Foss finally narrowed the language to Swiss Romany, which would be the last language anyone would even begin to try.

Finally the message, what little of it there was, took shape and even as quick as Foss had been to hit record, it still had not been fast enough to get the entire message:

"..........Protocol. Test subject."

Ok, what the hell did that mean? Thought Foss staring at the cryptic partial sentence and the transmission had been far too brief to attempt a location within the installation. As a matter of fact, if anyone, but him (and no false modesty prompted the assessment) had been at the COM board, they would have dismissed the transmission blip as an anomaly.

Chewing on his lip, Foss forwarded the Commander with the result and the very fact he did not query the decoded message told Foss that he was just as puzzled by the wording. With a quick flick of fingers, Foss setup a program to monitor the transmission frequency and record any future messages which would be sent to a secure ghost file. The Commander would expect no less of him.

Chapter 7

Commander Kolski muttered as he looked over the personnel files for the umpteenth time trying to find inconsistencies to pick out the mole in their midst or was there more than one? Crease? He was a new addition and an unknown, but his file was lack luster. He was only a grunt compared to the other men, but they had to try him since the transfer came from high up and Kolski had tried to refuse the man's assignment.

Stanton? What was Stanton up to? The man had been secretive recently completely out of character for him and Stanton logged nearly compulsive access to their extensive databases which made the Commander very nervous, but was he the only mole...or one of several. It seemed an obvious choice to suspect the man, but what easier way to hide than in plain sight; and he had the expertise to encrypt that transmission.

His eyes flicked to the VID screen, the Commander appraised the training in the special area setup to prepare for missions as men clung to walls or fixtures wearing similar suits to the one possessed by Bryn when they brought her to the Facility. Those suits were a marvel and quite ingenious. Most of the men were unidentifiable except Nighthawk; he was the only one that came close to using the bodysuit's potential and of course Bryn. None of the men exceeded her skill in that bodysuit, but Kolski wondered just how much was due to her slighter frame, then again, that could only aid her so far even if he did not want to be charitable about her abilities.

Bryn nearly drove him to drink with her intractability and one thing he hated to admit was that Nighthawk managed to get even more cooperation from her without direct or veiled threats. Kolski had to grudgingly accept they worked very well together.

The rest of the men, some of the best in the world, were very capable, but lacked the working relationship Nighthawk developed with Bryn. It was no secret she continued to stay in his quarters and more than a few off color remarks circulated about what happened behind closed doors, but Nighthawk never acknowledged the comments. Occasional probing from the Commander yielded little information. Nighthawk was a master of circumventing admissions; he never gave a straight answer to anything he preferred to keep private.

Occasional issues cropped up with Bryn, but it was usually due to unprovoked advances from one of the men hoping to score what they felt Nighthawk enjoyed, a smirk lit Kolski's face remembering she had slapped Crease quite hard for one of his suggestions. Apparently Nighthawk intervened before Crease could retaliate and one of the men taunted him about being lucky he escaped with no broken bones.

They would need to watch Stanton more closely even if his outward behavior seemed to change toward Bryn, now he essentially ignored her, but Kolski still did not trust him. If Stanton's skills were not such an asset, Kolski would have felt better tossing him elsewhere, but until they could find a comparable replacement that was not feasible.

Today the team would deal with unknown situations during training. The Commander had the area set up with pitfalls, some very dangerous, to test their ability to work together under duress and watched as a charge exploded. A structure began to break apart when the supports blew out, several men were in the way, but they would not escape without help and Kolski was impressed to see Bryn make unorthodox use of a scale dart. Her figure zoomed across the cord, sweep up to one of the men, and snagging the climbing clip on his belt before pulling him along with her, then she was off again into breaking structure.

One man still clung to the crumbling wall and Kolski swore when she leapt across the area with no climbing ropes or means of saving herself from a bad fall only to land clinging to a nearby wall. She threw a climbing rope to the man, but to Kolski's chagrin the idiot ignored it and attempted to climb his way out of the problem, a totally impossible solution, which would leave him injured.

He had to admit Bryn was made of sterner stuff as she jumped to almost nonexistent structure remnants, snapped a clip onto the man's belt and leapt off another angle then use a fixture to pull the man off at the last second before rubble covered him. The Commander's admiration gave way to rage when the rescued man was pulled next to her seeming to stumble and literally knocked her off the fixture in obvious bad temper. Nighthawk saved her fall, no other man could react that quickly and he caught her just shy of impact with the ground.

The Commander slammed his hand on the COM, "Into the conference room. NOW!" he roared.

The strong arms that saved Bryn from that fall had been unexpected because she had already tensed for impact with the ground from a relatively high place. When the man made it the rest of the way to the ground with her, Bryn knew it had to be Nighthawk even though she saw him grabbing another man at the time. During these training exercises she found they worked well together and was finding that she could trust he would be there if she ever needed help which was a novel concept to someone like Bryn after working alone for so long.

Why had the man knocked her off the structure? On a mission, it could jeopardize everything by a wanton act of that nature and one thing Bryn did not need impressed on her, this was not a game. When she was set on her feet, Bryn nodded over her shoulder in gratitude as she followed the other men to the conference room.

Soon as she entered the Commander's red face indicated fury to be unleashed so she sat down smartly and did not look at anyone else, she hoped her sensitive hearing could stand it or wondered if she would be penalized for covering her ears. Nighthawk took the seat on her left, but she only determined this by peripheral vision, Bryn did not turn to look at him, at least until his hand gently held her arm out of view of the others. She was not certain what he was trying to convey.

"What was with that lame brained stunt?" shouted the Commander.

Bryn winced as her ears rang and felt Nighthawk's hand squeeze her arm so she did not see the others all looking at Stanton in response to the Commander's ire.

"What part of teamwork don't you understand, Stanton?" snarled the Commander in a more modulated tone.

"I didn't need her help," said Stanton mulishly.

"I see. So you would rather she left you to spend time in the infirmary for at least a week?" The Commander snapped.

"I was managing on my own," said Stanton, his jaw jutting out.

"Ok team, Stanton doesn't need help in the future. We'll make certain you can identify him in his suit so you can apply your efforts to those in need of real aid," said the Commander with heavy sarcasm.

Everyone could see Stanton's face flush brilliant red, "I never said that, besides someone fell on me and it wasn't intentional," he began heatedly.

"Basically you did unless it's the help you want. None of you can pick and choose who or how the aid comes to you when the shit hits the fan and knocking that help off a building, just because it wasn't a man, is just asinine. Keep your head out of your pants," snarled the Commander not believing a word of the rebuttal and Stanton only gave a tight nod.

Bryn stood as fast as any of the men eager to put distance between her and the Commander. She felt Nighthawk's hand slip off her arm as she rose noting the man stayed seated as he often did at the end of conferences.

Soon as the door slid shut, the Commander said, "If I had a replacement for Stanton I would boot him. You will probably have to watch her back on missions because I don't trust that man not to throw her to the wolves. The fool would rather take an injury than help, just because it came from a woman. If he pulls a stunt like that during a mission, it could all go down the tubes."

Nighthawk looked at the Commander until he finished speaking, "It's no hardship to watch over her. She has my back as well," he murmured.

The Commander looked at Nighthawk across the table keenly. He was not certain he was meant to hear that last comment and began to wonder if there might be some truth to the rumors though no one could ever claim to have seen him treat Bryn differently.

Frustration colored Bryn's thoughts all the way back to her quarters, she felt like the proverbial "running in one spot and getting nowhere" during these training exercises. In an effort to clear her mind, she jumped into the shower and let it run longer than usual trying to wash the frustration away with the sweat. It helped, she thought; as she vigorously toweled herself dry.

Her stomach rumbled impatiently, if it had been a person, Bryn humorously imagined it tapping its foot and scowling at her for neglect. She tried to put her head through one of the sleeves initially in her haste to get to the cater unit and made a mental note to eat more during the day or this would be a common occurrence.

Instead of ordering several items, Bryn ordered and consumed one plate at a time to prevent a bloated stomach from eating too much too quickly and finding that she was overfull. Interspersing glasses of water in between also helped send signals to her brain to bludgeon her stomach into order until she finally sat back with a sigh.

Since Nighthawk had not returned yet, Bryn cleared the used dishes and sat at one of the data units, that interfaced with the Facility databases to examine the three dimensional hologram of the area where they would have her first actual mission. Old habits die hard and this was one habit she planned to keep: Staying prepared and knowing all choices available about her target whether entering or leaving.

Not long after she began her study, Bryn heard the sound of the doors open heralding the arrival of Nighthawk and the sound of his footsteps indicated he headed for the hygiene unit. He must have been as hungry as she had been because it did not take long for the odor of food items to scent the air, but she refocused on the diagram and real time images via satellite to continuing her preparations.

When two large hands gently came to rest on her shoulders, Bryn actually jumped in surprise she had been so involved studying the images and it took a little effort to force her attention back to the activity after the distraction. She jumped more violently when a breath next to her ear was followed by words. "Tell me what you're thinking?" said a soft, very sexy male voice.

Her mouth opened in shock for the voice could be no other than Nighthawk, but it was the first time she had ever heard him speak, to anyone, and her entire body stiffened to reflect her surprise. The first reaction Bryn was aware of was heat rising to her face at the sound of his voice, he was not faking that sexy tone it was his real voice. Her next reaction was confusion that he chose this moment to speak after nearly a year in his presence and that she had always seemed to know what he meant without words.

Words that finally stumbled from Bryn's mouth grabbed the first information that was foremost on her mind, "I...I always study everything about a job before ever making entry," she stammered feeling quite lame.

A sound of a chair scooting slightly told Bryn she missed him setting a chair behind her and that he was sitting looking over her shoulder which was one of the reasons she felt lame, he could see what she was doing just as well as she could.

An unexpected comment from him followed that explanation, "You know what I meant," he said and his hands squeezed her shoulders gently.

Somehow he perceived her frustration or maybe he noticed in the conference room and he just now decided to say something about it so Bryn decided to be candid.

"The training exercises seem pointless. I can't be part of a team when the team wants no part of me," she said trying to hide the bitterness she actually felt.

A sigh sounded close to her ear and Bryn felt his breath on her neck, he seemed to be considering her words as if weighing them or maybe assessing her.

"The training isn't pointless and the team has no issues with you, only one man. Don't let him discourage you," he said finally.

"I guess I sounded petulant again," she said with a snort.

He surprised her with a soft chuckle, "Not at all," he said, his tone told her that he was smiling, "Did you eat?"

"Yes, sir," she said tauntingly with a mock salute and heard another soft chuckle.

His hands squeezed her shoulders again, he seemed to have no intention of moving and Bryn thought he must be studying the images over her shoulder. So she decided to ask a bold question, but prepared for him to ignore her so she did not feel put down.

"Have you always been Nighthawk?" she said daringly.

Silence lengthened, but Bryn expected it and was not offended so she refocused on the images even though his hands on her shoulders were somewhat distracting.

"Yes," he said finally. "You can call me Ryan in private."

Her mouth opened, but no sound came out, she never expected an answer and certainly not his given name. The shock rendered Bryn speechless and she had no idea what to say even if she found her voice because this entire situation had a sense of unreality, this man speaking to her for the first time in nearly a year seemed positively chatty now.

"I remember you telling the Commander no one knew you as Bryn. What were you called if not that?" he said finally after a lengthy silence.

"I went by the name Shadow for my work," she expected laughter or scoffing announcing that name. "In normal life people thought me disabled and usually ignored me except for Donal, the man who gave me my sight, he was the only one who knew my real name."

"Do you prefer Shadow?" he said, his tone held no mockery to her surprise.

"I do for my job," and then she felt suddenly shy, an unlikely condition for her, "Bryn is fine in private."

It was even harder to focus on the images now and Bryn tried to bully her mind to pay attention, which failed abysmally.

"Why did you decide to speak to me after all this time?" she said unable to help herself even if it was an impertinent question.

"I had something to say," his response came so quickly she knew he had expected this question much sooner and from the sound of his voice, he was teasing her as well.

She spun her chair about to look at his face and the man actually sported a very attractive grin, Bryn made a sound of exasperation and shoved his shoulder as she stood up only to find herself reseated abruptly. He wore a half smile now and raised a hand to touch her chin affectionately before giving her a wink, "Get some rest," he said and she watched him vacate the chair then head to the other room.

One day the Commander called Bryn to his office and she proceeded warily wondering what other restrictions the man might heap on her. Soon as she entered the office, the Commander gestured her to take a seat, which Bryn refused still regarding the man warily expecting he had some dire announcement or that maybe he felt her performance was lacking.

With a frustrated sigh for her standing, the Commander stated, "You mentioned prior to the survival training you had not done any sky diving."

That statement was so unexpected that Bryn was unable prevent the shock she felt from showing in her expression. "No," she said.

"What were you going to do on the roof when we found you?" he said with surprise.

Her expression turned sardonic at his choice of words, "I was going to assemble a hang glider. The city provides ample warm air currents," she said stiffly, but suspected he knew this and that the men had gathered all her gear.

"Hmm, I see. Well you're going to need a crash course in sky diving then. It's a method of deployment we use regularly," he said.

Bryn struggled to hide her uncertainty. This was not a welcome prospect being out in the open with nothing to land on except the ground far below, no buildings to land on, no sides to climb and no control. A scale dart, one of her common pieces of equipment, would be completely useless in open sky.

So two days later, Nighthawk took her to the roof and the helicopter transported them to an airfield to her dismay.

"The first jump we'll make tandem so you get a feel for what will happen," said Nighthawk as he donned a parachute harness with an attachment for her in the front of him.

Even though she was beginning to trust this man, Bryn could not feel easy about this new experience and to her consternation Nighthawk picked up on her uncertainty.

"There's nothing to worry about, you'll see," he said squeezing her shoulder.

Her mouth went dry as they boarded a plane and it seemed no time at all before they reached the altitude to jump so that she began to panic, but Nighthawk calmly talked her through the process. She would have backed away from the open door on the plane if she had not been attached to Nighthawk by the tandem harness even though he tried to soothe her and when he jumped out into empty air, Bryn frantically grabbed at his arms.

"Take it easy. I won't free-fall long," he said into her ear though the wind whipped away his voice.

Then there was a massive jerk as the parachute deployed and their descent slowed to a more reasonable rate so Bryn felt her wildly beating heart begin to return to its normal rhythm once she accepted there was some control. The parachute they were using was of a rectangular design not the round type she expected and he was capable to controlling their speed of descent as well as guiding the parachute directionally. That calmed her further. She expected little to no control at all so this was a welcome surprise.

As training exercises continued, Nighthawk made certain she knew how to fall in case of bad landing, knew how to pack a parachute properly so it would deploy normally and eventually introduced her to a glide suit. Descending with a glide suit was initially a frightening experience for her since she found little difference between it and free fall, but eventually she managed to become inured to the sensation.

When at the Facility training, Bryn finally was able to pick differences in the men and identify Stanton so she could stay well away from him, if he complained about her the Commander would have proof she avoided interacting with the man.

The rest of the team had no particular issues with her just as Nighthawk stated so that when she was able to identify Stanton in his gear the sessions were basically trouble free and productive. Even the impatient Commander seemed pleased by their progress and performance no matter what pitfalls he could dream up.

During the briefing after the exercises, Bryn began to feel more confident about offering input by pointing out alternate strategies and suggesting several exit routes so gear could be left accessible if "shit hit the fan" as the Commander would often state. At times she was uncertain how the Commander felt about this information because Stanton always disagreed with any proposal Bryn offered, citing ridiculous or unrealistic reasons an idea would not work. At those times, Nighthawk would squeeze her arm surreptitiously as a subtle reminder to ignore the man and sometimes Bryn did need those reminders when she felt her temper rise.

Unfortunately, the Commander thought some of her input was over cautious so he brushed aside preparations that he felt would not potentially be of use and he flatly refused to allow her to leave the Facility to place gear in those areas herself. That was what happened today and Bryn woodenly stared at the table avoiding everyone's eyes feeling uneasy that she would not have her normal plans in place. They never gave her a chance to state she would retrieve all the unused gear, it seemed the Commander decided Bryn would use the opportunity to disappear and she knew that to be a flimsy excuse because he could have sent the team or Nighthawk to accompany her in that case.

Even Nighthawk's hand on her arm had little effect after such a dismissal meeting and Bryn popped out the chair before the other men soon as the conference ended to return to quarters.

The other men filed out of the room, Crease instead of Stanton wore a self-satisfied smile as if pleased that the Commander refused to use most of the preparations suggested by Shadow, as they now called her that is all except Crease surprisingly. She wondered if it was payback for slapping him, but he had deserved it. He lost no time disparaging the name after Nighthawk informed the Commander she had the right to go by her call sign just as several of the men did including him.

Soon as the final man left, the Commander looked up to find Nighthawk watching him with a posture of disapproval and he said impatiently, "Now what?"

"Don't be so quick to dismiss her suggestions. You asked for her skills to aid the team and then disregard her advice. You don't need me to remind you that she was never caught or identified," he said softly, but with an unmistakable warning in his voice.

"I think you spend too much time in her company. You're blinded by association with her if what most of the men say is true," scoffed the Commander, but he instantly regretted those hasty words as Nighthawk stood. His aspect seemed to change to threatening in the blink of an eye.

"Be very careful of accusations Commander. You went to a lot of trouble to obtain those skills and then you let jaded people like Crease or Stanton sway you which can only lead to potential failure," he said with a hint of bite in his soft voice.

The Commander noted Nighthawk did not deny the association, but he did subtly hint that no performance errors or failures had occurred which led back to him or the woman. Kolski let out a slow breath of relief when Nighthawk turned on his heel and left the conference room, he heard nervous shuffling either side of him so Kolski knew the two assistants were affected by that last confrontation.

On way to quarters, Bryn decided she was too angry to sit and review the data so she detoured to the exercise area of the Facility which held weight machines, tread-mills as well as a variety of other options. She had the feeling someone checked on her while her back was to the door and suspected it was Nighthawk, but she did not acknowledge it in her present mood. Finally her stomach would not be denied and Bryn began to feel light-headed so she returned to quarters hoping this was not one of those times Ryan would decide to break his silence. She did not think she could manage to be civil to him.

However, Bryn received a surprise when she saw no sign of Ryan in either room so she selected one item to eat before heading to the shower to rinse a very sweaty body which already assaulted her nose with an unwel-come odor. She returned to the cater unit once dressed in more comfortable clothing then decided to listen to music to calm her turbulent mind, she wanted a clear head for the mission and anger would only cloud her judgment.

Her eyes grew heavy sitting in the chair so the music had the desired effect and eventually Bryn drifted off to sleep still sitting in the chair. Much later that was how Ryan eventually found her before moving her to the sofa she used to get the sleep she would need for the mission.

Black of night descended as Shadow waited for the men to begin their part of the mission, she remained out of sight and listened for information through the ear bud, but for now all was silent. The rest of the team would make a covert entry through service tunnels supposedly unused since the eighteen hundreds.

Finally a voice said tersely, "We're in the tunnels," and that was her signal to move.

What Shadow did not expect was soon as she sighted the peripheral of the hundred and twenty story building they were to breach she picked up an unusual aura with her vision and knew this had not been part of the Intelligence gathered. It was highly probable that equipment used in the reconnaissance did not have sensitivity of her eyesight and Shadow was certainly not going to announce her discovery. An explanation would give the Facility far too much information about her abilities and could seal her fate as a permanent resident as too important an asset to lose.

Another thing the Intelligence did not seem to convey accurately was the absence of windows for a good twenty stories from the ground. Her careful approached allowed Shadow to see odd breaks in the aura running up the sides of the building in almost a hopscotch manner which she could negotiate. Soon as she touched the wall of the building, Shadow's sensitive fingers picked up an odd vibration, which increased the closer to the odd aura and tingled with a charge that reminded her off an ultrasound vibration on the skin. *An alarm of some sort?* She thought worriedly.

For a brief moment, Shadow's courage almost failed her. She did not like surprises and had she been the one to do her own reconnaissance, she would have been aware of the unusual aura or other surprises that might lie in wait. Was it possible that even with the technology at the Facility this building possessed devices beyond what they used?

Ascent slightly hampered by the aura, Shadow negotiated the irregular pattern and reached the windows without too much delay. That was when she noticed something else unforeseen: Odd wires running through the glass that emitted pulse charges and that was not good, she knew it would take all her expertise to circumvent such a safeguard if the men were unaware of the barrier. Would this problem deactivate when they shut down the security for the room that was her goal?

There was plenty of climbing left for Shadow before she would worry about that prospect which should give the men time to divert security to the room, which held the safe she had to breach.

Kolski watched the VID transmission from the team or at least the men, he grumbled sourly about that since the woman was not wearing any visor, but then she did not need the input they provided even if they had yet to figure out exactly what she could see. According to Shadow, she would be distracted or inhibited by such a device since she never used any during her previous career. So they were essentially blind to what she would be doing until beginning her actual breach and then she would mount mini Wi-Fi cameras to transmit her progress. He still did not like it.

Of course Nighthawk pointed out that the mission stood a greater chance of failure if they did not allow Shadow to operate as normal even if this entry would be more complex and dangerous to any of her previous "jobs." This would be an unusual assignment for her since the goal in question would not be a saleable item, but intelligence associated with a spy ring or so they told her. It also made this mission very dangerous because they were well funded and had security Shadow had not actually faced in her previous forays, one of which were special forces trained guards with automatic weapons.

Another worrisome factor was making the breach alone, not even Nighthawk could manage to accompany Shadow without getting in the way or so he said. So here he sat, the Commander no less, blind to what she was doing until Shadow mounted those cameras.

A separate monitor flickered to life to the right of the primary VID screen and Kolski thought, Finally! The men had tapped into the security system, which included the video surveillance and the Commander moved it to the huge wall screen, with the swipe of his hand, which nearly covered the entire wall of the conference room. One image split into a myriad of smaller pictures showing heavily armed personnel roaming all areas of the target building except for stairwells, which had a constant feed of video and each camera had motion sensors that instantly flipped to a moving object.

This was one of the main reasons they needed the woman; no one would stand a chance making their way in from a normal breach and there were so many fail safes, even the best of their digital experts could not loop the camera feeds to show a benign scene. All the guards' routines were intentionally sporadic so such a subterfuge would instantly be noted by security. Only the facade higher up on the building was not consistently monitored and under almost all circumstances would deter any would be intruder from risk alone.

As Shadow approached her goal, she mentally reviewed the equipment she carried in various pouches on her sides wishing there was less of it, but due to the complexity of this entry, she accepted it would be needed. Fortunately the side pouches easily contained the gear leaving her back free so she could use a special panel to secure her body as she climbed. Her mind kept returning to the advice the Commander dismissed and that could leave her with a potential situation where extracting her person might be impossible. That was why she worked alone, no one to blame, but her own failings if she had not done her preparation instead of relying on others, but Shadow pushed those sour reflections aside as she drew level with the target window.

Checking her timepiece, Shadow clung to the wall like a gecko and glanced at a window on the seventy-eighth floor in more detail rapidly sifting through her vision at the unwelcome pulses shifting through the wires in the glass. Only a minute behind schedule, so the men should have reached the trunk which fed the room security and diverted or shut it down, but...the wires in the window were in working order, not good. It was possible the wires in the glass ran off a different line since all the windows she passed had the same type of pulsing wires which meant the men probably knew nothing about the barrier.

Using some of the tin foil in one of her pouches, Shadow improvised a type of feedback loop to allow the pulses to continue through the wires once the window was no longer connected to wall of the building.

Then she began pulling out the special gear used to displaced the glass panes attaching one to each of the windows four corners, she carefully broke the seal about the glass and pressed the remote device in her hand. Each of the mechanisms simultaneously rotated pulling the glass away from the building yet holding the huge pane in place and Shadow slithered to one side and stepped on the sill of the window.

This was when she had yet another surprise. Instead of a clear room, beams of light crisscrossed the room detected by her vision that the team should have turned off and now what was she supposed to do? What the hell were the men doing? She thought fuming with impatience at such a lack of efficiency.

If she could have used the ventilation ducts, Shadow might have backtracked and continued up one more floor, but she knew from the Intelligence the ducts had a high voltage charge to prevent vermin, animal, or human from traversing unseen within the building.

Taking slow deep breaths, Shadow considered the choices before her: Back out and report the issue, wait to see if the men dealt with it or abandon the entire mission informing the Commander of the problem. Flicking through her vision allowed her to discover another disquieting observation: A misty turbulence at least waist high and nothing she had ever seen before from the wavelengths reflected or absorbed. A gas? Toxic or sedative? Whichever it was, Shadow could not take the risk to initiate contact or breathe it, not with the only aid far, far below her and essentially unreachable.

The improbability stung her pride awake. There had to be a way in and it could be the men faced obstacles deactivating the room's security, but what options did she have now? Shadow glanced up at the ceiling to see that with care, she could crawl across to avoid disrupting the beams and avoid the gas below. It would be tricky and she still had to avoid the motion sensors.

A snarled comment in her ear made Shadow flinch, "Where the hell are you, Shadow? Those cameras aren't in place," said the Commander's voice.

Twisting her lips in irritation, Shadow placed a special wireless camera to transmit her situation which was Nighthawk's idea and heard muted swearing of the Commander as he berated the men for her security situation.

Ignoring the voice, Shadow carefully shimmied up the wall and flattened her entire body as if she were crawling into a very tight space though she was actually on the ceiling with gravity working against her. It was tricky business, too.

"What are you guys playing at? That entire room is still live," demanded the Commander, moderating his voice so not to blast Shadow's sensitive ears.

"It should be down," said Stanton's irritable voice through the COM.

"Well it's not! I can see it for myself and...bloody hell!" swore the Commander as the camera picked up Shadow inching across the ceiling like a fly.

"What?" demanded several voices.

"Never mind! Just deal with that room security. We're behind schedule and Shadow is proceeding in spite of it," said Kolski wonderingly.

Crazy woman! Why is she continuing like that? If she fell...damn it to hell...the entire building would be alive with men running to her location. *Shit, shit, shit,* he thought and sweat beaded his brow realizing he had not truly appreciated the woman's grit or tenacity.

"Why is that security still up?" snarled the Commander a few minutes later.

Swearing came through the COM so that Kolski caught words like back up, fail safes, and heard Stanton order someone to another trunk line. With a mixture of respect and nail biting tension, Kolski continued to watch the woman work with a kind of fascinated horror as he considered the consequences she would suffer for failure.

Due to the unknown gas, Shadow did not dare alight on the floor as she might have in the past to access the security measures guarding information or item she was targeting. This presented an unusual solution that she never had reason to use: remain on the wall for the entire duration and work from an angle. Whatever function the item had she was after must pale in comparison to anything requested by past cliental. Never had laser beams been so dense in a room before and even if she had enough mirrors, Shadow would have taken hours to work through all the beams by which time a guard would most certainly check the room.

As the beams still remained intact, her hopes dashed that the team would deal with them in time and ignored the furious diatribe from the Commander at their lack of success; she could not afford any distractions now. Soon as her eyes settled on a large mirror in the room, Shadow had an unorthodox idea and crawled to it quickly noting she had room to climb down the wall without encountering any of the beams.

She removed a glass cutter from a leg pocket and began to systematically cut pieces of the mirror to secure them with special putty until it left the area about the safe clear enough for her to work. Letting out a slow breath, Shadow focused her eyes scanning every detail she had to bypass and felt her palms begin to sweat at the unprecedented difficulty she faced, especially clinging upside down. Again she placed another wireless camera to transmit her progress from this vantage point knowing both cameras would dissolve when a timer released acid from a small vial attached to them.

Odd, she thought, this room had no video surveillance with such extensive security, but Shadow was thankful for the oversight under the circumstances. Most likely between all the obstacles, their security was more concerned for anyone approaching from outside the room via the hallways and motion or sound sensors would prevent anyone from using free wall suspension. Drilling a rope hold would trigger the sensitive equipment by sound and vibration both, hence the confidence that security felt the room very secure.

After the painstaking diversion of the beams, Shadow examined her initial barrier in the form of a complex Chinese puzzle in three dimensions and she was already behind schedule. Fuming at the team in her thoughts, Shadow nearly made a blunder and halted, her heart racing at the escape of an error. *Make haste more slowly*, she berated herself in her thoughts.

The next obstacle was the standard glass plate under metal, so she removed a small portable drill from another pocket with a diamond tip to prevent the glass from cracking, child's play. Then the first real check, a retinal scanner…damn…intelligence said it was supposed to be a standard combination. If this was the way the Facility gathered data it was a wonder they stayed successful.

Various aspects of her vision told Shadow that behind the metal plate of the scanner had a failsafe in case an unauthorized user attempted to circumvent protocol, *exactly what I am doing*, Shadow thought grimly. Then something unexpected occurred, her optical implants did something she never had happen before, it displayed a mini holographic image of what Shadow suspected was the authorized retina. Somehow her visual ability adapted on its own just as it had when she was with Donal, but this time it superimposed on the scanner displaying the appropriate pattern and a minute click told Shadow she was past what should have been impossible. No time to wonder over it.

Time was not on her side and Shadow inched the small door open to reveal a charged door that should not have been live, but it was...*What the hell is the team doing?* She thought furiously and struggled to keep her cool.

With a variety of clips and wires, Shadow sent the charge away from the door so when it opened the current would still be continuous and not trigger the alarm due to grounding or a broken circuit. Time was ticking by fast and Shadow knew she had taken far too much time to get to this point and she was about to reach inside for a pouch which had been the goal of this entire venture when her eyes caught more beams inside the safe. She had to repress a groan because this would be much worse than the room she negotiated and Shadow privately damned whoever it was on the team that had responsibility for disconnecting all these barriers.

One thing Shadow knew for certain though, she would never state it to the Commander, whatever this supposed storage medium, it was a farce and all the electronic activity would corrupt digital information. Later, she would think about all that later.

Reaching into one of her pockets, Shadow removed rubber tongs to place tiny mirror slivers to redirect this set of beams in such an enclosed area, they had to be small to fit inside the safe and give her room to remove the pouch. Slowly and with great care, Shadow used the tongs to grip the pouch inching it out of the safe to avoid the mirror slivers, she barely took a breath as she cleared the opening before placing the item into its shielded case.

Pushing the small case into a secure pocket, Shadow began to back her way out of the safe's security knowing full well she would never be able to hide the damage to the mirror, which could be seen from the doorway. No matter how she cut the glass to avoid drawing immediate attention, any security worth their pay would notice something was off and these people were the best from what the Commander intimated.

Stowing each piece of mirror carefully, Shadow inched back up to the ceiling and knew her grace period was over, any minute an armed guard would check the room as part of normal rounds. A jingling sound outside the door sent a jolt of apprehension through her and she did the only practical thing, Shadow shimmed over above the door pressing against the wall as much as possible in hopes the guard would only look inside, not up, and then move on. There was a beep, as if the guard swiped a key card and the door opened underneath her.

Please don't look up, thought Shadow inwardly as a man's head poked slightly through the doorway and the man's head twisted quickly, he seemed to back out as if she planned for this eventuality. Since he never looked up, it almost worked, but unfortunately something about the big mirror caught the man's eye from the doorway and the beams of light crisscrossing the room suddenly winked out, worse some special field forced the gas away forming a path to the safe.

The man moved into the room and raised a radio to his mouth, Shadow knew the game was up and they would know there was an intruder. *Damn, damn*, she thought, *this guy is good*. So much for subtlety!

With no choices left, Shadow dropped lightly to the ground and sprinted out the open door. She rounded the first corner down the hall when the sound of automatic fire filled the area she just vacated, sending her heart to her throat in terror. It was the first time in her life anyone had shot any type of weapon at her, at least during a job, and there would be no way the men could help her.

The men stood silently at their exit point waiting for word from the Commander about Shadow's progress and if she purloined the item. Stanton fumed at their inability to alter the security measures about the room and as they diverted or shut down one pathway, another took its place, like a dike with too many holes to plug. It was not until he looked up that he noticed one of the men was missing and took note to see who the missing man was just as Crease popped back up from seemingly nowhere.

His eyes narrowed, not recalling at what point the man left the group. Where had he been and for how long?

"Where have you been?" hissed Stanton to Crease.

With a sneer, Crease said, "I was checking the security detail on the upper floors."

"For what reason? We already know their projected paths and timeframe of their sweeps. You risked their security cameras picking you up," said Stanton suspiciously.

"We shouldn't still be here, that's why," challenged Crease, his tone mocking.

Though that statement was true, something in the man's manner bugged him, but he had no time to dwell on those thoughts when alarms blared nearly deafening them, which meant only one thing, the woman had been seen.

"Shit," snarled Stanton. "We've got to go now!"

The alarm was spreading and they could not get caught no matter what was happening or where the woman was in the building, they had to trust she would use an alternate exit. That was the point Stanton noticed Nighthawk was missing, but he could spare no time to look for the man after issuing their retreat.

Kolski had his hands in his hair literally pulling at it when the alarms blazoned wildly as he watched Shadow run into the hallway outside the target room. He forced himself to watch what he thought would be a brutal end to her life, but she was quick, quicker than he realized when projectiles found an empty wall.

Unfortunately, as she turned the corner, two men were running from opposite directions in the new hall to intercept Shadow as she exited the previous hall only to be caught between the two of them. The only positive thing Kolski could see was the possibility of shooting each other kept them from firing at the fleeing figure.

The man Shadow was running toward took out what Kolski thought was a knife and threw in with deadly intent only to see the woman literally run up one of the walls in evasion arcing back down toward the floor as the weapon sailed by her. At that maneuver, the man she was running at slowed his pace to catch Shadow on the drop side as she descended toward the floor, but instead of dropping to the hallway floor, she planted her foot square into his chest forcing him down. Literally running over the man, he watched Shadow sprint down the hall toward what he knew was the stairwell, but another guard burst onto the scene from the same door.

Hunkering down, the man positioned himself to stop the oncoming intruder and Kolski stared in surprise to see Shadow skid sliding across the floor, as if she was stealing home plate in a baseball game, shooting straight through the man's legs. For some reason, the man doubled up and crumpled to the floor, but Kolski did not bother to ponder the reason watching Shadow finally hit the stairwell then jamming the door shut with her calf knife.

Guards all knew where the intruder was and flooded into the stairwell. Kolski watched in a state of high tension as they forced her up the stairs toward the roof.

Knowing the blueprints of the building well, she ran straight for the stairwell and planned to descend to meet the men when Shadow heard running feet ascending in her direction. That forced her to sprint upward away of pursuers climbing after her, Shadow had no time to worry if the team was at risk or already left, per the time table.

Good thing old habits die hard, she chanted in her mind. Shadow already fished a device out of her pocket to break the electronic lock on the rooftop door and pausing on her tired screaming legs, she laid the small box against the door watching the light switch from red to green. Soon as she was out the door, Shadow began to jam items on her person, including the mirror pieces, as well as rubble from the rooftop into the cracks of the door to wedge it until she felt an impact telling her at least one guard reached the door.

She sprinted away just in time as the sound of automatic fire broke the silence and holes appeared in the door as the guards attempted to shoot their way onto the roof to get her. Racing to the spot where the gear was supposed to be hidden, Shadow knelt down panting in terror as her searching hands finally found the false metal unit that hid the bulk she needed and ripped open the pack.

There was no point bemoaning this method of exit, Shadow seriously considered running to roof's edge and climbing down the building instead of jumping with a parachute. Quickly she donned the glide suit and clipping the parachute harness in place until the sound of the roof door crashing open sent her sprinting to the edge of the roof. With no other choice, Bryn leapt from the roof in free-fall knowing if she deployed the parachute too soon it would make her a sitting target and even that was not fast enough. Automatic fire sounded in a rata-tat-tat behind her, sending Shadow's heart into her throat from terror and barely cognizant of a sting in her calf until she yanked the ripcord, then she had a whole new set of problems.

Her speed did not slow and Shadow glanced up to see only the pilot chute had deployed, not the main chute, so she pulled another cord to activate the glide suit even though she knew it could not slow her enough to keep her alive. Manipulating the suit, Shadow angled back to the building attempting to use the windows to slow her descent and maybe even climb to the bottom until the building began to light up. Below her, the entire ground area became brilliant with light, *They radioed how I'm descending*, she thought in renewed terror and they hoped to catch her helpless or renew their assault.

Limited options faced her now, even if she did manage to stop her descent Shadow knew she could only climb up which was a death trap and her frantic gaze settled on a nearby power plant, she pushed away from the building using the glide suit to get as close as possible.

It was a stomach dropping plummet requiring Shadow to spread her arms and legs as wide as possible to slow her free-fall with the glide suit as she frantically seized the scale dart at her waist, aimed it at the roof of the power plant, and by sheer luck it took hold. Automatically, Shadow secured the cord at her belt and not a moment too soon as the world turned upside down when tension hit the cord snapping her back so hard, she slammed into the building façade. Lights sparkled in her vision and Shadow's right side felt severely bruised as she attempted to crawl to the roof with one functional arm, the other possibly broken. Helpfully the cord attached to the scale dart retracted as she climbed giving some added support so that she managed to reach the edge of the roof. What she had not planned on was the scale dart coming loose when she slipped and barely caught one of the building's outer lights to prevent an immediate fall, but her right arm did not want to work so she ended up hanging by only one hand which was quickly tiring. Every muscle began screaming in protest at the abuse she suffered thus far.

She needed both arms if she was going to climb up, but the broken or bruised one from her collision with the building quivered and refused to function after such a brutal impact. Shadow struggled to get closer to the building to crawl only to find her grip ominously slipping. Refusing to give up even in the face of the death she felt coming, Shadow finally lost her hold and closed her eyes resigned to her fate until a hand caught her extended arm in a vise-like hold.

Looking up in disbelief, she saw Nighthawk not understanding how he knew to be there. In her shock, Shadow failed to appreciate the raw strength it took to pull her up one handed on to the roof and soon as her feet hit the ground she sprinted across the concrete pushing the pain aside after being given a new chance at life. The glide suit resisted her running and the pilot shut slowed her down until the flapping ceased telling her Nighthawk had cut it away, but there was no time to remove the suit. Without hesitation, Shadow leapt from the roof to a lamppost of a street light and slid down it like a firehouse pole straight to the ground to sprint off again on an alternative escape route, but a strong arm curling about her waist diverted her course.

They were heading to one of the options that the Commander refused to sanction for escape gear, but Shadow knew she could not resist Nighthawk and in her weakened state she would need his protection. Sounds of rotors from helicopters came nearer which meant they were searching and Shadow suspected lights about the power plant had revealed her rescue. So it was possible they would be looking for two people now.

Nighthawk pulled her into an abandoned building that Shadow originally noted as an alternative and headed for a chute that she knew had been used for coal in a bygone era. He lifted her feet orienting her body inside the chute so she could slide to the bottom. Soon as she hit the ground, Shadow jumped aside to make room for Nighthawk's descent herald by a thud in the pitch black room which was followed by the sound of a zipper being pulled.

A light appeared and Shadow felt a flashlight shoved into her good hand, she bit off a comment that she did not need light and another flashlight appeared casting enough illumination that Nighthawk could locate the gear bag before heading for a sewer grate she knew was at the other side of the room.

Nighthawk quickly removed the floor grate and caught Shadow about the waist to lower her down before passing the gear bag to her after which he backed down replacing the grate as he came to leave no sign of their passing.

Shadow checked her timepiece noting that dawn was not far off and dressed as they were it would draw attention, especially her wearing a partially deployed parachute and a glide suit, from people already heading for work in the dusk before sunrise. Odors surrounding them were less than pleasant, but Shadow wryly reminded herself it was better than death as they negotiated rats and all manner of slimy refuse.

It was a struggle to hide her pain and weariness, but Shadow followed her companion without complaint until they reached a dry recessed area, which Nighthawk carefully investigated before setting the gear bag down. She stumbled trying to lift her weary legs just a few more steps attempting to wave off Nighthawk's assistance, which he ignored by pulling her over to the most sheltered spot as he proceeded to remove the parachute harness from her body. Then he gestured for her to sit.

He arranged one of the flashlights in a way to reflect soft illumination from the ceiling of their refuge and then handed Shadow a flask of water, which she took gratefully while her companion began to examine her useless arm. He must have decided the bones broke or fractured because he applied a special air cast once he removed the upper portion of the glide suit. As he finished with her arm, she passed the flask back to him so he could drink and accepted an energy bar in turn and though it seemed inadequate, it would have to do for now. How Nighthawk managed to appear on the power plant roof when she needed help most, Shadow still had no idea, but she was grateful to be drawing breaths instead of suffering imminent death.

"Thank you," she said very quietly so it would not echo though those two words seemed pathetically inadequate after he just saved her life.

She felt his finger touch her chin softly in acknowledgement before he fished another item out of the gear bag, which looked like a cellular phone and began to type out a text message about their delay. Leaning against the wall wearily, Shadow closed her eyes, too tired to even finish the energy bar, and dozed off leaving Nighthawk to handle contact with the Facility. The touch of his shoulder against hers woke Shadow slightly as Nighthawk settled against the wall. After that, she sunk into oblivion, accepting she was safe for the time being.

A gentle shake woke Shadow, but she felt odd, chilled, and sick as well as unusually sluggish though she knew her abused body would be worse for wear it should have just been stiff and painful.

"Something is wrong with me. I feel odd," she said very quietly, but her voice sounded fainter than it should have.

Aware of a light moving around, Shadow was not certain what Nighthawk was looking for until she felt him touch her calf, even through the glide suit, and she instantly heard the gear back zip open. Careful jostling of the glide suit told Shadow, Nighthawk completely removed it and she was cognizant he was wrapping something tightly about her calf. She felt curiously cold and detached, a floating sensation washed through her limbs.

The world seemed to turn upside down and Shadow was dimly aware Nighthawk had tossed her over his shoulder followed by the sensation of movement. She felt confused and unable to understand the reason he needed to carry her.

Reality faded in and out as Shadow was unable to account for passage of time until she had a vague impression of her body changing position to lay on something flat accompanied by voices she could not readily identify.

A woman's voice said, "I need help getting this body-suit off her, hurry."

Then a sharp prick in her left arm, followed by a man's voice, "Just numb the area. She's too weak to place under anesthesia that projectile shattered and we need to get those pieces out before we can repair the blood vessels. Once she is stable, we'll repair the broken bones."

She felt another prick, but this time in her right arm and felt a flare of annoyance, but Shadow could not seem to get her mouth to form the words.

There was activity around her calf again and finally the woman's voice said, "Let her rest."

In the conference room the Commander demanded, "What the hell happened? This mission should have gone quickly with minimal issues."

Stanton shrugged, "Maybe the woman isn't as good as you thought she was," and there was a nasty laugh, but he did not see who had made the sound, he had not intended to be derogatory.

On the heels of that comment, the door hissed open admitting Nighthawk and he seemed tense compared to his typical calm demeanor.

"Well?" snapped the Commander.

With deliberate movement, Nighthawk held out the encased pouch and the Commander relaxed as he took it, he did not miss the flexing jaw muscles of Stanton at the exchange.

"Now explain why that room's security remained active," demanded the Commander.

All the men looked at Stanton, he straightened defensively and bit off what he wanted to say, he knew the woman was not at fault, but he would never let anyone think he held any charity toward her.

"It should have been inactive. Whoever provided intel on the security matrix failed to mention the redundant backups in place," said Stanton with a sideways glance at Crease.

"Don't look at me! It was your incompetence," said the man scathingly.

At those words Stanton half rose in his chair to backhand the rookie for insolence until the Commander barked, "Sit back down Stanton. Crease, it was your responsibility to research those schematics. Your background is security systems in use and experimental," pinning the man with a hard stare.

"The fool woman tripped the alarms before we could neutralize them. She's sloppy and you heard him (referring to Stanton), maybe she's not that good," sneered Crease.

"Oh...you think so, do you? Let me enlighten you," drawled Kolski in a deceptively mild voice and glanced at one of the assistants to replay the recorded footage from the mini cameras as well as the surveillance video from the building.

It was a treat for Kolski to watch the stunned amazement on all the men's face with the exception of Nighthawk as he remained outwardly impassive as usual and did not seemed surprised at the woman's performance. As the recording progressed, the men collectively winced, including Nighthawk, when they saw Shadow slide beneath the guards legs and pummel his groin in passing, even the Commander found himself flinching watching it again. Well...it had effectively removed the man from pursuing her even if plenty of other guards filled that void chasing her up the stairwell where the video surveillance finally lost her exiting onto the roof.

"Damn it to hell," said Stanton finally into the silence following the recording, "She's certifiable. Why the ceiling?"

"No one knows yet. I'll know more once she can be debriefed," said the Commander barely concealing a smirk at the men's reactions.

"You had the gall to call her sloppy?" said Foss staring at Crease, "Especially after you went sneaking off on your own without a word..."

"What's this?" demanded the Commander.

Crease directed a murderous glare at Foss as Stanton confirmed the incident, "He claimed he was checking guard patrol on the floors above," he said thin lipped.

"You don't break mission protocol fool. The team responsibility was to deal with the security in that room why else patch into the surveillance to keep tabs on the guards," snarled Kolski furiously wondering just what the man had really been up to.

"Acting like a damn rookie...for all we know something he did tripped the alarms...," drawled Stanton obviously enjoying disparaging the other man.

Without warning, Crease launched across the table at Stanton, but Tank was faster and grabbed the incensed man with his ham-like hands that Crease could not disengage which left the man swearing impotently at Stanton's mocking expression.

"You idiot," said the Commander directed at Crease, "After he returned, just how long was it before the alarm sounded?" inquiring of the other men.

"Within a few minutes," stated Foss glancing sideways at the snarling man still attempting to reach Stanton unsuccessfully.

"What did you hope to gain if the mission failed? All the trouble it took to track down that woman and you nearly cost her, her life. It's a miracle she made it in let alone out of that building with the item intact and you sit her discrediting her for your own shortcomings," said the Commander scathingly.

Slowly he rose to his feet and leaned over the table toward the struggling man, "You're benched for the next missions," he said silkily. "We don't have time to deal with personal grudges." And here the Commander thought it would be Stanton at the root of the problem unless this lame brained move to discredit Shadow stemmed from her slapping him.

"You can't do that!" shouted Crease, his face red with fury.

"I can and just did. You should have been working with the team to deactivate the security in that room, but instead you sneak off on your own, completely unsanctioned by your team leader. You knew the most about those security schematics," stated Kolski flatly.

"There must have been backups we didn't know about...," began Crease hotly.

"I don't want to hear it. Maybe a hiatus will let you think more clearly about what you should do instead of what you want to do," enunciated the Commander very carefully.

As a snarling oath escaped Crease's lips, he managed to wrench free of Tank's implacable grip, or the man chose to release him, and he stormed out of the conference room without a backward glance. They all watched the man leave and soon as the door shut, Tank said, "How is she?"

The Commander glanced at Nighthawk, who chose not to comment so he said, "She was critical when she arrived. Lost a lot of blood from a leg wound, broken arm, and a couple of fractured ribs, but Doc said she should recover with rest." On another note he asked, "Does anyone know why she did not use the gear on the roof to get out of there?"

"She did use it. The parachute did not deploy properly," said Nighthawk flatly.

"Who packed that chute?" demanded the Commander.

"Didn't she do her own?" queried Stanton in surprise.

"Son of...do you know that for certain?" said the Commander through gritted teeth.

"She knows how to pack a parachute correctly, I made certain of that," said Nighthawk firmly and did not acknowledge Stanton's snort of disbelief.

Nighthawk leaned forward, "She made no mistake. I know how she packs so I will check it out. I'll know if she was the one who packed it," he said in a dangerous voice.

"What are you hinting at?" said the Commander narrowly.

"I'll see how that chute was packed first before I say anymore," said Nighthawk grimly.

Head in his hands, the Commander asked, "So how the hell did she get out?"

Every man looked straight at Nighthawk, "She jumped from the roof with guards shooting at her until she was far enough away then pulled her ripcord, but only the pilot chute deployed. She used the glide suit to angle back to the building to try to slow her fall, but she had to get away from the building before they intercepted her. She jumped away from the building still forty floors up and managed to set off a scale dart at the utility plant in free-fall which, unfortunately, it came loose when she tried to climb, so she had to catch an extended light on the power plant. If I hadn't been watching, she wouldn't have made it. I had to pull her up to the roof after the shock her body received. I placed gear in places she suggested in case we needed another route, the ones you shot down. Good thing I did because we had to use one," he said coolly though the thin line of his lips indicated his anger.

"Damn...forty floors...and no chute," said Foss in awe.

Nighthawk knew the only reason she took such a risk was because she was already dead if she did not, though he did not belittle the courage it took to make such a choice. He knew anyone else would have aborted that run seeing those beams still active, but Shadow trusted her team would do their jobs and they failed her.

"She should have backed off when she saw those beams...," began Tank nearly mirroring Nighthawk thoughts, but the Commander finished the sentence.

"She probably didn't think she had to if she trusted the team to do their job. It's hard to fault her for working alone before this," he said with a sigh and then to Nighthawk, "You were right. I apologize for dismissing her advice."

"It's not me you should apologize to," he said quietly.

Chapter 8

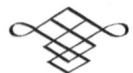

Dreams plagued Shadow escaping from the building and stuck helplessly in a death trap, she kept searching for gear she could not find only to face men with automatic weapons firing at her chest. It continued to replay until one dream mirrored her jump from the building and Shadow shot straight up as she saw the ground rushing to meet her.

A previously unfelt hand gripped hers tightly and another caught her shoulder as if in assurance she was safe, even though her pounding heart tried to say otherwise. Her eyes darted about to see the reassuring sight of the infirmary before she thought to look at the source of the hand on her shoulder.

The hand belonged to Nighthawk unsurprisingly and Shadow calmed further at his presence, but flinched at the flash of white from the corner of her eye when the doctor approached.

The man placed a thermometer in her ear and said, "Good. Your temperature is normal. It was too far below average when you arrived. Look at me please."

He flashed a light in her eyes checking for pupillary responses then moved on to check her reflexes as a woman walked over to take her blood pressure, which was thankfully normal.

"We can remove the I.V.'s," he said suiting action to words taping cotton over the needle sites, "You're to rest for two weeks and then return for a checkup."

"Two weeks? I feel fine," she said indignantly.

"That's what I said. Especially after your condition when you arrived here and the blood you lost. You had a broken arm and some ribs so you will notice some soreness in those areas from muscle trauma after bone repair. You can return to your quarters when you're ready," said the doctor sternly.

Great, she thought, *stuck in another hospital gown without any clothing in sight, typical.* She felt Ryan's gaze on her and refused to meet his eyes suspecting he just might tease her in remembrance of her very first visit. His hands supported Bryn as she slid off the gurney, which turned out to be wise when her stiff calf upset her balance though it was not painful exactly.

It was difficult to curb her irritation at Ryan's continued assistance though Bryn knew he did not intend to make her feel like an invalid, but thankfully they made it to quarters without encountering any observers for her exposed backside.

First thing she did was head to the hygiene facilities because she was certain the odor of the sewer lingered on her skin and hair, she paused to remove the cotton from her arms before standing blissfully under the warm water. Though it was still painful at times, her calf limbered up during the shower and she had to pat it dry carefully or suffer the backlash from the barely healed muscle.

Once she pressed her hair dry in a towel, Bryn's stomach began to rumble impatiently forcibly reminder her than the last thing she ate was part of a pathetic energy bar. Ryan had some snacks sitting on the table obviously anticipating her next goal and Bryn snorted in amusement, but found that the man was missing from the room.

After a stay in the infirmary, Bryn rested enough to feel fidgety so once her hunger eased she sat at the data unit to occupy her time and to see if another proposed mission listed enough information to study. At first the data could not calm her restlessness until she accessed the next mission preliminaries and saw that they would be on a different continent, but Bryn pushed that aside when she caught the time of year they expected to breach. Winter? They would be dealing with ice and snow...and what if they had to run, how would she survive separated from the others, if that happened?

Her only survival instructor had been Stanton, not her first choice to approach, but Bryn felt inhibited about asking Ryan, she did not know why and thought it might still be trust. Well...fruitless as it might be, she decided to ask Stanton and check the database for his quarter's location before leaving the room.

Taking a deep breath once she reached his door, Bryn pressed a button to alert Stanton to a visitor and the door hissed back within seconds revealing the man, who eyed her suspiciously before he said, "What?" Not that she expected him to waste courtesy on her.

"I need some advice. I just saw the preliminaries for the next mission. We never covered a survival situation in snow or even winter," said Bryn neutrally.

"Why don't you ask your cozy friend?" said Stanton waspishly.

It took effort, but Bryn did not flush or react to the insinuation, "Because you are my assigned instructor," she said stonily.

"I *was* your instructor," he stressed, "for one training exercise. It was an order; I followed it. I have no additional orders to help you further," stated Stanton with a sneering curl to his lips.

That was not exactly the response Bryn hoped for and she tried to hide sinking sensation in her belly at his

blatant refusal to give any helpful information, "I understand," was all Bryn said before the door slid shut in her
face. Even though she had expected him to be unhelpful,
Bryn berated herself for thinking the man might push
aside his animosity to at least give basic information.

No doubt she would meet similar resistance from
the other men Bryn thought bitterly and walked back
down the hall to head back to Ryan's quarters. Soon as
she arrived at the T-junction of the hall, Bryn glimpsed a
figure out of the corner of her eye and looked left to see
Nighthawk striding down the hall. Though she could not
see his eyes due to the visor, Bryn could tell he was not
happy to see her from the set of his jaw, lips thinned in
annoyance. Instantly, Bryn knew he did not approve of
her leaving his quarters as she attempted to head back to
his quarters, but it was not fast enough and found herself
tossed over Nighthawk's shoulder followed by a sharp
stinging slap to her backside. Obviously he took the
medical restrictions seriously and that she was to rest.
Since there was no point asking for release, Bryn fumed
at the man's high-handedness with only one comforting
thought, she was not bare assed to the world this time.

Though she was still restless the following day, Bryn
did not attempt to leave Ryan's quarters again or she
knew another rebuke would follow and probably just
as physically uncomfortable. Knowing the doctor would
not allow her near the gym, Bryn began to stretch to at
least limber up and perform some resistive exercises.

Annoyance seemed to roll toward her from Ryan at
one of the data units, but at least she was still in the room
so she felt there was little he could say about her activity.
Then Bryn stopped her exercise, she did not want to antagonize her only friend in the Facility and it was not his
fault she had to rest. She was acting petulant again even
if she never said a word.

Opting for sedate activity before she alienated Ryan,
Bryn sat in front of the second data unit and bullied

herself to focus on some of the new information the Commander made available about the next mission he was building for them. The COM blaring into the room made Bryn jump in surprise and the Commander's voice issued an order for Bryn to report to the conference room for debriefing which she did not consider a good thing.

Ryan reached over to press the COM button, "She's supposed to rest for two weeks," he said flatly.

"Damn it, I'm not telling her to report to the gym! Did you think I expected her to jog to the debriefing?" said the Commander dryly, "Just make sure she's here."

Obviously Ryan considered leaving the room at all unacceptable exercise, but since he had no rebuttal for that final statement, he gestured her to follow him.

"Are you always so implacable?" said Bryn.

"When others and you don't consider your welfare, yes," Ryan said with no apology.

Which told Bryn he had been assigned to watch over her and it had not been his choice, *I feel like an unwanted package passed around until it outlives its usefulness*, she thought bitterly. That was what she got for thinking of this man as a friend.

Kolski tapped the conference table irritably and wondered what Nighthawk's game was challenging him over a debriefing, he could not think even the Commander would escape Doc's orders on personnel health issues.

As the door opened, he saw the woman enter first and thought, *Finally*, until he saw her bad tempered expression and wondered just how uncooperative her mood was presently. All of the team was present with the exception of Crease, who was essentially suspended, for his shoddy performance, which nearly caused the mission to fail.

Once both Nighthawk and Shadow sat, Kolski called up the recording of the mission, beginning with the room entry and paused playback to show the security beams still in place.

"Why did you proceed when you could clearly see the team hadn't disabled security?" demanded the Commander.

They would not put this on her, thought Bryn repressively, "You brought me here for my skills," she said angrily.

"We could have returned," said the Commander flatly.

"Exactly. That would keep me here longer than I hope to stay," said Bryn acidly.

That rebuttal caught Kolski by surprise and he heard a snort of laughter from Stanton's direction, "I'm glad you're amused, but this is no laughing matter," he snapped and then to Bryn, he said, "Then why the ceiling? What if you fell?"

Fortunately, Bryn could see the barest shimmer of the gas on the recording so she could avoid drawing more attention to her vision, "Look, you can see a gas on the lower half of the room. I had no idea if it was toxic or even possibly a sedative. I did what was necessary to get to the safe," she said pointing at the frozen image.

Every one of the men leaned forward to study the image and Kolski muttered under his breath about the lack of this information going in and the fact he looked like a fool in front of everyone for that question. Of course, in light of that information, Kolski realized the woman would have used the ceiling beams or no beams.

Fast forwarding to the safe breach he paused where she drilled through the glass plate, asking, "And how did you know exactly where to drill through that glass without triggering the failsafe?"

"Practice," said Bryn unhelpfully.

Kolski fumed at the evasive answer and glared at Stanton again for his amusement, but obviously he was not going to get a better answer to his question.

Again he fast forwarded the image to the optical scanner, this was something Kolski had to know, "There is no way to get past an optical scanner short of bringing an authorized retina with you. This one even prevents a recorded image being used. How did you get past it?" Kolski demanded.

With a hard stare at the man, Bryn said, "You brought me here to help you on certain missions, not to reveal my secrets."

"I don't appreciate your attitude woman," snarled the Commander.

Stanton was enjoying himself watching Bryn confound the Commander and he had to admit she had guts stonewalling a man that could make her life far more miserable than maybe she realized. He was also enjoying the fact that her attitude was irritating Nighthawk from the flexing of his jaw muscles so maybe those two were not as cozy as he thought.

"I retrieved your package. And that was no storage medium for information. The electronics surrounding it would have formed enough of a magnetic field to wipe the data from anything and I don't appreciate being lied to," stressed Bryn goaded into saying what she previously intended to withhold.

Barking a laugh before he could stop it, Stanton inwardly admired the woman's intelligence and the fact the Commander underestimated her, she was no fool, this one.

With a start of surprise at the woman's assessment, Kolski glared at her for such an impudent retort before glancing at Nighthawk, noting the man was not happy with her attitude either and it did not help Stanton was underscoring the issue with his amusement.

"Do you have any more questions?" said Bryn icily.

"You're dismissed," snapped the Commander.

The men watched her leave stiff backed when the Commander indicated to them to remain sitting and soon as the door slid shut, he demanded, "Ok, who the hell put a burr up her ass today?"

Nighthawk stared hard at Stanton before he said, "She was coming from your quarters yesterday."

"Damn it, what did you do Stanton?" snarled the Commander.

"I didn't do anything. She came to me...," stressed Stanton, "for advice. That was all and then she left."

"What kind of advice?" said Nighthawk flatly as he leaned forward dangerously.

"I suggest you ask her," drawled Stanton thoroughly enjoying discomfiting the quiet man.

When the man rose threateningly, Stanton wondered if he had gone too far until the Commander barked, "Sit down," and the man sat slowly staring hard at him, "I suggest you speak to her. We need her cooperative for these missions," the Commander said obviously speaking to Nighthawk.

It was possible his attitude had irritated the woman, Stanton thought and he really had no reason not to help her if it got her out of the Facility sooner, he had not viewed the issue from that perspective. He would remedy the problem on return to his quarters.

Bryn stalked back to Ryan's quarters sufficiently annoyed by the debriefing as if the Commander expected her to give up trade secrets or be forthcoming about her vision capabilities. She might have to help them, but she did not have to give them any more information than absolutely necessary and soon as Bryn left the conference room, she could tell Ryan was annoyed with her.

Once back in Ryan's quarters, Bryn decided to listen to music to calm her frustration and used a headset to avoid conversation when Nighthawk returned which she suspected would be imminent. The first thing Bryn did was check the database to see if she had assigned quarters of her own, stupid really for her not to check that fact before and she wondered why Ryan never mentioned it.

Of course Bryn should have expected the music playing through the headset would mask Ryan's arrival in the room, but when two hands came to rest on her shoulders she jumped violently in her seat, completely unprepared for the contact. Panting slightly from the shock, Bryn ripped off the headset sensing confusion from the man behind her at the casual contact.

Her heart rate was beginning to return to normal only to quickly change again when Bryn felt Ryan's thumbs stroke down either side of her spine in what she could only call the beginnings of a massage and she jumped straight up out of the chair, this time, so abruptly the piece of furniture turned on its side.

"Thank you for offering, but that's not necessary," she said so fast all the words ran together and Bryn left the data unit quickly sensing an emanating confusion in her wake.

Shame and chagrin coursed through her simultaneously, she regretted such an abrupt reaction, but that contact was more intimate than she cared to admit so without a word Bryn walked out the door to her assigned quarters.

Her mind was in sufficient turmoil that it took Bryn twice to place her thumb on the slot to open the door, her mind turning over the comments circulating about her living arrangements. Once inside, she stared at the wall, uncertain of what to do next until her eyes roaming about the room noting it was half the size of Ryan's main room. A narrow bed folded from the wall, to one side a data interface, cater, and hygiene unit. Obviously the Commander did not waste prime quarters on her, particularly if she was only a temporary addition to the Facility.

To organize her confused thoughts, Bryn sat at the data interface and noticed a message from Stanton, of all people, to her surprise. Quick investigation revealed information on survival in the winter and snowbound areas, which puzzled Bryn after his reception when she asked for his advice the previous day.

That was all the thought she had time for when Bryn heard the door open, *so much for privacy*, she thought irritably and it seemed as far as she was concerned, entry could and would be overridden. Stubbornly refusing to turn around suspecting who came in, she felt a pressure of a presence at her back and unsurprised to hear Ryan say, "Ok Bryn, what did Stanton say to you that upset you?" he said quietly.

"He didn't say anything to upset me," she said, but keeping her back to him.

"I see. Then what's wrong?" He said pointedly.

"I'm tired of being manipulated. At least he's honest about his feelings. You can't tell me you volunteered to be around me," she said flatly.

What Bryn did not expect was her chair to twist about so fast she nearly fell off it and found herself facing Ryan, who had a stony expression on his face. She did not feel quite so confident now.

With his arms crossed and fairly oozing disapproval, Ryan said coldly, "I've done nothing to intentionally manipulate you unless you consider kindness a form of manipulation. Yes, I was ordered to work with you, but only after calling him," referring to the Commander, "out for how he treated you. I've tried to treat you with the respect you deserve."

Bryn could not meet his eyes, she felt doubly ashamed for taking out her frustrations on Ryan when he had attempted to make her stay at the Facility at least more pleasant.

"What is the real issue, Bryn?" said Ryan in a steely voice she never heard from him before.

"I don't like being forced to work when it isn't my choice," she said temporizing.

"You know what I mean," he persisted.

"I don't want to give truth to the rumors circulating," she said uneasily.

"It's more than that," he said to her dismay, "Who hurt you Bryn?"

Now how could he possibly know? Without meaning to do so, Bryn met his eyes only to see sympathy reflected back at her and then she was furious with herself for confirming his assessment.

"Why would you care? We aren't friends. I won't be here forever so there is no reason to get used to that much familiarity just to walk away from it all," she said flatly.

Those words produced a sigh from Ryan, "No, we aren't friends, I think we are more than that," he said to her utter confusion, "I do care Bryn. I don't deny it all started because I was ordered to keep an eye on you. It became more than that, at least for me. Why else did you think I never referred to your assigned quarters?"

"I don't understand," she said determined not to follow his meaning.

Instead of enlightening her, Ryan said again, "Who hurt you?"

Well so much for full disclosure she never intended to give. Ryan would make one hell of a lawyer the way he saw to the heart of a matter and having her innermost secrets laid bare was the most uncomfortable things she ever experienced.

Silence lengthened between them and Bryn hoped that would convey her desire not to discuss this particular point in her life, but Ryan just stood there waiting for her to comment. At that moment, she almost hated him for bringing back those memories she tried so hard to bury.

Uncertain if she could discuss the issue, Bryn began slowly and stammered through her story explaining her stupidity allowing someone like Vander near her. At her disclosure, Ryan took a seat on the fold out bed and observed her and Bryn wondered if he expected her to say more or if he was considering the information.

"I don't want to talk anymore," she said in rush hoping to end this encounter abruptly.

"Then you can listen," said Ryan quietly to her surprise.

"There isn't anything to discuss. I need to rest. It can wait for another time," she said practically babbling afraid of what he might say.

"For someone who said they don't want to talk you're certainly finding a lot to say," he said a little wryly.

Bryn flushed and looked away, "Look at me," he said softly, but Bryn shook her head.

That evasion did not work. A firm, but gentle hand, cupped her chin forcing Bryn to meet his eyes and he said, "You're not stupid. How could you possibly know anyone would contrive to seal their own house as a prison while they remained outside? Don't belittle yourself because of a deranged fool. You did well considering what was available, especially forced to search an entire house by hand in the dark and legally blind," he said in approval for her actions.

She attempted to jerk her head away, but he did not allow it and watched her face intently.

"As far as rumors, let them talk whether they get it right or wrong. They can't hurt you unless you allow it," he said patiently.

With a twist of her head, she attempted to avoid Ryan's gaze, but he said, "No, please look at me," pulling her eyes back to his.

"I would never hurt you Bryn," he said in response to her reaction, "but you already know that."

Bryn decided she did not want to hear anymore and stood abruptly to exit the room, which incited Ryan to pull her firmly back to the chair.

"Now the reason I did not refer to your quarters was that initially it was to keep an eye on you, but as I said that changed. I found I enjoyed you nearby and talking to you. As for the familiarity you mention, do you think I would let you leave this place alone? Give it time," he paused briefly, "just give me an open door to walk through. Take each day as it comes. Now, will you please come back with me," he said in a voice that matched the intensity in his eyes.

Unwilling to accept the meaning of his words, Bryn did not comment though she did nod and stand up to go back to Ryan's quarters in the interim, he had given her a lot to think about, not all of it comforting.

Once back in his quarters, Ryan surprised her by asking, "What did you ask Stanton?"

Apparently the subject came up in the conference room and as usual Stanton must have turned difficult, she should have suspected Ryan would figure out why she had been in that hallway.

"I asked for his advice about survival in the conditions of the next mission," she said warily.

Ryan looked irritated at that answer, "Why didn't you ask me?" he said.

"He was assigned as my survival trainer," said Bryn.

"You know as well as I do that was punishment for the confrontation in the gym," said Ryan all but growling.

Bryn stared at him in surprise, if she had to label Ryan's reaction she would call it jealousy, but that made no sense especially since everyone knew exactly what Stanton thought of her. When he saw her expression Ryan snorted and looked away before heading over to the data interface, Bryn decided to let the matter drop.

Without looking at her, Ryan finally said, "Get some rest."

A bleep at the data interface distracted Foss from mission preliminaries and he saw that it was the hidden alarm he set to track any unusual transmissions within the Facility; he accessed the storage file where the recording would go automatically. He kept the file well hidden under a bogus name and heavily encrypted since only the Commander had the privilege of a dedicated server.

The message was in the same format as the previous one, therefore, Foss could rule out the Commander as the source or it would have altered after he let his superior know of the first transmission.

His program decoded the message and Foss just stared at the content: *"Target exceeded expectations. Unusual perception noted. Death averted by unorthodox use of equipment."*

He felt the first stirring of alarm at these cryptic words because his mind jumped to the situation during the mission that nearly cost Shadow her life and even her quick thinking had left her badly injured. Foss' thoughts jumped to the conclusion that Shadow had been set up to fail to prove something to someone outside the Facility, but whom?

A few comments from the Commander recently indicated to Foss that his superior had contacted someone outside the Facility about Shadow though he did not think the man realized the impact of his muttered words and Foss had been certain to act as if he did not hear anything.

Though he kept quiet about it, Foss was not thrilled how they seized the woman, a civilian no less, to work on various missions and the security surrounding her meant that she was essentially a prisoner. You learned to keep your mouth shut when you worked for people who ran operations under the radar or you found your life conveniently shortened.

Nighthawk? Foss thought about that idea. The man certainly watched over Bryn, but not indifferently as Foss knew the man tended to operate and he sensed that he actually cared about her welfare. It would be difficult to speak to the man privately with all the surveillance, but Foss had a plan and sent a message to Nighthawk to meet him in the gym where it was only visual surveillance with no sound due to the nature of the activities in the area so it would seem just an invitation to work out.

Unsurprisingly, Nighthawk was waiting for Foss and so it did not appear they were just standing there to talk, "Let's spar, but I have something to discuss with you. I don't want to draw attention," said Foss quietly.

With the cover of working out, Foss explained about the transmissions and his suspicions telling Nighthawk that the Commander only knew about the first signal. Though the rhythm of sparring did not change, Foss could see his expression turned grim at the information as he considered the ramifications.

Then to Foss' surprise, Nighthawk said, "I suspected as much. The chute she had waiting for her was not the one she packed. Someone substituted her parachute, but the packing was too generic for me to trace its packing back to anyone."

"Would the Tabula be that ruthless?" said Foss warily indicating the governing body for worldwide Facilities.

Nighthawk did not comment for so long, Foss wondered if he misjudged the man, but he finally answered, "They can be as ruthless as necessary," was the disquieting response.

"They are going to try to keep her, aren't they?" said Foss uncertainly.

"It's highly probable after her performance on the past mission. The rest of us would have died in her place so that makes her a very valuable resource to them," said Nighthawk grimly.

"Shit," swore Foss quietly, "It's not right to hold her prisoner, but they are used to getting what they want."

"They are indeed," said Nighthawk flatly.

A few weeks later in the gym, Bryn practiced some martial arts on a long punching bag trying to divert her growing sense of discomfort at additional unseen surveillance she began to sense recently. It had bothered her so much she found herself whirling about suddenly while walking alone in the halls, expecting to see someone dart away, but Bryn never saw anything.

Working out hard helped her sleep at night instead of worrying over scenarios the Commander might have set up to watch her and Bryn knew since the mission, he had increased his monitoring of her actions. That meant anything she accessed in the databases or the Internet was most certainly cataloged and studied. One thing Bryn needed to do was contact Donal about the incident with the retinal scanner, but she did not dare send any request, any form of contact, or the Facility would eventually decode the attempt. If she approached medical about the recent headaches developing, they would perform intrusive test that could either damage her sight or reveal more about her capabilities than Bryn wanted anyone to know.

Sneaking out was not an option. With a GPS tag, they would catch her long before she made it to Donal and that was if they did not have the old man under surveillance as well. Now Bryn found herself jumping at shadows, a headache that was gradually worsening and a complete loss of privacy, she thought as she made her way from the gym to Ryan's quarters.

Barely eating after a shower, Bryn settled on the sofa to sleep though she tossed restlessly before falling into an uneasy sleep filled with odd dreams.

A gentle touch across her cheek roused Bryn to see Ryan sitting bent over her, his hand extended, but his sudden appearance jarred her to full consciousness and with a violent reaction she slammed against the wall in shock.

"Easy," he said as quickly catching a hold of her before she could injure herself with another drastic reaction.

"Ryan, why do you do that?" she said with more asperity than she meant.

"I like to watch you sleep," he said softly, "I'm sorry I startled you."

"It's ok. I didn't mean to sound so harsh. Just give me a moment so my heart returns to its natural rhythm," she said, but her tone sounding almost accusing to her own ears.

When he reached as if to touch her chin, Bryn flinched so badly her head hit the wall with an audible sound and a flicker of sadness crossed Ryan's features at that reaction as if he thought she did not trust him.

"He seriously traumatized you," he said unexpectedly obviously referring to her past with Vander.

Guilt at her reaction to Ryan's gesture shot through her, "I..." began Bryn in an attempt to brush off the statement regarding her instinctive response to a friendly gesture, but the words suddenly stopped.

His hand gently tilted her chin up as his eyes searched her face, "What is it?" he said with quiet encouragement.

"I'm scared. Someone is watching me and it's more than normal surveillance in the building. Whoever it is, it feels like they are trying to corner me," she whispered, words Bryn never thought she would utter, "and I have nowhere to run or hide."

With a swift move that made Bryn gasp in fright, Ryan's arms embraced her tightly and she instantly stiffened in terror feeling her heart pounding as if she was running from those automatic weapons she recently avoided.

"Shhh," he said quietly in her ear and that was when Bryn realized she was panting fearfully.

All he did was hold her which was a comfort Bryn could barely remember from anyone as her body shook from head to toe and her heart pounded so violently that her limbs seemed to pulse in time with the beat. Quiet strength that she always sensed in Ryan seeped through her and she felt the tension begin to fade from her body suddenly aware he was stroking her hair; she gradually relaxed into him burying her head into the hollow of his shoulder.

Shouting over the room's intercom rudely intruded into the moment and Bryn jumped in shock which resulted in a sigh near her ear from Ryan, but this time his reaction seemed to be exasperation at the interruption rather than her response.

"Where the hell are you Nighthawk?" said miniature-shouting voice of the Commander.

His arms seemed to release her reluctantly and Bryn saw Ryan grab his black hood placing it somewhat roughly on his head when she realized he was already dressed in his bodysuit. He snapped on his visor and strode out the door in the most purposeful manner she had yet seen from the man as her eyes followed him with some bemusement.

The Commander fumed with impatience toggling display around his desk until the door to his office opened followed by Nighthawk's entry.

"Where have you been?" snapped Kolski.

Instead of explaining, Nighthawk said, "Was there some appointment I failed to hear of?"

Something about the delivery of those quiet words left a subtle message hanging in the air, which said, "I am not at your beck and call," was causing the Commander to re-examine the man's arrival more keenly.

"You can't possibly have any commitments that I interrupted," Kolski said stiffly and then suddenly wondered about the "rumors" involving the woman.

Silence which emanated from Nighthawk was more telling than any words he could have used for Kolski hinting about personal time and it left a warning hanging in the air that told the Commander to let the matter drop.

"We have new intelligence about the next target. Satellite links are established so that we can start initial planning and this one will have even less room for error due to the conditions we face," said Kolski acting as if he could not have transmitted this information to quarters.

Somehow the silence of the man standing before him managed to convey that exact thought, *Why wasn't the information transmitted?* The Commander did not like the way it made him feel, the feeling of being tolerated. He was uncomfortably aware Nighthawk could choose to leave anytime he wished and what was worse; such a departure could seriously cripple the team. *Maybe I better check my arrogance at the door,* thought Kolski and that was a sobering realization.

"I'll make certain any new information is transmitted," said the Commander and then he instantly felt lame for saying those words though it was too late to retrieve them, but added, "She is to report to Tank for scuba dive training."

He looked back at his monitors in apparent unconcern after nodding dismissal to Nighthawk while inwardly berating himself for treating him as an extension of Stanton—a dangerous mistake.

A week later Ryan noticed Bryn wincing when he turned on a light at his desk and asked in concern, "Are your eyes hurting?"

Uncertain how to answer, Bryn was still worried that she could not trust this man, but the head pain increased to the point she was no longer able to tolerate it, "My head and eyes. Ever since the mission," she said uneasily.

"Let's go to Doc. You shouldn't have let it get so bad," he said reprovingly.

"He can't help me," said Bryn immediately and regretted her quick response.

Ryan studied her narrowly and said, "What do you mean?"

With no other choice, Bryn said dejectedly, "If it is my implants, only one man can do anything about it. I highly doubt permission to see him would be forthcoming no matter how I asked and he would never come here where his work could be observed and recorded."

Ryan turned thoughtful at her response and Bryn realized he had not expected the truth from her initially, he seemed satisfied that her words were true from his expression. *A good thing I was honest then if he can read me that well,* she thought with some chagrin.

"I might be able to help. We can't go to his building since they monitor it, but if we can get word to him to meet us in an unmonitored area, he won't have anyone staring over his shoulder," said Ryan carefully.

Bryn knew exactly why Donal was under surveillance: *It's in case I run away and they knew he would be high on the list of places I might seek refuge*, she thought bitterly. To help her though, it would be necessary to get word to Donal and she did not dare attempt to leave a message for him if they were monitoring his communications. Trying to send a coded message would instantly be noticed soon as she transmitted it which meant Ryan would have to initiate the contact and Bryn would have to trust him to some degree.

"There is no way I can get a message to him from here. Someone would notice," said Bryn finally unable to hide the bitterness in her voice.

A gentle hand gripped her shoulder, "Don't worry, I can do it without anyone knowing. I'll think of a way to get you out of the Facility with only me as your companion," said Ryan softly.

Two days later, Ryan told her to dress in normal street clothing and Bryn could only stare at him in disbelief that he managed to get the Commander to allow her to leave the Facility, however briefly.

"They are still going to follow us, aren't they?" said Bryn watching Ryan carefully.

"Of course, but they don't know what we plan to do. It will all seem benign to them no matter how they review it," he said so confidently Bryn wondered just what this plan entailed.

It felt very strange, after such a lengthy stay within the Facility, to be outside like a normal person as Bryn watched people bustling about shopping or taking lunch breaks from their jobs. To her surprise, Ryan led her to a public library that carried actual old style books and he said quietly, "As you've probably noticed the Facility doesn't allow full external access to the internet on your identification nor do the databases contain any form of entertainment reading."

Now she understood what he told the Commander and apparently this visit was to allow Bryn to obtain hardcopies of literature to read in her spare time, she mentally reviewed subjects to acquire before they entered the building. Once inside, Ryan indicated she was to peruse the selections and acquire at least some reading material to take back with them.

The library was quite extensive and Bryn took her time to examine the selection of books to pick out items of interest, she suspected the Commander might even check to be certain she read the literature.

About an hour and half later Ryan said quietly, "Decide you need to use the restroom and wait inside."

That suggestion startled Bryn so much, she almost gave herself away and asked Ryan how Donal planned to find her in the women's restroom, but she snapped her mouth shut. There were several women in the restroom and Bryn decided to take her time, wash her hands and face, as the women slowly trailed out. Enough time passed that Bryn almost decided to leave when an elderly woman came in and immediately turned to lock the door, which alarmed her instantly until she saw the other woman's face. It was Donal.

Bryn could only stare in utter shock wondering whose idea it was that Donal dress like a woman, but before she could voice her thoughts, Donal said, "We don't have much time dear. I got the message about the headaches, now tell me everything."

So Bryn explained the increasing pain, sensitivities, and what happened on the mission with the optical scanner, Donal only listened without interruption until she finished.

"Without my lab I can't be certain exactly what is happening, but I suspect the nanites have exceeded their programming and adapted. I wish I could take you back with me, but I don't want anyone to have too much information about your implants and I think you feel the same way. I'm going inject new nanites with adjusted programming in hopes they will divert the goals of the existing nanites, It's nothing to be afraid of," when he noticed her apprehension, "I think they are modifying abilities as you need them, but it's not something we want to happen without supervision," he said carefully.

Bryn nodded and knew the Facility would watch everything Donal did if he took her back to his lab, which would certainly give them too much information she would rather keep private. Donal pulled out a syringe from the handbag prop he carried before preparing Bryn's arm for an intravenous injection and then inserted the needle,

"Hopefully this will reduce the headaches dear. Try not to put any strain on your eyes for a while," said Donal quietly as he patted her arm.

Once Donal reassembled his items, he unlocked the door and left, Bryn waited about five minutes before following, she caught sight of Ryan nearby and nodded discreetly. After that they left with the reading she selected and returned to the Facility, Ryan never once asked what Donal did or said to her surprise.

Over the next week, Bryn found her headache fading and that bright light no longer bothered her eyes, which made it much easier to concentrate on the upcoming mission data. Sifting through the new information for the latest mission made Bryn feel far out of her depth since in the past she always worked within the confines of a populated city not the wilderness or extreme conditions. She briefly recalled her very first meeting with the Commander when he said they could offer her new and unique challenges enough to interest her, but this is not exactly what those words brought to mind at the time.

This time it was not the guards or their training that arrested her attention, it was the environment they would work in which would offer little in the way of concealment even if it were not for the daunting temperatures involved. Satellite images revealed ice and snow for many miles of uncovered landscape before any appreciable cover offered by trees appeared seriously hampering the possibility of alternative exit strategies. In spite of the encompassing information Stanton forwarded, Bryn still thought she would feel exposed even with the survival techniques extensively studied, but as yet unapplied.

A hiss from the door opening said Ryan returned and she was cognizant he sat behind her again watching the screen over her shoulder. "Why are you so tense?" he said in her ear.

Letting out a slow breath Bryn said, "There are no shelter or alternative places to hide. They would see us coming for miles and the nearest cover are these trees way over here," gesturing at the expanse of trees on the screen that was a significant distance from the goal.

Feeling a breath on her neck before he spoke, Ryan said, "What you can't see is the water under the ice in these images which your vision would show if you were physically there. We will probably enter over here," he used his fingers on the touch screen to scroll the image, "through a hole in this frozen river."

"Swim under the ice?" said Bryn sharply.

She felt his hand move to her neck before he said, "You don't swim?"

"Of course I swim," she said a little tartly to cover her uneasiness, "but we would die from exposure if I read these temperatures correctly."

"Not with the right gear. You never used scuba gear I take it," he said to her exasperation. Hiding something from Ryan was virtually impossible because he seemed to hear words she never said or maybe it was the omissions that gave her away.

"No," she said with a sigh.

"That's why we train. Tank is scheduled to teach you so there is no reason to worry," he said softly.

"It still won't change the fact that we will have little choice of alternatives to escape if an exit is compromised," she pointed out.

"We'll know more when we arrange the mockup of the area once we get all the data, but I don't deny we will probably have little room for error," he said, so she did not think he dismissed her concern.

Pursing her lips, Bryn touched the screen to scroll through the images and realized he was correct about limited data for now. They currently had no topography maps or scan of the ground about the area to indicate what might lie beneath, but that old habit reared its head to seek as many options as possible.

"You need to eat," he said in her ear.

Bryn turned to look at him, "How do you know I haven't already eaten?" she said piqued.

His expression turned wry daring her to think about it and his quick glance at the cater unit told Bryn he checked the usage which prompted her to say, "So you monitor me as well?"

"You don't eat enough as it is," he said ignoring her sarcasm.

"Trying to fatten me up for slaughter?" she said facetiously.

He chuckled softly, "That would never happen. You're far too active," he said pulling her out of the chair to guide her to the table.

"You say that now, but your opinion might change when I can't fit into my bodysuit," she said narrowly.

"It wouldn't hurt you," he said this time with a twinkle in his eye.

At his audacity, Bryn took a swing at his cheek only to find it intercepted by Ryan's hand before she came close to contact, "I promise not to stop you if I actually say something I deserve to get slapped for," he said with a grin.

With a sound of exasperation, Bryn said, "That will never happen. You don't need to say anything to make those kinds of thoughts known."

Outright laughter was the only response he gave to her comment, such a display was highly unusual and Bryn gave him a disgusted look before stabbing her finger at the interface on the cater unit.

Learning to scuba dive effectively took a great deal of practice, which began in a normal swimming pool with Tank constantly drilling information into Bryn's head about safety and emergency procedures. Several times she was lax checking her gauges resulting in a lengthy lecture about responsibility she had toward her safety, but eventually Bryn managed to succeed to the point even her exacting taskmaster could not fault her.

Though the sessions were tough, Bryn knew it was not only for her safety, but ultimately the team's safety when they faced a much more challenging set of conditions and there would not be time to remind her of protocol.

Today would be the first time they used the training area completely set up to resemble their target area and they would confront the actual conditions of temperature as well as iced over water. Wide-eyed in amazement, Bryn gazed about the area resembling a polar ecosystem, which looked exactly like the satellite images and the exposed skin on her face indicated they were facing the exact temperatures of the region.

The white suits they would all be wearing were not only capable for frigid water use, but also able to deal with the air temperatures without forcing them to change to heavier cold weather gear. What she found uncomfortable was the hood, which literally covered her eyebrows and her entire chin with an opening for her mouth, but she knew it was to minimize actual skin exposure to the extreme temperature. A protective mask would cover the remaining exposed facial skin leaving openings for the eyes, nostrils and mouth once they did not need their scuba gear any longer.

Once the exercise began, Bryn donned her mask which would be needed in the real situation to arrive at the river where they would cut a hole in the ice in the training area to swim up to their goal and she squatted next to the men to watch the procedure until they punched a large hole through the ice.

Though she never said a word during briefings, Bryn did not like the fact she would go first, but it would be necessary because of the initial barrier they would encounter where her skills would be needed to breach a security measure under the water.

Her scuba gear check went quickly from the constant practice and Bryn secured her air tank before she donned her goggles then slipped the regulator mouthpiece through the special slit in the facial mask. Reaching on top of her head, she clicked on the camera/light combination to allow the others to follow her progress and then jumped feet first into the frigid water.

After another quick check of her scuba gear, her flippers propelled her slowly forward and she moved her head so the light panned about in the eerie dark water until she caught sight of something totally unexpected.

Masses of bubbles blew from her regulator from the scream Bryn tried to utter and she violently propelled her body upward without thinking about the ice over head in her panic then blackness overtook her.

The men had donned their scuba gear nearly the same time as Shadow though they left the regulators hanging from their shoulders until needed and paused to watch her progress down what mimicked the frozen river they would ultimately navigate.

As the light passed over an object none of the men had a chance to see it clearly when clouds of bubbles obscured the camera to their surprise. It was not until the camera settled pointing to the bottom and her unequipped regulator floated past, that her scuba instructor, Tank, realized Shadow was unconscious.

"Damn it, she's drowning," he said shoving his regulator in his mouth, but Nighthawk was faster, he was already in the water before the man could move.

They all watched the monitor, which indicated the camera was moving back toward the hole in the ice until they could finally see it as Nighthawk pushed Shadow's body upward to the receiving hands of the men.

Soon as he pulled himself out of the water, Nighthawk turned Shadow on her side to let the water drain from her lungs before he began CPR and she coughed a minute or two later. What surprised the men was her reaction once conscious as she instantly panicked, her feet sliding on the ice back peddling from the hole into the water trying to stand babbling in terror about a corpse in the water.

Tank immediately checked her gauges to see if her mixture was too rich, but he looked at the others puzzled about Shadow's reaction when he found everything normal.

Her terror was so acute that Nighthawk had trouble restraining her, "There's a corpse down there, let go of me," she said wildly until he enveloped her with his arms.

"What the hell happened," said a miniaturized voice of the Commander.

"We're not certain. She said she saw something under the ice," Foss could not bring himself to actually say the word 'corpse' yet. "Did you place anything under there to leave surprises for us?"

"No, especially not for the first run. What is it?" said the Commander impatiently.

"A second, I need to check," said Foss as he assembled his gear and performed gauge checks.

With a splash he was gone and the others except for Shadow watching the screen as he turned on his camera/light combination and not much later they saw a stream of bubbles obscure the camera, but when they cleared everyone saw the grisly sight.

"Holy shit," said Tank, "Can you see who it is?" The new man on the Team, Hesney that the others called Hess, did not react at all as he stared at the video feed.

Foss moved forward at the question since everyone had earpieces and the submerged man finally waved his hand in front of the camera in a negative gesture telling them he did not recognize the body.

Tank said, "Commander, there is a body under the ice. Foss doesn't recognize it."

"What the hell...tell him to hold position while I suit up," said the Commander.

Shadow heard everything and began to push away from Nighthawk, "Let go of me I'm fine," she said, but he only pulled her tighter against him and murmured in her ear, "Take it easy."

The Commander arrived in short order skidding slightly on the ice in his haste to get to the spot and looked at the monitor in disbelief, he swiveled on all the men still above water, "Is this some sort of joke one of you pulled?" he demanded looking straight at Stanton.

Tank, the designated team leader for this mission said, "No way boss. None of us would screw with mission prep and besides that," he pointed at the monitor, "is not funny in any sense of the word."

"Did you do this?" said the Commander directly to Stanton and completely ignoring Tank's words.

"No! What would I have to gain?" snapped Stanton irritably.

"Get it out of there and to Doc to determine who it is," said the Commander tightly and not at all mollified by Stanton's denial, he would not put it past the man to pull such a stunt.

At those words, Shadow said loudly, "Let go of me, I need to take a walk. I'll be fine." Although the men thought they could determine that odd quiet before hysteria sets in as she pulled free of Nighthawk and headed toward the exit.

Because of the temperature in the training area and the extensive time it took to arrange the conditions, the men cut away more ice to allow for the frozen body to be removed since the original hole would have been too small to negotiate with a stiffened length of body.

Foss pulled the corpse to the larger opening, but it took two men to lift it out and support it to the infirmary with swearing Kolski in their wake before he turned toward his office to await the result of Doc's examination.

Before he made it to his office however, Kolski saw Shadow coming down the hall toward him and ruefully thought the woman probably never saw a corpse or used lethal force in her entire life given the type of jobs she regularly did before this, whereas the men on the team were almost all ex-military. Every one of the men had killed someone in their life and seen plenty of bodies. Even if Shadow might eventually need to confront the reality of death that way, Kolski would not be heartless enough to spring it on her like that without some warning ahead of time.

Soon as Shadow came closer he noticed her pallor matched her suit and though sensitivity was not one of Kolski's qualities he said, "Call it a day. We can pick it up tomorrow," surprising himself with those words of consideration.

"No sir. Every day of training lost means less preparation. I'm ready to continue," she said tonelessly.

"Very well, as long as you're certain," said the Commander and watched her nod before passing by him.

When Shadow returned, all the men seemed highly surprised and even more so when she said, "I'm ready to continue," before donning all her scuba gear again.

In silence they watched her perform gauge checks, click on her camera and jump back into the water to continue her interrupted progress until she reached the first barrier. At that point, the rest of the men hit the water to continue the training run which went so smoothly even the Commander was impressed.

Soon as the team began to wrap up for the day, Kolski decided to contact the infirmary to see if they had more information on the unidentified body and Doc took his call, "This man was garroted and I can tell you this man is from our Facility from DNA and fingerprints. Due to the condition of the body presently, I can only postulate time of death, which will no doubt surprise you. That man has possibly been dead at least two weeks possibly longer," he said.

"How is that possible? It would have decayed and someone would have noticed," said the Commander in confusion.

"You've had that area in preparation for over a month. This man, Jason Stapler, was due take leave for a month. I suspect soon as he was killed, someone dumped his body into the cold water before the ice completely formed. I can be close to his time of death because you would have been apprised if he had not shown for duty prior to his leave," he said significantly.

"Shit! So he had to be killed off duty?" demanded the Commander.

"That is my conclusion Commander and his right thumb is missing which unfortunately means someone probably accessed some areas they shouldn't have. Because of the freezing of the tissue and immersion, I can't tell if the digit was removed post mortem or not," said Doc grimly.

"Thank you," said the Commander as he signed off.

Impossible! How could someone get a body into the training area without alerting security when they had surveillance in every corner? Someone had to time the murder perfectly and have somehow altered or deactivated the video coverage for the particular area. What could someone hope to gain leaving a body there? Was this someone's idea of a sick joke? *Actually*, he thought, *it is a clever place to hide a body and it stayed frozen hence a window of doubt regarding the perpetrator.* There was no time for this stupid foolishness and then

Kolski's mind jumped to Stanton who would know everything about the Facility and how to circumvent security if need be, but there was no proof. Though the man seemed deranged, he was far from stupid or useless and he could access most of the information about the missions. Kolski had to check what areas were accessed before and after the dead man's leave started.

Pressing a button brought security online, "Yes, sir?" said a voice.

"I want all records for the last month reviewed for unusual activity. Not just coming and going, but inconsistent entries, gaps of unexplained time lapses in recordings. And I want a comprehensive report on everything Jason Stapler accessed over the past two months. One last thing, remove any access Stapler had, reset the entry code to the training area, and forward me the new one," said Kolski flatly.

"Yes, sir," said the voice.

In the time he spoke with security Kolski wondered if that body was placed in the training area was meant to terrorize Bryn and Stanton would have known the mission procedure that she would be the first person to enter the ice.

Walking rapidly to quarters, Bryn felt like she was in a bubble and ruthlessly pushed away the image in the water when it attempted to surface in her mind. She was barely aware of simple actions of showering, dressing, or eating and did not remember any of it as she pushed herself to review the mission parameters to keep some sense of her sanity.

Blinking at the monitor in surprise, Bryn could not remember sitting in front of it and the sound of the door opening distract her to look over her shoulder at Ryan entering the room, but she turned back to the data not really seeing it.

A pair of warm strong hands touched her back and Bryn barely reacted, she was not even certain how long she had been sitting there as Ryan began to run his thumbs along either side of her spine in an effort to ease tension she did not acknowledge.

Uncharacteristically, she did not even sense his concern when there was no lessening of the tension of her body under his attempted ministrations. When her chair turned toward him, Bryn could see Ryan watching her face before he pulled her into an embrace, which she attempted to wriggle away from instantly.

When she did not calm, Ryan leaned back and to Bryn's utter shock he kissed her on the lips, she immediately began muffled protests with her arms flailing which he blocked effectively, uninterrupted. It was not until she calmed somewhat that he desisted and Bryn pounded her fists into his shoulders furiously saying, "What are you doing?"

"You needed a distraction Bryn. You might not feel it, but your tense as a board and white a sheet," he said quietly.

"Let go of me. I've had enough surprises today," she snapped, but instead of release Ryan embraced her again.

Her last words brought the glaring image she recalled under the ice into full clarity and Bryn began to sob wildly into Ryan's shoulder gasping for breath unable to stop the burst of emotion that threatened to consume her.

Soon as she felt calmer, Bryn pushed away from him so she could find something to wipe her face and to hide the fact she was quite angry about the way Ryan distracted her so she would open up.

"Do you want to return to your quarters Bryn?" he said tonelessly.

That question nearly made Bryn spin in fury until she forced herself to admit Ryan was only trying to help her and never meant to be pushy by kissing her. It actually had the intended effect of forcing her to release her shock from the earlier experience in the water. Not once did he invade her privacy and always gave her space when needed, friendship when she felt lonely, and comfort as needed.

"No," she finally whispered.

"As I told you before, I brought you here initially because the Commander made you my responsibility. I watched over you so you wouldn't get injured trying to leave or by other people attempting to stop you," he paused for a moment then said, "I meant what I said before, I want you to stay because I enjoy you being here."

His hand touched her arm gently and Bryn did not jerk away so he moved closer, but did not pull her into an embrace, he seemed uncertain about her mood. Soon as she raised a tentative hand and touched his arm he finally pulled her into a hug, she relaxed against him before placing her own arms about his waist.

He released her momentarily to lead her back to the chairs so they could sit. She looked up into his face to find him watching her in an assessing manner before pulling her against him again and she sighed at the comfort it gave her.

When his lips found hers, Bryn jumped in surprise, but unlike the previous kiss, this one was very tender, even loving and she found the sensation completely unexpected. A sensual feeling coursed through Bryn which Ryan picked up immediately and he lifted her into his arms heading for the room where he slept.

Without altering the kiss, Ryan laid her on the bed and stretched out next to her. He touched her cheek when he stopped kissing her, looked at her with a smile and said, "Not yet, darlin. I won't take advantage of your state of mind."

She looked at him startled not for the content of his words, but the Irish brogue he said it, "Where did that accent come from?" said Bryn curiously.

"Where do you think it came from?" he said teasingly with a twinkle in his eye.

He kissed her softly again and then said, "Get some rest, my little Shadow."

Soon as he rolled to his back, Ryan pulled her against him and planted a soft kiss on her forehead when she heard a whisper in her ear, "I love you, Bryn."

Chapter 9

It was a moonless night as Foss glanced at the rest of the team surreptitiously as they all prepared to board the helicopter which would take them over the border to set them all within striking distance of their target. That meant no one could risk being caught or they would be labeled a terrorist with essentially no rights or hope of release from the country's central law enforcement which did not bother him personally, it was business as usual for the men. It was for Shadow that concerned him.

This kind of breach was far outside her experience, not the difficulty of the entry, but the risk involved if she were caught and it could mean her death which was not a risk she was trained to accept as part of the job. Foss realized his concern was unusual, but then he had a chance to work with Shadow on types of skiing she would use as necessary and found her a very intriguing person; if he was not so certain Nighthawk had an interest in her he might have tried his luck.

That explained the reason for his concern for her, even with the established escape routes if, "shit hit the fan," as the Commander was always fond of saying, happened, this landscape was not conducive to hiding with its wide open spaces and snow covered ground showing every footprint.

Another thing that bugged him was this new man Hess replacing Crease, at least for this one mission. Out of the corner of his eye, Foss saw the man leaning against the wall smoking a cigarette acting completely unconcerned with the mission and that annoyed him to no end, he seemed lax at best in training. During training Hess always talked, but never really said anything, he reminded Foss of a politician and he performed tasks halfheartedly. Foss did not trust the man, but he kept those thoughts to himself.

"Get the gear stowed," called Tank disrupting Foss' thoughts.

Foss barely suppressed a grin when Hess attempted to help Shadow with her gear and was neatly intercepted by Nighthawk, it was the first time he noticed the man's expression change and it was wariness. At least the idiot knew better than to tick off Nighthawk, he thought, but then so did the rest of the team, even pain-in-the-ass Stanton.

While they were airborne, Tank passed out assigned ear buds that contained a GPS tag to transmit back to their command post over the border. They were making an illegal entry into the target's country from a country they entered legally to prevent alerting certain individuals of the team's presence. Some of the team had a past globally and a few of them would trigger alarms in the target country when DNA was scanned, hence the illegal entry, but not all countries performed such checks, like the one the team entered legally. Even the DNA scan was not an advertised check requirement and few knew of the practice, but the Facility did. All of this meant they essentially did not exist and it could lead to death, or worse than death in some cases; they all knew the risks.

Trees stood like silent sentinels in the blanket of snow beneath them, Shadow helped Stanton scoop out snow at the base of one of the tree trunks so they could stash extra gear to avoid revealing their presence if someone happened to patrol the area. An added fortune was the wind blowing enough to cause the snow to drift, which would hide signs of their presence; she was thankful for her suit and could only feel the wind's pressure instead of wind chill biting her skin.

Listening to Shadow's advice altered the entry point through the river ice so the hole would be shielded by the tree cover making it less likely to find a patrol strolling by so far from their target. Due to the increased distance to their goal, they had to carry two small tanks of oxygen instead of one, but the river ran deep enough to prevent ice or debris from blocking their way.

Scanning the region about her with her eyes, Shadow blinked between modes checking for unusual light frequencies, heat sources, or movement. All their suits hid their body heat from any detection equipment, satellite, or detectors fixed to the local area. Refocusing nearer at hand, she had trouble locating some of the team since their suits blended in with the snow so well and it was not until they passed a tree that she could see them.

"Here, take this," said Stanton handing her an unusual knife, "It converts for multiple uses. You said you don't carry weapons, but I have a bad feeling about this place. I want that back though, so don't lose it!"

Shadow stared at him a long moment, but Stanton had looked away so she was uncertain why he would give her anything, even a loan unless he remembered what she said during the survival training.

A touch on her arm from Nighthawk distracted her. He indicated they were ready for her to prepare to dive and Shadow donned her flippers and air tanks while checking her gauges, but this time she waited to turn on the camera until after she jumped into the water.

Propelling through the water quickly, but staying cautious, Shadow slipped through the water for at least thirty minutes before reducing her speed to approach the barrier carefully. Soon as the light shined on the barrier, Shadow waited until she received a signal through her earpiece before she began to work disarming it. Practice made it a smooth process.

Now Shadow took greater caution blinking various states of her vision before advancing slowly and found the first hiccup, which appeared to be a recent addition, but fortunately she was prepared. A touch on her legs startled her, but she knew it was Nighthawk hovering nearby and she suspected he entered the water soon after her.

Finally, they made it past all the technical barriers until they reached a plain old-fashioned iron grate and this time it was Foss' turn as an underwater torch flared up so he could cut a hole for the entry team. Shadow slipped through first and surfaced pulling off her air tanks moving ahead to divert beams from being broken by the passage of the men following her, she had been told to leave the mirrors in favor of covering up their underwater escape.

Foss and Tank slipped by her and before Shadow could follow a hand caught her arm with a vise-like hold; "Go back," murmured Nighthawk.

She shook her head vigorously and his hold increased painfully, "They may need me," she said very quietly.

"I want you to stay safe," he murmured nearly nose to nose with her.

"If I was one of the men you wouldn't be saying that," she shot back quietly and not exactly excited at the prospect especially with Stanton remaining on guard outside.

His hand tightened more and then loosened, but he kept his hold pulling her with him, she did not need to see his face or hear his voice to sense his irritation. They moved along the hall with no noise until Shadow's sight picked up another trap that should not be there, she jumped forward with a gasp wrenching her arm away from Nighthawk barely managing to catch the two men's belts before they triggered it.

Dropping to her hands and knees, Shadow examined the trap and decided it would be faster to step over it than disarm it since it was low enough. She ran a colored string far above it so the men would not accidentally trip it and they continued, although something did not feel right—Shadow did not like these new things appearing after all the research they did. This time Shadow moved ahead blinking and adjusting her vision as she went until she saw something odd, she held up her hand to warn the men behind her.

The area of the installation they were aiming for had no electronic clutter of expected security that should surround their goal; someone had moved the main surveillance trunk elsewhere. The installation expected attack in the quarter so she backed up and pulled Tank down to whisper in his ear.

"The target is no longer there. Someone expected us to hit that room," she breathed.

She slipped ahead to the active site where the most electronic security emanated in her visual range ignoring the old goal and what she found was not good, it would impact their timeline to penetrate it so Tank had to make a decision to retreat or try anyway. Quickly relaying that information, Shadow waited to see what the call would be and Tank gestured her forward to continue. It took all her cunning and experience to get past all the pitfalls placed in the new spot, she was sweating with tension by the time it was safe to wave the men inside.

After that, Foss worked quickly tapping into the security video and communications trunks which should not have been in this area while Shadow continued to restlessly scan the installation, flicking through various wave lengths, even x-ray. That was when she saw a room her sight could not penetrate, *lead?* She thought and decided it had to be the explanation, not much else could block x-rays, so she was sure that was the problem. What was hidden in that room? It was not part of their goal nor did Shadow recall any mention of the room's existence in the mission parameters and she muttered her discovery to Tank.

The man swore quietly and she felt the same way. This mission was not going according to plan and after the hiccups they encountered on her first mission, research had been extra careful which meant changes had recently occurred.

When Foss signaled he was ready and covered up the access point to the building's surveillance trunk, Shadow's thoughts diverted back to her duties. After carefully surveying the building again, Shadow started forward toward their goal and felt Nighthawk's firm grip on her arm, he apparently made a point not to lose her.

Schematics which had told them where they would obtain the particular item they were after were obviously inaccurate once Shadow came close enough to examine the room without the visual clutter of superimposed rooms. The safe they should find in the room was not there nor could Shadow see evidence of it in any of portion of the extensive installation, which only could mean one thing: It was in the room she could not penetrate with her vision.

Though the men never asked how she knew any of this information, Shadow suspected they had done some guessing, but she did not think the Commander or Nighthawk had ever discussed the information gleaned about her initially. Again, her thoughts diverted back to the job at hand when Tank decided to proceed and they all followed her to the room in question since the only way to determine if the safe was there would be to enter and physically see it. They were losing precious time and even though Shadow hid signs of their passing as they backtracked, it would not be possible to hide everything with their timeline shot.

Soon as they approached the special room, Shadow determined it was a very ugly situation with the kind of security waiting for them at the door. Some of the technology she never encountered before and only read about which could be lethal if Shadow made one mistake, she carefully surveyed the barriers aware the men waited tensely behind her. To get a better sense of what she would be dealing with, Shadow removed a glove, tucking it into a pouch to keep from losing it and spread her fingers as wide as she could hovering over the mechanism. What she found made her uneasy.

A field seemed to be in force about the mechanism that would probably sound some sort of alarm if breached and as she moved her hand about she felt it encompassed the entire door. Nothing they brought could deal with such a measure or produce a counter field to fool the system and she was about to tell the men this when her arm began to tingle.

Completely diverted, Shadow watched her hand as the tingling increased to the point it felt like her arm was waking up after being asleep and then suddenly a light under her palm began to glow; she had to bite back a gasp of surprise. One of the men was not so quick and behind her came a gasp, though Shadow could not determine who made the sound.

Shadow had no time to ponder this anomaly, she just watched moving her hand back over to the mechanism that apparently opened the door and nearly jumped in fright when it suddenly flared then vanished. The field had been disabled to her confusion, but she proceeded to work on the mechanism and when the door finally slid open, she did not dare look at the men.

Slipping inside did reveal a safe and, thankfully, the room did not have much additional security since the owners probably thought the door was significant protection. Accessing the safe seemed relatively straightforward and she moved out of the way so that Foss could retrieve the item, which no one had discussed with her. That thought irritated her, but then Shadow was not a regular member of the Facility and she decided it could also be for her protection to know as little as possible, however before Foss stowed the item, she caught a glimpse of an unusual aura. It was possible no one, but her could see it.

Foss signaled that he completed the retrieval and Shadow made her way back to the door to check for guards since the room prevented her from seeing anything outside, a fact that made her very uneasy. She slipped out of the door and surveyed the building very carefully, but nothing moved or seemed out of place so Shadow gestured for the men to exit when a wave of uneasiness hit her. Her hand flew up instantly and the men halted into a tense crouch.

Suddenly, Shadow felt one of the men stumble against her and an arm came out of nowhere holding a weapon of some sort sending the rest of them into silent action.

A hand grabbed her arm fiercely, "Get him out of here," hissed a voice, but she knew it had to be Nighthawk.

Her eyes found the wound on the man's shoulder that she identified as Foss. Blood stained the surface of his suit rapidly, descending to his hip, and Shadow immediately pressed her hand on the wound, pulling the injured man with her. She could not waste time worrying about the others, she knew the protocol, "They were not to get caught," and Foss had the item on him so he was the priority.

A figure leapt out of nowhere at her and Shadow pulled Foss down before she let go of him then launched at the figure, whose face was covered, immediately relieving the person of the weapon. Then Shadow proceeded to beat the attacker senseless and grabbed Foss again to lead him back to their entry point. The cold water would slow the bleeding until they could reach the helicopter medic.

As rapidly as she could, Shadow helped Foss don his scuba gear placing a bandage beneath the strap to help stop the bleeding, but before she could acquire her own gear, noise came from behind.

"Can you manage on your own?" she hissed to Foss.

"You need to come to," insisted Foss.

"I can't. Someone is coming and I won't have time to get my gear on. It's important you get out," said Shadow grimly.

"Shit," snarled Foss, "I need to stay and help."

"You can't help me if you bleed to death," she snarled back at him. "Go, I'll get out another way."

And that was that, helplessly Foss watched her fade away knowing she was correct.

Back at the command post men were swearing as they watched the feeds from the team's cameras and the pirated video from the installation, it was chaos with shadowy figures materializing from everywhere.

"What the hell is going on?" demanded the Commander since he could see the same video feeds as the command post.

"Unknown sir. Those figures just began popping out of the shadows like they were waiting for the team to exit that room. So far we haven't heard any COM chatter from the target building," said one of the men.

"Mute everyone's ear buds from our side. The last thing they need is distractions from our random comments and it protects us if any of them are caught," said the Commander grimly.

"Yes sir!" came the immediate affirmative to the order.

Kolski fumed with impatience and wanted to know what the hell had happened, but it was obvious from the video feed none of the team in the building was in a position to respond which only left Stanton outside. He was only able to see as much as the rest of the command post.

Soon the feed labeled Foss and Shadow's cameras separated from the rest, they could all see the bleeding wound on the man's shoulder via her camera as Shadow fought their way through a figure to the entry point. Kolski groaned when he heard their discussion and imminent interception, but he grunted with respect at

Shadow sending the wounded man on since he had the item on his person.

"Activate Stanton's ear bud," barked the Commander and then said to the man, "Stanton, get Foss to the helicopter once he gets to you and start loading gear. It looks like the others will have to take an alternate way out of the building."

Video feed showed Stanton helping Foss from the icy water soon as the injured man managed to get back to the ice hole and immediately escort the wounded man to the helicopter so that the medic could remove the projectile. Kolski's eyes shifted between the various feeds only peripherally seeing the medic close Foss' wound and Stanton retrieving gear. Sound began to transmit as orders flew through the installation's security COM and Kolski clenched his fists when he heard orders to capture the team for interrogation. Swearing and snarling flew back in response to that order about the devastation the team heaped on their would-be captors, which forced a grim smile on the Commander's face.

Then words came clearly through the installation's COM to all observing, "Separate out the woman and kill the rest. She's the one we're after," snarled a voice, which sent a stab of coldness through Kolski. Even if she was shorter, how did they know? Wearing modesty protectors, all of the team looked generically like men, even Shadow, and that meant these people knew beforehand that she would be there which left Kolski undeniable proof there was a mole in the midst of the Facility.

Would the Tabula go that far to secure her? Kolski thought uneasily knowing the Drury oversight council could display a brutal ruthlessness, if necessary. He had been careful not to forward any unusual information to them so that he could honor his word to the woman about leaving the Facility. Even the mole would have no firm evidence and then it dawned on Kolski: They were not satisfied with his reports and probably wanted to perform their own tests.

"Remove mute from all the ear buds, NOW," yelled Kolski slamming his hand down on the table.

"Done sir," came an almost immediate response from the command post personnel.

"All of you get out! Foss and the item are safe," snarled Kolski to the team and then, "Mute them again just in case."

One of his assistants put all the video up on the wall screen and Kolski began to pace watching the chaos ensue as more security converged toward the male team members while two men attempted to head off Shadow. Kolski's hands nearly pulled his hair out as Shadow literally collided with the men sent for her, not that it did them any good as the Commander watched her demolish the two men with barely a pause. His respect increased considerably for her skill, which she had intentionally not displayed within the Facility.

When one of the men that encountered Shadow began screaming into his COM unit about the woman, if it was a woman, disabling him and his partner, Kolski had to grin; she was not going to be easy to catch especially from his own experience.

The darkness seemed to aid Shadow in a way it did not any of the men which further confirmed to Kolski her eyes were nothing like the rest of the people around her now or in the Facility. She moved as if in broad daylight through the installation, neatly avoiding men from the sounds they made which most people would never hear until too late.

Suddenly, Shadow seemed to turn a corner and disappeared from the pirated video feed and Kolski felt a cold stab in his gut until the building's pirated COM chatter began to go crazy; they had obviously lost sight of her as well. He relaxed again.

Screaming over the COM indicated the men had escaped the installation with a contingent on their tails and Kolski demanded, "Open a line to the helicopter!" Then to the helicopter he snarled, "The team is coming in hot!

You need to lift off even if we have missing team members. We need to minimize losses and hope the others don't get caught!"

Feeds from the body cameras told Kolski that Nighthawk and Tank made it outside, but Hesney's was mysteriously dark, either not transmitting or destroyed which either meant the man was captured or dead. It also showed Shadow was still within the building via GPS, but the camera seemed to be facing a blank space that made no sense though she had not been captured, at least yet, he reminded himself sourly.

The helicopter's video picked up the two men running to it and even Kolski could see the blood stains on their suits as he ground his teeth in fury because this breach should have been smooth and straightforward. Instead, the building's security had lain in wait for his team.

A shriek broke his through his thoughts, it came from the buildings pirated COM and a voice snarled, "Dolts!" it said, "You let them get the shard! How the hell did they get in? Stop those men and find that woman, now."

Kolski smiled grimly, whoever had been expecting them seriously underestimated the team or maybe it would be better to say they did not know anything about Shadow's capabilities. That meant it still could be Tabula involvement, but Kolski did not think it had the right feel to an operation they might run, he would keep an open mind just in case.

Again he was distracted when the helicopter pilot yelled over the COM, "Strap in for rapid lift off," and saw the vehicle ascend with abnormal speed while its cameras were trained on men below finally reaching its take off point firing impotently into the air.

"Damage medic?" demanded Kolski to the medical person on the helicopter.

"Foss took a wound in the shoulder with significant blood loss. He'll need rest, but the shoulder is repaired. Nighthawk's wounds were minor and just needed sealing. Tank took several projectile wounds, some blood loss and internal damage, which are also repaired, he will need rest as well. Hesney and Shadow are both still MIA sir, but all other team members are accounted for," said the medic with forced calm.

"Nothing we can do about it now. They know protocol," said Kolski flatly, he was unhappy, but hid it.

It was never good news to have personnel dead or missing in hostile territory and his eyes flicked back to the pirated video feeds noting a frenzy search ensued in the search for Shadow, though she remained unavailable. Hesney's ear bud said he was still within the target building, but GPS static so Kolski said to the command post, "Make certain Hesney's ear bud remains muted on our side, but I want you to record anything his microphone picks up. We don't know his status yet. Do the same for Shadow. Prepare to send a hovercam into the area."

Kolski did not know how much the team had heard from the men attempting to kill them or if they knew Shadow was the one they were after, but they would soon find out back at the command post when able to view the pirated video and COM from the building. That presented another problem. He could not have any men rushing off to do some rescue for missing team members, especially with satellite images showing swarms of men searching the surrounding area of the target installation.

"Once the team has returned to the command post, I want it locked down and no one is to leave unless I give the order. We can't risk another incident and potentially compromise this country for harboring us. For now they can only guess where we have gone since the chopper flew below radar and can hide from satellite recon," said Kolski flatly knowing he would get resistance and mostly likely from Nighthawk.

It was not long before the stealth helicopter landed at the command center. Team and crew entered to find doors sealed behind them to their surprise except for

Nighthawk, he marched straight to the COM practically slamming it with his fist.

"Why are we under lockdown?" snarled Nighthawk to the surprise of all the men in the room, they never heard him lose his cool before now.

"You know exactly why. I don't want any heroics to retrieve missing team members. Take a look at the satellite recon for yourself. The entire area is swarming with patrols looking for signs and they already found the river entry point," snapped the Commander.

The rest of the men watched Nighthawk warily as he turned to the monitors to assess the situation and locations the GPS showed of the missing people, he could see both were static at that moment.

Finally the Commander's voice demanded, "Did any of you see what happened to Hesney? He's been stationary since security attempted to pin you down."

"Unknown sir. I saw him head down the hall following Foss and Shadow. That was the last I saw of him," said Tank wearily.

"Did you order him to help Foss?" snapped Kolski.

"No sir, but everything got hot too quick to say anything to him so I thought he made a run for the gear to get out," said Tank irritably for the missing man's unreliability.

Just then one of the men at the monitoring equipment swore, but they all saw why, the ear bud/GPS combination and camera, which belonged to Hess disappeared as if destroyed and the Commander said grimly, "I saw. We will have to assume Hesney is dead if they found the ear bud and camera."

"And Shadow?" said Foss tensely.

"From what we could see during the fighting, it appears she is hiding. You can play back the recording to see for yourselves, but so far we can't determine exactly where she is concealed," said the Commander with a sigh.

After viewing the recording, Foss walked over to the schematics of the target building suspended in a three dimensional holographic display to see if he could glean where Shadow might be hiding from the searching building security.

"You should be resting," insisted the medic when he noticed Foss leaning on the table for support during his observation.

"I can rest when I'm dead," said Foss flatly and the medic tossed up his hands in futility.

Then to the men at the interface controls, "Put Shadow's GPS into the hologram schematics and the heat signatures of the installation security," said Foss abruptly, which attracted Nighthawk's attention immediately.

"Is that some sort of ventilation duct she's in?" said Tank looking over Foss' shoulder.

Foss snorted, "Explains why they can't find her at the moment. I was wondering if she pulled the ceiling stunt again," he said dryly.

All of them could still hear various orders and counter orders via the installation's pirated COM link with men's voices increasing in desperation to locate Shadow since the perimeter guard did not record her exiting with the men.

"Why didn't you make her go with you?" demanded Nighthawk suddenly.

It took some self-control for Foss to meet Nighthawk's glare, "You know as well as I do no one makes Shadow do anything she doesn't want to do, not even you. I tried to get her to leave, but we had company and she took off," he said pointedly with no apology.

Though Foss felt far from comfortable making that assessment, Nighthawk did not respond and only his lips pressed thin in disapproval, he apparently acknowledged the merit of the explanation. Such a comment from the quiet man told Foss he accurately guessed the man's feelings for Shadow and that he made a wise choice not to approach the woman with any interest that was not work related.

"She's on the move," said Tank suddenly drawing all eyes back to the holographic schematic.

The holographic display indicated Shadow entered a hallway and the men turned back to VID to watch what she would do next now out in the open, though they could tell little about the hall in the dimness other than it was currently devoid of body heat.

The pirated COM came alive with chatter and one voice said, "Release the widara to track the woman."

The men in the command post looked at each other puzzled by the term 'widara' but they knew whatever it was could not be good news for Shadow who was trying to find a way out of the installation.

"Shit, shit, shit," swore Tank as they all watched a mass of heat signatures heading to cut her off, "Should we say something to her?"

"She knows," said Stanton suddenly and the other men's heads swiveled in his direction, they had forgotten he was there because he had been so uncharacteristically quiet.

"She might know, but there is nowhere for her to go," snapped Foss irritated at Stanton's clinical observation.

A voice stood out over the pirated COM, "The widara has the trail, stay with it," he demanded.

Shadow meandered away from her pursuers and even if she knew where all of them were, the men could see the situation turning dire as various separate groups converged on the area herding her into a corner of the installation.

When Shadow's camera seemed to go blank the men swiveled to the holographic display to see she was in the same general area and Foss said approvingly, "She's on the ceiling. Smart move if she's going to do what I think."

They watched as a one group passed by her signal, almost as if they ran over her, and literally collide with the other searching groups that expected to pin Shadow between them. In spite of the tension, several of the men grinned at the shrieks from men grappling at each other expecting one of them to be the intruder.

With that distraction, they saw Shadow's signal move away in the opposite direction she had been running putting distance between her and the installation security.

"You know that's going to piss them off," snorted Tank with grim humor.

A voice came over the pirated COM, "Back this way. The widara has the trail," it snarled.

"You've got to be kidding? We just came from there," snapped another voice.

"Well, she got by you then," said the first voice waspishly.

"Who the hell is this person? Are you even sure it's a woman?" snarled the second voice. "Those others didn't give us this much trouble."

The men in the command post actually heard the Commander bark a laugh via his link at the quick exchange recalling Shadow's elusiveness to their mind when they attempted to track her down.

All eyes returned to the VID and watched the security heat signatures in hot pursuit of Shadow's signal and a section of the group split off in another corridor to trap her between them. Soon as the two groups began to approach each other, the movement in Shadow's camera indicated she dropped to the ground.

Swearing men stumbled over her body careening into the oncoming group and the first voice they heard shrieked in rage, "Bring up the lights. Now!"

Everything became blindingly clear in an instant showing men looking about each other wildly attempting to locate their elusive quarry which was sprinting back in the direction she had run originally. The corridor had collections of ancient armor standing in nooks along the wall and weapons from various eras mounted on the wall in display, a fortune in collected historic items worth a king's ransom.

"What the hell is that?" said Stanton when he caught sight of a covered hunched figure among the men moving with an unusual gate.

Leaning forward, all the men stared hard at the cloaked figure unable to see anything recognizable exposed, but they could tell it was bipedal whatever it was and more than one of them grew uneasy. It did not take a leap of logic to know this was probably what those men called 'widara.'

Though not as tall as her pursuers, Shadow outpaced them even if it was no more than terror of capture until one of the lead men threw something at her legs that tripped her up and caused her to stumble. Her loss of momentum allowed some of the men to catch up to Shadow, but they soon regretted laying hands on her, as she became a whirlwind of arms and legs, tossing her bigger adversaries about like children.

"Damn...she held back the night we grabbed her," said Tank in astonishment.

"You think?" said Foss sarcastically and noticed Stanton's jaw muscles flexing at Shadow's display they were all watching.

"Damn it to hell," shrieked a man and then into his wrist unit, "Are you certain this is the person we want?"

A new voice came over the COM, "Subdue her, him, it, or whatever and capture," it snarled.

That was when the cloaked figure surged forward and what reached out of one sleeve made a few of the men at the command post recoil from the VID: A black tentacle-like appendage reached out to snare Shadow by the arm.

Though none of them could see its features, the posture of revulsion in Shadow's body gave them enough of an idea they did not want to see what was under that hood. The thing, the widara, was obviously strong the way it pulled her, but fueled by desperation or pure terror, Shadow grabbed at Stanton's loaned knife.

In a frantic slash, she severed the black tentacle and the sound that came over the pirated COM was an unearthly "screeeeing" shriek, which did not sound even remotely human. The cloaked figure lurched and thrashed, men near it cried out in fear and pain, as it appeared to lash out in agony before launching at Shadow for injuring it.

Its leap caused the hood to fly backwards off its head and one man at the monitors in the command post began retching noisily onto the floor at the twisted nightmare revealed. It might have been a man once, but no longer, hair bristled out of the bulging eyed head that reminded them of a spider, which sported a pincher mouth adorned by fangs.

It sunk those fangs into Shadow's right arm which she threw up to defend herself from its sudden assault and maddened with fear, Shadow launched the creature away from her with both legs and in the same motion grabbed a long lance-like weapon from a wall display. She barely had time to bring it to bear before the widara launched at her again.

In its maddened state, the widara never saw the weapon and impaled its body on the short ancient lance with a shrilling ululation, "screee" which Shadow dropped as if it burned her.

"Bitch," shrieked one of the men, but he was too afraid to pass the thrashing creature to do anything about Shadow fleeing from him.

Back at the command post, white-faced men watched the pirated VID as the creature thrashed in the throes of death and Shadow ran toward a glass window on an upper level only to dive out of it, fists first, arms extended. After that they only had her camera and GPS to track her progress since Shadow was no longer within range of the pirated VID stream.

Kolski stared at the VID speechless and as white-faced as any of the other men even though he was safely ensconced within the Facility, *my god*, he thought, *what the hell was that thing*. The Tabula certainly did not indicate his team would be up against anything unusual and it was possible they did not know. With that thought in mind, the commander contacted his liaison to the Tabula to explain what had happened and what they saw in the installation though he was discreet about the exact situation around the encounter.

His contact was silent for so long, Kolski wondered if he disconnected until he finally said, "The fools used the shard. Has your team witnessed anything else strange?"

"No. They have exited the installation under the circumstances, but have retrieved the shard," stated Kolski, he did not want to be anywhere near that artifact.

"See that they do not become curious," said the contact and then added. "Did the creature touch or bite any of your team?" demanded the voice flatly.

"It may have bit the woman in the chaos," said Kolski evasively.

"If so, she is already dead. Withdraw the team immediately since you have secured the artifact," said the voice dispassionately.

"No!" exclaimed the Commander involuntarily. "We never abandon anyone we know to be alive."

"Did you not hear me? The woman is already dead. There will be no cure if bitten," snapped the voice.

"We don't know for sure," Kolski lied, "I said it was possible, but inconclusive. She is currently free and making her way to a rendezvous point so the woman seems far from dead or wounded," he insisted.

"The first indication you have the woman is affected, your orders are to abandon her and you will leave immediately," snarled the contact before breaking the connection.

After forwarding a message to the command post to make preparation to depart, Kolski wondered what exactly they were now involved in and if their previous retrieval was something just as dire. One thing for certain, he did not think even Stanton would just abandon the woman no matter what her condition and Nighthawk would just go AWOL if he, the Commander, attempted to hint at abandoning Shadow. Just like that, the Tabula would cast her aside, but then, if she was affected by some incurable poison, all anyone could do for her would be to watch her die, he thought with an audible sigh—such a terrible waste.

Shadow hit the snow rolling, winded by the impact, but she did not have time to worry about trivial things like gasping and ran from the horror of what she had just seen. Right now she was on the wrong side of the installation and did not dare attempt to circumvent the area with who knew how many security personnel chasing her. The last message via her ear bud told the team to get out immediately, but it felt like every guard in the building had homed in on her and not the men, a ridiculous thought really. Shadow knew the men were in just as much danger as she was and it was not time to be selfishly centered on an improbability as she saw it.

Alarms hooted behind her from the installation and search lights roved about trying to locate Shadow though, thankfully, her suit would not show up against the snow, but her shadow would give her away. Then there were the tracks in the snow she was leaving in her wake even with the stiff breeze blowing.

In the distance, Shadow picked up movement and flicked through her vision as she ran to see cable cars moving far above the snow up into the higher altitude and that presented her with an idea, but her first order of business was a backup gear site. Shadow was not certain whether or not she would have found the gear stash if it had not been for her vision since so much snow drifted over the spot.

With studied haste, she began to dig out the gear donning the parachute harness as soon as she pulled it out and continued digging until she revealed a fanny pack, cross country skis, and poles. Now that she had the skies, Shadow toyed with the idea of heading back toward the drop point until the sound of motors reached her ears telling her snow vehicles followed her trail.

Sufficed with terror of capture again, Shadow took off in the direction of the cable car suspension, following down slope to get to the destination point where it would drop off or pick up passengers. Thankfully, the sloping land helped her gain speed, not that Shadow had any delusions of out running motorized vehicles, but initially they would think she was on foot, which she hoped gave her a margin of safety.

Soon as Shadow skied around a hill she saw the depot where the cable cars stopped and started which was surrounded by a small town when rooftops also came into view. That was a stroke of luck for her because the men pursuing her might assume she attempted to blend into the residents, which might stall them further.

Nearby the building which the cable cars catered to passengers, Shadow saw outdoor supports with skis all stacked in rows as if their owners found it easier just to level them overnight to be picked up in the morning. *Perfect*, she thought with relief, no one would know which pair might be hers or if she left any there with the all the muddled tracks from other skis from tourists or residents in the town.

Carefully surveying the terrain for observers, Shadow glided up to the racks and removed her skis, setting them with the others along with her poles that would encumber her. Then listening closely for voices, she slipped around the building where it was most trampled to hide her own prints among the others. There were some people chatting inside a lighted room, probably they had been skiing at night or came to visit the town for the evening and beyond them was another door, which no doubt led to the cable cars.

If she went inside, her attire would be instantly noticed and remembered which was not what Shadow wanted, but if she tried to board one of the cable cars as is, people would definitely remember her. Nearby the door she was peeking in was a row of coat hangers with some coats on the hooks either belonging to people present or forgotten during the day by their owners and that gave her an idea.

Ducking below the window sill, Shadow slipping around to the opening that serviced the cable cars and heard a couple of men talking in a Germanic based language, she breathed a quiet sigh of relief noting their backs were to her. A fierce wind blew inside the building coming down off the peaks and Shadow ducked down again, slipped up to prop the door open enough the wind would catch it before slipping back around to the other door.

She almost was not fast enough when the wind caught the door and it opened with a terrific bang causing everyone inside the room to jump and turn around to see what happened. Immediately, Shadow slipped inside and snagged a coat, put it on, then pulled up the hood just like she came inside from out of the cold. It did not matter if they saw her legs since many people wore close fitting ski pants and it covered the parachute pack.

Wrapping her arms about her body as if chilled, Shadow noticed a burning in her right arm, but brushed aside the irritation and made her way to the door leading to the cable cars. One of the men turned around as she came outside again and walked to a cable car to hold the door open, she nodded her thanks then sat on the bench like seating lining the edges of the car. A few people followed her outside to take the cable car, which Shadow suspected stopped at another resort town higher up the peaks.

The door of the cable car clanged shut and it lurched forward suddenly as one of the men pulled a lever. About a hundred yards from the depot Shadow heard motors roaring up to the town of snow driven vehicles coming from the direction she had escaped and instantly tensed in fear she could be trapped. No one stopped the cable car's rise to the peaks, but Shadow could hear a heated argument with the men at the controls with the arrivals probably questioning them about someone of her appearance.

For almost thirty minutes the cable car continued upward until Shadow could see the dark maw of the next depot where it would let off passengers, but when it lurched to a stop sixty feet away, she knew the men below intended to search this cable car. A couple of people gasped at the sensation from the abrupt stop and began to babble, some in English, wondering if they were stuck or the motor, which ran the cables failed. Below them was a good seventy to hundred foot drop, which was enough to injure her if she attempted to exit the cable car, but Shadow knew she had to do something or those men would trap her and potentially hurt the innocent people with her.

It was too late to worry about people remembering her now and Shadow jimmied the door open while a man grew shrill with panic at her activity, she discarded the coat so she could haul her body up onto the roof of the cable car. People in the car began to converse in shock, but Shadow ignored them and laid flat on the roof to avoid detection if anyone was watching the car when it was brought into the depot. If she were lucky, they would be over confident that their quarry would be trapped in the car and not pay much attention to the arrival, certainly not looking on the roof of the transportation.

While she waited, the burning in her arm renewed its presence, but accompanied by twinges of pain and Shadow finally looked at her right forearm to see two blackened holes in her suit oozing blood mixed with a smelly yellow substance. The coldness in her belly had nothing to do with the weather when Shadow realized that was where the creature in the installation bit her and now she was probably poisoned in some way.

The cable car finally lurched forward and Shadow ignored her arm for the time being as she waited for the depot to grow closer until it was about six feet away, which was when she jumped onto the roof of the building. She had only moments to act and ran across the snowy roof, peeking over the opposite side to see a variety of motorized snow vehicles telling her the pursuers were waiting to receive the occupants of the cable car. It was a relatively short drop so Shadow jumped down and appropriated a snowmobile, opening the throttle full force as she took off willy-nilly over the snow toward the general direction of her original escape had she left the installation with the team.

"Pan out on Shadow's camera so we can see more and launch that hovercam. I want to see exactly what is happening," demanded Kolski impatiently after the woman smashed through the glass window of the installation.

After that order, all the men remained quiet except for the tapping of keys on the interface adjusting for data feeds into the command post. They watched as Shadow reached one of the gear stashes, equip herself, and then take off in a totally unexpected direction, Nighthawk literally launched over to the satellite feed to assess the area.

"What the hell is she doing?" fumed the Commander, "None of you were to head toward any towns to prevent risk to the civilians."

"Check the satellite image," directed Nighthawk. "You can see the thermal images of people heading in her direction and from their rate of speed, they are using vehicles."

"Damn it," snarled the Commander. "They want to catch her badly if they are risking civilian involvement."

"They could think she has the shard," said Foss grimly, "Or intend to use her to trade for it."

"Possibly, but I'm not certain that is the entire story," said Kolski evasively.

At the Commander's words, Tank gave a sideways glance at Nighthawk and both men exchanged knowing looks since they overheard the order to catch Shadow so, apparently, had the Commander. They all continued to watch as Shadow skied into the town right up the cable car depot and Tank made comment of approval when she hid her skis in plain sight along with the others in the rack.

When Shadow circumvented the building and peered into the door of the lounge with people inside, "What's she doing?" exclaimed Foss suddenly, "She can't think to go inside dressed in that suit with a packed parachute on!"

None of the others commented and they continued to watch as Shadow skulked around the building, prop open the side door slightly before dart back to the original door just as the wind caught the side door. Foss gasped in surprise as Shadow slipped inside the lounge, donned an unused coat, and pull the hood up before any people in the building even knew she was inside.

"Never stops thinking, does she?" the Commander said drolly which the others greeted with snorts.

They all watched as she boarded a cable car like any normal resident or tourist though unfortunately followed by other people and just caught sight of Shadow stowing her mask since it would be remarkable.

"Shit, shit, shit," said Foss when the cable car eventually lurched to a halt before the next depot, "It's too high for her to jump and she would be a fool to sacrifice her parachute."

The atmosphere in the command post turned grim when it appeared Shadow was finally trapped until she spurred to action and every man leaned forward to watch what she was going to do. Panicked voices came through Shadow's ear bud from the other passengers in the cable car as the woman jimmied open the door, removed the coat, and replaced her mask followed by her climbing out of the cab onto the roof. The camera appeared to go blank, but they knew that Shadow was lying down on the roof to prevent her profile from showing if anyone from the next depot would be watching the cable car come inside.

Sound through Shadow's ear bud told them when the cable car lurched back into motion and then she suddenly stood up just in time for them to see the cable car barely feet from the depot as she made a magnificent jump right onto the roof of the building. Their view could see as she peered over the opposite edge of the building so they could see all the vehicles of people waiting for the cable car to arrive. No one expected what happened next as Shadow jumped from the roof, acquired one of the snow mobiles and head off at high speed in to the snow bound forest bordering the town. The men watching knew there was added difficulty navigating at night and the terrain contained steep inclines or dropoffs at that altitude.

It was an interesting move since it prevented larger vehicles from chasing after her, but the men had seen enough snow mobiles in their brief glimpse to know Shadow would have sufficient pursers.

"Get that hovercam in the area, stat!" snarled the Commander.

"Pull up the topographical map of the area," demanded Stanton out of the blue.

"What are you thinking?" snapped the Commander over the COM.

"I'm not certain just yet," said Stanton repressively in spite of who he was talking to.

"They're after her," said one of the men at the interface watching the thermal images chasing Shadow's GPS.

"Damn, she must have eyes like a hawk the way she is weaving in and out of those trees," said Tank incredulously.

The satellite thermal imaging showed some of the following heat signatures had halted, but the men were unable to tell the reason though most guessed it was due to accidents at the speed they needed to pursue Shadow. Another sound superimposed over Shadow's snow mobile engine and the men realized the pursuers had put a helicopter in the air to follow her movements, which only incited her to stay undercover of the evergreen forest.

"Shit, those idiots are hovering too close to that upper ridge," snarled Stanton suddenly.

"Care to enlighten the rest of us?" snapped the Commander sarcastically.

"There has been heavy snow fall recently and it built up on that ridge. The sounds and down draft from those rotors could trigger an avalanche," Stanton replied.

"Is there any way to tighten the satellite image so we can see what is going on?" fumed the Commander.

"Sir, with no moon, we won't see much except for thermal images. We'll lose the satellite before daybreak even if she manages to keep them off her back. No... wait, the hovercam is there now," said one of the men at the interface and the Commander demanded a better image.

Finally, they had an encompassing view of Shadow's situation as she barreled through a forest to elude her less acute pursuers which evidenced by the satellite images as thermal signatures halted, sometimes abruptly, in her wake.

A voice came through the pirated COM link at the installation, "Whoever this individual is they are taking out a lot of our men trying to catch them and they don't want to be caught," it snarled in fury.

The response to the frustrated voice made nearly all the people listening at the command post turn grim, "You shouldn't have to wait long. That venom will slow her down soon enough and you will need to get her back here for the antidote before she dies."

Of course none of the men could see the Commander's black expression at the word 'antidote' after he had been led to believe there was no cure if any of his team had been bitten and once more, Kolski suspected Tabula involvement. Why else abandon the woman if there was a cure they denied?

Now the question would be: Did Shadow have enough time to get free of her pursuers before the venom disabled her? The Commander could not authorize a mission across the border with the odds against them.

Suddenly, Stanton swore vociferously and Tank muttered, "My god," as they witnessed the unthinkable via the hovercam when a wall of snow separated from the ridge from the helicopter flying too low to locate Shadow.

"She can't out run that..." said Foss trailing off helplessly as everyone watched the wall of snow gaining speed and debris consisting of boulders, ice, and trees.

The hovercam kept pace with the Shadow, but it was obvious from the various views they had that the wall of snow was gaining on her and began to overtake the men pursuing by the cries through the pirated COM link.

"What is she doing?" said Tank uncertainly as they watched Shadow wrap something about one of the handles.

"Lashing the throttle?" guessed one of the men at the interface.

"Insane! The woman is insane," exploded Stanton when all of them saw Shadow crouching on the snow mobile seat angling it toward a sheer cliff.

Every man, including the Commander, griped tables or chairs until their knuckles were white, leaning forward as if in the situation with Shadow, breathless and waiting to see what she planned to do in this desperate situation. Edges of the avalanche had caught up to her and the hovercam showed everyone mists of snow spray beginning to obscure Shadow's crouching figure when suddenly the land fell away from the snow mobile. At the precise moment, Shadow sprang away from the vehicle, which dropped like a stone, but her body still had the momentum of its forward impetus and suddenly the hovercam lost sight of her.

"Where the hell is she?" demanded the Commander urgently.

Her GPS tag indicated she was in the same general area and one of the men repositioned the hovercam enough for everyone to realize why they momentarily lost sight of Shadow: Her parachute deployed jerking her body upward abruptly. This parachute was made to parasail and would allow her to glide for a long distance which could get her over the border, but it was not to be that easy.

"Damn it! That chopper has seen her and they're going to try an aerial snag," said Stanton suddenly, his face close to one of the monitors.

"If they create too much downdraft, it could fold the chute and she'll drop like a stone," spat Foss furiously at such a maneuver.

"She knows," said Tank suddenly. "Her speed is increasing and she's dropping altitude fast."

With a suddenness that made most of the men jump, the hitherto silent Nighthawk launched at the secured door, "Open it, NOW," he all, but shouted.

"I said no rescue missions," roared the Commander in response to Nighthawk's words.

With an advance that made the nearest man at the interface recoil, Nighthawk approached the COM, "She's coming in hot and will make it over the border. She's going to need help since she's wounded and poisoned," he hissed threateningly.

It did not take much for Kolski to realize the man would get his way even if he had to take out the entire command post and the last thing he wanted was Nighthawk making a mission out of confronting him later. That man scared him, even as Commander and he could admit that privately.

"Take a small crew. DO NOT CROSS THE BORDER FOR ANY REASON! Is that understood?" snapped the Commander and all the other man did was nod tightly.

"I'm coming," said Foss immediately and then he wilted to the floor as the medic removed a hypospray from the man's arm.

"I think not," murmured the medic before quickly gathering gear and stuffing into a bag as he followed Nighthawk.

"Stanton, you didn't have an injury. Go as back up just in case," said the Commander needlessly as the man was already walking in that direction.

It had been a risky gamble trying to outrun the avalanche and Shadow barely had time to feel a modicum of relief when the sound of helicopter rotors impinged on her ears, she knew what they would attempt to do.

From her study of the topography of the area where the team made the breach, Shadow knew where the borders of the countries lay and used the parasail to head to the uncertain refuge of host land in which the command post resided. Since the pursuing helicopter would obviously attempt to snatch her from the sky, Shadow began to lose altitude at a faster rate than advisable knowing that her only protection from the air vehicle would be the tree canopy. This course of action was a double edged sword, so to speak, since it also presented a dangerous problem for anyone using a parachute and could leave her tangled within trees branches making Shadow an easy target.

A terrible shooting pain coursed up her injured arm that made Shadow aware that a scale dart previously through her thigh had not been quite so bad after all. Dread settled over her when she realized that the thing that bit her had done more than cause a wound and there would be no aid nearby to help, if anyone could help with the injury. Chances were the people at the installation knew exactly what happened to her and Shadow was relatively certain that was the reason no one attempted to shoot her even now, exposed as she was in the air. That meant only one thing to her terrified mind: They wanted to capture her.

Helicopter rotors sounded much closer and Shadow knew she had only one desperate chance to escape these men, which could also kill her if she made a mistake. They were following her over the border confident in the knowledge they could seize her before she managed to make a safe landing so Shadow changed the rules.

Buckled into the parachute harness it would be easy for the helicopter to snatch at the parasail with little effort so Shadow began working clips and buckles loose above the evergreen treetops. Not for the first time did she resent being in an environment that left so few options, which normally existed within the city.

When the downdraft from the helicopter's rotors began to cause the parasail to jerk wildly, Shadow just managed to work the last buckle free noting the treetops literally brushed the bottom of her boots. A massive jerk told her that the men had seized the parasail and Shadow allowed her body to sink down folding her arms up freeing her body from the harness so that she fell instantly into one of the waving evergreen trees beneath her feet.

Cries of rage and impotent fury followed her crashing descent among the branches, but Shadow could not spare a glance upward as she tried to avoid the bludgeoning branches checking her fall until she managed to halt her descent. With a more controlled descent, Shadow then proceeded to climb quickly out of the tree before the men in the helicopter decided to rappel down as she had done with Stanton so many months ago.

Fortunately beneath the evergreens there was very little snow on the ground so Shadow could make some speed until her body began to feel strange and the land seemed to lurch about her as if she had been spinning in a circle too long. At that point, Shadow was not certain if she trusted her perceptions when sounds of a second helicopter came to her ears and the one following seemed to recede just as she broke out of the line of

trees. She had just enough wit left to realize leaving the
tree cover was probably not wise before her legs buckled beneath her and tremors ran through her body as if
she had the chills. Pain Shadow never imagined seemed
to course through all her limbs and then she felt a pair
of strong arms, she looked into the swimming features
of Nighthawk managing to mutter, "Help me," before her
focus was gone.

While the hovercam transmitted Shadow's plight
back to the command post, the helicopter carrying her
rescue headed to the area to intercept her and chase off
the pursuing helicopter. They could see and hear the entire situation from a feed sent by the command post and
Stanton muttered, "certifiable," when they saw Shadow
slip from her parachute harness.

"Get Doc on the line," said the medic into his wrist
unit, "I'm going use a vitastat unit to transmit her condition to him. If she is poisoned, he should be able to
suggest a counter-agent to bind the toxin and prevent
any more damage than she's already suffered."

The pursuing helicopter came into sight and seemed
intent to continue its chase until their pilot barked a
string of orders as if he belonged to the host country's
military sending the other chopper veering off back the
way it came in a hurry. Minutes later they saw Shadow
stumble from the trees into the open and the pilot landed
so fast, it knocked his passengers off their feet.

Barely hampered by the rough landing, Nighthawk
catapulted from the helicopter seeming to leap to the injured woman, who was now unable to stand, scooped
her up, and appear to teleport back to the helicopter before anyone else could move. Once in the helicopter, the
pilot shot back into the air as the medic slapped a thin
metal square onto Shadow's neck before saying urgently,
"It's on Doc. She's in a bad way. What can I do for her?"

A groan of dismay sounded in response, "Damn it,
there is some exotic toxin at work I've never seen before,

but it is similar to several I know. Make a mixture of...,"
and he rattled off several compounds hurriedly. "Put
something between her teeth quickly so she doesn't
swallow her tongue. If she isn't convulsing now, she will
be," said Doc grimly.

"Doc...this is poison," said the medic in dismay about
the mixture he made at the doctor's instructions.

"Yes, yes, I know. Some poisons are fought with
poison. The two bind together and become inert. Don't
hesitate, she's already been exposed too long and the
damage will be bad enough," snapped Doc.

By now Shadow twisted and moaned in pain unable
to fight the onset of the poison any longer and the medic
said, "Hold her and put this between her teeth. It's going
to be rough."

Nighthawk pried open her mouth to insert a roll of
leather as Stanton grabbed Shadow's feet and the medic
struggled to inject the solution into her writhing body,
but when he did, the reaction was immediate. Almost
instantly Shadow began to convulse, her body going
rigid and thrashing, foam forming at the corners of her
mouth, which took both Nighthawk and Stanton to subdue sufficiently.

"Damn it, whatever that toxin is, it is interfering with
the neurotransmitters regulating her muscles. Give her
a muscle relaxant, but start with a low dose first and
watch her breathing. I want her back here ASAP before
her heart gives out," ordered Doc.

The Commander's voice jumped in, "Does anyone
need a medic any longer back at the command post?" he
said.

"No sir. They just need to rest," answered the medic
instantly.

"Head straight to the jet. Bring Nighthawk with you.
The chopper can return with Stanton and we'll send the
plane back to pick up the rest of the team," ordered the
Commander.

This jet was not what past history would bring to mind when planes were in their infancy, this jet literally arced through the atmosphere and made the journey in an hour, which had a helicopter waiting to return to the Facility. It was only an hour and thirty minutes later that Nighthawk delivered Shadow to the infirmary with personnel seething about in preparation to treat her.

"You can't help here. Go rest," said Doc when he noticed Nighthawk sitting nearby.

All Nighthawk did was stare at the man and remain immobile so that the physician sighed shaking his head before returning to Bryn.

Once Shadow had stabilized, Doc examined data puzzling over the toxin, which had affected her, she should be dead if the timeframe from the initial poisoning was correct not that he wished her such a fate. People fought off disease not poison which by the very nature of substances made them so lethal yet somehow this woman had held an unknown toxin at bay for a while which made no sense.

Sighing, Doc rubbed his tired eyes and now he had to determine just what damage Bryn had suffered, what could be repaired or if it could be repaired. More than the neurotransmitters had been effected, her nerves had taken damage as well and Doc had a small partial respirator unit on Bryn's face to assist her breathing. What had bitten her? He thought examining the two blackened holes on her arm.

Movement distracted him when Doc looked over to see Nighthawk waking from sleeping in a chair, but the man ignored his stern glance, "How is she?" he asked quietly.

"She's holding her own right now, but her body suffered damage from the toxin. I will assess what I can repair," said Doc uncertainly.

"She might not recover?" said Nighthawk quietly though his anxiety evident.

Doc assessed Nighthawk narrowly, he knew the man had originally been assigned as the woman's caretaker particularly after her initial arrival at the Facility and subsequent reaction to her relocation had made her dangerous. Now he wondered at this man's concern, could it be he also did not agree with the manner the young woman had been restrained?

"I don't know. Changes are taking place in her body I cannot account for. I'm reluctant to begin treatment at the moment," said Doc truthfully since he noticed some spontaneous healing which should not have occurred.

"What changes?" insisted Nighthawk.

Doc sighed, "She should have died from that toxin before anyone had a chance to help her due the chemical composition, but somehow she managed to survive long enough to get to the medic. The treatment could have killed her, but did not which puzzles me. Then I've seen some spontaneous healing and a body cannot heal from this kind of damage, not without help. That has stopped however and I don't know if I can repair the rest of damage," he said noting the tension in the other man.

"May I see all the data you have on her condition?" said Nighthawk suddenly which surprised Doc.

"You're welcome to review it, but I warn you, it's grim reading," said Doc wearily wondering why the other man would make such a request.

With those words, Doc left the man to review the data wishing he could offer the Nighthawk more hope and knowing what the Commander would say if Bryn stayed on a respirator. They did not manage patients who did not recover which would portend a grisly fate for the young woman that he did not want to contemplate.

Chapter 10

A brief flare a light illuminated Donal Meany's face as he used a fine laser weld on a special device that he created when placed under the skin of a person could regulate the immune system of people afflicted with autoimmune diseases. It was one of his latest accomplishments.

A knock sounded on his laboratory door startling him, Donal never had visitors since the young woman had been seized from his life and that thought grimly reminded him that she was probably held against her will. Financial support still came to him, but at what cost, Donal wondered and he was reluctant to notify anyone, as he had no idea where she could be or who might have her. A misstep could endanger her further.

The knock sounded again and Donal made his way to the door cautiously, he peered at the surveillance monitor to see an unknown man dressed casually, seemingly alone. Taking a deep breath and wondering what trouble appeared on his doorstep, Donal opened the door slowly to see a tall man with piercing grey eyes. Everything about this man said he was dangerous and it was too late to close the door.

"May I come in," said the man in a quiet voice that made Donal start with recognition.

Standing back and opening the door wider, Donal gestured the man inside watching him keenly after recognizing his voice knowing this was the man who had arranged for him to see Bryn when she had headaches.

Donal was uncertain what to say to this man, "Would you like some tea or coffee?"

"No thank you. I need your help," he said without preamble.

Warily Donal regarded the man wondering just what kind of help he needed, but apparently his expression suggested enough of his thoughts that the man handed him a small portable drive, which he took uncertainly. Walking over to his interface, Donal plugged in the drive and the grim reality of Bryn's condition flickered vividly before his eyes.

"My god, what did this?" said Donal in horror.

"It's better if you don't know," came the response, "She can't recover though our lead doctor never actually said that, but he doesn't have the technology to fix this kind of damage."

"Very few are even close to fixing such injuries," said Donal in evident distress as he turned to look at the man.

That was when he realized the other man was actually as distressed as he was and he had missed it initially in his assessment so he came here because he worried for Bryn just like he had when he contacted Donal previously.

"Then you can do nothing for her?"

Pain was in that voice Donal noted, pain of loss of someone dear and he realized this man loved Bryn, coming here as a last resort in person, to get any help possible.

"I can help her, but if I go to her, it will reveal more than others should know about her," said Donal struggling with the dilemma of saving someone who was like a daughter to him.

"Tell me what to do and then I will do it. I will make certain no one knows," came the fierce response.

Donal assessed this man, he meant what he said and that he would protect Bryn any way that he could, besides it would be the only way or people would know about the real link he had with the young woman.

"It will take me some time. I will have extensive programming to affect the repairs she needs to recover. After that, it will only need to be injected," said Donal watching the man's expression closely.

"Is there anything I can do to help?"

The man was sincere in his offer, Donal realized, "Unfortunately what I need to do is beyond your skill, but if you don't mind menial work, I would appreciate some food and tea," he said.

To Donal's surprise, the man instantly rose to perform the request with no questions or distaste and he watched bemused as the man rummaged about to prepare food on hand. It was many hours later that Donal finally looked up wearily as his visitor deposited yet another cup of tea that he completed the programming of the nanites. Carefully he placed them into a saline solution and used a syringe to prepare them for injection before capping the needle carefully.

Turning around Donal looked at his visitor, "This will repair her damaged cells. It is best injected into a vein if at all possible and I ask you make certain this syringe is completely destroyed after you're finished. Please let me know how she recovers," he said handing over the syringe.

"I owe you a debt I am not certain I can repay."

"Her recovery is all the payment I would ever want. She is like a daughter to me," said Donal and noted the man nodded before he left.

Kolski made his unwilling way to the infirmary to get news about the woman's condition. Past events made him uncertain if COM transmissions might be monitored and he did not want the Tabula to know anything until he was ready to tell them. As he arrived at the infirmary door, Kolski hesitated wishing he could avoid seeing the woman, but he had to know for the future of missions he had planned or what assignment the Tabula might send his way.

With a sigh, the Commander pressed his thumb into the reader and the door opened, he immediately saw Doc at one of the data interfaces looking drawn with fatigue. The head physician looked up at him and any hope Kolski had for good news quickly fled, he realized Shadow's condition must be critical.

"I can already tell you don't have good news," said the Commander in greeting.

"No though I wish I did. She's managing to hold on and in truth she should be dead after studying the toxin. Right now she needs assistance to breath and I'm uncertain how much repair I can make to her autonomic nervous system. The larger peripheral nerves present less challenge, but her involuntary processes..." said Doc trailing off significantly.

"We had no warning any of the team would be exposed to such a toxin or we would have taken precautions," said the Commander grimly.

"No doubt you would have, but that doesn't help her now. I will do what I can. Even by some miracle she does recover, it's highly doubtful her body will be the same after such damage. I'll know more later," said Doc with a sigh.

Kolski nodded and noticed, with some surprise, that Nighthawk was nowhere in sight which was highly unusual over the past two days. On the occasions he contacted the man since his return, Nighthawk had refused to leave the infirmary and insisted answering question via the COM to the Commander's irritation. Once back in his office, Kolski noted security logged Nighthawk as leaving the Facility over eight hours ago and left no word of his plans or estimated return further annoying him.

Pressing a button, the Commander contacted security, "I want to know the minute Nighthawk returns and inform him to report to me immediately," he snapped.

"Yes sir," came the response.

With nothing else to do, but wait, the Commander turned his thoughts to the Tabula and what he would tell them about Shadow's condition, wondering if he could find himself censured for her rescue.

The first thing Bryn was aware of was an empty blackness, she could not hear, feel, see or smell anything and she began to wonder if she was dead. Slowly sound impinged on her senses, but it seemed dim or distant and then a scent reached her nose that reminded her of the infirmary so she attempted to open her eyes. Blackness frightened her at first thinking she was blind, but when Bryn attempted to deliberately blink, she realized her eyelids did not open and let out a quiet breath of relief that chances were she still had her vision.

Soon she found that hearing and smell were the only options she had and when Bryn attempted to open her mouth to call out she was unable to open her mouth or even move to draw attention.

A voice spoke suddenly and if Bryn could have jumped in surprise she would have, "You can't do anything for her so you might as well get some rest," said a male voice that she thought might be Doc.

"I can rest fine right here," said a voice that Bryn recognized as Nighthawk.

"Listen to me. I haven't seen you eat and I don't care how resilient you are, sleeping in a chair is not rest," said Doc's exasperated voice. "Watching her is not going to change anything and we have monitors on her to let us know if there are any signs of improvement."

"Like that?" said Nighthawk's voice pointedly.

Bryn heard hurried footsteps and then silence for possibly a few minutes before Doc's voice said, "I don't understand. Her vital signs are stronger and there is increase electrical activity in her nervous system. It doesn't make any sense when I could not repair her autonomic functions."

Doc called several names and Bryn heard hurried footstep approaching, "Run some tests. Check her perceptions regularly. According to these readings she is conscious."

Fingers snapped near her ears, but Bryn was unable to flinch, "She heard that, see this brain wave?" said a new male voice she could not identify.

The sound of footsteps came closer and Doc's voice sounded in Bryn's ear, "Young woman, I know you can hear me and I can see you are straining to move. Stop trying or you could cause more harm. I have you in a temporarily induced paralysis to prevent all your muscles from contracting after the damage your nerves suffered from a toxin. You are improving, but if I allow you to move the pain and trauma from the spasms could affect your organs, especially your heart. I am going to sedate you, but soon as tests show your nerves are sufficiently repaired, I will gradually reduce the paralysis and sedation," he said softly.

At the word, "sedation," Bryn tried to fight her way out the stupor to argue against the course of treatment frightened of losing consciousness, but was unsuccessful as sounds began to fade away. Her next awakening was to silence, not even the rustle of clothing or footsteps and the thought took hold someone had moved her. Bryn began to panic and struggled to throw off the lassitude gripping her body, fear burning away the sedation until a massive spasm coursed through her body, she cried out at the sudden intense pain.

A voice in her made Bryn jump again since she had not heard anyone, "Relax darlin. Don't make any sudden movements," said Ryan very softly.

All Bryn could do was groan in response feeling like a coward to succumb to muscle spasms, but nothing compared to her entire body wrenched in agony, not even the worst spasm she ever had in her calf or side. Then suddenly she realized something covered her eyes as she attempt to look in the direction of Ryan's voice, but Bryn was unable to lift either arm to pull at the cloth with muscles in her limb protesting any active movement.

The sound of a door opening followed and hurried feet approached her, Bryn felt a sharp sting in her upper left arm accompanied by a soft hiss of what had to be a hypospray.

"You got the jump on us young woman. I meant to bring you out of sedation slowly, but it seems you are adept at fighting the effects. I've just given you a muscle relaxant to counter those spasms. Unfortunately the lactic acid built up in the muscle is going to make you feel extremely stiff for several days. I'll do what I can to minimize it, but the best option for it is physical therapy," said Doc's voice sounding a little exasperated.

"Why did you cover my eyes?" demanded Bryn.

"I didn't want any visual stimuli to make you flinch. That's one reason I have you isolated in a room, so sound would not do the same thing," said Doc irritably.

A sound of feet retreating slightly and then Doc's voice called, "Davidson, get in here. Looks like I need you to start sooner."

More footsteps approached and Doc continued, "Work in sections and don't let her move more than small areas to start."

Another male voice spoke, a soothing one that Bryn thought she recognized, "I'm going to touch your left hand to begin with and work from that point."

"You're the medic…" said Bryn trailing off and the man she now knew as Davidson chuckled.

"Yes. Nothing wrong with your hearing is there?" he said with a tone of amusement and Bryn thought she heard Ryan snort.

When the Commander insisted on seeing her after a few days of physical therapy, Bryn was not surprised

since she had not technically been debriefed after returning from the latest mission. Several times since waking
the past week she wondered why the man never came to
the infirmary, but attempting to tease information about
the final outcome of the mission from Ryan met with no
success and Doc had been less forthcoming. Probability
was high that Doc refused to allow the Commander to
question her until he was satisfied Bryn had sufficiently
recovered and no doubt found Ryan a formidable ally.

Arriving at the conference room door diverted Bryn's
thoughts from Ryan, who had rarely left her side, a fact
that seemed to annoy Doc greatly. When the door opened,
Bryn took a step backward uncertainly at the sight of the
full room as she had not expected the rest of the team's
presence in the room and looked accusingly at Ryan for
not warning her of the situation. All he did was place a
hand on her lower back and gently guide Bryn into the
room completely ignoring her irritation.

Ignoring Ryan's initial offer of a seat, Bryn reasoned
inwardly that it was not really that many people, but just
unexpected to see the other team members which was
when she realized one person was missing: Hess. A hand
gripped her shoulder gently and Bryn jumped in surprise
aware Ryan was still waiting for her to sit so she sat stiffly, feeling a deep wariness about what this discussion
might portend.

The worrisome part of the discussion was not what
the Commander or the men said, but what was left unsaid and it yelled a silent warning to Bryn. Someone was
after her and either the men did not know who it was or
knew, but would not tell her or maybe it was them trying
to infer it was an outside threat.

Finally Stanton turned to her with a sneer, "So why
did you let us capture you?" he said scathingly.

"I did not let any of you do anything," said Bryn tightly, furious the situation at the installation forced her to
reveal more skill than she intended which were confirmed by the next words.

"We saw your display in that installation or did we catch you off guard that much you just ran scared?" said Stanton condescendingly.

Stanton barely had time to jump to his feet Bryn moved so fast across the table, her hand struck him flat in the solar plexus which sent him reeling against the wall gasping for air, the hint hanging in the air that if she had meant to harm him he would be dead already. The rest of the men, with the exception of Nighthawk had jumped to their feet defensively.

With Stanton gasping motionless before her, Bryn said in a deadly quiet voice, "I am not a killer, but that does not mean I don't know how to kill. I prefer not to harm people so I ran when we first met," her face turned mocking at those words, "Whatever that thing was…it meant to kill me and I will defend myself with deadly force if necessary."

Slithering back across the table, Bryn resumed her seat still watching a now white-faced Stanton, his jaw muscles flexing furiously as he glared at her balefully. The other men returned to their seat gingerly though the Commander looked accusingly at Nighthawk for his lack of reaction or response to her threatening maneuver.

"What are you playing at?" demanded the Commander of Nighthawk.

With an arched eyebrow, Nighthawk said calmly, "If she meant to hurt anyone, she certainly wouldn't have waited until she was in this room. If Stanton is going to continue to goad her then he is going to get his hand slapped at some point."

Foss snorted a laugh at the idea that Bryn's reaction could be synonymous with 'a slapped hand,' but Nighthawk did have a point, Stanton never lost an opportunity to needle her and it had been satisfying to watch her knock him down a peg.

After a repressive glare at Foss, the Commander said, "You will refrain from further displays Keane and Stanton you will keep your smart ass comments to yourself in the

future. We have more to discuss than irrelevant personality conflicts."

Tank commented into the awkward silence, "Shadow
did a hell of a job especially separated from the team and
faced with that...that...thing. Granted she took inordi-
nate risks, but what choice did she have?"

"There were no other choices," added Nighthawk
looking at the Commander's sour expression.

Uncomfortably aware the Commander was staring at
her, Bryn refused to meet his eyes and squirmed slightly
at the praise from Tank, he had a normal tendency to be
taciturn so his approval caught her off guard.

Suddenly the Commander said, "You're dismissed.
Keane stay where you are, I want to speak with you
alone."

A sense of tension from Nighthawk told Bryn that
the request had been unexpected, but to her puzzlement,
the Commander truly meant to speak to her alone and
glanced significantly to his aids, they seemed surprised
as well. The men filed out of the conference room and
the door shut leaving the room in a lengthening silence,
which Bryn refused to be first to break, she could still
feel the Commander watching her.

"What I am about to say next you need to listen to
and just do it," said the Commander flatly.

Bryn looked at him with a stony expression as if daring him to force her to do anything and saw him look
back at her impatiently.

"You're eyes are bothering you. Blurriness comes
and goes. You have trembling in your muscles and odd
pains you can't account for," said the Commander flatly.

At those words, Bryn stared at the Commander in
unfeigned shock and wondered if the man had been
drinking or might be having a seizure, she opened her
mouth to comment, but he held up his hand to forestall
her.

"Damn it just listen and do as I say unless you prefer to stay here for an indefinite period time," snapped the Commander.

That got her attention and the last thing Bryn desired was to stay in this Facility a second longer than necessary.

"You're to tell Doc this and make certain it's believable. He does not answer to me and his reports are seen outside of this Facility," said the Commander significantly.

Coldness washed through Bryn hearing those words and though he never actually said it, she felt that the man was hinting the Facility answered to a higher authority, some person or people far more dangerous than he was. What she did not understand is why he was trying to help her after the way the men brought her into the Facility and it made her wonder if something had happened or changed. Worse yet, he was telling her alone which meant he did not trust anyone else, not even Nighthawk.

"Doc asked me to attend physical therapy once a week after today," said Bryn slowly.

"Temper what improvement he sees," said the Commander shortly.

Her mind worked quickly, jumping around for possible explanations and settled on the probability that the Commander would report the toxin limited her usefulness, which Doc would corroborate if she followed the advice. Bryn looked up at the Commander noting he watched her sort through her thoughts and he nodded as if he sensed she came to the correct conclusion.

"You're dismissed," said the Commander, "And," Bryn paused to look back at him, "...trust no one," so she left very thoughtful.

Stanton stalked back to his quarters furious with Bryn for embarrassing him after he made a valid observation though he refused to admit, even to himself, that he could have been more diplomatic about the assessment.

One thing for certain, she was no plain thief, not trained to fight like that, and it galled him to think that any woman had gone easy on him during a capture, she could have cleaned their clocks probably even decked Nighthawk.

That thought cheered him slightly, but Stanton had to know more about this woman and how she could learn to fight a tornado personified. Skill like that at her age could only mean Bryn had been trained practically from the time she could walk and regular families just did not go to those lengths to educate children.

When he reached his quarters, Stanton immediately sat at the data interface and keyed in 'Bryn Keane' through various levels of search function, including law enforcement. What results those searches finally returned puzzled him more than answered the questions he had so Stanton began to dig into the background of her guardians. The parents came to a suspiciously dead end, but the uncle, now there was some interesting information and Stanton began to hack into the Interpol database to glean more information.

When the conference room door slide open, Bryn received a shock not to see Ryan standing there waiting for her, particularly after hovering about the infirmary and literally shadowing her anywhere she went after Doc released her. She was about to turn down the final hallway to Ryan's quarters, when the sound of someone hammering on his door stopped Bryn and she peeked carefully into the corridor to see Crease using his fist.

Immediately the door slid open, not that it surprised Bryn given the manner Crease sought attention instead of using the buzzer and with her hearing a question came from the man to Ryan, "I want to speak to Keane," he said in a sneering voice.

"Why do you want to speak to her?" said Ryan coldly.

Fortunately Bryn's hearing was extremely acute so she could hear every word very clearly, as if a normal person were standing next to the men.

Crease snorted derisively, "I don't need to explain my reasons to you. She can make up her own mind whether she wants to speak to me or not," he said snidely.

"I said, why?" repeated Ryan in a soft dangerous voice.

"I don't answer to you," said Crease unwisely, "I want to speak to her."

Almost on the heels of those defiant words, Crease collided with the other side of the corridor, obviously hit by Ryan and Bryn decided it was time to intervene before something more dire occurred to the visitor.

"Stop Ryan," said Bryn practically skidding to a stop at the door and interposing her body between the two men.

"Get in the room Bryn," said Ryan, but she ignored him.

Turning to look at Crease, Bryn saw his eyes glittering malevolently at Ryan as he wiped blood from his nose, "I came to ask you if you wanted to go top side for a break," he said glancing at her, "However your roommate didn't tell me you weren't here."

"Stay away from her," said Ryan in tone than made the hairs on the back of Bryn's neck stand up.

From the corner of her eye, Bryn could see Ryan looking daggers at the other man for asking such a question, "I think under the circumstances it would be better I don't accept. Thank you for the offer," she said politely.

Fixing his eyes on her coldly, Crease said, "Don't be fooled by him. It's his fault you're here in the first place," and with a malicious glance of triumph at Ryan, he left.

Bryn stared after Crease in confusion and then turned to look at Ryan for an explanation, which is when she saw the bleak expression on his face.

Uncertainly, she entered the room and turned to Ryan after the door slide closed, "Is that true? What he said about me being here?" said Bryn neutrally.

At his hesitation, Bryn felt a sense of betrayal first and then fury that Ryan had probably manipulated her the entire time, especially keeping that information from her. Before Bryn even realized what she was doing, her hand collided with Ryan's cheek with a resounding "smack" and it never dawned on her that he made no effort to evade it.

Shaking with fury, Bryn snarled, "All this time you've been manipulating me and using my feelings to control me. Not once did you ever tell me you were behind them bringing me here."

Those words stung a response from Ryan, "No! I would never use you."

"So you just conveniently used protestations of your own feelings to pacify me," snapped Bryn.

"No! I told you the truth. I meant every word," said Ryan intensely, "When we attempted to find you we didn't even know you were a woman. We waited to watch you at one job so we could study you and I was told to follow you until you ended up in that hotel. We recorded all the interrogations and people leaving, but we were looking for a man."

Ryan rubbed the back of his neck before continuing, Bryn used her vision to observe his heart rate and so far he was telling the truth even if she did not have to like it. Recalling the night in question, she had sensed someone following and berated herself for overconfidence dismissing the incident even if she had taken precautions in case.

"When no one could determine who our target was after all those interrogations, the Commander had us in the conference room watching all the recordings over and over to check for inconsistencies. I saw a blind woman and pointed you out. The information we got from the hotel was Jean Easley so the Commander researched that information and found you were a local. I pointed out that is was odd that a local woman would stay at a high priced hotel, especially a handicapped woman."

Damn, thought Bryn, *I never thought anyone would go to those lengths or even notice a blind woman, but then again, these men are not ordinary people and likely some of the best operators in the world.*

"Even at that point we thought you might be an intermediary or go-between, not our actual target given your apparent disability. Your disability would give you a very slick cover for a contact though. So the Commander located your residence, had you followed and that was when we saw the meetings with Dr. Meany in the park even though you both made it seem casual. After that we went to him and began asking questions thinking he had contact with the target, which was when he sent you a scram signal. After that we couldn't even locate you. Basically you know the rest."

Bryn watched his heart rate critically, Ryan was telling the truth and the succession of events made sense, but she was still angry over the entire situation. It was so unfair. Ryan would not meet her eyes now and looked so dejected which forced Bryn to remember that he had been doing his job recalling they had called her "he" after they first captured her.

How could she blame him for an observation? The summations were all very logical just like any research she would have done on a target and Ryan had attempted to ease her circumstances in the Facility ever since she arrived. The night he first kissed her, Ryan could have seized the advantage he had, but chose not to do so and had not even alluded to further intimacy; he continued to show respect for her privacy.

Ryan looked so lost and sad, even bereft right now that it actually distressed Bryn since he had always seemed so strong which incited her to lay a hand gently over his abused cheek. He grabbed as if she threw him a lifeline and pressed her hand against his cheek thankful she understood or at least believed him.

"If I had known it was you, I never would have brought attention to the recording. I never thought he would stoop to keep anyone, man or woman, a prisoner here. It's been torturing me ever since I saw you in the infirmary after we brought you back here," said Ryan in a soft anguished voice.

"Why did being a woman matter?" said Bryn hearing words Ryan did not say.

Ryan sighed, "A man had a higher probability of accepting the offer to work with us. As a general rule men are more resilient to the rigors the team is normally exposed to hence the reason we thought you a man. Most women would not attempt the life you lead," he said quietly.

It was the truth, Bryn could hardly consider herself a normal or average woman when she was blind and certainly not once she regained her eyesight, especially with her training. Until Donal gave her the implants, she had not even known what color her clothes were and had kept the same items since college days, which her aunt had bought her.

"I'm sorry I hit you," said Bryn soberly when she could still see the mark on Ryan's cheek even with her hand over most of it.

"You don't need to apologize. It's nothing I haven't felt I deserved. If anything I should apologize to you being forced to work in this place like a slave," said Ryan softly as he squeezed her hand on his cheek before releasing it.

To Bryn's surprise Ryan walked over to the data interface and sat down, silence hung in the air and Bryn sensed he was not in a good mood so she kept her distance for a while before deciding to approach him.

His mood made her so nervous that when she reached out to touch his shoulder she was about to snap her hand back until Ryan's hand swiftly grabbed it making her jump in surprise, "Why were you annoyed with me earlier? It wasn't because I went to the briefing," said Bryn in an attempt to distract Ryan from his dour mood.

He glanced at her with a set expression before saying cryptically, "You were correct, but I didn't have to like it."

Unable to place the context he referred to, Bryn said, "I don't understand."

"When I told you to swim back during the mission, you said if you had been one of the men I wouldn't have told you that. You were correct and I didn't like it. I don't want to put you at risk," he said quietly.

"I sensed you were annoyed," she admitted.

"Not with you darlin. I don't like to see you in danger and even before this I didn't like it. Watching you jump from that building during the first mission was hard enough especially knowing I could do nothing to help you. I thought all I could do was watch you die," he said bleakly.

"Did you get hurt?" she said worriedly.

"Just cuts, nothing to bother me," he said and pulled her against him.

Hesitantly, Bryn ran her hand through his hair and he smiled up at her before pulling her down to his lap kissing her on the cheek.

"Someone leaked information," she said suddenly.

"Aye they did," he said, his Irish coming out.

"How are Foss and Tank?" she said uncertainly since she had not had an opportunity to speak with either man.

"They're fine. Foss would have been a lot worse if you hadn't stopped his bleeding," he said rubbing his hand up her back.

He was not really looking at her so she knew something was bothering him, but he would tell her in his own time unless he had reason to not involve her. She leaned into him effectively distracting him from his thoughts and Ryan looked at her with a twinkle in his eye before he kissed her lightly on the lips. Just then, the COM unit blared with the Commander's voice. "Damn him and his timing," said Ryan uncharacteristically.

He seemed ready to ignore it until Bryn said, "We can't just ignore him," and she tried to get up until she noted the frustration on Ryan's face, "I'm not using it as an excuse."

"Stay here," he said, "I'll speak to him."

"I want to speak to Keane. I know she's there," said the Commander's voice irritably when he heard Ryan's voice.

When Bryn answered, the Commander said, "Have you been to the infirmary since we spoke?"

"Not yet. Physical therapy doesn't start for several days yet," said Bryn curiously remembering the man's last words in the conference room.

"All right then and remember what I told you," said the Commander.

Before she could sign off, Ryan intervened, "I'm taking some personal days and so is Shadow so we'll be out of contact," and then broke the connection.

He turned to her prepared to continue but Bryn said, "We can't just cut him off like that!"

Again he sighed in frustration, "You need to think of yourself once in a while Bryn," he said.

Ryan turned toward cater unit and ordered something to drink so she said, "I'm sorry I upset you."

He walked over to her and reached out to stroke her chin, "It wasn't you darlin. You rarely upset me. His timing has caught us several times and I'm just frustrated we lost the mood that's all," he said quietly.

Bryn reached up to his cheek and he caught her hand to bring to his lips, she shuddered at the sensation, "That's not fair how easily you can do that," she said trying to sound severe, but he only grinned as his hand lightly followed her arm making her throat catch.

He tilted her chin up for a kiss that made the previous one pale in comparison and Bryn found herself swept up into his arms again this time with no one to interrupt them.

The next morning did not begin precipitously when a pounding on the door woke them, Ryan actually swore before he growled out, "If he's," referring to the Commander, "doing that I'll punch him."

"Ryan, please don't do that," said Bryn urgently.

"Stay here," he said with a quick kiss on her lips.

Though Bryn was in the room she could hear all the words when the door swooshed open.

"You better have a good excuse for that noise," said Ryan dangerously.

"You turned off your COM," said Stanton.

"I'm taking personal days. Leave a message," said Ryan in that same soft dangerous voice.

"Personal days? Since when? Or does it have something to do with *her*?" snapped Stanton, slurring 'her' into an insult.

"Stay out of my personal life," said Ryan warningly.

"I came to retrieve my knife I loaned her," sneered Stanton.

"That could have waited," snapped Ryan as he balled a fist.

"I actually am going to need it tonight. I have plans," drawled Stanton as if he enjoyed taunting Ryan.

At those words, Ryan actually cocked his fist until Bryn ran from the bedroom saying urgently, "Ryan, please don't."

"Get back in the room Bryn," said Ryan without glancing at her.

Instead of complying Bryn hurriedly grabbed the for-mentioned knife and held it out for Stanton, "I'm sorry, with everything that happened I forgot about returning it," she said contritely.

"It's not a problem, but I am going offsite in a few hours," said Stanton with unaccustomed charity though he looked at Ryan in a sarcastic manner before turning on his heels to walk down the corridor.

Silence hung in the room like a heavy smoke; Bryn could feel actual anger emanating from Ryan who was normally calm and contained. He finally turned toward her and said, "There was no reason that could not wait for a few days."

"Well he did only loan it to me. If it's a tool he uses often I can understand wanting it if he's going offsite," she said uncertain why Ryan seemed so angry.

With a sigh he said, "He could have used a substitute and he must be leaving for personal reasons because there isn't any active missions."

"Well...instead you should think of thanking Crease," she said drolly to divert him.

"Why would you think of telling him something like that?" said Ryan in confusion.

"Because it would have upset him after he attempted to influence my opinion of you," she said.

"I don't follow you on this one," he said uncertainly.

"Well he seems to be pleased with the negative effect it had when he told me it was your fault I was here, but imagine his expression if you thanked him because it brought us closer," she said with a grin.

Ryan just looked at her for a moment and threw back his head filling the room with his laughter; he walked over to Bryn still laughing and hugged her.

"Ah me," he said through his laughter, "I love you Bryn. It would almost be worth it to chase him down and say that."

"You may get the chance in the future, you never know," she laughed.

Chapter 11

Stanton exited the public transportation he used to get to the town where Keane's guardians previously resided. Too much of the information surrounding the death of her aunt and uncle made no sense, at least until he stumbled on information connecting Jimmy Keane's father to the Agency, an organization reputed to monitor subversive activities. What did not seem to jive was Jimmy Keane was not listed or rumored to have any connection with the Agency at any time and the little gossip Stanton managed to ferret out in his search said the man had been estranged from his father. Then why kill him? Police still listed the case as open, but cold with no new leads and he noticed some editing had been done to the public file and he wanted to know why.

A sudden feeling of being watched made Stanton turn around abruptly and he thought he caught a shadow slipping away quickly, but was uncertain as it happened so fast. After that his suspicions were aroused so Stanton acted as if he were being followed to see if he could catch that illusive tail he glimpsed.

Whoever was back there managed to stay out of sight and most people might have shrugged of the encounter as paranoia, but Stanton knew to trust his instincts with the life he led. However, he continued to his initial goal: The house where the Keane murders occurred.

Unsurprisingly after passing years, the house had a new occupant though Stanton wondered if the resident had any idea about the house's history. Many people would refuse to live in such a place, particularly in the kind of neighborhood Stanton surveyed about him, the kind where crime rarely existed and a murder would definitely be greeted with dismay.

Since he was a direct person, Stanton decided to approach the resident, but posing as a potential home owner in the area and that he wanted to check the history in the neighborhood having heard rumors about this particular house. What he was not expecting was the door to be answered by a man with a scruffy beard smoking a joint openly and yet dressed in relatively new jeans, t-shirt, and loafers.

"Yeah?" said the man belligerently.

"Sorry to bother you, but I'm looking to buy a house in the area and heard there are rumors about something happening in this house. I wanted to determine the truth and if there have been any problems since," said Stanton is his fake guise.

The man snorted, "Ha" in obvious humor, "You mean the murders? I knew their daughter at college before the bitch sent the cops after me for some misunderstanding. You might say karma caught up with her wouldn't you? I told her something bad would happen if she ran from me and her damn parents would never let me talk to her or tell me where she lived," said the man nastily evidently enjoying the thought of the Keane's suffering.

Though he was no saint, Stanton found this man's enjoyment over Bryn's loss perverted and then to come live in the very house where the tragedy occurred, spoke of a warped mind, *no wonder she kicked the moron to the curb*, he thought.

Hiding his true thoughts, Stanton said, "Ah, so they caught the killers. I guess things have been pretty quiet since then."

The man grinned nastily, "Oh they never caught anyone. The bitch ran and hid or so they said when I asked around. Thought she would appreciate me after her hard luck. Cops wouldn't tell me where she went, kept saying they didn't know, but that detective knew all right, the bitch. And yes, things have been quiet around here," he said scornfully.

Stanton had to refrain from punching the twisted fool not that he carried any sentimentality for Keane, but he was not twisted or degenerate like this man and to think anyone would want to live in a house where they even had a connection with the people who died there was just wrong.

All he said was, "Thank you for your time. Seems like a decent neighborhood," and left to see what the local police would tell him.

For his trouble all Stanton learned from a reticent Detective Medina that the murders were still open, but a cold case, just like he read previously and that no one knew where Bryn Keane could be located. Something told him the detective might know more than she revealed, but nothing Stanton could say brought any more information to light. So Stanton left the precinct and that was when he was certain he had someone tailing him, he decided to turn the tables on whoever it was.

The door of Kolski's office slid open and he looked up to see Nighthawk regarding him, but he was unsurprised since he sent for him.

"I want Doc to replace Shadow's GPS tag with something new. It will transmit vital signs as well and it seems we need to watch her health most of all," he said with no preamble.

"I don't think it's necessary, as a matter of fact, I think we should remove the one she has. She won't run if that's your concern," said Nighthawk pointedly.

Kolski looked up at the man speculatively recalling Stanton's raving about Nighthawk spending some rest days with Shadow, but as the man normally spent a lot of time around the woman since he made him responsible for her so anything else was conjecture.

"It's not a matter of trust this time," he said not certain Nighthawk would believe that statement or not.

Silence from Nighthawk confirmed he did not consider it the truth so Kolski went on, "Stanton is AWOL. He left during your short leave and did not return. When security checked his quarters, a significant amount of items were missing and they think he managed to circumvent some protocols to acquire gear. Chances are good he knows about the next mission and he could lay in wait to cause problems. I know you don't need reminding about the last mission. Shadow saved our collective asses and nearly died even though someone warned the target," said the Commander candidly.

Another silence lengthened, but this time Nighthawk seemed to be considering the words until he finally spoke, "If that is the case, we should tag the entire team. I agree she is at risk, but so are the rest if he is our leak and gets an opportunity to isolate someone. She is more likely to trust the reason for the tag if we all get one after the threat you made when she first arrived."

Kolski sighed, he remembered his words, which he now regretted and Nighthawk knew the woman so she would probably not greet the replacement with any joy after that first meeting. He should have listened to Nighthawk about how to handle her, but it was water under the bridge and he had a valid point about the rest of the team if Stanton saw an opportunity.

"That makes sense. I'll let the men know so you can discuss it with her," said the Commander and Nighthawk nodded before turning to leave.

Bryn was considering information at one of the data units in quarters when the door hissed open to admit Ryan, she glanced over as he pulled off his hood and visor, but he was not looking her direction.

Returning her gaze to the display, she heard a chair set next to her a few minutes later and glanced over to see Ryan assessing her, which meant he planned to discuss something.

"We need to head to the infirmary for a brief visit," he said carefully, but his eyes searched her face.

She raised an eyebrow in response and a subtle request for more information.

"We need to get a GPS tag," he said and saw the expected flash of anger on her face.

"I already have one. The Commander made that perfectly clear the first day he spoke to me," she said in hard tone.

Ryan extended his hand to her chin touching her gently, but Bryn was not moved to relax. Her initial arrival to the Facility was indelibly burned into her mind as well as the veiled threats tossed at her to gain cooperation of her skills assistance.

"This is a different type darlin," he said gently, "It is capable of monitoring vital signs as well and we'll all have one."

Those words calmed her somewhat since such a device did have merit after all her past injuries on missions, "I guess that makes sense given my record," she said drolly.

"It pissed me off he tagged you especially since I blamed myself for your capture," he said crossly.

It pissed her off too. Bryn could still find the anger at hand every time she thought about that night they brought her to the Facility, but anger was unproductive at this point.

"Talk to me darlin," he said with quiet plea at her abrupt silence.

She knew her expression must have been remarkable because Ryan sighed in regret and looked away, she wondered if this is what had been on his mind on and off in those unguarded moments she watched him

"I was angry too about that and I guess it still makes me angry if I think about it," said Bryn truthfully.

From his expression Bryn could see that he was not certain she truly had forgiven him when he had revealed his involvement over a week ago.

"I wish I could change what happened darlin," he said quietly.

After a lengthy pause, Bryn said with forced calm, "You were doing your job Ryan. It wasn't personal. It was the thought you used my feelings to manipulate me so I would cooperate that made me so angry," but she was unable to prevent a single tear rolling down her cheek.

"Never! I would never do that Bryn. I could never toy will your feelings or manipulate you that way. I love you and I did not say that to you so you would work for him! I always tried to give you the respect the others denied you, but I never expected to fall in love. I challenged him that day he threatened you and told him he was wrong to do that. That was when he made you my responsibility," he said, but this time all the calm detachment was gone.

It was the first time Bryn ever saw the varied expressions of fury, guilt, and pain from Ryan, she knew he was being honest with her and the fact she thought he used her seemed to upset him most of all. Bryn realized she loved him too and that she never told him.

Again Bryn reached up and placed a hand on his cheek, "I believed you when you told me. I wasn't withdrawing anything from you."

Ryan repeated the process of pressing her hand against his cheek, but this time so hard it was painful and closed his eyes almost as if he did not believe she forgave him.

It took Bryn a little while to master her emotions before she asked the most pertinent question, "Why do we need a GPS tag?" she said in a more civil tone.

Ryan sighed, but did not release her hand and opened his eyes, "I was told just before I returned that Stanton is AWOL. Security says he managed to abscond with some gear and the Commander thinks he could target the team while we are on a mission if we ever become separated. He won't expect us to be tagged so if he does manage to do anything, a team can be sent to retrieve someone in crisis," he said.

"He is bound to know I have a tag. If I recall he led some missions and probably had access to that information," she said pointedly.

"Yes, he knew you had one. This time however, if you agree, I plan to ask Doc leave the current one so that only the team will know about new one. He will think to check for one, but not two," he said.

"By that you mean you expect he will be looking for me specifically if he can get to me," she said homing in on the real reason.

"That's what the Commander thinks, but we can't rule out he might try for anyone if he can," said Ryan temporizing.

"What do *you* think?" she persisted.

Ryan snorted and gave her a half smile, "You're a little spitfire," was all he said squeezing the hand he held and Bryn took that to mean he agreed with the assessment or he would not have mentioned two tags.

Though it was not high on her places to be, Bryn sat in silence as the doctor began to implant GPS tags on the team, she at least felt more amenable to the idea that the men were being subjected to the same procedure. She coughed to hide a laugh when Foss leapt off a gurney swearing after pop of the device sounded shooting the tag under his skin, but the other men were not so charitable laughing and Tank sniping comments at him for his reaction.

"Don't be such a girl!" laughed Tank and then he coughed when he saw Bryn watching him.

"Sorry Shadow," he said a bit more soberly. "That wasn't a dig at you."

"Oh I know. I nearly laughed myself so I'm glad he's glaring at you instead of me," she said with a snort of amusement.

And Foss *was* glaring at him with an expression clearly indicating he hoped Tank suffered any number of undisclosed humiliating encounters.

With Foss' reaction in mind Bryn steeled herself for the process especially since she would awake for this implanted tag. To her surprise, Doc placed this one in her hip where she could get access to it to remove the tag at some point, painful as that might be without help and Bryn did wonder where the other tag was located. *Probably in my back*, she thought which made sense if originally the Commander did not want her able to dig it out initially after he mentioned it during their first confrontation.

"Why the hell does she need two of them?" demanded Tank soon as the doctor implanted the second tag.

"Just a precaution and this one is different, it transmits vital signs," stated the doctor, but the narrow-eyed look Tank gave him told Bryn he was not mollified by the answer; however, it indicated no one informed him of any suspicions.

Training exercises were smooth and this mission was not supposed to present the risk level of the previous missions, so they were optimistic about efficient speedy completion. The unusual part was the building and area it was located had historical background. Bryn never breached such an old structure that looked like it belonged in an old horror movie with its mildew stained ashlar walls displaying old fashioned fixtures that she suspected were reproductions. It reminded her of a tall castle because it had towers with conical roofs, though from their intelligence, the inner structure contained state of the art security.

What pleased Bryn were all the alternative options available for escape routes. Even if they were quickly compromised, there would be enough buildings near enough to offer choices that would confuse pursuit.

Before they set out, Ryan gave her a special earpiece very different from what they normally used, that fit directly into the ear canal which would act as an invisible miniature microphone and speaker so the team could hear what was going on if they were separated. Apparently these had been newly developed to offset interference normally encountered by high tech equipment emanations they were usually facing which they never disabled since it did not interfere with the actual target of the missions.

These devices would be a unique experience for Shadow. It was not long before Tank ordered everyone to head to the chopper and they piled into a van with everyone checking personal portable gear on their person. Their base of operations had been leased for them under the guise of a temporary business venture since they would not be close to the Facility and it made Shadow uncomfortable in its rundown state. In her previous work, she always stayed in nice hotels and never had to eat reconstituted freeze-dried food. She was careful not to mention this glaring difference though because the men would have eyed her askance as a pampered socialite compared to their average day.

They would make a window entry this time, highly unusual for a team breach, but the roofing material was reported to be old-fashioned ceramic shingling which could break or slide easily sending anyone of them to their death. There were no large subterranean access points that could accommodate the men and using explosives to get through the concrete would alert sensitive security equipment, hence the unorthodox entry.

Her sticky pads on the bodysuit did not like these old walls and Shadow ended up relying on rappelling cords, scale darts and old fashioned rock anchors to ascend to the bailey. What confronted them rather than a normal window, the best access point had old stained glass. This presented a unique problem since they could not use special suction cups to remove the glass with all the lead forming a design throughout and they had to remove the entire window, secured by rope, to be lowered inside the bailey.

This marriage of new and old architecture made this particular mission a unique challenge, technology would only get them so far until they managed to get inside. Shadow fretted inwardly about the time it took to actually secure the window especially as a displaced window would certainly arouse curiosity of any roaming security. She was used to getting in and out of a target in the time it took for the stained glass to finally be secured.

The men kept eyes open for exterior patrolling guards as Shadow slipped into the building disarming alarms while Nighthawk followed to be her eyes when she was in the room with the target. They were after a microchip this time, or so the Commander explained, but he did not divulge any additional information, such as why this particular chip was important or what it contained and, in a way, it encouraged Shadow that he still viewed her as temporary personnel.

Though the technology was state of the art, old buildings like this one unnerved Shadow because in her past research, older structures did not adhere to the more current building codes, which meant blueprints were generally inaccurate or unavailable. It left a glaring possibility that such structures could contain hidden rooms or passages as described in the annals of history and her skin crawled at the thought someone could be watching, which their intelligence could not reveal.

An uneasy feeling made Shadow hesitate and she wondered if her previous worries made her paranoid yet something did not feel right, a quick glance at Nighthawk was enough to let him know what she was thinking. His body subtly changed indicating he took her warning seriously and Shadow knew he was scanning the area with various modes of his visor while she worked on a door into the room that held the safe.

Due to the age of the building, security existed in certain rooms instead of the overall structure though there were general alarms and surveillance cameras mounted. Shadow knew Foss had put linked video on a feedback loop, but it was spot surveillance that concerned her, the kind only mounted in special areas that could only be accessed right at the camera. That was if she found them all, Shadow knew just how cleverly video could be hidden in innocuous items that even her sight might not detect.

Therefore it was not surprising when security beams crisscrossed the room once Shadow breached the sealed door and she did a critical sweep with her eyes to detect other signs of security such as hidden video. Unfortunately, if surveillance was there, it was very well disguised.

Mirrors for the beams took time as the room had a heavy amount of crisscrossing lines, but Shadow finally made it to the safe. This safe would have a very fiddly painstaking process to circumvent and she set to work immediately hoping her fingers would not cramp from all the fine movements and adjustments she had to make.

Finally after about thirty minutes, Shadow breathed a quiet sigh of relief as the last barrier clicked open and using rubber tongs she carefully extricated the microchip. Soon as she slipped into her arm pouch, Shadow began to back out of the safe re-establishing the security until she was able to start removing the mirrors. Folding the last mirror, Shadow was placing in a pouch when the sound of shattering glass reached her even on the fourth floor, immediately alarms screeching followed the noise.

Swearing sounded in her ear, but there was no time for questions, Shadow saw guards running down the hall on a lower level and they looked up seeing intruders. Quick as thought, Shadow slipped out the microchip and shoved into one of Nighthawk's sleeve pouches since he would have the strength expertise to get free trapped by larger men, he had the physical size she lacked.

Returning to the safe's room was pointless because breaking the beams would release gas to render an intruder unconscious so at Nighthawk's gesture she fled down the hall to a room they had originally entered.

Soon as she dashed into the room she saw that a barrier had slid down covering the open window to her horror. After examining it quickly she located a spot, if she drilled carefully, it would be possible to bypass security protocol and open the steel barrier. That gave her an idea and she pulled out a drill trying to bore into the masonry accurately yet quickly muttering at such a contradiction in goals. Perspiration beaded on Shadow's forehead knowing she had no room for error and Nighthawk could be trapped waiting to hear she was safely out of the building.

Finally the drill bit made a hole in which she exchanged it for a special saw attachment, which under normal circumstances would be pointless to use due to the sound. Once Shadow carved a hole large enough for one of her mirrors, she slipped into the hole to break the beam of light and voila, the steel barrier over the window retracted. It was necessary to secure the mirror and leave it behind to allow Nighthawk to exit.

She pulled out the round special scale dart launcher, like she used to use, and punched an expanding anchoring hook into the wall next to her then loaded it again after she attached a cord to the current hook. Another shot at a wall across the street, but she aimed slightly lower and heard a fainter thunk as the hook imbedded.

Unfolding the special wheel with handlebars, Shadow snapped it onto the cord and whizzed over to the next build where her sticky pads worked much better allowing her to slither up the wall to the building's roof.

"I'm out," she said for the men's benefit so that was one less person they had to worry about.

The building she was on currently had a girder type structure bridging it to the building on the opposite side and Shadow jumped up to begin walking very aware there was not much below her to catch if she fell.

Breathing a sigh of relief Shadow jumped off the girder onto an abandoned building and ran across the roof to take the internal stairs down now that she was far away from the gathering forces behind her.

Soon as Shadow hit the final step, people materialized literally from all sides and she found herself ducking and spinning to avoid close quarters of grasping hands; she knew these were not people from the Facility. They did not run missions in this manner.

With at least six people, presumably men given they were all larger than she was, Shadow could not hope to evade every searching hand and when one brutally caught her arm she instantly broke the offending hand. The yell of anguish announced the person male and his companions swore sulphurously when they realized one of their numbers was out of action.

These men were not novices or easily caught off guard and tightened in circle about Shadow until a flash of something crossed her vision and secured about Shadow's throat. Instantly Shadow's hands flew to her neck to feel a chain that she managed to catch before it drew tight enough to garrote her accompanying her effort with a variety of devastating kicks, even one over her shoulder. Rather than release, her actions incited the very strong assailant to bodily force her toward a wall to take away her ability to kick.

Shadow could not use her arms to lash out or she would black out, so as soon as she was close enough to the wall, she ran up it to flip over the man's back freeing her neck from the chain. Now she had all her limbs free.

"Filthy bitch," snarled the man and the chain began whistling through the air as he attempted to strike her with it.

What none of the men knew was Shadow could clearly see yet they wore masks and similar visors men at the Facility wore so they probably could see nearly as much as she could. Her feet kept shooting out battering the man's head and chest until she caught the whirling chain allowing her to spin under his arm using the loose end to nail him across the face. He screamed in pain. Instinctively he dropped the chain to grab his face and Shadow spun back around dealing a flat-handed blow to his chest putting her entire body weight behind it. He flew backwards off his feet and crashed into the wall, Shadow was about to turn on the other attackers to see another masked figure enter the fray, but oddly the person set upon the four able bodied men left.

Instead of seizing that opportunity to run to another exit, Shadow systematically disabled her attackers not trusting the new addition and once the intruders all hit the floor, she faced the newer figure.

When he paused, presumably another man, Shadow turned to take advantage of his hesitation, a voice issued from him that stunned her, "Not that way fool. I saw them come in from that direction. Come on, this way," he waved an arm in the indicated direction, "Don't forget the mission," said Stanton's voice.

"Is this your idea?" spat out Shadow.

"No, it damn well isn't and I don't have time to explain. Move...Now!" snapped Stanton grabbing her arm directing her toward the rear of the building.

Shaking her arm loose, Shadow followed him at a dead run scanning everything ahead and saw, to her dismay, a trip wire that Stanton obviously could not or did not see.

"Stop! A trip wire," she shrieked and her vision flickered wildly as she located the explosives.

However, it was too late and his swearing said Stanton heard the warning, but they were running so fast, Shadow was not certain she could have avoided the wire had she been the first one into the corridor. Time seemed to slow almost as if Shadow watched a movie frame by frame as the flare of light hit her eyes temporarily blinding her in the current infrared mode and then came a deafening sound that made her ears feel invaded by twin knives.

Stanton seemed to vanish before her eyes and something hit Shadow hard on the head before it felt like a great hand literally pushed her from behind frontally slamming her into an unyielding surface. Blackness overtook Shadow's sight and she had time for one brief horrible thought: She lost her sight again. Shadow was unconscious before she hit the ground.

Back at the target, Nighthawk drew the guards to him so the other two men could get out now that they knew Shadow made it and soon as he heard from his companions, he systematically disabled guards to follow Shadow's exit from the building.

Nighthawk was whizzing across the cord when he heard weapon fire. As he reached the wall, he had to take evasive action instead of climbing to the roof immediately where he would have been a sitting target. Once he slipped out of the line of sight, Nighthawk slithered up to the building's roof knowing that the guards would expect him to come down.

When a voice yelled, "Filthy bitch," all the men knew Shadow had encountered someone unforeseen and Nighthawk streaked to the girder knowing she would be in the next building. It was slower work than anticipated especially since he could not afford a fall and even though he knew Foss and Tank would converge on the area, he had no idea how long it would take them. Then all of them heard Stanton's voice, "Not that way fool. I saw them come in from that direction. Come on, this way. Don't forget the mission," and wondered if the man mentally snapped. Foss, Nighthawk, and Tank's thoughts the same, Stanton jumped Shadow and he was attempting to separate her from the rest of the team.

Finally, Nighthawk cleared the girder and was in a dead run for the internal stairs of the abandoned building when he heard, Shadow yell, "Stop! A trip wire," and Stanton snarl wordlessly. He felt an explosion from underneath and it was one of the few times he could remember losing his calm on a mission.

The stairs ended up a mass of twisted metal at the second floor with various holes in the floor and he knew he had to be careful in case Shadow happened to be on the first floor or he could knock rubble on her or incite a point of the weakened building to collapse.

It seemed to take hours, but in actuality about thirty minutes once he finally got down since leaving the target and Nighthawk began searching the area worried that Shadow could be under rubble unconscious. He could not let himself think she might have been crushed and it was bad enough to accept she was probably severely injured.

No bodies, no cry for help, or heat signatures could be found even when the other two men converged on the scene, so Nighthawk reluctantly broke COM silence to request Shadow's GPS location and the other men waited to locate her body.

When her senses began to return, Shadow felt someone, she assumed to be Stanton, dragging her by a leg, but she was still too dazed to do anything about it, her ears were ringing so badly she was not certain she would be able hear anything. A shaft of fright pierced her; *did I lose my hearing?* She thought fearfully and then she wondered where Stanton was dragging her, but any attempt to speak did not produce any audible words as far as Shadow could tell.

Why would someone cause an explosion in such a small enclosed area when they could suffer the backlash as well? Why accost her at all? It could not have been the security from the target because they never had time to get to the abandoned building and that was if they knew she would be there.

Then she was not certain if she opened her eyes because blackness greeted her and this time she felt a wave of terror, it was possible the explosion damaged her implants, now she was blind as well.

The dragging stopped and her leg was dropped unceremoniously, she felt a hand grab her right wrist to place some sort of cuff on it followed by a metallic sound. Next, Stanton began pulling everything out of any pocket or pouch on her person, but she was uncertain what he was looking for until her foggy mind jumped to the microchip. That made no sense, Stanton knew protocol and that she always turned over acquisitions back at the Facility and then a scream of rage penetrated the ringing in her ears.

"You bitch! Where is it? What did you do with it?" shrieked a strangely toned voice and it certainly was not Stanton. Kicks connected with several parts of her body following the scream of rage and then stopped briefly, she felt the man grab her left arm and turn her over to expose her back. It seemed he was running something over it and then he stopped at the spot behind just under her shoulder blade for some reason. *Was that where the first GPS tag was located?* She wondered. Pain of something very sharp piercing the skin of her back made Shadow cry out in agony even in her dazed stupor and then what sounded like stamping before he grabbed her arm to shake her.

"They'll never find you now," snarled the odd voice, which was followed by repeated backhand slaps to her face until she lost complete consciousness again.

Consciousness returned slowly for Stanton, but even injured, he was careful not to give any sign of his returning senses and a voice impinged on his abused ringing ears, "You bitch! Where is it? What did you do with it?" It sounded like someone speaking through a voice modulator.

When Shadow cried out in pain, Stanton nearly gave himself away and wondered if someone were torturing the woman for the item she retrieved which she apparently hid or was unsuccessful obtaining.

Another voice spoke over what sounded like someone being beaten, "Don't kill her. You said she was mine," yelled a vaguely familiar voice, which Stanton could not place.

"Shut up you fool. I have to retrieve the item or this is all pointless," said the modulated voice.

"Well no one can talk unconscious," said the vaguely familiar voice, "What about that guy? Wouldn't he know?"

"Don't play games with me. He wasn't part of the breach moron," said the modulated voice.

"She was alone with him for short time," said the vaguely familiar voice logically.

Wordless swearing followed the retort and Stanton suddenly felt his clothing searched though pretended to be unconscious yet nothing was found for the trouble.

"Hey where are you going?" demanded the vaguely familiar voice.

"We got company. Leave if you know what is good for you," said the modulated voice.

Stanton sensed that one person left and then heard the second voice snarl, "Wake up bitch. You thought you would get away from me after all this time? I told you I would make you sorry if you left me again and I will kill you as promised."

Immediately Stanton opened his eyes and saw a figure leaning over an unconscious person holding what appeared to be a knife from a glint on metal, he ignored searing pain in his body to kick the weapon from the man's hand. In the time it took Stanton to reach the threat, he found someone had attached electronic restraints to his wrists and he received a hefty zap of electricity when he attempted to separate his wrists.

Swearing furiously, he stood facing the other man and recognized him from the house he visited checking on Bryn Keane's background. He had no idea what the hell the man was doing there, but Stanton did remember turning the tables on the person that was tailing him and the individual met with this man. The Commander was going to have an apoplexy over this situation. Using his legs, Stanton disabled the man just as three men came rushing into the room.

When Nighthawk requested Shadow's GPS, the men expected her to be under the rubble and the pilot's response surprised them, "She appears to be moving north which is odd. That area she's in now is out of bounds for the escape routes listed in the mission plan. Go two streets west Nighthawk and you'll be on the same road," said the pilot.

Knowing Shadow could be seriously injured, Nighthawk took off running, discarding stealth because he had an uneasy feeling she was in great deal of trouble, which was confirmed when they all heard a male voice shrieking in rage through Shadow's earpiece. At the sound of blows connecting with a body, Nighthawk set his jaw even though Shadow never cried out, but it made him wonder if she was conscious until he heard her scream in pain.

A man's voice carried to them through the earpiece, "They'll never find you now," and the pilot announced, "One of her GPS tags disappeared."

It could not be Stanton, he either lay injured and unconscious in the rubble or was dead, but only someone who knew to look for the tag would find it so quickly and Nighthawk was thankful he convinced Shadow to have the second implanted. Everyone then heard an unmistakable sound of someone being slapped and Nighthawk heard Tank snarling with the rage, even as they all ran to converge of the point of the last GPS tag.

"You're right there," said the pilot through their earpieces.

They started to advance into the building and Nighthawk threw up his hand for them to halt, they instantly understood, if they all rushed it the guy might kill Shadow outright before anyone could intervene. She stood the best chance if only one person entered and the other two men knew by common consensus, except for Shadow, Nighthawk superseded them all in stealth as they watched him slip away without a sound. He would call them if needed.

Any sound of reinforcement could mean Shadow's instant death and Nighthawk knew it, he refused to admit she was already dead and tried to convince himself the man would want her to suffer after hearing the beatings. The tag only told them she was in this building not exactly where she was, her suit would hide her body heat and he wondered if the unknown man wore a similar suit.

The addition of a new unfamiliar voice and the content of its words electrified them all, "Don't kill her. You said she was mine," followed by a brief conversation with the original voice which told them time was up. Someone knew they were coming and threat to Shadow's life was imminent.

What Nighthawk suspected was the man would probably go underground or at least the lowest level to avoid anyone accidentally wandering in from the streets so he took the gamble to seek Shadow in the lowest levels of the building.

His heart pounded in his chest with worry that was slowly turning to dread when he did not locate Shadow until his visor picked up a thin trail of blood, but it seemed to end at a wall then Nighthawk realized that a piece of old drywall was for show. Easing the dry wall to one side revealed a hidden stairway that descended even lower than the floor he was on which he first thought was the lowest level of the building.

The floor beyond the fake wall was extremely dingy and Nighthawk could not pick out a blood trail from the littered floor containing rats' nests, crumbled plaster and other debris, but he soon found he was in the correct spot when sounds of a voice carried through the earpiece that seemed to echo up the dingy stairs.

The new male voice yelled, "Wake up bitch. You thought you would get away from me after all this time? I told you I would make you sorry if you left me again and I will kill you as promised."

It took great effort for Nighthawk not to race down the stairs hearing those words, but he knew the man was too close to Shadow to stop him from harming her until he heard sounds of unmistakable fighting.

Slipping toward the voice like a ghost, Nighthawk paused carefully to use a mirror to check around a corner and saw two figures fighting, one lashing out with legs as if his arms were restrained blocking access to a crumpled figure on the floor. At the unmistakable sound of fighting, Nighthawk heard soft sounds of the other two men slip up behind him.

In the commotion, the three men rushed in just as the partially restrained figure dealt a disabling blow to the other man and his form slumped to the floor unconscious. When the partially restrained figure turned toward them defensively, the three men recognized him as Stanton looking distinctly worse for wear.

"About time," swore Stanton at their arrival, "Someone get these damn things off me," referring to the electronic restraints.

"What the hell are you doing here?" demanded Tank ominously as Foss worked on the restraints and Nighthawk examined Shadow's limp form.

"Nice to see you, too," said Stanton sardonically. "No time to tell stories with some unknown element out there which might get reinforced and she needs Doc A.S.A.P. Of course, so do I, thank you for asking."

As annoyed as Tank was, he saw Stanton had a point and aided the battered man while Nighthawk scooped Shadow up in his arms.

"Someone grab that guy. He's in the middle of this and I know the Commander will want him questioned," snapped Stanton tossing Tank's assisting arm to one side.

Diverted, Tank tossed the unconscious man over his shoulder and followed the others out of the dingy basement warily expecting an ambush at every corner, but their path remained clear. They traveled as fast as Stanton could manage and finally reached the helicopter where Davidson, the medic, greeted them.

"Forget me," said Stanton waving the medic away, "She needs you more than I do," gesturing at Shadow's limp form.

"Shit, she's going into shock. Get in the air on the double," yelled Davidson to the pilot.

"Should we divert to a hospital?" said Tank after securing his unconscious prisoner.

"They can't help her now," then to Nighthawk, "Put her heels on your shoulders, we need the blood back toward her heart. Someone toss me a thermal blanket," said Davidson as he worked to stabilize Shadow.

It took several hours to get back, even directly cutting through airspace by flying under the radar, and Nighthawk jumped from the chopper with Shadow, ignoring the medic's furious shouts, before it came to rest running to the elevator.

After one look at Shadow's battered body, Doc said, "My god. We need to get that suit off immediately," and proceeded to cut it off.

Doc had just directed Nighthawk to move Shadow to the CAT scan to see what injuries they were dealing with when Stanton staggered in assisted by Davidson followed by Foss and Tank.

"Saints preserve us. What have you've done now?" said Doc in exasperation when he caught sight of Stanton's obviously broken bones.

Since Shadow needed his attention more than the injured Stanton, Doc directed other staff to see to the man's needs while he viewed the CAT scan to see broken bones that needed no medical degree to identify.

"Royce!" yelled Doc, "Into surgery with me, now," then to Nighthawk, "You'll have to wait outside the clean room."

When the COM blared with the Commander's voice, everyone collectively jumped and Stanton began swearing in pain such movement incited, "What the hell is going on? Tank? Are you there? Where is my status report?"

Tank marched over to the COM, "We haven't been cleared by medical sir. There were injuries," he said.

"Injuries?" said the Commander incredulously, "How? This was a straight forward mission."

"Sir, I can give you a rundown once medical clears me. We also have a guest in the brig which I'll explain soon as I get there," said Tank.

At first the men all thought the Commander dropped the connection, but after a lengthy paused he said, "I'm not going to like this, am I?" and then he broke the connection without waiting for an answer.

Stanton snorted and winced from the pain incited while Foss gave a low humorless chuckle at the expression on Tank's face as he turned around, it was obvious the man was not looking forward to any briefing over this mission details. Nighthawk ignored them all as he kept watch on the clean room where Shadow underwent surgery.

Doc was not surprised to see the Commander the following day since the uninjured men would have given him basic facts about the injured team members and prepared for a confrontation regarding Stanton.

First words from the Commanders mouth were, "How is Shadow?"

"I don't know how she survived long enough to get here. We counted fifteen broken bones, which are all mended now and sealed all the internal injuries. I don't even want to guess what she went through. Most of the swelling will have to subside on its own though we will use cold packs until we're certain there is no possible reoccurrence of the internal bleeding. If that goes well we can finally administer anti-inflammatory drugs. She won't be able to see at first not because we think her implants are damaged," he added quickly sensing concern, "but because her eyelids are swollen shut. We can't rule out possible damage to the implants, but until she can actually open her eyes we won't know for certain. I will keep you updated once she comes around," said Doc.

"And Stanton?" said the Commander coldly, "I want him transferred to the brig soon as possible."

"Well you will have to wait. I want to be certain he has completely recovered before you place him somewhere like that," said Doc belligerently.

Kolski bit back want he wanted to say and instead said, "How long has he been here?" referring to Nighthawk with a gesture.

"Since the team returned, but he needs to eat and rest. He won't listen to me so if you have any other motivation for him it would help before he ends up ill," said Doc irritably.

However intervention was not required soon as Nighthawk caught sight of the Commander and he approached purposefully with a request, "I want to speak with you alone."

"That's good because part of the reason I am here was to have you come to my office and I didn't think you would accept it over the COM," said the Commander caustically.

Kolski left the infirmary without checking to see if Nighthawk followed trusting that if the man had something to discuss he would be on his heels and he was not wrong once they reached his office.

"You might want to sit," said the Commander pointedly indicating his news might not be welcome.

Nighthawk's eyebrow rose in query at the Commander's opening statement, but he sat and gave the man deference to start the discussion with his news.

Passing a digital pad to Nighthawk, the Commander said, "It seems you have been recalled and that we may no longer avail ourselves of your service."

Kolski watched as a stony expression settled on the other man's face when he took the digital pad and perused the information, not an unexpected reaction with Shadow still recovering in the infirmary. Since Nighthawk was on loan to his unit Kolski could hardly protest the order though the man did have a few days of leeway.

Once Nighthawk finished reviewing the information, he passed the digital pad back and gazed at the Commander with his piercing grey eyes, almost as if he was looking inside the other man.

Those eyes made Kolski far from comfortable at the best times and thankfully the other man usually wore a visor, but not today which took most of his self-control not to fidget uncomfortably at the regard.

"Then let me make my thoughts plain under the circumstances. I have one request before I leave: Let her go. She has suffered more than any man since I have been with you and far more than she should have had to endure as a contract specialist. If I find out that you have kept her here, I will bring resources to bear to deal with the matter," said Nighthawk dangerously.

Kolski cleared his throat hurriedly, "I intended to. Though I don't know why, it seems the Tabula can't see her gone fast enough. Of course I pointed out that she was hardly in a condition to leave, but I told them I would inform her once Doc releases her. They made inference that she was more trouble than she was worth," here he laughed cynically at the Tabula's whims, "forgetting they were responsible for most of the trouble," he said.

The startled expression on Nighthawk's face afforded him some compensation enduring the man's earlier scrutiny and he said, "I suspect they are not aware of your opinion."

Kolski snorted humorously, "You knew that before you said it. It does strike me as poetic they realize their error, but no doubt they will pass it off as my fault. On another note, will you take her with you?" he said.

A fleeting look of pain passed over Nighthawk's features so quickly, Kolski almost thought he imagined it and then the man said, "You of all people know that isn't possible if I have been recalled. Besides, once she knows she is free, she will probably want to forget she ever met any of us."

Kolski was not so certain that was an accurate statement, but Nighthawk knew the woman better than anyone else and it was possible she would take off the second she knew freedom awaited her.

Nighthawk stood and turned before leaving the office, "Don't tell her I asked that you release her," he said.

"As you wish," said Kolski inwardly bemused by the request.

Aiden Keane reviewed information in his office when a signal indicated an encrypted transmission arrived; he paused to read it and grunted with satisfaction at the content. It had taken years to get the information on the secret group known at the Tabula and he had drawn on his covert connections as well as considerable resources to find them. A well placed friend had informed him his granddaughter had been seized against her will by people posing as law enforcement after an anonymous group began to subsidize him in her absence.

Although the routing codes for the funds were untraceable, they had a stroke of luck when a younger man came to Donal fearing for Bryn's life from an exotic toxin that not even the eminent doctor and scientist had ever seen. On the special drive the man handed over to Donal were codes that finally led to discover the covert Tabula and once he could trace them, Aiden spared no expense to force them to release his granddaughter or suffer extreme consequences.

This transmission confirmed that she would be released soon, but Aiden was concerned to see that they were waiting for the top physician to consider her healthy enough to depart the Facility and dreaded to imagine what had happened to precipitate her latest injuries. Thankfully she soon would have freedom to live her life as she chose.

Hovering on the edge of consciousness several days later, Bryn was uncertain if she was dreaming or not because every time she thought she opened her eyes nothing, but blackness greeted her and she could not understand why at first. As her mind began to sharpen, flashes of memory came back to Bryn and she attempted to sit up which was accompanied by a painful lassitude inciting her to groan.

A voice that sounded faraway said, "She's coming around," though that barely made sense. Her mouth opened to call out, but she was not even certain the words left her lips when she tried to say, "Ryan," until a whispered voice spoke in her ear.

"I'm here darlin," he said and she felt his hand gently grasp her own as it lay on the bed.

"I can't see," she breathed fearfully.

"You're eyelids are swollen shut. Doc doesn't want to give you an anti-inflammatory meds until he's certain you won't start bleeding again," he said quietly in her ear.

That information calmed her fear somewhat for the moment since it explained the blackness of her eyesight and then her mind cast back to the mission about who attacked her.

"Who?" she breathed.

"Now's not the time for that darlin. Just rest," he said gently followed by a soft kiss on the cheek and she knew he would not give her any information until he was ready.

"They'll see," whispered Bryn aware of the infirmary personnel.

Ryan snorted quietly in her ear, "Let them see," he said and that was that.

By the following day, Doc decided Bryn could deal with the anti-inflammatory meds and the rest of the pain fled quickly, her swollen eyelids eased enough so she could see light and shadowy figures moving. When she mentioned this Doc said, "Your eyelids are still swollen. Give it a little time and then we can check to see if the implants suffered any damage."

Her eyesight improved though Doc told her since her skull had been fractured it was possible sharper images might take time to surface if she noticed fuzziness, but at that moment in time Bryn was just grateful to see the world semi-normally. Ryan stayed near her once she woke and occasionally she had to shoo him away to rest when the Doc tattled on him about his lack of sleep or regular meals, it was one of the few times she finally was able to tease the sharp witted man.

"I have my own monitor to keep track of you," said Bryn mischievously and Ryan gave her a look a pure disgust before he left the infirmary with her laughing at his departure.

Doc only kept her in the infirmary for few days to be certain she suffered no complications, "You're to report to the conference room," said Doc after he was satisfied with the results of her latest tests.

Bryn slipped off the gurney so fast that Ryan flinched as if he intended to help her and suspected the man had been about carry her to the conference rather than allow her to walk.

"Walking will do her good," said Doc when he noticed the other man's aborted movements.

They made a brief stop at Ryan's quarters so Bryn could change into something more than a medical gown and she could tell he was hovering, she looked at him in exasperation, but his expression held no apology.

Continuing to the conference room Bryn stepped back in alarm since she had not expected a formal debriefing, but berated herself for her surprise, of course they needed to hear from every team member.

When she noticed Stanton's absence, Bryn said, "Where is Stanton?"

"In the brig," said the Commander shortly.

"I can't begin a debriefing without him here. He came to help me," said Bryn insistently and not at all disconcerted every single man was looking at her.

The Commander looked far from happy and he practically punched the COM, "Bring Stanton to the conference room on the double."

"Didn't he tell you what happened?" said Bryn insistently.

It was Tank who answered, "We never really gave him a chance. He was AWOL and then interfered with a mission."

"He didn't interfere," insisted Bryn and she realized how unlikely it seemed that she would be the difficult man's champion, particularly the way everyone was looking at her.

Stanton arrived in short order looking very bad tempered and took a seat so Bryn began recapping the entire mission including the last she could remember about a man searching her.

"And what do you have to say for yourself?" snarled the Commander at Stanton.

"About time you asked," said Stanton obviously fuming.

"You expected more? Taking off with no word whatsoever, not even to check in and then show up on a mission you were not supposed to have information on. You're lucky to be alive," snapped the Commander.

"Well then let me enlighten you now," snarled Stanton. "First, I wanted to find out more about her," indicating Bryn, "because given her chronological age, the degree of her training would have to start when she practically learned to walk. Why train anyone, especially a girl, that hard? And you can't tell me we don't have some sort of leak and I knew it wasn't me. It could have been any of you except for her and why would I tip my hand before I knew who to trust. Someone knew a lot more about Shadow than we obviously did to go to the lengths they have so far to secure her on missions that should have been secret."

Some of this information disconcerted Bryn to have her life set out before these men, albeit a small amount and the fact Stanton managed to trace back enough history on her to dig further into the past.

"What makes you think we can trust you?" said the Commander almost biting every word off.

"Oh please," began Stanton sarcastically, "I may be an ass, but I'm not a traitor. If I wanted her dead I could have left her to those fools during survival training and made up a believable cover story that you could have corroborated by their presence in those woods. I'm also not stupid. Why the hell would I show up where any of these guys could break my neck and leave me to rot? I followed someone there; I didn't get intelligence illegally."

Now he had everyone's attention, Bryn forgot about being uneasy Stanton poked into her past and waited breathlessly to hear just who he managed to follow into an active mission, it had to be someone from the Facility.

"Well? Who was it?" demanded the Commander for information they all wanted to hear.

"I don't know. I could never get close enough without breaking my cover," said Stanton in disgust.

"I see and we're supposed to believe you?" said the Commander incredulously.

"You will when you hear where I followed the guy from. I went back to her relatives' home where she grew up…" began Stanton, but the Commander interrupted.

"And just how did you access classified data?" demanded the Commander.

Stanton looked at him as if he was an idiot, "Her relatives' murders are a matter of public record. You have called her Keane in front of us numerous times so it wasn't hard to make a search for a girl by that name that had been listed as legally blind. Remember, you had us do that much research on her trying to catch a thief we thought was a man."

The Commander had the grace to look abashed that his indiscretion had given Stanton and anyone else enough information to seek Bryn's history.

Continuing after an uncomfortable silence Stanton said, "I located the house and the guy you have in the brig was living there. I posed as a potential home buyer checking on the neighborhood history concerned about crime. He never came out and said her name, but he knew her from attending the same university until he ended up dropping out because of a misunderstanding, he called it. I could tell he was a slimy sort of person the second I saw him and that sick bastard moved into that house because of those murders hoping he might catch her coming back at some point."

At this point it was Bryn who interrupted, "What man is this? He said he went to the same university? I never kept in contact with anyone," she said in confusion.

In answer to her question, the Commander called up a hologram of the man in the brig and Bryn was no wiser as she did not recognize the individual, how could she? She had been legally blind during those years of study.

"What is his name? Remember, I wouldn't have been able to see anyone during that time," Bryn reminded the Commander.

"He has refused to give us any name and we haven't run a background check yet," admitted the Commander.

"Have him brought here. I wager he will recognize her and she will recognize his voice," drawled Stanton, "I realized I had a tail when I got to that area. So I turned the tables on whoever it was and he actually met with that guy. He seemed to know whoever was tailing me, but I couldn't get close enough to see anything or blow my cover. I wanted to see where this guy went when he finally left and he led me right back here. If I had come in then I wouldn't have been able to watch for unsanctioned activity. I had a suspicion someone had been playing with the security footage or you would have had reports long before now."

The Commander looked shaken by that information and called for security to bring the man in the brig to the conference room, Bryn had a very bad feeling about all this. It was not long before the conference door slid open to reveal the man from the brig flanked by two guards and the Commander signaled the escort to wait outside.

Immediately the man gave voice when his eyes identified the Commander as person in charge, "I demand to see an attorney. You can't keep me locked up without charging me with anything, I know my rights," he snapped.

The second the man opened his mouth Bryn knew exactly who he was and found Stanton staring straight at her reading her body language so she had no way to dissemble, pointless really when the man caught sight of her.

"You're behind this bitch?" screamed the man before he lunged at Bryn.

Tank was faster even if all the other men were on the feet in reaction to the man's attempt to get to Bryn and the huge man's hand literally closed about the neck of their visitor.

"Who is this?" said the Commander sternly and looking straight Bryn.

"Tell them bitch and I'll make it my mission to see you dead however long it takes me," shrieked the man.

Ignoring the raving, Bryn said, "When I knew him, he was called Vander Da'well. He probably still has an outstanding warrant for assault back in the university town where he attempted to imprison me."

Vander renewed his efforts to get to Bryn until Tank squeezed his hand hard enough Vander began to choke and finally had to cease his efforts.

Then he caught sight of Stanton, "She sent you to do her dirty work?" Vander spat out.

"Hardly. I was doing my own investigation and found some very interesting information. Who was the man that came to see you the same day?" said Stanton coldly.

"Ha you think I'll tell you anything? I know my rights and I want a lawyer," snapped Vander confidently.

To Bryn's surprise the Commander laughed mirthlessly, "We aren't police. You've stuck your nose into operations that if I want to, you can disappear forever and no one will ever know what happened to you. Here you have no rights unless I give them to you which means the more you cooperate the better the chances are you live and then if you're successful, we might consider release."

Such a statement shook Bryn to her core when she realized just how much power this man had over her and whether or not she would continue her life, she felt Ryan's hand slide over her forearm in reassurance at her reaction.

Vander looked about wildly when the content of the words finally sunk into his thick head as if he might find a way to escape and his expression settled into one of abject terror when he accepted that he had no choice.

Wild eyed, Vander finally spoke "I don't know who he is. He always kept his head covered and wore dark glasses. I only recognized his voice. He paid me for information, anything I knew about the Keane family and said if I ever told anyone he would kill me."

Bryn noticed Stanton was carefully watching all the men in the room even the Commander's assistants and suddenly realized he was looking for signs that they might recognize Vander, but as far as she could tell no one batted an eyelid.

"What did you tell him?" insisted the Commander.

Bryn listened to a skewed version of her college days and regurgitated information she gave Vander about her family, but nothing of real consequence that she could see.

"…and he wanted to know why that guy…" pointing at Stanton, "had come by the house. I told him what the liar said to me," said Vander glaring malevolently at the man.

Before the Commander could comment on the information, Bryn said, "Tank, you can let him go."

"What are you up to Bryn," murmured Ryan immediately in her ear.

Ignoring Ryan, Bryn stood and walked over to Vander eyeing him with disgust agreeing with Stanton's assessment of slimy, *had Greg tried to tell me this all along?* She thought.

"Why would you move into my aunt and uncle's old house?" said Bryn quietly.

An expression of triumph lit Vander's features as if he won a point in a game, "You would come back there someday. I told you I would find you if you left and I will hunt you down eventually," he sneered confidently.

"You're welcome to try, but you might regret meeting me one on one," said Bryn quietly and she could suddenly feel tension in the room, "I'm fine, let me handle this," to the rest of the men.

"You lied about being blind," Vander sneered.

"Actually I didn't lie at all. I was lucky to meet a doctor able to fix my sight a few years ago not that I have to justify my actions to you," drawled Bryn tauntingly and waiting for what would come next.

Fast as Vander moved, she was faster and intercepted Vander's fist when his fist attempted to connect with her face, an audible crack of bone with an accompanying scream followed.

"Bitch, you broke my arm," yelled Vander clutching the wounded arm.

"There are two hundred and six bones in the human body. That's one. I gave you the benefit of the doubt in college in spite of what people said about you, but no longer! Your actions speak volumes and if you *ever*," she paused for effect, "...bother me again...remember the other two hundred and five whole bones you still have," said Bryn coldly and stared Vander in the eye even though he topped her by at least seven inches.

Never before had Bryn threatened anyone using her training, but Vander received a long overdue reality check and she wanted to be certain he realized continued harassment would be dealt with harshly. She watched as he shrunk from her as if he had never seen her before this moment.

The Commander called security back in and directed them to take Vander back to the infirmary and then said to everyone else in the, "You're dismissed except Keane, stay where you are."

Bryn sighed suspecting a reprimand was imminent and felt Ryan squeeze her shoulder before he left the conference room, she watched the Commander warily.

"It's good to see you looking better. You had a pretty rough time and because of that I wanted to speak with you," he said neutrally.

Her wariness increased and her distrust must have shown in her expression as the man made a small smile to her surprise, certainly not an expression of rebuke.

"You've done more than I could have ever expected for this team so I wanted to tell you that you are free to go, no strings attached. And this belongs to you," he slid the microchip across the desk she had on her the first day she arrived, "Do whatever you originally planned with it. No one will know from us that you had it in your possession."

SHADOW OF IRELAND 293

All Bryn could do was look at the man as if he were a new kind of creature and then she surreptitiously pinched herself just to check to be certain she was not dreaming.

"The only thing I must state is you will have to leave any technology behind we provided you with except for the bodysuit you arrived in, but I reaffirm there are no conditions pertaining to your person. When I said you are free to go, I mean it. You can leave anytime, day or night and no one will stop you, he leaned over and handed Bryn a card, "If you ever decide to return, feel free to call this number we would be glad to have to you back at any time," he said with a smile.

She reached out and took the card mechanically and he placed the microchip in her hand along with it then he looked away at whatever had occupied him before she walked into his office. Woodenly she stood and left to return to quarters and found Ryan was not there so she sat briefly to think trying to sort out what just happened.

One thing the Commander was not was a prankster, so what he told her was no joke and he meant it, she could leave, just walk out without a glance back. A stab of pain pierced her stomach at the thought of leaving Ryan, but she now realized the only thing they ever had in common was this Facility and this was his way of life.

Though he mentioned leaving with her, Bryn cared for him too much to put Ryan in a position to choose between his life and her. Relationships failed because one partner sacrificed something they never wanted to give up and the bitterness felt by the partner who left it behind, Bryn had heard enough about such incidents listening to people. It was time to leave before he returned so he would not feel pressured into a decision to go with her and Bryn knew it was for the best even if it broke her heart.

One thing she could not do was leave without saying something even if it was in written form and wrote out a farewell by hand that she left on the table.

I've been released from the Facility and I couldn't leave without saying something to you. I know you would follow me, but I care for you too much to force you to choose between me and your way of life. I will always love you, Bryn

With that Bryn left the Facility without a backward glance tears stinging her eyes.

The Commander and Nighthawk watched Bryn via the monitors as she entered the lift out of the Facility, "I kept my word. She didn't know you spoke to me," said Kolski, but the other man only nodded.

A sound of the door told the Commander that Nighthawk left, he felt his wordless sense of loss as Bryn left and wondered why he asked for this, but it was not his business to ask.

Chapter 12

Bryn had no clear idea of where she would go after the years of forced servitude and her mind was filled with the thought of freedom so she did not attend to her surroundings, an error she was soon to regret. A grey van screeched to a halt next to her and five men jumped out instantly grabbing her. Bryn was taken by surprise due to her ruminations, which gave her little time to fight back and before she could summon significant resistance, she felt a sharp pain in her back followed by the senselessness of unconsciousness. In her fading thoughts, Bryn knew she had been drugged and barely recalled the hood pulled over her head.

Consciousness returned slowly, but Bryn was aware of lying on something cold and hard before noticing a vile taste in the back of her throat, she groaned involuntarily moving very stiff muscles since whoever grabbed her had not been gentle. An accented male voice spoke nearby, "Tell the boss she's awake," the inflections reminding her of Ryan's brogue when he had let his guard down speaking to her at times in the past. However, the voice was definitely not Ryan.

A hood was roughly pulled off her head and Bryn found herself yanked unceremoniously to her feet by a rough hand on her left arm that maintained an implacable grip, she was far too drugged to fight, actually barely able to stand. Her so called companion literally dragged Bryn through the door of the room she had been laying in and down a hallway, but she was still too dazed to take in much of her surroundings. She knew they must have used something to keep her docile if it was taking so long to wear off so Bryn decided to play along feigning more weakness than she really felt to keep them from drugging her again.

As her mind slowly gained clarity Bryn wondered if one of the mysterious hierarchies behind the Facility had had her captured, at odds with the Commander's decision to let her leave and brought her back. Eventually she could hear voices growing closer as the person dragging her approached a door and with a single knock, the voices subsided until one uttered, "Enter," so that her companion opened the door. Again the person dragging her pulled Bryn through the door and literally threw her onto the floor without regard to any injury she might sustain by such handling, she made no effort to roll or otherwise avoid the fall lest she give away her recovering status.

As she laid there, another accented male voice spoke, "Looks just like her mother," he said with a sneer sounding in his voice. At those words, Bryn's rage began to burn away the drug in her system recalling her childhood when her parents fled in the family car to avoid people chasing them even if she never knew why then.

"Wake her up," snapped the voice and someone literally threw a bucket of cold water on Bryn.

Grasping at the shock, Bryn then groaned and struggled to her hands and knees, still feigning more lethargy than she actually felt knowing surprise would give her an advantage, doubly so if these people had no idea of her background.

A rough hand grabbed her upper left arm again and slammed Bryn into a chair making her vision swim slightly before her eyes settled on the man in front of her. Since he was sitting Bryn could not exactly gage his height, but estimated the man was about five foot ten inches, he might have been handsome if it had not been from the cold dark eyes that resembled empty tunnels, and he had high cheekbones in a slight gaunt face. His hair was jet black though there was grey beginning at the temples, same colored heavy eyebrows and mustache framed his face giving him a brooding expression.

Her eyes flicked about to look at other people in the room and settled on the last person she expected: Ryan. A wave of betrayal and coldness coursed through her body at the impersonal expression on his face, as if he did not even know her especially after he once assured her that he would never use her.

When the man in the middle spoke, Bryn's eyes riveted back to him, "I've searched for you a long time and now I want that information Rory gave your uncle," he said openly sneering.

Bryn did not bother to answer, she had no idea what he was talking about, but knew this man would never believe her from the expression on his face. If Uncle Jimmy knew this man, he certainly never mentioned it and even if this man had visited the house, Bryn knew that being blind she would never recognize him and had never heard him speak before this moment.

The man's expression turned mocking, "That bitch mother of yours was my wife and ran off with one of my men when she was pregnant. No doubt they filled your ears that Rory O'Keefe was your father, but I know the truth," he said maliciously as if discovering a long lost daughter were little more than a mild curiosity.

One thing for certain, this man was not her father or would ever be even if it was the truth and she did share his DNA, Bryn stared back at him defiantly daring him to make his words true.

"You have more backbone than your sniveling moth-er. It must come from my side since she was a coward," he continued to mock.

Those words stung Bryn to a response, "You will nev-er be a father of mine," she said softly, but quite clearly.

Her words satisfyingly wiped the mocking smile off the man's face and he literally launched at Bryn back-handing her across the cheek in one broad motion which made her nose begin to bleed, she looked up at him as she calmly wiped the blood from her nose with the back of her hand.

"Where is that damn chip?" he snarled threateningly.

"I have no idea what you are talking about," said Bryn coldly.

The man next to her chair, the one who dragged her into the room said, "We found this on her, boss," he said extending his hand with the chip Bryn had on her before the Facility seized her.

One thing Bryn knew for certain, that chip had noth-ing to do with her father or uncle, but of course this man did not know that so Bryn did not blink as she stared back at the man.

"Finally this is over," said the man with that mock-ing expression back on his face, "The damn Agency has been breathing down my neck for too many years. Now I know they don't have anything on me."

Bryn wanted to look at Ryan and struggled with her-self control not to permit such weakness, he had sold her out to this monster and no amount of studying him would ever explain such a betrayal. At this point she did not care what this ogre he worked for had in mind, besides death would be a far less painful outcome that what she suffered right now.

"Put her back in the room," said the boss man with a negligent wave of a hand.

Again, Bryn felt the rough hand on her arm, but did not resist as he dragged her back to the room and threw her inside before slamming the door. Now that she had her senses back, Bryn looked about the sparse room to see a portable chemical toilet in one corner, which explained the odor assailing her nose. There was not even a bed or any running water so she surmised this was probably never a guest room wherever it was and though Bryn could tell nothing of the building's location, she suspected it had been some abandoned building by the general ambience. There were no windows, the ventilation was high up the wall and Bryn was not wearing her special suit to cling to the walls even if the shaft was big enough for her body. Other than a central video fixture in the middle of the ceiling, there was an apparent lack of technology, but with only two ways out of the room, it added another level of difficulty and the door was likely to remain guarded.

Retreating to the corner furthest from the chemical toilet, Bryn curled up and pondered the matter, anything to avoid thinking about Ryan standing in that room with an indifferent expression on his face.

The sound of the door opening woke Bryn from a fitful doze, but she pretended to be asleep, she could hear soft footsteps approach, but remained relaxed and if she was lucky, she could disable this man so she could run. Unfortunately the footsteps stopped far enough away that Bryn knew the man would have enough time to react to any surprises, he was wary so they must know something of her background she thought to her annoyance.

A voice electrified her, "Darlin, it's me. I never expected to see you here," said Ryan's voice quietly.

Bryn's eyes shot open in fury, "Don't you talk to me. You sold me out to these people. You said you would never use me? Pah! Liar! You've been manipulating me from the start," she spat out.

Ryan squatted down his expression hurt, but Bryn did not care, he was a good actor if he managed to maneuver her into this mess and of course he would have told them everything about her background. The fact he was there now meant they were ready to deal with her and even if she could overcome him, Bryn knew it would be at a great cost to her physical wellbeing since Ryan had never attempted to injure her previously. Of course that had all changed now.

"You can choose to believe me or not Bryn, but I did not sell you out. I had no idea you would be here or that they intended to grab you. I would have told you to stay at the Facility or recommended leaving a different way," he muttered.

"So you've been working for these people all along. That's why attempts have been made to grab me. I thought someone was watching me at the Facility, but little did I know it was in the same room," said Bryn coldly.

"Not all is as it seems," breathed Ryan cryptically leading Bryn to believe someone might be listening, "Now isn't the time for explanations."

"Ha, you can't lull me that easily," said Bryn scathingly.

"There is more to this than you're aware of. Your family had connections they kept from you," continued Ryan barely audible, but he knew she could hear him.

"What a fantasy you expect me to believe. My parents or my aunt and uncle never did anything to anyone and they were not spies," snapped Bryn.

"No, they were not spies, but your father used to work for Kendall, the man who spoke to you, and turned against him. He helped your mother escape, changed their names and hid in North America. Your uncle was already living there," said Ryan.

"He wasn't really my uncle. He and his wife were just friends of my parents. They told me to call the aunt and uncle," said Bryn sharply.

Ryan shook his head, "No, he really was your mother's brother and they never told you. He helped your father and mother hide with new identities, but they couldn't tell you that Bryn. It was to protect you," Bryn snorted in disbelief, but did not interrupt, "Kendall believes your father gave your uncle a chip just in case anything happened to him."

There was a sound outside in the hallway and Ryan paused in his muted story, it was some elaborate fantasy he expected her to believe and she did not know why he persisted, he got what he wanted.

"Leave me alone. You got what you wanted from me so telling me some fairy tale isn't going to make any difference now," said Bryn coldly.

There was definite pain in Ryan's eyes now and Bryn almost felt guilty, "Listen to me, everything I told you was true. My feelings are true. I've never lied to you Bryn, not once," he said intensely.

"Then why leave me here? Why don't you help me get out?" sneered Bryn.

"Why do you think I came in here? The only reason you're still alive is he believes you are his daughter. When he finds out that chip has nothing he expects on it that might not even matter. I can't just march you out of the room. I know you can see the guards through the wall," his gaze challenged her to deny it, "but even if we got past them, this man is no fool and has a private army at his disposal. Don't think he would care too much if he shoots you," said Ryan grimly.

"Then you better go curry some more favor with your employer," said Bryn offhandedly.

"Damn it Bryn, don't act like this. You know I care and don't want anything to happen to you," growled Ryan quietly.

Bryn refused to look at him. His story was too convenient and she wondered if the man already knew the chip was useless by sending Ryan in here to charm information out of her and if Ryan thought she had what he needed, he was just as delusional.

Ryan leaned forward as if to caress her cheek and Bryn spat out, "Don't you dare touch me."

More noise came from the hallway and Ryan stood suddenly, he gave her a glance that was hard to decipher before he slipped from the room. Bryn tried to tell herself to forget Ryan, but the boiling feelings of hurt and betrayal in her stomach would not go away yet refusing to admit she still loved him after what he had done.

His visit, however, gave Bryn a lot to think about if any of the information was true regarding her family and if true, how Ryan could possibly know such information. As much as it annoyed her, Bryn made a comprehensive scan of her environment to verify Ryan's claim about the impossibility of escape and found he spoke the truth. She refused to consider the other information as truth, a childish stubbornness, she knew.

What chip was that boss man referring to? Uncle Jimmy would never have given her anything that could be deemed dangerous even if it was important and Bryn could not believe her parents would sanction such a choice either. That meant if Uncle Jimmy had such a chip, he either hid it or made alternate plans in case anything happened to him, she thought shrewdly and then a thought occurred to Bryn. To her growing dismay she realized that even if her aunt and uncle had a will she had gone into hiding long before anyone could contact her of its existence which meant her uncle could have left instructions of some sort. Due to the manner her guardians had died, the detective informed Bryn all the assets had been frozen as standard procedure and not once had she thought to check back after the detective warned her to limit all contact with her past. Of course Bryn knew she would never tell that odious boss man, inferring he was her father, of such a potential link to the sought after microchip. Or did he mean the recent microchip? She wondered. If that was the microchip in question, then she had stolen it from the people her uncle meant to safeguard the information, but how would she have known? Well she certainly would not be able to obtain that microchip for love nor money, as the old saying went and Uncle Jimmy was fond of quoting.

Again Bryn considered the advisability of escaping on her own in spite of validating Ryan's words about the men within the building, but without her gear, she would be incredibly vulnerable and they took her satchel containing her old bodysuit. That much was obvious since the microchip she had in her possession when the Facility seized her was also in the satchel before one of those men presented it to their boss. A depressing thought struck Bryn: Ryan would be ready for her to make any sort of bid for escape and would either stop her or inform the boss man of her tendencies so that the guard outside would be double that of normal. Her eyes flicked about the building again and noted the well placed surveillance which she had no hope of eluding without gear, she finally felt the first stirrings of defeat that had become all too common stuck at the Facility.

Doc grumbled as he returned to his office in the infirmary to forward data the Commander needed to review when he halted in surprise to see the only woman, regular personnel in the infirmary, sitting before his dedicated interface. A place she was not supposed to be and she knew that even without the hunted expression on her face, he immediately hit the alarm for security.

The Commander could be an annoyance, but Doc could not fault the almost immediate response to the alert, "Take her to the Commander. She has been accessing classified information and I will forward which files soon as I review the interface," said Doc as security strong armed the woman out of his office.

What Doc found was not good and disturbing. All the files referenced Bryn Keane (aka Shadow) and what's more, there was evidence the information had been downloaded. How long had the woman been accessing the information on Shadow and who was she sending it to? Well that would be up to the Commander to find out and Doc was quite familiar with methods which could be used to loosen anyone's tongue.

Kolski found himself pulled from quarters by the alert and ran to his office demanding information, "What the hell is going on?"

"Alarm from the infirmary sir," said the duty security man.

"Details?" demanded Kolski for he knew no teams were out or anyone currently in need a treatment.

"Doc is on a secure COM link for you sir," said the man and immediately switched to the channel.

Doc's breakdown on the files accessed and downloaded stunned Kolski especially after he released the Keane woman, added to that he never suspected someone in medical would breach ethics to become a mole. It could not be the Tabula because they knew all the information accessed since Doc reported directly to the board of directors and with growing fury, Kolski had to admit they had more than one infiltrator. Their prisoner definitely indicated he spoke with a man and as yet undiscovered.

"Shit," he exclaimed out-loud and slapped his hand on the COM, "send someone to the brig to check on the prisoner on the double," he had a sinking feeling just what security would find.

Damn, damn, thought Kolski, someone had been just waiting to make a move and the COM link opened, colored by inventive swearing, told the Commander what he already guessed, the prisoner had been executed. Someone was cleaning house.

"I want all surveillance pulled immediately inside and outside the Facility for the past six hours. Report any alterations or discrepancies," said Kolski seething, wishing he had thought to do this sooner, but had thought with Shadow gone, so was the potential trouble.

In the interim, security dragged the woman into Kolski's office and she was obviously resisting, struggling to free her arms without success.

"Who do you work for?" snarled Kolski, but the woman returned his gaze defiantly, "No matter we have methods no one can resist."

Again Kolski pressed the COM, "Davidson, bring your IG kit to my office," he said and saw the woman visibly pale so she understood what was coming.

In an apparent faint, the woman slumped and her escort shook her upright when Kolski saw her begin to foam at the mouth, "Shit!" he roared, "Get her to the infirmary," and then he punched the COM, "Doc, she's trying to suicide, poison I think. They'll have her there in a flash."

This was serious business if someone was cleaning house and one of the discovered moles was actually attempting suicide to prevent interrogation, Kolski wondered who the hell these people worked for to go to such lengths.

It could not have been even five minutes before Doc was back on the COM, "She's gone," he said grimly, "It was a designer poison meant to prevent rescue. Any antidote triggered a cascade of a mutated toxin. She was already dead the second she took it."

Kolski swore sulphurously, he ran a tight unit, had the best technology and still someone managed to infiltrate one of the best black ops units in the world with more than one person or turn them once they were in place. Some group had enormous resources and people as skilled as anyone currently contracted at the Facility, it was a sobering thought.

The COM alerted Kolski again, "Sir, I've forwarded several anomalies to your interface and a video someone attempted to delete. It's ugly," said the man grimly.

Yes, it was ugly. The information showing altered surveillance records was bad enough and someone managed to fool his best men even Foss, but it was the recovered video that made Kolski ill. It clearly showed Shadow leaving the Facility and she barely got a hundred yards away when she was accosted, seized, and tossed in a nondescript grey van by five men capable of subduing her quickly, there was nothing he could do to help her, he did not even know who they were dealing with or where they had taken her.

Calling the core team to the office, Kolski displayed the video to the three disbelieving men and reiterated he had no idea who had taken the woman or where they would hold her.

It was Foss who interjected, "I know how to find her," startled Stanton, Tank and the Commander looked at the man for an explanation.

Devin Mulcahy positioned his surveillance so he could inform his employer when his granddaughter Bryn Keane was released from the building found to locate a unit known as the Drury, Facility which had been essentially holding the woman against her will. He had been there for two weeks waiting and giving Aiden Keane daily updates that so far his granddaughter had not emerged from the building, at least as a free woman.

He leaned against the wall of the building where he set up when Devin caught sight of movement that revealed an average height woman with reddish golden hair and he knew that Bryn Keane had finally left the target building. His motion to contact Aiden Keane of the event was arrested when a nondescript grey van screeched level with the woman and at least five men jumped out to accost her. It all happened so fast that Devin never had a chance to aid the woman telling him the pickup had been well planned and professional.

With grim certainty he knew who those men must report to and Devin had just enough time to throw a special tracking device which stuck to the van before he unhappily reported the situation to Aiden Keane.

So it was with sinking spirits Aiden Keane received the message about his granddaughter from his most trusted friend and did not need Devin to confirm what he already knew: Liam Kendall had found Bryn at last.

Bryn decided these men had kept her for several days based on the infrequent supply of food they deigned to feed her, which she had to eat by hand since they wisely omitted any type of flatware that could be used as a potential weapon. The only concession to civility was a plastic tray instead of eating off the floor.

After his initial visit, Ryan remained absent so Bryn tried to convince herself that was a relief even if she could not shake the sense of betrayal that he was here and probably instrumental in her capture. Every time she recalled his words, Bryn instantly dismissed them as ridiculous and felt it was most likely some faction associated with the Facility hierarchy that did not want to let her go.

With little else to do, Bryn used her vision to survey the building of her prison watching and timing patrolling men, locating surveillance as well as exits. She was in no mood to be charitable when Ryan's comments proved glaringly true about the boss man's private army or the impossibility of escape, but she refused to give up. Every place Bryn ever assessed in her past always had some weakness and she had to be missing something, something these men had not thought of and she could use against them to escape.

After several frustrating days of monitoring her surroundings, Bryn was rudely interrupted by the sound of the door opening, but did not bother to look and smelled food from where she sat. The men were cautious when bringing meals and rarely entered the room, but even when they did, it was only a step or two through the doorway.

"Slide the tray here if you want to eat bitch," said an Irish accented male voice heavy with scorn.

This was the ritual, slide the tray to be removed and they left the food laden tray on the floor inside the doorway. Bryn thought about rebelling, but she knew they would take the food away as punishment and she needed her strength if she was going to escape so she slid the tray noisily across the floor in the appropriate direction.

Once alone, Bryn retrieved the food and ate while continuing to think. Her eyes settled on the ventilation duct, which was just large enough to accommodate her body, barely and wondered if she dare try to use it. Certainly it was high up the wall, but Bryn noticed it was close enough to a corner of the room so that she could use adjacent walls to scale up by using hands and feet with opposing pressure. The downside of such a plan would be the obvious way out of the room and it would not take the men long to guard exit points she could use so that they only had to wait for hunger or thirst to drive Bryn out into the open. Sighing in frustration, Bryn rolled her eyes upward in exasperation only to freeze when her sight settled on the ceiling and the space above it. The ceiling material was very old fashioned, squares set into a framework covering the entire room, but what meant most to Bryn was that those squares were not solid. Each one was a cut square unlinked to the rest, which could pop out of the framework and she swore savagely to herself that she had missed this over the intervening days of monitoring. The space above the ceiling was nearly high enough to allow her to stand upright, what a fool she had been to neglect it in her initial search no matter how confused the drug had made her.

Swearing at his failure again, Cormac, one of Liam Kendall's men, was attempting to break the encryption on the microchip removed from the woman recently captured. He rubbed his tired eyes resulting from hours of staring at his interface trying to think of another option he had not considered yet or face the Boss' wrath. Liam Kendall did not accept delay or failure and punished those people that followed either result quite brutally.

After running a special algorithm, he finally managed to break part of the encryption and what he saw was not good news. Nothing Cormac saw on his screen had anything to do with Liam Kendall or at least as much as he knew about the organization and the Boss' was likely to explode with rage when he realized the information he sought might still be discovered by his adversaries.

So it was with great trepidation Cormac transferred the information to a digital pad before presenting it to his Boss, but as soon as he walked out of the room, alarms began blaring throughout the building. Men literally bumped into Cormac twisting and turning him from the myriads of shoulders clipping his person so that he found himself looking about wildly trying to understand what was happening.

In the security hub set up in the building, two men muttered in conversation as their eyes flickering about the multi-screen surveillance display reflecting either inside or outside the building, one screen devoted to the captured woman's room.

One of the men waved his companion silent as his eyes settled on the room with the woman where he saw her stand and gaze into the monitor with a mocking expression just as they caught sight of a plastic tray in her hand that guards normally left with food. With a blinding fast movement her hand holding the tray flung the item straight at the module and the screen went black which set both men to swearing as one hit the alarm.

"What the hell is going on?" snarled Liam Kendall over the COM to the surveillance room.

"Boss, the bitch threw something at her monitor and it's gone," said one man curtly.

"Damn chit," then COM wide through the building, "Get in that bitch's room immediately," roared Kendall.

It was easier said than done as men at the woman's door said via COM, "She's jammed the door somehow Boss!"

"Idiots! Break it down!" snarled Kendall.

The sturdy door took a great deal of effort and three men to finally pry it open enough so they could slip in

one at a time which was when they noticed the ventilation duct cover on the floor. "She is the ventilation shaft,"
said one man over the COM.

"Seal off both ends before she gets to a junction,"
roared Kendall knowing they never installed any video
or sensors in the old duct work. "Then start dismantling
segments until you corner her."

All the men knew better than to lag following orders and with amazing speed began dismantling the duct
work only to find no woman, even the dust inside had not
been disturb by anyone sliding through it.

"She's not here," shouted a man in frustration until
he realized the duct work occupied only a portion of the
area above the ceiling, "She's in the ceiling!"

Soon as that information was relayed back to Kendall
he screamed, "Seal the exits and windows!"

Men scrambled to do as ordered while several others began to prod ceiling panels aside searching for the
woman, two men actually climbed in the recess to physically search, possibly grab her. Elsewhere in the building
other men had the same idea which was how Bryn found
her way to the exit blocked and decided to confront her
problem directly by changing course toward the room
where she could hear the boss man screaming.

Unfortunately some man began popping out the ceiling squares near her and Bryn was not able to get any
closer to her goal when the man used something to snag
her loose pants, literally yanking her to the floor. His
sneering visage changed in an instant when Bryn landed
on her feet like a cat and proceeded to annihilate him
with a series of blows he never dreamed she could deliver deeming her female, therefore too weak to resist. Of
course even that brief of a pause allowed other men to
see her and they quickly converge onto the area only to
suffer the same fate as the first man. Bryn knew she had
nothing to lose any more so she fought with desperation.

Instead of running to the exit, Bryn immediately
turned back toward her goal where the boss set up his

conference room which she figured out by the gathering of men over the days since her captivity. What she did not expect was the palm scanner to gain entry if the door was not opened from within and without her equipment, she was not going to be able to get into the room nor did she want to attempt any chance of her body adapting to the situation. Any change in her body could leave her exposed and weakened, not to mention potentially revealing more information to that wretched boss about her capabilities.

Sounds behind her told Bryn men were communicating her location to others and she would soon be overwhelmed by sheer numbers so she used the corner of a wall again with opposing pressures of hand and feet to climb back through the ceiling. It was the only way over the door.

Once over the room, Bryn jumping through one of the panels and hit the floor about twenty feet from the boss man preparing to rush him, she got only a few steps before several things happened. There was a sound of something metallic sliding before a body hit her so hard it winded her which simultaneously accompanied a searing pain in her side as she found herself literally under the body of a man. It was then she recognized Ryan's strained voice whispering, as if he was in a great deal of pain, trying to explain something to her. What she had not seen or taken the time to assess, the boss man's chair contained a variety of traps, which he could launch or use against people approaching him and all could be lethal. Ryan had taken the brunt of the injury to protect Bryn, but the projectile had passed through him enough to penetrate her side.

Bryn slid from beneath Ryan feeling his blood soaking through her clothing and knew the man was seriously injured if he was bleeding so badly, even though she was bleeding her injury was a nick by comparison. With more care, Bryn assessed the situation in more detail maintaining her distance from the boss man.

"Fool!" screamed Kendall at the prone figure of Nighthawk, "I didn't need your help!"

"Boss you didn't see what she did to the men outside," said one of the men that burst through the door urgently before handing him a digital pad so that Kendall could review the recorded footage.

Kendall snarled at what he saw, "Damn O'Keefe planned this hoping I would grab the bitch of a daughter and turned her against me," he seethed ignoring the man bleeding on the floor.

Nighthawk's whispered information warned Shadow to rein in her anger and use her cunning as she took inventory of the traps in the raised chair that launched the barbed spear-like projectile that Nighthawk had deflected from its lethal course. Now the man lay wounded, probably fatally, but he warned her to ignore him as if she had never been acquainted to give the Boss the impression he had attempted to help him rather than her. Yet another person she cared about was dying again, being ripped from her life by this man and he probably had killed everyone else in the past, she would end him for his treachery it did not matter if she died anymore.

With narrowed eyes Kendall watched the woman pace back and forth like a predator faced with an unseen barrier, her eyes glittered through the long lank strands of hair reminding him of a horror movie about undead. Her gaunt figure from captivity and dark circled eyes added to the image so that the blood leaking down her side from the graze faded into the background.

How did she know to keep that distance? Her eyes never left him and she continued to pace as if looking for weakness or waiting for him to become vulnerable, slowly his fury began to change to fear. Realization stuck him forcefully that she had not attempted to vacate the building, she came straight for him and he wondered if he had played right into his enemies' hands by seizing his so-called daughter.

Grinding his teeth, Kendall cursed Rory O'Keefe in his mind. The man prepared for every contingency and knew that someday that he, Liam Kendall, would come face to face with this woman in the belief she was his daughter. He did not need to review the recorded security footage again to know the woman was extremely dangerous, far more dangerous than his men as improbable as that fact was to him as he watched her pace testing for weakness.

It was the sound of an explosion that broke the tableau and the COM shrieked building wide, "We've been breached!"

"Boss you got to leave now," said another man in the room.

"Kill her," snarled Kendall as he backed toward a secret exit.

The man was too slow to raise the weapon and with impossible speed, Kendall saw the woman seize a hold of the man, knock the weapon from his grasp, grab a knife which she threw with incredible accuracy into his, Liam Kendall's, shoulder. It would have been his chest had he moved a fraction slower.

Another man ran into the room just as the first man wilted to the ground, *probably dead*, thought Kendall as he pressed the hidden button for the concealed exit and since the woman whirled to face the new threat, she did not witness his exit.

Frustration welled up in Bryn after dealing with the second man to see the boss had disappeared and she did not have time to search as other men came into the room to confront her. These newer men were not foolish enough to approach and spread out leveling weapons at her, fast as she was it was not fast enough to avoid all the projectiles that stung her body.

It was the end as far as she knew and no one would help her or care if she died on one of the floors in this building. Forced to one knee from pain, Bryn struggled not to give up when the men facing her collapsed to the floor revealing three men behind them in familiar garb which could only be the Facility, but barely had time to consider that as numbness spread through her body.

One of them ran up to her as if to carry Bryn, but she diverted him by pointing to Ryan, "He's dying, help him first," she did not even know if he was still conscious.

The larger man joined the first and slung Ryan over his shoulder before the first man turned to her, Bryn staggered to her feet to follow when another man appeared dressed in regular street clothing pointing a weapon at the men.

"She's to come with me," he said in an Irish brogue, "I was sent to secure her safety."

All three men took a defensive posture and Bryn said gritting her teeth in pain, "I won't go with you."

The man's brilliant blue eyes flicked to her and back the men before he said, "I'm a friend of Donal's."

Anyone spying could have figured that out, but soon none of them were given a choice when a heavily armed contingent of men descended with high tech weapons and gear demanding, "All of you come with us. Resist and you will be stunned."

The man in street clothing holstered his weapon, his lips pressed together in disgust and the three men from the Facility saw enough not to resist, but Bryn would have disappeared had her body not decided to give out. She crumpled to the floor in a daze before feeling a pair of strong arms scoop her up and begin moving, but to where Bryn had no idea.

Everything was hazy for Bryn, but at one point she thought there was a great deal of arguing going on in reference to her before someone cut off the discussion indicating that she needed surgery and in a portion of her mind she wryly thought she must have spent half her life in a medical environment.

Men silently watched as the gurney with the injured woman rolled away. The room was crowded with a variety of individuals, three of the men: Tank, Foss, and Stanton stood with crossed arms offering no comments at all. Of course through their ear buds the Commander heard everything.

"Who do you three report to? What were you doing in the building? You interfered with an operation that has taken us years to plant an undercover operative in that organization," fumed a brown hair, brown-eyed man in high tech combat armor holding a helmet under his arm.

Unknown to the man, the Commander relayed information via the ear buds the three men from the Facility wore and told them to give the questioner a number to call, Tank wrote the number before holding out the piece of paper to the questioner.

"What's this?" snapped the armored man irritably.

"If you call you will have your questioned answered. None of us are authorized to speak of our assignment," said Tank evasively.

"Of all the…" snarled the armored man before looking at the dark haired, blue-eyed man who had been insisting the woman leave with him, "I haven't forgotten you either."

Devin Mulcahy's eye brow rose staring back at the armored man and said nothing as yet, but he knew he had an ace in the hole that would be a shock to this unit.

Muttering, the armored man punched buttons on an interface to connect to the proffered number and the Commander obviously expecting the call, answered immediately saying, "Please place this on a closed COM."

With an irritated movement the armored man slipped an over ear COM unit, "OK who is this?" he demanded officiously.

"I'm Kolski of the Drury Facility and who are you?" said Kolski flatly.

"Jenson of the Agency, southeastern region. Why are your people interfering with an operation that took us years to plant an undercover operative, which has now been compromised I might add," he snarled.

"We did not interfere with your operation, at least not intentionally. Men in that building seized one of my contract operatives and we of course did a standard retrieval of our asset! We had no idea who grabbed her or why she was seized, but as she is on contract with us and her seizure could have been related to a security breach we suffered," snapped Kolski.

Jenson snorted derisively, "If that is so then why do I have a lone man here claiming he was sent to retrieve this woman?" he demanded.

"I have no idea who that man is, but I can tell you there have been attempts to seize the woman during several of our operations and this could be yet another ploy. If you ask the woman, herself, she can clarify her status and whether or not that man is known to her. I suspect he is not," stated Kolski pointedly.

"She's in no condition to question at this moment, however, once she is, the woman will be debriefed about her presence in our operation. What did she do for you?" demanded Jenson authoritatively.

"I am under no obligation to reveal my modus operandi any more than you are yours sir," said Kolski obstinately, "and anything my operatives do in the course of their contracts is classified information. I can assure you she was not sent into your operation and can prove she was seized. Give me a place to send a video file so you can see for yourself."

Jenson relayed pertinent information to a special e-mail account and opened the file to see Kolski was indeed telling the truth about the woman's seizure. Facial recognition of the five men responsible for grabbing the woman indicated the men worked in the Kendall organization, but why they would seize this woman remained a mystery.

"So you have no idea why these men seized her?" said Jenson suddenly pensive.

"None or why repeated attempts have been made during our operations to secure her," drawled Kolski in triumph, "So if you would please release my operatives and return the woman with them for treatment of her injuries."

Jenson uttered a furious denial, "Not until she is debriefed here. She may have vital information that may aid us to recover our operation," he said.

"You already have an operative in place or so you said. She is one of my contract operatives," said Kolski dangerously.

Jenson's voice turned scathing, "We did have one in place, but this fiasco cost us that hard earned benefit. He is no longer capable of aiding us and that woman is in the middle of this somehow," he said.

"I know who the operative is. He was on loan to us for several years and I know he is capable of almost anything," said Kolski hotly.

"Not if he's dead," said Jenson grimly.

At those words, the three Facility men stood straight their expressions disbelieving and they could hear the Commander swearing through their ear buds since he left the two way communications open for them to hear the conversation.

Kolski finally gritted out, "I think you are lying so you can keep the woman. My operatives indicated he was alive when they removed him at the same time as the woman," he snapped.

The men saw Jenson's face purple, "He was dead on arrival. Some projectile was stuck through his spleen and he bled out before anyone could aid him," he snarled, "That is why we need to question the woman, we need to know what happened! Your men can leave, but the woman stays until we are satisfied with her account of the situation!"

Kolski gathered his thoughts before dismay at Nighthawk's demise could take hold, "I will make certain she is released. You have not heard the last of me until she walks out of there," he said flatly before disconnecting.

Jenson felt his temples throbbing and turned on the three men, "Out! Out of my sight unless you can tell me more of what occurred than you already indicated!" he ordered.

To Jenson annoyance the three men looked at one another as if sharing hidden thoughts before turning to leave the room and then he looked at the single man left, who was lounging almost negligently.

Finally Jenson demanded, "How do you fit into all of this?"

"As I told you before, I was sent to secure the woman's release, but from those men initially," indicating the three men from the Facility. "I was waiting outside when five men took her in a grey van which I managed to plant a tracking device on before it left. That is how I ended up in the middle of your operation: I went to retrieve her," said Devin coolly.

Jenson narrowed his eyes, "According to the man I just spoke to, you are not affiliated with him and he claims the woman does not know you. As a matter of fact, he says there have been repeated attempts to seize her from his operations. If the woman does not know you, you will find yourself sitting in the brig," he said flatly.

Devin crossed his arm confidently, "Oh she won't know me on sight or in any other manner. We were never introduced, but there is a mutual acquaintance that can verify I was assigned to protect her and if that is not enough, my employer will certainly have verifiable evidence," he said smoothly.

Jenson looked at the man suspiciously, "Who is this so called acquaintance?" he said.

"Donal Meany," stated Devin calmly.

Snorting Jenson said, "Never heard of him. Who is your employer?"

Devin let a small smile cross his face, "Aiden Keane. Lord Aiden Keane and that woman is his granddaughter," he said silkily as Jenson face paled at the name.

That could explain Liam Kendall's interest if he knew that information, but how the hell did the woman end up an operative and with such people as the Drury Facility? Suddenly Jenson was not certain he wanted to know the details or if Aiden Keane would let anyone ever hear the details of the entire situation.

Though Jensen did not like it, he had accommodation assigned to Lord Keane's man, who never named himself, since he would not leave and Jensen was not about to let him go anyway until he managed to verify the claimed connection.

Several days later Jenson demanded of the lead doctor, "I need to speak to the woman. I'm getting pressured for holding her from higher up."

The doctor was unmoved, "She is still weak," he said.

Fuming with impatience, Jensen said, "Then why did you say her rate of recovery is so surprising?"

Pulling his shoulders back the doctor enunciated clearly, "That woman should have died from all those wounds. I have no idea why her body did not bleed out, but understand this: Her body suffered significant trauma. Had that been one of your men, he would have been dead before anyone arrived to help!"

Jensen thought he knew what was up, "You cannot keep her for study. We have to release her as soon as she can be moved and it sounds like that's possible now. I need to question her before that happens," he stated flatly.

When the doctor's expression tightened in anger, Jensen knew he had been correct and the man wanted to study this woman's physical anomalies, already word had spread about her ocular implants no one had ever seen before during her examination.

Unwillingly, the doctor stepped aside and allowed Jensen to pass to the guarded room where Shadow was being monitored. Two guards nodded at him before Jensen entered the room, but soon as he opened the door, he stopped in surprise to see her standing looking at a wall as if it might be a window. After retrieving surveillance footage from the building Kendall's organization occupied, Jensen made absolutely certain this woman could not use any weakness to get out before they had a chance to question her. If he had not seen the footage, Jensen might not have credited the devastation wrought by the woman on Kendall's men and a brief segment indicated she had wounded the man without concern for her own life.

His entry into the room brought no reaction or change in the woman's stance, but Jensen knew she was aware of his presence especially with the training she had displayed on those recordings.

Jensen decided to announce the reason for his visit, "I need to question you before you leave here. You were in the middle of a sensitive operation that had taken us years to infiltrate and now we have lost that gain due to your presence. I have seen the video of your capture so I realize you were taken against your will, but what I want to know is why Liam Kendall would care to seek you?" he said suspiciously.

Bryn felt her jaw harden at the insinuation, "I want to see him," she demanded ignoring the question.

Jenson said coldly, "You want to see Liam Kendall?"

Bryn whirled faster than advisable and nearly fell as she spit out, "Nighthawk! Where is he? I know he came here. He will answer your questions."

Jensen stiffened in anger that this woman was demanding anything from him, "There is no one to question any longer. The sooner you answer my questions, the sooner you can leave. What reason were you seized?" he said coldly though he did not understand the swift emotions fleeting across her face.

Bryn thought about being obstructive, but her heart ached so much she did not have the strength to act stubborn, all she could think about was Ryan was gone and that he died to save her life. Another person she cared about taken from her by that awful man.

In a dull voice Bryn said, "I don't really know what he wanted. He claimed he was looking for a chip that my father had, but he never gave me anything or did my uncle before their deaths. I had an unrelated microchip on me that they seized, but it had nothing to do with him, of that I am certain, so I don't know what chip he was referring to. After that they left me in a room barely feeding me and I finally got tired of waiting when I suspected he was going to kill me anyway so I planned to die fighting."

Jensen digested the information slowly. Soon as the unnamed man claimed a connection with Lord Aiden Keane and that this woman was his granddaughter, he had the Agency get background so he knew about Fiona Keane's marriage to Liam Kendall and her subsequent disappearance from Ireland in the rumored company of Rory O'Keefe. Lord Keane had turned over the information about Samuel and Elizabeth Smith which was the aliases that Rory and Fiona had lived under for ten years before an ally organization of Kendall's caught sight of O'Keefe accidentally which lead to the two people's death. It left their daughter legally blind and in the care of Lord Keane's son who had been living in North America with rumor that he was estranged from his father. A cover story that ultimately did not save him or his wife when Kendall decided to track down Fiona's daughter and Jensen suspected that Kendall believed the woman was his daughter. Unbeknownst to this woman, Lord Keane had arranged for her to go into hiding due to the manner of his son's death to protect her and the tenor of the information indicated that she had no idea there were any living relatives.

One thing he wanted cleared up, so Jensen said, "How did you know our operative? We observed you interacting on the recovered surveillance."

Bryn felt her jaw flex in anger, "At his previous assignment which you can check without my help and I suspect you know already," she said coldly.

"Why did you ask for him?" demanded Jensen.

"Because he tried to help me, though I suspect you already know if you have the surveillance!" snarled Bryn from physical as well emotional pain.

Jenson had to suppress a flare of rage as the woman's clever words and making him feel like a dimwit, but instead of commenting, he left to apprise Lord Keane's man that he could take her whenever he was ready. He had seen enough of the disagreeable woman.

Bryn was not certain how much time passed when the door of her guarded room opened again, but instead of medical personnel or the irritating questioner, it was the man from the building who tried to separate her from the Facility men.

"It's time to go, Miss Keane," said the man who on closer inspection had very dark hair and eyebrows that made his brilliant blue eyes even more vivid. His Irish brogue sent a shaft of pain through her as a reminder of Ryan.

"I am not going anywhere with you. I don't know you," said Bryn flatly, she did not care if he was well built or taller than she was.

"You've no need to fear me. As I mentioned before I am a friend of Donal Meany and I will take you to him for now," said the man with forced calm.

Bryn crossed her arms rigidly, "I can find my own way to Donal without your help," she said coldly.

Instead of being combative, one of the man's eyebrows rose obviously wordlessly questioning that statement before he said, "In your present condition you would be vulnerable and these people want you to leave today."

Then instead of adding more argument to his cause the man pulled out a cellular phone, placed a call and handed it to Bryn as if that would resolve her questions, she hesitated to take it, but finally reached for it.

Soon as she placed the cell phone to her ear, Bryn said warily, "Hello?"

"Ah, Bryn, I am so glad to hear your voice. A friend said you would come here soon as your health improved," said Donal's voice.

"I don't know this man and I have no reason to trust him," said Bryn glancing over at the man.

"His name is Devin, my dear. He has been trying to help for some time. He'll make certain you get here safely," said Donal soothingly.

"I can get there on my own, Donal," said Bryn stubbornly.

Donal sighed on the line, "My dear, I know you've been through a lot and I also know you are recovering from yet more injuries. Please let him accompany you so I can be certain you're safe," he pleaded.

"I guess I will see you soon then," said Bryn tonelessly before handing the cell phone back to the man she now knew as Devin.

Chapter 13

Donal watched over Bryn worriedly thru the passing weeks. She was so forlorn and sad, but he could not seem to draw her out no matter how sympathetically he attempted to discuss her mood, if he had to label it, he would call her mood grief. It made no sense, she should be glad for her freedom from those people that had taken her for their own ends and he knew Aiden had been furious once he realized the situation. Due to the monitoring that had been in place, Donal had been unable to contact his longtime friend to explain the situation and with Aiden's connections with the Agency, he could not risk exposing the man to an unknown source.

Devin had not been able to shed light on Bryn's mood either, he like Donal, thought the woman would be overjoyed to have her freedom from the men who used her skills to further their own aims though the man offered a guess saying that something Liam Kendall had said to her might be the cause. Donal knew via Aiden that the notorious criminal had been the reason for both his friend's daughter and son's deaths including their other family members; Bryn had only escaped their fates by sheer luck.

Finally, so concerned that Bryn had not even left his lab, which was completely unlike her, Donal decided to contact Aiden and see if what he thought about revealing his relationship to the young woman. So far Donal suspected that Aiden hid his relationship to Bryn to protect her, but he could not bear to see her so withdrawn and listless.

Checking about carefully to be certain Bryn was well out of earshot given her sharp hearing, Donal dialed Aiden's private number in Ireland, which was immediately answered by Aiden, "What's wrong?"

Donal sighed, "Aiden, Bryn is very sad and withdrawn not at all what I expected from her after leaving that place. I wondered for a week or so if her injuries might be bothering her, however all her checkups were better than normal. Devin is of the suspicion Liam said something to her when he had her captive, but if so, I cannot get her to speak about it. She's grieving over something," he said worriedly before adding, "Now might be a good time to let her know about you."

Aiden sighed in turn, "Kendall buggered off and from what I've heard from the southern headquarters she wounded him. He's going to be out for blood this time. I think initially he only let her live because he thought she might be his daughter, but after her performance, the man will be afraid of her and I suspect he means to have her killed now. After her ordeal at his hands, I'm uncertain if she will believe I am her grandda," he said despondently thinking of everything Bryn had gone through in her life.

Donal inhaled sharply, "Do you think she is still in danger here?" he said urgently.

Aiden paused thoughtfully before saying, "I think she is still in danger, but Kendall won't know where to find her even if he still has someone watching Drury. They won't let her come back there anyway, but he doesn't know that or I believe he doesn't at this point. Apparently he managed to slip a few spies in their midst and I don't know if they identified them all. Their Commander has kept the situation with Kendall very quiet and only sent three of his trusted people to retrieve her that day so no one will know where to check for her," he said.

"Aiden, some of them knew about me before they caught her. Liam might try to find her here," said Donal with trepidation.

"Not with Devin there. He would send people to check or observe anyone coming or going and you said she has remained inside besides, I suspect Liam left the country after that breach of his safe house," said Aiden.

"If she decides to leave, Aiden, I won't be able to keep her inside and she won't listen to Devin either. She wouldn't even come here with him and only relented because I asked her to let him keep her safe. Do you think she might be safer there?" said Donal.

Aiden sighed, "She sounds so much like Fiona and that means we can't force her to do anything. As much as I hate it, we are going to have to manipulate the situation to get her to come here and you will need to start by encouraging her to go outside to help you with small things. It certainly isn't healthy for her to stay inside so much either. I'll discuss options with Devin," he said.

"I'll see what I can do. There are always groceries," commented Donal thoughtfully.

It had been over six months since Bryn left the Facility and there was emptiness in her heart now and a sense of loss she could not seem to come to terms with no matter how she tried. Looking out across a park from a café, Bryn could hear several people talking around her, but one conversation caught her ear though she never meant to eavesdrop.

"How did you get your injury?" said a woman speaking to another woman in a wheelchair.

The disabled woman was quite beautiful with sleek black hair, porcelain skin and brilliant green eyes, she sighed slightly at the question but gave the other woman a stoic smile.

"I used to work for a commodities firm and I went out to lunch with a few co-workers one afternoon. We were waiting at a crosswalk on the way back to the company building when someone lost control of a vehicle and rammed right into the crowd waiting to cross," at this Bryn winced, "I don't remember much about the actual accident though people filled me in later, but I was one of three who survived a crowd of fourteen people."

"I woke up in a hospital unable to feel my legs. Even with company health insurance I spent all my savings on medical bills and then my company told me they were laying-off people. I was one of the people cut and though they never said, because they couldn't legally, people believed it was because of my disability."

"That's just wrong!" said the other woman. "Did you get an attorney?"

"I couldn't afford it any longer. I had no job and my savings gone. The company was very careful how the dismissal was worded and even when a friend had someone look over the document, they said unless someone from the company actually admitted the true reason I would never win," said the disabled woman with a sigh.

"I'm so sorry. I shouldn't have asked," said the other woman contritely.

"Oh, please don't worry. I manage now. It may have done me a favor anyway. I have a lot less stress in my life and in some ways I actually take time to live," she said with a brilliant beautiful smile.

The story tugged at Bryn's heart. She had been like this woman though the circumstances were different. She was not born blind, but lost her sight at ten years old in a freak accident. Her parents had died in the accident, which left her blind though their life insurance managed to cover an operation to grant her minimal sight. She was still considered legally blind however. Then out of the blue Donal stopped by her one day and spoke to her, it was then her life truly changed after hiding in anonymity. He offered her a chance to completely regain her sight with the cybernetic implants that fused to her optical nerves and she remembered the day when she opened her eyes to see the world she remembered as a child.

That feeling still brought tears to her eyes. Of course Bryn could easily pay for this woman's spinal repair, but she suspected that like her, this woman would not welcome charity after the way she came to terms with her disability. Though her job as a thief made her wealthy, the Facility fee for her services surpassed what she already put aside to Bryn's astonishment, so that she would never have to work again and that was a good thing. After losing Ryan, she felt no desire to do anything anymore as if her passion for life left her and she just existed doing odd errands for Donal now, but maybe she could help this woman after a fashion without making it seem like charity.

The disabled woman left and Bryn followed slowly behind her until she turned into an old fashioned travel agency which was the kind of work based on commissions, odd in the era of their current technology where people could research anything over the internet. It must seem like bare subsistence now after being in the corporate world, but her face seemed light and happy, she waited a few minutes before entering the agency.

A bell rang in the back of the shop and the disabled woman rolled around the corner smiling when she saw Bryn, "Please sit. How can I help you?" she said.

"I'm not certain. I've never really traveled for pleasure," said Bryn candidly.

"My name is Donna," she said smiling.

"I'm Bryn," she said holding out her hand.

"What a lovely unique name! Where does that originate from?" said Donna.

"I honestly don't know. I never had the chance to ask my parents," said Bryn.

"Well let's check the internet! You never know what you might find out," said Donna with a grin.

"Well it seems to be of Irish origins. Have you ever considered visiting the country?" said Donna smiling.

This woman was quite good at what she did in this small shop so Bryn knew she must have been a force to be reckoned with in the corporate world though the thought of Ireland brought back memories of Ryan.

"Actually I've never been or had a reason to go there. I guess it's possible my family came from there, but I don't remember much about them. They died when I was ten years old. That was when I lost my sight," said Bryn conversationally.

"You're blind?" said Donna in amazement and then, "Oh my, please forgive me. It's just I couldn't tell because you seem anything, but blind to me," her face was now red.

"Oh, no apology needed Donna. I'm not blind any longer. I had the good fortune of meeting a gifted man who helped me of his own accord or I would be blind still," she said quickly to assure the other woman.

"That's so wonderful! There aren't many people in the world like that anymore," she said a little wistfully.

"So, tell me more about Ireland," said Bryn to distract the woman for the moment.

There were not only brochures, but also books she gave Bryn to borrow and then she wrote down all manner of websites to investigate all the while discussing guided tours to solo exploration of the massive island. It was nearly overwhelming the amount of information Donna retrieved in such a short space of time.

"Do you mind if I look over all of this for a little while? I don't know where to begin and from the looks of things, I'll need to spend months to see everything," laughed Bryn.

"Please take your time. There are seasonal things you may prefer to time your trip for and you're right it could take months just to scrape the surface of all there is to see," said Donna echoing the laugh.

It did not take Bryn as long as she thought to peruse the information and Ireland appeared to be a beautiful place, besides she could do with a vacation which would help Donna as well. At least that is what Bryn told herself instead of admitting the underlying reason it all reminded her of Ryan. If she went on a trip, it would remove the temptation to wallow in grief. It had been a struggle these past months to get out of bed or to leave on errands for Donal and her spirits were so low, Bryn had considered calling the Facility to speak with anyone who would talk to her just to feel closer to Ryan's memory.

Returning the next day, Bryn waved at Donna soon as she entered the agency, "I think you're right Donna. It sounds like a wonderful place to go and I haven't really had a vacation in a long time," she said sitting in front of the woman.

"That's grand!" said Donna with delight.

They began preparations and Donna gave a great deal of good advice, especially when Bryn did not want to end up in area's inundated with tourists, she preferred the freedom to move about in a less regimented or restricted touring of the landscape.

"Then I suggest allowing me to book a private guide who can take you 'off the beaten path,' as you might say. That way you will get opportunities to see and do things that not many tourists ever get to experience. How long do you think you want to stay? I can possibly get a jump on organizing a visa for you," said Donna with a smile.

Bryn tugged at her bottom lip in thought, "I don't really need to be back here in any timeframe and from what I've seen so far, it will take some time to get a good exposure to the country," she said.

"I can help you set up a longer visa than most tourists get. That way you can have an open-ended return ticket," said Donna enthusiastically.

"That sounds like a good idea," commented Bryn thankfully.

Once all the arrangements were finalized, Bryn chose to fly first class since she could take a special jet to reduce the travel time considerably and before she left, she said to Donna, "Here is a number for a special person named Donal. He is the man who fixed my sight. If he can't offer you any help, he will know someone who can. Don't worry about money just tell him I recommended you. He helps people because he loves to," handing her a card with a number.

"Oh, Bryn," said Donna her eyes filling with tears, "You don't have to do this."

"And you didn't have to help me plan this trip as extensively as you did. I know what life is like when a part of you is taken away and I'm glad to help people whenever I can, to find the hope I was given back," she said squeezing Donna's arm before she left.

Her flight to Dublin was uneventful and negotiating customs easy due to Donna's help. Soon as she headed for baggage claim, Bryn saw a relatively handsome black-haired man hold a card with her name, "Bryn Keane," and suspected he was the guide arranged by Donna. Soon as she approached, the man's brown eyes widened in surprise, but the reason for the expression eluded Bryn and he cleared his throat gesturing her to following him to the baggage area.

The baggage carousels began to move not long after they both arrived which eventually began to fill with luggage, Bryn snagged at only two small luggage pieces since she only brought enough to change and wash along with a couple of nice items in case she needed them. If she needed more, Bryn knew she could always buy additional items.

"Travelin' a bit light aren't you Miss?" said her guide.

She shrugged, "I can always wash things and if it's not enough, I can buy items," she said with a smile.

Baggage in hand, her guide politely nodded for her to follow him to customs, but Bryn had the impression he kept glancing at her surreptitiously and wondered if she looked too American or if something might be on her face given the man a reason to stare. After clearing customs, he led her to a vehicle and she nearly entered on the wrong side since she was not accustomed to the passenger seat on the left side of a vehicle.

They drove in silence for a while until Bryn could not stand not knowing why the man kept glancing at her, "Do I look odd or have something on my face you've too polite to mention? I get the impression you see something about me that is different," she said finally, but tried to inject some humor in her voice.

"No Miss. I'm sorry it's just…well…I was expectin' someone a bit older than you from the arrangements made," he said a little uncomfortably.

That surprised her since he would have her visa and passport information so he had to know her age, not that she was old by any means, but she was no teenager at thirty two. "I guess I'm confused since I know the agent sent my information unless something did not make it through correctly," she said in a puzzled manner.

The man cleared his throat, "Aye it arrived just fine. No offense meant, but you don't look your age and I thought for a moment I had the wrong person when you walked up to me. You look like you might still be in a university," he said and bright patches of red appeared on his cheeks.

Bryn laughed, "Thank you. I can accept that. People could say much worse I imagine," she said humorously.

He cleared his throat again, "Beggin' your pardon, but there is nothin' worse to say about a lady that looks like you," he said with another glance at her, this time admiring which made Bryn blush.

First stop was a beautiful bed and breakfast in outer Dublin close to the sea where the proprietor was a friendly older man that directed her guide to the room she would occupy in the lovely old building. The proprietor told her some of the history of the building as her guide deposited·her luggage and then invited her down for a traditional tea.

One thing immediately apparent to Bryn was that Irish people were extremely friendly and full of wit so that she enjoyed her first evening so much that she nearly forgot her sadness. The bed and breakfast actually had a portion devoted to a pub and she could hear impromptu music accompanied by a variety of voices. The singers were very good and so was the music as she sat entranced by the melodies.

Her guide caught sight of her and waved Bryn into the pub offering to buy her a drink, "What will you have?" he said.

Bryn immediately shook her head, "I don't drink, but thank you for offering," she said.

Her refusal fell on deaf ears, "Fergus pass a half o'pint of stout over," said her guide and then to her as he handed it over, "This is good for you. Brewed the old way! Me mum used to give t'me when was ah was ah bahbee."

Bryn wanted to refuse, but did not want to insult her guide or server so she sipped the stout and it tasted like a heavy beer in a way though earthier. It actually had a better taste than she remembered of beer back in North America, but it was not something she would drink often or in quantity like most of the people in pub seemed to be doing.

Though she preferred to sit and listen, Bryn was drawn into conversations swirling about the pub and before she knew it, the man behind the bar was calling time. Her legs felt like lead as she negotiated the stairs with her guide solicitously escorting her and even tired as she was, Bryn suspected he might be hoping for more. However, she thanked him politely claiming the time difference caught up with her when she realized lost a good six or seven hours since North America besides she privately admitted was not ready to see men that way right now.

"She's in Dublin now. I arranged the guide to be Seamus so he can make certain she doesn't end up in the wrong places or anywhere Kendall might come across her," said Devin as he watched Bryn get into a car with her guide.

Aiden said, "Good! Hopefully she can relax and forget the past back in North America, at least for a while. It's doubtful Kendall will look for her over here even if she used her given name. He will think I intend to keep her far away as possible and set up his spies around Drury or Donal's building. Only you, Seamus, and I know she is here," or so he thought.

"I'll still keep an eye on her just in case. She's too sharp to fool if he starts acting like a guard instead of a guide especially if you want her to enjoy the time here," said Devin.

"Yes, please keep an eye on her. Bryn needs to have as normal a time here as possible. The last time her life was normal was before Fiona died and she deserves to vacation like anyone else," said Aiden with a sigh.

Her guide told Bryn to call him Shay, short for Seamus as he took her about Dublin to begin her tour of Ireland showing her so many things relating to the ancient history of the Irish people from old historic buildings, monuments, castles (renovated, restored and still used), areas along the coastline, and myriads of pubs. He certainly knew where all the pubs were, Bryn thought humorously.

It was after a particularly long day when Shay brought her back to the bed and breakfast that her visit took a strange twist of circumstance. She went up to her room to bathe and did a double-take in her room when she noticed a beautiful red rose on the bed which Bryn knew had not been there that morning. It could not have been there that long since it was not wilted.

After bathing and changing, the proprietor's wife came to Bryn's room and invited her to take a traditional tea with her family and friends visiting for the evening. Downstairs, the proprietor introduced her like a visiting family member and all the people present. They were so friendly it amazed Bryn, especially after the suspicious city people back home.

They all ate little cakes, scones, and tiny sandwiches on an antique service accompanied by several pots of heavenly tea chatting about all manner of things including Bryn's adventures in Dublin thus far. No one seemed in a hurry to leave and before long a huge dinner was prepared for everyone including other guests with an amazing variety of old fashion foods that Bryn had never eaten before like cockle soup, brown soda bread with fresh butter, hunter's pie (a main dish with lamb), Irish stew, and a detectible apple pie for desert.

"It's a good thing I'm doing a lot of walking or I would gain weight from all this wonderful food," said Bryn humorously to the people at the table and they all laughed at her comment.

After dinner she asked the proprietor, "Did you leave a red rose in my room?"

"No Miss. You say you found one?" said the older man curiously.

"Yes, lying on my pillow. That's why I thought you or one of your staff left it since I didn't leave the door unlocked," said Bryn a little uneasily.

"I'll speak to them all tomorrow to be certain. Maybe someone clipped one of the rose bushes in the garden and left it for you. I notice Shay watches you as well as a few other men, it could be they asked one of my staff to leave it for you," said the proprietor patting her hand.

Bryn berated herself for being suspicious knowing Shay might have done something like that even though she made a point of not encouraging his interest and decided to stop looking for problems that were not there. A rose was hardly a threatening gift!

The following day after the proprietor spoke to his staff as well as Seamus, the guide decided to contact

Devin Mulcahy about the situation regarding the unauthorized entry into Bryn's room.

Seamus made the call outside the bed and breakfast
so no one would hear as he waited for the connection
speaking his concern to Devin, "You told me to contact
you if anything unusual happened. Last night Miss Keane
mentioned someone left a rose on her bed even though
she locked her door that morning. The proprietor asked
his staff and me if any of us left the rose, which we did
not though I told him I didn't think it was something to
worry about to keep him from upsetting her," said Shay
uncertainly.

"Shite!" said Devin, "No one saw anything or anyone
that shouldn't be there?"

"Not a thing though it was only a rose," commented
Shay.

"No one's been approaching her have they?" snarled
Devin wondering if the man had been lax in his duties.

"No one other than a few men in the pub which isn't
surprising when you look at her and they haven't been
rude or pushy, I watch to be certain," said Shay carefully.

"Keep a sharper eye out, but don't act different or she
will see it and ask questions. Continue to take her places though you might want to change towns to give her
different sights. Work your way toward Thurles and we
can set up more surveillance just in case," ordered Devin
before disconnecting the call.

Devin then called Aiden Keane to apprise him of the
anomaly, "It may be nothing. Some man may have asked
one of the staff to leave the rose and they are afraid to
come forward," he said.

"But you don't believe that," stated Aiden thoughtfully.

"It seems unlikely, but then Kendall wouldn't leave
a rose. He would have left a much direr message," commented Devin.

"True. Well if someone is watching her then Shay
bringing her closer to me will allow us to set up more
extensive surveillance without alarming her. I can have

it in place ahead of time so she won't notice new people suddenly in places," said Aiden.

Bryn walked in the lovely garden behind the bed and breakfast smelling the sea on the breeze, though it was getting late, she did not want to sleep so soon after such a big meal. Sounds came from the main building from people who had not left yet and she had to smile: The Irish certainly enjoyed celebrating any occasion. What she did not expect was a hand coming to rest on her shoulder and she reacted instinctively seizing the arm in a judo move so that a body went sailing over her to land on their back with an expiration of air that said the person just had the air knocked out of their lungs.

Her attention had been lax with the commotion in the building and she had not heard the person come up behind her, but when Bryn finally looked at the person, she saw it was Shay to her dismay.

"I'm so sorry," said Bryn contritely as the man sat on the ground gasping for air.

Unable to speak momentarily, Shay waved away her apology, but Bryn felt totally embarrassed she reacted so strongly in a friendly environment and hoped it was only a residual response to her former life, not uneasiness from anyone around her in Ireland. *Maybe that red rose left by an unknown person put me instinctively on edge*, she thought uncertainly.

Shay finally stood back up looking at Bryn cautiously, "I shouldn't have surprised you like that Miss Keane. Of course if I'd known I would eat dirt the second I touched you I might have called out first," he said humorously to alleviate any embarrassment.

Bryn felt her cheeks burn, "My parents sent me to classes when I was a child and I guess it stayed with me," she said to explain away any curiosity the man might have before any questions began.

"I've been warned," was all Shay said with a small smile.

Actually Bryn was sort of glad it happened so that it might add another reason to keep Shay from becoming too interested in her romantically and though he had not been pushy, he certainly did not bother to hide his interest.

"Actually, I came to ask if you would like to continue moving through the countryside and stay in different towns or villages. It will be easier to see those areas without so much travel time," said Shay cheerfully.

Bryn thought about that and it made sense. The further they wandered the longer the commute and she wanted to see everything the traditional way, not the high speed transportation that made her stick out, as she began to notice, in outlying villages. Another added bonus was it would put distance between her and whoever left the rose on her bed, as she was not ready to have another relationship in the immediate future.

"I like that idea. I'll be ready to leave in the morning since you apparently have a plan," said Bryn humorously and Shay gave her a mock salute accompanied by a grin before he returned to the building.

Shay stopped in villages only a few days before moving onward and Bryn enjoyed the history he recounted about each area, but one note of unease haunted her, she felt someone was watching her. It reminded her of the time in the Facility when she felt the additional surveillance and it came from another source. Bryn never caught anyone staring at her other than Irish residents who could tell she was not from the local village, even though she had acquired some Irish clothing to blend in, however the villages were small enough people probably knew all the residents.

Soon she began to notice at least five or six men, intermixed with other residents, which seemed to be busy, but Bryn could not determine what some of them were busy doing, almost as if it was for show and she felt a stirring of warning as she watched those men narrowly.

However, none of them ever approached, looked at, or talked to her, which was an oddity since the majority of Irish people she had met were very friendly and curious about her.

Chapter 14

It had taken a while, but Devin finally managed to sneak up to a man they marked that had been following Aiden Keane's granddaughter and it had not been easy, the man seemed to fade away at the first hint of anyone approaching him.

Devin pointed his weapon at the man's head from a safe distance before saying quietly, "Move and you're dead."

The man seemed to freeze, but Devin could not see his face as he was wearing a hooded pullover and he was certainly not going to get any closer after the trouble it took to corner this man.

When the man seemed to stiffen, Devin added, "I suggest you don't try anything clever. There are men all around me with you in their sights and we know you've been tailing a woman. There is someone who wishes to speak to you and if you want to live longer, you would be wise to come with me."

For the first time the strange man spoke, "And if all the men come with you, who will watch over her?" he said in a quiet voice though Devin thought he heard a hint of sarcasm.

"She will not be alone," said Devin stiffly at the implied insult about his carelessness.

All the man did was nod and wait for direction from him which irritated Devin because he did not like how calm and collected this man behaved as if sure of himself. Hiding his irritation, Devin told the man to walk in front of him occasionally telling him to turn right or left until they approached a black SUV with tinted windows.

"Please get in," ordered Devin after several men arranged themselves within the vehicle as an added precaution.

As Aiden Keane lived in the Thurles area, they did not have very far to drive and arrived at his estate within twenty minutes. The strange man did not comment at all during the journey, not even to ask where they were going or whom they were going to see which miffed Devin somewhat at his indifference.

With several men in tow, Devin guided the man to Aiden's private office and pressed the intercom to announce his presence before the secure door opened, he gestured the man inside alone knowing Aiden could stun the man if necessary.

Aiden looked at the man Devin finally cornered in Thurles that he and his men had determined was following his granddaughter, he seemed oddly unconcerned which warned him to take great care with security precautions. A stun field surrounded his desk if the man made any attempt to attack him.

Aside from his concern, Aiden saw no reason to be impolite, "Please sit," he said hoping the man might be more cooperative with pleasant treatment.

The man sat lithely indicating to Aiden he was very fit and he used the shadow of his hood to great effect preventing his features from being clearly seen or recognized which made him wonder why the man was hiding. It was obvious the way he carried himself.

"Please tell me why you are following that woman?" said Aiden in a polite conversational voice.

The man's head tilted up slightly and he caught the glimmer of eyes, "Because she is not safe, even here," he said in a quiet voice.

Aiden looked at the man keenly and said, "I see. How do you know this? For that matter how do you know her?"

A sound, like a soft snort came from beneath the hood, "I worked with her for several years and a lot happened to her in that time that told me she was not safe there or possibly anywhere," he said almost coolly.

"To my knowledge that would mean you are part of the Drury Facility. What is your name so I can verify who you are?" said Aiden in the same vein.

His head tilted up again and the man's eyes glittered from beneath the hood, "I was with her when the Agency brought us all into their southern region operations. As for my name, you can call me Patrick Kelly though that is not what anyone ever called me there. Most of us went by call signs or nicknames. As for contacting them, well you might say I've been burned for taking off on my own to watch over her," he said quietly.

Well that explained the man's secretiveness if Drury burned him and from what Aiden found out about their Tabula, they were as ruthless as the Agency could be when they decided to act or his granddaughter would not have been captured. Devin did mention three men supposedly from Drury which attempted to free his granddaughter from Liam Kendall's clutches and that they demanded she be turned over to them when the Agency seized all of them. A fourth unknown was injured, assumed to be one of Kendall's men. Of course Devin would not allow the Drury operatives to remove Bryn after orders to see that she was free of Drury and yet, he did recall Donal mentioning her depressed state once she arrived at his home again. *Could she have planned to return there?* He wondered.

Feeling the man watching him as he sorted through this information, Aiden finally said, "If you know her so well, why not approach her? Surely she wouldn't expose you if she knows you."

This time, his snort was clearly audible from beneath the hood and he said, "And put her in further danger if anyone questioned her or was watching her in case I met with her? Now that would be selfish of me, wouldn't it? Besides, after her experiences at the Facility, I can't imagine anyone associated with it would be a welcome sight to her," he said wryly.

All plausible information and sensible precautions especially if people were looking for a burned operative it would certainly endanger his granddaughter, but why would this man care when most people sought as operatives were ex-military or even assassins by trade.

Regarding Patrick shrewdly, Aiden said, "Why would you care what happened to her? I know the kind of people who work for places like Drury. The Agency looks for similar traits in operatives and caring or compassion is certainly not some of those traits."

Silence lengthened in the room and Aiden could feel Patrick staring hard at him, sensing he was angry at the challenge.

"I want to make one thing perfectly clear. None of us knew we brought in a woman especially the way she injured some of our men. Most men would never pursue such a trade or take the risks she had been taking on jobs that we tracked over time. Once most of us knew about her, we thought she should be released if she did not want to work with us, but someone higher up decided they had to have her skills for several key missions over the years she stayed there. In spite of her situation, she did her damnedest to help us even when it nearly cost her life in several situations. Some of us that were there will never forget that and I, for one, don't want to see anymore happen to her especially after those men seized her right out in the open," said Patrick biting off the last word.

With a feeling of consternation, Aiden returned Patrick's gaze wondering just exactly what his granddaughter had been doing prior to her tenure at the Drury Facility because Donal never indicated the kind of risk this man was hinting. Out of necessity, he could not keep up with too much information about his granddaughter lest a spy in his house manage to purloin the information or intercept the coded correspondence from Irene via Devin. Jimmy could not actually contact him to keep up the appearance of estrangement for any observers inside or outside the estate and of course there had been no contact with Fiona at all once she fled Ireland. What did Fiona and Rory plan for their daughter? Aiden considered possibilities and wondered if both his granddaughter's parents worried that she might come face to face with Liam Kendall someday. If Fiona worried about such a possibility it was plausible that she asked Rory to seek special training for the girl, but Aiden could not believe she would condone anything with the amount of risk Patrick was intimating. Suddenly he realized he did not really know his granddaughter at all, much of her life was blank to him and that saddened Aiden.

With sudden perception, Aiden said, "It was you that left the red rose in her room!"

Surprisingly Patrick looked away and nodded, "I did though maybe I made a mistake. I never meant to alarm her, which is what must have happened if you know about it," he said with a sigh.

"It's possible she thinks one of the staff left it there as a token of one of the men that frequented the pub there," said Aiden.

Patrick snorted again, "Highly unlikely. She is not lulled easily by convenient explanations. That much I know after years in her company on missions. It was almost like she had another sense entirely," he said dryly.

If that was true, his granddaughter knew about his men watching her and that would probably alarm her further from what Patrick just mentioned, Aiden had to concede he knew very little about the young woman compared to this man.

"If I let you walk out of here, what did you plan to do?" said Aiden curiously now.

Patrick's hooded head swiveled back to him, eyes glittering in the shadows, "What I was doing before: Watch over her. I know that she is still in danger since the Facility never caught all their moles and from an overheard conversation at the southeastern Agency, it sounded like their target got away," he said.

Running a hand through his hair, Aiden sighed for the truth of that last sentence because Liam Kendall did get away and if Drury did not catch their leak, there were now two potential sources of danger for his granddaughter.

This story could be convenient so Aiden decided to test Patrick, "If you are truly burned, there are ways I can check without giving you away if you will allow a DNA test. Once I confirm your story there are a few things you should know and maybe I can help with your current status, that is, if you agree to it," he said.

Silence lengthened again, but Patrick was still watching him, maybe weighing the worth of his words or honesty until he finally said, "I'll trust you then to check the DNA and not turn me over to Drury or the Agency because you are trying to help her."

The answer surprised Aiden. He had not expected such an answer and wondered just what his granddaughter knew about this man and if she trusted him to such a degree that he was betting his life on her.

"Until I can verify the information, it would be better if you remain a guest here," said Aiden appraisingly.

All Patrick did was nod in agreement knowing he had little choice.

In truth what Aiden found was proof of Patrick's words and that a man had been burned by the Drury Facility and the Agency, the DNA profile listed him as location unknown, but highly sought after within North America thus far. Apparently they did not know he had managed to leave the country which pointed at his resourcefulness and that was not surprising if he had significant training in black ops as most field operatives must have. Also as he mentioned, no listing of a Patrick or any other name other than a general description that fit the man, who sat in his office several days ago. Given the degree of electronics used in this age, there was no such thing as redacted files when someone could just easily hit a delete key, but there were obviously history gaps. Again expected given the classified nature of any missions. What it came down to was if Aiden trusted this man enough to release him and to make that assessment, he would need to speak with him again at length this time.

So he sent a polite request for an extensive meeting with Patrick Kelly, actually when Aiden thought about it, a very Irish name though the man spoke with an American accent, of course that could be faked. To make the meeting more relaxed, Aiden had dinner served in his office in preparation for Patrick's arrival even though the dining room would have been more appropriate, but his office was still the most secure place on the estate. He knew no surveillance equipment would work within its walls thus preventing any spies in his household from gleaning information from this unusual conversation.

When Devin showed Patrick into the office, Aiden finally had a better look at the man as he was now wearing clothing provided instead of the hooded pullover. He was not a huge man though tall, well built, dark haired, curly to his shoulders, with a mustache and dark eyes, but again, Aiden discounted most of what he saw, particularly eyes and hair because they could be easily changed.

His face had some scarring and swellings whether real or added for effect, he did not know.

"Please sit we have a lot to discuss. I hope your stay has a least been comfortable," said Aiden politely.

The expression on Patrick's face was almost mocking, "It was better than prison," he said.

"Well as to that, I managed to have your burn order confined to North America, so as long as you don't return there, you should be able to have some sort of life. If you need arrangements for a visa or other necessities, perhaps I can help," commented Aiden conversationally as he began to pass food to Patrick.

A searching glance from Patrick greeted those words as he took proffered dishes, "You must have a great deal of pull with highly placed people. Neither Drury or the Agency are easily intimidated," he said.

With no false modesty, Aiden said, "Yes you could say I have my 'fingers in a few pies' as the old saying goes."

Patrick snorted with some humor before saying, "What more do you want from me?"

"One way I was able to force them to leave you alone was to infer that you would be in my employ," Aiden watched Patrick stiffen, "Of course that is if you are willing. If you choose otherwise they will not learn that from me," he said.

Patrick's eyes narrowed as he paused over his food, "Why would you do that for me?" he said suspiciously obviously expecting some other angle to ensnare him.

Aiden pressed his fingers together into a steeple and gave Patrick a frank look, "Because you have been trying to protect my granddaughter," he said plainly.

For the first time Aiden saw Patrick lose some of his detachment as his face paled slightly before suspicion formed in his expression, as if, he was being toyed with for some reason. He could see the question form in the younger man's face whether he said the words or not, Patrick wanted to know who he was.

"She never mentioned any living relatives before. We found out at Drury that both her parents and guardians died. There was no mention of any other relatives because the police were looking for them after her guardians died. We did that much research on her when we found someone was trying to harm her," stated Patrick flatly.

Aiden smiled slightly, "First, she never knew about me which was for her safety. Second, her parents lived under assumed identities to protect all of them, which unfortunately failed after nearly eleven years. Third, my son and his wife adopted her to hide the fact she was my daughter's child because we did not want Kendall thinking she was his daughter and seize her. My son lived as if estranged from me to protect his family, but somehow Kendall figured out that she was alive and where she was which I believed happened because of a spy within my own house. After that, I helped a Detective Medina to hide her from everyone and only she had any idea where my granddaughter could be found. Thankfully, the detective was clever and put an altered case file in her computer and files because we believe Kendall sent men to acquire my granddaughter's whereabouts. They were foiled. Yet again, I believe he located her because of a spy in my house and try as I might, I haven't been able to root him out. He's been too clever. So you can see why I have not announced my existence to her and handpicked men I trust to secretly meet you in Thurles. They were not told anything until they were well away from the estate," he said.

Finally Patrick came out and said it, "Who are you?"

Watching the man keenly, he said, "My name is Aiden Keane," and the man's face changed to an expression of recognition at the name.

"Then she really is Bryn Keane? We wondered since we could find no past information on her parents," said Patrick.

As Aiden thought about it, he realized some key facts, "I guess technically she is Keane since Rory and Fiona never had a formal union to avoid attention. She is actually Rory's daughter, confirmed by a paternity test my daughter had done after Bryn was born. Apparently Kendall did enough to research to find Bryn's birthdate, which was only about six months after Fiona slipped out of his grasp. Of course no one, but Bryn's parents and my son's family knew this in North America at the time and Liam only found out about my granddaughter after his men caused the accident which killed her parents. They actually thought she died as well and I did the best I could so that people believed that publicly. She suffered grievous injuries in that accident and came close to dying."

Sighing he continued, "Her blindness was a devastating truth for us all. Of course, I could do nothing to help her financially and they will not perform experimental surgeries on children. Then with her body growing and changing, even if I had been able to help, any permanent fix would have to wait until she was an adult. My son could not appear to afford such an expensive surgery once she reached her eighteenth year or it would have announced contact with me no matter what appeared on the surface. It was difficult to know I could do nothing without endangering her. Once my son died, I helped to relocate her in a city where an accomplished friend had retired so that he could give her the help she needed."

A glimmer of understanding lit Patrick's eyes, "Then you know Donal Meany," he stated.

With a nod, Aiden said, "Yes. We have been friends a long time and spent early years at school together until our chosen professions diverged our schooling. Of course, Bryn does not know of the connection and I have been very careful about anyone here knowing of the connection except for one man. However, Donal did not explain the risks Bryn seemed to be taking and based on your earlier comments when we first met, they were considerable risks if Drury was interested in her."

A hint of a smile crossed Patrick's face, "He may not have known exactly what she did. At Drury, she was quite cagey about revealing any experience and the Commander even pressed her for details at one point. I believe her response was, "You brought me here to help not to reveal my secrets," he said.

Smiling, Aiden said, "Ah she sounds so much like Fiona. I could never force her to do anything and would only succeed in prompting the opposite response from her if I tried," then more soberly, "That is how she ended up with Liam Kendall. I tried to warn her away from him."

"Do you have a picture of your daughter?" said Patrick suddenly.

Hesitating, Aiden appraised the man at such a request and realized he was trying to determine the validity of his claim of Bryn as his granddaughter so he reached behind him for one of the digital prints on his bookshelf of Fiona after attending university. Handing over the cherished print, Aiden watched Patrick closely. If the man truly knew Bryn, he would see the uncanny resemblance to Fiona and, in his own way, Aiden could take measure of the man as he was apparently doing to him.

An expression of startled recognition crossed Patrick's face telling Aiden the man truly had met his granddaughter, "They could be sisters they look so much alike," he said.

His manner changed abruptly and Aiden could see Patrick believed everything said after seeing the image before handing it back.

With a sigh, Aiden replaced the image on his desk, "Perhaps you can tell me why Bryn was so unhappy when my man brought her back to Donal's home after the latest situation since you seem to know her better than I do. He could not explain why she was not glad to be free from Drury," he said.

At that question, Patrick's face hardened, "The Captain of the team that took us all to the southeastern operations told every man taken in their raid that night and no doubt her, a man she worked with died after they waylaid us. They were very close though some speculated a great deal more between them," he said flatly.

All Aiden could do was stare at Patrick for that information initially before saying sadly, "My granddaughter has lost too many people she cares about and if what you say is true, it explains a great deal about her mood. Donal thought she was greeting over something," when he saw Patrick watching him closely he clarified, "A manner of speech we use for grieving. She would only speak to Donal and would not acknowledge the man I sent to watch over her. Bryn has lost more people close to her in twenty-two years than most people do their entire lives."

Sadness seemed to cross Patrick's features at those words and the knowledge appeared to shake him significantly Aiden observed. *For an operative, the man seems far too compassionate to kill on orders or ignore situations where people might be suffering unless of course this man also had some relationship with Bryn,* he thought.

"Were you close to her?" said Aiden after noting the man's reaction.

"Not as close as I wanted to be. It would be frowned on at Drury and she probably did not see me the same way. I couldn't blame her for that after working like an indentured slave for years," said Patrick sighing.

Making a sudden decision that he had planned for, Aiden reached in his blazer pocket and removed a high tech COM unit to hand over to Patrick, who looked at it startled before taking it.

"What it this for?" said Patrick uncertainly.

"Whether you choose to work for me or not, I am releasing you. I know you will return to keep an eye on Bryn and since you have her best welfare at heart, I want you to be able to contact me if there is a need. Based on

things you have described, I suspect she has already noticed my men watching over her and is no doubt alarmed
by them given her past history. One person stands a better chance of watching over her without unsettling her
unduly," said Aiden pointedly and then added, "I gather
you have an alternate way of locating her?"

For the first time, Patrick openly grinned, "You could
say that, but I will save that for another time, at least
once I know she is safe," he said.

Chapter 15

A sound of a lock clicking roused Bryn instantly, she did not bother to check to see who was entering in dead of night since that would cost valuable time, instead she needed to get out of the room and instantly headed to the window. It took great care to raise it, maddeningly slow, so that whoever was jimmying her door lock would not hear and resort to breaking the door down. Once a sufficient gap opened, Bryn slipped through not bothering to change from the light shirt and shorts she wore.

Barely noticing the damp chill that clung to her skin, Bryn quickly and noiselessly traversed the slanted eave in her bare feet before dropping to the ground silently. She had to bite back a gasp as rocks bruised her feet. It suddenly dawned on her, *Where can I go*? and that thought nearly choked her with terror. In the city, where she lived in North America, there had always been some place to run or hide, but this village was small with few options to conceal a person trying to stay unnoticed.

People in rural Ireland maintained livestock unlike the city environment she was used to, so Bryn decided to find a barn or stable to slip into until daylight. However, Bryn had only passed a few buildings when she distinctly heard the swish of clothing behind her. Whoever was trying to enter her room probably succeeded and the partly open window would be the only logical place she could have gone in the middle of the night when most people would be sleeping. Deducing that would not take a rocket scientist and someone obviously circled about the bed and breakfast to see if they could catch sight of her.

Was this one of the men she marked as Shay moved her from village to village? Or was this someone else, like men from the boss man that grabbed her off the street, Bryn never did get any disclosure about that situation. Apparently the man who questioned her after seizing the three Facility men, Nighthawk and the man Donal called, Devin, did not feel she deserved any in depth explanation of his so called operation she disrupted.

Pressing against one of the buildings, Bryn froze at the sound of muttering behind her that anyone, but someone with acute hearing like hers would miss, so she knew there was more than one person trying to find her. A crunch of shoes on gravel ahead of her told Bryn they were attempting to cut her off which left her only one option: Out into the moors that she knew nothing about. Shay gave her some information about the moorland type areas where farmers let sheep roam, but there were pitfalls such as bogs and deep crevices within the rockier areas, sometimes hidden by shrubbery unless you knew what to look for, he had said. Of course Bryn did not have a clue what to look for regarding either hazard had it been daylight and certainly not at night even though she attempted to scan the area with various modes of vision.

As a visitor unfamiliar with the terrain, the last thing these people following Bryn would expect would be that she go out into the moors, so that is exactly what she did. Due to her sensitive hearing, it was not long before Bryn heard swearing behind her in the distance when the people attempting to pin her between them realized she had somehow eluded their trap.

Faintly the words drifted to her, "The crazy bitch must have headed into the moors," though she could not tell the gender of the speaker, she had little doubt it was male as most women would not usually choose to perform such duties or work for people that would make them accept such a task.

There was a grim determination in Bryn's mind now and she suspected her pursuers just might follow her, which she soon confirmed by electric torches waving about behind her. They could not know about her eyes and her abilities see much better than a normal individual, which gave her a margin of potential escape. Her pursuers would assume she could not get far stumbling in the darkness and that was her advantage, not much of one granted, especially with the cool damp night, barefoot, and unprotected from the elements.

Things became worse when thunder rumbled in the distance and the men behind began to curse increasing the speed of their search, which drove Bryn at more reckless speed than she wanted to take in unfamiliar territory. Not to mention she was bruising and scraping her feet horribly, every toe felt abused, but she dare not slow down.

Thunder came closer and Bryn deviated at right degree angle from the men in case they began to wave their electric torches further ahead. Unluckily or maybe luckily, the land rolled away suddenly sloping downward and Bryn was unprepared from continuing to glance behind which precipitated her rolling over rocky broken ground adding even more bruises to her body.

She lay there curled into a ball biting her lip to stifle groans of pain suspecting the sound would carry in such an open space which was confirmed by words filtering to her, "Did you hear something?"

Galvanized by the query, Bryn made it to her feet somehow and pushed her abused body onward again changing direction in case her pursuers managed to get an idea where they heard her fall. Blood pounded in her

ears from fear and tension at being so exposed and unable to hide effectively. If she could only determine it was
only two people, Bryn considered standing her ground
and fighting, but she knew from her recent experience
that was highly unlikely. Besides, she had no idea what
sort of weaponry they had, which could disable her and
unlike the mountain installation, she was not cornered.
At least not yet…

Then it happened, she should have expected it, but
Bryn had allowed fear to cloud her mind and was not
paying attention where she was going instead of what
was happening behind her. From one second to the next,
Bryn took one running stride and instantly found her
body in something cold, thick, and wet all the way up to
her chest. One thing Shay never mentioned was what to
do if you ever fell into a bog, which is what she guessed
was exactly what happened to her. Soon as she attempted to move toward the closest edge, Bryn felt her body
sink to the shoulders and froze instantly. Now she was
totally helpless, she had no skills to deal with this predicament, no one to call except people who wanted to
capture her, leaving her with two choices: die or let her
pursuers capture her. No one else would know where
she went or where she was.

For the first time in her entire life Bryn encountered
something more frightening than being blind, completely
at the mercy of something that had no mind, no emotion,
and no remorse. Panic threatened to consume her until a
whispered voice literally made her jump.

"Catch my belt," the voice whispered and Bryn could
see it fall just within reach, "Move very slowly, don't jerk
your arm or you will sink more," added the voice.

With painstaking slowness Bryn inched her hand
closer to the belt as advised attempting to keep her panic
under control, so far she only saw one person, a man by
his size, and she could handle one man if he turned out
to be one of the pursuers.

Once the man felt the tension on the belt, he began to pull her to the edge until he could catch her arm and then pulled Bryn out easily telling her this man was quite strong; a disquieting discovery.

"Come with me," he whispered, "They aren't far behind."

It could have been a ruse to disarm her, but Bryn knew she had little choice and surprisingly this man had a North American accent, not Irish, besides he offered potential escape. She noted he wore some type of eyewear which probably gave him some ability to see in the dark from the sureness he seemed to know where he was going other than that he appeared dressed in general Irish clothing common to what Bryn had seen in the residents.

A crack of thunder overhead followed by a drenching rain made her companion swear softly, but from Bryn's initial point of view, at least it would help wash mud and grime from most of her body. That positive thought was quickly replaced with dismay when she began to shiver violently as the rain cooled her body rapidly. She had nothing to help retain her body heat until the man literally pulled off the high-necked sweater he was wearing before forcing it over her head.

"It's wool so it will retain heat when wet, but keep moving," he whispered grimly, "Try to warm your body. We need to find shelter, preferably a place with a fire before we both die of hypothermia."

"You should have kept the sweater," whispered Bryn back.

"I have more muscle mass that you, I generate more body heat, and I'm dressed bettered for the climate than you are currently," was the whispered retort and all quite true.

Irritated that this unknown man might think she was a fool, Bryn whispered tartly, "I didn't plan to be out here. I wasn't given a choice nor did I have time to acquire appropriate clothing."

The man actually snorted in amusement to Bryn's disgust, she suspected he did not believe her, but now was not the time for a heated discussion that might be overheard. She would set him straight in more secure surroundings.

Even though it continued to rain, the sky began to lighten somewhat telling Bryn she had been running for some time now and following an unknown man that could potentially lead her straight into more trouble. Ahead Bryn could see what looked like a barn and apparently her companion could also see it as he changed direction toward it obviously hoping to provide shelter against the elements. Soon there was enough light, whatever eye gear the man wore he removed stowing it in a pocket of his shirt before entering the barn.

To Bryn's annoyance the man caught her arm, pulling her just inside the door out of the weather before holding up his hand in an obvious command for her to wait there until he checked the area. *Like I'm some helpless woman*, she snarled in her thoughts forgetting just how this man found her.

When he returned, he gestured her to follow him to an area filled with straw, "Take off your clothing and crawl into the straw. The longer you keep wet clothing on the quicker you will lose body heat," he said as if it was the most normal thing in the world to do for any woman to strip off all her clothing in front of a strange man.

"You'll pardon me if I climb into the straw first before I remove my clothing," said Bryn sarcastically.

The insufferable man actually coughed a laugh, as if she would not know it for what it was and shrugged before stripping off his own clothing not all perturbed that he did not know her. *Men!* She thought repressively which brought to mind Ryan and her ire was replaced with a stab of pain.

"Rub your limbs to help circulation, unless you need help," he said and though Bryn could not see his face, the tone of his voice said he was grinning.

Knowing he was baiting her, Bryn did not comment, but her mind was turning over a few surprises for this arrogant excuse of a man. She watched as he lay out their clothing to dry, if that was even possible in such damp air and no sunshine refusing to let her eyes wander in spite of noticing his well-muscled upper body. From what she could see of his features he had shoulder length dark curly hair, a similar colored mustache, and possibly dark eyes though it was hard to tell in that light. She looked away quickly as he began to turn in her direction.

Unable to understand why this man aided her, Bryn asked, "Who are you? Why did you bother to help me? How did you even find me?"

"My, my, we are inquisitive," he said drolly as he worked his way into the straw and began chaffing his limbs.

"I guess that means you decided not to answer," said Bryn fuming inwardly.

"And when did I say that?" said the man with laughter in his voice.

"I'm certainly not going to beg for answers," said Bryn repressively.

A soft laugh from the man, made Bryn grind her teeth that in some way she seemed to be amusing him with about every word she said unless he just enjoyed taunting her.

"To answer your last question first, I've been keeping an eye on you for a while because you haven't been safe, even here. I know you had no choice about running tonight, I saw them slip into the bed and breakfast and there were four more men outside. I don't know how many actually went inside. I suspected you would use the window so I was waiting. When they headed you off, I knew you only had one choice: The moors. Not the wisest course, but as you said, you had little choice and it worked, they never expected you to go that way. So I followed you before they started their search. I almost said something to you when you fell, but you jumped up so fast and started running, I never got the chance. When you disappeared from view suddenly, I thought you stepped into a crevice. Scared me that you might be seriously injured or worse and when I found you, your circumstances were hardly any better. You would have died out there if those men never looked in that direction unless that was your plan to avoid capture," he ended sardonically before adding, "Actually I think I answered question two and three."

Bryn was not certain whether to be angry or not, he actually sounded impressed by her tenacity, but subtly mocked her questions.

After a lengthy silence, he said, "As for whom I am, it might be better if you get some sleep first before I discuss that with you."

That comment completely puzzled Bryn, she could not understand why sleep would make any difference, but the man said no more and seemed to settle into the straw to sleep.

Waking was not a pleasant experience for Bryn, every part of her body felt like someone had taken a hammer and bludgeoned her with it, she was stiff, but worse, chilled to the bone. She felt ill, now she was stuck with a man she did not know and men chasing her, if she went to a medical facility, anyone could find her easily.

Movement nearby brought her to full alertness and she noticed the man was clothed though without his sweater, when he noticed she was awake he tossed her clothing to her. To her surprise, he turned away allowing her to dress and did not move until he heard her moving out of the straw. He handed the sweater back to her barely damp though he did not look at her.

Bemused, Bryn asked, "How did you manage to dry the clothing without a fire?"

"Using the straw and some old blankets I found," he said quietly not sounding the brash person from the previous night, "How are you feeling? You look pale."

"I feel like a tenderized piece of meat," said Bryn facetiously that incited a soft laugh from the man noting he kept his face averted.

"To answer your first question from earlier, you might want to sit down. I have a lot of explaining to do if you let me," he said still facing away to Bryn's confusion.

"I doubt I'll need to sit," said Bryn tartly.

Sighing the man turned toward her, but two obvious differences glared out at Bryn, he had no mustache and his eyes...HIS EYES...were piercing grey just like...and Bryn screamed as if she had seen a ghost. Throwing her body backward into the straw Bryn turned to run and did not realize she was trying to scramble up the inside barn wall bloodying her fingers, scraping her knees all the while screaming.

Powerful arms enfolded her and instead of an unfamiliar American voice she heard Ryan's voice...it *was* Ryan's voice, kept pleading, "Easy darlin, you're going to hurt yourself even more than you are. Please calm down."

Alternately screaming and weeping, Bryn kept struggling until she had no more energy, her body weakened by illness and injury. He was real, he was touching her, but why did he let her think he was dead?

Angry, hurt, relieved and a variety of other emotions took over, Bryn sobbed out, "Why? Why did you let me think you were dead?"

Ryan sighed in her ear, still holding on tightly, "I didn't know they told you I was dead darlin, not until recently. I was going to come to you, but there was a complication, I'll explain if you will hear me out and stay calm. You're already bleeding and I don't have anything here to care for your hands or knees."

In response, Bryn relaxed and Ryan cautiously released her until he was satisfied that she would not repeat her attempt to climb the barn wall in a blind panic. He turned her to face him though it felt strange to look at him with black hair as she started to reach for it and jerked her hand back as if burned.

A look of sadness crossed Ryan's face at her reaction and he sighed obviously feeling she would not forgive him, but he began to explain, "When they brought us all back to the southern region headquarters, I wasn't conscious anymore and had no idea where I was initially. They only treated my wounds enough to keep me alive and did not completely heal me so I suspected what that meant. They were deciding if I was useful anymore," that comment chilled Bryn, "And they wanted to debrief me first. I knew they would have any surveillance footage because Kendall's men wouldn't have had time to delete it. I knew they would see me deflect that barb intended for you, but they would also hear the comments about protecting Kendall. They would have seen the footage about you. Since people from the Facility were attempting to remove me, I think they felt it compromised my position if any of Kendall's men saw it. They told me I should have let you die," here Ryan's jaw muscles flexed in anger, "but I would stop that dart again if put in the same situation."

Bryn clapped a hand to her mouth in horror; Ryan looked at her puzzled, "It was my fault," she whispered agonized, "I told them you saved my life when I insisted upon seeing you. That's when they told me or hinted actually, that you died. I probably sealed your fate the second I said anything about you."

Ryan reached out tentatively and rested a hand gently on her knee, "No darlin, I think they had already made up their minds by the time they talked to you. Besides, Kendall would know that wound was fatal without treatment and that the breach would grab any men left. It is doubtful he would ever trust any of his men once they were seized."

"However, I overheard that one of the doctors was going to try to keep you for study, but the Commander at the Facility was using all his resources to get you out. Apparently there was another man there that had a trump card in your favor and they had to release you to Dr. Meany. Soon as I knew you were free of that place, I slipped out half healed knowing I didn't have long to live," he sighed.

"I couldn't go to a hospital, the Facility, or even Dr. Meany. The first two places they would have found me easily and I didn't want to put Dr. Meany in harm's way with a burn notice on me."

"Burn notice?" interjected Bryn in confusion.

"It's what they do to rogue agents in many organizations. It means termination by any force necessary to any other agents that find the rogue agent. The Facility would have to comply with it so I was a dead man if I ran there. I had to hide so I could heal the old fashioned way, but I tried to stay close as possible to you without being too near that I would endanger you or Dr. Meany. By the time I healed enough, you left the country and I knew you wouldn't be safe abroad, especially if Kendall left the country, too. It wasn't easy getting out of the country with every kind of agent looking for me to claim the bounty because they know how to look for disguises. Once I did get out and managed to get to Ireland, I caught up with you at the first place you stayed. People were already watching you there though so I couldn't just walk in and announce my presence to you. I had no idea if they were Kendall's men or agents who suspected I might come to you waiting to pick me off and you with me. I did manage to slip in one evening, but I think I frightened you," he gave her a sheepish look, "when I left a rose."

Bryn sighed in relief at least *that* was explained, "At first I thought it was my guide or one of the men who came to the pub," she said humorously, "until I asked about it then paranoia set in."

A hardened look crossed Ryan face at the mention of Shay, "That one has hopes," he said flatly.

Hesitantly, Bryn reached out to the hand on her knee, covering Ryan's hand and squeezing it, "He never had a chance. He came out one night in the garden to discuss moving to different villages, but instead saying anything first, he put his hand on my shoulder. Needless to say, he ended up spitting dirt out of his mouth," she said ruefully.

That information gave Ryan the broadest grin she had ever seen on his face and his tension eased immediately, he had been jealous of Shay and Bryn could not really blame him due to the circumstances that kept him from getting close to her.

"I planned to contact you once you moved to another village, but some men protecting you waylaid me and brought me in for questioning. They only let me go once they were satisfied I was there to help you and that is where you need to go once we get out of here. There may be different people, other than Kendall, who are trying to get at you darlin and we need more help," said Ryan earnestly.

"If they are trying to help, then why didn't they contact me?" said Bryn suspiciously.

"Because they didn't think you would trust them and run. If you left the country it would be harder to protect you," said Ryan.

"So they sent you?" said Bryn warily.

"Not exactly, I had my own agenda, but I am satisfied they do mean to protect you," said Ryan confidently.

"Back up a minute, you said you had a 'burn notice' on you. You made that sound very encompassing, what is going to happen to you here if they find you?" demanded Bryn.

Ryan paused as if gathering his thoughts before saying, "It is revoked in Ireland courtesy of one of your benefactors here. As long as I stay in Ireland, no one will touch me," he said evasively, but it explained why he did not want her to leave the country.

"And who is this benefactor?" pressed Bryn.

"It's best that you hear it from them," parried Ryan skillfully.

Bryn fumed, "Why are you refusing to answer?" she demanded.

Ryan actually rolled his eyes, "First it isn't my place to tell you. Second, you don't need anything to worry about right now, especially until after we get some help," he said.

"Anything to worry about?" her tone incredulous, "You mean like slipping from a window in the middle of the night with nothing but a t-shirt and shorts because people are breaking into my room and proceed to chase me across the moors in the middle of the night? Or, falling into a bog only to be pulled out by a strange man? Of course, I had nothing to worry about when a cold drenching downpour eventually led to a barn with a strange man who told me to take off all my clothing before crawling into a pile of straw. Then that same man, the following morning, reveals he is someone I care about that I thought was dead, which scared me half to death since I thought I saw a ghost! You certainly have a warped sense of worrying me," said Bryn sarcastically.

Ryan stared at her for a second or two after such declaration and threw his head back laughing until tears rolled down the insufferable man's cheeks; she never had seen him laugh like that, ever.

"Ah me, Bryn," he gasped out, "How I've missed you and your sense of humor."

"I wasn't trying to be funny," she said taking a swipe at him with her free hand which Ryan grabbed grinning.

Suddenly he turned serious when Ryan caught sight of her bloodied fingertips, "We need to find a farm house and get some help to take care of these scrapes before they get infected. Are you hurt anywhere else?" he said as his eyes roamed over her exposed skin.

His lips thinning at the sight of the livid bruises on her exposed skin told Bryn he was unhappy about her condition, but all she said was, "I can manage," until she tried to stand, she instantly crumpled to the floor from a stabbing pain in her feet after one foot settled on a small stone.

Before she could stop him, Ryan grabbed one of her feet and hissed a curse at the lacerations he found, "Damn it Bryn, it looks like someone took a knife to the soles of your feet. You aren't going to walk anywhere," he said in tone of no compromise.

"But...but..." she began to sputter.

"People will stare? And they won't stare if I drag you by your feet? Of course I can always throw you over my shoulder, you should be used to that," he said drolly.

"Just where did this brash personality come from all of a sudden?" snarled Bryn impotently at man she once considered so serious.

Ryan actually snorted in amusement, "We were under surveillance almost constantly at the Facility. In spite of our relationship I still had to be careful about what they saw between us just as you knew you had to do the same. You never want people like that to know too much about you, especially in that line of work. I suspect there is a lot no one knows about you either darlin, especially me," he said pointedly.

"So you're saying there is a whole other side of you I don't know?" said Bryn suspiciously.

Ryan grinned and did not even try to deny it, "Most definitely. Here I don't have to keep up appearance to protect either of us. You aren't going to distract me from carrying you either," he said.

Suiting actions to words, Ryan stood, caught one of Bryn's arms, pulled it about his neck and put an arm about her waist and under her legs before lifting her with ease. Irritated though she was Bryn knew she had no recourse because he would toss her over his shoulder if she gave him trouble, she knew he was not just teasing her about that reminder.

As he negotiated the barn door burdened with her, Bryn toyed with his hair, "What did you do to your hair?" she demanded.

Ryan snorted, "It's only dye darlin, it can change back or it will grow out. I couldn't leave it the same with people looking for me," he said.

"Something is different about your face, too. You didn't have some of these scars or swellings," she said worriedly.

"Enhancements I can remove. There are many ways to disguise features, but unless a surgeon actually changes your bone structure, some facial recognition programs can still flag you as a possible suspect. I couldn't go to anyone like that so I had to be creative. Besides if I changed too much, you might never believe it was me before I could find someone to reconstruct my original features," explained Ryan.

Daylight was actually fading to Bryn's surprise, "We slept most of the day?" she said uncertainly.

"We needed it. It was a long night. If we don't find a warmer place tonight I'm worried you're going to get ill," said Ryan grimly.

Bryn sighed, she had not fooled Ryan a bit, he could tell she was not feeling well and no argument was going to stop him even if he had to keep walking in darkness to find them a safe haven.

"You can't carry me all night," said Bryn tartly.

Ryan snorted, "You still haven't been eating enough. Actually you're lighter than the last time I carried you so it seems you do need someone to look after you," he said pointedly.

Bryn sputtered, "That's not true! Especially here! They've been stuffing me with so much food each place I stop I must have put on at least ten pounds since I've been here," she said indignantly.

"Then you must have been far too thin before you arrived," concluded Ryan grimly, his tone indicating he knew why she had not been eating because she had been grieving over his supposed death.

Hiding something from Ryan was nearly impossible so Bryn gave up trying to defend her eating habits or lack thereof and silently fumed until her acute sight identified a structure that looked like a house in the distance.

"I think there is a house up ahead," she said though Bryn felt mortified at the thought of approaching the homeowners in her bedraggled condition.

The sun was just touching the horizon when Ryan approached close enough that Bryn saw an older man outside working about his house and picking vegetables from a garden, at least until he looked up at their approach.

"Lawks!" the man exclaimed or something that sounded like that to Bryn as he had a very heavy accent "Is dhe lady hurt young man?"

"I'm afraid so and we were lost on the moors last night caught in that storm," said Ryan ruefully, his accent much stronger than Bryn ever heard him use.

"Shite! Um beg yehr pardon miss," apologized the man for his outburst, "Come inside, m'missus will help clean yeh up young woman and yeh both must be famished."

The man moved very surely for his years, obviously fit and opened the door calling for his wife urgently, "Maggie, got a couple here been lost in dhe moors last night during dhat storm," said the man.

A grey haired slender handsome woman came out of another room with a cry of horror, "Flynn get some chairs near dhe fire, dhey must be chilled to dhe bone," said Maggie as she bustled into another room only to returning with heavy blankets.

"Mam," said Ryan respectfully, "my lady has cuts that need attention, could we bother you for some hot water and remedies you have on hand?"

After tossing blankets about them both, Maggie pushed between them, "Let me see dear," she said kindly holding out her hand.

Bryn could refuse nothing to this kind woman and held out her hands, Maggie gasped in dismay, which turned to horror when Ryan indicated her knees as well as her feet.

"Yeh poor thin," moaned Maggie, "Flynn, get me some basins, she needs to soak dhose feet to get dhe dirt out of dhose cuts before I seal dhem," to Bryn she said, "Yeh've got splinters in yehr fingers," she reached for a tweezers-type instrument before beginning the process of removing the slivers of wood from Bryn's skin.

Flynn placed a basin on the floor for Bryn to soak her feet and one on the table in which Maggie placed her hands once she removed all the slivers then she began cleaning the scrapes on her knees.

"Really, I can clean those scrapes, you're being far too kind," said Bryn embarrassed.

"Girl, yeh look too peaky to sit upright," said Flynn grimly as he placed the back of his hand on her head, "She's burnin with fever Maggie."

With a gasp Maggie bustled over to a beautifully carved cabinet and removed a bottle, she placed a cup on the table before pouring a measure of dark liquid into it, "Drink dhis dear, it will help dhe fever and stop dhat illness in its tracks. Tastes horrible, but it works!" She said proudly.

That warning in mind, Bryn knocked back the dark fluid into her mouth and swallowed quickly, she gasped as her throat constricted as if on fire feeling her eyes pop with a very bitter aftertaste.

"What was in that?" croaked Bryn, her eyes watering.

Flynn chuckled, "A bit o'Irish whiskey in dhat. Dhe alcohol dissolves dhe ingredients even after all dhe technology out dhere, alcohol is still some of dhe best medicine," he said with a grin and a wink at Ryan who was also grinning at Bryn's reaction.

Maggie touched Ryan's face carefully and looked into his eyes, "You seemed to handle dhe weather better o'course yehr dressed better dhan yehr girl. What possessed yeh to let her outside like dhat?" she said disapprovingly.

Ryan introduced them both then told the couple more than Bryn thought he would and it made sense, besides these people deserved the truth though she hated that look of dismay on their faces that anyone could harm another person is such a way.

"My lord, girl, if he hadn't followed yeh…," said Flynn his expression ashy.

"I'm afraid we made free with one of your barns in the wee hours for some shelter from the rain," said Ryan ruefully.

"No need t'apologize boy! Yeh had a need. Yeh both need to stay dhe night and on dhe morrow I'll take yeh both into town. Yeh need to see a physician girl, just to be sure. Dhat remedy is all around good, but it doesn't cure everyt'in," said Flynn warningly.

Maggie was tsking at the bruises on Bryn's skin, "I can't do anyt'in about dhose unfortunately dear. I'm afraid dhey'll have to heal dhe hard way," she sighed.

"You've both done enough already!" exclaimed Bryn urgently.

"We're about to eat supper and yeh both need to eat from dhe sound o' dhat story. We have more'n enough," said Maggie as she bustled off to what was probably the kitchen.

"Let me see dhose hands girl so I can put lotion on to heal dhem up," said Flynn holding out his hand and Bryn obediently offered each hand to him.

"I'll let yer man get yer knees and feet so he doesn't t'ink I'm making free with me hands," teased Flynn his eyes twinkling.

Ryan laughed as he took the lotion from Flynn and then applied to her knees before moving to each foot so that the pain of the cuts mercifully faded, he was about to stand to remove the basins, but Flynn stopped him.

"Nay boy, I'll take care of dhat. Yeh just rest with yer girl. Yeh both need it after dhe night yeh've had," said Flynn as he whisked away the basins heading toward that same door that Maggie used.

Bryn stared into the fire until she felt a gentle hand cup her chin and looked over to see Ryan searching her face, "You look a lot better after drinking that remedy, tired, but more color in your face," he said relieved.

It was not long before Maggie came bustling out with dishes, Irish stew made with fresh vegetables, fresh salad, fresh brown bread with heavenly rich butter, Flynn deposited some sort of ale in front of Ryan though Bryn declined in favor of water.

When they were done, Maggie brought out tea and what she called a pudding, which Bryn knew back home people would call a cake, but instead of sugary frosting, she had used whipped cream. It was decadent and very good.

"My compliments to your cooking Maggie, if I may call you Maggie," said Bryn hesitantly not wanting to offend.

"Bah we don't stand on ceremony here me dear," snorted Maggie humorously, "If I may be so bold, yeh look like yeh could use some sleep in warm bed. First let's get yeh in a warm shower and clean dhe moors off yeh. I'll give yeh somet'in to wear while I clean dhose clothes. On dhe morrow I'll give yeh some old t'ings to keep yeh warm until yeh get to dhe village in the morn," she gestured Bryn to follow her.

Flynn and Ryan watched them go before Flynn turned to Ryan with a grin, "I've never seen a man more in love dhan yeh boy. She's a rare prize dhat one. Got grit to her even if she's not from Ireland, but from dhe look of her she's Irish stock come home," he said.

Ryan smiled back at the older man, "Oh she's the most important thing in the world to me. You're right, too, she's Irish stock come home and now I hope to convince her to stay. We haven't quite talked about that yet," he said uncertainly.

Flynn pondered that last comment as he surveyed Ryan, she trusts yeh, but I can see she's like a wild t'ing yeh can just pin down. Remember dhat and she'll stay by yehr side, force her and yeh will push her away. I have a daughter a lot like her, can't tell her to do a t'ing. I can tell yehr girl's been through a lot, it's in her eyes and she needs yeh," he said solemnly.

"You're so right. No one can force Bryn to do anything or she fights back. She can be quite fierce for a little thing," said Ryan half in admiration, half rueful.

Flynn chuckled and shook his head, "Yeh'll do fine. I can tell yehr not married, at least not yet and we're not so old fashion dhat we'll keep yeh both separate if yeh plan to stay dhe night with her. Unless yeh don't t'ink she will agree," he said inquisitively.

Ryan hesitated a moment, "I'll stay with her. In part I want to be near in case your remedy didn't catch everything and that fever comes back in the night. The other reason is I don't want to let her out of my sight especially after she was forced into the moors," he said.

Flynn patted his arm and made no comment, he refilled their tea before chatting about inconsequential things while Maggie was busy helping Bryn get ready to rest.

Bryn was nearly asleep when a gentle hand cupped her chin and a soft kiss touched her cheek followed by Ryan's soft voice, "Darlin, are you ok if I sleep in here with you? I trust these people, but I don't want to leave you alone, not after how long it took finally get close to you."

For answer, Bryn pulled hand to her neck hugging it to her like a pillow and Ryan chuckled softly before crawling into bed next to her; she immediately snuggled against him with a sigh of contentment.

The creak of the bedroom door roused Ryan instantly, he immediately shielded sleeping Bryn until he was certain of the person entering who turned out to be Maggie, she called softly, "Are either of yeh awake?"

"I am Maggie. Bryn is still asleep," said Ryan relaxing and yawning.

"Let her rest a bit longer dhen. I'm makin breakfast for yeh both before Flynn takes t'dhe village. I have yehr clothing here all cleaned, a pair old wool trousers one of me daughters left behind, for Bryn t'protect her legs from dhe chill and stout coat she can use 'til she gets t' her t'ings," said Maggie leaving the clothing on a chair by the door.

"Thank you, Maggie. I wish there was some way to repay you both for all your kindness," said Ryan seriously.

"Nay boy, we were glad of dhe company and pleased t' help yeh both. If dhere is anyt'ing wantin, it would be another visit from both o' yeh some time," said Maggie with a smile before closing the door again.

While Ryan was dressing Bryn woke groaning a bit from stiffness, "Maggie brought your clothing in and left you a few things to get you back to the village. Breakfast will be ready soon and then Flynn will take us back. Are you feeling alright?" he said walking over touching her face to check for fever.

"Stiff mostly, but I expected it. I don't feel ill if that is what you are asking. Whatever Maggie gave me to drink last night zapped any cold that was trying to take hold," said Bryn snorting with amusement and heard Ryan chuckle.

By the time they left the room, Maggie had porridge, eggs, bacon (which looked more like rashers of ham than what was called bacon in North America), fried tomatoes, and that wonderful brown bread with butter setting on the table accompanied by hot tea. It all tasted fabulous and felt just like sitting at home with her guardians so long ago, Bryn missed them terribly all of a sudden.

When they were done, Maggie lent Bryn an actual handmade coat of embroidered felted wool, it was beautiful and she would be sure to send it back with Flynn when they reached the village. No doubt Maggie either made it herself or it was passed down to her from her relatives.

Maggie hugged them both as if they were family, Bryn felt a lump in her throat; it had been so long that she felt such security or warmth of relations. She thanked her for such wonderful hospitality. Bryn inwardly vowed to do something for the couple when she could even though they never once alluded to any recompense.

Flynn had a modern vehicle as well as horses, but since Maggie had no shoes that would fit her, it left Bryn wearing socks so he decided a traditional cart ride to the village would not be wise. "Another time young Bryn, I'll take yeh about dhe old way when yeh got some stout shoes t' protect yehr feet," he said with a smile.

Once in the village, Flynn pulled up to the bed and breakfast and Bryn removed the coat Maggie lent her, passing it to the older man, "Thank you for all your help. Please thank Maggie for lending me this beautiful coat," she said gratefully.

"We were glad to help Bryn. Yeh both take care now and stay outta dhe moors," said Flynn shaking his finger at them before he drove off.

Even with the socks protecting her feet, Bryn still felt the bruises as she began to hobble toward the entrance of the bed and breakfast when Ryan intervened by scooping her up to her embarrassment. He managed maybe two steps before Shay marched out with a hard expression flanked by two men, one of who seemed familiar and Bryn felt Ryan stiffen defensively.

"What did you do to her?" demand Shay flatly.

Tension increased in Ryan so much his arms felt hard; Bryn intervened, "He didn't do anything. I know this man. Someone broke into my room two nights ago and forced me into the moors. If he hadn't followed to help me I probably would be dead in a bog," she said.

Her quick defense of Ryan rocked Shay back on his heels with a fleeting look of disappointment on his face telling Bryn the man's interest was still there and the tension in Ryan said he noticed though he relaxed somewhat at her defense of him.

One of the men next to Shay, the familiar one, leaned over to whisper to the guide who grudgingly nodded which was when Bryn recalled where she had seen the man before: Devin, the man who took her to Donal from the place where they told her Ryan had died.

Her eyes narrowed suspiciously as she looked at him, but Devin did not attempt to speak to her directly, he probably knew she would refuse to speak to him or trust him.

"If you don't mind, Bryn needs to get inside so she can acquire her clothing," said Ryan pointedly.

Shay's eyes narrowed at the familiarity that Ryan used her name and his shoulders slumped slightly, he probably read all the signs of Ryan's feelings noting Bryn accepted him passively after tossing him, Shay into the dirt, not long ago.

Though she suspected Ryan could not hear, Bryn's acute hearing caught Shay speaking to one of the men, "How long has he been with her?" his voice filled with heavy disappointment, "There was no sign of him when she got here and she never mentioned him."

Another voice answered almost too low for Bryn to hear, "It's a long story, but best in private," said a man and they either moved out of range or chose another venue for discussion.

Ryan set Bryn on her feet inside the door where the floors were smooth and in some places carpeted, the proprietor hurried over to her, "Miss I'm so glad to see you. We found your room broken into and you missing. We feared the worst and called the Garda, but no one could find you. I'll let them know you've returned. They would like to question you in case you were robbed. Please check all your things to be certain," he said urgently.

"I'm so sorry I was part of the reason for any damage to your property," said Bryn ruefully.

"Responsible? Hardly miss, how could you be? Sometimes ruffians come around and they like to target tourists thinking they have a lot of money or they are foolish enough keep it in their luggage. That was why I was glad you placed your passport and any other valuables in our safe even if thievery is not usually common around here. People will mark tourists at the airports and watch them if they think they might get easy pickings," said the proprietor with some annoyance about the criminal element that all countries deal with to some degree.

Ryan followed her to her room, it was in disarray, but Bryn had little more than clothing except for toiletries after placing any money or documents in the proprietor's safe. Unfortunately, she did not think they were looking for money or even her passport, more likely they were hoping for clues of her plans or even her possible whereabouts when they lost her in the moors.

"Get your things together darlin, I want to take you where I know you'll be safe and if you want the guide to keep showing you around, he can work out from that spot. I'll behave around him," said Ryan, a little irritation in his voice at the thought of Shay's company.

"I saw, Ryan. I know he isn't happy you're here. I was never interested in him, please believe me," began Bryn hurriedly until Ryan placed a finger on her lips.

"I know darlin, I saw how you acted with him. You were polite, but didn't encourage him and he saw it too, even if he didn't like it. Men can be stubborn if they want something bad enough," said Ryan half smile.

Bryn snorted in disbelief, "Can be?" she said incredulously and Ryan chuckled his eyes twinkling.

While Bryn changed her clothing and packed, Ryan attempted to neaten the room, righting any turned over furniture or straighten a rug, he slung the smallest of her luggage pieces with strap over his shoulder as she finished before capturing the remaining small bag. As she followed him down the stairs to get her passport, travel documents, and money, Bryn wondered what transportation Ryan intended to use to take them to this safe place he mentioned.

Men in uniform were waiting downstairs that the proprietor introduced as the Garda, apparently local law enforcement, and they proceeded to ask questions about unlawful entry into her room.

Seeing no reason to prevaricate, Bryn told them everything, as she had no idea who the men were and it was always possible they were thieves or at least she let the Garda believe that without involving her prior history.

Several people moved closer to listen and more than a few gasped in horror about the bog where Ryan finally located her then began to drift away after she explained about Flynn and Maggie.

"Miss Keane, you're lucky this man followed you. Even in these times people still occasionally die in bogs. It doesn't seem anything was stolen so other than damage to the building, there isn't much to hold against them. I understand why you didn't wish to get close enough to observe any faces, but we certainly wish you had," sighed one of the uniformed men.

Since she had nothing else to add, the Garda resumed speaking with the proprietor and Ryan led her out of the building where Bryn instantly noted the man she knew as Devin was waiting with a vehicle. Her suspicions roused instantly.

Bryn halted mutinously, "No!" she defiantly as the Devin held the door open for her.

Devin's face hardened briefly, "Miss Keane, I have done nothing to harm you. My goal has always been to help you even when you didn't know it back in North America. I am not one of the people hunting you," he said flatly.

"You only pulled a weapon on me and people trying to help me while I was wounded. You would have left him," indicating Ryan, "to die," she practically snarled.

A flash of anger crossed Devin's face, but then he seemed to consider what she said from her point of view and suddenly nodded, "I see your point given those circumstances and the state of your injuries though understand I had no idea of your connection to this man at the time. All I knew is that Drury Facility had essentially kidnapped you and held you against your will for years per Donal Meany. He told us what he thought happened to you, but it took us a long time to track down what organization actually had you. It seems this man left us a clue to help, but of course I did not know that at the time either. If you will come with me there is a lot more you will finally understand and maybe get most of your questions answered," he said more politely.

It was not until she felt Ryan grip her shoulder that Bryn finally relented and entered the vehicle, Ryan stowed her luggage before he slid into the seat beside her.

"Is Shay not going to come with us?" queried Bryn noting the guide's absence.

Devin glanced in the rearview mirror as he settled behind the steering wheel, "You won't need a guide for this trip, but if you still would like him to show you around," here his eyes flicked to Ryan, "I will notify him later," he said.

Suddenly, Bryn realized that Shay had been put in place to keep an eye on her too, she fumed inwardly and felt Ryan squeeze her arm as she struggled to speak civilly to Devin, "So he was one of my unknown guards, too?" she said stiffly.

Devin sighed, so Bryn knew her tone was only marginally polite, "He is a guide of sorts and knows the country well. We know he is trustworthy and that he would keep an eye on people around you for suspicious behavior," he said.

"Did you manipulate me to visiting Ireland?" demanded Bryn her temper flaring.

"Miss Keane, I don't deny we wanted you to come here and Donal was hinting for you take a vacation. We considered manipulating you, I don't deny it, but circumstances actually worked out strangely enough. It was hard to protect you in North America or you would not have lost your relatives so tragically. And before you think Donal Meany was party to any conspiracy, he had been living in North America before you were born pursuing his research. He just happened to be a contact we have known for years and when you needed help, he offered as friend of the family. He's a good man that would not manipulate anyone," said Devin succinctly.

An honest answer was completely unexpected and it left Bryn speechless, but it also left her with more questions than she started with which she suspected Devin would not answer from the set of his jaw. Oddly, Ryan had returned to the taciturn man she was familiar with and had not uttered one word, he only touched her to reinforce his support allowing her to talk or maybe vent would be a more appropriate term.

"I apologize for being rude," said Bryn as neutral as possible, but Devin only nodded in mute acceptance and did not offer any more conversation during their drive.

Chapter 16

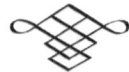

Devin had a lot to think about on the drive to the Keane estate, he fumed inwardly at the sneering hints and in some cases outright accusations from Bryn Keane, he had known Fiona Keane well, even hoped to marry her at one time. Her daughter could be a nearly identical twin not just in appearance, but personality, though actually Bryn seemed even fiercer than he remembered of Fiona. Though his anger made him unwilling to be charitable, he had to admit Bryn had been through a great deal more than her mother ever had and had even less chance at a normal life since she was ten years old. He felt a brief stab of sympathy for Shay, it was obvious the man he knew as Patrick Kelly was in love with Bryn and Shay had been desperately attempting to get her attention, but she cared deeply for this man with her, it was obvious. Sighing, Devin realized that except for Donal, this man had probably given Bryn the only connection to any sort of secure feelings since Jimmy and Irene died.

Of course Bryn could not know of his history with Aiden Keane or with her family and to have his loyalty or integrity questioned by this girl irritated him immensely, if he had only known of her connection with this man,

Patrick Kelly, before he pulled out that weapon...too late now. He would have to earn her trust the hard way unfortunately.

They pulled up to the Keane estate and Devin noted with irritation, Bryn's suspicious expression was back on her face; he opened her door politely, however allowing Patrick to get her luggage. Surveillance remained hidden, Devin had messaged ahead to keep any additional men from being present to avoid spooking Bryn after the way she responded to seeing him as well as her ordeal in the moors. That blasted Patrick had to be one of the most resourceful men he had ever seen to have managed to save Bryn from that situation in the moors when his own men did not even catch a whiff of trouble until the unknown men had already entered the bed and breakfast. It stung Devin's pride about his job and he felt he failed Aiden by letting those men get that close to his granddaughter.

Once inside the grand old foyer, Devin directed Bryn and Patrick to a sitting room to wait so that he could inform Aiden not only of their arrival, but all that had passed, including his granddaughter's reactions on the way here.

"Make yourselves comfortable. I'll announce your arrival and return to guide you through the house," said Devin quietly before leaving the room.

Bryn glanced about the sitting room of the grand old castle she saw as they drove up, it had many ancient antiques, old leather bound books, and exquisite art probably collected for generations.

She was aware Ryan sat watching her still uncommunicative and wondering why he reverted to his Nighthawk persona, as she decided to style it, but she did not ask, partially because she did not think he would give her a straight answer. He seemed to be waiting for something.

Aiden noticed the long awaited arrival of his granddaughter on the monitors wavering between uncharacteristic anxiety about meeting her finally and impatience for news after hearing of the disturbance in the outer area of Thurles. A knock on his office door indicated Devin had arrived to bring him news and impressions of Bryn since bringing her to the estate, he pressed the button to allow the door to open.

A grim faced Devin walked in, instantly alerting Aiden that something had not gone as planned and his friend was more than a little irritated, but he waited until the man sat, offered him glass of whiskey, which was gratefully accepted.

Aiden folded his hands and waited until Devin began to speak, first explaining about the forced entry into Bryn's room, "That blasted Patrick must be one hell of an operative. He got wind of it before we even suspected and managed to catch up with her in the moors. Good thing he did because she might have died in a bog," he added grimly.

He continued to explain what happened after, the storm and the older couple that helped them, how Bryn fled with hardly any clothing to protect her from the elements until she returned with Patrick to the village.

"Ok, old friend, what has you so on edge?" said Aiden quietly.

"She wouldn't get into the vehicle with me! As if I was some man of Kendall's organization," said Devin indignantly.

"Did something happen that made her suspicious of you?" queried Aiden carefully.

Devin sighed and explained about the breach on Liam Kendall's safe house, the men from Drury there to help her, and about Patrick in the process of dying from an injury before he pulled a weapon on them all. At least until men from the southern region Agency showed up.

"Ah, so she thought you intended to leave the rest to their fate," said Aiden shrewdly.

"We didn't know that Patrick was important to her. I don't know if Donal even knew so why would I concern myself with collateral damage? Apparently he was the one she was told died by the Agency Commander," sighed Devin in frustration.

"I see. It seems Patrick did not tell us the entire story either and he cleverly worded his conversation with me making certain everything he said was true. Resourceful man indeed," Aiden mused.

"Poor Shay is devastated soon as he saw them together and you'll see for yourself, he's in love with Bryn. She never said a word to anyone or hinted, but then, of course, she thought he was dead. I'd like to have been a fly on that wall when he told her he was alive," snorted Devin caustically.

Aiden raised an eyebrow at that rejoinder in polite query, "Oh Bryn's a fierce one, got her mother's temper and then some. She was snapping and snarling at me part of the way here like I bent the world about her to force her to Ireland. I just told her we considered manipulating her visit, but circumstance fell in our favor so we didn't need to do anything. That at least quieted her, I don't think she expected an honest answer, but she figured out Shay was set to watch out for her. I had to jump in about Donal before she accused him as he was probably the most innocent party in all of it," added Devin irritably.

"And you're upset she doesn't trust you?" said Aiden carefully.

Devin's jaw worked until he spat out, "Yes. If I had known about Patrick before I entered Kendall's safe house or that she had come to some understanding with some of those Drury agents, I would never have drawn my weapon," he snarled.

Aiden sighed. Devin had been with him a long time and came close to being a son-in-law until he interfered with Liam Kendall's intentions toward Fiona pushing her straight into the foul man's hands. It was hard for his friend to feel like an outsider to Aiden's one remaining relative.

"Give her time, Devin. She's been through too much and has had precious few people she could trust that are still living. Losing her parents in that accident and then finding Jimmy and Irene dead, it would take its toll on anyone. She barely had a chance to grow up," said Aiden attempting to placate his friend's ire.

"I know, I know," sighed Devin, "And I guess it's hard to see her too. She could be Fiona's twin and I do still miss her."

"Did you want to join us for lunch?" said Aiden cautiously.

"No, but thank you, she will talk more freely without me present and I would advise you to have your initial discussion in here. I think there is a lot we don't know about her and that dratted Patrick," said Devin crisply.

"Then if you would be so kind as to have them send lunch up before you bring them to the office, I would appreciate it," said Aiden understandingly.

"I'll do that," said Devin with a nod.

Aiden sighed as his friend left, Bryn's mistrust hit him hard and he suspected the man regarded Bryn like the daughter he never had, Devin had been crushed when Fiona ran to Liam Kendall out of spite. Yet never once had Devin said a disparaging word about Fiona abandoning him and since then, he never chose to offer marriage to another woman.

When the door to the sitting room opened, Bryn whirled defensively, but only saw Devin and he said, "Please follow me. Lunch will be waiting. Leave your luggage and someone will move it to a room for you," he said a little stiffly.

Bryn felt a trifle ashamed at her reaction to his entry, Devin seemed to take her mistrust of him as a personal slight and she had been rude in the vehicle so when he brought them to a door preparing to knock, she said politely, "Thank you," his smile was slightly sarcastic as if recognizing her words had been an effort to utter.

In answer to Devin's knock, Bryn's sharp ears picked sounds of series of locks as if this door was built to prevent a determined entry to her surprise making her slightly uneasy, as if they might be entering a prison. Ryan's hand resting on her waist squeezed in reassurance.

As the door opened to admit them, Bryn noted a beautifully laid table set elegantly as any five star restaurant with food all carefully covered to keep warm or cool depending on the particular dish it contained. An older man stood to greet them, something about him was unsettlingly familiar, but Bryn could not understand why, she was certain she never met this man before in her life. He was distinguished, handsome, as tall as Ryan with a subtle strength about him, and dressed elegantly compared to the Irish people she had met thus far, he had allowed some grey to show in his hair instead of dying it. Though he was older, "old" did not really apply to him, he seemed vigorous and suspiciously muscled though not as much as Ryan by any means, but enough that it did not seem to fit with his cultured appearance.

"Please sit and join me for lunch. We have a lot to talk about," he said and Bryn started at the sound of his voice, it nagged at her memory even though he spoke with an Irish brogue.

As she sat, Bryn's enhanced eyes saw a set of digital photographs displayed on a handsomely carved bookshelf with an entire shelf dedicated to memories in an old fashioned way, but it one picture that stunned her. She knew the person even though it had been twenty-two years: it was her mother smiling out at the person taking the photograph.

Bryn lurched back to her feet in fury, "Where did you get that picture of my mother?" she demanded furiously, "Is this some elaborate trick?"

Normal eyes would never have seen the subject of the photograph at the distance Bryn now stood, but in her shock and anger, she had given the man more information about her vision that she ever intended.

Instead of storms of denials or attempts at fabricating a reason for the photograph's presence, the man acted completely unexpected to Bryn's surprise, he stood calmly and went to the shelf to retrieve the picture. He returned with it and handed it to Bryn without hesitation and she took it mechanically though warily.

"That is a photograph of my daughter when she was only nineteen after she was accepted into university. I took that myself and it is one of my most cherished possessions," said the man quietly, but very sincerely.

His heart rate never changed, he was telling the truth or believed he told the truth, Bryn amended, as she looked down at the beloved face of her mother in a happier time. Without realizing it, Bryn's hand caressed the beautifully carved frame until a drop of moisture appeared on the glass from a tear she did not remember shedding.

"Mom," she whispered in anguish, her loss felt keenly as if it had been yesterday and then her mind finally processed what the man said "my daughter," which could only mean the man before her was her grandfather or else he was claiming that her mother was his daughter for some unknown purpose of his own.

Voice cracking, Bryn croaked out, "Why didn't she ever tell me about you?"

Aiden sighed, "Please sit and I'll explain," he said sadly.

Bryn sat as the man explained about Liam Kendall and why her parents fled to North America, which was to protect the unborn child, her daughter from a life under the dreadful man.

"I blame myself for the travesty of that situation. When Liam kept trying to woo Fiona even though she was already engaged, I lost my temper and told her to stay away from him. She ran straight to that horrible man out of spite and all I could do was help her once she realized the mistake she made. Had I kept my mouth shut and ignored the man's efforts, you would have grown up with a normal family, but it's too late for regrets now," said Aiden bitterly.

"My son Jimmy had gone ahead months earlier after a staged argument and rumored estrangement so he could set everything up for Fiona and Rory, with Devin's help, to change their names, arrange false passports, acquire a home and a job."

Bryn was back on her feet pale as death, Uncle Jimmy! That is why this man seemed so familiar, he had his voice even with an Irish brogue and the similarities were there in the older man's face. She was not even aware Ryan had moved, carefully supporting her as if she might faint from the knowledge she just surmised.

Her grandfather, for she knew it truth now that was who he had to be, did not ask her to sit again, kept explaining and his expression turned so grim it made him look much older than he had appeared earlier.

"Neither of them could contact me lest Liam Kendall suspect any sort of connection and begin searching for Fiona again. He never knew she was pregnant, but you were not his daughter, the man you knew as your father, Rory O'Keefe, was your biological father, Fiona had a paternity test even though he never asked for one."

"Everything went according to plan for nearly eleven years. Through Devin, Jimmy secretly kept in touch, but I knew I would never see either of my children again unless Rory could give us enough information to seize Kendall permanently. All those years, Rory documented Liam Kendall's operations, carefully encrypting it and eventually passing it to Jimmy, but before my son could get the information to Devin, someone from an ally organization recognized your father, even disguised."

"After all that time?" said Bryn woodenly without realizing she intended to speak.

Aiden sighed, "We managed to convince Liam Kendall your mother died, fictitiously of course, in Ireland from a vehicle collision, but he suspected Rory ran and that man never gives up until he gets what he wants. Anyone

Liam Kendall had any connections to receive information about your father, that he was wanted alive and returned until someone finally caught sight of him or thought they did. That was enough for Kendall."

Bryn watched her grandfather close his eyes against a memory before he began again, "Devin had returned here to do a few things for me feeling your family was secure after so long, then we heard Kendall's men had already reached North America. He didn't have time to get back before they found your home and I'm sure you remember the situation clearly without any more reminders from me."

"So that man *was* responsible for my parents' death!" Bryn spat out.

"Sadly yes and he moved so quickly we never had the chance to stop him. That was when he found out your mother had been alive when his men transmitted the accident to him and that you existed. The men thought all of you died and we made certain that summation was corroborated publicly and had a funeral for three deaths. Once Jimmy adopted you, we thought the worst was over and Kendall would leave all of you in peace, but he knew Rory had stashed information about him somewhere, probably on a chip of some sort. His men took a computer from the crash, we found that out later of course, but Kendall was able to recover little. What he did manage to recover confirmed Rory had collected information on him, however."

"And then he came for Uncle Jimmy and Aunt Irene," quailed Bryn and this time Ryan did have to keep her from falling as he set her back in the chair still clutching the photograph of her mother.

"It wasn't Jimmy he was after Bryn. Kendall isn't a stupid man, but it took time for him to draw a correlation between you and the young girl in your parents' accident. That of course led him to believe Rory had hidden the information with you or on you, possibly an implant under your skin or even that you knowingly had a special encrypted chip with you. Since Jimmy had told Devin you were spending the day after the local holiday with them, Devin was not nearby when those men arrived and they thought you would be there like most other families gathered. It is something Devin regrets deeply, but no one can foresee all outcomes."

"They were tortured!" whispered Bryn, "Uncle Jimmy recorded a message to warn me, the police said he had hidden it in his pocket."

The grey pallor on her grandfather's face said he knew all this and had suffered each loss with her even if she had never known at the time.

"I knew you were in grave danger and being blind, you could not adequately protect yourself so I worked with that Detective Medina 'off the books' as she called it and we managed to get you into hiding. I suggested the city where Donal lived since he is an old school friend and I knew he would probably be the one person who could help you regain some use of your eyesight after such severe damage."

Bryn was very quiet for a long moment, she looked down at the happy picture of her mother wishing fleetingly for things she could never have before glancing back up at her grandfather. A bit of guilt at her treatment of Devin surfaced, he had been watching over her a long time just as he said and it must have been a severe reality check for the man to know he failed to protect the rest of her grandfather's family. She understood why her grandfather and Devin never came forward to speak with her, they were trying to protect her and keep that Liam Kendall man from locating her. She wondered just how much of this Ryan knew or if any of this was news to him too.

Her mind returned to the reason the man was chasing her and Bryn said, "Neither Dad or Uncle Jimmy ever gave me any chip or told me to keep anything special for them. I assumed it was in Uncle Jimmy's assets they froze because of the murders. When that man grabbed me he kept going on about a chip and I had no idea what he was talking about. They found a special data chip on me, but that was for another job I did."

"We'll talk about that later dear. For now eat something and relax. I would like to finally get to know the granddaughter I never thought I would get the chance to meet," said Aiden wistfully, he meant what he said.

All the food was well prepared and only partially Irish style as her grandfather asked about her childhood experiences, school, and her activities just like any normal grandparent though he raised his eyebrow slightly at the martial arts training.

"Mom said she wanted me to be able to take care of myself," said Bryn a little defensively.

Aiden sighed a little, "I'm not surprised actually after I heard about some of the treatment Liam heaped on her while she was still in Ireland," he said in a tone that indicated he did not disapprove, but he had only been surprised.

She talked about college though left out the incident with Vander, uncertain if her grandfather knew about it or not and soon as she told him about her first job, he beamed fondly at her.

"I was so proud of you when Devin told me. Both of your parents were quite intelligent, but blind you graduated with a master's degree when most people still were struggling with the undergraduate work. It was a great accomplishment with such a disability."

Bryn had the impression Ryan was soaking all this information in and that he seemed surprised about her schooling, he must not have researched that information or it was deemed irrelevant during the Facility background check.

"Donal said you were a great help to him after he worked on your eyesight. You helped him get funding and equipment donations that furthered his work," said Aiden, his manner pleased.

Bryn heard Ryan snort a laugh and her grandfather turned to the silent man finally, "And just what do you find so amusing Patrick?" he demanded quietly.

"Patrick?" demanded Bryn instantly glaring at Ryan.

Ryan looked at her with a grin, "My full name is Patrick Ryan Kelly. My father is Patrick, or Paddy, as some people use here in Ireland. My family always called me Ryan," he said with almost a wicked twinkle in his eye.

Looking back at her grandfather, Ryan said humorously, "Bryn *was* those donations and funding."

Aiden looked back at his granddaughter narrowly, "Oh? Donal said you worked at a little place nearby," he said.

Bryn squirmed slightly glaring at Ryan watching her, "I acquired items for him when I could and sold objects to get the funding," she prevaricated.

Her grandfather was not fooled for an instant, "*YOU* stole those items?" he demanded.

Bryn felt her cheeks heat and saw Ryan was enjoying the entire scenario, "Only from people who stole ideas or equipment rights from other people or firms. Objects of art stolen from the original owners and I returned them for a fee," she said stiffly.

Aiden put his forehead in his hands before looking back up at his granddaughter, "Did Donal know any of this?" he said.

Bryn glared repressively at an amused Ryan, "No, I never elaborated," she said.

Aiden turned suddenly to Ryan, "And you, you clever devil, missing some contacts, a mustache, and a North American accent. Where do you fit into all of this?" he demanded, "Work with Bryn indeed! Not as close as you wanted to be! No wonder they were scared of you when they thought you had gone rogue."

Ryan seemed unabashed, "I never lied to you. I learned long ago my life depended on just how much information an opponent had about you. I was trying to protect her, but I never knew that she thought someone she cared about died, not until after I arrived here. I had to slip out from the southern headquarters still injured because they saw no reason to heal me completely if they planned to terminate my employment."

Aiden observed Ryan narrowly and asked, "How much reconstruction did you have done?"

"Only superficial, I could hardly approach a surgeon for a deeper change. Besides, if I changed too much, Bryn might not believe who I was," stated Ryan.

Aiden snorted, "That and the first place agents would look for you would be at any reconstructive surgeon legitimate or off book," he said with a hint of sarcasm, "And you met Bryn, how?"

Ryan was unfazed by the sarcasm and continued, "I was on loan from the Agency to Drury when we became aware of a thief so skilled no one could locate him or corner him. It took us years of research until one of the men stumbled on an Internet notice board where a potential client posted using weak encryption. It took us awhile, but we finally decoded the board yet even then we weren't certain it had anything to do with the person we sought until one of the posted items was reported missing finally. The thief was extremely clever, resourceful, and totally elusive. Never bragging or leaving calling cards when others were trying to claim they were responsible and he let them which told us he was confident in his abilities."

"We had to set up surveillance to see what kind of person we were dealing with and it took months because the thief didn't take just any job, he was very selective. He never rushed out to acquire the agreed upon item, he planned so carefully we thought we would never catch sight of him. Finally, after months of monitoring a target we finally saw him, crawling up a building like a lizard in a suit hiding body heat, slipping in and out of that building like a puff of smoke. It was impressive, so quick and slick, not one mistake. I was told to follow to see where the thief would go, to observe only, but I wasn't certain if he saw me at one point when he climb through an upper story hotel window."

"Men watched the hotel and Drury sent agents in to question people and gather evidence. They found nothing for their trouble, it drove the Commander crazy and we kept reviewing all the footage of people who left the hotel and interviews until I noticed an anomaly," here Ryan sighed regretfully, "A blind woman in a high priced hotel. She could have been wealthy, but I checked, surprisingly she was a local and listed as working in a modest job, not a socialite, so it made no sense for her to stay in such a place. We suspected she was a go-between for the man we actually sought and being blind would be a great cover for a drop since she was listed as legally blind. We followed her, which ultimately led to Donal Meany, we investigated him, but couldn't determine where he fit in or even if he was part of it. They would meet in a park and talk, but never said anything important if they thought anyone was close enough to hear. We almost discarded that avenue until a check of missing high tech equipment with the same lack of signature, the kind a scientist would find useful even if it was never listed on the Internet board. That was when we knew there was a link."

Bryn groaned in dismay, she had not been careful enough or they would never have known about Donal.

Ryan glanced at her, but he was not amused any longer, he seemed to sense her regret, "Drury sent men to question Dr. Meany about Jean Easly still with the belief she was the go-between for the thief and him. Then he sent her a scram signal and we lost her. We had no other option, but to watch the Internet board for more activity and even if Dr. Meany had known of the board, we never mentioned it so he would not be able to pass the information along. Another few months passed and the thief eventually responded, so the Commander set up an operation to catch the thief, this time so he could present the offer of a contract or so I believed at the time," his nostrils flared in anger.

"We forced the thief into an error so he would take the quickest way out where we would be waiting. Once he got to the roof of the nearby building where we were waiting, some of the men attempted to seize him and found they had made a mistake assuming it would be an easy catch. Half the team was disabled within a minute and the next thing we knew, the thief literally dived off the roof and grabbed a flag pole further down like he was some sort of Olympic gymnast, totally unconcerned that it was several hundred foot drop below. Next, he was up and running down one of the ledges like it was a broad path until our chopper was in the air. Then he began to climb lower until a three story high ground mounted flagpole came into view, he literally dove off the building until one of the team did the unthinkable and used a climbing dart to stop him. It pierced his thigh and we pulled him back up to the roof to secure him. It wasn't until we reached Drury's infirmary that we found out it was Bryn."

Aiden stared at Patrick in morbid fascination with the growing sense of horror about what his granddaughter had been involved in and knew Donal could not have had any idea she was taking such risks.

"Good lord, Bryn, what were you thinking? What was your father thinking teaching you such skills or arranging for you to learn them? I know it had to be Rory because Fiona would have no clue where to begin. You could have been killed! Do you know how many organizations were looking for that thief to use as an asset?" he demanded, "It was only a matter of time before any of us found you."

"I did what I needed to do," said Bryn uncomfortably.

Aiden threw up his hands and rolled his eyes in futility gesturing for Patrick to continue, "Everyone was surprised we brought in a woman. The doctor treated her wounds and I was sent to bring her to the conference room to discuss the contract work, but she had other ideas," Ryan snorted humorously, "Even barely recovered and befuddled with sedative, she nearly destroyed the infirmary to get out and nearly got by me if her recently healed leg had not buckled."

"Understandably, she was uncooperative due to the way we brought her in and refused to consider a contract unfortunately," said Ryan grimly, "The Commander or maybe it was the Tabula, refused to take "No," for an answer and they used what was tantamount to blackmail to force her cooperation by invoking Dr. Meany's name. I was assigned as her caretaker when I protested the situation and tried to keep her safe against potential reprisal or injury if she attempted to escape. She is more accomplished than any of us dreamed, but she suffered a great deal during that time. The Agency recalled me to resume my place in Kendall's operation since he arrived back in North America, but before I left, I demanded they release Bryn. I had originally planned to leave on my own and take her with me until the recall came, obviously I could not take her there. Had I known Kendall was after her though, I would have moved her myself instead of finding her tossed on the floor in front of me while I was undercover amid an army of men."

Aiden stared at Patrick a long few minutes and felt the desire to immediately forbid his granddaughter from any such future activities, which took all his self-control to keep from uttering, he knew what effect it would have after what happened with Fiona.

Reorganizing what he really wanted to say, Aiden finally turned to his granddaughter, "My dear Bryn, please have more thought for you safety now. Donal told me about that toxin which apparently Patrick here sought help to cure as you were dying. I know you can't discuss the situation, but I was terrified I would lose you too. I want you to have a chance at a normal life, one you were denied so long ago, but I accept you are your own person and obviously active. If you wish to stay involved, albeit in a less hazardous way, you are welcome to work with me as I know you have other skills that will not require you to breach hostile targets," he sighed, but hoped Bryn would not consider his offer a demand.

Bryn stared at her grandfather impressed, he made an effort not to couch his feelings in the form of a demand obviously concerned for her and she glanced at Ryan, who appeared thoughtful.

"And Ryan?" she said glancing to the man at her side.

"Pat...err Ryan as it were, had an offer that he has yet to answer so I don't know his decision," said Aiden surveying the younger man.

Ryan glanced at Bryn uncertainly, "Before I make any plans, I want to visit my family. I've been gone a long time and obviously could not keep in regular contact with them. My first priority was to see that Bryn was safe before anything else," he said quietly.

"You're going to leave me here?" demanded Bryn furiously.

"Darlin, you will be safe here. Our adventure on the moors should show the risk you face wandering about alone when you have people searching for you..." but Bryn launched to her feet, clutching the photograph, not quite concealing tears rolling down her cheeks and raced to the door.

"Let me out," she yelled furiously, pounding her fist on the door, which would not budge and had no obvious way out until the clicks of locks or bars moving heralded the door opening, she ran out.

Aiden frowned at Ryan, "You hurt her, why? I can tell you love her, but you intentionally made her think you brought her here as some sort of duty," he said in displeasure.

Ryan expression was sad and confused, "She isn't certain about her feelings for me. What I want she must want also and if she doesn't it will only torture us both," he said quietly.

"And what exactly do you want from her," snapped Aiden angrily.

"I've wanted to be with her for several years now, but she never actually told me how she felt or if she planned to stay in my life. I won't force that on her or hound her for something she isn't prepared to give me. I want to marry her, I have wanted to marry her for several years, but obviously, I couldn't pursue such a goal with her trapped in Drury," said Ryan candidly.

Aiden reorganized his thoughts, Ryan knew Bryn very well and that he could never force a relationship with her, but how could the man not see his granddaughter feelings for him?

"That young woman loves you Ryan," said Aiden flatly.

"I want to be certain she knows that and not love the idea of me when I was the only man she could turn to," said Ryan not put off in the least by Aiden's comments.

"You are referring to Seamus, her guide, aren't you?" demanded Aiden.

"He is one yes, but she now has options, a chance to interact with more men of her own choosing, not forced into their company. The last thing I want to see in her eyes is the wish she had moved on after being with her for years, but if she won't be happy with me then I want her to find someone she can find happiness with," said Ryan with barely concealed agony for what he was doing.

Aiden paused this time in understanding, Ryan was giving Bryn the chance to go free if that was what she wanted, "You love her that much you would stand aside for another if you thought that made her happier?" he said in wonder.

"I do, with all my heart," said Ryan unable to hide his pain from the other man completely, "I know you will keep her safe and she needs time to think now that she knows I'm available. Time in peace, not running across moors forced to rely on me. She may never forgive me for leaving her here anyway."

"Don't under estimate her boy," said Aiden sternly, "She is a lot like Fiona and my daughter rarely changed her mind unless someone tried to force her in the opposite direction. Even when she married Kendall, she never loved him. Devin had been my daughter's intended and how I wish I had left matters alone," he ended ruefully.

"That is exactly why I am doing this, I want her to choose me and fight for what she wants and if she doesn't, then I have to accept the feelings I hoped from her were never there in the first place. That I was deceiving myself with a delusion," said Ryan wistfully.

Aiden sighed in futility, he understood what the man meant yet it warred with the pain his granddaughter was dealing with at the thought this man was walking out of her life. His reasons held merit, especially since Bryn had not been given a choice about Ryan's company in the past. There was a possibility he was correct, Bryn was comfortable by continued association and not exploring other options.

Ryan stood, "I will keep the COM device you gave me so you can always contact me. If she asks for me, let me know and I'll come. If I work for you and she decides to finish with me, I can perform at a distance to make it easier on her," he said quietly before taking his leave of the office.

Devin sat in thought while Aiden Keane dined with his granddaughter and the man known as Patrick until sometime later he heard pounding on the office door, as if someone were trying to break out. Alarmed that something had gone wrong with the meeting, Devin leapt toward the door only to be nearly knocked over by a distraught Bryn clutching something in her hands, but she was alone. Hesitating, Devin could hear the two men speaking in low voices so he waited outside knowing Aiden's surveillance would show him on the monitor. It was not long before the man he knew as Patrick also left, but he passed Devin by without a word and continued down the hall.

Confused, Devin entered the office to see Aiden looking unhappy still sitting at the table set for supper, his employer glanced up and beckoned him to a seat before explaining what happened toward the end of the meal.

"Just like that, he is going to walk away from her?" demanded Devin incredulously, "I don't believe it, not the way he looked at her."

Aiden explained the rest of Ryan's words and Devin sat back into the chair dumbfounded, "He wants her to have a chance to know other people to be certain of her feelings," he said quietly.

Devin snorted, "Shay will be pleased, but he doesn't stand a chance, not the way your granddaughter just left this room," he said.

"He makes sense, Devin. She's so much like Fiona and he knows exactly how to handle her, probably better than either of us ever will. No one wants to feel that someone they love is settling for them by default and he loves her enough to let her make that decision," said Aiden unhappily for Bryn's pain.

"Before all of that, did everything go smoothly?" said Devin changing the subject slightly.

Aiden stared at Devin in consternation, "If you only knew what she had been up to and what she hid from you. Donal never knew a portion of what she was doing, he would have had heart failure," he said in amazement proceeding to explain Bryn's activities after Donal restored her vision.

Even hard to perturb Devin stared in bold-faced shock at the information surrounding Bryn's secretive activities, "Everyone was looking for that thief for years. We couldn't even manage to get close to approaching the person as an asset. It had to be luck they stumbled across a link to her. I had no idea Rory trained her like that or arranged for her to learn such skills and I doubt he ever thought she would apply them in such a way. All this time it was your granddaughter...and we thought it was a man!" he sputtered unable to continue.

"Patrick, who prefers to be called by his middle name Ryan, it seems, did not disclose much about her accomplishments or abilities, he may not even know the full scope of them. Even Donal isn't completely certain how Bryn's eyes have developed only relying on her to indicate if she had any problems or report unusual adaptations. Of course once they seized her, Donal made certain to avoid the subject at all costs and kept any information about her in his head so no one could hack or steal it. I suspect Bryn is full of many more surprises and my friend have the men be very careful with her, from things Ryan did not say and some of what he did, she is a very dangerous woman," warned Aiden.

"That slip of a woman?" said Devin almost laughing.

Aiden held up a finger for attention, "What is your impression of Ryan? As an adversary?" he said musingly.

Devin grew quiet, "A very dangerous man. When we cornered him I had the feeling he was quite capable taking on more men than most, which is why I kept men spread out and at a distance. Even then, it's my belief that he allowed us to take him out of curiosity and had we been a threat to your granddaughter...well...we might have all regretted it, if we survived at all," he said cautiously.

Aiden described Bryn's capture and initial tenure in the Drury infirmary, Devin whistled in surprise and disbelief that a woman could make an impression on Ryan in such a state.

"I had no idea, none at all," stammered Devin worriedly, "She could have hurt you Aiden before she knew you were her grandda."

"I don't think Ryan would have let that happen. He was watching her like a hawk at first, prepared to stop her. I heard some comments about Kendall's safe house breach during a meeting I thought were an exaggeration. I'm going to have them send me a copy of the seized surveillance footage to review," said Aiden picking up his dedicated land line.

It did not take long for the request to receive an answer and Aiden was decrypting the files with Devin in the room before bringing it up on a two-way monitor on his desk so they could both view it. Both men witnessed the devastation Bryn wrought on Kendall's men instead of trying to escape and making a beeline for Kendall, seeing a person they now knew as Ryan shield her from a projectile meant to kill or disable her. They saw Liam Kendall's arrogant face turn to fear confronted by Bryn looking like the aspect of a creature from a horror movie, silent and predatory. Finally they witnessed her attempt to kill the man just as the safe house was breached and then some of the remaining men of Kendall's riddling her body with various projectiles as Bryn gave no thought to her own life.

"Those three are the ones from Drury," said Devin in a voice devoid of emotion just before his own countenance appeared on the monitor pulling a weapon on them just prior to the arrival of the Agency contingent.

"My god, Aiden, she's lethal, almost unstoppable. If that's what Fiona and Jimmy's deaths did to her, I have no words to apologize for failing to protect them. Shay could never handle her, I don't think any normal man ever could," said Devin feeling the first tears roll down his cheeks since Fiona's death.

Aiden knew Devin might never reconcile what he felt Bryn had become, but he had to try, "My friend, you did not do that to her, Liam Kendall did. Need I remind you that she did not resort to such measures until she felt her death was imminent or Ryan would have certainly commented? Drury would never have brought her in after witnessing a performance like that for any amount of money. Dangerous as Bryn is, I do not believe she is a cold-blooded killer nor would she kill anyone unless she had no other choice. I saw that much in her tonight," he said soothingly as possible.

Devin removed a handkerchief to wipe his face, "Why did she run into the moors instead of retaliating?" he said.

"I thought about that. I suspect Bryn uses confrontation as a last resort based on her most recent choice of career. Also I think she refused to risk people around her, possibly intended to lead any pursuers away to protect innocents in the village. She still has a conscience Devin, you needn't worry about that." Aiden referred to the monitor, "I believe she was going to die fighting for her life like any cornered person or animal would do on instinct. I repeat, you did not cause her irreparable harm," he persisted.

"What do we do now that...Ryan has left...at least for the time being?" said Devin.

Aiden sighed, "Let her think, sort through her feelings and try to relax. If Shay is still willing, maybe continue to show her about Ireland, with precautions in place obviously. Let Bryn handle his interest, don't warn him off or we'll be interfering with her life," he said and Devin nodded.

For days, Bryn sat on a window seat looking outside wondering if she would be allowed to leave her grandfather's house or castle though she never asked during meals because he tried to keep them involved together, like a normal family. Her grandfather did not seem perturbed by her silence and would talk about the area, friends, or relations, even showing her old family histories and photographs.

One day during breakfast, her grandfather asked, "Would you like to continue touring Ireland?"

"I was under the impression it was not safe," said Bryn quietly subdued.

Aiden sighed, his granddaughter seemed so wan and bereft, but she never asked about Ryan, as the man requested, so he did not call him yet if her demeanor did change soon, he just might call anyway.

"Devin will send people ahead to check everything out and keep their distance. Shay will be happy to continue if you're interested in seeing more of the country. There is no reason for you to stay in the house staring out of the windows or at the walls. I know you exercise in the gymnasium, but there is more to life than that," said Aiden firmly.

"I would like to see Maggie and Flynn please," said Bryn quietly.

Aiden cast through his mind trying to recall who those people were until Bryn noticed his confusion, "The couple that helped me after I was lost in the moors," she clarified.

"Ah, the Connells, yes, I can arrange for Devin to take you for a visit if you like," said Aiden.

Later, Bryn found she was in a vehicle alone with Devin as they drove to the opposite side of Thurles where the Connells lived, but there was no conversation most of the way, until she finally said to the man in the seat next to her, "I owe you an apology for the way I treated you. I really did not know you looked after my family for so long and what you must have felt when they died, too. My grandfather said you almost married my mother and that Uncle Jimmy was a good friend of yours."

Devin was silent for a moment and realized Bryn truly meant the apology, "You couldn't have known and you weren't supposed to for a lot of reasons, the largest part was in hopes you might have as normal a life as possible. I won't deny I was angry after your family trusted me for years and you completely discounted me. I thought about some of the things you said and had I been in your shoes, I doubt I would have been any more accepting of some stranger confronting me with a weapon in the middle of a war zone. I had no idea you had an understanding with the Drury Facility or I would have approached the entire situation differently," he said quietly.

It was not long after those words that the vehicle arrived at the Connell home and Bryn left the vehicle

without waiting for Devin to open her door, she saw
Flynn outside working in the garden. He grinned and
waved gesturing her to come over until he realized he
did not know the man with her, Flynn glanced at her in a
startled way, but made no comment.

"It's good to see yeh girl. Yehr lookin much better and
warmer," teased Flynn with a twinkle in his eye.

They chatted a bit while Devin waited in the background until Flynn shooed her off to the house to see
Maggie. He waited for her to go inside before approaching Devin uncertainly.

"What happened to Ryan? Dhe girl looks so sad,
please tell me not'ing happened to him?" said Flynn in
anxiety.

Devin answered discreetly, "He traveled to see his relations so she could spend some time with her grandda.
They never had a chance to meet until recently," he said.

"Her grandda? Which would be who?" said Flynn
narrowly.

"She didn't know until she left here, but her grandda
is Aiden Keane," said Devin cautiously.

"Shite! I would never o'guessed dhat. What dhe hell
was she doing in dhe moors dhen?" demanded Flynn.

Devin discreetly explained again guessing that Flynn
Connell thought people had marked Bryn as wealthy and
may have attempted to extort money for her if they knew
the name of her grandfather.

After a little more discussion, Flynn invited Devin
back toward the house, but both men stopped outside
when the sound of sobbing reached their ears accompanied by heartbreaking words from Bryn's mouth.

Bryn opened the door to the Connell house tentatively and called for Maggie, she came out of the kitchen her
face lighting with a huge smile when she saw Bryn. The
woman walked up to her and hugged Bryn as if she had
been one of her own daughters, "It's so good t'see yeh,

girl. We were talking about yeh dhe other day wondering if yeh'd both return t'visit us," said Maggie smiling.

"Is yehr young man outside wit' Flynn?" she asked kindly.

At that question, tears began to flood down Bryn's cheeks to Maggie's alarm and the older woman enfolded Bryn in her arms, "Dhere, dhere pet, what's happened?"

"He left, Maggie. Once he took me to meet a grandfather I didn't even know I had and said he was going to visit his family he hadn't seen in many years now that I was safe," sobbed Bryn.

"I didn' know yeh had relations near here," said Maggie in a soothing voice.

"Neither did I. I thought all my relatives died years ago," said Bryn.

"He'll be back pet, I've never seen a man more in love dhan dhat one," said Maggie patting Bryn's shoulder.

"He didn't say he was coming back Maggie. He told my grandfather he wanted to make certain I was safe before he left," wept Bryn.

Maggie sighed, "Bryn, did yeh tell dhe boy how yeh feel about him?" she asked softly.

"He knows," sobbed Bryn.

"Dhat's not what I asked pet, did yeh say dhe words t'him?" insisted Maggie, "Men can be daft buggers girl and dhey aren' good wit' hints. Yeh got t' tell dhem plain out right."

Images flew through Bryn's mind and she sobbed even harder, the only time she ever alluded to her feelings for Ryan was in a brief note left in his quarters, she never once uttered the words, "I love you," to him though he frequently had said them to her.

"He doesn't think I love him, does he? Because I was a fool not to say it and he's gone now," said Bryn in shame, weeping at her stupidity.

"Now, now, yeh don't know he t'inks dhat dear. It could be he's givin yeh space to t'ink and if he does have family, he does have dhe right t'see them if it has been a long time. It sounds like he was given yeh time t' get t'know yehr grandda too," said Maggie soothingly.

"Here, sit down pet and let me get yeh some tea. All's not lost, yeh can still tell him dear and I bet he'll come running, no fear he'll stay away. We saw how he looked at yeh," smiled Maggie gently.

Her breath shuddering, Bryn sat and Maggie returned with tea as well handing her an embroidered handkerchief to dry her face just as the two men came inside. Maggie supplied both of them with tea before joining them at the table with little cakes and Flynn proceeded to tell his wife who Bryn's grandfather was.

It seemed the Connell's knew of her grandfather and the entire Keane family history, both speaking admirably about them.

"We owe prosperity to dhis area because of yehr family Bryn," said Flynn smiling, "From way back in dhe old days. Dhey were always good people, kept others from starving in bad years and helped manage dhe land."

Devin checked his watch after a couple of hours of chatting, "Miss Keane, your grandfather is expecting you back for lunch I can let him know if you want to change your plans," he said politely.

"Nay, nay," said Flynn urgently, "Spend time with yehr grandda Bryn, we'll be here when yeh want to come again. Don't take family for granted!"

"Thank you both for letting me visit again and you Maggie for letting me cry all over you," said Bryn ruefully.

Maggie patted her hand gently, "Come any time yeh need to talk pet. Remember what I told yeh," she admonished after giving Bryn a hug.

Devin remained silent on the drive back to her grandfather's home and Bryn did not feel inclined to talk instead, she berated her stupidity in silence for assuming Ryan knew how she felt about him.

Surprisingly Devin joined them for lunch, but Bryn did not enter any discussion and kept her eyes on her plate thus missing the two men exchanging significant glances during the meal. They waited until after she excused herself from the table and left the room before beginning a completely different conversation.

Aiden glanced once more in the direction his granddaughter left and said, "What happened? She looked upset when you returned."

"It seems Bryn was talking to Mrs. Connell and though I didn't mean to eavesdrop, Mr. Connell and I didn't want to interrupt them so we waited outside for a convenient moment to enter. She is still very upset about Ryan leaving and Mrs. Connell finally made her see she hadn't really told him how she felt. I suspect that now Bryn is in a quandary of how to contact Ryan after Mrs. Connell told her she needed to speak to him," explained Devin.

"I'll let him know, but I want to give it a little while longer so he at least has a chance to spend time with his own family before any big changes which are bound to occur in both their lives as soon as he knows she wants to see him. He intends to marry her and I suspect he will want to make preparations along those lines with his family before he arrives," Aiden mused.

"In the meantime, I'll see if she will do some more sightseeing with Shay so she isn't sitting about fretting," said Devin wiping his mouth with a napkin before rising from the table.

A few days later Bryn was in the gym working and a man named Quade made his regular stop for a visit, he apparently was another relation, a second cousin or something from her grandmother's side of the family. He was handsome enough dark eyed, black haired with a mustache and not much older than her, but there was something about the man that bugged her, a furtive air about him as well as slightly narcissistic. His opinion of his appeal put her off and he made no secret of the fact he thought he would be a good match for her.

Ignoring him, Bryn continued to work out struggling with the dilemma of how to contact Ryan after she stupidly ran from the room without bothering to ask where he was going or if she could call him. If she lost the chance to be with him, Bryn knew she could only blame herself for her childish behavior.

When Devin walked in, Quade's attitude changed abruptly looking at the newer arrival narrow-eyed before choosing to leave the gym without further comment though Bryn noted Devin watched the man leave.

To her surprise, Devin asked, "Is he bothering you Miss Keane?"

"Nothing excessive, but he seems to have a high opinion of himself," she said sardonically.

Devin snorted, "He does at that. Your grandda doesn't turn away family, but if he gets out of hand, please let me know," he said courteously.

"Did my grandfather need something?" said Bryn pausing since Devin usually relayed those requests to her.

"No, Miss Keane, I thought you might like to get out for a while and see more of the country. Shay is available and fresh air does the body good," said Devin.

Since her visit with the Connells a week ago, Bryn had not felt like going anywhere once she realized she had no way to contact Ryan and had been wracking her brain to figure out some way to track him down. Unfortunately, the surname Kelly was as common as the name Smith in North America and Ryan never indicated, at least to her, what part of Ireland his family lived. Ireland was big enough to be daunting when it came to searching for people and Bryn knew very little about the country.

Sighing, Bryn decided Devin's suggestion had merit and maybe it would clear her head for fresh ideas. A part of her secretly hoped that Ryan might actually be watching out for her and that she might catch sight of him, but another more rational portion of her mind that she chose to ignore, told Bryn that he would not be there as he always had been in the past. It made her feel exposed and she hated it.

Finally she nodded, Bryn headed back to her room to shower and change before meeting Devin in the huge foyer where Shay was also waiting. The guide's attitude had shifted to a more distant cordiality to Bryn's relief, but she felt a twinge of remorse that he might have been hurt initially discovering Ryan. Those thoughts mocked her now due to Ryan's absence.

In spite of her sour mood, Bryn did enjoy being outside and tried to give Shay the attention he deserved when pointing out landmarks or discussing history of an area with a silent Devin in their wake. They stopped for lunch in a quaint little pub filled with the usual friendly Irish people and more than few flirting men, though they were polite, Shay seemed to know quite a lot of people.

Soon as the sun began to descend, Devin pointed the vehicle back toward her grandfather's home until they arrived on the scene of an accident and Devin had to slow the vehicle. In the back seat, Shay jumped out of the car as if to help, but Devin bellowed, "Get back inside," to Bryn's shock and then instantly she knew why, it had been a ruse to stop them as Shay melted to the ground with a wound in his chest.

Immediately, Devin jammed the accelerator shifting in reverse, a breaking of glass followed by a hole materializing in the windshield said the men ahead were firing some sort of weapon at the vehicle. To Bryn's horror, Devin was hit in the shoulder, but he never slowed the vehicle's speedy reverse even when blood began to soak the left side of his shirt, she reached over to put pressure on the wound that he could not stop to do, before he bled to death.

"We aren't going to be able to get away Miss Keane. I suspect there will be men behind us soon enough, we've got to abandon the vehicle before they see us and that might not even help. Damn it, I should have made certain men cleared both ways before we traveled, I was care-less," snarled Devin furiously.

"You can't run with this bleeding, you'll never make it," said Bryn shakily.

"Under the seat, a first aid kit, grab it before we get out. We'll have to make do and hope that they can't com-pete with your eyes in the dark. That may be the only thing that saves us because they won't know anything about Donal's work to help you. Get ready, when I back the car into those hedges, it should hide it for a short while and force them to search," said Devin shortly.

"They were hoping to use the darkness to their ad-vantage then?" said Bryn, but Devin only nodded and maybe that was why they went after her in the village. They may have assumed the storm prevented them from catching her and Bryn quailed at the thought they may have been correct. She could have potentially put the Connells in danger.

There was a loud crunching and snapping of wood as Devin rammed the vehicle into a thick bunch of hedg-es, at a distance no one would probably be able to tell, but up close Bryn knew the wood splinters or damaged greenery would be a beacon once someone arrived.

"Out Miss Keane, we have to get distance from the vehicle before they catch up. I've picked a place with as much cover as possible, but Ireland isn't known for extensive forests and we won't have time for much first aid," said Devin urgently.

Devin took over keeping pressure on his wound as he gestured Bryn before him until he found an area that would leave no sign of their changed direction. Once they were concealed again, he halted briefly to allow Bryn to help him bind his wound.

"Don't leave even a scrap of tape or gauze. They will broaden their search when they can't locate us quickly and we don't want them to have any possible clue to our direction," ordered Devin when Bryn finished checking that nothing was left in evidence.

Soon light failed completely to utter darkness other than starlight, "I'll have to rely on you now, we don't dare use any form of illumination," said Devin as he secured a hold on Bryn's arm for guidance since he was unable to see anything, Donal must have told her grandfather enough about her abilities for this man to know.

An image of Shay with that gaping wound in his chest haunted Bryn, "He's dead isn't he," she whispered hoarsely.

Devin sighed beside her, "I'm afraid so Miss Keane. Even if he didn't die immediately they would finish the job to avoid witnesses. Don't you dare blame yourself for that incident it was my fault for not sending men back before we returned. They would have warned us to take another route," he said softly.

"You can't stop everyone. Apparently they still think I have information they want unless this is someone else I am unaware of," commented Bryn quietly.

"You're grandda said you were sharp," sighed Devin, "We think we've had a spy in the house for many years, but don't know his agenda, not completely. There is some connection with Kendall, but it doesn't explain everything. Stop here Miss Keane, I'm going to send a message to Aiden now so he knows what happened and they can locate my GPS. It will still take him time to get men mobilized and a vehicle to us. We'll have to keep moving in moment."

Back at the Keane estate, Aiden was extremely worried that Devin and his granddaughter had not arrived prior to full dark, he kept checking his secure COM for a message to explain the delay. Finally it came and Aiden's jaw hardened at the grim reality when Devin told him about the vehicle being waylaid and Seamus' death though Bryn was unharmed, at least for the moment. It had to be their spy from the timing; only someone in the house would know that Bryn was out sightseeing in the general area.

Aiden sent back a private message that he would send people to help immediately and he barely finished when his grandnephew, Quade, sauntered into the room even more cockily confident than usual.

"Uncle," said Quade with a barely veiled sneer.

"I don't have time for a chat Quade, something has come up I need to attend to," said Aiden turning toward his office, but his nephew intercepted him with an unpleasant grin.

"You'll attend me right now Uncle if you want to see your precious granddaughter alive," said Quade with a nasty smile.

Coldness washed through Aiden, he never guessed he had a snake so close to him as well as part of his family and Quade knew Devin was nowhere close by or he would not be so confident, surreptitiously he activated his COM hoping one of his men might hear.

The hardest thing Ryan ever did in his life was to walk out of that castle without Bryn even if he did it for the right reasons, but he had to know if she really wanted to be with him and not just a convenient companion in her life. He had not lied, Ryan did need to see his family who still lived near the west coast and had not seen him in almost twenty years even though he did try to keep in touch as much as his job had allowed. Too much contact could have put them at risk, like now that he was considered a rogue agent in another country, which easily could have followed him to Ireland. Thankfully, it had not due Aiden Keane.

Eventually, he found his way to Kerry and the town where he grew up. Ryan stood outside the bed and breakfast his family had run for several generations, watching his father chatting with one of the other local men. It felt odd to be standing there gazing through the looking glass.

Ryan walked up to the two men talking, "Da," he said softly and his father turned to him startled.

"Ryan?" said his father with a startled shout, "What the hell did yeh do to yehr hair?" His father engulfed him in a bear hug.

"Becca," roared his father calling to him mother, "Get out here!"

His mother froze in the doorway, her eyes wide in disbelief, "Ryan?" she whispered before throwing herself at her son weeping, "What did yeh do to yehr hair," she alternately sobbed and laughed.

It felt like his parents practically carried him inside announcing to people friends or strangers that their son had come home after all the years he had been away. They had never asked why he did or pestered him for explanations, they accepted whatever he did their son could not discuss.

"Are yeh only home for a visit or yeh back to stay boy?" demanded his father.

"I'll probably stay in Ireland Da, I've been offered a job in Thurles that I'll probably take soon, but I wanted to see you and mum first," said Ryan quietly.

His mother pulled him to a table, delivered a meal and wiped her hands before grabbing his face to look at him intently, "Paddy, he's got a girl. Where is she Ryan? When do we get to meet her?" she demanded.

At the saddened expression on his face, his mother gasped, "Yeh left her behind? What were yeh t'inking! How could yeh just walk away from her like that?" she said furiously.

"Now isn't the time to talk about it mum," said Ryan evasively and his mother relented at his subdued response glancing in concern at his father.

"Eat, eat, yeh look too thin," said his mother in a change of subject.

Ryan picked at his food though his mother was an excellent cook, but he had no appetite and listened to his parents filling his ears with stories about family or people he had known years ago.

"Paddy," said Becca suddenly, "Send someone to clean up the garden, I was comin to tell yeh that when Ryan showed up on the doorstep."

"I'll do it mum," said Ryan and his mother began to sputter until his father lay a hand on her arm.

They watched him go in concern, "Something has broken that boy's heart," said Becca softly.

"Yeh t'ink his girl refused to follow him?" said Paddy softly.

"I don't know, but even as a youngster I've never seen him like this no matter how disappointed," said Becca worriedly.

A few days later, Ryan made an effort to hide his feelings so his parents would not worry and joined a cele-bration they prepared as a welcome home for him which included distant family as well as old friends. Several women tendered offers, but he politely declined to their consternation and to the surprise of some men present.

Becca came up behind one of the more persistent women, and pinched her arm, "Yeh leave him alone Aoife, he's got a girl," she said firmly.

"Then where is she?" demanded Aoife, "I don't see anyone with him and the years been good to him."

"Never yeh mind girl, just leave him be," said Becca repressively.

The following week became much quieter for Ryan once the novelty of his arrival wore off and he helped his family about the business never mentioning he was hoping to get a call from Thurles. As the second week came to a close, Ryan began to despair that the call he desperately hoped to receive might never come and that maybe Bryn would not forgive him for walking away without her. That was when he wondered if he had made the worst mistake of his life.

Ryan decided he had to know once and for all just where Bryn's feelings stood so he approached his par-ents, "I need to head back to Thurles about that job Da, Mum. I may stay in that area, but I'll be close enough to visit more often unless I'm traveling," he said not disclosing his entire reasons for the departure.

"Do what yeh need to son," said Paddy, "Please be careful."

His mother did not say anything, she only hugged him before Ryan went upstairs to get some rest, but when he got into his room, he distinctly heard voices to his confusion until he remembered the COM unit Aiden gave him. Ryan practically leapt the table where he left the device eagerly anticipating the call he hoped for, but stopped in stunned amazement at what he heard.

Aiden's voice sounded strained however it was not talking to him, but an unidentified male, "What have you done with my granddaughter?" he demanded.

"Nothing yet, but we'll have her soon and you'll agree to our marriage," sneered the unidentified male voice.

"My granddaughter already has someone and I already contacted him. It is him she will marry, not you and you're a fool if you try to cross him," said Aiden's voice coldly.

"Not if you want her to stay alive. Liam Kendall still wants her badly and the bounty on her head will bring people from all over the world once they know she's here. He'll leave her alone if you turn the operation over to me," said the unknown male voice in malicious amusement.

"If you think the council will let you replace me, you're delusional Quade. You don't have the experience or the training and certainly not the reputation. Betraying your family will most definitely reduce any small chance you might have had to zero. All these years it's been you feeding Kendall information, you bastard," snarled Aiden.

"I had to get rid of Jimmy and Fiona to be certain you couldn't hand over the estate to them even if you managed to hide that chit of granddaughter from me for so long. With your backing, the council will reconsider when you make me an heir and to be certain you comply, your granddaughter will be my wife. They'll have her soon enough I heard," laughed the cruel voice of Quade.

Another set of voices were audible through the COM as if from another communications device, but Ryan could not hear what was said until the Quade voice shrieked with rage, "What the hell do you mean you can't find her?"

A voice male voice said clearly, "One of the men stayed in the vehicle and backed it down the road at high speed. We shot him, but they got away. We found the vehicle pushed into the hedge, but they aren't close by so they managed to get away before the sun set."

Ryan did not wait any longer, he pocketed the COM and put a watch-like device on his wrist before running downstairs, "Da, I have to go. Unexpected emergency at that new job, I'm sorry," he said without waiting for response running out the door.

In the darkness, Devin and Bryn also heard the confrontation, though muted to avoid the sound carrying, as Devin swore luridly knowing that Aiden was exposed unable to get to the safety of his office. They never suspected Quade and the man had been allowed too close.

"Is he going to kill my grandfather?" said Bryn fearfully.

Still swearing, Devin said, "No Miss Keane, he doesn't dare. Quade has no support of the council and he needs to use you as leverage to get Aiden to do what he wants. He knows Aiden will never risk his only grandchild or any family for that matter. We never suspected him since he was family. If Aiden could get to his office, he would be safe, but Quade knows that unfortunately."

"Why is he allowing us to listen?" said Bryn anxiously.

"He didn't have time to notify any men about us and he's hoping someone is listening that will be able to help, but I think Quade has sealed Aiden off from outside aid or he wouldn't be so confident. The bastard can use the GPS to find us so I have to destroy it," snarled Devin.

They heard other voices speaking as if by communications or COM indicating they could not find a GPS signal and Quade shrieking about losing Bryn and Devin, Devin laughed nastily that Quade was partially scuttled, at least temporarily.

"Where would they go?" demanded Quade obviously to Aiden.

Grim humor in Aiden's voice afforded Devin and Bryn some minute pleasure, "How could I possibly know? I have no idea where those men tried to waylay them," he said silkily.

"Tell him to give her up, now," shouted Quade.

"I can't do that and I won't do that besides, I have no way to contact them when all they were doing was sightseeing," snapped Aiden.

"I don't believe you, damn it. You always have a way to contact Devin," said Quade with a certainty.

"When he's traveling for me and performing errands yes, but not when he here locally and why would I need to contact him when he is usually home? He won't come out of hiding after being waylaid now and he will probably contact the council on his own," said Aiden pointedly.

"Miss Keane, we need to get moving again. He's going to push those men to search hard, he knows it is the only way Aiden will give in and we can't let that fool get any leverage," said Devin urgently.

Bryn could tell the constant moving was taking its toll on Devin due to his injury, he had lost a lot of blood and then there was the trauma his body suffered. His risk of infection increased every hour even though she had cleaned the wound with basic first aid supplies and she could not carry him if he collapsed, at least not far. If she left him and those men found him, she knew exactly what would happen so it was not an option even if he decided to send her on alone. At some point Bryn knew she would not be able to continue either, no food or water and certainly no sleep, while the men trying to find them could rotate in shifts.

"What are we going to do when the sun comes up? We'll be seen easily where the land opens up," said Bryn worriedly.

"We may have to find a river and hide under the embankment. Can you locate one by any chance, in the dark?" asked Devin.

Bryn paused flicking through modes of vision assessing the topography and the likelihood of where river would flow based on the time she spent with Stanton training in the wilderness. It took a little time, but Bryn thought she located a likely area and veered in that direction leading a weakening Devin with her until her acute hearing picked out the sound of water flowing over stone.

Devin eventually heard the water, "Brilliant, Miss Keane. We need the water and we can locate a spot to conceal us from any searchers during the day. The land is so broken about here they will never believe we could get this far in the dark and probably search the wrong areas for us," he said almost happily.

"Devin...please stop calling me Miss Keane, I feel like an old school teacher every time you say it," said Bryn irritably.

In spite of his pain, Devin actually coughed a quiet laugh, "If that is what you want then with your permission, I'll call you Bryn," he said.

"Thank you," said Bryn dryly, "Since we are stopping, I should check that wound unless you think it will start bleeding again."

Devin seemed to hesitate, "It's what is called a through and through. There isn't anything in there anymore Miss...uh...Bryn. Until I can see a physician it's best to leave it alone or it will start bleeding again," he said.

"What about infection?" persisted Bryn.

"You did what you could with that kit. Using the water here might actually cause more problems in an open wound," he pointed out and Bryn had not considered that aspect.

"Is there anything I forage? I don't know what is edible in Ireland," said Bryn ruefully.

"Not this time of year, Bryn. It's probably possible to find some sorrel if you know what to look for, but there wouldn't be enough of it. We might be able to catch some fish, but it will leave us too exposed to try during the day and I don't advise getting wet this time of year either. Help will come eventually. Water was the larger worry and we have that now," said Devin.

"So how do you plan to hide here?" asked Bryn.

"It needs to be lighter for me to see that so we'll have to wait until closer to morning, but the principle is to crawl under the foliage that is growing down over the embankment in spots. We'll have to be very careful not to disturb any mud or leave any sign just in case they eventually search this far. I hope Aiden will manage to get help to the general area before that happens," said Devin.

Bryn did not comment on that assessment as she felt it was highly unlikely as long as Quade was confronting him and preventing him from getting into the secure office, but she suspected Devin was trying to be positive for her sake. Those years at the Facility taught Bryn to be more of a realist and the outlook was grim, odds favored Quade while her grandfather was isolated from his staff, especially with no GPS to find them now.

Chapter 17

Given his burned status with any previous resources, Ryan had no choice, but to use public transportation to return to Thurles knowing he could not contact Aiden Keane directly. His mind prioritized options as the landscape swiftly passed by without noticing the pristine country side which Ireland returned to after many years of clean up and removal of dilapidated homes or decaying non-historical buildings. Unlike the public transport of an earlier era where it would take hours from Kerry to Thurles, Ryan reached the Tipperary County in less than a half an hour.

The first priority would be to get to Aiden Keane as his friend and bodyguard was unavailable. With Devin in Bryn's company she at least had some additional protection and continual monitoring of the COM told Ryan that Quade's men could not locate her even if he could, in the dark. If he made a beeline to Bryn, he also might lead men searching straight to her and he had no resources to defend against an undisclosed amount of opposition, he would need Aiden Keane.

Risk entering the Keane estate would be high as Ryan did not know the layout or placement of any surveillance and coupled with those odds, he had no idea who was loyal to the Quade man or Aiden Keane. There would be a chance even Aiden Keane's men would deny him entry if they were cut off from their employer and Ryan did not want to potentially harm people Bryn's grandfather might need.

Pulling special goggles from a pocket to aid him, Ryan began his approach of the estate checking ceaselessly for surveillance, heat signatures of people, and electronic clutter. A few items acquired from his father's workshop would be all he had to work with, like a small can of spray paint, tape, and a few other simple tools.

A roving guard made him freeze, the man had exited a nearly hidden door and Ryan slipped up to it before it completely shut tensing in case he triggered any motion sensor activated security. There was none to his relief, apparently the door was known only to very few and probably not used except in darkness when it would not be easily noticed, he had to mute the COM when voices began to speak again.

"Call for food," said Quade coldly, "Tell any staff about your predicament and they'll die."

"You would hurt my cook or the kitchen staff when they are not armed or even involved?" said Aiden flatly.

"Don't take me for a fool Uncle. I know they are loyal to you and would try to get word out of the castle to some of your friends," Quade sneered rudely.

Aiden did not deign to respond to that assessment and he would not risk any defenseless staff, no matter how loyal, so he called via house intercom to bring a meal to the upstairs library. It was an unusual request, but Aiden had eaten there on occasion, usually with an old friend visiting though he tried to couch the request in words that would warn the kitchen staff not to ask questions. Their safety depended on it.

Within thirty minutes there was a soft knock on the door and Aiden said, "Enter," with forced calm noting

Quade made a show of perusing a book though he knew his nephew was watching carefully.

One of the kitchen staff entered, eyes darting about and Aiden made a small hidden gesture to check the man's questions that Quade would not be aware of which also told the man not to do a thing.

"Thank you Nevan," said Aiden pleasantly as if he had been entertaining a friend, but he knew Nevan was aware something was wrong. Thankfully, Quade's narcissistic personality blinded him to subtle cues in people's body language and his self-absorption deemed others beneath his notice.

Nevan backed out of the room with a nod and closed the door quietly. Quade immediately moved to the food seemingly ignoring anything Aiden might do which possibly meant his nephew had men within call and did not fear any action his Uncle could attempt.

"Not eating?" mocked Quade as he sipped a glass of wine he just poured.

"It's not the food, but the company that made me lose my appetite," said Aiden sleekly.

Quade's expression blackened at the insult, "Be careful old man or your granddaughter will suffer for your smart mouth and I'll make sure you watch," he snarled.

Aiden nearly smiled, he certainly would love to see Quade try to harm Bryn one on one, and it would be quite entertaining to see her trounce this arrogant little berk, but he made no comment.

Ryan caught sight of a man carrying a covered platter, the scent told him it was food and he suspected exactly where it was going even if he no longer could listen to the COM to gain more intelligence. The man moved through a maze of halls contained within the castle, at odds with where someone might normally deliver a meal and he slipped after making no noise. Keeping his distance, Ryan noticed the man eventually stopped before a closed door and melted into the shadows to avoid the man catching a glimpse of him, but he would wait until the man came back in that direction.

There was only a barely heard comment before the man left the room and came back in Ryan's direction, soon as the man passed he felt Ryan's strong arm about his neck accompanied by a hand over his mouth.

"Not a word," hissed Ryan in his ear, "Is Aiden Keane in that room? Just nod."

The man froze with tension, but he nodded before making a hand signal to indicate there was more information, Ryan hesitated suspiciously before muttering very softly in the man's ear, "Shout and you're a dead man," and the man nodded in obedience.

In a soft whisper, the man said, "Lord Keane is there with his grandnephew. Something is wrong, but he gave me a sign to do nothing so I believe he is in trouble."

This man could be playing him but Ryan needed more information, "Is he injured?" he growled quietly in the man's ear.

"Not that I could see. He rarely eats in this library unless an old friend is visiting and he certainly does not socialize with his nephew," whispered the man grimly, "Are you here to help him?"

Ryan ignored the question initially, "Tell me the lay of the room, where the other man was standing, what I would see if I open that door, and is there another entry into that room?" he breathed softly not loosening his hold on the man a millimeter.

The man stiffened suddenly and Ryan tensed, but the other man seemed surprised by the question instead of considering escape, "Yes," he almost said too loudly in wonder, "It's very old and concealed from back in the old history of the castle. It's a passage that leads to one of the old historic rooms where Lord Keane displays artifacts from his family heritage. He showed me once when I was a boy when my parents worked for the Keanes and I can show you if you are going to help him," he whispered urgently.

Not willing to trust this man in case he was telling him what he wanted to hear, Ryan snarled quietly, "Show me. Alert anyone or lead me into a trap..." he left the threat hanging.

The man nodded vigorously, Ryan released him, but stayed close as the man's own shadow following him through the maze of halls, and they had to slip into a darkened corner when an unexpected man rounded the end of one of the halls. Soon as he was well past their hiding spot, the man continued until he led Ryan to a room filled with a treasure trove of historical artifacts.

Ryan pushed the man through the doorway first before entering and closing the door, he jammed an old ornate dagger between the woodwork and door to wedge it shut, as they had no key to lock it. A quick inventory of the room for surveillance incited Ryan to spray black paint over several camera lenses just to be safe, always keeping the man in sight for any movement that might indicate he would warn the household.

"Show me," said Ryan in a dangerous voice, his meaning clear he referred to the hidden passage.

The man did not hesitate and walked straight to one of the walls to an alcove containing an ancient burnished suit of armor, he ran his hand carefully down the wood on right edge. Ryan heard a soft "snick" and the wall offset slightly which indeed revealed a hidden opening, with a silent gesture, he indicated the man was to precede him into the passage.

They had to feel their way along the passage with care so not to create noise or echoes. There were steps, twists, and turns and Ryan noticed openings along the walls indicating other potential exits. His suspicions roused wondering if the man was leading him to Aiden Keane or into a nest of men loyal to the man called Quade until one last turn, the man stopped silently in front of an opening. Voices carried through to them both and Ryan listened warily.

"Where is Devin going to take her, Uncle? They can't hide forever or they'll starve," snarled Quade voice.

"Devin will do what he must and he will adjust as needed. I won't know where they will end up and yes, they could starve if they stay out there too long," said Aiden seeming unperturbed.

"Call him in or maybe I need to start hurting some of the staff to make my point?" snapped Quade's voice.

"I can't call him in, I told you before I have no way to contact him and if those men chased them into crags or moors, I have no idea where they will end up," said Aiden's voice coldly, "Injuring the staff isn't going to make any of that less true."

Quade's voice began swearing vociferously and he began yelling, apparently into some sort of COM, "Get more men and spread out. They could be hiding right under your noses."

Ryan advanced, but the man with him tugged at his sleeve indicating he knew where the latch was located, so Ryan followed his hand carefully to the protruding piece of metal and waited. Soon as Quade's voice began to yell again, Ryan flipped the latch as softly as he could.

Aiden's concern was growing by the minute as his nephew goaded men into a frenzied search for Bryn, especially with Devin wounded, the odds against them increased the more men Quade sent into the area.

His nephew paced yelling into the COM taking no more notice of his Uncle for the moment and Aiden continued his silent ruminations until he caught a slight movement against the wall. Instantly he knew what it was, the secret passage, and realized Nevan had to be there, Aiden suppressed a groan of dismay hoping the man was not going to pay with his life at the hands of his nephew.

Quickly averting his eyes lest Quade see him staring, Aiden desperately tried to think of a way to warn Nevan to retreat when everything seemed to happen in a blink of an eye. One second Quade was raving into the COM and the next he was lying on the ground immobile at the feet of Patrick Kelly with Nevan peeking into the room from the passage.

Aiden nearly collapsed from relief, "How did you know?" he said faintly his relief was so acute.

Ryan pulled out the COM Aiden had given him and the older man realized he must have hit the wrong button which broadcast to Ryan's COM instead of his men's devices in his haste when Quade surprised him.

"Lord Keane, are you alright?" said Nevan urgently.

"I'm fine Nevan. I owe you a great debt for bringing this man through that passageway. Do you know how many men my nephew has in the house? What about my people?" said Aiden hurriedly.

"I don't know my lord. There are some men in the house, but I don't know their loyalties," said Nevan worriedly.

"Go back to your duties. Don't rouse the staff, I don't want anyone to get hurt. I need to assess the situation, but first I must get to my office. Go back through the passageway, make certain it stays concealed, check it carefully before you leave the room and act like nothing is wrong," ordered Aiden and Nevan nodded obediently before closing the passage door.

Turning to Ryan, "I've never been so glad to see anyone in my life at this moment," he said to the younger man.

"I heard enough to know your man Devin and Bryn are in trouble. First, we need to get you to your office and I need more adequate supplies. What do you want to do with this man?" said Ryan the last question held dire threat.

"He needs to be restrained until I can determine exactly what he has been up to and who he is in contact with, so bring him with us. There is a room we can lock him in until I get control of this situation," said Aiden.

Ryan hauled the man over his shoulder, but halted Aiden's progress until he checked the hall and preceded him out, Aiden directed the younger man in a quiet voice down the various halls or up occasional stairs to his office and safety.

Before they reached the office however, Aiden said, "Put him in here."

"Do you have any restraints?" asked Ryan.

"You'll have to improvise. I don't dare call for any right now," warned Aiden as he watched Ryan tearing stripes of cloth from the unconscious man's clothing to provide some sort of restraint.

"Does anyone else have the key to this room?" said Ryan warily.

"No, but the door can be forced. Only my office is fortified against entry and I don't want him there potentially privy to any plans we make," said Aiden irritably as he wished he had made another provision though he never considered he might have to restrain someone of his own household.

"You realize it might be better to remove the threat," Ryan pointed out.

Aiden sighed, "Yes the thought crossed my mind, but I need more information I suspect only he has and we might be able to scare it out of him, if not, I may condone torture," he said grimly.

The two of them continued to Aiden's secure office and the older man sealed the door before heading straight to his shielded computer, flicking through the various surveillance monitors shifting them to the large panel wall for Ryan's benefit. On one monitor, he brought up the general blueprints of the castle to allow the younger man to get an idea of the layout, as he would need it to leave the premises. There was no one else that he could trust to send for Devin and Bryn.

Aiden moved to his panic room and opened a walk in safe where he selected a set of keys to hand to Ryan before reaching into another cabinet to secure a black duffle filled with gear. Soon as he set the duffle at Ryan's feet, the younger man unzipped it to take inventory of items he had to work with and grunted in satisfaction when he found a high tech visor, an improvement over his Drury visor and probably a prototype of some sort. He would need more complex data input than the goggles he was using.

Ryan noted Aiden seemed to be assessing his build before he opened a drawer and removed a black suit, which he also handed to the younger man, "It'll hide your body heat though it might be a little tight. I don't know what equipment Quade provided to those men, but they have some type of hand weapons from my last communication with Devin before he went silent. I can only give you the general area prior to Devin destroying his COM GPS so Quade could not locate them," he said.

"I can locate Bryn," interjected Ryan to Aiden's surprise yet confirming his earlier suspicion.

"And how, may I ask, can you do that?" said Aiden narrowly.

"I'll explain once we both know their safe, I give you my word. Right now it would lead to more questions than we have time to discuss," said Ryan deferentially to let the other man know he did not disregard the other man's request.

Aiden nodded silently in agreement that there was little time for questions and he turned back to the surveillance monitors, "Ok, look here," he pointed to an area of the castle blueprint, "This is where we are. It looks like Quade moved my men, how I don't know, and left this entire section unguarded, probably people loyal to me he wanted out of the way. You should be able to slip through easily and get over the wall. Once there, go north about two hundred meters and you'll find a special undetectable hover vehicle those keys are for it since I don't have your thumb print or DNA on file. It runs almost completely silent and will not reflect any light they may be using to locate Bryn and Devin," he paused hesitantly,

"It contains a kit of current meds and treatment options. Devin is wounded, I don't know how seriously, but he did not indicate Bryn was in any distress."

Ryan listened without any more comment, nodding at the various points until Aiden finished speaking and he started to turn toward the door until the older man caught his arm.

"Ryan, she wanted to contact you. Devin took her to the Connell couple's house, the people you stayed with after leaving the moors, and he inadvertently overhead Bryn crying to Mrs. Connell. She truly never realized that she made a mistake not speaking of her feelings for you until Mrs. Connell pointed it out. I had hoped to give you a little time with your family before I sent word, but I never planned to involve you in a situation like this. Please be careful, it would be a final blow to Bryn if she loses you," said Aiden, his distress evident.

A smile lit Ryan's face briefly and he squeezed the older man's shoulder in gratitude for those words before heading toward the door as Aiden released the locks.

Sunlight reflecting off water dazzled Bryn's eyes as she looked out through a screen of foliage growing over the embankment of the river where Devin finally chose to hide soon as it was bright enough for him to see. The exercise had taken its toll on the man's injured body in his weakened state and he dozed fitfully beside her, she did not dare rest lest the men searching for them stumbled upon their hiding place.

During the night and most of the morning, Quade's furious voice issued through Devin's COM at the failure of the men to find some trace of their quarry. Her grandfather had been silent for a while, Bryn worried about his safety, but trusted that Devin understood the situation better when he said Quade did not dare risk harm to Aiden just yet, so she decided that her grandfather probably was resting.

It was late afternoon when Bryn's acute hearing caught sounds of men arguing in the distance and she reached over to wake Devin carefully so he would not jump, his eyes opened immediately.

"What is it?" he whispered.

"Men arguing, but they aren't very close. It seems they reached the river though," said Bryn quietly.

Devin cursed and then winced as he attempted to re-orient his injured shoulder, "They may decide to check the embankments, but they have to know which way to look and they could still walk right by us," he whispered, "Did you rest?"

"I'm fine," said Bryn shortly and her stomach rumbled audibly.

"That's not what I asked Bryn," whispered Devin sternly, "I can keep watch for a while."

Bryn refused to acknowledge the offer and Devin glared at her irritably, but they were in no position to debate over differing opinions yet something told her that the man would have more than a few words for her at later date.

The voices did not get appreciably closer and the sun began to sink toward the horizon, but Bryn knew their situation was slowly turning dire when they both heard Quade yelling about sending more men to the general area. Eventually, someone would think to search along the entire river once they had sufficient number of searchers, as there were only so many places they could possibly hide in such an open area.

Instead of arguing, Devin finally whispered, "I'm turning off the COM. All we need is Quade to begin screaming again and one of those fools get close enough to catch the sound on a breeze," she nodded in agreement.

For second night, darkness settled around them and Bryn noted Devin slept fitfully again, she examined his heart rate as well as other physiological factors her eyes were capable of assessing. What she found was worrying.

His body showed signs of an infection, his temperature and heart rate had increased, his skin clammy to the touch, and he did not wake as she touched him. Devin had maybe a day or two before his condition became life threatening.

A small sound interrupted Bryn's thoughts. She froze as a light wind rustled the foliage covering their hiding spot, wondering if some wildlife gravitated to the river for water or food. Carefully scanning the areas of the river she could see, Bryn found no men though she saw a rat moving along the opposite side of the river looking for edibles, possibly it made the soft sound she heard. Acute hearing could be a curse when in a situation like this.

So when a hand grabbed her mouth and a powerful arm circled Bryn's upper body pinning her arms, she was caught completely by surprise with no chance to warn Devin.

"Quiet," hissed a voice in her ear, "There are men close enough to hear a scream."

Bryn stayed frozen, uncertain why this person was warning her until the voice muttered, "Are you alright darlin?" She practically wilted in relief and tears sprang to her eyes that Ryan must have felt rolling down her cheeks to his hand.

The arm about her became a hug against his body and his hand moved from her mouth to press her cheek against his before he pressed his lips softly against her forehead.

"He's hurt," whispered Bryn very softly, "and he's getting worse."

Ryan released her and moved toward Devin removing a small kit from a pouch on his arm, he had something that looked like a hypospray, but he placed a hand firmly over the injured man's mouth before using it.

Almost instantly Devin roused and lashed out until Ryan hissed, "Quiet, men are near enough to hear if you aren't careful," then he froze.

"What did you do to me?" demanded Devin in a whisper though Bryn knew he could not tell who was helping them yet.

"Something for your pain and I'm going to give you something for infection until we get you to a physician," whispered Ryan suiting words to action.

"Who are you? You should be back at the estate with Lord Keane," hissed Devin furiously and obviously thinking Ryan was one of her grandfather's loyal men.

"Aiden Keane is fine and in his office. He sent me to get you," whispered Ryan, "Can you walk? We need to get out of here."

Devin grunted softly, obviously irritated and wanting to ask more questions, but he was no fool to question the danger of their situation since one additional man, in his mind, was not a big improvement of odds.

"Bryn," hissed Devin, "Are you alright?" as if he did not completely trust the new man.

"I'm fine," she whispered back and saw Devin only then begin to move after the assurance.

Devin needed help to negotiate the embankment even with a painkiller so Bryn hung back to give Ryan room to assist the wounded man, once up, she saw Ryan reach down offering his hand to her.

After pulling her up silently, Ryan directed Devin, who he knew could not see in the dark and Bryn realized he was wearing a similar visor to the one he had used at the Facility, so he could also see where he was going. They seemed to be heading toward a dark bump that Bryn had trouble identifying until they were very close and found it was an unusual vehicle that she had never observed previously. The presence of the vehicle seemed to quiet the rest of Devin's suspicions which told her that the man recognized the vehicle as belonging to her grandfather and she watched his hands grope for a catch to open a door.

Ryan pulled her to his side and lifted her in behind the driver or pilot's seat, Bryn could not determine what to label it before he climbed into the vehicle himself, but when he started it, she was not even certain it was running it ran so silently, even to her ears.

Once inside the vehicle, Ryan used a more normal voice, "Where is a physician you and Aiden Keane can trust?" he said.

Devin swore luridly, "Patrick Kelly?" he shouted in the enclosed space making Bryn's sensitive ears ring, "How in the hell did you get here? Scratch that how in the hell did you even know?"

"Do you really want to sit here until those men stumble on us?" countered Ryan dryly.

Devin swore again, "There is a man in Thurles, an old friend of Aiden's and Donal's, we can trust him. He won't send word to Quade or any of his men. Let me see where we are so I can direct you," he said flatly.

A light on the dashboard of the vehicle illuminated their GPS location and Devin said, "Head east from here if you can circumvent those men, if not, this is where you need to get to," he pointed to a building, though Bryn could not tell where it was in relation to the village or her grandfather's home from their position.

"Men to the right," hissed Bryn before the vehicle could move and Devin swore.

"They can't see this vehicle and it doesn't make much noise, but they may see the movement. If they suspect we've managed to get away, they'll start searching the medical facilities and questioning the physicians, damn it," snarled Devin.

"We don't have a choice unless you can trust a different physician in another village," stated Ryan.

"We can't risk it. If Quade's men threaten someone I don't know well, they could hand us over and it would be difficult to blame them," growled Devin.

Ryan said no more and the vehicle seemed to leap over the rough ground in a blur though Bryn could tell they were not taking the direct route, which could be in part to fool anyone that noticed the movement. They reached the village outskirts, but instead of driving into the village straight to the physician, Ryan drove the vehicle into a cover of shrubs and opened the door. He reached in to help Bryn while Devin exited the vehicle and all three of them moved off toward the village slinking quietly in the shadows of buildings, foliage, and gardens.

When they reached the physician's building, Devin tapped quietly on the door, waited, and repeated the taps in a certain sequence until the door was opened by a man that reminded Bryn of Donal though his grizzled hair had a sandy blond cast.

"Devin?" said the man quietly in surprise, "What has happened? Is Aiden ill or injured?"

"Daig, I'm sorry to do this to you, but we're in a spot of trouble. I'm the one who needs treatment and we shouldn't stand out here for long," he said significantly.

Daig hurriedly gestured them in looking out behind them before shutting the door and led them into a room with medical equipment, he turned on an examination light before swiveling it toward Devin.

"Shite, Devin, that's a big wound. What happened?" demanded Daig as he literally pushed the wounded man to the table after removing his shirt and began to remove Bryn's attempt to bind the injury.

While Daig examined the wound, Devin tersely gave the salient points of their predicament though he paused at one point hissing in pain as the physician cleaned the wound more thorough than Bryn had.

"Is Aiden safe," said Daig anxiously, but Devin glanced at Ryan, who nodded and then continued, "You're lucky, only a few smaller blood vessels nicked though there's an infection and it's too late to prevent scarring so you'll have to get any scars removed later," he said reaching for an instrument to run over the wound. Bryn watched in fascination as new skin began to cover the hole in Devin's shoulder.

Once Daig completed the process, Devin grabbed his bloody shirt and attempted to leave the table, but the physician snapped at him, "Stay where you are!" He placed another device against Devin's throat that made him swear irritably.

"That infection is in your body, red blood cell count is down, and blood sugar too low, it's a wonder you managed to walk in here unless you had pain medication," said Daig emphatically, again glancing at Ryan, who nodded again.

Devin sighed irritably as he donned his bloody shirt gazing at the physician caustically as if this was an old dialog between them, but he waited patiently until Daig administered additional treatment in the form in hyposprays.

"We need to leave my friend. I must get back to Aiden..." began Devin, but Daig waved his hand in a cut off gesture.

"You're staying here," he pointed to the floor, "until I'm certain that infection is receding. You can't help Aiden if you drop dead on him no matter how tough you think you are," said Daig flatly.

"Daig, Aiden has no one to watch his back and it's my job to do that," insisted Devin his temper rising, but his words checked when Ryan's hand came to rest on his opposite shoulder, Bryn knew exactly what it conveyed.

Ryan turned to her then and said, "Bryn, please stay here, I want your word on it."

"What! That's..." began Bryn, but Ryan caught her chin in his hand, his eyes hard, he was asking, not telling her...

"You're exhausted. It's all over your face and your probably only in marginally better shape than Devin. A tired body and mind makes mistakes, mistakes none of us can afford, especially your grandda," said Ryan in hard tone, "Your word Bryn!"

Bryn opened her mouth to argue until she felt Devin's hand on her arm, he knew Ryan was correct even if he did not like it either, she started to nod, but the warning in Ryan's expression brought the words to her lips, "I promise to stay here," she practically growled.

With no other comment, Ryan pulled her into a crushing hug and tilted her head up surprising Bryn with a bruising kiss on the lips before releasing her to leave without a backward glance.

Still standing where Ryan left her, Bryn heard the front door of the building close indicating Ryan was gone when Daig said, "Alright girl, let's check you too," as he placed the diagnostic unit on her neck.

Hyposprays with her name on them pressed to Bryn's arm as Daig muttered imprecations about people taking care of their health though he knew from Devin's recital that there had been no options.

"Come with me I have rooms for you and I don't need to remind either of you not to set foot outside until I say differently," said Daig repressively as he glanced over his shoulder at them both.

Devin snorted sourly and Bryn pressed her lips together as they followed the physician to rooms next to each other, he bid them good night as he continued down the hallway.

In darkness, Quade distantly heard an incessant word, "Boss," over and over until his wits began to clear only to realize his wrist and ankles were bound. Snarling in fury, he tried to remember exactly what happened, but all he remembered was yelling at his men over the COM to increase the amount of men searching and then nothing. He could not understand how his Uncle managed to get the drop on him, Quade made certain to keep his distance with a table always between them and he was certain Aiden had not moved. So what the hell had happened?

Barely managing to touch his ankles, Quade realized Aiden had not used regular restraints because they felt like cloth, but he had no idea where his Uncle had put him. It took him painful agonizing minutes before he could pull his arms around his legs, feeling at one point that he dislocated his shoulders.

Groping with his numb hands, Quade finally located the COM unit, "Are you there, damn it?" he snarled into the COM.

"Yes Boss, what happened? We've been trying to reach you since last night," said a man.

Quade swore vociferously, he had lost an entire day because of the old man, "The old man got the drop on me somehow so it's safe to say he's barricaded in his office," he snarled, "He's tied me up in one of the rooms, but I don't know which one. One of you track my GPS and get me out of here before he gets the council on us."

Some other voices swore through the COM, "Boss, he's recalled some of his men we can't get inside and several of us are already dead."

A battering on the door of his room said at least one of his men found him, "Someone found me, keep those fools busy and distracted until I can get off the grounds," snapped Quade.

Aiden listened to the chatter with a grim smile, he needed his nephew to believe he was escaping so he could learn more information and had already planted a hidden transmitter on the man to track him. It would only be a matter of time before Quade destroyed the COM knowing his Uncle could tap into it and monitor everything.

The council already knew of Quade's actions and the breach, but so far Aiden found his nephew had not been able to access much in the way of classified data, which the council confirmed. Agency council experts were already tracing the information Aiden gave them about Quade's suspected link to Liam Kendall now that they knew to look in such a direction, but Aiden suspected there was even more to his nephew's agenda. It was not just the Keane estate, but some bid for power, possibly attempting to fund an autonomous organization, the Keane wealth would be a convenient source of capital.

"Lord Keane," came a quiet voice over his personal COM startling Aiden.

"Ryan?" said Aiden immediately.

"Aye," said Ryan, "I have news."

"Take care coming in, my men are after Quade's people," said Aiden carefully waiting to give full disclosure in private just as the younger man was doing.

It was not long before the office door surveillance showed Ryan waiting outside to Aiden's amazement finally comprehending the elite abilities this young man possessed as he opened the door.

"Young man," said Aiden severely, "They made a huge mistake in North America forcing you to go rogue," as Ryan entered the room and the door secured behind him.

Ryan grinned at the older man knowing his manner was a compliment as he approached a chair across from Aiden to deliver his news.

"Devin and Bryn?" said Aiden immediately.

"Safe," said Ryan as he sat, "Devin had me take them to a physician he called Daig and said you trusted him."

Aiden sighed in relief, "Yes, he's an old friend of both Donal and I. How did you manage to keep Devin from storming out of there?" he added with a hint of amusement.

Ryan snorted, "Daig took care of that. Ordered him to stay," he said.

Aiden was not fooled, the only reason Devin even listened to Daig was he knew Ryan would come to guard his employer's back and that was praise coming from his old friend, Devin trusted no one. He must highly respect Ryan's abilities, not that Aiden could blame such a conclusion after witnessing some of the young man's skill.

"Which is the only reason you left Bryn there," said Aiden shrewdly.

"Under protest," said Ryan dryly and Aiden snorted humorously.

Aiden cleared his throat, "Quade is making his escape," Ryan tensed and he held up his hand, "I arranged it. We want to see where he runs and what he plans to do. I planted a transmitter on him since it will only be a matter of time before he destroys the COM he knows we can track," he said to placate the younger man.

Chatter from Quade and his men came over the COM, "Boss we think the woman got back to the village," both men froze as Quade screamed, "Search all the medical facilities and physicians, Devin is wounded so he has to get treatment. He won't let the woman leave his sight until he delivers her to my Uncle."

Ryan snarled wordlessly and leapt for the office door almost before Aiden could release the lock, he stared at the monitors with grim disgust that Quade still planned to grab Bryn even with Keane guards harrying him.

A determined pounding on Daig's front door woke Devin immediately and he knew someone was attempting to break the door down, without thought, he ran to Bryn's room, scooped the dazed and exhausted woman into his arms.

Daig ran in, "Follow me," he said in a quiet urgent voice.

They entered a storage room and Daig pressed a concealed area on the wall allowing a previously hidden panel to slide silently open, "In now," and Devin slipped inside as the panel silently slid shut.

Devin sat on the floor cradling Bryn to him, "What..." she began groggily, but he placed a hand over her mouth.

Daig mussed his hair, rumpled his clothing, and shuffled to the door as if dragged from his bed by the pounding. Opening the door, he saw four men dressed in black to match the night and pretended to stare at them stupidly, "Is someone injured," he said muzzily.

Instead of answering, one of the men said, "Do you have any patients? Especially anyone that came to you today for treatment of any wounds?"

"My good men, it's two o'clock in the morning! Even if I had any patients at the moment they would be sleeping and I certainly would not disturb them at this hour," said Daig indignantly.

"Did you treat anyone for anything today?" snarled the man.

"Not today," said Daig stiffly.

"Two of you check every room," snapped the man pushing Daig to one side.

"Here! What is this all about?" demanded Daig.

"We're looking for two fugitives that escaped after killing a man on the road yesterday," said the man officiously though Daig knew none of these men represented any legitimate authority, but he did not admit that.

"Oh, I see. I understand the urgency then, but I've treated no injures in several days, only minor illnesses however I'm hardly the only physician in Thurles," said Daig pretending to appear scandalized by the thought of murder.

The two searchers returned, "Nothing," said one of them and the first speaker swore before leaving not even bothering to apologize for their behavior.

Daig sighed quietly relief, *What have you got yourself into this time my friend*, he thought in reference to Aiden Keane.

Devin froze as men came into the storage room he could hear them tossing items around obviously looking for something and swearing. The noise roused Bryn and he breathed, "Shhhh," in her ear then felt her body stiffen as she recognized danger nearby, Patrick had been wise to leave her if it took this long for her to come to her senses.

To his surprise, Bryn pressed against him for security confusing him, especially after the way she had been trained and Devin found such a change hard to reconcile after seeing that footage of her attempting to kill Liam Kendall.

They could hear the men searching other rooms and then that noise gradually faded when Bryn made a quiet comment, "I'm never going to have a normal life, am I?" she whispered in such a wistful way it pulled at Devin's heart.

The tough exterior, her stubbornness, it was all to hide the pain of a little ten year old girl that had her life torn from her in moment, left blind with little hope, and later to find the last family she knew murdered.

Devin hugged Bryn to him like the child he never had, rocking gently and kissing her forehead softly, she sighed and fell asleep in his arms finally trusting him completely, his eyes closed soon afterward.

The sliding of the wall panel instantly woke Devin, but when it opened, Ryan was there with a relieved expression and the light in the room indicated daylight so immediate danger had passed. Ryan knelt on one knee to take Bryn out of his arms. She had to still be exhausted if the noise of the panel had not woken her and Devin watched the man tenderly kiss her on the lips.

"I heard," said Ryan indicating the previous night's search.

"She does love you, you know," said Devin quietly.

Ryan sighed looking at the other man, "Her grandda told me about the Connells. I had to make her think about what she wanted. The hardest thing I ever did in my life was walk away that day," he said quietly.

"In some ways she's still a scared ten year old girl," sighed Devin, "She asked me if she would ever have a normal life last night," he said sadly.

Ryan swore softly, "I'm going to try to do my best, but I don't think she would be happy with what some people call a normal life. She's is too active, intelligent, and adventurous, but it can be a damn sight better than she had to live these past several years," he said and then asked, "How are you feeling?"

"Much better, but Daig will really tell me how I am feeling," said Devin with snort of amusement that made Ryan grin.

Ryan stood to allow Devin to get to his feet and they all left the storage room, Daig intercepted them in the hall pointing down toward the treatment area wordlessly, Devin gave him a mocking salute. The physician glared at him for his levity where his profession was concerned and Ryan laughed softly behind him.

Soon as Daig seemed satisfied with Devin's condition, he indicated Ryan lay Bryn on the table, "She must have been more exhausted than she admitted," he frowned as he examined the diagnostic unit.

The cool touch on her neck of the diagnostic unit roused Bryn and she launched into explosive action when the unfamiliar surroundings registered to her eyes, she became a whirlwind of arms and legs.

At the first hint of Bryn's reaction, Devin pulled Daig as far away from Bryn as the room would allow before she inadvertently harmed the physician leaving Patrick to subdue her and he was glad he did.

Acting purely on instinct Bryn lashed out in perceived defense of her person and she was fast, in some cases faster than Patrick, Devin noted as the man dodged in attempt to grab her without hurting her. The younger man stumbled several times as Bryn connected with his body until he finally hit one of the walls hard enough to daze him and suddenly the woman seemed to process her surroundings.

Gasping in horror, Bryn said in anguish, "I'm so sorry Ryan," and rushed over to him.

"It's ok darlin, I didn't want you to hurt Daig when you reacted to strange surroundings," gasped Ryan trying to get his wind back after his meeting with the wall.

At that explanation, Bryn whirled about in dismay, "Did I hurt either of you?" she groaned out.

"No Bryn, we're both fine. I knew better than to stand nearby the second you exploded from the table. I made certain to take Daig with me," said Devin humorously, "Though I thought young Patrick might benefit from a few knocks."

Ryan snorted a laugh as he rubbed some of his bruises and winked at Bryn to ease her distress, "We've been overdue for a sparring session. I'll regain some points later," he said.

Daig finally found his voice, "So, who was protecting who last night Devin?" he said wryly.

"You're full of yourself today Daig," said Devin dryly inciting Ryan to laugh.

"If you're sufficiently awake now young woman, I would like to finish your examination," said Daig with a raised eyebrow.

Bryn flushed beet red and the two observing men grinned humorously as she resettled in the table so Daig could continue reading the diagnostic unit.

Soon as he finished, Daig said, "I want both of you to eat immediately. I called ahead to Aiden to let him know to expect you and a list of your needs today. Devin, you're to rest another day and then can resume normal duties, young Bryn you need to eat and you should be fine, though I suggest you wait several hours before any sparring sessions."

Bryn stared at the physician bemused, he had a very dry sense of humor and Devin glanced at him narrowly, Ryan only chuckled shaking his head as he moved toward the door.

Aiden was waiting literally in the grand old foyer for them to arrive obviously relieved beyond words at the sight of them safe and relatively whole until he noticed a change in Bryn's expression soon as she stepped through the door. Bryn's face paled as if she might be sick and silent tears coursed down her cheeks to everyone's initial confusion.

Aiden folded his arms about his granddaughter at a loss, hugging her for the first time since meeting her, but finding the silent tears more heartbreaking than hysterics, even Ryan stared in utter confusion.

"My dear, what's wrong?" said Aiden urgently, "Are you ill? I can call Daig to come..." but she shook her head.

"Shay..." whispered Bryn hoarsely and Aiden closed his eyes in sorrow knowing his granddaughter witnessed that death.

Devin sighed regretfully and explained to a very confused Ryan, whose face hardened perceptibly when it became clear what was upsetting Bryn, Ryan may not have been fond of the fact the man liked Bryn, but he never wished any harm come to him.

"Bryn, my dear granddaughter, it was not your fault. Please don't punish yourself for other people's poor actions. My men caught the culprits," said Aiden trying to sooth her tears.

"All he tried to do was help...," croaked Bryn, her throat constricted.

Aiden sighed and continued to hold her; time would heal the pain. Life was not fair and unfortunately Bryn had seen more than her share of those examples in life, they had to find something else for her to focus on.

"Come dear, Daig insisted that you eat and I know that's probably the last thing you feel like doing right now, but its doctor's orders," said Aiden gently keeping an arm about his granddaughter's shoulders and leading her into the formal dining room.

Aiden seated Bryn on his right, kissing her forehead gently before he sat at the head of the table. Ryan took a seat to Bryn's right before leaning over to kiss her cheek tenderly, and he noted she squeezed the young man's hand in acknowledgement in spite of her distress. Devin claimed the seat on his left just as Nevan and another staff member brought in the meal, quickly arranging the dishes, pouring wine, water, or a preferred beverage.

"Thank you," said Aiden to his staff and they bowed slightly before leaving the room.

Rather than tip toe around the subject, Aiden questioned Devin about the entire incident, though he noted his friend was careful illustrating certain details in front of Bryn which he would no doubt clarify later. Ryan listened silently as if digesting the information occasionally touching Bryn on the cheek or stroking her hair in reassurance saying more than words could convey, noted Aiden.

As Devin's tale continued, Aiden noted Bryn began to relax that horrible hunched hopeless posture which began to fade even quicker once he reached the part about Daig, humorously illustrating the thrashing Ryan received at Bryn's hands when the physician startled her out of sleep.

"Better him than me," said Devin with a sly look in Ryan's direction, though Aiden knew Devin to be quite accomplished in a variety of self-defense forms.

"You should take a turn sparring with her," drawled Ryan wickedly out of the blue.

Aiden had to laugh at the expression on Devin's face, "A good way to sort out differences I believe you once told me, my friend," he said taking his own poke of levity.

"I see," said Devin narrowly glancing between the two men.

"Actually, it does everyone good sparring with different people, that's how you learn to adapt," said Bryn suddenly shocking all the men, "Unless of course you enjoy terrorizing physicians."

There was a moment or two of silence and Ryan threw back his head laughing uncontrollably as tears rolled down his cheeks from his mirth, the other men soon joined him.

"Ah me Bryn," said Aiden wiping his cheeks with napkin, "That must be your father's sense of humor. Fiona was never quite so unexpected."

"So young man, have you thought about that job?" said Aiden after finding some semblance of control.

"I have. I really have few other options and I've told my family about it. I mentioned I would probably stay in the country more unless you require me to travel," said Ryan glancing at Bryn.

Devin looked at Aiden, "Even with half the abilities I've witnessed in him, he would be an asset. Do you know that cheeky devil came right to us under that embankment by the river even after I destroyed the COM GPS?" he said wonderingly.

For some reason Ryan looked distinctly uncomfortable Aiden thought and then remembered something the younger man said in his office when he presented him with the equipment to find the two stranded people.

"Ah yes, Ryan you mentioned you would explain that later when I told you Devin destroyed the COM GPS. You said it didn't matter because you could locate Bryn," pressed Aiden.

Bryn's head swiveled in Ryan's direction and noted he began to rub the back of his neck as if embarrassed about something regarding her grandfather's comment.

Ryan sighed, "After we seized her at Drury and she refused to cooperate, the Commander didn't trust her not to run the first chance she had so he had medical tag her with a GPS so we could find her," he said.

"What?" demand Aiden in outrage.

"A man cut it out of my back with a knife after the explosion so no one could find me," said Bryn inciting even more outrage from her grandfather.

"Someone cut it out with a knife?" demanded Aiden his face red with fury.

Ryan cleared his throat, "I can't go into details about mission specifics, but as you know we also had at least one leak in the Facility. On several missions, there were attempts to separate Bryn from us and that was one of those times. It had to be someone from the Facility to know about the GPS tag because we all had them so they would transmit vital stats given some of the incidents we encountered," he said.

Bryn froze suddenly, "The second tag, I forgot to go to medical before I left…, and you knew that somehow," she turned to Ryan glaring at him, "That's how you kept track of me all this time," she said.

Ryan looked at her in mute apology, but it was not his fault she forgot to go to medical to have Doc remove the tag in her hip and then she suddenly realized, "That's how the Facility found us in that building with Liam Kendall's men," she exclaimed.

"Aiden," said Devin quietly and his friend's angry expression swiveled on him, "Contemptible as the reason was for putting the first tag there, it has actually benefited her in manner of speaking. It isn't uncommon on hazardous missions, even for the Agency, to do that for recovery purposes. If he hadn't found us out there, Quade would probably have her by now."

"Well it bloody well won't stay there any longer," snarled Aiden furiously until Bryn laid hand on his.

"No, please leave it for now. Devin is correct and I would have lost Ryan completely if it hadn't been there, he wouldn't have known where to find me and I would still think he was dead," said Bryn quietly.

Aiden forced himself to calm down at his granddaughter's calm acceptance and Devin's logical comments it was just the thought of his granddaughter being tagged like some animal that incensed him.

"Now I have a question to redirect," said Devin sardonically, "How did you know what happened here to come back? Aiden wouldn't have had time to notify you before Quade cornered him."

"Ah that was my error, but it worked to our benefit," interjected Aiden to Devin's surprise, "I gave him a COM unit when I offered him a job so I could contact him. When Quade cornered me, I thought I pressed the button to transmit to the men so they would hear what was happening, but I must have activated Ryan's COM instead. He heard almost everything and came back to help."

Devin grunted, "Good thing you did," he said dryly.

"Actually," commented Ryan, "I was coming back the next day before that happened to talk to you about that job and to have a long talk with Bryn," he glanced sideways at her, "I couldn't take being there without her and my mother is pestering me to bring her home," he rolled his eyes.

Bryn felt like her heart might burst when Ryan said that he intended to return anyway, she thought he might never return and felt like a double fool after the things Maggie said to her.

Aiden looked at the resourceful young man in consternation, "Are you saying you plan to take my granddaughter away after I just managed to get what family I have back together again?" he demanded.

Devin coughed a laugh, Aiden glared at his friend, but waited for an answer as he watched Ryan narrowly.

"Actually no, only for a visit. I told my family I would probably live here in Thurles because of the job and the fact you might hunt me down if I tried to take her away," said Ryan drolly.

Bryn laughed at the expression on her grandfather's face before she could clap a hand over her mouth to stop the sound, Devin was not so restrained and laughed quite merrily at his friend's expression.

Aiden glanced at his friend repressively, "I recall some of your plans...did you intend to execute them during your visit or here?" he demanded.

"What plans?" said Bryn suddenly confused.

Suddenly Ryan had the air of trapped animal frantically searching for a way out, "I hadn't decided since I still had to have a talk with Bryn..." he trailed off at Aiden severe regard.

"And a very long talk with me it seems," said Aiden fiercely.

"What plans," demanded Bryn insistently, "Talk about what?"

Both men ignored her though and stared at each other, "My office young man, right now," said Aiden flatly.

Ryan rose from the table soon as her grandfather stood and both men left the room to her irritation, she turned to Devin, "What's going on?" she demanded.

Devin grinned, "I'd say a territorial dispute," he said humorously.

"About what?" demanded Bryn again.

Devin chuckled, "You'll hear soon enough," was all he said before he too left the table leaving Bryn to fume in confusion.

Aiden marched into his office not bothering to see if Ryan followed him until he reached his desk, the other man shut the door and stood with his legs braced as if preparing for a battle.

"You will not marry my granddaughter without me present," said Aiden spacing out each word.

"I never planned to do so," said Ryan quietly.

"So just exactly are some of the finer points of your plans?" demanded Aiden flatly.

"I don't know if my parents can come here, they own a demanding business and I've spent so much time out of their lives, I don't want to exclude them from something this important," said Ryan uncertainly, "They wouldn't have been safe before this and now, I can be close enough to them so at least I can visit on occasion. They are good people sir."

Aiden sighed, he did understand that a life of black ops agents cut out family ties for obvious reasons to protect both parties involved and he recognized that this was an attempt to bring some normalcy to Bryn's life by pulling her into a family surrounding. Ryan was not attempting to exclude him, but he, Aiden, might need to compromise so that the young man's family also had a chance to share in such a happy event with a son they had seen so little of for many years.

"So you are considering a ceremony where you parents live I take it," stated Aiden.

"It would solve a large problem for them leaving their business unsupervised," said Ryan.

"Just what is this business?" asked Aiden.

"An old bed and breakfast that's been in the family for several hundred years over on the west coast in Kerry," said Ryan, "The Wind and Gull."

"Ah yes, it has been there a long time hasn't it? Isn't it considered a landmark?" Ryan nodded, "I see what you mean about a demanding business, people go there from all over the world," Aiden mused thoughtfully.

"You have no siblings to help out?" queried Aiden.

"I have a sister, but her husband travels a lot, though she does help out when they are in the country. She can't run the business on her own. Other relatives help as well since it's a family business, but then if the ceremony is here, it excludes the rest of them," said Ryan pensively.

Aiden sighed, most of his family was distant except for Bryn leaving that bastard Quade as his next nearest relation, other than that there were only close friends, some like family, but most of them would be able to travel. It was not as if it was the old days anyway, even a trip to Kerry would be traversed quickly and such an establishment would have board available for visitors. Besides, he could arrange a reception in Thurles to include those unable to travel to Kerry, which was the art of compromise.

"I see your dilemma and understand more than you think about family which is why I reacted so strongly about you taking Bryn away," said Aiden.

"I know sir. I've not lost my family and you only have Bryn now," said Ryan softly.

"Well, before anyone can consider plans, I believe you still have some talking to do with Bryn and if she agrees, your parents should meet her before you consider discussing arrangements with them. No doubt given their schedules, I imagine they will need time to make arrangements particularly for visiting family from both sides for any type of ceremony, wouldn't you say?" commented Aiden.

"I could be getting ahead of myself since Bryn obviously has say in this. And yes, my family would want to meet her before anything permanent occurs. They will want to make a celebration of it so it will take time to plan around their business commitments and booked reservations," Ryan agreed and added, "However, I do intend to live in Thurles. I won't take Bryn away from you sir."

"Alright young man, see that you don't, she's all I have left," said Aiden quietly, "You do realize she is my heir, don't you?"

Ryan opened his mouth soundlessly, as if the thought had not actually occurred to him and his eyes widened in incredulity, "Does she know that?" he said uncertainly.

"Probably not," mused Aiden, "I guess I need to have a long talk with her as well it seems."

Given her irritation with the men's evasiveness, Bryn made the only logical choice to vent her frustration and went to the castle's gymnasium. It was not until she heard Ryan calling her name that she noticed her clothing drenched with sweat from several hours of intense practice and turned to look at him irritably.

"From your expression I might come out on the worse side of a sparring session with you this time," he said humorously.

"Care to see?" she challenged keenly.

A grin spread across Ryan's face, but before he would start, he pointed at protectors, which even he donned to Bryn's surprise and she regarded him warily suspecting this was going to be a brutal session.

"Did you stretch?" asked Bryn as she rolled her shoulders to work out some earlier tension from her workout.

"While I was watching you," he said in amused tone.

Bryn froze indignantly and said, "Just how long were you watching?"

"About an hour," said Ryan with a sly grin, "I thought it might be better to let you tire more before I took my chances."

"HA!" exclaimed Bryn, "Not from what I remember!"

"I seem to recall you hiding a great deal of your competence until that installation in the mountains," he taunted as he took an offensive stance barely giving Bryn chance to prepare.

They danced about dodging, striking, weaving, knocking each other backwards, down, and even tossed each other onto the mat, "Are you holding back?" fumed Bryn as she pressed Ryan harder.

However, Ryan would not level any blows where his greater strength could potentially injure her even with the padding on, like her head, neck, or lower rib area, not that it inhibited him at all. Then he caught her off guard with a double sweep on her legs putting Bryn flat on her back and before she could spring to her feet, Ryan pinned her to the mat with his greater weight deflecting her twisting limbs attempting to dislodge him.

At her increased struggles, Ryan cheated and kissed her passionately completely shocking her to stillness until her mind unfroze; she began batting at him with her padded hands in fury at such a maneuver. Instead of stopping, he pulled off the pads on his hands and pinned her arms to the mat continuing uninterrupted to Bryn's disgust, she protested through the kiss in indignation.

When she finally wrenched her lips away, Bryn snarled, "What are you playing at?"

To her surprise, Ryan did not answer, his piercing grey eyes searched her face and something in the candor of that gaze made her uneasy, she suddenly decided it was time to take a shower. She wriggled out from underneath him yanking off her padding angry and confused in turn at Ryan's odd behavior during a sparring session.

Bryn did not make out of the gym before a powerful arm circled her waist keeping her in the gym, "Let go of me Ryan, I don't know what's gotten into you," she snarled.

"Please stay," he said quietly in her ear.

"Are you going to stop acting silly so we can spar then?" said Bryn irritably.

"We're not going to spar, we're going to talk," said Ryan from behind.

"I'm really not in the mood to talk, let go Ryan," snapped Bryn.

"Please Bryn," this time there was plea bordering on pain in his voice that surprised her and she did not know why, they had been sparring, it made no sense.

She stopped her struggles wondering if that was bothering him, "I don't understand. You and my grandfather leave the dining room talking in riddles, completely ignoring me, and now you say you want to talk," said Bryn uncertainly.

"There is reason I was coming back Bryn even before I came to get you and Devin. Your grandda wouldn't let me speak to you about it until he talked to me first. Now will you listen?" he said still holding her off the ground.

Suddenly, Bryn felt very nervous and she did not know why, she remembered a similar tension to his voice back at the Facility, the day he followed her to those assigned quarters, he had made her uneasy then, too.

Possibly due to the stillness of her body, Ryan decided to set her on the ground as a sign she acquiesced to his request to listen.

"I told you the truth when I left to visit my family. It had been nearly twenty years since they had seen me, but it wasn't the only reason I left," said Ryan quietly, "I needed you to think about your feelings Bryn, about what you wanted from me."

Everything Maggie said to her came flooding back to Bryn's mind, the older woman had been correct with every word and Ryan now wanted to know where he stood, it explained the pain in his voice. It came to Bryn suddenly that Ryan was worried and confused, he did not know how she felt about him, not for certain, the fact he was there meant he wanted to be with her, yet now the unspoken question hung in the air: Be with her in what capacity?

He turned her to face him and Bryn instinctively resisted, but Ryan got his way, he cupped her head between his hands forcing her to look at him.

"What do you feel for me Bryn?" he asked softly.

It felt like another voice use her mouth, "I love you Ryan. I have even before I left the Facility, but I didn't want to make you choose between me and the life you had. That wouldn't have been fair to you."

Ryan seemed to sigh part in relief, part exasperation, "Did you ever consider there had never been anything to choose from for me? That the life I wanted was with you darlin?" he said intently.

"I...I...no I guess I didn't," stammered Bryn, "I barely had a choice, so I didn't think you did either."

Ryan actually did sigh in exasperation this time and looked at the ceiling still cupping her face in his hands, "Why didn't you ask me? I told you how I felt many times, unless you believed I was manipulating you in spite of the fact I told you otherwise," he said.

"I was afraid of the answer," whispered Bryn, "That it wasn't real."

Ryan swore, "Darlin, I was going crazy trying to figure out how you felt. I would have taken you out of there the second I knew you wanted to be with me, even if we had to hide the rest of our natural lives from people. I tracked you down here and you still held back, why?" he said.

"I don't want to lose anyone else," it came out in wail of despair Bryn never felt coming.

Ryan wrapped his arms about her trembling body, "Damn it, I should have realized," he said sadly realizing the truth of Devin's words about Bryn still being part frightened ten-year-old girl. When she thought he died, it scarred her more deeply that he imagined.

"I'm going to be near from now on darlin, working for your grandda," said Ryan gently.

"I'll have to go back home eventually, Ryan," said Bryn suddenly realizing her home was half a world away and a place Ryan could no longer go.

"Who said you have to go back?" challenged Ryan.

Bryn looked up at him and opened her mouth, but no sound came out for a moment, "I'm not a citizen here, I can't legally stay," she said finally.

"I think your grandda might take exception to that and maybe you don't realize the authority wields here, I don't think you have to worry about leaving, unless you want to of course," said Ryan searching her face again, "Besides, there are other options to stay."

"Like what?" demanded Bryn at the sudden twinkle in Ryan's eyes as if he was teasing her.

They were interrupted by Devin at that point, obviously to Ryan's exasperation from the expression on his face, "Supper is soon, you might want to change," he said humorously nodded at their bedraggled appearance.

Bryn pulled away from Ryan and ran to get clean not checking to see if Ryan followed her, once she was out of the gym, Ryan commented to Devin, "You're timing is appalling," he said sarcastically.

"I see," said Devin an eyebrow raised, "You still have time I think, unless you think you've scared her away."

"Don't even joke about that," said Ryan repressively to the other man's surprise.

"Is something bothering her?" said Devin in concern.

Ryan explained briefly and Devin sighed, "So you were right about the scared part of her and she thinks she has to leave Ireland because she isn't a citizen," he added.

"That will never happen, Aiden would personally kill every official if he had to," said Devin facetiously.

"I was about to offer another option when you displayed bad timing," said Ryan irritably, but Devin snorted a laugh.

"Makes haste more slowly my friend. Don't overload her with shocks. Let her get comfortable with you around again and meet your family. Try some normal pass times so she can relax or you will scare her off," said Devin more seriously before leaving the gym and Ryan followed with a great deal to think about.

Chapter 18

Aweek had passed since the night her grandfather had frantically searched the castle for Bryn the morning after the discussion in the gym with Ryan. It was not as if she had been hiding. One of the staff informed her where Ryan's room was when he inexplicably had not arrived at her own room after their talk earlier that day in the gym. He had seemed surprised Bryn came to his room, but uttered no word when she climbed into bed with him and promptly fell asleep yet Ryan only lay next to her cradling her body against him through the night.

There had been a moment of guilt for her grandfather and Devin's worry when they heard she was not in her room or anywhere else in the household until Devin approached Ryan, to request his help, only to find Bryn asleep in his room. The entire week, Bryn found her footsteps leading to Ryan's room when he continued to inexplicably avoid her room and she was too uncomfortable to ask why.

Every night, Ryan only curled up next to her with little comment and fell asleep to Bryn's growing confusion so that she began to wonder if something she said in the gym earlier that week had offended him in some way.

Her frustration returned and Bryn predictably sought the gym to exercise rigorously which was where Ryan found her today after she had woke alone in his room. She was aware he arrived, but he made no comment and began to stretch apparently preparing for his own routine exercises.

Bryn could not stand it anymore, she whirled about to face him demanding, "What did I do wrong?"

Ryan seemed genuinely surprised by the question, "What do you mean?" he said in confusion.

Her gaze fastened on his eyes fiercely, Bryn wondered if he was dissembling or teasing her initially, but his eyes held no humor, there was no sly expression on his face and she felt suddenly embarrassed about announcing the subject matter.

"Never mind," said Bryn suddenly preparing to turn away and resume her exercises rather that delve into an intimate conversation that she was certain would give her answers that made her uncomfortable.

"No," said Ryan firmly, "Not after that question or the look on your face, what do you mean?"

"It's nothing!" snapped Bryn fuming.

Of course that evasion would not work and Ryan took several strides toward her instantly closing the distance, he caught Bryn's arm when she attempted to leave turning the encounter into an impromptu sparring match.

"Enough Bryn," snarled Ryan as he pinned her irresistibly to the floor, he had a bloody split lip, colored cheek, and his patience was gone, "What the hell is the matter with you?"

Too angry to prevaricate, Bryn spat out, "Why wouldn't you come to my room?"

The anger on his face changed to unfeigned surprised and a brief flash of emotion passed over Ryan's features she could not identify before he said, "You never asked me to."

"I don't remember asking you at Flynn and Maggie's house," snarled Bryn.

Ryan snorted in disbelief, "No, I asked you if it was all right, if I recall. That circumstance was not exactly the same situation either. This is your grandda's home, *your* home, and I'm a guest here," he said.

"A guest?" said Bryn incredulously; "You think I would show up in your room if you were only a guest?"

"This isn't the Facility Bryn, I'm not your caretaker anymore, and you're a free person with the right to choose how you spend your time awake or asleep. You did not invite me to your room and though I have many faults, entering a woman's bedroom uninvited is not one of them," said Ryan sternly.

"Did you ever think to ask?" fumed Bryn throwing his words back at him.

Ryan's face hardened briefly, but he saw the humor of the situation from the twinkle in his eyes, "Touché, you little spitfire," he said humorously.

"Why?" insisted Bryn as Ryan released his hold on her, she watched him stand and he stretched his hand toward her to off assistance, which she took to stand up.

"I wasn't and I'm not going to pressure you Bryn. We have been separated for a better part of a year and the dynamic changed drastically, like I said, you now have a choice. You deserve to make that choice. You've had precious few opportunities to exercise that right since you were a little girl from everything Devin and your grandda have told me. If you want me to stay with you, all you have to do is tell me that," said Ryan gently.

"Yet you let me walk into your room and invade your privacy..." demanded Bryn.

Ryan actually laughed, "Invade my privacy? Oh I hate every minute you stay in my room," he said facetiously, "And I believe you were invited and if that wasn't obvious enough, consider it a standing invitation."

"Then why did we only sleep?" demanded Bryn, but her face flushed brilliant red at such lascivious statement leaving her lips.

Ryan threw back his head and laughed, his entire body shaking with mirth, "Again, I received no invitation," he said in a voice rippling with his laughter.

Bryn shoved him away fuming and opened her mouth to say he never had any invitation before, but words froze in her mouth, she thought back about her actions in the Facility. In a manner of speaking, she did tender the invitation and Ryan had actually delayed accepting the initial offer, sensitive to the fact she had been traumatized at the time.

His finger came up wagging at her, reminiscent of the rebuke when she attempted to challenge him again after the initial confrontation in the infirmary when at the Facility, "And don't you dare try that on me again...that I could have asked," said Ryan with a sly expression.

Bryn crossed her arms in consternation, the man was insufferable and she had a good mind to plan some sort of torment for him, but she knew the fallout would never be in her favor; Ryan was far too quick witted.

Devin and Aiden were watching the monitors in the gym within the office highly amused by the conversation between the two young people though both men had a fleeting concern initially when Bryn heaped significant punishment on Ryan's body in unreasoning temper.

"He certainly does know how to handle her," snorted Devin humorously.

"That he does. A very patient man all things considered. She's injured him more than he's letting her see," Aiden observed.

"His family raised him well. There aren't many men who wouldn't seize the advantage over a beautiful woman if given a chance," said Devin impressed by Ryan.

When Bryn's eyes settled on Ryan's split lip, she felt deep remorse, "I'm sorry I hit you," she said ashamed by her actions.

"It's nothing to worry about, but if I get a choice next time, I would prefer to use the padding," said Ryan humorously.

Bryn sighed a little sadly and Ryan's humor vanished instantly as he pulled her into his arms gently, she felt him kiss the top of her forehead.

"When were you planning to visit your family again? You didn't get a chance to see them for very long," Bryn murmured into his shoulder.

"They know I will be working here darlin. Besides, if I show up without you next time, my mum just might disown me," said Ryan quietly, but he felt Bryn stiffen at those words, "What bothers you about that?" he added.

"They probably won't like me," whispered Bryn.

Ryan snorted in disbelief, rolling his eyes, "I seriously doubt that would be possible," he said dryly.

"Until they see that I cover you with bruises and split lips," snorted Bryn and Ryan laughed softly.

"My mum would probably find that entertaining," teased Ryan, "and Da would make certain to tell every friend or guest on the premises."

"Premises? Guests?" said Bryn curiously leaning her head back to look up at Ryan's face.

"My parents, actually my family, own an old bed and breakfast over in Kerry near the coast. It's been in the family for generations and people come to stay there from all over the world so it keeps them busy," he felt Bryn stiffen again, "Alright, now what is it?" he said.

"It sounds like there are a lot of people," said Bryn uncertainly.

"And that is a problem, how?" pressed Ryan.

"I guess I'm not used to crowds," stammered Bryn.

"When I first arrived, you were visiting pubs and other sites surrounded by plenty of people, a lot of them talking to you, especially men," said Ryan calmly, "Don't worry so much darlin."

Aiden sighed at the later part of the younger people's conversation and looked at Devin, "You mentioned Fiona schooled Bryn at home, correct?" and the other man nodded.

"So she didn't have the normal childhood interactions which I understand was to protect her and keep Liam Kendall from potentially finding out about her," said Aiden.

"Jimmy and Irene really had little choice, but to school her at home once she was blind Aiden, but at least she did go to university and meet people," said Devin.

Aiden's expression hardened, "At least until that bastard cut her off taking advantage of her disability," he said flatly and Devin agreed ruefully. They could not interfere in that situation no matter how incensed they had been over it.

"Of course then most people ignored her because she was blind so she really didn't interact with many people and once Donal restored her sight, she spent her time mostly with him until recently. She really had been cutoff Devin…" said Aiden sadly.

"Give her time Aiden. She'll relax," said the other man.

"I plan to visit my family next week Bryn, I want to bring you with me to meet them," said Ryan suddenly.

"I…I…" stammered Bryn uncertainly.

Ryan sighed in exasperation, "I swear no one has eight arms or three heads," he said facetiously.

"Very funny," said Bryn irritably.

"Please think about it," was all Ryan said before he released her to continue his exercise routine.

That evening a knock on Ryan's door startled him, thinking it was Bryn, he said, "Come in."

To his surprise, Devin stood in the doorway, but it could not be anything urgent or he would have used the COM unit.

"Did you need something?" said Ryan with a raised eyebrow to indicate his puzzlement at the other man's appearance.

With a droll expression, Devin said, "Not exactly. I came to speak to Bryn, but I can see she isn't here."

"What made you think she would be here?" said Ryan narrowly.

Devin snorted incredulously, "Remember where we found her a week ago after searching for her," he said dryly.

"That doesn't necessarily mean she would be here," said Ryan a bit stiffly, "Did you check her room?"

"After your discussion with her in the gym? I believe you called it a standing invitation," said Devin humorously.

"You're monitoring me?" demanded Ryan.

Devin sighed for patience, "Do you think Aiden would allow lax security within these walls after what Quade did? He won't let anything happen to Bryn again and you sir, are still an unknown quantity to us," he said pointedly.

"If he doesn't trust me why let me go?" said Ryan flatly.

"You know and knew if he didn't trust you, he wouldn't have released you after you first met him. Aiden made the mistake once not knowing people about him well enough; he won't make such an error again. He also wants to know his granddaughter better," said Devin succinctly.

"He could sit and talk with her instead of monitoring her," said Ryan wryly.

"Does she tell you everything or do you learn by observing her? Bryn doesn't say much of herself any more than you do. Given your careers, it's a wise precaution," said Devin tersely.

"Ryan sighed, "Point taken. As for Bryn, I assume she is in her room for now. I actually thought it was her when you knocked," he said.

Devin quirked an eyebrow at the idea of Bryn knocking on Ryan's door, but did not comment on it, instead he said, "Excuse me then, I need to speak with her briefly."

Leaving Ryan's room, Devin heard the door close, though he was surprised to hear footsteps following him and humorously wondered what was on the other man's mind.

Knocking on Bryn's door, Devin watched Ryan position himself at his side, almost defensively, furthering his amusement until they heard, "Come in," from within the room.

Soon as Devin opened the door, he gaped in shock at a small array of equipment surrounding Bryn as she sat on the floor and completely forgot about the man next to him.

"And when did you manage to get all that?" demanded Devin.

"This week," said Bryn stiffly, "Is there a rule I can't buy what I choose?"

A glance at Ryan said he was stunned seeing the equipment so apparently he knew nothing about Bryn's acquisitions either.

"Just where did you think you would be using all of this?" said Devin gesturing at the very high tech, lucrative equipment.

"Is this the reason you both are here, to complain about my buying habits?" said Bryn sharply, her body stiff in preparation for a confrontation.

Devin knew that posture too well from Fiona and that he better change the subject before he entered a battle of wills he would not win.

"Actually, no, your grandda wanted me to find out if you needed anything you might have not brought with you, but I think he had an idea along the lines of clothing or personal items," said Devin wry grin.

"And you Ryan? Did you finally come to ask?" said Bryn tartly.

Ryan glanced at Devin bemused, "Ask what?" he said.

"Apparently not," said Devin with a laugh as he caught Bryn's reference from monitoring her conversation with Ryan in the gym.

"What?" demanded Ryan dangerously, his eyes narrowing at the other man.

"As you are standing at the door, I thought you might be waiting for an invitation," said Bryn as she comically wagged her finger in Ryan's direction as a reminder of the discussion in the gym.

Ryan stiffened and crossed his arms, "Alright, did you two set me up for this?" he said impatiently.

"Why would Devin even be involved, unless of course, you involved him?" said Bryn slyly.

Grumbling, Ryan turned on his heel and stalked back down the hall with Devin struggling to hide a grin at the other man's discomfiture, he would never relax completely with Bryn always honing her wit.

After Devin left, Bryn walked into Ryan's room just as he was beginning to change for bed, she hesitated uncertainly realizing she had not knocked, especially after teasing him earlier. He paused, but then gave her a twist of smile, winking at her before continuing unembarrassed.

"You didn't have to leave, you know. You're always invited," said Bryn carefully, uncertain of Ryan's mood.

Ryan looked at her with a smile and gestured her closer before giving her a kiss on the forehead.

"Of course if you aren't going to give me an invitation to stay…," said Bryn cheekily as she began to back out the door.

Ryan slipped behind her too fast to manage another step and closed the door firmly, "You little…, you have every invitation you can think of," he said with amused impatience.

Later, head resting on Ryan's chest, Bryn opened her eyes and saw an antique clock across the room on a dresser: It said five o'clock in the morning, they had been up most of the night.

The even rise and fall of Ryan's chest made her wonder if he fell asleep, Bryn pushed her torso upright to look at his face and his eyes opened with a lazy smile.

"I think your grandda will be expecting us for breakfast darlin so we need to keep an eye on the time," said Ryan.

As they arrived in the dining room, Devin took one look at Ryan's face and laughed which made Aiden look up from something he was reading and he grinned at the expression on Ryan's face.

Bryn blushed furiously at the other two men's amusement, but the two men only chuckled as unabashed Ryan sat next to her running a caressing finger across her cheek.

"Can you spare Bryn next week so she can meet my family," said Ryan suddenly as he gazed at Aiden.

"Just a visit?" pressed Aiden to Bryn's confusion.

"On my honor, sir, just a visit," said Ryan seriously and Bryn knew she was missing something important, but could not figure out what it was.

Bryn noted her grandfather's gaze flicked to Devin for some reason and then back to Ryan so that she was under the impression some silent agreement had just been made. What kind of agreement, she had no idea.

As if the silent exchange never occurred, Aiden said, "Did you plan to surprise them or let them know your bringing her?"

Ryan paused thinking for a moment, "My mum will twist my ear if I surprise her, but I think Bryn might prefer a chance to meet them without half my relations showing up greeting her the second we arrive," he said glancing sideways at her catching Bryn's wince at the thought of a mass of people she did not know converging on her.

In an apparent change of subject, Devin said, "Ryan I noticed you haven't sent for any luggage. Did you need me to send someone for it?"

Ryan snorted a laugh, "I don't have any. I wasn't in a position to carry much and keep a low profile. Hazard of the job you might say. I never really kept much in the way of possessions over the years," he said.

Aiden interjected, "Well you're going to need more clothing than a few shirts and socks working for me young man. Your family will think I forced you into slavery if not," he said severely.

"Granddad, just pick things out for him or it will never get done," said Bryn rolling her eyes comically.

"Now wait a minute," said Ryan indignantly, "I'm capable of acquiring my own clothing."

Bryn looked at him archly, "As long as you can press a button for it as I recall back at the Facility," she said in mock distain to older men's amusement.

"That's not fair! We had a certain dress code to maintain," said Ryan seemingly unaware that Bryn was teasing him.

"I'm surprised your mother allowed you to return without a new shirt," Bryn said continuing to torment him, enjoying herself.

Ryan's eyes narrowed suddenly, "All righ' yeh little divil," altering the pronunciation of 'devil' saying the entire sentence with a strong Irish brogue, "Two can play this game," he said repressively before looking at the other men, "She can hardly talk, have you seen what's in her suitcases? They aren't even proper suitcases, more like handbags."

Bryn stiffened indignantly, "How could you possibly know what is in my suitcases," she said irritably ignoring the size reference and realizing they were entertaining the older men quite thoroughly.

"If you recall a rose…" said Ryan playing his trump card.

"You looked through my luggage?" demanded Bryn indignantly.

"I needed to be certain no one placed a transmitter or surveillance on you," said Ryan unabashed at his invasion of her privacy under those circumstances, "It's not like I hadn't seen your lingerie before."

"Ryan!" exclaimed Bryn scandalized noting the gleam of triumph in his eyes.

It was only then she noticed the other two men were consumed with mirth listening to the two of them parry words and Bryn knew Ryan won that round, blast the man.

Once the meal finished and Aiden had one of his staff present grumbling Bryn with a digital catalog of clothing before the older man asked to speak to Ryan privately.

In the office, the first thing Aiden said was, "I haven't enjoyed a meal that much in long time. You keep her from focusing on the pain and hurt she's suffered, I thank you for that young man."

Ryan grinned, "I actually enjoy bantering with her. I love her sense of humor," he said.

Aiden grinned back, "Yes, she is quite unexpected and refreshing isn't she? You'll need to keep your wits sharp with her," he said humorously.

"Don't I just know it," said Ryan rolling his eyes comically.

"On a more serious note, I have something I want to give you, aside from a digital catalog as well," Aiden's eyebrow rose in amusement at the disgusted sigh from the younger man, "That is close to my heart and that I want Bryn to have," he said.

All amusement left Ryan's face realizing the other man was very serious and he listened patiently for the Aiden to continue.

Aiden reached inside his desk and pulled out an old-fashioned ring box, he paused to look at it as if stirred by memories before handing it to Ryan, "This belonged to my wife and Devin was to give it to Fiona, but sadly that did not happen. I give it to you to offer to Bryn because my wife would have wanted her granddaughter to have it, that is, when you finally ask her. I don't know if it needs resizing and it would be difficult to inquire without alerting Bryn to your plans initially," he said.

Ryan opened the ring box to see diamonds winking in the light and gasped, "Sir...how can I take something like this? Why don't you present it to Bryn? It would mean a lot to her I'm certain, especially with its history," he said dumbfounded at such an offer.

"It would mean even more if you gave it to her Ryan, unless of course, you already picked out a ring that I'm unaware of or you prefer to make your own selection," said Aiden uncertainly.

"NO, no, I haven't picked anything out and it would be an honor to give her something like this, but sir, it deserves to come from you, something this precious," stammered Ryan feeling unbalanced.

"Then please take it...for me. You're going to become part of my family too," said Aiden softly.

Ryan sat speechless from shock that this man was honoring him as family barely knowing him and did the only thing he could do, he nodded accepting the precious offer.

Aiden returned to his business-like manner once Ryan placed the ring box safely in a pocket, "Devin will follow, but keep his distance. Quade may still attempt to approach her and of course Liam Kendall is still at large with the belief Bryn has Rory's data about him. Unfortunately, if she does, neither Rory nor Jimmy left clues how to find it. His presence will also help safeguard your family just in case," he said.

"Devin doesn't need to remain hidden sir. He's welcome to visit since you regard him as family and he treats Bryn like his daughter as it is," protested Ryan.

Aiden smiled, "Yes he does and believe it or not he loves her like a daughter, too, though I don't think he would ever tell her that. His presence would be noted by outside parties if he goes with you as a guest and that will cost him some effectiveness. He doesn't resent it, actually he tends to prefer working that way," he said.

"Did he tell you want she said at the physician's?" said Ryan suddenly.

Aiden searched his memory and looked quizzically at the younger man, "She asked him if she would ever have a normal life," said Ryan sadly.

"Yes, I remember, he did mention that. We'll try to help her find some balance, but I think you know as well as I do, she is not the sort of woman who will ever be happy cooking, shopping, or other considered normal activities that women in general enjoy. Her life is shifting right now and we need to let her find the balance best for her Ryan," warned Aiden.

"I said something similar to Devin," sighed Ryan.

"Meeting your family is a step in that direction, just remember your word," said Aiden firmly holding up an admonishing finger.

Ryan snorted a laugh realizing the other man was taunting him and saluted facetiously.

Bryn looked out at the country side speeding by as Ryan drove a vehicle loaned to him by her grandfather, along with some new clothing he insisted that she have as his granddaughter. When her grandfather had a true account of her luggage, not just Ryan's teasing, he refused to let her go another day without remedying the situation and the only satisfying portion of that discussion had been Ryan did not escape either.

She glanced over at him driving, his hair returned to his normal shade of dark blond and cut shorter, the physician, Daig, had removed the enhancement Ryan made to his features so that now he looked like Bryn remembered him at the Facility. He seemed to be thinking; even distracted enough that he did not even notice her glance.

The coast appeared in the distance, at least to Bryn's eyes and she caught the flash of sunlight on water as wind blew clouds across the sun so that random shafts of light struck the wavy surface. Foliage appeared shorter, hardier probably because of the nearly constant winds from the sea, and there were even fewer trees than around Thurles, but Bryn saw rolling grassy hills dotted with color as wild flowers poked through the grass.

As buildings and homes came into view, Bryn noted that many were white washed, all clean, tidy, and most with well-maintained gardens. Of course, as Ryan told her people came to this area from all over the world, it made sense all the residents would put forth the effort to present a welcoming atmosphere.

Ryan did not have to tell her what building he was heading for once they were in the town, and it was a town, not a village, because she had never seen a bed and breakfast so large. The sign read, The Wind and Gull, with a hand-painted picture of a seagull that had stylized paint impressions of wind blowing. It was a beautiful building of old mortared stone; even the road about it had the cobblestone restored so that it looked like you were walking into a different era. There was an attached pub just like several of the places Bryn stayed at previously, obviously very popular with local residents as well as guests from the amount of people entering or sitting outside at tables.

She was so busy looking around, Bryn was taken by surprise when Ryan stopped the vehicle in a parking area nearby the bed and breakfast, and suddenly she was not so certain she wanted to get out. Of course, that tactic did not work with Ryan, especially when she made no move to exit the vehicle so he moved around to her side and opened the door offering Bryn his hand.

Bowing to the inevitable, Bryn took his hand swinging her legs out of the vehicle, wind whipped strands of hair, which escaped her braid, across her face. Ryan placed an arm about her shoulders after closing the vehicle door and guided her toward the main entrance of the building. People barely spared them passing notice, either the individuals were guests that did not know Ryan or locals that failed to recognize him, which brought to mind the last time he visited, his hair had been black and longer.

Laughter and song issued from the pub portion, Bryn could hear the impromptu instruments from local residents, and they were all happy sounds. They avoided the pub initially as Ryan's guiding arm directed Bryn toward a beautiful reception area where an older man was chatting with people, gesturing about the building as if explaining the history. Bryn noticed the man was about Ryan's height, of similar build and though not anywhere as close to as fit as Ryan, he was certainly not fat. It was not until the man turned toward them that Bryn saw the same piercing grey eyes and knew this man had to be Ryan's father, she froze on the spot in surprise, but the man initially only had eyes for his son.

"Ryan!" he shouted in surprise, "Yeh divil! Yehr mum is going to be furious yeh sneaked back without warnin her," and that was when his father's eyes followed Ryan's arm to her. His eyes widened in shock and darted back at his son in consternation.

The tableau froze as Bryn and Ryan's father looked at each other, until Ryan said, "Da, this is Bryn Keane, Bryn this is my Da, Patrick Kelly."

"Shite, Ryan," exclaimed his father in dismay, "Forgive m'language Miss Keane," he said in a brief aside before looking back at his son, "Yer mum will never forgive yeh for not lettin her know ahead o'time yeh were bringin yehr girl."

"Da, I wanted her to meet you both before the relatives descended on us. I know mum will tell everyone to be here and even I found it overwhelming a few weeks past when everyone stopped in," said Ryan quietly.

His father sighed in exasperation, "On yehr head be it when yeh see yehr mum," said Patrick before turning to Bryn.

After his shock, Patrick spoke to Bryn with com-
mendable charm offering his hand to her, "It's a real
pleasure t'meet yeh Miss Keane. Becca, me wife, knew
the second she saw him," indicating his son, "he had a
girl and she was right. I apologize me wife isn't by m'side
to meet yeh, she wouda been had there been any warnin,"
he said mercilessly glaring at his son.

Bryn had to laugh, Ryan's father was going to make
him suffer and now she might have an ally or two to torment him.

Ryan glanced sideways at her for the outburst, "I can
see I have more than mum to worry about," he said to his
father, who was sharped witted and caught the reference
with a grin.

To Bryn's surprise Ryan kept her pinned to his side
and did not remove his arm as his father gestured him
to follow, no doubt to find his wife, "I hope yeh can stay
a bit Miss Keane. People would like to meet yeh," said
Patrick as they walked.

"Please, call me Bryn. I feel like an old school teacher every time someone calls me Miss Keane," she said
urgently.

Patrick laughed, "Bryn then. Yehr from North
America from yehr accent, right?" he said.

"Yes, but my grandfather lives in Ireland. I was raised
in North America," she said.

"We get a lot of visitors from North America so don't
feel outta place. Are yeh just visiting yehr grandda or yeh
comin back home?" said Patrick conversationally.

Bryn hesitated, "I don't really know. I'm not a citizen
here," she said uncertainly.

Patrick glanced sharply at his son who returned the
gaze passively, but he made no comment and kept his
thoughts on Bryn's last words to himself.

"Becca!" roared Patrick making Bryn jump in shock.

A slender, very pretty woman about Devin's age
poked her head through a doorway and she had shoulder
length dark blonde curly hair, which reminded Bryn of

old paintings of damsels in her grandfather's castle. Her eyes were brilliant blue and missed nothing soon as they settled on Ryan.

Instantly her manner became daunting, her hands flew to her hips and those blue eyes seemed to emit veritable sparks of fire, "Just like that, yeh come back without lettin me know yeh divil and with yehr girl! She must think I've got no manners at all not meetin her at the door! I raised yeh better than that Patrick Ryan Kelly," snarled his mother.

His father cleared his throat, as if to introduce Bryn, and his mother cut him off with a gesture, "Oh no yeh don't Paddy! Yehr not going to help him outta this," she snapped.

Bryn heard Ryan take a deep breath, "Mum, this is Bryn Keane, Bryn this is my mum, Becca Kelly," he said with more poise than Bryn thought she would have under those daunting blue eyes.

Becca's eyes softened when they shifted to Bryn, she held out her hand, "I'm so pleased to meet yeh Miss Keane. I only wish I greeted yeh properly. I told him he shouldn't have left yeh when he came back the first time after twenty years, but at least yehr here," she said with a smile that slipped from her face the second her eyes shifted to Ryan.

"Please, call me Bryn," she said quickly.

"Bryn then and yeh must be hungry. It's nearly lunch time," said Becca peeling Bryn away from Ryan still regarding her son fiercely.

The two women moved ahead and Patrick laughed merrily at his son's discomfiture, "I did warn yeh," he said.

"Da, she's a bit uncomfortable around crowds of people. You know people will come running soon as mum tells them about Bryn, I wanted to give her a chance to relax before that happens," said Ryan carefully.

"I'll talk t'yehr mum, but shite, Ryan, yeh could have told yehr mum that before yeh came," said his father shaking his head.

"Actually, I wasn't certain when I could convince her to come," said Ryan.

Patrick groaned, "Please, tell me yeh didn't just drive her here without warnin her either! If yehr mum found out yeh did somethin like that..." he trailed off.

"No, no Da, I wouldn't do that to her. I asked her grandda in front of her so she knew," said Ryan quickly.

"Yeh asked her grandda? Ryan...she's a grown woman," said Patrick halting to stare at his son.

"It's the first time he's met her Da. This visit to Ireland I mean. I didn't think I should just drive off with her when he's the only family she has left in the world," said Ryan carefully.

"Her parents are gone?" said Paddy in concern.

Ryan nodded, "A long time now," he said quietly.

"Why is she just meetin her grandda then? That makes no sense," said Paddy in puzzlement.

"She never knew about him Da. Her parents died when she was a little girl," said Ryan.

"That's harsh," Paddy sighed, "O'course yeh would want to ask him if that was the case. Is he all alone with her here right now?" he said worriedly.

"No, people work for him and he has many friends in Thurles, but I had to promise to bring her back," said Ryan ending with a hint of humor.

Paddy snorted, "I just bet yeh did," he said, "And from the way yeh look at her, he made sure yeh weren't goin to jump into anythin without him knowin either."

Ryan looked at his father in consternation and the other man laughed heartily, "How could you know that?" he demanded.

"I'm a father," said Paddy humorously, "I can see what yehr plannin, and it's all over yehr face. Why do yeh think yehr mum is so angry? She sees it too."

Both men heard Becca calling them to eat, she kept shooting disapproving glances at her son during the entire meal for just the four of them making Ryan realize he had underestimated his mother.

People swirled about Bryn most of the day and night, but there was never more than two or three that would speak to her at a time which she wondered about after Ryan's pronouncement of crowds of relatives. A few people Becca introduced turned out to be relatives though occasionally the odd guest or two happened to stop for a chat when they knew she was from North America, she found it more pleasant than her previous worries.

Out of the corner of her eye Bryn could see a pretty small dark haired woman watching her with pouty lips and a sour expression on her face. Oddly enough she never introduced herself nor did Becca or Patrick seem to glance in her direction, strange for generally friendly people.

Men would stop and chat with her animatedly but inexplicably vanish looking uncomfortable though Bryn never saw the reason why; she certainly never said anything rude to them. Patrick stopped by to hand her another glass of water, when Bryn decided to ask about the anomaly involving the men.

"Mr. Kelly...am I saying something inappropriate that some of the people are hurrying off after barely chatting?" said Bryn a little worriedly.

Patrick clicked his tongue, "Paddy, Bryn...please... call me Paddy. Mr. Kelly was me Da," he snorted, "And no yeh didn't say anythin, it's Ryan looking daggers at them. He has a way about him that can chase the paint off the walls if he wants too," he said humorously.

"I see," said Bryn glancing about trying to locate elusive Ryan who apparently placed himself to watch her strategically at a distance.

"And don't let Aoife's stares bother yeh. She's in a mood over Ryan since he first come back and ignored her," added Paddy, which Bryn took to mean the sour small woman.

Actually, Bryn felt tired and had been struggling to maintain her presence out of politeness so she was not really worried about any stares, just the idea she might have offended some of the local residents who knew the Kellys.

Becca bustled up irritably, "Paddy, the girl's tired, yeh should have shown her upstairs," she said catching Bryn's arm gently before saying to Bryn, "Yehr things are upstairs dear, come with me."

Paddy rolled his eyes as his wife brushed him aside watching the two women move off and caught sight of Ryan immediately move in the same direction only to find Aoife barring his way.

Pressing his lips together in annoyance, Paddy noticed Aoife glance after Bryn leaving with a sort of triumph and began to flirt shamelessly with Ryan. Her expression changed to alarm, Paddy noticed in amusement though he could not see his son's full expression and knew Ryan gave the woman one his looks. His son certainly was a master at saying a lot without opening his mouth as Ryan stepped around Aoife without a pause and Paddy watched as her face reddened with fury before she stalked toward the exit.

Becca showed Bryn into a beautiful room decorated with a mixture of modern and old fashion design with modern conveniences, but they barely arrived when Ryan literally materialize by his mother's elbow, startling her.

"Ryan! Don't do that!" snapped Becca after she jumped violently in surprise at the sudden appearance of her son, "Yeh didn't need to come up, Bryn can rest fine on her own," she added tartly.

Bryn opened her mouth to comment because she knew it was more than just wondering where she went, but a glance from Ryan stopped her, she realized then that his parents probably knew little about his work. Of course that would make sense and her grandfather was in essence tied directly to that aspect of both their lives, mentioning the recent difficulties would only alarm his family.

"I'm tired too mum, it's been a long day," said Ryan quietly.

Becca sniffed irritably and continued to show Bryn about the room chatting about things relatives said that met her until she began to move toward the door, she touched Bryn's cheek fondly, glared at Ryan and backed out the door closing it.

"They don't know about your work, do they?" said Bryn quietly and Ryan shook his head.

"Even if most of it wasn't classified, they would only worry. It also keeps them safe," said Ryan even more quietly.

Bryn decided to bring up a different subject, "Why were you terrorizing people speaking to me? I thought I did something to offend them until your father told me you were somehow chasing them off even from across the room," she said irritably.

Instead of looking at her, Ryan avoided her eye, "Talking to you wasn't what was on their minds," he said flatly.

Bryn fumed inwardly, "There were several women in your direction that obviously didn't have talking on their minds either. I didn't chase them away," she said indignantly.

Ryan glanced at her narrow-eyed, "*You* have nothing to worry about," he said.

Bryn bridled at those words, "You didn't trust me?" she snapped.

"I trust *you*, I didn't trust *them*," said Ryan adamantly.

"I can take care of myself Ryan," snarled Bryn.

Anything else that she thought about saying froze on her lips when Ryan fully faced her with a hard expression on his face and she had no idea why he was reacting this way.

Then out of the blue, Ryan said the last thing Bryn thought she would ever hear, "I didn't like it," he snapped.

She could only stare at him for such a statement, it was probably the closest Ryan would ever get to admitting he was jealous and he meant it, his entire posture was defensive.

"I wasn't intending to irritate you by talking to people. Your parents introduced most of them," said Bryn more civilly now she understood his reaction.

In a calmer voice, Ryan said, "I know that darlin.'"

"What's bothering you?" said Bryn eyeing him critically, "You've been quieter than usual."

Ryan turned to face her again, "Nothing is bothering me. I've only been thinking about the job your grandda offered me," he said.

Bryn did not believe that was the entire story, but it was a plausible explanation as her grandfather had been discussing duties before they left and a variety of responsibilities, he offered no additional comments though as he changed clothes and walked over to the bed to stretch out. Pressing him would not get answers, Bryn learned that long ago so she sighed and removed her shoes before stretching out next to him.

Ryan was propped up on his left side watching, his eyebrows rose in surprise, "You're going to sleep like that?" he said fingering her shirt as he looked down at her.

"Is that a problem?" said Bryn narrowly.

That was when Ryan's eyes narrowed, he seemed to be trying to determine if she was teasing him or in a bad mood since he seemed more talkative that usual.

"You're angry about those men running off?" he said defensively.

"I'm not angry, at least not anymore," said Bryn in exasperation, "Initially I thought you inferred I was untrustworthy, but I understand now."

"Was it Aoife? Did she say something to you?" demanded Ryan suddenly, his eyes flashing and his body stiffened.

Bryn sighed throwing her head back on the pillow, "No one said anything to me Ryan, if you are referring to the woman that kept staring at me. Your dad told me to ignore her," she said.

"Then why are you wearing those clothes to bed?" demanded Ryan defensively.

Bryn sat upright to face him, "What is bothering you Ryan? I've never seen you so touchy," she demanded before adding, "I'm tired and it was more effort than I felt like expending to undress, that's all."

Like a thunderclap a realization hit Bryn, because Ryan had been up late nights speaking with her grandfather or Devin about responsibilities or duties which included the man named Quade as well as Liam Kendall, they had not had any private time together.

"I'm sorry darlin, I guess I'm a bit tense. I'm not used to crowds like this just for entertainment or relaxation. Most of my off duty time was spent alone until you came to the Facility," said Ryan with a sigh.

"Is that all that is bothering you?" said Bryn suspiciously.

To her surprise, Ryan actually looked away embarrassed, embarrassed for the first time she had known him. Movement on the sheet drew Bryn's eyes and she saw Ryan's hand crawl over to hers, he clasped her fingers gently caressing and tender.

"I love you so much, Bryn. I don't know how to show you anymore, I'm at a loss. Sometimes I'm not certain you want me that way, when I touch you," said Ryan in a voice so low that even her ears nearly missed what he said.

Simultaneously, Bryn felt warmth and a stab of concern, the warmth about his feelings, but the concern that she had done it again, left him feeling uncertain where he stood in her life.

"Even after all the bruises I've given you, you still want to keep me around?" said Bryn trying to ease Ryan's mood.

Her words had an unexpected result, Ryan's head snapped up and those piercing eyes fastened on her eyes. She was taken aback at the intensity, he was in no mood to joke. He moved so fast Bryn barely had time to gasp and stiffened her body uncertain what to expect only to be engulfed into his powerful arms receiving an intense, loving kiss.

"I love you Ryan, forgive me for not telling you enough," she whispered in his ear a little while later.

At her words, he kissed her again in a lingering way, "My little shadow," he murmured through the kiss.

Paddy Kelly walked out into the garden just as the sunrise peeked over the horizon breathing in the brisk morning air, he made his rounds to check what weeding, repairs, pruning, or picking needed to be done. He paused gazing over the crags toward the water, wind tousling his brown hair and froze when he caught a movement on the steep rocks, Paddy gasped in horror, "RYAN!" he bellowed in alarm.

His son must have been downstairs because Ryan raced out of the building within seconds, his body tense as if preparing for some sort of confrontation.

"What's wrong Da?" said Ryan urgently looking about expecting to see someone threatening his father.

Instead of answering, Paddy pointed toward the crags, his arm trembling violently, fear on his face as if he had seen a ghost or something too horrible to voice. Ryan ran toward the area his eyes searching frantically for what could bring such a terrified expression to his father's face, when he saw a person with reddish golden hair climbing one of the steepest most dangerous cliffs near the Inn. It was Bryn... he knew it without recognizing her face or her figure.

Ryan relaxed and had to bite back laughter at his father's expense because he could understand why the older man was so terrified, he had no idea about Bryn's background or abilities.

"It's ok Da. She'll be fine," said Ryan keeping his voice neutral with great effort.

"FINE? Fine? Ryan, that's over a hundred meter drop if she slips. She's not using any safety gear and there's barely enough light t'see where she's puttin her hands or feet," said Paddy indignantly at his son's calm acceptance of serious risk to a woman he knew his son loved fiercely.

"She has a lot of experience Da, it's ok. She knows what she's doing," assured Ryan.

Paddy could not credit his ears, "That's normal activity for her?" he demanded.

"In a manner of speaking," said Ryan finally allowing a grin to show.

"Don't yeh dare tell yehr mum or she'll faint dead away," said Paddy worriedly.

It was too late, "Tell me what Paddy? What were yeh yellin about? Yeh probably woke half the guests," said Becca joining them looking at her husband disapprovingly for his early morning disturbance.

Paddy groaned in horror at the thought of his wife's reaction to a woman, her own son's intended, climbing the crags in the dim shadows, but to his chagrin, his dratted son actually found humor in the situation. He watched in dismay as Ryan pointed Bryn out to his mother.

Her first reaction was completely expected, Becca gasped in horror and grabbed Ryan's arm in alarm when she perceived the reddish golden haired woman climbing. Then she froze, watching in fascination as Bryn scrambled up the rock like another person might easily walk up a flight of stairs.

"She's been doin that a long time," said Becca in wonder to Paddy's consternation.

"She has," agreed Ryan.

"Yeh two act like yehr talkin about the weather," growled Paddy repressively, "She could be killed out there."

"She looks far from dead to me, Paddy dear," said Becca drolly and Ryan laughed at his father's expression.

"If it really bothers you Da I'll ask her to choose another spot," said Ryan more seriously.

"Choose another…she shouldn't be doin it at all!" said Paddy indignantly, "I would think yeh would be more concerned for her safety."

"I do care Da, but Bryn is who she is. I won't ask her to change when I love her the way she is," said Ryan quietly.

Paddy huffed, prepared to take another tack until he caught the warning expression on his wife's face and amended his words, "Please tell her to be careful," he said before walking back toward the Inn.

Becca watched her husband leave a little concerned, "Don't take him the wrong way Ryan. He really likes yehr girl and doesn't want anythin to happen to her. Yehr Da has a bit of an ol'fashioned idea about women, but I could see yehr Bryn is no lay about when I met her, she has strong hands, there's muscle on her arms," she said.

"I didn't take it the wrong way mum. I don't blame him for being worried, I worry about her too, but Bryn isn't a person you can order about, she will choose black if you try to force her to choose white," said Ryan slightly amused.

His mother snorted a laugh, "No, I could see that in her too. She grew up in North America, but she's all Irish. I'm proud of yeh for scein it in her. Yer a good man, son," she said patting his arm before following her husband inside.

Bryn made her way back to the Inn, climbing over less broken crags and rock, the sun was higher now, she could hear people in the distance so she knew guests were waking up preparing for breakfast. Instead of the road, she cut through the back of the huge garden and noticed Ryan's father picking at some bushes off to one side, he looked up apparently catching a glimpse of motion from her appearance.

To her surprise, his normally friendly expression appeared wary and Bryn wonder what she had done that Ryan's father would look at her in such a way, he nodded a greeting, but did not speak. She suddenly felt uncomfortable, like she committed some offense, but had not known the rules before she broke them.

As she moved closer on her way to the building, Bryn noticed he was picking berries, no doubt to offer guests for breakfast so she offered to carry some of them inside for him.

"That's not necessary, but I appreciate yeh askin," said Paddy neutrally, not his usual genial voice.

Puzzled and uncertain, Bryn continued into the building and ran upstairs to take a shower before breakfast since Ryan's parents usually ate that meal privately with them, she had a strong desire to make a good impression after Paddy's odd behavior.

Whatever impression she hoped to make however, it was not what occurred because Bryn noticed breakfast seemed a bit strained on Paddy's side of the table and Becca gave her husband an exasperated glare. Ryan seemed to sigh quietly for some reason that eluded Bryn.

The awkward situation was interrupted when one of the staff approached Becca apologetically for interrupting their family time, "Mrs. Kelly, something is wrong with the computers, we can't get into the guests bills and several want to leave," said the woman urgently.

Grumbling, Becca said, "Not again! Those technicians shoulda fixed that the last time. Probably tryin to keep us comin back by only patchin it and not really fixin the problem. Did yeh call them?"

"Yes Mrs. Kelly, but they said they can't come for a few days," said the woman worriedly.

"I can help," said Bryn before she could sensor her words or think about the wisdom of making such an offer.

The way Ryan's parents hesitated made Bryn wish the ground would swallow her up and she did not know why, Paddy's expression preceded what she knew was about to be a refusal of her assistance, when Becca cut him off, "If yeh truly think you can patch it until they get here, we'd be yehr debt girl," she glared repressively at Paddy.

"She can do more than patch it mum, believe me," said Ryan pointedly his eyes sliding to his father.

"Come with me then girl. We're goin t'have a riot if people can't get their bills," said Becca standing hurriedly.

Ryan watched them go and turned to his father, "Da, what are you doing? Bryn thinks she has upset you, I can see it and she's confused. Is this all because of her climbing the cliff?" he demanded.

"Women shouldn't be climin cliffs Ryan, not like that and what are yeh goin to do when she falls? What if she does that when she carryin a bahbee?" demanded Paddy.

Ryan struggled to keep his temper, "Da, I don't think she would be that irresponsible. Besides, it's far too soon to think about children and in our work, it might not be possible," he said unwillingly.

"What!" said Paddy outraged, "No children? That's not natural or is that her decision?"

"There's been no decision Da, it's a fact. I can't tell you about our work, just like before," said Ryan still struggling to keep his voice even.

"Yeh mean...yeh mean...she *works* with yeh?" demanded Paddy paling since he had an inkling of the risky work his son could not discuss.

"That's how I met her Da," said Ryan carefully watching as his father look deflated and defeated.

"I didn't think they would let women do t'ings like that..." Paddy trailed off and then added sadly, "I'd hoped yeh came back to have a more normal life."

"Da, if that was what I wanted I would've stayed here and worked with you. Please don't think I take everything you did for me as a boy for granted or the life you gave me growing up, but I had to find my own way. I like my life. I never thought I would find a woman who could be part of that, but somehow I did, please don't make her suffer for the choices I made," pleaded Ryan.

Paddy sighed, "I didn't mean to make her uncomfortable son, and I didn't know she did *that* kind of work. I started worryin seein her on the cliff that she wasn't serious about yeh if she could take risks like that and the way yeh love her, I was afraid to see yeh hurt," he said.

"Is that what this all about? You thought she was toying with my feelings?" said Ryan incredulously.

Paddy looked distinctly uncomfortable, "Well…after seein her on the cliff, it made me wonder if she didn't care what yeh t'ink or how yeh'd feel if she got hurt," he said sheepishly.

Ryan laughed, surprising his father, "Da, she cares. She would do anything for me," inwardly recalling how Bryn made certain he had been pulled dying from Liam Kendall's safe house even believing he might have betrayed her.

"I won't ask her to be anyone other than who she is. She wouldn't be happy and I enjoy the life I have with her. What about Oona, Da? Hasn't she decided to start her family?" said Ryan inquiring about his sister who traveled with her husband.

Paddy looked irritated, "She's too busy seein the world, she says. She's too much like yeh, enjoys runnin about instead of stayin put like a normal family," he said.

"Da, give her time. Most people don't have big families like they used to and you want her to be happy, I know you do," said Ryan in placating voice.

"Well I guess I should be grateful yeh will at least be in Ireland now," grumbled Paddy, but Ryan knew it would take time for his father to come to terms that neither of his children had a traditional outlook regarding family.

"I'll be able to visit more often Da. Mum will skin me if I don't," said Ryan humorously elicited a weak smile from his father.

Becca watched Bryn miraculously fix her computer issues in half the time of the previous technicians they had used before and found herself fuming about her husband's attitude toward the young woman. She knew Paddy had an old fashioned outlook regarding women and family, but his own daughter was gallivanting about the world with her husband so he should be more tolerant.

Her husband was proud of his son, but Becca suspected he secretly hoped Ryan had come home to take up the family business, which she knew would never happen, her son had other ideas for his future. She did not have to ask what was going through Paddy's mind seeing Bryn on that cliff, he immediately thought of her being pregnant and doing activities like that, risking an unborn child. Ludicrous when Bryn was obviously an intelligent woman and with the technology the society enjoyed, she suspected it would be a long time, if it happened, before Ryan had any children. That idea would upset Paddy because he would think Ryan should order Bryn to start producing heirs. That thought made Becca snort inwardly, Ryan had a better measure of Bryn than his father, and no one would ever force that girl to do anything, not with the fire in her personality.

"You shouldn't have any more problems now unless you buy another system or use new software," said Bryn finally, "You were right, they never really fixed it and probably hoped it kept breaking so they would get more business."

"I knew it," said Becca irritably and then she beamed at Bryn, "Thank yeh dear, yeh saved us from having a riot among the guests."

"If there is time, I can make it more efficient for you before I return to my granddad's home," added Bryn, "but only if you want me too," she said glancing around for Paddy.

"Oh that would be wonderful Bryn. We haven't had time to work on something like that as busy as we get," said Becca in true gratitude.

As Bryn's fingers flew across the keys, a rough voice carried to her, "I'm looking for Bryn Keane," she instantly dropped to the floor looking for a way to slip out noting Becca's amazed expression at her actions. Apparently the speaker had not been as close as he sounded for the confusion on the other woman's face.

A wary female voice answered the man hesitantly, "Sir if you have questions about guests you'll have to speak to the proprietors," she said.

Becca must have caught that response even if she did not understand Bryn's reaction because she stepped in front of her crouched figure pressed against the counter offering more concealment.

Worried Becca might turn difficult and incite the man to potentially cause trouble, Bryn tugged at her skirt so the woman would look down before making quick gestures to say she had gone out.

"You the proprietor?" said a male voice with a sneer that Bryn guessed was now speaking to Becca.

"I'm one of them," she said, but not asking why the man wanted to know.

"I'm looking for a Bryn Keane," said the man in a heavy voice that nagged at Bryn's memory, but she could not imagine why and she dare not attempt to get a glimpse of the man.

"Well sir, we don't keep track of guests comin and goins, but I believe the woman yehr askin for is out seein the sights," said Becca stiffly.

"Did she check out?" snarled the man in anger and Bryn caught Becca's leg in warning not to anger the man further.

"I don't believe so," said Becca.

"Check," ordered the man menacingly.

"I'm sorry sir, but unless yehr the authorities we don't give out guest information and yehr not from our Garda," said Becca flatly and Bryn wanted to groan in dismay.

The only hope was there would be too many witnesses for the man to actually add physical coercion to his demand.

"Is there anyone with her," snapped the man, "Or is she alone?"

"Again sir," said Becca sternly, "Yeh have no right to guest information. I must ask yeh present me with some legal authorization for the information or leave the premises."

"Be careful bitch, you have no idea who you're dealing with," hissed the man more quietly to hide the fact from anyone around Becca that he was threatening her.

Wisely, Becca did not answer to Bryn's relief as she breathed out a silent sigh of relief and wondered how anyone had tracked her here; she never meant to put Ryan's family at risk with her presence. Certainly her grandfather would have mentioned it if he thought such trip unwise or potentially hazardous to innocent people.

Though Becca did not look down at her, Bryn heard her speak softly, "Lawks, girl, what have yeh and me son gotten into?"

Someone must have gone to get Paddy and Ryan because within minutes Bryn heard Paddy demanding to know what happened, Becca explained without using her name obviously worried about people with unknown agendas listening.

A voice she barely recognized as Ryan's snarled, "Where is she?" He was very quiet even if it did not lessen the menace conveyed.

In an instant, Ryan was squatting next to her, his eyes grey daggers along with the most dangerous expression Bryn had ever seen on his face, it made her quail.

Holding out his hand, Ryan said flatly, "We're leaving."

His mother began to sputtering as Ryan physically pulled Bryn with him, not even giving her a chance to use her own feet, toward the back stairs straight to their room.

Becca and Paddy followed them into the room, "Yeh practically just got here," said his mother outraged.

"I can't talk about it Mum," said Ryan without turning around, bite in the tone of his voice.

Bryn's heart sank at the conflict of emotion's on Paddy's face, he probably was wondering what sort of snake his son had brought into their home potentially risking their guests. To attempt to apologize seemed pathetically inadequate and Bryn knew she could never elaborate enough to satisfy anyone, she finally realized how cut off she was from regular normal people. Her attempt to fit in like a vacationing tourist had all been a sham, Bryn had to accept she would never have a normal life.

Clutching at her suitcase, Bryn paused before Becca almost bereft of words, "Thank you welcoming me to your home," she said finally trying to hide her distress, but tears sprang to her eyes when Becca hugged her tightly.

"Yehr welcome back any time dear," said Becca trying to act stern, but her eyes were bright with tears.

That was all Ryan gave her time for as he snatched Bryn's arm pulling her with him out of the room with only a nod of farewell for his parents and then they were out of the Inn, into the vehicle speeding back toward Thurles.

Chapter 19

While Aiden reviewed some Agency council business, he tried to ignore the absence of his granddaughter and the loneliness he felt, even after such a short time with him her presence had filled the old castle.

"Aiden," said Devin's voice on the COM so suddenly that Aiden jumped in alarm.

"We have a problem," continued Devin's voice grimly, "Someone showed up asking for Bryn Keane and tried to bully one of the proprietors."

Aiden barely masked a groan, this was supposed to be a pleasant visit to meet Ryan's parents, not a situation that would put innocents at risk, "Which means they're headed back herc, I take it," he sighed.

"Yes," said Devin's voice, "Ryan looks like he could chew stone and…I think it was a blow to Bryn from her expression."

"I imagine it was, Devin. That was supposed to be an opportunity to have normal interaction and relax, but apparently my blasted grandnephew isn't going to back off. I thought we put enough pressure on him to leave her alone for now," growled Aiden furiously.

"Aiden…I don't think this is Quade. The man looking for her had a North American accent, it could be Kendall, but…" paused Devin.

"You don't believe that either," finished Aiden uneasily.

"It's best we talk with Ryan and Bryn about this. I would be only guessing and they might have some insight," commented Devin.

"I'll see you soon then," said Aiden pensively.

In Aiden's office, later the same day all four of them gathered to discuss the man who had been asking for Bryn, the other two men mulling over Devin's hypothesis that this man with the North American accent, might be an unrelated party with no connections to Quade or Liam Kendall.

"Why would anyone else even care?" insisted Bryn.

To her supreme annoyance all three men shared meaningful glances, but it was Devin who answered her demand for information.

"Bryn, you may not know it, but your reputation is worldwide. There are organizations out there that consider you a prime asset and would do almost anything to secure your skills," said Devin pointedly.

Bryn snorted in disbelief, "They don't even know who I am. When I did any work I was disguised or was until the Facility people grabbed me," she said dismissively.

Devin sighed in frustration, as if she was missing some obvious point, "No, they didn't know it was 'Bryn Keane,' but they were aware of a thief with unmatched skills that could remain invisible. The fact you eluded so many organizations trying to locate you only increased their desire to have you. No doubt they thought you a man, at least until Drury seized you," he said carefully.

"I can't imagine they wanted to advertise they had me," said Bryn belligerently.

"You're not thinking Bryn," said Devin harshly, "They didn't have to advertise after some of the jobs Drury pulled with you on their team and you're missing another key point, they had at least one spy in their midst. Someone planted there or activated because of you. What do you think they did with information about you?"

Bryn felt like someone slapped her, of course people would sell important information, but she never considered herself important enough to be worth notice, which was what Devin was trying to point out. People did think she was that important.

"Bryn," said Aiden quietly, "Until I knew you were that same person, the Agency here had still been looking for you. We collect extraordinary assets into the organization to further our agendas and we recruit people like Ryan or others you worked with at Drury. Sometimes we lend assets between organizations."

"I'm not doing anything for people to notice anymore," insisted Bryn.

Devin sighed again, "You don't understand Bryn they already know you have the skills. These are not organizations people just retire from or quit their jobs. If you had not been the person Drury sought, you wouldn't have lived long," he said unwillingly.

Bryn felt blood drain from her face, the Facility had not been going to release her and her mind jumped to Ryan's predicament, 'burned,' meaning a terminated asset. In her goals to help Donal, she had become marked throughout the world even though she stayed hidden, did not boast or flaunt her skill, people still noticed...the dangerous organizations like Drury knew the difference between people claiming credit and the real operators.

"So you're saying there are people that still would grab me? Why did the Facility release me then, if that is the case?" demanded Bryn.

"Because of me, Bryn," said Aiden softly, "I threatened to bring the Agency down on them for detaining you once Devin was able to locate your whereabouts. I believe even Ryan here had been attempting to broker a deal for your release."

Bryn's head swiveled to Ryan furiously, "And you just hid that from me?" she snarled.

"Darlin, I didn't know if I could succeed. I had no idea of your connections with Aiden Keane or I would have used that to my advantage. I knew you didn't want Dr. Meany endangered if they decided to use him as leverage or it might have resulted in your death if you attempted to protect him," said Ryan plausibly.

"If you managed to force them to release me Granddad then other people must know that, surely they will leave me alone if you could make people like the Facility let me go," said Bryn pointedly.

"Legitimately? Yes, but only if they acknowledged they had you or a similar spy revealed your presence, but we now suspect we are dealing with an individual or variety of individuals attempting to broker you off, shall we say, like a piece of stolen art. In spite of your considerable skills Bryn, there are ways to force capitulation with the array of technology available, even you know that. You were extremely lucky Drury chose not to enforce such methods which you can probably thank their Commander for in this circumstance. I was given to believe he did not want to work with a woman, but others will not share such prejudice," state Aiden succinctly.

"What spy told you they had me?" demanded Bryn uncertainly.

"Actually it wasn't a spy Bryn," said Devin with a glance at Ryan, "Donal received a special drive with your health vitals when you lay dying from an unknown toxin. He of course handed over the drive to me and we searched it for clues of your location, which we found. We suspected the information had been left there intentionally to help you and soon as your grandda traced the information, he began the process of securing your freedom."

Bryn looked at Ryan knowing he could have been the only one who had any idea that Donal could help her after arranging the meeting with the scientist at the library to help with her headaches.

"You did that intentionally?" demanded Bryn still watching Ryan.

"I did. I was hoping to find anything or anyone who could help get you out before they killed you on a mission," here Ryan hesitated uncertainly before continuing, "Foss intercepted internal transmissions that indicated some of these hazardous situations had been arranged to test you. If you died during such testing, they were not going to be too concerned thinking that maybe you were not the one they sought. The Commander was not part of issue, but he knew about it and was trying to locate the leak," Ryan looked at the floor, his expression bitter, "but you acquitted yourself to such a high standard when any other member of the team would have died, that I'm certain people intended to steal you from Drury, against your will. That's why I had to get you out of there and then I was recalled to my organization. Before I would leave, I demanded the Commander release you, but oddly enough, he said his superiors ordered him to let you go. He never explained why or he might not have known, but I suspect your grandda was the reason," he concluded.

"So that Liam Kendall truly was only after something he thought Uncle Jimmy gave me?" said Bryn uncertainly.

"Yes, Bryn," said Aiden, "He knew nothing of your other activities and probably didn't care. Liam Kendall has no use for women as assets and would never have believed you competent in anything, for him women only serve a very basic purpose."

"Of course," added Devin with grim satisfaction, "He found out his mistake when you went after him. We reviewed the seized surveillance footage and the devastation you created, it was probably the first time in Kendall's sorry life that a woman scared him..." he paused to edit his comment, "voiceless."

Aiden snorted briefly in humor at Devin's alteration of a more crass comment and noted Ryan's lips twitched in humor as well in spite of the seriousness of the discussion.

"So what is the real reason we are having this discussion?" demanded Bryn suddenly making certain the men did not divert her.

The men collectively sighed and Bryn knew she was not going to like whatever it was they were planning just from the expressions on their faces.

"Unfortunately Bryn, you will need to have protection so you can't be isolated again. I will disseminate word with other organizations to stay away from you, but it will take time and that won't stop independent operatives from attempting to secure you," said Aiden unhappily.

"No," snarled Bryn, "I will not have my movements monitored. I can take care of myself."

Devin rubbed his hand over his face in frustration, Aiden sighed irritably, but Ryan said nothing, he only narrowed his eyes at her rebellion.

"Unfortunately Bryn, you're not going to get a voice in this. You're all the family I have left and I mean to protect you whether you accept that or not. Of course, I will try to impact your freedom as little as possible, but I will not stand by and let someone steal you away from me," said Aiden sternly. It was the first time her grandfather presented a formidable and threatening aspect.

Bryn knew she would do well to remember that her grandfather was no ordinary man and carried a great deal of authority worldwide which made him a force to be reckoned with in any confrontation. She had to pause for a moment to finally understand that her grandfather was a dangerous man or he could never have forced the Facility to release her, he would get his way.

After a long significant look at his granddaughter, Aiden turned to Ryan, "I would like you to address the issue of these independents. It may take some time, but when the rumors of inability to reach Bryn eventually circulate, they may finally leave her alone as long as she remains in Ireland," he said.

"And if I want to go home?" said Bryn bridling furiously.

"You are home Bryn," said Aiden quietly.

"This is not where I grew up. I can live where I choose and I have an open ticket back to North America," began Bryn heatedly.

"And return to what Bryn?" this time it was Devin who interjected a comment.

Bryn opened her mouth angrily, "I...I..." but she could not form a plausible argument, she could mention Donal, though suspected her grandfather would, if he had not already done so, mention to the scientist his granddaughter's previous activities acquiring his resources. Donal would never allow that to continue and might even have a severe lecture for her to underscore when he told her to reinvent herself, he never meant for her to risk her life.

"Then I will help Ryan with these independent operatives," snapped Bryn.

This time Ryan spoke, "No you won't," he said flatly, "They would know you are running about Ireland and attempt to corner you."

Bryn jumped to her feet in fury, "You can't stop me," she snarled, "I'll know when you leave."

It happened so fast Bryn could not react; Ryan was seated one second and the next his arm was about her throat, blackness followed, but her last remaining conscious thought was that Ryan would be gone when she awoke.

The suddenness of Ryan's movement caught even Aiden and Devin off guard, they both jumped in alarm until they witnessed Bryn wilt unconscious from pressure on her carotid arteries.

Aiden looked at him with a mixture of anger and confusion as he scooped up Bryn's limp form, "You shouldn't have done that," he snapped.

"You never would have stopped her sir. I've seen her like this before. This way she can't follow me and she'll be safe, or safer than running around the Irish countryside with men hunting her at every turn," said Ryan regretfully.

Devin sighed ruefully, "He's probably right Aiden. Fiona could be the same way, I know you remember," hating the reference that Aiden's daughter ran to Liam Kendall and the pain that cost the other man and then to Ryan, "She's going to be in a fury against you for this, you realize that?" he said.

Ryan sighed, "She'll be alive and safe with both of you. She may not forgive me. I would gladly accept her hating me the rest of her life rather than disappearing as a slave asset and not be able to locate her again," he said, but the other men saw the agony those words cost the him.

"You can hurt her so easily...walk away from her after you know the way she feels about you," snarled Aiden angrily for the suffering he knew Bryn would endure at what she would see as betrayal.

Ryan stared at the older man, "No, I cannot hurt her so easily. I can barely stand the thought of what I just did, but I would sell my life for her, and I will if necessary, to know that she is safe. I love her enough to let her go if that is best for her," he said quietly.

Both men stared at Ryan knowing he had not made the decision to disable Bryn without considerable thought of the consequences, he knew she might never speak to him again.

It appeared even Ryan had underestimated Bryn's fury when she finally regained consciousness as she refused to speak to Devin or Aiden, would barely eat, and hardly slept. The two men watched helplessly as Bryn stayed obsessively in the gymnasium exercising or honing her skills until she could barely stand each day.

Aiden offered her invitations to dine, but staff said she would only shake her head and shut the door to her bedroom, Devin kept incessant watch over her based on Ryan's suspicions that Bryn would slip away the first opportunity she had.

"She's going to get ill," said Aiden to Devin several weeks later watching surveillance, "She can't keep up such activity with no rest and barely eating."

"She's knows we can't force her Aiden. Remember what Ryan said about her initial tenure at Drury, she was prepared to starve to death at one point and there wasn't a thing they could do about it, even in these days. Forcing nutrients can only be done for so long before the human digestive system shuts down, likely that clever girl knows that too," said Devin sighing with futility.

"The only positive thing I can see is she hasn't attempted to leave the premises," Aiden mused wondering what was going on in his granddaughter's mind.

"We don't dare relax surveillance on her even now," said Devin direly and Aiden knew he was right, Bryn was too clever and skilled, even Ryan admitted he did not know the full extent of her abilities. Aiden wondered if anyone ever would.

Bryn stalked through the castle completely aware of all the surveillance with her eyesight, even though she could trust Devin, Ryan, and her grandfather, old habits die hard and she only revealed a small portion of her skills. Donal would have told her grandfather and Devin what test results he had from previous examinations, but it had been years since that occurred. Donal had not examined her eyes again once Devin brought her from the southern Agency headquarters he had only done a basic health check to monitor her healing.

Of course, they suspected things, even Ryan, but she knew they could not even imagine the truth unless she chose to reveal it. If they thought they could and would keep her any place she did not wish to stay, they were going to find out their error as she used the time over the months to test the surveillance, her guards and plans. They would be aware of her data usage, checking maps of Ireland, topography as well as populated areas, but Bryn knew how to plan, how to be patient, it was what made her so accomplished and brought notice to her activities in the past.

The men did not seem to realize she truly could take care of herself even with the technology available, but then, she reminded herself, they worked with limited knowledge of her abilities. No matter how many of those independent operators who sought Bryn managed to corner her, they would lose quite spectacularly, even if they managed to secure her. The Facility slowly came to that realization and this time, they could not threaten Donal!

Her grandfather and Devin had the resources not to become victims like Donal had, Ryan had the skill and strength so no one could use those men as leverage to coerce Bryn so she was free to retaliate at will. They would not know she was gone until it was far too late to do anything about it.

Aiden Keane reviewed encrypted reports forwarded to him by Ryan, as Devin did the same in the office after the months the younger man had been ferretting out the independent operatives. He had been very successful, but the tone of the reports indicated he was not foolish enough to believe that he managed to get them all, the more skilled and resourceful individuals.

"He's a hell of an operative Aiden. They made a huge mistake burning him in North America over protecting Bryn from that dart. Kendall might not have trusted him again once he thought one of his men had been seized, but damn, he has other skills and abilities you don't just throw away. It's difficult to find men like him," said Devin wonderingly.

"I agree. I've been working on rescinding that burn notice in North America, but that southern Commander is still in a snit over what he keeps calling, 'breach of protocol,' and I wouldn't be surprised if the man went after Ryan himself if he returned to North America," commented Aiden perusing the data.

"He would never leave her Aiden, even if she refuses to talk to him. He'll stay near her no matter where she goes," said Devin looking up at his friend.

Aiden sighed, "She's so angry with him, but then he knew she would be. I wish we could get her to see past that temper. That man loves her so much he would die for her, but she doesn't see it or refuses to acknowledge it if she does," he said.

"She still won't speak to him or contact him?" said Devin sighing.

"No, even after he made an attempt to send her a message," said Aiden slapping his had in irritation on his desk, "She can't be so foolish as to throw away her life like that. They are made for each other, I don't think any other man could ever handle her or would even want to and she doesn't appreciate that,"

"She needs to let go of her anger first Aiden," said Devin unhappily.

"I just hope she has the chance and nothing happens to him. If he were killed during his work, she would be consumed with guilt over making him suffer like this," said Aiden worriedly, "and I can't ask him to be anyone he is not any more than we would do that to Bryn."

A voice over Aiden's private intercom interrupted them, "Lord Keane, we cannot locate your granddaughter anywhere on the premises. She is not in her room and we have reviewed all surveillance, we don't know where she is," said a man's voice.

Devin groaned, "She's left the estate. There is no point looking for her here. That clever girl has been testing our weakness, studying us and she'll be certain no one can follow her," he said furiously.

Aiden slapped his hand down flat on the desk again, "We have got to try. She doesn't know Ireland so we have the advantage on her. She can't elude us forever. I'll make certain she can't fly out of the country or use any form transport to get across the water to Great Britain, once those doors are closed, it won't be long," he snapped extremely irritated with his granddaughter.

"You better let Ryan know. He will probably want to work on locating her too especially if she removed that GPS tag and he might have some ideas, or will once he stops swearing about what she did," growled Devin.

"She hid her skill very well damn her and this is probably her way of shoving it in our faces that she can take care of herself," snarled Aiden as he placed a call on Ryan's secure COM.

Ryan remained silent as he received the news, if he was swearing, as Devin predicted, he was doing it mentally, until he finally said in a tight voice, "Locating her will be much worse this time. Before, she had no idea people were after her or their capabilities, this time, she knows a great deal, particularly what we have available to track her and she could stay away to prove a point. If Bryn doesn't want to be found, I don't think anyone will find her. Did she remove her COM GPS?"

"Yes," growled Devin, "Did she remove the GPS planted on her?"

"I don't know, unless she figured out a way to shield it, but since I can't track it, it is entirely possible she did remove it," came the grim response.

"She won't get out of the country, I'll make certain of that," fumed Aiden mentally wishing he could deliver an old fashioned spanking to his granddaughter even if she was a grown woman.

"Do you think she is doing this to prove a point?" demanded Aiden via the COM to Ryan.

The other man was silent so long that Aiden and Devin wondered if he closed the connection until he said, "I think that is part of it, but not the entire reason. I suspect she is going after those independent operatives," he said finally, "And she is capable of doing it from the little I've observed of her abilities."

"No!" exclaimed Aiden in horror, "If they can't take her, they may decide to kill her."

The silence on the COM said that Ryan considered that aspect and Devin looked at Aiden worriedly, they could only search for her now.

Finding those operatives looking for her was proving more of a challenge for Bryn than she cared to admit, even to herself, and she had to conclude that it was possible her skills were not sufficient in this realm of expertise. At least not unaided with minimal technology at her disposal as when she was at the Facility there was access to vast amounts of data, which she might have had at her grandfather's home and of course, if she returned there, they would probably lock her away.

The way they monitored her activity, they would have suspected her goals, which was why Bryn had been careful what kind of data she acquired. Taking any digital units with her would have allowed her grandfather to track her via any uplink she used so that had only left her with a COM unit he had given her. She had been certain to remove the GPS from the COM unit mindful of her experience with Devin and secure a special shielding material over the one in her body though Bryn considered digging it out.

She noticed Ryan had attempted to call her, no doubt her grandfather had notified him and there had been an call attempted from Devin, but she suspected that once the connection completed they could trace her without a GPS, hence their reason for initiating the contact. So she had ignored both calls.

Gathering her items together, Bryn prepared to move again as darkness fell, that was her advantage and since the men would need special gear, it made it nearly impossible for them to track her. People would never remember seeing her nor would Bryn attract attention moving through the darkness when most people shunned the night.

Her COM vibrating unexpectedly made Bryn jump in surprise, she looked at it in annoyance thinking the men were doggedly attempting to get a response from her on the chance she would speak to them so they could locate her.

To her surprise, it was not a code she recognized, so she tapped a few buttons to get the origin of the call and it came from Kerry confusing her even further, which could only mean Ryan's parents unless he was attempting to trick her.

Her mind raced trying to determine if Ryan would go to such lengths, but then she decided he would not do that, he was a direct actionist and did not rely on others to take action for him.

Devin? She mused. Possible, but then she discarded that idea as well since Devin or her grandfather would not involve Ryan's family in a potentially dangerous situation particularly if operatives still searched for her. It had to be an actual call from Ryan's family, but why?

For the barest instant, Bryn considered dropping the call, but another portion of her mind did not want to offend Ryan's parents when they were not responsible for his actions. Yet were they attempting to locate her and pass along that information? Finally Bryn became disgusted with her suspicious thoughts, unkindly labeling two very nice people that had welcomed her into their home even if the situation had been a little awkward. With a sigh, Bryn pressed receive and took the call.

Aoife sat in the Wind and Gull pub listening to the swirl of conversation sourly, a few of the women chatted about Ryan Kelly and how much he changed. "He's so handsome," gushed one woman further souring Aoife as she remember that woman he brought with him as if she, Aoife, was not good enough.

When they were teenagers, Aoife tried to get Ryan to take her with him when he decided to go abroad, but he had told her he was not ready to settle down and left a few days later without even saying goodbye. However, she waited and he came home again twenty years ago much improved, but he ignored her in favor of a few offers made by some other women, she had been furious. The only positive aspect was Ryan never promised any of those women anything and they had tried to get a commitment out of him.

Now he shows up with a North American chit and kept all the men away from her like she belonged to him, it was not fair, fumed Aoife inwardly, *she is not even that pretty!* Or so she tried to convince herself.

A voice distracted Aoife from her sour reflections when she heard a man with a North American accent asking, "Do you know where I can find Bryn Keane?"

Immediately she turned around to see who had spoken, Aoife identified the man when he asked the same question closer to her, but the man he asked shook his head, so she decided to find out what this man wanted. Maybe he was a boyfriend from North America come to take Bryn Keane away and that would suit her perfectly.

Approaching the man, Aoife noticed he was tall, dark haired with hazel eyes, he had a hard expression with a jutting chin that she associated with a belligerent man, but she ignored his appearance before tapping his shoulder.

"What do you want to know about Bryn Keane?" said Aoife curiously.

"I was told she could be found here," said the man gruffly.

"She's not here, but I know people that can probably find her or get her to come here," said Aoife crystalizing a plan in her head.

"Don't mess with me woman. If your lying, you'll find out I'm not a nice person," said the man coldly.

For a brief instant, Aoife shuddered, "I'm telling the truth, but first why do you want to find her?" she said hesitantly at the dangerous expression on the man's face.

"I came to take her with me, away from this country. She doesn't belong here," said the man evasively.

Aoife almost sang with joy because that was exactly what she hoped for, "If you are telling the truth about taking her away, I'll take you to the people that can find her. I hope she never comes back once she's gone," her voice thrummed with hate on the last comment.

The man silently assessed her before shrugging his shoulders, "it's the truth. I will take her away," he said purposefully.

"Good!" said Aoife exultant, "Come with me."

It was all she could do not to run so excited was she at the prospect of having Ryan all to herself again and led the stranger toward the rear of the Inn where she knew both Becca and Paddy were tallying the day's business.

"In there," said Aoife triumphantly.

The man turned on her menacingly, "You first and you stay until I say otherwise," he snarled quietly.

Feeling a bit less confident, Aoife pushed the door opening without knocking and saw Becca glance up, her expression turned annoyed at the interruption.

"We don't have time for chatting Aoife, please come back another time..." but Becca did not finish when she saw the man behind the woman.

"Yewh!" exclaimed Becca in alarm, "I asked yeh to leave months ago and I know yehr not a guest here."

At those words Paddy looked up, his face hard, "Out sir, me wife asked yeh to leave before and she had her reasons," he said flatly.

Instead, the man shut the door facing the two proprietors, "You once acted like Bryn Keane was a guest here, but I've learned that you actually know her and can ask her to come here," he said sleekly.

"We don't know what yehr talking about," said Paddy in a flat voice, "We don't know any Bryn...Keane...yeh said the name was?"

The man whirled on Aoife, but she was looking at Paddy, "You're lying, Patrick Kelly! I sat in the Pub while you introduced the chit to people like she was some long lost relative. I saw her with my own eyes!" she snapped furiously incensed that Ryan's parents would protect someone they barely knew.

In a stride, the man closed the distance from the door to the desk and backhanded Paddy so hard his nose began to bleed, "Don't you dare play games with me," snarled the man, "Or you might find more than that happens to you."

Aoife crossed her arms defiantly looking angry, but pleased with herself.

"You're going to call Bryn Keane and tell her to come here. You won't tell her the real reason, but you better make it believable and if you try to warn her with clever words, you can watch your wife die slowly in front of you. Refuse, she'll die and I'll make sure you live to suffer with the memory of it," growled the man flashing a knife.

"Aoife, what have yeh done!" said Paddy white-faced.

"He'll take her away then Ryan will be mine like he should have been," said Aoife, her eyes sparkling maliciously.

Becca had never been so angry in her life and recklessly said, "He'll never take yeh for any amount of money. It will always be her even if it takes him the rest of his life to find her again."

Aoife's eyes blazed and she rushed at Becca trying to scratch her face as the unknown man laughed nastily, but Paddy shoved the enraged despicable woman to one side.

"You," said the man pointing at Paddy, "Be sure you only contact the woman. Anyone else shows up, your wife is dead, understand me?"

"Why? Why do yeh want her so badly?" demanded Paddy.

The man grinned, "She's worth a fortune. You have no idea what people are willing to pay for her," he said unpleasantly.

"Slavery," spat Paddy knowing even in the modern age people still sold men and women into slavery for a variety of reasons.

The man laughed, "Slavery? Hardly! You don't know anything about her capabilities and apparently she never mentioned any to you, but you would think your son might have given you a clue," he said with a hateful smile, "Now call her."

Paddy looked up the code that Ryan had given him, his fingers trembled as he punched in the numbers and then there was an attempt to make a connection, "She's not answering," he said.

"Keep trying until she does. If she doesn't answer, neither of you is important any longer, so I suggest you don't give up," said the man dangerously.

Hand trembling, Paddy suddenly heard Bryn's voice, the man held up a warning finger, "Bryn, how are yeh? I called to see if yeh would come visit since we didn't get much time to chat last time, Becca will glad to see yeh," his voice broke and he prayed Bryn would not notice.

"Paddy, I don't have much time at the moment. It could be a while," said Bryn's voice.

Paddy nearly panicked when the man closed his fist indicating he better find some enticement to get Bryn there or Becca would be dead, "Just a short visit Bryn. I need to apologize for the way I acted last time, yeh didn't deserve that and I would feel better if I could say it to yehr face even if yeh can stay only a few hours," he babbled.

Tension crackled in the room when Bryn hesitated, Paddy was about to give up his wife for lost when Bryn said, "I can do that Paddy, but I can't stay long."

"Thank yeh Bryn. We'll see yeh soon," said Paddy breaking off the connection as the man tried to stop him.

"Fool, you should have asked when she was coming here," snarled the man, but when Paddy attempted to reconnect, the man slapped his hand away from the COM, "Don't try it or she'll suspect something if you sound too eager, or was that your plan?" he added raising his fist.

"I didn't think about it. I was thinkin more of that knife yehr wavin in our faces," said Paddy flatly.

The man swore again, but Becca could not be silent as she looked with undiluted pity at Aoife, "Yeh sad, sorry little girl," she said.

Aoife shrieked in outrage and made another attempt to attack Becca until the man pushed the enraged woman to the door, "Enough out of you, you're going to bring people in here shrieking and shouting. Get out, I don't need you anymore, but keep your mouth shut," he snapped shoving the irate woman out of the room.

"Now we wait and you better hope Bryn Keane comes sooner rather than later," sneered the man.

Bryn pondered the call from Paddy and how he seemed so uncomfortable, but then if he felt awkward about the last time she visited that would account for it. What did not make sense was the flare of panic her ears picked up in the tone of his voice when she attempted to delay her visit, he almost seemed scared. Her perceptions must be really disjointed after meeting with her grandfather, Devin and Ryan, when they made her so angry as if she could not take care of herself.

Traveling that distance would present a problem because Bryn knew she would have to use public transport and that would probably be the first place her grandfather would search for her. Golden reddish hair was remarkable even in Ireland so she would be noticeable during the daylight and easily spotted by those that knew what to look for which left her one option: Disguise.

A wig would only be available in a larger town or city so Bryn acquired a hat that would hide her hair tucked inside and sit at the hairline to cover the color, she also acquired an oversized coat that would make her appear bulkier than usual. Those small changes would have to do for now, she really did not have time and if she delayed her visit, the men just might decide to check the Inn. No doubt Paddy would inform his son of her potential visit if he saw him before her arrival so that made delay risky since he could intercept her.

Nervous though she was, Bryn found the travel to Kerry almost boring as early in the morning people did not speak much either still tired or reading news before they arrived at their respective jobs. No one even glanced her way so Bryn began to relax, more confident that her grandfather had not sent any men to wait on a chance she might visit.

Again old habits reasserted as Bryn finally exited the transportation nearest the Wind and Gull, she flicked through her vision to check for anomalies, but was unable to use the infrared spectrum due to the sunlight. She did not notice people acting differently or as in the Thurles before she ran into the moor, men appearing busy doing nothing.

People were leaving homes for work, beginning to tend gardens, feeding livestock, and other normal activities she witnessed on her first arrival to the town. Her wary nature still made her approach slowly, appearing to look in shop windows or market stalls all the while her eyes roved about the area. Finally, Bryn berated her suspicious nature reminding herself Ryan's parents had never done anything to earn such an attitude from her.

Taking a deep breath, Bryn finally entered the Inn, staff bustled about bringing trays to the buffet for guests and guests, yawning, walked toward the dining room and no one took any notice of her. Continuing forward, Bryn's eyes roved looking for signs of Becca or Paddy knowing they would be about directing staff for the day, preparing bills for customers who would check out that morning, or making other arrangements.

Oddly enough, she did not see either of them especially since they should be expecting her to visit even if she never disclosed an arrival time, which was in part just in case her grandfather or Ryan intended to lure her. The only other place Bryn could think of was the elaborate gardens, she recalled Paddy picked fruit and vegetables for the Inn meals, no doubt Becca did when necessary too. So she continued through to the back of the Inn via the main hall that any guest would use so as not to attract attention of wandering in a place staff normally used and someone notice her.

The sun was up higher so Bryn had limited use of some modes of vision or the glare would have blinded her so she had to wander the entire garden to physically check for Paddy and Becca. She found no one to her surprise and began get an uneasy feeling.

A pounding on the office door made Paddy and Becca start from the uneasy doze they adopted when fatigue had set in and they were forced by the unknown man to sit in chairs.

"Open it! Slowly," hissed the man quietly retreating so that he would be behind the door as it opened.

Feeling trepidation, Paddy stood and opened the door a crack, but it was Aoife, she pushed her way in nearly knocking him down, her eyes roving over the office looking for the unknown man.

Soon as she saw him, Aoife said excitedly, "She's here. I saw her go out back in the garden. She's wearing a big coat and a hat is covering her hair, but I recognized her."

Becca made a sound like an angry cat, but the man ignored her, "You," prodding Paddy, "Take me out there and you," indicating Becca, "remain here. If you try to alert anyone, I'll kill your husband," said the man.

Pushing Paddy before him, the man closed the door noting Aoife followed them out, "You stay here and watch the door in case the woman tries anything. Let me know if she does," snapped the man.

Aoife looked indignant, "I want to watch you take the chit away," she whined.

"Do what you're told," snarled the man, "I don't need any more complications."

Paddy burned with anger glaring at the woman in disgust; she had to be delusional to think Ryan would ever look at her with any other expression, but loathing once he found out her part in this affair.

"Move," prodded the man rudely.

With no other choice, Paddy proceeded to the garden wishing there was something he could do to help the young woman, but he would never get the chance and he knew this man made no idle threat he would kill Becca without thought. Maybe, just maybe, Aoife would not listen and follow to watch, he knew his wife well enough that she would call anyone that she could for help once she had the chance.

When they entered the garden the man said, "Call to her, but watch what you say," snarled the man quietly before he faded into the shrubbery.

Hating himself for what he was being forced to do, Paddy called, "Bryn? Are yeh here?" He repeated the call and saw movement off to his left, just like Aoife said, she was wearing a big coat that made her look bulky and a hat that covered all her hair, he might have passed her on the street easily without knowing her. How could he warn her?

"It's good to see yeh," said Paddy haltingly, but he widened his eyes in an attempt to warn Bryn.

A crashing rush sounded from the shrubbery, but to Paddy's amazement, Bryn moved so quickly she was a blur; almost as if she materialized in another spot, forcing the man to come to a stumbling halt to change direction.

Bryn's eyes widened when she saw the tall man turn to face her, it was Hess, the man that went missing during the mountain installation mission so she knew he had been one of the spies. Now she understood why the voice asking for her seemed familiar during her last visit.

"Alright bitch, you're coming with me. There are some people who want to meet you," sneered Hess, "I don't know how you got out of the installation it was supposed to be a trap for you. I would have had you if that damn Nighthawk hadn't decked me. It seems you impressed a lot of people managing to escape."

"Hess you're a fool if you think you can make me go anywhere," said Bryn coldly whipping off coat and hat so she would be uninhibited.

Hess laughed mercilessly, "You think I'm alone? There are men covering you now. We can do this the hard way or the easy way. Maybe we can start by cutting this one," indicating Paddy, "down to size. Seems he's a friend of yours," he said nastily.

Paddy interjected, "Don't worry about me just get out of here…" he began.

"Shut up," snarled Hess as he launched at Paddy, but Bryn was quicker though not quick enough to spare Paddy a slashed arm, she had deflected the killing blow however.

Paddy gasped stumbling backward grabbing his arm as blood soaked his sleeve, "Bryn, please run he'll kill yeh," he groaned.

"Get inside Paddy, please," said Bryn never taking her eyes off Hess.

"Runaway old man I only want her," laughed Hess nastily.

All Paddy could think about is his son's girl being kidnapped or worse and what it would do to Ryan if he lost her after the way his son looked at this woman. He staggered backwards wondering if he could use one of the garden implements as a weapon or to at least distract the man so Bryn could run away. A metallic clanking told

Paddy he stumbled into some of his old fashioned garden tools, ones passed down through generations, he had never bought the robots some people used to do basic garden tasks. He enjoyed doing them by hand.

His hand closed about one round smooth handle that turned out to be a hoe and Paddy had the idea to advance to threaten the man until something froze him with shock: Bryn seemed to morph into a whirling dancing figure of arms and legs deflecting the man's attempts to grab her.

Hess backed away in fury and activated his COM, "Stun her or trank her," he snarled into his wrist.

Paddy heard the response, "She's too fast. We might hit you," a voice said.

"Wound the old man," said Hess his eyes sliding to Paddy maliciously.

Somehow Bryn intercepted whatever those concealed men intended for him, but Paddy felt sweat of terror bead on his forehead when there was a spray of blood from Bryn's side and dots of her blood liberally decorated his shirt.

Hess roared in frustration, "Fools, she's worth nothing dead," he said.

Finally, Paddy accepted something his son said to him, *I won't ask her to be anyone other than who she is. She wouldn't be happy and I enjoy the life I have with her*, and realized he had no right to judge her, he had been wrong. Apparently his son knew Bryn had more than rock climbing skills, but true to Ryan's nature he tended to keep his own council about what information he divulged.

Watching Bryn now, Paddy knew he stood no chance of protecting her against these men and that left him with one choice, "Bryn," he yelled and tossed her the hoe before dropping flat to the ground to get out of line of fire.

"You bastard," Hess screamed when the hoe sailed through the air into Bryn's hands.

Paddy kept looking over his shoulder as he crawled away with grim satisfaction as Bryn used the hoe to great effect, the man shrieked for support to disarm her and for others to tranquilize or stun her.

"Trank her, trank her," yelled Hess to the men undercover.

"We did. Several times," bawled a voice, "Can't you see the tags? She's not dropping."

Bryn was beating Hess and one of the men who ran to help him, black and blue, she smiled grimly at them when the tranquilizer had no effect, she knew why even if they could not know the reasons. It was the nanites Donal programed for the toxin and they must have recognized that the substance was intrusive because of the stress on her body so they were neutralizing every dose.

"Wound her then until she is weak from blood loss," snarled Hess finally.

"Are you sure? We might not make it to a med facility in time," bawled a voice, "Wouldn't it better to try to grab her another time?"

"I'm sure," snapped Hess, "We'll never get another chance. She'll be under such a tight guard we'll never get close again."

The time had come to take more drastic action, these men were not going to leave so Bryn knew her next actions had to be severe, but she did not want to kill these men on the Inn's grounds. It could cause no end of issues for Ryan's family business.

The hoe whirled like a thing alive and the man who attempted to help Hess dropped like a stone with a split head, he might have a fractured skull, but Bryn could tell he was still alive. Suddenly, agony ballooned in her shoulder, a quick glance told Bryn it was a sort of projectile that expanded once it entered he skin, intended to cause massive tissue and blood vessel damage. She cursed mentally that she moved too slow.

Since the men undercover were the greater threat Bryn raced to the foliage on the right, her eyes easily picking out their hiding spot, in five strides she leapt feeling pain rip through her skin on her left arm and leg. One man cried out in pain when she broke his arm, he dropped his weapon just as the hoe came from the opposite direction connecting with his chin rendering him unconscious. The second man dropped his weapon soon as he saw the fate of his cohort and tried to run, but Bryn used the end of the hoe to snag a leg, she brought him in and whirled, her foot connected with his temple, he went limp. That left Hess.

"Damn it to hell bitch," snarled Hess once odds were even, "If I can't have you then no one will."

Bryn smiled grimly, but did not take his skills for granted, if he had been good enough that the Commander used him at the Facility, he would be competent and capable of extreme lethal force. Hess raced at her, Bryn parried his blows hand or foot, but she knew she was weakening and he was not bleeding or significantly wounded. Time felt like it was standing still except they whirled, parried and shifted moving through the garden fighting for advantage or Hess would attempt to take her. The finder's fee for her must be fabulous if Hess was willing to risk grabbing her in populated area with so many potential witnesses so the men had been right, grudgingly Bryn had to admit it. People wanted her badly and were prepared to do almost anything to secure her.

A stream of curses issued from Hess when he could not get through her defenses nor was she obviously weakening enough to him to take risk that might result in him joining his other cohorts in unconsciousness. Round and round the blows took them, at one point Hess thought he had Bryn until she sprang back up to her feet before performing a backflip to get out of his reach, but losing the hoe in the process. Vaguely the sound of sea impinged on Bryn's ears, they had come near the drop offs and cliffs where a rocky path cut through so people could go down to the water, it seemed Hess was moving that way, possibly to escape.

Whirling around him, Bryn blocked Hess from the path, if that was his goal, and he began swearing again, obviously worried now that someone alerted the authorities. Suddenly, there was a dull, "dong," sound like metal hitting an unyielding surface and Hess collapsed to the ground revealing Paddy, his right sleeve soaked with blood, holding an old fashioned shovel.

Paddy managed to get back to the Inn once Bryn disabled the men in the shrubbery, but he could not abandon the young woman to an uncertain fate and grabbed a shovel hoping he might have a chance to aid her. Out of the corner of his eye, Paddy noticed someone watching from the shadow of the doorway and realized it was Aoife, *good*, he thought, *Becca will get help*. Aoife was staring in dismay at Bryn's performance, no doubt realizing that she stood no chance of overcoming her perceived rival if Bryn managed to win free of these men, Paddy ignored the foolish woman.

Blood on his arm caked as the wound clotted, the cloth buckled oddly from the blood dried in the cloth, but Paddy spared those discomforts little attention as he watched Bryn fighting with the last man. It was nail biting tension and Paddy could see by the sun at least an hour, probably two, had passed with Bryn wounded and bleeding, he knew she had to be weakening as he felt weak from his less serious wound.

As the two people whirled about Paddy followed, careful to stay out of sight of the man or become a casualty that Bryn might not be able to prevent any longer. With grudging admiration, Paddy conceded Bryn had impressive skills as she gracefully moved about the man parrying his blows so that she seemed to dance.

When the two moved closer to the cliffs, Paddy had a more difficult time hiding, but the man did not seem to look about him any longer, he seemed more concerned with Bryn so that when she forced the man to turn his back in the direction of the Inn, Paddy saw his chance.

He ran out swinging the shovel, which connected with the man's head and he wilted to the ground unconscious.

Bryn seemed confused standing their looking at him, Paddy noted she was so pale and knew she needed a physician, but before he could take a step forward, a shriek sounded behind him. A push from behind sent Paddy to his knees, he dropped the shovel to catch his fall just as Aoife ran past him, arms outstretched and she shoved Bryn backward toward the cliff's edge forcing her over. Unfortunately for Aoife, she had too much forward momentum and tumbled over as well screaming until it was suddenly cut off.

Bryn stared stupidly at Paddy unable to register what happened, he looked pale and worried. Unexpectedly there was a shriek of rage and Paddy reeled forward onto his hand and knees dropping the shovel to catch his fall revealing a red faced woman behind him that ran at Bryn, her arms held out in front of her. Before she could react, the woman literally shoved Bryn backward off the edge of rock face, but the woman's weight shifted too far forward and with a scream of terror, she tumbled over the cliff.

Somehow Bryn managed to catch one of the ridges in the stone face, but her right arm was useless because of the damaging projectile and the rock below too smooth for a foothold. She was weakening from blood loss and a sudden clarity hit her.

Images flooded into her mind faced with imminent death, what she had done to Ryan, her grandfather and Devin, but Ryan most of all. In a temper she had alienated a man who loved her so fiercely that he risked his life and his job to save her, followed her across the world to protect her. In a childish temper tantrum she pushed Ryan away, denounced him, when he had been right all along and she refused to listen, arrogantly confident in her abilities. Now she hurt him far more severely than any injury she ever sustained.

As her fingers continued to slip, Bryn screamed, not from fear of death, but for the pain she caused a man she loved and now she would never get to apologize for what she had done to him. Her sight began to fade, her body numbing and Bryn thought, *Death is the lesser pain, it's peaceful*, which was her last conscious thought.

Sick with horror, Paddy knew Bryn had been forced over the cliff as well, a terrible scream welled up filled with despair that nearly made him choke with fear, but before he could check a flash of movement ran by him so fast that he flinched defensively. Then before his eyes, Paddy saw his son lunge half over the edge of the cliff only to wriggled back clutching an arm followed by Bryn herself.

Becca came up beside him terribly distressed moaning over his wounded arm, but Paddy only had eyes for his son pulling a limp Bryn into his arms and running back in the direction of the Inn which he hope meant she was still alive.

"I'm all right Becca. The physician will fix me up in a trice," said Paddy soothingly to his wife.

"I was so scared, Paddy. I thought that man would kill yeh once he had what he wanted and then poor Bryn, what he planned to do to her," sobbed Becca suddenly, "It woulda killed Ryan to lose her."

"I take it yeh called Ryan. Does her grandda know yet?" said Paddy wincing as he moved his arm; his fall had caused the wound to bleed again.

"I don't know. I didn't know his code and Ryan only told me to use his in an emergency," said Becca, her body still trembling.

"I'd say this qualified as an emergency," said Paddy drolly.

Becca looked at her husband sternly, "This is no laughin matter Patrick Kelly. Yeh coulda been killed and Bryn...I hope she will be ok...the look at Ryan's face when he ran out..." she said hesitantly.

"Did you call the Garda?" Paddy sighed for what was coming next.

"Just before I came outside," said Becca uncertainly.

"Well not just because of these men, but...Aoife fell over the cliff trying to push Bryn off," said Paddy grimly.

Becca gasped in horror, "No!" she groaned, "She tried to kill Bryn? Her family will be shunned and it wasn't their fault!"

"I'm not goin to tell the Garda the real reason she fell Becca. I'm goin to let them think it was the men tryin to push Bryn and she got in the middle of it to spare her family the shame," said Paddy unwillingly.

"If those men saw, Paddy..." said Becca fearfully.

"They didn't pet. I hit the last one with a shovel so only Bryn and I knew, now yeh," he sighed, "Such a terrible waste. I knew she followed Ryan about as a boy, but I never realized she was so obsessed. I wouldn't believe she was capable of such a thin until I saw it with me own eyes."

"Yeh got to tell Ryan what happened Paddy, he'll keep the knowledge in his head," murmured Becca and Paddy nodded letting his wife help him into the house to check his wound.

An unexpected softness brought Bryn to full consciousness, she tried to identify scents and thought she smelled the odor of food cooking, as she opened her eyes sunlight in the room indicated it was midmorning. Glancing about the room at the décor reminded Bryn of the Inn so she was still in Kerry, but could not remember climbing up the cliff, if anything, she expected to be dead.

The sound of movement drew her eyes and she saw Devin shifting in a chair reading so that meant her grandfather knew where she was.

"Is granddad angry with me?" said Bryn, her voice sounded hoarse to her ears.

Devin's' head jerked up so he had not realize she was awake, "A bit yes. He is trying to keep you safe, the way he never could in the past. You're the only family he has left Bryn. He doesn't want to lose you too," he said quietly.

"I'm used to taking care of myself. I didn't like anyone telling me how to live my life," said Bryn with a hint of stubbornness.

Devin sighed as if for patience, "He wasn't telling you how to live your life. He wanted you to live, survive, and to do that he needs to make certain provisions to keep people from bothering you. If you had had a little patience, we would have dealt with the problem and not involved innocent people," he said.

That last comment cut Bryn to the quick even though she knew Devin was not accusing her of placing the Kellys in danger, she had though just by visiting the first time which of course Ryan never expected such a result or he would never have brought her.

"I've caused enough problems here. I should return to North America," said Bryn feeling depressed.

"What will that achieve Bryn? Like we asked you before, what will you go back to? You have family here. I watched you grow up through the years, like the daughter I never had and I see no reason for you to return unless you're worrying about Donal," said Devin shrewdly.

"He's my friend. They frightened him and kept him under surveillance because of me," said Bryn in shame.

"Donal isn't going to stay there forever Bryn. He plans to return here. Part of the reason he went to North America was to do research, but then he stayed on after the accident so once you reached maturity he could help restore your sight," then noticing Bryn's expression, "Oh, he benefited doing research so you were not the only reason he decided to work there for a while," said Devin pointedly.

"Where is Granddad?" said Bryn suddenly.

"He's resting. He was up all night watching you. It was a close call since you lost so much blood. He'll be glad you woke up," said Devin moving closer to the bed, "Doctor's orders are to rest even though they gave you synthetic blood. It kept you alive, but your body still needs to replace it for you to recover completely."

"I'm sorry," said Bryn looking away, "For leaving and worrying both of you."

Devin reached out to stroke her hair with a sigh, "I know Bryn. You did scare us though. Mr. Kelly told us what happened so we know you didn't run here irresponsibly. We didn't even know someone would use the Kellys in such a way or your grandda would have placed men nearby to keep them safe. He has now, though if word gets out about your latest adventure it may discourage most of those operatives," he said, "They were all in bad shape."

"Mr. Kelly? Is he ok? Mrs. Kelly?" said Bryn worriedly.

"They're both fine. Mr. Kelly had a nasty slice, but it was easily sealed. He lost some blood though not nearly as much you. Physician has him resting for a few days. Mrs. Kelly was never injured," said Devin.

"A woman pushed me…I just remembered…" said Bryn suddenly.

"Enough talk about negative things Bryn," warned Devin firmly.

"I imagine the Kellys can't see me gone fast enough," said Bryn tears misting her eyes.

Devin sighed and sat on the edge of her bed, "That's not true. If you hadn't come that man would have killed them as useless, they said so. From what Mr. Kelly said, you're the reason he's alive. He said they tried to kill him twice and you protected him. The Kellys are both very grateful to you," he said encouragingly, but noting she never asked about Ryan.

Bryn sighed again, she could not bring herself to ask about Ryan, she did not feel she deserved to know anything after her childish behavior, she felt Devin brush her hair back gently, "Get some rest," he finally said.

Once Devin was certain Bryn fell asleep, he left the room knowing Ryan would be waiting to hear news, he had been pacing all night, but refused to go into her room in case he upset her.

"Is she awake?" demanded Ryan quietly when he saw Devin shut the door.

"She was. She's asleep now," said Devin noting the man's shoulders sag when he did not add any information about Bryn asking for him.

"Is she doing better," said Ryan quietly not quite masking his pain that Bryn did not ask for him.

"Give her time Ryan. She loves you and yes, she looks better," said Devin sympathetically.

"She may never forgive me," he said bitterly.

"You did what was necessary to protect her and she knows that even if it made her angry. We both know she isn't a killer no matter what she attempted to do to Liam Kendall. How do you think it would have affected her to be with you and see all those operatives you killed that were looking for her?" reminded Devin.

Ryan looked at the other man, "No, she isn't a killer. She still didn't kill those men here even after all they tried to do to her and my da, but I think that was in deference to my parents," he said.

"Oh?" said Devin waiting for elaboration.

"Because of their business, they rely on tourism and people being killed on the premises would have incited rumors, possibly affected their reputation. Bryn thinks about things like that where I wouldn't have wasted a thought about tossing each one over the cliff," ended Ryan grimly.

"She started to ask about that woman that pushed her over the cliff…" Devin halted his words at the burning fury on the younger man's face.

"Da told me what happened and had I been here, it might have been the first time I killed a civilian. She not only hurt Bryn, but she risked my family," snarled Ryan dangerously, "I've never put them in jeopardy my entire career and then some foolish bitter woman does it on a whim."

"Let it go Ryan. Anger isn't going to change anything now and your family is safe. Aiden is making certain it stays that way," said Devin holding up a placating hand knowing it was his feelings over Bryn's refusal to see him previously that was a root of the anger, if she had just asked about Ryan.

"Get some rest Ryan it will improve your mood. If there is any change I'll let you know, I give you my word," he added.

Her next awakening, Bryn saw her grandfather, guilt assailed her at the grey expression of worry on his face and remembering what Devin said about being the only family he had left.

"I'm sorry Granddad," whispered Bryn unable to raise her voice more due to a constricted throat.

Aiden's head jerked at the sound of her voice and relief flooded his face, "It's good to see you awake. You gave us all quite a fright Bryn," he said moving to her beside to sit on the edge of the mattress.

"I apologize for behaving so childish. I've been used to taking care of myself for a long time and I guess I resented anyone interfering without considering the merit of your arguments," said Bryn softly, tears leaked down her cheeks.

Aiden made an impatient sound as he pulled out a beautifully embroidered handkerchief and began dabbing her cheeks, "Bryn dear, you would not be your mother's child without that streak of fire in you. Under the circumstances, it seems that had you remained at the castle, the Kellys might not be safe so it appears circumstances exceeded our plans. I don't deny I was angry. As for my actions, I behaved arrogantly, too accustomed to people obeying unquestioningly, even Devin and that was wrong. Everyone needs to be challenged occasionally if for no other reason than to make them think about the decisions they are making. I've been without family too long and forgot that not everyone is at my beck and call," he sighed.

"Devin doesn't act like he's at your beck and call," said Bryn a little dryly.

Aiden snorted, "Over the years our relationship has altered to a respectful friendship on both sides, but he still doesn't question my actions or decisions the way I should be at times," his face altered to disgust as he added, "Quade would question me, but it was usually more of the nature of complaints not a logical argument."

"Has he bothered you again?" said Bryn.

"No, he doesn't dare with the Agency alerted to his activities, but it doesn't mean he isn't capable of mischief," said Aiden flatly and then his expression altered touching Bryn's arm with an unusual tattoo on the inside of her upper arm which was normally hidden by regular clothing.

Bryn glanced at her grandfather's hand at his fingers moved over a tattoo she had since she could remember, he turned her arm out so he could see the entire design.

Aiden mused thoughtfully, "How long have you had that tattoo, dear?"

"I'm not certain. It was there when Donal restored my sight. I don't remember when or where I got it," said Bryn pensively.

Aiden sighed his face lighting, "I think we found out where Jimmy hid that information from your father. It's seems Liam Kendall was right that you had the data all along. That's a special tattoo my dear. Clever Jimmy, he knew I would be the only one that would recognize the design as our ancient crest in Keane family tree and no one else would think of it as anything, but a mundane piece of art. Back home I have a special scanner that will be able to read the fractal patterns within the design," he said triumphantly.

I guess it's a good thing I was injured then or you might not have seen me in a sleeveless shirt," said Bryn drolly.

That comment wiped the smile of Aiden's face, "That is never a good thing Bryn no matter what good came of it," he said sternly and then he added in a change of subject, "I think you need to forgive young Ryan dear."

That comment wiped the amusement off Bryn face, "I'm not angry at him anymore. I understand why he did what he did even if I didn't like it. I don't deserve to talk to him after the way I treated him," she said hoarsely.

Aiden sighed in exasperation, "Girl, your being foolish. That man has been dying a little bit each day he's been separated from you. Don't talk nonsense about deserving to speak to him when he would break the door down if you sent for him. I'm not going to tell you what to do. This is something you have work out for yourself, but a word of advice, don't throw away something so special on foolish guilt or anger," he said firmly as he stood, "Get some more rest dear."

Chapter 20

Four days later the physicians stopped by again, "Well Miss Keane, you're doing much better. You don't need to stay in bed any longer, but I want you to keep to light activity for five days to give your body a chance to adjust so no climbing rock faces or martial art exercises. Walking is fine, light gardening, and things like that, then you can resume your normal activities with care," he said patting her hand.

"Thank you," said Bryn her eyes flicking to her grandfather's relieved expression.

As the physician left, Aiden said, "I need to return home dear. Unfortunately I have pressing business matters, but I recommend you stay here for a while," his gaze inferred she had unfinished business of her own, "and relax. Devin will be here if you need anything," he leaned down to kiss her forehead before leaving.

Bryn sighed and began to dress into appropriate clothing in preparation to facing the Kellys after the horrible mess yet she just hoped they could forgive her for the situation.

It was not long after making her way downstairs that Bryn caught sight of Becca, she braced herself for harsh words, but soon as the other woman clapped eyes on her, her face lit with such joy, Bryn nearly stumbled in confusion.

Nearly colliding with her, Becca grabbed Bryn into such a tight hug she felt the air squeezed from her body, "I'm so glad to see yeh up and about. We didn't want to come up when the physician insisted yeh rest in quiet. I can't thank yeh properly for savin me husband girl! Paddy told me what yeh did for him," she said in Bryn's ear.

"I'm so sorry about all the problems. I hope your guests weren't too alarmed by the entire ordeal," said Bryn in a choked voice.

Becca leaned back to look at her in exasperation, "Come with me so we can talk without so many listenin," she said grabbing Bryn's arm firmly.

Leading Bryn into an office, Becca shut the door before turning around and planting her hands on her hips, "Now yeh listen to me girl. None of that was yehr fault and actually not many guests knew anythin happened thankfully. Those that do, think there was an accidental fall from the cliff because someone didn't read the warnin and crossed the barrier. The Garda took those men away and the guests think they had a drunken brawl so there is no harm there. Yeh did more good than any harm and the harm was to people that deserved it," her head nodded decisively, "which was to those horrible men," she said sternly.

There was a light tap on the door and Bryn jumped, Becca opened it to reveal Paddy, "I heard yeh were escortin Bryn to the office and I wanted to speak to her," he said before engulfing Bryn into a bear hug to her utter amazement, Becca grinned fondly at them.

"Yeh saved our lives girl. I can't ever thank yeh properly for that. It wrenched me heart to lure yeh here," Bryn felt Paddy tremble, "but that man was gonna kill Becca," said Paddy hoarsely.

"You didn't have any choice Paddy. I'm just sorry I was the reason it all happened to either of you. I exposed you both, your staff, and your guests to terrible danger for which I am so sorry," said Bryn in a choked voice.

Paddy leaned back, his expression irritated, "Bah girl, yeh didn't do that. Me son brought yeh here, it's not like yeh traipsed through the door with all this mischief in mind. Yeh barely talk as it is. I owe yeh an apology for me attitude the first time yeh visited," Bryn started to interrupted, but Paddy said, "No, yeh listen to me girl. I'm old fashioned, Becca will tell yeh and I always thought women should stick to the old ways, but yeh proved to me, if that had been the case, we would probably both be dead now. I was wrong, even if admittin that leaves a sour taste," a grin crossed his face to let her know he was joking, "so I ask yeh forgive me for me foolishness."

"There's nothing to forgive," said Bryn quietly, "I'm hardly normal."

"Now, now don't yeh start that girl!" growled Paddy as Becca made a sound of dismay, "We like yeh just the way yeh are so remember that if yeh remember nothin else!"

Paddy emphasized those words with a bone crushing hug and Bryn felt tears spring to her eyes, Becca batted at her husband to release Bryn so she could dab the tears on her cheeks with a handkerchief.

"Great oaf, yeh nearly crushed the girl," scolded Becca tolerantly.

Another tap on the door, made Bryn jump again and Paddy opened it for one of the staff, "I'm sorry to interrupt Mr. Kelly, but a man named Devin asked me to give this note to Miss Keane, he said it was important," said the woman handed over a folded piece of paper.

Taking the note in confusion, Bryn wondered if this was something her grandfather sent to apprise her of a development and opened the note reading a puzzling message:

Walk where to roses bloom, breath where the foun-
tain bubbles, seek the arbor where secrets lay, and you
will find the land will welcome you home.

All she could do was gape at the note. It made no
sense unless someone was playing a joke, but Bryn knew
Devin tended to be very serious so what was he up to
with this? Was this something her grandfather arranged?

"Does this make sense to either of you?" said Bryn
finally passing the note to Paddy who passed it to Becca,
both looked completely puzzled.

"Maybe somethin yehr grandda arranged," said
Paddy pensively.

Bryn hesitated warily perusing the note again for a
hidden meaning especially after recent encounters she
was understandably suspicious.

"I think yeh'll be ok girl. Yehr grandda would never let
anythin happen to yeh," said Becca encouragingly though
Bryn missed the glance she exchanged with Paddy.

Bemused, Bryn nodded absently, Paddy opened the
door wider for her and she followed the hall toward the
one of the doors leading to the massive garden, as the
note hinted, stealing herself for the memory of the confrontation. The sea breeze ruffled her hair, bringing the
scent of salt mixed with flowers so instead she relaxed
breathing deeply until the sound of the fountain bubbling
came to her sensitive ears. Bryn wandered through the
lovely paths until she finally saw the fixture, its water
glistening in the sunlight and then off to the right, she
saw an arbor previously unnoticed in her initial visit to
meet the Kellys.

Curiously, she moved through the climbing roses
surrounded by three additional arbors creating a sort of
courtyard and saw a pedestal with a lone candle on it
to her surprise, flickering though most of the greenery
blocked the full force of the draft. This anomaly thoroughly baffled Bryn and she approached it wondering
why Devin would place a candle outdoors where it could
be impractically blown out.

To her surprise, a red rose flanked the saucer style candleholder and as she reached for the flower, she found another note she had not first seen because of the subdued light, she had had no reason to use her alternate vision modes.

Carefully removing the envelope, Bryn opened it and saw the words:

"Marry me"

Bryn gasped in amazement, a variety of emotions ran through her wondering why Devin would leave such a note and she could not understand how she misread his intentions all this time. What would her grandfather say? Did he know?

Because of her distracted state, Bryn did not immediately register the noise behind her until it occurred again, she whirled about in alarm and nearly fell down from what she least expected to see. Standing there was Ryan looking at her with those piercing grey eyes scanning her face for some sign of her thoughts; Bryn dropped the note unable to credit what she was seeing until she finally was able to speak. "How long have you been here?"

"Darlin' my mum called me after my Da was forced to trick you into visiting them. I almost didn't make it in time to grab you off the cliff and even that almost wasn't enough," he said softly.

"But...but why didn't you let me know you were here?" she blurted out incredulously.

"The physician wasn't certain he could save your life after losing so much blood. Your grandda wanted to send for Dr. Meany, but the physician said he wouldn't get here in time so they collaborated through a COM. They wouldn't let you have any visitors other than Devin and your grandda to avoid stressing you," sighed Ryan, "I waited outside your room, but you never asked for me."

Bryn was consumed with guilt over those last words, "I didn't think you would want to see me again after the way I treated you. I was angry, but I also acted irrationally, I didn't realize that until I thought I was going to die," she whispered then glanced at the note that had fallen from her fingers.

With a gesture Bryn pointed at the note, "Why did you wait until now to say anything?"

"You weren't ready to hear what I wanted to say. When I tried to lead up to it, you would push me away, but I understood why from some things you mentioned before, you don't want to lose anyone else. It nearly killed me when I put you in that headlock, I knew exactly how you would feel once you came to and I wondered if you would ever forgive me, but I couldn't lose you Bryn. You have no idea how dangerous those operatives are and were. I couldn't let you follow me to see what I was going to have to do to stop them. I didn't want you to see a monster when you looked at me," he said quietly.

"Do you enjoy hurting people?" demanded Bryn suddenly.

"Of course I don't enjoy it. I did what I was ordered to do or what was necessary," said Ryan stiffly.

"Then why would I see you as a monster?" insisted Bryn impatiently.

Ryan sighed and looked at the ground, "Because you aren't a killer Bryn. You might have come close to it, but you never killed. Witnessing it leaves a mark on your soul almost as much as committing the act. Those people were not going to stop without lethal force. The fact those men survived attempting to kill you and my parents proved you were not prepared to take those measures. I would have had no reservations tossing each and every one of them over the cliff," he said with certainty that chilled Bryn slightly.

"I might have," said Bryn tartly, "I didn't want to ruin the reputation of your parents' livelihood. It's hard to hide the fact people are killed on your doorstep. It seems my granddad managed to deflect the worst of it from what your mother said."

Ryan sighed, "It's convenient to say that when you aren't faced with the reality darlin', but it's a moot point right now," he said.

"Then if you thought I might see you like that, why the note?" said Bryn raising her eyebrow.

"I told you I loved you. Did you think I was lyin' darlin'? I can't live my life without you so I had to try even if you refused me. I came close to asking you several times, but something always interrupted the moment. If it's not what you want, I'll keep my distance even if it will eat me alive. It's you I want and no one else," he emphasized.

"So you pulled Devin into your scheme?" demanded Bryn.

"No, he offered when I didn't know how to approach you. I thought you were still angry with me and wouldn't accept a direct request to talk," he said a little sheepishly.

Bryn made a telling point, "How can it work when I will have to return to North America at some point. I'm not a citizen and you're restricted to Ireland from what you told me before," she said a little sadly.

"Not if you answer that note," said Ryan intently.

"What do you mean by that?" said Bryn suspiciously.

"You can stay as my wife and become a naturalized citizen," he said taking a step closer.

Bryn nearly took a step back in alarm at the intensity in Ryan's face, "You could accept me beating on you every time I lost my temper?" she babbled nervously.

A slow grin lit Ryan's face, "I would look forward to it," he said insufferably.

"Does my granddad know about this?" she said suspiciously.

"Actually, he does and gave me this to give to you," said Ryan with an air of triumph as he went down on one knee to Bryn's shock as he presented an old fashioned ring box in his outstretched hand.

Bryn felt the blood drain from her face as she reached out mechanically to take the little box, fingering it until she opened it to see a dazzling flash as the array of cut diamonds caught the candlelight and the daylight and gasped at the delicate beauty of it.

"I couldn't wear this all the time, I would damage it," stammered Bryn without thinking about what she said.

"You don't have to as long as you wear my wedding band, I can make certain it's plain," said Ryan quietly still on one knee.

Her hand trembled, when Bryn realized she was home, truly home and launched at Ryan to throw her arms about his neck which succeeded in knocking both of them over so that they both ended up sprawled on the ground.

Ryan chuckled, "Is that a yes?" he said hugging a squirming Bryn to him.

"If you can forgive me for the way I treated you, then it's a yes," murmured Bryn into his chest.

"There's nothing to forgive darlin' I hated myself for using skills against you like that. Your grandda wasn't very happy with me either, but I knew it was the only way to keep you from following me," sighed Ryan kissing the top of Bryn's head.

"And your parents? What do they think?" said Bryn tentatively.

"They knew I planned to ask soon as they saw me the first visit it seems. Da said he could see it in my face, I have no idea how," snorted Ryan humorously.

"Is that what some of those cryptic remarks were about to my granddad?" said Bryn suspiciously.

Ryan laughed out loud, "Yes, I was warned not to slip away with you to a private ceremony somewhere without his knowledge or to take you away from him," he said in amusement.

"I see," said Bryn irritably, "And of course you didn't want him to hunt you to the ends of the earth?"

Ryan laughed again, "No I didn't because he is one person that would probably find me," he said with a grin.

"Well I guess your parents deserve to know all this," said Bryn philosophically.

"Yes and ready yourself for a celebration this time. They will call all the relatives and friends for certain. And…we need to tell your grandda or he'll twist my head off. He agreed to the ceremony here because my parents are so busy and would plan something later in Thurles for friends and distant family there," stated Ryan.

"I see," said Bryn sarcastically pushing away from Ryan indignantly, "All of you seem to have made considerable plans without informing me!"

"Come on darlin' it's not that bad. He is your grandda so of course he's going to make plans for your future since you have no one else. Let him do this for you. It was just as hard on him to lose his own children as it was for you to lose those same people. He couldn't be a part of their lives or do the things regular parents do like sending gifts or visiting. Your grandda needs you more than you realize," said Ryan with quiet plea reaching up to stroke Bryn's cheek, watching her face as he lay on the ground.

Bryn sighed, she needed to stop being so selfish and self-centered, of course her granddad would have suffered the loss of her mother and Uncle Jimmy, then to be denied the ability to acknowledge them because he was trying to keep them safe had cut him off completely. He missed the normal things grandparents enjoyed like watching grandchildren grow, giving them gifts, celebrating holidays. Ryan was correct, her granddad was all alone too and he was trying to make up for time he could never spend with her as a child, to bring his family back together again.

"Are you still going to be running around the countryside when all of it is over?" said Bryn avoiding Ryan's eye.

"Until we're certain you're safe, darlin', probably. I'll be careful Bryn, I promise," he said gently this time running a caressing hand up her arm.

"And I can't come with you?" she said with plea in her voice.

Ryan sighed, "If they found out you were out there with only one man, they would home in on you and we couldn't take a bunch of guards with us or we would be noticed," he said regretfully.

"I understand," she said dejectedly, "I miss you when you're gone."

Ryan pulled her down into his arms, "I always miss you too darlin'," he said lovingly.

"I guess it keeps me from being a distraction," said Bryn trying to find humor in the situation.

"It certainly will do that," laughed Ryan.

Bryn sat back up and opened the little ring box again before turning it to Ryan with a raised eyebrow, he grinned at the subtle hint as he removed the ring to place on her finger, it was a little loose, but it would not fall off.

Ryan then pulled her left hand to his lips and kissed the ring then he sat up, "Let's tell your grandda, Devin, and my parents," he grinned.

When they arrived inside, Becca was busy directing staff to prepare the dining room for lunch until she turned and saw them, her face lit up so happily that Bryn thought the woman must have personal radar to know Ryan gave her the ring. To Bryn's utter surprise, she ran not walked, up to them and pulled Ryan's face down to kiss him before turning to hug Bryn.

"It's about time," she chortled, "The way he's been moping about Bryn...well I know yeh'll take good care of him," she said fondly.

"Paddy, PADDY," Becca basically shrieked making both of them jump in surprise, Ryan looked at his mother in wonder as if he never heard her like that before.

Paddy came running and looking worried, not that anyone could blame him after recent events, he calmed when he saw nothing out of the ordinary or at least until Becca grabbed Bryn's left hand to wave under her husband's nose.

At first he stared at the ring in silence and then roared in delight, making Bryn jump again, before pounding his son's back enthusiastically nearly knocking Ryan down to Bryn's amusement.

"About time! Yeh shoulda seen him Bryn...like a lost puppy," snorted Paddy.

"DA!" said Ryan in obvious dismay and Bryn had to laugh.

Her laugh cut short when Paddy engulfed Bryn in a bear hug forcing air from her lungs with an 'oof,' and Ryan had his turn to laugh, especially when Becca began to bat at her husband for squeezing the life out of her.

When Paddy released her, Bryn jumped again as Devin appeared at her elbow a grin on his face too and found herself in another hug, but considerably more reserved that Paddy's hand been.

"Your grandda is going to be happy Bryn and it's about time you stopped that boy's suffering," said Devin in amusement.

Bryn heard Ryan snort and his parents' chuckle at Devin's words, "I hear you had a hand in it sneaking that note to me," she said tartly as Devin released her.

"He didn't think you would talk to him even after what I told him," said Devin shaking a finger at her, "You need to work on that temper of yours."

"Why did yeh think that Ryan?" said Becca narrowly, apparently suspicious.

Bryn had to bite her lip to keep from laughing at the alarm on Ryan's face, he glanced in a panicked way at Devin, his father and then back at his mother.

"I can't help you with this one," said Devin ruefully stepping out of the line of fire, Bryn decided to join him to avoid the backlash.

Ryan cleared his throat several times, glancing at his father in dismay, "I...uh...put her in a headlock to keep her from leaving her grandda's house," he said hoarsely.

Paddy's eyebrows shot up in surprise and then he too sidestepped away from his wife as an angry yowl escaped her lips, Bryn decided that her first impression of Becca's temper had been inaccurate, she was truly scary now.

"Yeh flamin great oaf!" Becca smacked Ryan so hard on the cheek everyone could see the handprint left behind, "Yeh don't treat any woman that way I taught yeh better than that. Yeh could have hurt her. Yehr lucky she decided t'speak to yeh again even luckier she accepted that ring from yeh. If I'd a known yeh done somethin like that, I'd a told her to say NO," snarled his mother, her eye sparkling with fury.

If Bryn had not seen it with her own eyes, she would never have believed it, Ryan seemed to wilt in chagrin before his mother's anger, a man that faced all the danger she had witnessed literally folded at his mother's diatribe. He did not even attempt to justify his actions.

"I know mum. I never expected her to speak to me again either. I love her so much and I didn't want any more to happen to her. I was wrong to do that to her," whispered Ryan in agony that tore at Bryn's heart, "I can't live without her, I had to protect her."

Becca's face was still blotchy with anger, but Ryan obviously said the right things in the right way because she began to visibly calm down though she was breathing rather fast, "Yehr still a great oaf, but I know how much yeh love her. I saw the first time yeh got here without her just don't yeh ever do somethin like that again!" she snapped.

Bryn cleared her throat, "I'm not innocent either. I've gotten angry at him before and used martial arts on him," she winced.

Becca snorted, "HA! He probably deserved every blow. It's good to know yeh can give him a thrashin when he needs it," she said in a satisfied way.

Bryn gaped in shock, Ryan had said his mother would say something like that, Paddy chuckled and Devin grinned as he scratched the side of his nose, "After seein her in action, I'd say yeh better watch yehrself boy," added Paddy humorously knowing his son would never retaliate.

"Oh she keeps him on his toes from watching the gym surveillance at her grandda's home," interjected Devin slyly.

Becca nodded satisfied, "Good, yeh keep doin that girl," she said.

Ryan looked at his father in consternation, Paddy only shook his head chuckling and held up a hand to forestall whatever he thought his son might say, "I can't help yeh out of this boy," he said.

"I'm going to contact your grandda Bryn. He'll want to know when you plan the ceremony and so he can make plans for a celebration in Thurles. You might as well get out and find a dress or he'll pick one for you," said Devin.

"I don't need a dress!" said Bryn indignantly.

Devin sighed, "If you think your grandda is going to miss walking you down the aisle, you have a rude awakening coming. So get shopping or I promise you, he will do it for you," he warned.

Ryan actually grinned at Devin's words as he knew Bryn rarely wore anything, but basic attire consisting of pants, shirts, sweaters and a variety of sturdy footwear or special body suits.

Watching Devin walk away, Bryn said, "I never owned a dress even as a little girl and there was no point when I was blind."

Becca chuckled, "I can come with yeh if Paddy doesn't mind keepin an eye on thins," she said.

Paddy snorted at those words and waved his wife away, he glanced at his son once the women were out of earshot, "Luck boy, it coulda been much worse," he said.

Ryan breathed a sigh of relief, "I know Da. I thought mum was going to disown me. I've never seen her like that before, not that she didn't have a reason...I should never have done that to Bryn," he said quietly.

"No, yeh shouldn't have, but I understand why yeh did it after everythin I saw. Son," Paddy laid a hand on

Ryan's forearm, "Yeh can't protect her from everythin even though I know yeh want to. If the situation hadn't been so bad, it'd been a treat to watch her. She's amazin."

"Yes she is," murmured Ryan his eyes following Bryn.

Aiden received a call from Devin later the day he returned from Kerry, "He's finally done it," he said cryptically.

"You're obviously in a good mood to start off like that," said Aiden repressively at the levity in the other man's voice.

"Ryan finally gave her the ring," clarified Devin a grin in his voice.

Aiden nearly shouted with joy, "Finally! That man was going melt away if she refused to talk to him any longer," he said happily.

Devin coughed a laugh, "He told his mother why Bryn hadn't been speaking to him. I think all of us scattered for that fallout. For a formidable man, Ryan is no match for Becca Kelly," he said humorously.

Aiden laughed heartily, "That would have been something to see. That clever devil needed a check or two, not that Bryn isn't capable of giving it to him," he said.

"I sent her out to get a dress, she tried to refuse until I told her if she didn't you would acquire one for her and if she thought you would miss walking her down the aisle, she had a rude awakening coming," laughed Devin.

Aiden chuckled, "I noticed she had nothing like that anywhere or did she order any type of dress or skirt. Just this one time she can manage. I suppose Mrs. Kelly went with her?" he inquired.

"Yes, which is good for her not having many women in her life lately," said Devin a little ruefully.

"Very true," sighed Aiden, "I'll make some plans for a celebration here later for friends and family though I will inform them about the initial one in Kerry if they would like to attend. Let me know when the Kellys settle on a day they can arrange."

Aiden straightened his suit jacket, running his hands down his sides to smooth the material and adjusted his old style cravat before going to his granddaughter's room. Becca Kelly had finished arrangements for the wedding ceremony within six weeks of Bryn's recovery though his thoughts turned humorous that it might be to prevent his granddaughter from getting away from her son. Another humorous note via Paddy Kelly was that Becca had sent Ryan away to stay with relatives while she made all the preparations forbidding him from the Inn until the day of the ceremony even though Paddy had commented Ryan had already been avoiding Bryn suspecting his mother might invoke such a rule.

Leaning down to his luggage, Aiden pulled out a long velvet box and placed it in his pocket before turning toward the door, it was almost time to escort Bryn downstairs. Arriving at her room, he tapped lightly on the door and heard, "Come in," from Bryn and turned the knob only to stand in stunned amazement.

Aiden had not seen Bryn's dress though Devin assured him Becca informed him of the purchase, but there she stood in ivory silk and satin, simple elegant glowing in the morning light shining through the window. Her hair was full of living flowers and baby's breath, woven into her tresses, probably by Becca, in an old elegant whimsical style, she looked stunning.

"You'll take Ryan's breath away dear. I've something for you before we go," said Aiden softly pulling out the velvet box to drape a necklace of large emeralds surrounded with diamonds set in gold about his granddaughter's neck.

"Granddad! This is too much!" said Bryn aghast at such an expensive gift.

"I wanted to give you something special at least this once. I know you probably won't wear jewelry often, but you should have something," said Aiden waving away her concern, "It's time we head downstairs toward the garden."

The garden had been the logical choice for the gathering as the guests would be using the indoor facilities and Bryn had actually preferred the idea, not that he was surprised given his granddaughter's nature.

When he led Bryn outside, Aiden heard a sigh of admiration whisper through the guests when they caught sight of her, but Aiden was curious to see Ryan's reaction and focused on him. The younger man's eyes nearly popped out of his head, he seemed to waiver slightly until his father laid a steading hand on his shoulder with a grin.

It took great effort for Aiden to lay Bryn's hand into the young man's hand, he just got his granddaughter back only to give her away again though he did remind himself she would still live with him. Filled with emotion, he watched the ceremony noting Becca wiping her eyes and Paddy's proud smile, Ryan seemed almost too amazed to speak his vows the way his eyes stayed riveted on Bryn. There was a huge cheer when Ryan kissed his new wife and they exchanged rings.

People surged around to congratulate the new couple, Aiden observed quietly until he noticed Devin at his elbow, "She's breathtaking," commented Devin in admiration, "I think Ryan nearly fainted when he saw her," he added humorously.

Aiden chuckled, "I noticed that too," and then he asked, "Are all the arrangements made?"

"Yes, the men are in place at the retreat so they can relax during their honeymoon without looking over their shoulders. I don't think they've had much time together without something happening so they deserve the rest," said Devin watching the couple speaking to a variety of people.

"Yes they do need some time alone. Make certain the men remain hidden unless absolutely necessary. I'll leave you to explain when you drive them out. I hope Bryn understands," Aiden sighed.

"She will even if it irritates her initially Aiden. Even if she had grown up normally, she has to understand that being your granddaughter comes with some concessions, she still would have needed guards once the relationship was known," Devin pointed out.

"True, but she's so much like Fiona. You remember how Fiona hated having guards, especially socially. Even though Bryn is more than capable of defending herself, I still don't want to take chances," said Aiden and Devin nodded wordlessly.

They watched Bryn walk over to a table and suddenly appear if she was removing the skirt of her dress, Aiden exclaimed in dismay hurrying over when he saw revealed elegant ivory silk trousers that were obviously part of the outfit.

Soon as he was close enough to his granddaughter, Aiden said irritably, "So I see this is how you managed to work your way around wearing a dress for the entire day."

Bryn sighed, "Granddad, this is how they sold it. Even Becca thought it would be more convenient, particularly moving about the garden. I didn't want the skirt to get stained by grass or dirt and she said it still appeared bridal like this."

Stepping back, Aiden circled his granddaughter critically and grudgingly conceded that the outfit appeared suitable for a wedding reception, she would need freedom for any dancing that the Irish enjoyed during celebrations.

"It's still beautiful. I enjoyed seeing you in a dress, you looked so lovely. Maybe we will have to reserve such attire for gatherings in the castle where you don't have to worry about soiling material so easily," Aiden mused.

"I'll wear a dress for you if the occasion calls for it granddad, but I ask if you can please avoid it as a daily requirement," said Bryn cautiously.

Aiden chuckled cupping his granddaughter's chin, "It's a bargain my dear," he said affectionately.

A hiss came to both of their ears suddenly, "Move behind the hedge or I'll shoot you both."

Bryn stiffened, but Aiden placed a hand on her arm cautiously, "Don't warn anyone or say a word just move," hissed the voice.

Both of them circumvented the hedge to find Quade waving a weapon of some sort, he gestured with the threatening hand for them to keep moving away from the crowd of guests to a quiet part of the massive gardens.

Once they were far enough away, Quade sneered, "I finally have her. You thought I'd given up didn't you Uncle? She's coming with me until you sign the estate irrevocably over to me," his eyes surveyed Bryn's body with a leer, "Or maybe I'll keep her. Move," he indicated Bryn with a wave of the weapon.

"You have no idea what you're up against Quade," said Aiden coldly, "She's just married and if you think her husband will sit idly by and let you keep her, you're delusional. As a matter of fact, if you think even I'll let you take her, you're sadly mistaken."

"I can achieve the same effect by shooting her," Quade sneered, "I'm giving you the more palatable choice."

A rustle in the hedge heralded the appearance of Devin and Ryan, Quade however, grabbed Bryn's arm pulling her with him waving the weapon around her head, "Stay back," he snarled, "Or I will shoot her," he kept yanking her backwards watching the three men.

To Devin and Aiden's surprise Ryan began to murmur barely above a whisper, "Bryn, don't do anything with him facing the crowd or a stray discharge could hit an innocent person. Try to wait until he's facing another direction."

"Can she actually hear that?" hissed Devin in amazement.

"Yes," breathed Ryan, "Her ears are very sensitive."

"Donal's work?" inquired Aiden softly never taking his eyes off his granddaughter.

"I don't know. Maybe because she was blind so long…" breathed Ryan also never taking his eyes off his wife.

They could not tell for certain if Bryn actually heard her husband's low words until Quade made an error shifting his body so that the weapon pointed away from the crowd of guests in the garden. Instantly the weapon arced away from the hateful man and Bryn turned on him in fury, Ryan attempted to move forward, but Aiden laid a hand on his arm, "Don't Ryan, it's your wedding day. If anything needs to be done, Devin will take care of it," he said.

The three men stiffened in outrage when Quade attempted to strike Bryn, but she moved so fast he only swiped at empty air, Aiden watched his grandnephew's eyes widen in shock. Then Bryn began to speak in an angry voice that all the men could hear, "You horrible man," a resounding crack as she backhanded him, "That's for trying hurt my granddad," she snapped.

Again Quade made attempts to strike Bryn to no avail and she backhanded him again hard enough to make him stagger, "That," she enunciated implacably, "is for hurting Devin."

With a roar of rage, Quade threw his arms wide and jumped at Bryn only to find he was sailing through the air to land on his back gasping for air, he struggled to his feet, his face red with fury.

One more time Bryn approached and this time, with the flat of her hand, she struck his cheek so hard that Quade's nose spurted blood, "And that is for Shay. A kind man who did not deserve to die at the hands of a spineless creature like you," she snarled dangerously.

Suddenly, Aiden worried Bryn might do the unthinkable, "No, Bryn," he said softly, "Let him go. Don't dirty your hands with such scum. This is your wedding day, spend time with your husband and let Devin handle this."

When Bryn froze, Aiden knew that his granddaughter had heard his soft words. The other men saw fear replace Quade's arrogant expression when he realized that Bryn could easily deal with him before he turned and ran away. Devin vanished from his side and Ryan leapt to his wife pulling her into his arms literally lifting her off the ground kissing her face.

"Come," said Aiden quietly, "Both of you will be missed and you have guests to attend to."

"Lord Keane," began Ryan as he set Bryn on her feet.

Aiden waved at him impatiently, "We're family Ryan. Call me Aiden please," he said.

Bryn had her head against Ryan's shoulder when he said, "Sir, please don't tell my parents what happened."

"No, they've had enough to worry about for a lifetime," Aiden sighed.

"Thank you sir," said Ryan in relief.

Bryn noticed her grandfather's expression become irritated by Ryan calling him, "sir," but she suspected her husband might be teasing him subtly.

"Young man," began Aiden in annoyance, but Bryn interjected softly, "He's teasing you granddad."

Aiden paused to glance at Ryan sharply and noticed the younger man's lips twitch, "I see," he said flatly though he winked at Bryn in spite of the tone of his rejoinder.

They did not get a chance to say more because Becca bustled over to them looking relieved, "We've been lookin for yeh both. Yehr Da wants to do a toast before people eat," she said.

Paddy toasted his son and new daughter-in-law emotionally wishing them a long happy marriage, which was seconded by a roar of voices from the crowd of guests all raising their glasses. Becca announced the food was ready on the beautifully decorated buffet and traditional Irish music began in the background accompanied by the swirl happy conversation, Bryn noticed her grandfather approach Paddy, shaking his hand chatting amiably.

As the day progressed Bryn and Ryan changed into informal clothing in preparation to travel to the retreat that Aiden surprised them with, he handed them a formal document in an envelope, "Here, a wedding gift for you both," he said.

Ryan took it hesitantly and passed it to Bryn to open, she looked at her grandfather curiously before opening the envelope to pull out the document, and soon as she read it Bryn gasped shoving it at Ryan so she could hug her grandfather.

Usually imperturbable Ryan began to stammer, "Sir...Aiden, this is too much! It isn't necessary, particularly since we will live at the castle," her grandfather had given them both an exclusive villa.

"Nonsense, I wanted you both to have somewhere private to go. As much as I enjoy having you at the castle, I know you need time alone on occasion, though you will always have guards around you, Sorry about that dear," he added to Bryn, "but as my granddaughter even without your skills you are at risk and by association so is Ryan. They will stay out of site so you both can truly relax without always looking over your shoulders," said Aiden.

"I understand granddad. Devin pulled me aside to explain. He said mom never liked it either, but it kept her safe," said Bryn ruefully.

"Good, I'm glad to hear that you understand. There are people out there that are not particularly fond of my position or my authority, not only that it makes you a target for ransom as you are my heir dear," said Aiden patting his granddaughter's hand.

"Does that mean Devin will be with us?" said Bryn curiously.

"Yes, but after he drives you, he will stay out of sight unless you need him." Aiden handed her a wrist COM and said, "I had this made for you Bryn as a precaution whenever you leave the castle. It contains standard GPS linked to Devin's unit and mine, like the one Ryan has. Of course, you may use it in a nonemergency situation, but I wanted you to have it in case of emergency as well," he said.

"Thank you granddad," whispered Bryn emotionally hugging her grandfather.

"No need to thank me dear, you're my family," here he surprised Ryan hugging him thumping his back affectionately before letting him go, "Just keep safe, is all I ask," he said.

Devin walked up to them with a sideways smile, "Well now Mr. and Mrs. Kelly are you both ready to depart?"

"Anytime," said Ryan with a huge grin for the Mrs. Kelly reference, he certainly seemed pleased noted Bryn.

The vehicle Devin directed them to, was obviously meant to transport people in more luxury given the room inside as he humorously gestured them into the back seat like a chauffeur noting Ryan's wicked grin. Of course Ryan took full advantage of such an accommodation pulling protesting Bryn across his lap and passionately kissing her as if they were alone completely ignoring his wife's muffled words.

Bryn wrenched her lips away, but Ryan nibbled on her neck, "Ryan! Devin is in the vehicle! It's rude," even as she shivered in delight from her husband's efforts as they sped through the Irish countryside.

"He's not naïve darlin'," murmured Ryan to Bryn's horror obviously unconcerned there was an observer.

Devin chuckled heartily to Bryn's embarrassment.

Suddenly, there was a deafening "BOOM," Bryn's ears rang painfully as the vehicle skewed and rolled forcefully off the road. Once the vehicle began to roll, she was violently ripped from Ryan's strong arms and tossed about the canopy like a child's toy. Pain blossomed all over her body from severe battering, as she had not been strapped in like the men. In a daze, she could smell burning foliage, metal, plastic, and a variety of other unidentifiable scents, Bryn desperately tried to listen for sounds of life from her companions, but her ringing ears prevented anything other than normally audible sounds to reach her ears. Her body stunned, Bryn could not seem to move, she thought she heard a hiss and then something shattering the canopy, her mind jumped to the thought someone saw the accident, so they might be trying to help.

Finally able to open her eyes to slits, Bryn saw movement of arms and strangely enough the arms led to a masked face, but they seemed intent on Ryan's form, cutting away the restraints with a knife that flashed in the sunlight. Her mind tried to make sense of that, but could not and all Bryn could understand was someone was trying to take her husband away from her.

The individual, which had to be a man from the ease he began to pull Ryan's body from the vehicle, yanked at the still form of her husband without regard to any injury he might have sustained burning away Bryn's stupor from outrage. Apparently this man was not concerned with her or Devin as he succeeded in separating Ryan from the twisted remains of the vehicle.

With supreme effort, Bryn ignored her pain and climbed from the vehicle noting the man never looked behind him, obviously he felt that he had nothing to fear from the other passengers deeming them unconscious or dead. Bryn's mind quailed briefly over the thought Devin might have died, but she had to help Ryan, his need was more immediate as he must be alive otherwise the man had no reason to take him.

Dropping painfully to the ground, Bryn saw the man dragging Ryan to another vehicle, its back facing toward her as she staggered to her feet to stumble in the same direction. The man succeeded in shoving Ryan unceremoniously into the opening, again without regard to his injuries, before sprinting about to the driver's side. Despair washed through Bryn, she was not going to make it time to stop the man as she noticed the canopy close and heard the sound of the engine start. Unable to close the distance quickly enough Bryn made a last desperate leap, ignoring the pain torturing her body, and caught ahold of a projection on the vehicle body just as it whisked away.

Bryn held on for dear life, without the protection of the canopy, the wind was buffeting her body like a living thing from the speed of the vehicle so she did all she could to pull close and press her battered body close to the vehicle's outer skin. Again despair washed through her, Bryn felt her body giving out, what little strength she had was ebbing quickly and then without warning her hand slipped, she found her body tumbling over the broken ground beaten severely again.

That was when she noticed the ringing in her ears subsided somewhat and heard the vehicle decelerating, of course she realized that was why she survived the loss of her grip, had the vehicle been at the original speed, she would probably be dead. Sunlight dazzled her eyes from the west so she knew it was beginning to set as Bryn oriented her head to search for the two men, she still could not locate their body heat with the sun in the sky, but she did see movement in the distance. Now she had to be careful, stealth was of primary importance.

Ryan groaned, awakened by something cold hitting his face, when memory of the accident impinged on his sense, his head jerked up instantly looking for his wife, but all he saw before him was a masked man. That was when he realized he had restraints on his wrists and ankles, an attempt to move sent a wave of agony through his injured body then he knew they were electronic restraints and he had no hope of escaping them.

Where was Bryn? What did he do with her? Had she already been delivered to a broker?

"Where is my wife? What did you do with her?" snarled Ryan.

The man laughed, he was wearing a modulator, which instantly reminded Ryan of the last mission at Drury, the man that had taken Bryn and nearly caused her death.

"I'm not interested in Bryn Keane. It's you I've been after for a while now. It was one of the best days of my life when that burn notice circulated," said the modulated voice.

"It isn't in effect here," growled Ryan realizing he had been careless and let down his guard.

The man laughed again, "That may be, but I personally don't care. I've been hoping to have a chance at you even before it circulated. I don't care who your father-in-law is, he can't protect a dead man and I might have a fringe benefit of your delectable wife," he said maliciously.

Ryan attempted to jump at the man for the reference to Bryn, but the jolt from the restraints stopped him instantly, "Stay away from her," he snarled.

"You won't know what happens to her or what I do to her," said the man nastily as he pulled out some sort of hand weapon that fit into the palm of his hand to place against Ryan's chest.

In a glance, Ryan recognized the weapon with a stab of coldness, it fired a special charge of tiny metallic slivers that ripped apart skin and organs; survival rate for the victim was less than five percent.

The man yanked off his mask and he stared briefly in stunned amazement: Crease! Random information clicked into place suddenly and Ryan snarled, "You sold her out on her first mission! That's why Stanton found you missing."

Snorting derisively, Crease said, "I was ordered to by the Tabula. They didn't want to waste time on her if she wasn't the right person."

"So they sent you after her again on that last mission," Ryan spat out in fury.

"Actually they didn't," sneered Crease, "I planned to take her from that fool once he was done with her, she was always mine. You just kept getting in the way.

Ryan felt his temples throbbing with rage, "She will never belong to anyone and if you think she will have anything to do with you, you're delusional."

Without deigning to respond to the insult, "I'll give my regards to you lovely wife when I take her," Crease sneered leaving his victim with the worst pain he could devise as he pressed the weapon to his prisoner's chest.

Bryn, he thought with agony, *I'm so sorry*, knowing his wife would never see him again as no help would get to him fast enough to allow him to be in that five percent. An attempt to reach the wrist COM indicated the man removed it at some point, now no one would know where to find his body.

Pain blossomed in Ryan's chest, but the man's final words actually hurt worse knowing he could not protect his wife any longer when in his fading sight, Crease suddenly wilted to the ground after a loud crack.

Miraculously Bryn was there, sobbing over his broken body, "Ryan, help is coming, stay with me. Please don't leave me alone."

"Darlin'," he whispered, "Don't watch me die. Walk away, it's too late to get any help."

"No, no," shouted Bryn wildly her eyes flicking through various modes to examine Ryan's wounds.

The wound in Ryan's chest was terrible, whatever the man used had been meant to minimize survival of the victim from the torn muscles and organs she detected, she could only think of one option that might keep him alive long enough. She grabbed the knife from the other man's calf sheath, sliced her hand deeply and let the blood run over Ryan's chest wound hoping the nanites would help keep him alive long enough once they entered his body.

As the sun faded, Ryan's pulse began to slow, Bryn screamed in agony just as sounds of vehicles approaching reached her ears, people began to cluster around them, someone pulled her aside as they placed Ryan in an emergency cocoon. Immediately, they whisked Ryan away, Bryn could not understand questions people were asking her as she swayed on her feet.

One of the men ran a diagnostic unit over Bryn's wavering body, "She's badly injured, quickly get another cocoon," and there was another scramble that Bryn was barely aware of as her sight went black.

Aiden Keane left the wedding celebration shortly after his granddaughter and arrived home in a pleasant frame of mind, he went to his office to review any pending business including the arrangement for another reception in Thurles. His relaxing evening was shattered abruptly by the agonized voice of his granddaughter, "Granddad, we need help...please," her voice begged and then followed by a wail,"Noooo," and the connection went dead.

For a heartbeat, Aiden froze in horror, before hitting his COM yelling, "DEVIN! What's wrong? What happened?"

There was momentary silence that sent coldness washing through Aiden when Devin did not instantly answer and then, "Aiden," groaned Devin weakly, "We had some sort of accident, an explosion. Bryn and Ryan aren't here, I just came to."

"I'm sending people for you," said Aiden immediately while trying to squash the terror he felt for his family.

"Send them to Bryn and Ryan first, Aiden," said Devin weakly, "It sounded urgent. They can swing back for me. And...send medical support, if I'm injured so are they."

Aiden checked his GPS coordinator and found only two signals, both far apart, he expelled a breath worriedly, one was Devin's, the other Bryn's, but what happened to Ryan's? Slapping a hand on a broad message band to his men, Aiden issued emergency protocol giving the coordinates telling them to go to Bryn's first and once they dealt with the situation there to swing around to the other coordinates to attend Devin.

A bad feeling hit Aiden and he decided to take further action so he picked up his land line calling a number swiftly, which was thankfully answered immediately, "Donal, I need you to come sooner than we planned for the reception. There's been some sort of accident, but I don't know the particulars. I have a bad feeling about it and your expertise could mean life or death for my family. Get here immediately! I'll have a transport waiting to bring you to Ireland and then on the Thurles," he said urgently.

"I'll be there Aiden, soon as I can," said Donal in evident worry before disconnecting the call.

The next call was to Daig, "My friend, you're about get two or three seriously injured people on your doorstep. I've sent for Donal, he'll be here soon. I think it's bad," said Aiden his voice trembling.

"My god, Aiden, what happened?" said Daig urgently.

"I don't know for certain. At the moment all I know is there was a vehicle accident, but not what caused it," said Aiden agitatedly.

"I'll be ready for them. Tell them to forward the information to me so I can be prepped for the injuries and I know who will need attention first," said Daig quickly.

"I certainly will," agreed Aiden and soon as he broke the connection, informed the men racing to the aid of the injured people to coordinate with Daig.

Devin sat on the ground with his back against the twisted remains of the vehicle trying to recall what happened, he felt impotent fury that even with all the precautions they had taken clearing the route that someone still managed to waylay them. Though he did not state it was an attack outright to Aiden, Devin was no fool, that crash was no accident someone planned that explosion and did it almost faultlessly. The area was chosen to avoid witnesses or the chance someone would call in the accident too soon and then the fact that two injured people had been removed, but he did not understand why Ryan would be missing. Bryn yes, but Ryan, no, and if his condition was any gage, neither person had been in shape to wander off on their own.

Devin's thoughts mocked him. How could he fail Aiden again? The last of his family had been in his hands to protect yet someone still managed to get to them, he

still keenly felt the loss of Fiona and Jimmy. He had false-
ly assumed they were safe years ago, such a mistake he
lived to regret, now Bryn, she was like a daughter to him,
she might be potentially in the hands of some broker preparing to sell her to the highest bidder.

It was dark now, the sun had set and in the distance
Devin thought he heard a vehicle. As the sound drew
closer, he was certain and heard it stop nearby followed
by several men squatting near him as one ran some sort
of a diagnostic unit over him.

"You're pretty banged up Devin, but nothing life
threatening fortunately. You need some bones and a few
lacerations mended. We're going to strap you to a board
for now, you have cracked vertebrae and we don't want
them to move," said the man with diagnostic unit, but
Devin was too tired to recognize the voice.

"Relax, sir, let us move you," said another voice.

Devin allowed his body to go limp even though the
pain of shifting his body made him want to tense and
then he was flat, some of the pain faded as they strapped
him down.

"The others? Bryn and Ryan?" said Devin wearily.

"They've gone ahead to the physician sir," said a man,
but Devin detected a worrisome note in the voice.

"Bad?" inquired Devin.

"Lord Keane asked us not to discuss it sir," said the
man uneasily.

Devin swore and knew it was bad…very bad if Aiden
did not want anyone talking about it so something else
had happened and until Aiden decided he should know,
he would remain ignorant. With nothing else he could do,
Devin subsided as the vehicle took off toward Thurles.

Via constant communication, Donal kept updated
through Aiden and he arrived in Thurles barely forty
minutes after the first contact his friend had sent such
special transportation for him, but instead of the Keane
estate, his escort delivered him to Daig's surgery.

At Donal's knock, Daig literally jerked the door open, "Their almost here. One of the men's heart kept stopping that's the reason for the delay. He's bad Donal, very bad and I don't know if we can help him," said the physician worriedly.

"Fill me in on the vitals my friend so we can get ready. I've brought some of my new developments with me so that could help tip the balance," stated Donal as he followed his friend listening to details before they arrived at a data unit transmitting live vital feeds.

"My god, what did this?" said Donal with shudder at the damage to the heart, lungs, and major blood vessels.

"Some sort of weapon they recovered. The projectile shatters to cause maximum damage to minimize survival rate," said Daig grimly.

Donal looked at the data helplessly, "How is he still alive?"

"We have no idea, but his heart restarts when they stimulate it so they are keeping him alive, barely," said Daig.

"We have to get all those slivers out or they will work their way into other areas. The heart muscle needs repairs and the lungs, set up the artificial heart and lung so we can bypass the injured organs. We have to stop his heart and breathing to make those repairs, but even then...I don't know if he can survive the trauma shock, there is only so much a body can take," said Donal uneasily.

"We'll do our best," said Daig firmly.

They continued to monitor the updates on their patients, Daig told them soon as they arrived to bring the critically wounded man into the operating theater since the other patients stabilized. In moments after that request, the door burst open delivering Ryan into their hands and the two physicians hooked up the artificial heart and lung so they could begin removal of splinters.

As they split the chest cavity open, massive damage greeted the physicians' eyes appearing more like ground meat that a human body, "It's a travesty that weapons like this exist," said Daig grimly.

Donal did not say anything, he was quickly removing splinters when he noticed something odd, "Daig, give me a magnifier," he demanded.

"What did you find?" said Daig urgently.

"Something strange, vessels are repairing spontaneously," Donal mused.

"Impossible!" insisted Daig.

"Hand me a diagnostic unit," said Donal thoughtfully and passed it over the injured man's discarded shirt.

"What is it?" said Daig uneasily.

"Oh Bryn, you clever girl," murmured Donal with a sigh of relief.

"What do you mean?" demanded Daig.

"I'll explain later my friend, let's help this man first. The faster we work the better chances of his survival," said Donal holding his hand in apology for the evasion.

Even with the technology available, it took the physicians two hours to remove all the slivers from Ryan's chest and mend the damage to all the affected tissues so all they could do was wait, it was up to Ryan's body now.

A commotion from another room, followed by an emergency signal sent the two physicians running to see Bryn, apparently conscious struggling and screaming for her husband.

"Sedate her, sedate her," yelled Daig, "She's exacerbating her injuries."

"It took several doses to finally subdue Bryn to Daig's surprise he was worried they might stop her heart with so much sedative, "We could kill her with so much sedation."

"I'll explain as we work on her, she's not as critical as her husband," so Donal proceeded to explain the gist of the procedures he performed on Bryn to a fascinated Daig which gave the woman her sight back and at one point repaired damage from an exotic toxin, "The nanites will fight sedation under duress."

"Amazing Donal, have you marketed it?" said Daig in wonder.

"No, Bryn has been my only subject. There is a possibility of misuse of the technology that worries me. That brings me to her husband, she obviously cut her hand to pour blood in his wound, and the nanites would have acted on their programing, which would start repairing the tissue. Clever girl must have realized it was the only option to save him. That's why he did not completely bleed out," explained Donal.

"Amazing. I guess you have two subjects now, one indirectly," said Daig dryly.

Donal snorted examining Bryn, she had a few severely broken bones that needed to be set and mended, lacerations that needed sealing, and a large amount of bruising, but she would recover rapidly.

They moved to their last patient, a very taciturn Devin who barely acknowledged their presence, he submitted passively to treatment hardly flinching even when they set and mended several broken or fractured bones. Both his eyes had spectacular shiners, which echoed a number of other bruises over his body.

"You have a concussion Devin," commented Donal flicking a penlight in each eye, "We'll need to monitor you overnight."

Devin ignored information about his own heath, "How is Bryn?" he growled.

"Some broken bones, lacerations, bruises, and a concussion, she isn't critical any longer. She just needs rest," said Donal encouragingly.

Then with a flat stare, Devin demanded, "Her husband, Ryan?"

Daig sighed and Donal ran a hand through his silvering hair, "He's in bad shape Devin. Time will tell if his body can recover from the trauma shock. You don't need the details right now. Tomorrow you can review all the data yourself, but for now you need to rest," said Donal.

"Tell Aiden to contact his family. They should be here if he might not make it," said Devin biting off each word.

"I'll do that now," said Daig quietly.

Aiden rushed over to Daig's surgery after contacting Ryan's parents, it had been one of the most terrible calls he ever made informing the Kellys their son was dying and that he had a slim chance of survival. They had been too stunned and grief stricken to ask what happened, he said he would send someone for them.

Once at Daig's surgery, Aiden asked, "Can I see Devin or is he forbidden to talk right now?"

"He was told to rest, but something is eating at him, we can't even get him to stay in bed. Maybe talking might help Aiden," said Daig helplessly.

When Aiden entered Devin's room, he sucked his breath sharply at the expression on his friend's face, it was lined with bitterness and self-loathing, and he had never seen the man look like this in their entire acquaintance.

"Devin, you should be resting," said Aiden quietly and his friend whirled about at the sound of his voice.

"I failed you Aiden," spat Devin bitterly, "My complacency cost Fiona and Jimmy their lives, now Bryn is injured and may lose her husband because I let my guard down."

"Devin, you did everything possible. You cleared that route twice. I'll have men comb over it in the morning, but I suspect something was launched at you from a distance or the men would have picked up on it. How would anyone know someone would use a weapon made for a battlefield? Especially near populated areas, not to mention how could they manage to get it into the country? Ireland banned such things and uses technology to scan the entire country to catch smugglers, so it had to have been brought in recently. None of this is your fault," enunciated Aiden firmly.

"I barely remembered what happened," snarled Devin, "Ryan was teasing Bryn and the next thing we know there is an explosion. I remember the vehicle spinning and tumbling after that I must have blacked out. I have no idea how they got out of the vehicle or where they went afterwards. Bryn's voice on the COM is what woke me, she sounded so scared Aiden."

"I know, but she is alright," soothed Aiden.

"She won't be if Ryan dies. It will crush her. What happened to him? Daig or Donal won't tell me," snapped Devin.

Aiden sighed, his friend was not going to let this go or rest until he worked the anger out of his system, "All I know is when the men arrived, they found a dead man with a broken neck and Bryn crying talking to Ryan. Donal and Daig said some sort of weapon that used a splintering projectile inflicted the wound in his chest, designed for minimal survival rate. They repaired his wounds now they have to wait to see if his body can overcome the trauma shock."

Devin began snarling, "An assassin's weapon. They were after Ryan this time, but you rescinded the burn notice in Ireland, so who was that man?" he demanded.

"We don't know yet. Donal will run DNA test tomorrow and we'll compare them against the legal visitors into the country and against other countries databases. I suspect he was illegally in this country if he brought such weapons with him. Once Bryn is able to talk, she might shed some light on the situation," said Aiden quietly.

"Now will you please try to rest? Self-recriminations aren't going to change anything and you don't deserve it. You've done more for me over the years than I could ever dream and I have no reservations about your competence."

"I felt so helpless," sighed Devin suddenly, "I wanted to go to her Aiden and I couldn't."

Aiden sighed and walked over to the other man to place his hands on his shoulders, "I know that, she knows that, so please stop punishing yourself. She was probably just as worried about you."

Daig walked in, "Good you're calmer, but I want to give you a sedative. You need to rest tonight," he held up a warning finger when Devin opened his mouth to argue, "We won't let you see any of that data unless you allow the sedative!"

At that threat, Devin sighed in frustration, but he lay on the bed before Daig administered the hypospray, almost immediately Devin wilted with relaxation and his breathing became even.

"Thank you for talking to him, he needed to calm down. He is going to be in pain from all the bruising tomorrow as it is," said Daig, "and the Kellys are here," he added quietly.

Aiden steeled himself for the interview with Ryan's parents, hoping that somehow the young man would pull through and wanting to encourage the Kellys.

Becca saw him first, "Aiden, what happened? Yeh said he was hurt bad," she said her voice trembling.

"We aren't certain what happened, but he had a terrible chest wound. I had the best physicians I know work on him. Now it is up to him to overcome the shock his body received," said Aiden quietly.

Paddy was grey faced and seemed incapable of speech, Becca's hands flew to her mouth with tears leaking down her cheeks, "And Bryn?" she choked out.

"Also injured, but not as badly so she'll be all right with rest," said Aiden.

Becca nodded tearfully, "Can I sit with him?" She said hoarsely.

"Come with me," gestured Aiden.

Paddy froze in the doorway of Ryan's room obviously shocked by the pallor in his son's face, Becca bustled in and set a chair next to the bed so she could hold her son's hand, Aiden did not know what to say to offer any comfort. Then Becca began to sing, her voice so beautiful and haunting, she sang in Gaelic, an ancient lament,

Aiden felt his throat close as he too found release in tears.

A dream nagged at Bryn persistently, telling her to yell, scream, or anything to be heard as she felt a crushing weight pressing down on her, suffocating relentless until she thrashed awake, breathing hard, her body damp with sweat. She was alone, some place she did not recognize and jumped out of bed only to have her legs fold like accordions as she crumpled painfully to the ground, she crawled toward the door ignoring the abrasions developing on her knees. In the doorway, Bryn grabbed at the woodwork to pull herself up, she staggered unsteadily into the hall with one insistent goal: She had to find Ryan. He had to be alive, he must be alive, and she could not accept the alternative.

Pain wracked her body, even though bones were mended, lacerations sealed, only time would take the bruising and stiffness away, added to that was a distressingly keen headache. She passed another doorway, sensing Ryan was not in there, but Bryn barely moved any further when a strong arm circled her waist.

"Stubborn woman, you should still be resting," said Devin's voice behind her.

"I've got to see him…please," pleaded Bryn ending in a sob.

Devin's sigh frightened her, he did not tell her not to worry and Bryn choked on the fear threatening to consume her, he scooped her up into his arms before continuing down the hall. A sound of another voice, clicking a tongue in disapproval, came to Bryn's ears, "She should be resting," it was Donal.

Bryn began to weep openly now, shaking her head and she heard both men sigh, "You won't keep her in bed unless you sedate her again. She has a right to be there Donal," said Devin quietly.

Devin began to move again and finally he negotiated another doorway, Bryn's heart nearly stopped when she caught sight of the deathly pallor in Ryan's face. When Devin carried her closer, Donal placed a chair by the bed, but soon as Devin set her in the chair, Bryn crawled into the bed clutching at her husband.

A gasp from behind told her that was not what the men had planned, "Bryn, dear you can't stay here like that," said Donal urgently.

"I'm staying unless *he*," referring to Ryan, "sends me away," snarled Bryn through her tears.

There was another gasp and then Becca's voice, "Yeh leave her be. She'll do him more good than harm. He'll know she's near!" she snapped.

"But..." it sounded like Daig's voice that she remembered.

Paddy's voice interrupted him fiercely, "Let her be! People can still hear and feel in comas yeh told me yehrselves. It'll give him somethin to live for."

Bryn rubbed her face against Ryan's chest to dry her tears, she felt a hand stroking her hair even though she was not certain who it was and then a soft singing began, lovely sweet and haunting, in a language she did not know. It soothed her in a way that platitudes could not.

A running song weaved through his mind as Ryan dreamed until suddenly his eyes opened and he realized the singer was next to him, sweet, beautiful and in Gaelic, a song he remembered from his childhood. His eyes shifted toward the sound to see his mother, her eyes closed griping his hand and her lips moving in song, "Mum...," he whispered.

"Ryan?" said Becca her song faltering in amazement, "It's good to see yeh awake," fresh tears sparkled on her cheeks.

It was hard to talk, but Ryan managed to get out the word, "Bryn?"

"She's fine son. Look on yehr right, she's sleepin. Let me wake her," said Becca.

"No, let her rest," he struggled to say quietly, "Is she hurt?"

"If yeh mean when she was brought here, I think so, but she's fine now," said Becca hesitantly, "I don't know the tale, I didn't ask."

Ryan nodded and sighed, relieved his wife had not been taken by Crease though he had questions, he knew it would be awhile before he was allowed to ask them.

Aiden poked his head in Ryan's room just as he spoke to his mother and went to find Paddy, who was resting in a chair, he shook him awake, "Your son's awake," he said and the man launched out of the chair.

Following Paddy back to Ryan's room, Aiden stayed by the door respectfully as the man rushed to his son's bedside, both parents looked as relieved as he felt, it was a good sign the young man was conscious.

"Da," whispered Ryan as his father approached, Paddy stroked his son's head tears of wordless gratitude on his face.

Ryan noticed Aiden at the door, "Tell him to come in," he whispered to his parents.

Becca gestured to Aiden and he approached the bed, "Devin?" whispered Ryan.

"He's fine Ryan. He suffered more of an emotional beating to his pride, but it wasn't his fault," said Aiden.

"Not his fault," whispered Ryan shaking his head slowly.

"Enough," the voice of Daig came from the doorway, "And no more talking, he needs to rest. He's not stable yet," the physician approached with a diagnostic unit to check Ryan's current vital signs.

The others watched tensely for an update as Daig swiped his finger through the diagnostic units various modes peering critically at numbers until he sighed almost happily, "Amazing, he's much improved. I guess you were both correct about leaving Bryn here with him.

There is still a risk, but not as much as it was several days ago."

The observers all sighed in supreme relief, "Becca," said Paddy, "Get some rest. Yeh haven't closed yehr eyes since we got here. Ryan isn't gonna want to see yeh get sick watchin over him."

Becca looked about to argue, "Rest mum, I'll be ok," whispered Ryan, so she relented though glared at her husband.

"Ryan," said Daig, "I'm going to give you a light sedative. You still need to rest to heal."

Aiden left Paddy by his son's bedside and moved to a private area to speak to Devin on the COM, "He's awake Devin," he said and heard a heartfelt sigh of relief that he shared.

"I guess the Kellys were right to leave Bryn in there," Devin mused.

"It seems so," agreed Aiden, "Any updates?"

"The dead man didn't get into the country legally as you surmised which accounts for the illegal weaponry. DNA profile had a match in North America which led to Facilities run by the Tabula, his last assignment was Drury, but apparently he was on leave and they had no idea of his activities here. Whatever he was up to was not sanctioned by them and I tend to believe the story, they don't want to be at odds with the Agency. They won't confirm or deny if the weaponry belonged to them however, but then I'm not surprised, arsenals are usually classified. I asked them if there was a possibility the man was acting on the burn notice in North America for Ryan and they said that was not a sanctioned operation either since it was not in effect in Ireland. They could have known Aiden, but if so, they're denying it, again expected," Devin reported.

"Hmm I wonder if the southern Agency headquarters Commander had a hand in this. He was certainly in a snit over Ryan, but I'm not certain he would hire someone from Drury or if we could prove that. Since Ryan is awake and if he continues to improve, he might be able to give us a better understanding unless the man was after Bryn. Ryan would have given his life to stop anyone from taking her," Aiden mused.

"Aiden...he was in no condition to kill that man. Reports said he had electronic restraints on his wrists and ankles when they arrived at the scene," said Devin hesitantly because of what he was inferring.

"You believe Bryn killed the man," said Aiden blatantly.

"It's the only explanation Aiden. Once Ryan received that wound, he would not have been able to kill anyone even without those restraints. She may not even remember doing it from the sound of her emotional state at the time, she probably acted instinctively to save him," state Devin.

Aiden sighed, "I guess we'll deal with the fallout of that when it happens. Under the circumstances, she was justified and chances are it was the only way she remained out of the man's clutches especially if he was a Drury operative. In a wounded state, she would have been no match for him in one on one confrontation, but again, we won't know the story until we can talk to them both and right now, we don't want to stress them," he said.

"I agree," said Devin, "I'll send the reports encrypted to your secure server. No doubt the council will need a full brief on all this."

"Unfortunately," said Aiden grimly.

Bryn felt someone shake her awake, she irritably batted at the hand, but it persisted, "Bryn," it was Donal, "You need to move around to keep your circulation healthy and to heal. You can come back after you eat something."

"I don't want to be away in case he wakes up," grumbled Bryn.

"He woke last night," said Donal.

"What? Why didn't someone wake me?" demanded Bryn angrily.

"He wouldn't let us Bryn," said Becca, "I was goin to, but he stopped me and said to let yeh rest."

"Why isn't he waking now?" said Bryn worriedly.

"Daig sedated him so he would heal Bryn. Don't worry, he's improving and in part thanks to your quick wit," said Donal approvingly as he held out his hand to support her.

"The nanites?" queried Bryn.

"Yes, clever girl. They kept him from losing all his blood," beamed Donal.

"It was all I could think of," choked Bryn tears running down her cheeks suddenly.

"Now, now Bryn, yeh calm down. He's gonna be alright. Yeh go for a walk and eat! I'll see yeh when yeh get back. They make me move and eat too so yeh can't escape either," said Becca dryly glancing at Donal.

Bryn snorted, "Yes they are an insistent bunch aren't they," she said drolly.

"Bad patients, both of you," said Donal shaking a finger at them both as he chivied Bryn out of the room.

Ryan woke later and instantly felt Bryn missing from his side, his eyes riveted to his mother, "Where is she?" he demanded his voice stronger.

His mother clicked her tongue and rolled her eyes, "One of the physicians made her exercise and eat. I suspect the last thing yeh wanted was to see her ill from watchin yeh," said Becca sharply as she tossed back the same words Paddy had used on her.

Ryan sighed, "No, I didn't, but I wanted to talk to her," he said.

"Don't get yehr knickers in a twist. She'll be back and she might have some words for yeh too," said Becca tartly.

"Oh? Why is that?" said Ryan curiously.

"She wasn't happy yeh wouldn't let me wake her last night," snorted Becca.

"Ah, I see. Mum if she didn't wake with us talking then she was tired. She's a very light sleeper," Ryan said defensively.

Becca snorted, "It's not me yeh gotta convince."

Diag entered the room carrying a tray, "Good, you're awake. I timed the sedative well. Eat all of this young man. Nutritional assist help only so far, your digestive system needs to have food and since your mother is here, we can see if you might walk to the privy with some help. I suspect you'll want that catheter removed," he said.

Ryan gave his mother a wry look and she chuckled while Diag pulled out a diagnostic unit after depositing the meal on a swing table next to the bed, he began to mutter wordlessly.

"Just amazing, you've improved so much. Either it's those nanites or your wife has a very healthy effect on you sir," commented Diag.

Becca laughed, "It's his wife. Yeh should have seen him before he got the nerve to ask for her hand. I've never seen a man sufferin so much as this one. It changed him once he got that ring on her finger."

Diag snorted humorously and Ryan gave his mother a sour look as he put food in his mouth, she patted his shoulder gently with a grin and wink.

Bryn walked in to see Ryan sitting up and eating, he did not even hesitate to shove the swinging table to one side and hold out his arms for her, Daig barely managed to get out of the way in time for Bryn as she launched into her husband's arms.

Daig chuckled, "I see what you mean," in an aside to a grinning Becca.

"Are you all right darlin'?" murmured Ryan into Bryn's ear and holding her tightly.

"I am now," said Bryn kissing his face which Ryan promptly reoriented to his lips for a very passionate kiss.

Daig cleared his throat, "You need to eat sir," he said pointedly.

Bryn gasped and pulled away, "Don't you dare leave," said Ryan sternly.

Bryn moved only far enough away so Ryan could swing his meal back in front of him, "How are you feeling?" she said anxiously to her husband noting that horrible grey pallor was gone.

"Much better now that you're here," he said with a twinkle in his eyes, Becca snorted a laugh.

Soon as Ryan finished his meal, Daig said, "Ok young man, swing your legs to the side, and Mrs. Kelly help me support him to the privy."

"I can help," insisted Bryn.

"Not just yet," said Daig, "Your body is still recovering and I don't want you carrying any weight if he collapses."

Which of course initially Ryan did, his legs shook and wobbled badly, only his mother and the Physician kept him from completely hitting the ground with more than his knees.

"Why are my legs wobbling so much," said very frustrated Ryan.

"Both your legs were broken young man, compound fractures pushing into your muscles. It will take a little time for the muscles to function properly. Once you get back to the bed, I'm going to have to sit on the edge flexing your legs to get them used to moving again. You'll have some pain, maybe some spasms, but that's to be expected," explained Daig.

Bryn could sympathize from her initial awakening and stayed back to allow them to get to the privy in the room, Becca stepped out to allow Ryan some privacy, but the physician remained with him. On the return trip, Ryan was muttering curses and his mother was tartly reprimanding him for his language so that Bryn had to laugh, Daig snorted humorously at the exchange until they finally delivered him to the bed.

Daig pulled over a chair and began to massage Ryan's legs to help the circulation, explaining the exercises he wanted Ryan to perform as he flexed his leg, knee, ankle, and toes.

"Can't Bryn massage my leg?" said Ryan with a sly glance at his wife.

Becca made a scandalized sound and Daig looked him sternly, "None of that young man! Not for a while. Probably the last words you wish to hear, but that is too much activity."

Ryan looked like he ate a lemon whole, Bryn struggled to keep a straight face knowing her husband was in no mood for levity after such a pronouncement, though the fairer side of Bryn realized they missed their wedding night. He did have some reason to be disappointed.

The following day, Devin stopped by and Bryn raced across the room throwing her arms about the man so firmly he staggered from the impact, "I'm so glad you're ok," she murmured into his neck.

Devin noted Ryan's expression turned defensive at Bryn's display of affection; inwardly he snorted humorously at the younger man's possessiveness before he released the young woman.

"Down boy," said Devin looking straight at Ryan grinning, "I know whose wife she is."

Becca laughed at her son's expression as Devin walked over the bed, "You look much better. You gave us all fright. If you're up to it, I'd like to speak to you in private about a few things," he said glancing at the two women.

That request did not appear to please Ryan, but he nodded with a sigh and after a brief kiss, Bryn joined his mother, "A walk will do us some good," said Becca over her shoulder.

Devin made certain the women were out of Bryn's earshot before he began speaking, "As you probably guessed I want ask some particulars about what happened and didn't want to upset your mother or Bryn, though we will have to get information from Bryn eventually. So far she's refused to talk about what happened."

Ryan sighed, "I barely remember her being there. A man woke me and I had electronic restraints on so I couldn't do a thing. He was taunting me about the burn notice and I stated it was not in effect here. It turned out it was personal, I knew the man from Drury. We had a confrontation over Bryn there and actually Bryn slapped him hard once for a lewd suggestion. He made comments like he might go after Bryn next, but I had no idea if he had her with him right then. He must have taken my COM so I couldn't warn anyone and I thought no one would ever find my body, especially when he pulled out that weapon. I knew I had no chance. I'm not totally certain what happened after he used it. I remember pain, I heard a crack I think and then suddenly Bryn was there crying, telling me to stay with her that help was coming. I told her to walk away so she wouldn't see me die, but that's all I remember until yesterday."

Devin rubbed his chin, noting that Ryan's story agreed with his suppositions, "We are fairly certain Bryn killed the man, most likely in a fit of panic to save you. I'm not certain she even remembers what happened or she's blocking it out," he mused.

"Crease is dead?" demanded Ryan.

"Yes his neck broken and as far as we can ascertain, his visit was not sanctioned. He was in the country illegally as you might guess from the weaponry used and the Tabula will not confirm the weapons belong to them, not that we expected them to. We finally found the rocket launcher he used from over a mile away so we would never have picked up his hiding spot on a normal clearance run. Do you think he was here for Bryn like other operatives?" said Devin.

Ryan sighed, "I don't know. He may have eventually turned her over once he was done with her or he might have killed her. Did he touch her at all?" the question came out in a snarl.

"You mean did he rape her? No, she wasn't assaulted. She must have surprised him from behind because with her injuries she would not have been able to take him one on one in a confrontation. So he either did not know she was right there or he thought her too wounded to do anything which we won't know until she talks about it," said Devin.

Ryan laid his head back on the pillow sighing in relief about Bryn, "Maybe she'll tell me what happened, but I don't want to ask in front of my parents," he said.

"Your Da already returned to Kerry. I guess he had a large party coming in and needed to be there so I suspect your mum will return soon to help out. Maybe we can ask Bryn then," said Devin and Ryan nodded.

Two days later, Daig released Ryan to return to the Keane estate, "I'll be by to check on you in a few days, but if you feel any negative change at all, notify me. Slow exercise like walking, lengthen time slowly and soon you will be back to your normal routine," and then with a glance at Bryn, "Mind you get sleep as well."

Bryn laughed at Ryan's expression when he heard that last comment, "Oh I can sleep in a separate room if necessary," she taunted and her husband glared at her to the amusement of the physician and Devin.

When they arrived home, Aiden was there to greet them, he wrapped his arms about his granddaughter, "I'm so glad your home," he said before releasing her to do the same thing to a very surprised Ryan.

Aiden sighed suddenly, "I hate to do this now, but we need to get it over with Bryn. Let's head to my office for privacy," though his gesture included Devin and Ryan.

Bryn felt nervous at her grandfather's solemn mood once the office door shut, she felt Ryan sit very close to her, which only heightened the feeling, and apparently everyone else knew what this discussion entailed.

Instead of sitting behind his desk, Aiden moved his chair out so the atmosphere would seem less formal and hopefully relax his granddaughter noting the wary expression on her face even in the proximity of her husband.

"My dear, we need to talk about the accident. I won't ask you to repeat it again, but we need to know what happened and it seems you're the only one who can answer the questions we have. Can you explain everything you remember?" said Aiden cautiously noting the flicker of emotion flitting across Bryn's face; he knew this would not be easy for her.

Bryn stiffened at the request, there was nowhere to run and evasion would not work, she jumped slightly when she felt Ryan began to stroke her hair, he whispered, "It's ok darlin' get it over with."

Rubbing her palms along the thigh of her jeans, Bryn licked her lips nervously, "I…I…remember an explosion. I was the only one not wearing a restraint so I tumbled about the canopy. I remember smelling burning plastic and plants. I didn't know if either of them was dead when I heard the canopy shatter, I couldn't seem to open my eyes at first, but I thought someone saw the accident and came to help. When I finally opened my eyes, I saw someone in a mask dragging Ryan out of the vehicle, it made no sense, but he didn't seem to notice me. I crawled out of the hole and saw another vehicle, which is where that man was dragging Ryan; he didn't look like any sort of medical personnel so I stumbled after him. I had no idea what I would do, but then he managed to get Ryan into the vehicle and run around to jump inside himself. I panicked, worried about Ryan, but the vehicle started so I had to leap and catch a handle on the outside before it took off," here Aiden gasped in horror.

"Bryn…" he groaned, "The turbulence alone could have dashed you to death. No wonder your wounds were so much worse than Devin's."

The other two men sighed helplessly for the risk Bryn took, but said nothing, she knew they were correct yet she really had no other options, "I don't know how far he drove, but when he started slowing down, I lost my grip," she winced at the various exclamations of dismay, "he stopped only a little further away and pulled Ryan out of the vehicle, I saw the restraints so I called for you Granddad until I saw the weapon he put at Ryan's chest. I forgot about talking to you and jumped on him to push him aside, but it was too late," tears streamed down her face at the memory of Ryan's mangled body, "whatever he wounded Ryan with was horrible, his chest was mangled. I did the only thing I could think of, I cut my hand to put my blood in his wound because of what Donal did for me, and I thought it would help. I remember telling Ryan to hold on that help was coming, but I knew he was dying," she sobbed, "Then people began showing up and I blacked out."

Ryan pulled her into his arms murmuring reassurances as he glanced at the·two other men significantly silently inferring Bryn did not remember killing anyone and hoped they would not say anything.

The men were silent for a few moments and then Aiden said, "Donal said your blood did help Ryan, it was a clever idea. He told me about the nanites, but didn't go into the details how it helped to repair your vision. I'm just glad all three of you are safe. On another note, since your honeymoon was interrupted, I thought we might as well prepare a reception here for friends and relatives that could not attend in Kerry, particularly with Donal visiting. If there are any guests you would like to invite please leave the information with me. And Bryn...I will acquire your dress for this. No pants outfit under the skirt this time," he shook his finger at her, "I'll make certain it's comfortable besides you won't be outside for this event."

Ryan chuckled at the reprimand, Devin tried to hide a grin and Bryn sighed, she had promised her grandfather that she would were a dress whenever he deemed the occasion called for it.

"Now you two," making a shooing gesture at his granddaughter and her husband, "Go spend some private time together, it's long overdue," said Aiden firmly.

Ryan had a broad grin on his face as he scooped his wife up into his arms, obviously not feeling any residual effects from his injuries and Bryn looked back at her grandfather's amused expression with chagrin.

The two men watched Ryan negotiate the door with his wife and Devin commented, "Any wagers that he listens to Daig about not overdoing the activity?" Aiden snorted a laugh and declined knowing the young man would undoubtedly push his resources.

After Ryan essential kept her captive in the bedroom for several days, Bryn asked to speak to her grandfather privately so he invited her into the office and closed the door watching her curiously for such a meeting.

Clearing her throat, Bryn said, "You mentioned that if we had any guests we wanted to invite to let you know," she handed him a note with six names listed.

Soon as Aiden looked at the names and the comments Bryn had beside them, his eyebrows rose to the hairline in utter amazement, "Are you certain about some of these? Did you discuss this with Ryan?" he demanded.

"Yes, I'm certain and no I didn't discuss it with him. Other than Donal, they are the only friends I really had when I needed them," said Bryn quietly, "I understand if you prefer to omit them."

Aiden sighed, "You do realize Ryan might be unhappy about this? Devin will certainly be irritated after the trouble it took to track you down," he paused at the defeated expression on his granddaughter's face, "I'll see what I can do dear. You have the right to invite people," he said finally hoping to erase that forlorn expression of Bryn's face.

Bryn left the office knowing her grandfather's comments had merit and decided to head to the gymnasium as it had been too long since she exercised or worked on her skills. Of course it was not long before Ryan came in search for her, she was not exactly hiding the invitation list from him, but Bryn did not want to explain her reasons, afraid she might look pathetic.

"Darlin' why didn't you tell me where you were going?" said Ryan as he approached.

"I'm just exercising and I don't remember Daig mentioning you were allowed to do more than walking just yet," said Bryn dryly.

Ryan snorted, "I can work on light weights and focus techniques," he said though his eye narrowed at the evasion.

"At least I can tell him I reminded you when he scolds you for pushing his orders," said Bryn humorously though she should have known her husband would not be diverted since he never was back at the Facility.

"What's bothering you darlin'?" said Ryan pointedly.

Bryn sighed, frustrated she could not seem to keep her thoughts private from Ryan, but then he did worry about her and always had, "It's not easy to forget what happened, Ryan. Thinking you were going to die right there in my arms and that I was going to lose someone yet again, I didn't even want to live if that happened," she said quietly.

Powerful arms encircled Bryn from behind, "Bryn, I don't expect you to ever forget. One thing that ran through my mind was I broke my promise to you, to be careful, and that very thing that kept us apart was happening again. I prayed in my mind that you would forgive me. The thought of leaving you like that hurt far more than any wound I received," said Ryan in an agonized voice.

Tears leaked silently down Bryn's cheeks, she knew he meant everything he said and the situation had not been his fault besides there had been no way to predict such an event. It was still possible he could die in the future working for her grandfather and Bryn knew she had to accept the possibility even if the thought terrified her.

Ryan was not suited to working like a regular average person, not with the skills he acquired over the years, just as she was not suited for such a life and her grandfather had to accept that about her.

"It wasn't your fault. I know that and I realize neither of us will ever have what regular people consider normal jobs, risk will always be there. My grandfather has been living with such worry longer than I've been alive and he will keep worrying even now," said Bryn in futility.

Ryan kissed her temple softly, "Yes, the risk will be there darlin', but less than before as I can't leave the country anymore, not that I want to since you are here. I think you'll find your grandda will adjust the work we do, but still use our skills, it would be wasteful for him not use his resources," he said quietly.

One of the staff walked in announcing, "Mr. Kelly, the physician is here to see you," he said formally.

Ryan sighed in disgust this time and Bryn had to chuckle in spite of her depression, her husband swatted her backside for humor at his expense, she grinned at him before continuing her exercises.

The next day, Devin arrived at their bedroom door early and Ryan answered the knock to see the older man with a garment bag, which he presented to Bryn with a grin that bordered on a smirk, she unzipped it warily to see forest green material.

With a sigh, Bryn said, "I don't have any shoes…" but before she could finish the sentence, Devin handed her a pricy looking shoe box, his eyes twinkling with humor.

Ryan coughed a laugh, but his smile slipped from his face when Devin pulled another garment bag into view, he knew better than to comment though his expression appeared disgusted as he too was the recipient of a shoe box.

"Is granddad going to extremes for this reception?" demanded Bryn irritably.

"Not by his standards," said Devin grinning, "Don't worry I ended up with a new suit as well. He's going to be entertaining some very important people, not just friends and relatives so that's the reason for the high end clothing. You'll have to get used to this on occasion Bryn due to his position."

"Ok, ok, but under protest," said Bryn futilely, "I did agree to wear dresses when he deemed it necessary. May I get my hair trimmed before all this happens?"

"One of the staff is a hairstylist so when you're ready, let me know," commented Devin before leaving them alone to hang their new clothing.

"You're not allowed to laugh at me," warned Bryn watching her husband narrowly.

Ryan snorted, "Why would I do that? The last time you wore a dress there was nothing to laugh about, you looked beautiful," he said seriously even though Bryn blushed.

"It's strange for me to do things like this after a life of anonymity," Bryn sighed though she smiled at Ryan as he stroked her cheek affectionately with a finger.

Chapter 21

Day of the reception dawned and Bryn found the castle bustling with activity so much so that she was dodging staff until she finally followed them to a huge ballroom where they were arranging tables at the perimeter of the room. It reminded her of a restaurant with the flower center pieces, soft lighting and the place settings, a raised dais at one end of the room appeared to be for a small orchestra from the arrangement of chairs.

A hand on her shoulder made Bryn jump, "What are you doing down here?" said Devin's voice behind her.

Turning to face him, Bryn said, "I was curious what everyone was doing. People seemed to be dashing about when usually I hardly see anyone."

Instead of commenting, Devin placed an arm about her shoulder's and guided her away which ultimately led to her grandfather's office where to her surprise, Ryan was also waiting, but looking unaccountably sheepish.

"She was watching the activity in the ballroom," commented Devin as he removed his arm from Bryn's shoulders.

The door to the office shut and Aiden gestured Bryn to sit noting his granddaughter had turned wary, "Bryn, there is going to be a slight alteration tonight. I'm going to be escorting you," he said.

Bryn launched back to her feet with a fierce expression, "Why?" she demanded.

"For several reasons, one, so some of the guests will see the association and back off any attempts or plans to acquire you, two, so Ryan can move about unmarked to observe for potential operatives that might have slipped into the reception so that he can identify them," said Aiden honestly, knowing better than to deceive his granddaughter.

"If Paddy and Becca come they'll think I'm embarrassed to be seen with my own husband!" said Bryn in outrage.

Ryan cleared his throat, "They already told me they won't be able to come, darlin'," he said quietly.

"That won't stop other people from wondering," said Bryn indignantly not all mollified by Ryan's seemingly calm acceptance of this plan.

"The guests only know I'll be introducing my granddaughter since we decided not to make this a wedding reception," said Aiden carefully.

"I see," snarled Bryn, "When was I going to know this was not a wedding reception after what I was told in Kerry?"

Ryan sighed looking helplessly at the other two men; it did not help Bryn's ire to observe that her husband apparently told her grandfather that she would react in her current manner which soured her further.

It was Devin that diverted her, "What is really bothering you Bryn?" he said pointedly.

Bryn turned a withering look on Devin, but the man did not flinch, she really wanted to slap him for cutting right to the point, "I don't want to be the center of attention! I spent my life living under the radar and now you're going to parade me in front of people I don't know, even use me as bait," she spat out.

Ryan had the grace to look ashamed, Devin's lips thinned at her response as if he had not expected that answer and her grandfather sighed before running his hand through his hair as if uncomfortable.

"Would you do this for me Bryn? I want to do all that I can to see you are safe and letting some of these guests see our association will make them think twice before grabbing you anonymously. They may still approach you directly with requests for your assistance, but at least you would have the option to decline this time," pleaded her grandfather not even attempting to deny the reference, 'use me as bait.'

Though Bryn did not like the idea, she sat back down crossing her arms and only nodded in response to her grandfather's request, she refused to look at Ryan or Devin still irritated with all of them.

Suppressing another sigh with extreme difficulty, Aiden said, "Thank you. I'll send someone to help you with your hair for this evening and he can help with makeup if you wish. I don't have any women employed at the moment, but since you will be here I will interview for someone at a later date."

"I don't need any help, but thank you," said Bryn tightly.

"Tonight you will Bryn. This reception will be along more elegant lines and since Becca can't be here to help, you will at least need assistance with your hair," interjected Aiden softly.

"May I leave now?" said Bryn narrowly and jumped to her feet when her grandfather nodded.

The men waited until she was out of the office before Aiden said, "All right young Ryan, you were correct, I should have said something to her sooner. I never realized just how much she abhorred attention. Most people would enjoy it when denied attention for so long, but it's as if she embraced the anonymity."

"If you think about it Aiden and what Ryan has told us, she had to embrace it performing those jobs she did over the years. It's the main reason no one could locate that thief, no desire for attention or credit for anything and we might still be looking for the thief if Drury hadn't grabbed Bryn first on a minor error of a client," commented Devin.

Ryan looked at the floor briefly then glanced up at Aiden, "I'll come down after you escort her so no one will associate me with either of you. Are you going to track the number of invitations or just let people enter if they can present one?" he said.

Aiden mused over that question for a few moments, "Let them enter even if we have more than we sent out, it will help if they think security is lax and we might catch someone off guard. I think it is unlikely anyone will try anything overt though, not with so many important people present or it could be tantamount to suicide for the fool," he said.

Bryn stalked back to the bedroom fuming about the men making plans for her without including her or asking her opinion, she was not thrilled that a man with a black handled blocky case was waiting patiently for her and knew why he was there after her grandfather's comments.

"Mrs. Kelly, my name is Abban, your grandfather sent me to style your hair and help you with your makeup," he said politely.

Bryn nodded and struggled a moment so that she would speak civilly to the man, it was not his fault her grandfather made the recent unilateral decisions without consulting her.

"Thank you. I don't wear makeup however," said Bryn neutrally.

Abban pursed his lips, "Mrs. Kelly at least tonight you will want to wear some and you will see why once some of the guests begin to arrive. I'll wait out here for you to change into a robe. You won't want to pull any clothing over your head once your hair is finished and you have makeup on your face. I recommend that you step into your dress," he advised.

Grumbling inwardly, Bryn entered the bedroom and closed the door. Fortunately she had showered earlier that day so she removed all her outer clothing and donned a robe before opening the door to admit Abban. Standing to one side, Bryn waited for Abban to arrange the room instead of taking a random seat knowing he would just ask her to move anyway and she did not trust herself to remain polite with anymore requests.

From somewhere in his case, Abban produced a folding stool and placed it in a clear area before politely gesturing for Bryn to sit down. For a long hour and a half Bryn sat there as Abban trimmed, styled, wove, and arranged her hair, she never remembered sitting still so long in her life, at least conscious. Before she could protest, Abban began to apply makeup and it was all Bryn could do not the grind her teeth in fury that she would be presenting an aspect to people that did not even remotely resemble her true self. Apparently her grandfather told the man to proceed with any arrangements necessary and it would not be fair to take out her frustrations on Abban just because he was following his employer's orders. However, she was going to have a stern discussion with her grandfather after the reception!

"Thank you for your patience Mrs. Kelly," said Abban as he began to place items back into his black case, "Oh and Lord Keane asked me to give you this," he handed Bryn a square velvet box the size of her hand with a note attached.

These should coordinate with your necklace, the note indicated and Bryn opened the velvet box to see gold earrings both with large emeralds surrounded by diamonds, she managed to suppress a gasp that her grandfather had again spent a significant amount of money on jewelry that she would rarely wear.

"I'll wait outside the room while you step into your dress so I can attend to the closure," said Abban with a small bow as he backed out of the bedroom shutting the door.

With a sigh, Bryn pulled out the shoe box first dreading the thought of opening it and seeing extreme high heels, but thankfully once she removed the lid there was only a pair beautiful black and forest green silk flat heels. The last thing she needed was to break her neck in front of a bunch of people.

Slipping on the shoes first, Bryn opened the garment bag and stepped into the off the shoulder filmy shimmering forest green dress which was fortunately lined since she would not be able to wear a brassiere. She walked to the door holding the dress up with one hand while opening the door for Abban wondering where Ryan was until she decided he was probably avoiding her after she lost her temper earlier. *Coward*, she thought repressively refusing to acknowledge that he might dress later so he could arrive among the guest unnoticed, she was not feeling very charitable at that moment.

The worst part about the dress, at least for Bryn, was the corset type lacing that Abban tightened to hold the bodice against her torso instead of a zipper which would make it difficult to remove the dress again without aid. *Well I won't have to worry about support of missing lingerie*, she thought sardonically.

"Thank you, Abban," said Bryn politely though her actually thoughts tended toward ripping off the dress and jumping out the nearest window.

"Lord Keane will be here shortly. Have a good evening Mrs. Kelly," said Abban with another small bow before he left the room.

Since her grandfather was obviously expecting her to wear the jewelry, Bryn donned the gifts of the earrings and necklace not even bothering to check her appearance in any mirror; too disgruntled about the entire evening. She just wanted it to be over and even forgot about the guest list she had handed to her grandfather.

Instead of waiting in the bedroom, Bryn moved into the hall and began to pace, it seemed like hours, but her grandfather actually arrived at the end of the hall within fifteen minutes of Abban's departure dressed impeccably in a dark grey shimmering rough silk suit with a snowy cravat pinned with the Keane crest.

Bryn crossed her arms impatiently and waited for him to draw closer, not really paying attention to his expression still too irritated by the entire plan the men had made particularly since they never allowed her input.

"You look lovely Bryn," murmured Aiden in quiet amazement at his granddaughter alteration, he noted that Abban had outdone himself arranging her hair and applying cosmetics which only enhanced her remarkable features. The off shoulder bodice of the dress fit snugly enhancing Bryn's trim figure ending just above the hips transitioning into a floating silk organza nearly to her ankles and long fitted sleeves accentuated her fit arms all the way to her wrists. She was so lovely that the jewels she wore paled by comparison.

Very formally Aiden offered his right arm to Bryn to her obvious surprise, she took it hesitantly and he could tell her keen mind was turning over many thoughts, which mostly likely related to the reception.

Bryn noted that her grandfather chose a stairway she never used before which led literally into the ballroom though she heard music playing long before she knew where the staircase led. She bit back a gasp at the transformation of the room from her earlier observations, it was quite elegantly decorated. As they moved toward the main entrance into the ballroom, Bryn noticed quite a few elegantly dressed people out in the hall talking and understood they had been waiting for their host to arrive to greet them. Her grandfather took position at the doorway inside the room keeping her placed on his right side just as one of the staff began to announce each set of guests or individuals depending on how they arrived at the estate.

Her grandfather welcomed each person, but his initial introduction of her as, "Bryn Keane," nearly made her protest out loud until a thought stopped her, *He's trying to keep Ryan and his family anonymous*, which made sense after what Hess had nearly done to Becca and Paddy. It also made Ryan invisible to the majority of the guests.

Bryn did not look at faces, she just shook hands and nodded welcome with a socially correct smile on her face fuming inwardly about politics, but that is what her grandfather's job entailed. Soon the ballroom began to fill and her grandfather abandoned his post by the door so he could mingle among the guests, though Bryn did note there were occasionally new arrivals. The people her grandfather intended to impress or maybe daunt would be a better term, must have arrived if he was not concerned with the newer additions to the reception.

At the sight of Flynn and Maggie, Bryn excused herself from her grandfather's side and moved to welcome them, she was glad they could attend, but wished they did not seem so uncomfortable, not that she could blame them.

When Bryn touched Maggie's shoulder, she actually jumped as she turned around and her expression changed from worry to utter surprise, "Bryn? Bryn is dhat yeh?" she said uncertainly.

"It's me. For the record, this was not my idea," said Bryn gesturing at her outfit and hair.

Flynn was still goggling, "Girl, I woulda past yeh on the road dressed like dhat! Yeh look like yeh walked outta a magazine," he said a bit breathlessly.

"Yeh look so beautiful, but where's Ryan?" said Maggie worriedly.

Bryn sighed, "My granddad has him performing some duty or other. You might see him mingling off in a corner somewhere," she said irritably.

"Ah I see," said Flynn pursing his lips thoughtfully, "I didn't realize he was workin for yehr grandda."

Maggie caught her left hand and beamed, "Ah see yeh married him though," she said.

"Yes even though we had a few disagreements leading up to it. The wedding was at his parents' bed and breakfast in Kerry. They were too busy to make arrangements here in Thurles, but it is a beautiful spot they have and the garden is magnificent," commented Bryn.

"Ah good yeh got t'meet his family!" said Flynn with a smile.

One of the staff came over, bowing to Bryn, "Miss Bryn, Lord Keane is asking for you," he said formally.

Suppressing a sigh, Bryn said, "Please excuse me, Flynn, Maggie, it seems I also have duties tonight."

Maggie gave her a gentle hug and Flynn squeezed her arm, "We might not stay long Bryn. We don't tend to stay up until dhe wee hours," said Flynn apologetically.

"I understand, you don't need to apologize," said Bryn with a smile before she left them.

Bryn appeared at her grandfather's side, "I'm here granddad," she said quietly.

Several men were speaking to Aiden and he was aware they instantly noted his granddaughter's appearance though they seemed to regard her with supercilious distain as if they did not credit rumors they heard prior to arriving.

"I find it highly unlikely that this woman was responsible for anything that thief accomplished," sneered one of the men quietly.

Bryn took more time examining these men, all tall, well-built and reminded her strongly of men she had seen at the Facility, but they were not people she knew. Most of them had dark eyes that reminded her of bottomless pits and just as merciless so these must be representatives of at least one organization her grandfather was intending to warn.

The men seemed to form a crescent about them, almost as if blocking the view of the other guests and then one man suddenly made an offensive move only to find

out his error. Instantly the one man found himself on his
knees, the other men attempting to grab weapons found
those weapons missing, on the floor and Bryn shielding her grandfather from any further action they might
perform.

Aiden had a brittle smile on his face, "That was a
foolish thing to do. You're lucky there are guests or you
might have found you were missing more than weapons,"
he said in a forbidding tone.

Every single man viewed Bryn with a good deal more
respect, so she realized they had been testing her, the
man rising from his knees pulled out a special device and
ran it over his wrist, flexing his fingers thoughtfully.

One man said to the other who had ended up on his
knees, "Fractured?" and the man nodded.

"This was not the place to perform such a test even if
you had been justified," said Aiden sternly.

To Bryn, the man whose wrist she fractured said,
"Would you consider working for us?"

"I work for my grandfather," said Bryn flatly.

"I see," said the man in a steely tone looking at Aiden,
"Does the Agency intend to share its asset?"

"You misunderstand sir, she works for me privately,
not the Agency," said Aiden flatly, "She is my heir and my
family, not an organizational asset."

Another man said coldly, "We are given to believe she
worked for Drury so you apparently traded on her as an
asset."

"I did not! Their operatives stumbled on her wounded and seized her without knowing her background. She
worked for me indirectly and they had no right to avail
themselves of her skills, which is why she is no longer
there. I know you have confirmed this," said Aiden tightly, obviously angry at the challenge.

One man's eyes flicked to her left hand before Bryn
could hide it, "She's married. Who is her husband?" he
demanded.

Aiden smiled mockingly, "It is not necessary for you to know such information nor will you find public record of it," he said sleekly.

The first man growled, "How can you waste such an asset? There is no one like her in the world!"

Aiden held up a stern finger, "Let me be perfectly clear, how my granddaughter chooses to use her skills is up to her though I do advise her to consider all avenues carefully. During her tenure at Drury, she suffered in a way few operatives ever experience and survived so I will not condone anyone attempting to force her into any environment not of her choosing. Anyone who attempts to acquire her will suffer severe retribution not only from me or my contacts, but Bryn herself. You've seen an example tonight, how would you like to have someone so dangerous looking for a way to make your organization pay for infringing on her rights?" he said in dire warning.

Each man's eye glittered angrily, but they took the point, "What hold did Drury have over her to gain cooperation then?" demanded one man finally.

"They presented her with an offer *she chose* to accept with a stipulation it would be a temporary contract," said Aiden coldly, "Ask her yourself."

"And if we presented a contract?" said the first man swiveling his gaze on Bryn.

"I am not accepting any contracts. At the time, I worked for my own goals and finances prior to meeting my grandfather," said Bryn pointedly.

Ignoring her words, the man said, "Will you review contracts sent to you?"

"My grandfather will review them," countered Bryn trying not to grit her teeth, "Please excuse me," she stalked away before she did irreparable harm to one or more of the men.

Aiden watched his granddaughter walk away before turning to the men, "My granddaughter has a temper and you have unwisely stretched her patience. You cannot force her into anything, if you try, you will find severe consequences awaiting you. I know you heard enough of what happened to Liam Kendall to understand just how dangerous pressuring her can be. Present your contracts to me if you wish, but if I deem the danger too significant, she will never see them. Send operatives to secure her and you will lose those assets permanently," he warned angrily.

Two of the men swore quietly, three remained coldly silent, but he first man said glacially, "I guess that explains a great deal. Thank you for your invitation Lord Keane," and the group turned on their heels to leave the ballroom.

Bryn felt her heart racing and her face flushed from anger, Devin had been correct about people looking for her, they also did not want to take no for an answer either. Her eyes roved about looking for Ryan or at least trying to pick him out of all the people when she halted her gaze at a familiar figure she had not seen in over a year. Instead of walking up and speaking to him, Bryn wickedly decided to startle him with a hug in greeting.

The man stiffened in surprise and physically grabbed her shoulders pushing her away looking down with utter shock, "Who the hell are you?" said Foss maintaining his hold on her shoulders to keep her at a distance.

His eyes widened, eyebrow nearly reaching his hairline, "Shadow? Shadow? Is that you?" demanded Foss.

Bryn grinned up at him, "Who else were you expecting, a tavern maid?" she said drolly.

"What the hell are you doing here of all places?" demanded Foss just as a huge man walked up behind him.

"Shadow?" said Tank incredulously.

"Attending a reception I believe," said Bryn facetiously, "You might as well call me Bryn or people are going to stare at you both."

Foss looked over his shoulder at Tank, but Bryn could not see his expression, Tank raised an eyebrow before saying to her, "Don't you dare call me Ernie or

Earnest, just leave it Tank or I'll make it so you can't sit for a month," he said repressively.

"Want to bet on that, about sitting for a month?" said Bryn dryly.

Foss grinned, "I think I would bet on Bryn. You can call me Jason if you want, but I probably won't answer to it," he snorted a laugh.

"Did only the two of you come?" said Bryn curiously glancing about her.

"No, the Commander is here somewhere and believe it or not, Stanton. No clue why Stanton cared to come to something like this unless he was just curious," said Foss.

"Oh? Where is Stanton?" said Bryn looking about more carefully.

"Next to that statue with the shield," indicated Foss cocking his head in that direction.

Bryn looked back at the two men with a mischievous expression before she walked over to where Stanton stood with his arms crossed eyeing the guests with a disgruntled expression on his face. Without hesitation, Bryn slapped Stanton's right arm and the man jumped before turning on her with a severe expression, hand on his hips literally looming over her, "What the hell was that for woman?" he snarled.

Bryn copied his position, hands on her hips and stared up into his face until his expression changed to one of complete surprise, "Keane?" he demanded.

"Who else were you expecting?" said Bryn still staring up at him, hands on her hips.

"What the hell are you doing here?" demanded Stanton.

"The same thing you are, why?" retorted Bryn.

Foss and Tank stood watching, grinning so much at Stanton's reaction to Bryn that their cheeks hurt, it was a treat to see the man get some flack after the hassle he had given Bryn at the Facility.

A quiet voice distracted them from this scene however, "And what are you two doing here?"

Foss and Tank whirled about to see a tall man with piercing grey eyes, "Nighthawk?" said Foss in shock.

"But…that Agency Commander said you died," insisted Tank quietly as he looked about for potential eavesdroppers.

Ryan looked at the two men grimly, "He said that because they were deciding whether or not to terminate me for the situation in that building," he said quietly, "Hence the burn notice when I slipped out."

"Shit! We wondered about that," said Foss quietly glancing furtively about, "It certainly made Crease happy and then he went missing, AWOL in fact."

"He tried to make it personal," commented Ryan quietly.

"Damn, the fool tried to take you on?" said Tank in quiet amazement.

"Nearly did if it hadn't been for Bryn," said Ryan grimly.

Both men realized what Ryan meant without clarification and glanced at each other, Foss began, "Is…"

Ryan cut him off quickly, "She doesn't remember and I never told her," he said quietly indicating they better not tell her either. On another subject, "Just why are you two here?"

"Actually four of us, we received invitations," said Foss, "Why are you here? Did you get an invitation?"

Ryan sighed and glanced around until he located his wife, "Bryn. I should have known. I wasn't invited exactly, I live here now. One place the burn notice isn't in effect," he explained.

"You work for Lord Keane?" said Tank interestedly.

Ryan nodded, but he had eyes for his wife obviously tormenting Stanton, "I can't believe she had her grandfather include an invitation to him," he said irritably.

"Her grandfather?" said Foss and Tank in unison.

Ryan grinned, "I thought seeing, "Keane," on the invitation would clue you in," he said.

"Well that explains why the Commander let her go and that southern Agency Commander. Why didn't she doing anything sooner if she was related to Aiden Keane?" said Foss curiously.

Ryan said, "She didn't know he was her grandfather," and proceeded to explain the salient points.

Both men looked at Ryan in consternation once he finished the explanation, "So you followed her here obviously. Why would Lord Keane invite us after what happened at Drury?" demanded Tank.

"He didn't. I'm fairly certain it was Bryn," said Ryan with a sarcastic expression.

Foss glanced at Tank before saying, "That makes even less sense after the way we brought her in and then everything she went through especially with Stanton."

"I guess you'll have to ask her," said Ryan shrugging his shoulders, he was just as confused, "I'm even more surprised she's talking to him."

Foss grinned wickedly, "Did you see her walk up to him?" he said, but Ryan shook his head.

"She slapped his arm and he started scolding her without knowing who she was at first," snorted Tank humorously.

"I see," said Ryan grinning, "I wished I hadn't missed that," now he too was watching Stanton looming over Bryn with disgust on his face and she had copied his position no doubt further irritating the man.

"Well go ahead, say it, I know you're going to explode if you don't," said Bryn sarcastically glaring up at Stanton.

"Say what woman? What the hell do you mean now?" snarled Stanton nearly bent nose to nose with Bryn.

"Some rude comment about how I'm dressed," said Bryn narrow eyed.

Stanton actually looked surprised for a heartbeat before he recovered his expression, "Why would I care?" he said disdainfully.

"HA! Because you've never been at a loss for words before when it came to harassing me," snarled Bryn quietly, but to her surprise, Stanton glanced about carefully as if he did not want anyone to hear what he planned to say.

Though he kept the disgusted expression on his face, in case anyone was watching Bryn decided, his eyes changed so that only she could see it, they actually twinkled with humor, even respect, "Because I have nothing rude to say. You look beautiful," he said very, very quietly.

Bryn stiffened straight up in utter shock, of course anyone watching would think Stanton had said something impossibly rude, she had to give him full marks for his ability to deceive even the most hardened observer.

"So that was all an act?" said Bryn just as quietly back glaring at Stanton seriously now, not for fun.

"Hardly, I still believe a woman should not be in a place like the Facility. No matter how skilled she is, it's inviting trouble for a multitude of reasons that I don't have to list, do I?" said Stanton caustically.

"So then why the knife and baton in the gym?" snarled Bryn quietly noting Stanton's eyes narrowed.

"I never said I was perfect. I lost my temper and made a mistake, not that you can comment after a few things you did or said during debriefings," drawled Stanton quietly, but pointedly.

Aiden walked up to a man he knew was the Commander from the Drury Facility, a guest on Bryn's list oddly enough, confirming Devin assessment of some sort of arrangement between his granddaughter and some of the personnel.

Holding out his hand, "I'm Aiden Keane," he said formally.

The Commander hesitated uncertainly, "Kolski," he said shaking the proffered hand.

"I'm actually surprised to see you accepted the invitation," said Aiden curiously.

"Probably as surprised as I was to get it," said Kolski humorously.

"Ah, you can thank my granddaughter, Bryn, for that," said Aiden with a small smile.

Kolski's eyes widen, "I wondered when I saw the invitation. I guess it explained why my superiors could not see her gone fast enough," he said dryly.

"Apparently you came to some arrangement with her or I would not have received a list with your names on it," commented Aiden interrogatively.

Kolski snorted, "I honestly can't say. She was not easy to work with and could be disruptive until a contract operative decided to watch over her," he said a little irritably.

Aiden snorted in turn, "She does have a temper, but you could hardly expect less from her after the way she was, 'acquired,' yes?" he said narrowly.

Kolski sighed, "We thought she was a man initially or I would have steered clear of her, not that that would have helped with others looking for her. It was only a matter of time before they stumbled on a similar inconsistency," he said.

"True, we were looking for her as well thinking she was a man. You were going to release her though before I contacted your superiors, why?" said Aiden intently.

Kolski glanced about until his eyes settled on Bryn confronting Stanton, "In part because of what she went through and the fact we had one or more leaks resulting in attempts to snatch her off missions. She was no longer even marginally safe. Another reason was the contract operative: He insisted and intended to force the issue though I tended to agree with him. My superiors intended to abandon her to her fate on one mission," he said grimly.

"The toxin?" said Aiden quietly effectively shocking Kolski.

"Damn, you're well informed," Said Kolski uncomfortably, "That situation was highly classified."

"Let's just say I found out through less orthodox channels. I gathered her performance superseded your expectations?" queried Aiden.

Kolski snorted again, "Any of the men would have died in similar circumstances, so yes she did. Some of those situations had been set up to test her from an outside source which obviously led to them attempting to snare her," he said quietly.

"No doubt," commented Aiden dryly, "This man she is speaking to now, they do not seem to be on friendly terms so I'm confused why his name was on her list."

Kolski turned an incredulous expression on Aiden, "No more than I am when you told me she gave the list with our names. They were constantly at odds with each other. I even forced him to take her on a training mission to resolve their differences though I'm uncertain how much that accomplished. They seemed to have some sort of truce even if they taunted each other, but in my opinion, his attitude was for show. I think he respects her and didn't want anyone else to know that," he mused.

Aiden actually laughed in amazement, "A training mission together? That I would have enjoyed watching after the trouble she's given one of my people," he said.

"I can only imagine," grinned Kolski.

"Were you aware one of your former operatives came here to address a personal grudge?" murmured Aiden carefully.

Kolski turned to him slowly, "We've had one missing, but no word about him. You confirmed this?" he demanded quietly.

Aiden cleared his throat, "With your superiors and DNA," he said quietly.

Kolski expression turned threatening, "Where is the slag?" he growled.

Aiden glanced at Bryn before answering, "My grand-daughter doesn't remember doing it, but she killed the man protecting her husband," he said carefully, "He had severely injured them both and one of my men in the process with weapons smuggled into the country."

Kolski swore explicitly though quietly, "That explains some shortages, but to take on Bryn was ballsy after some of the things I witnessed," he growled.

"I don't think he was very concerned with her at the time after the injuries she sustained though what he ultimately planned to do to her we will never know. Apparently another one of your past operatives intended to seize her to broker her off to the highest bidder, she called him Hess," murmured Aiden watching the Commander interestedly.

"Son of a...we thought he died during a mission. Damn it, now I wonder how many infiltrators we haven't caught," snarled Kolski quietly, "What happened to that one or did she deal with him too? I would love to get my hands on him."

Aiden smiled grimly, "That one I will be glad to release to you. She only disabled him to protect an innocent business from poor publicity," he said, "He had several other men with him, but you will have to examine their files to determine if they are people you have any links to."

Kolski sighed, "She hasn't had an easy time of it has she?" he said ruefully.

"No, she hasn't, but it was the near fatal injury to her husband that almost broke her," Aiden sighed.

"I gather her marriage is a recent occurrence?" inquired Kolski softly.

"Yes and I believe you know her husband. I've kept it out of the public record however to protect his family since they were some of the people threatened in the attempt to acquire her," said Aiden glancing sideways at Kolski.

"I have a suspicion, but don't confirm it. Crease was after one person in particular though at the time we thought he was dead. It also explains some of the missing equipment since the man had no hope in a one-on-one confrontation with his target, he would have had to injure at a distance. I should have suspected the southern headquarters lied about his death, especially when that burn notice circulated," said Kolski in disgust.

"Have you arranged for lodging yet since your arrival?" inquired Aiden in a change of subject.

Kolski hesitated uncertainly, "Not exactly, but I noticed an Inn or two in the town," he said.

"It's not necessary there is plenty of room here for your stay which I suspect will be brief knowing of your superiors as I do," said Aiden his eyes sliding over to Bryn.

Kolski sputtered incoherently at first, "That's not necessary. Especially after the past history we have with your granddaughter," he said almost embarrassed.

Aiden grinned, "I'm curious to watch the dynamic between your people and Bryn, particularly from her discussion with the man she is speaking with now," he said humorously.

Kolski breathed out worriedly, "Lord Keane, there was an incident between them where she was injured. I don't want to invite trouble with you," he said.

Aiden cocked an eyebrow at the Commander, "I don't think that will be an issue or the current situation would have exploded by now and the fact that her husband is watching instead of interfering," he said with a small smile.

Later that night, Bryn made her way back to the bedroom, but before she arrived at the door she found Devin waiting, his arms crossed and watching her closely.

Soon as she drew near to him, "I know you are responsible for four of those invitations, what were you thinking?" demanded Devin.

"Why does it matter what I was thinking?" said Bryn irritably as she attempted to move by him, but Devin grabbed her arm.

"Those people kept you a prisoner for years and you invite them as guests?" snapped Devin with no patience at all, "You met some of the other people tonight, the ones they exposed you to!"

"According to you, my own actions exposed me before anyone caught me even if no one knew who I was," said Bryn glaring up at him.

"Why?" Devin demanded not put off.

"Besides Donal, they were the closest things to friends that I had," snarled Bryn.

Devin's eyebrow rose in surprise, "Friends? How did you come to that conclusion?" he insisted.

"They did try to protect me on missions and, before you arrived with your weapon, they came to help me by choice after the Commander released me. They were not there for any mission, of that I am certain and as they are here, you can easily verify that," growled Bryn.

Devin could only stare at Bryn for that piece of information, he had not known those men had come there to help her and had assumed they arrived to retrieve her back to Drury, he believed that the release might have been a sham or at one point she managed to sneak out.

"That's the first time you mentioned this information. I thought they had come to take you back to Drury," said Devin neutrally.

Bryn heard footsteps behind her and knew it had to be Ryan, she wondered just how much he heard of the conversation or maybe confrontation would be a better description.

"I did not invite them to irritate you or to throw their presence in your face. Goodnight," Bryn sighed as she proceeded to the bedroom.

"Did you know they had come to help her?" demanded Devin once Ryan was closer and Bryn was gone.

"No, not initially, but then I wasn't in any condition to think at the time. Once I woke in the southern head-quarters, they did not elaborate on people present when I was removed from Kendall's safe house," said Ryan thoughtfully.

"I could tell you weren't exactly happy they are here," said Devin pointedly, "Especially when she hugged the one man."

Ryan snorted, "It wasn't their presence so much as the fact she hugged him. I admit I'm possessive of her. I never thought I would find a woman I could spend my life with until I met her," he said a little defensively.

Devin grinned at that explanation, "And it doesn't help she's so independent I gather," he said humorous-ly at the other man's narrow eyed assessment, "You do know that Aiden has offered them rooms here, don't you?"

"No, I didn't know that," said Ryan a tad sourly to Devin's increased amusement.

"You've never had anything to worry about, Bryn doesn't look at other men even if they do look at her," said Devin quirk of an eyebrow and slight smile.

"I know, but Foss, the one she hugged, was interest-ed in her during her tenure at the Facility. It drove me batty wondering if she might prefer him at some point," grumbled Ryan.

Devin coughed a laugh, "I'll let you get some rest before I end up on the wrong side of your temper," he grinned before walking back down the hall.

Bryn was struggling with the ties on the corset bod-ice when the door to the bedroom closed. Ryan could tell that she was upset as he helped to undo the laces and soon as the bodice was loose, she moved away from him. She could feel confusion emanate from him at her reaction, Bryn felt ashamed she was letting her irritation with Devin carry over to her husband.

"Are you still upset because I didn't escort you?" said Ryan quietly.

Bryn sighed, "No, not after listening to some of the conversations my granddad had with several people. I knew he was ultimately trying to protect your family and keep you anonymous," she said with her back to him.

You act like you don't want to be in the room with me," said Ryan sounding confused and a little hurt.

"It's not that. I just don't feel like talking," said Bryn.

Out of the blue, harsh words issued from her husband, "Do you have feelings for Foss?" said Ryan dangerously.

At such a question Bryn whirled about in shock, "No! I've never had romantic feelings for him. If you are referring to hugging him, I did it only to shock him because I knew he wouldn't be expecting it," she said flatly.

Ryan would not meet her eye and proceeded to undress, carefully hanging his suit though his motions indicated he was angry or maybe, Bryn mused, it was jealousy.

"Why didn't you tell me you wanted to invite them before handing a list to your grandda?" demanded Ryan thinly veiled fury as he faced her fully unclad.

"Because I didn't want you to take it the wrong way, like you are now," fumed Bryn, "You act like I gave him the list to upset you and I didn't!"

Without looking into a mirror, Bryn began to remove jewelry as well as pull at the pins and combs holding her hair in place with her free hand, she was aware the hand trembled as she laid the items on a dresser. Why did he automatically assume she would show interest in other men? It was like he did not trust her or he believed she might wantonly hurt his feelings with no regard to their marriage or his feelings for her.

Fury bringing tears to her eyes, Bryn faced away from Ryan, "Why do you trust me so little or think I would seek other men and entertain feelings for them? I would never have agreed to marry you if I did not love you, but it seems you doubt that as well," she said as her voice broke.

Ryan sighed behind her, but Bryn still could not look at him, "I'm sorry darlin'. I'm possessive of you and...," he paused before adding uncomfortably, "I guess I'm jealous of every man that looks at you. I'm only the second man you've ever allowed close to you and the first one was a poor excuse of a relationship after what he did to you. I keep wondering if you will wish you had a chance to meet other men. It's the reason I left you here before I went to see my parents initially, I wanted to give you a chance to be with other people like Shay or even Devin, if that is what you wanted. I couldn't stand being away from you, I was coming back to find out your feelings for me even if you sent me away."

Bryn turned on him furiously forgetting the tears on her cheeks, "Devin? What would you think I would see him that way? Or even Shay? Devin is my parents age, not that he is old per se, but he's always treated me like his daughter," she said flatly.

Ryan's lips twisted, "Devin isn't much older than I am Bryn. By today's standards of longevity, he is still young if you think about it and a lot of men in Ireland tend to wait to marry until they are at least fifty or sixty years old, sometimes later, especially when people tend live over one hundred and ninety years or more," he said uncomfortably.

"What do you mean Devin's isn't that much older than you?" demanded Bryn.

"Darlin' where did you think I learned all my skills particularly after meeting my parents? I wasn't raised like you when your Da started training you practically soon as you could walk. I had to learn those skills after I left my parents' home and take time to hone them. When I told you I hadn't seen them in twenty years, that wasn't the first time I had visited them after I left home," said Ryan carefully.

This time Bryn stared hard at Ryan, she never considered him much older than she was and he certainly did not look it, of course, as he pointed out the era they lived in had remarkable technology to maintain youthfulness for a long time. Even her grandfather did not look old and the only sign of his greater age was the sprinkling of white in his hair that he chose to display for his own reasons, his skin had no wrinkles or lines at all.

"Why is age supposed to matter," said Bryn finally.

"I never said it should, but you can't deny I've had more years to be with other women even if they were passing encounters. I was able to see what I didn't want in a long-term partner and actually never thought I would ever have a wife or find anyone that complimented me. My job certainly is not family oriented. You never had the same chances. You didn't even see me that way when you arrived at the Facility or probably even considered it. The day you nearly destroyed the infirmary made me appreciate you and I admired your spirit in the face of the odds against you. I was hoping to get to know you better not only because I found you fascinating...I wanted you. When the Commander made you my responsibility I was inwardly thrilled. After a while I was going crazy trying to figure out what you thought about me, you would hardly talk so I watched and even though Stanton had hurt you one day, I was pleased you finally spoke to me. Unfortunately you never seemed to regard me any differently than the other men and I knew Foss had become interested in you so I did everything I could subtly to keep the others away from you," said Ryan with complete openness.

Bryn stared at him for such a long explanation. Ryan was never extensively chatty even once they reunited and it was amazing to hear all those words come from his mouth, yet to know he had been keeping the other men away from her for personal reasons back in those years at the Facility was a considerable shock. Categorizing his experience based on his parents' background, Bryn knew Ryan had to be at the very minimum fifteen years older than her, probably more like twenty or twenty-five years which explained his defensiveness about Devin. After that last mission, she recalled Stanton's comments in the debriefing, *"because given her age, the degree of her training would have to start when she practically learned to walk,"* and he had been correct that for a woman or man it would be unusual to train an operative at such an early age.

"Why do you continue to think I'm not capable of making my own decisions about who I love and want to be with, whatever my experience?" snapped Bryn irritably, "If I was uncomfortable getting married, I would have told you that, not string you along to hurt you. Or is that something you did to women in the past?"

Ryan looked irritated now, "No, I never made promises to women or gave them any offers. I was certain not to keep seeing the same person twice so no woman would think they had a claim on me," he growled.

Turning her back to Ryan, Bryn carefully removed her dress and hung it before donning a long shirt. She could feel annoyance emanating from her husband that she hid changing her clothes from him.

"If you prefer to see other women I can't stop you," said Bryn before she could stop herself.

For the first time since knowing him, Ryan began to swear explicitly and vociferously, she knew uttering those words had been a grave mistake.

"Why the hell would you say that?" demanded Ryan furiously, "If I wanted other women I certainly wouldn't have asked you to marry me or is this retaliation for my jealousy?"

"I didn't mean for it to come out like that," said Bryn quietly and feeling a stirring of agony within her, "I feel I don't satisfy you enough or meet your needs the way you seem to get upset every time I talk to a man. I guess I thought another woman might make you feel better."

Ryan grabbed her shoulder hard enough to leave a bruise and spun Bryn about in white-hot anger, both hands gripping her shoulders so hard she definitely knew there would be bruises in the morning. He shook her furiously, his face hard, but Bryn saw tears in his eyes and felt them in her own eyes.

"My god Bryn, how can you say that? After everything I just said to you? I've never once felt unsatisfied being with you and I'm not just speaking of the intimacy. You don't truly understand how much I love you or you would never had said those words. I don't want other women, not for any reason or there would have been no point asking you to be my wife. Do you know how scared I was when I slipped away from those southern Agency headquarters that you might have remembered to remove that GPS tag? That I might never find you again? I knew nothing about your grandda and I couldn't go back to the Facility or talk to Dr. Meany to ask about you when operatives were looking for me in every corner of North America. I've waited all my life for someone like you and I'm not about to let another man get ideas about taking you from me," said Ryan angrily as he forcefully shook her.

Words would not come for Bryn, she knew Ryan was truly upset in a variety of ways and she was annoyed tears flowed down her cheeks unchecked she had never been weepy before or let emotion rule her. When she could not seem to speak, Ryan engulfed her in a crushing hug that left Bryn's feet dangling at least six inches off the floor, it was then she realized that she had thought Ryan had been attempting to put distance between them ever since he agreed that her grandfather escort her to the reception.

Unable to move her arms, Bryn could only touch Ryan's sides as she buried her face into his neck so he would not see her weeping, she felt him kiss her cheek tenderly without lessening the fierceness of his hug.

Ryan sighed softly, "So that's why you're uncomfortable when I touch you, you think you don't satisfy me?" he said, but she only nodded into his neck, "Believe me you do just fine," he snorted humorously.

"All I've really done is to do things for myself, practice skills or martial arts. After my parents and guardians died I've never spent much time with people until Donal and then at the Facility," whispered Bryn.

Ryan sighed understanding Bryn had been cut off from most interaction with people, especially children as she grew up which was where so many people learn social behavior. To protect her, her parents had carefully kept her away from people so Liam Kendall would never get any information about her existence.

"It's time to stop that habit of isolating yourself darlin'. Before it was necessary, but not anymore you have people who care about you, family and friends that no one will take away from you again," said Ryan gently in her ear.

"Some of those people are still after me. They wouldn't take no for an answer tonight even when granddad threatened them and they asked who my husband was before I could hide my ring, I shouldn't have worn it tonight. They are looking for a way to blackmail me just like what happened with Donal, they could still take everything from me again," wailed Bryn softly.

"What?" demanded Ryan furiously before he set Bryn down gently and began to throw on regular casual clothing, he kissed Bryn tenderly on the lips, "Stay here darlin'," he added before he stalked from the bedroom.

Aiden had been filling Devin in on the evening's events when they heard a pounding on the office door and the monitor showed Ryan waiting outside which meant Bryn had not forgotten some pertinent portions of the reception. The fact Ryan was there meant his granddaughter was a great deal more concerned than even he, Aiden, had realized.

Locks barely finished opening before Ryan stalked into the office and marched right up to Aiden's desk, "They are going to try for Bryn again, aren't they?" he snarled without any form of greeting.

"Please sit Ryan," said Aiden carefully and once the younger man was seated, he proceeded to review the evening.

"They threatened her or they wouldn't have mentioned the ring," said Ryan flatly.

"There is no public record of your marriage Ryan, I made certain of that just in case so they can't trace anything back to your family or even you," said Aiden raising his hand in a placating gesture.

"You still don't understand, Bryn thinks they are going to try to take everything from her again, family, friends, and me," snapped Ryan leaning forward, his face hard as stone.

This time Devin sighed, "We never considered *that*, did we? If she faced some of these people and heard the veiled hints and warnings. Of course she would think she would lose everything again after what Kendall did to her and we never thought to ask her to remove the wedding band for the evening because of her earlier reaction about you escorting her," he said ruefully.

"They asked if they could submit contracts to her..." began Aiden, but Ryan launched out of his chair.

"You think they wouldn't seize her just as the Tabula tried to do? Attempt to force her to work for them in even more dangerous conditions? For all we know some of these other organizations were responsible for those tests which nearly killed her and they will continue to use or test such a lucrative asset as her. Any contract they submit to you will be as dangerous as anything she faced at Drury and I won't allow my wife to suffer such abuses," roared Ryan furiously, his temper finally snapping.

"Calm down, Ryan. I appreciate your sentiments and share them. I also warned them that any attempts to seize her would cost them their assets permanently and they are aware now why some have already gone missing," said Aiden raising his voice.

"Ryan," said Devin cautiously, "We won't ever let anyone get close to her and given her skills, anyone who tries will find out they have no hope of controlling her if you recall your parents' business and the man she killed already."

"I intend to forward footage of a relevant portion of Bryn's confrontation with Liam Kendall and his men at that safe house in North America, edited of course per Agency protocol, but they will see more than enough to quell any desire to force her to do anything. Have you seen any of the footage?" queried Aiden.

Ryan sat back in his chair breathing a little fast, "No, I never saw her escape from the room they held her in. The only portion I can recall is her dropping from the ceiling and blocking that projectile so it wouldn't kill Bryn after that I really wasn't in any condition to observe much," he said.

"Then watch this from the point of view of an organization hoping to capture her and think what Drury would have done had they seen this," commented Aiden as he displayed the footage from the time Bryn disabled the security camera in her cell of a room.

As they both had seen the footage before, Aiden and Devin watched Ryan for his reaction to Bryn's performance, he began to sit straighter in unfeigned shock until the part where she attempted to kill Kendall, his expression turned to dismay watching her body hit with various projectiles even though she destroyed some of the men.

They both watched Ryan turn pale as the footage ended, he took him a minute before he commented, "She was preparing to die because of me. She didn't even try to protect herself and anyone seeing that footage would think she was a monster, an uncontrollable killer. If I'd known my presence there would have turned her into that…" they could see his evident distress, "I would have risked everything earlier to get her out somehow. Promise me please, never show her this," he said his voice shaking with varied emotion.

Devin sighed, "When I first saw that footage, I blamed myself for not protecting her parents or Jimmy and his wife sufficiently. I thought their deaths had done that to her and that she lost her sanity," he said uncomfortably.

"You both should not blame yourselves. She thought she was going to die and I believe intended to die fighting. She isn't a monster Ryan or those four men would not have survived in Kerry so she still has a conscience, but…other organizations will not know that about her. What do you think the Tabula would have done if they saw Bryn perform like that?" said Aiden shrewdly.

"They wouldn't have wanted her anywhere near the Facility and probably would have considered her unstable or uncontrollable," said Ryan with understanding of the point Aiden was attempting to make.

"That is the impression I want to leave with all of them so that the attempts to seize her will vanish and if they forward contracts, they certainly will want to refrain from inciting a performance in that footage," said Aiden with a grim smile, "So try to get some rest and not worry too much."

Ryan nodded feeling some relief with the plan and left the office in a better frame of mind than he arrived, but soothing Bryn would not be as easy, he never wanted her to see that footage if he could help it.

When Ryan arrived in the bedroom, he realized he should have known Bryn would be too agitated to rest, he found her pacing and her face was drawn with worry.

"Darlin' your grandda has the situation under control. Since I never had a chance to talk to him about his conversations earlier, I didn't know how he was going to handle these people. He has plenty to threaten them with and they won't dare bother you though it could take a little time to disseminate the ultimatums among the organizations. I'm satisfied it will stop eventually," said Ryan quietly which seemed to relieve his wife.

Sitting on the edge of the bed, Ryan watched Bryn after her earlier reaction to his entering the bedroom and realizing now why she had closed up, she felt insecure or threatened, probably both.

"I'm sorry I was distant to you earlier," said Bryn softly looking at the floor, "I guess I was worrying about some of those people talking to my granddad."

"Understandable given the things you've gone through darlin', but you can talk to me, I hope you know that," said Ryan quietly.

Feeling a bit ashamed taking out her mood on Ryan earlier, Bryn approached him where he sat on the bed, she could hardly blame him for thinking something else was wrong the way she pushed him away soon as he entered the room. Once she was close enough, Ryan caught her hand and began to caress it, but that was all, he just kept watching her face; he could read her so well it was uncanny.

"How do you always seem to know what I'm feeling?" said Bryn quietly, her eyes still on the floor.

"I've studied people a long time darlin' and you for years now, body language can tell you a lot about a person's thoughts or what their next action might be. I don't always know what you're thinking, especially if it involves complex ideas. I have to ask about some things and on occasion my jealousy gets in the way where you are concerned," said Ryan with a sigh at his last comment.

"In hindsight, I can see you don't have interest in other men, even if I don't like the way they watch you or talk to you, but it doesn't mean I like it any better. Of course, I need to remind myself I don't own you and you're not a possession," he added ruefully.

Bryn suddenly sat on one of his thighs and put her arms around Ryan's neck, "Ryan, I hope I don't do anything to upset you when I talk to people," she said quietly in his ear.

Putting his arms tightly about his wife, Ryan said, "No, you don't do anything wrong darlin' it's just one of my faults that I've rarely had to deal with until I met you. I love you so much and I don't want to share you with anyone, which is asinine of me, I know."

Bryn leaned back to look at her husband and said, "I love you, Ryan," as they fell back onto the bed.

The next morning, Ryan woke smiling and reached over beside him and found the bed empty, Ryan sat upright in consternation, he never felt Bryn get out of bed let alone heard her leave the room. Usually he was a very light sleeper.

A knock on the bedroom door disrupted his thoughts about Bryn's current location and Ryan pulled on a pair of pants before opening the door.

"I'm sorry to disturb you Mr. Kelly, but Lord Keane asked that you join him and his guests for breakfast," said Nevan with a small bow.

"Nevan isn't it?" asked Ryan and the man nodded, "You don't happen to know where my wife is, do you?"

Nevan nodded briefly, "She ate much earlier sir and retired to the gymnasium to exercise," he said.

Ryan sighed in disgruntlement he wish Bryn had awakened him, "Thank you. I'll be downstairs in a few moments. Are we eating in the main dining room?" he said and Nevan nodded again before he left.

Dressing for the gym so he could join Bryn after breakfast, Ryan leapt down the stairs three at a time to check the dining room and he carefully noted all four visiting men were present to his relief, he still did not trust any of them where his wife was concerned. Not that they would hurt her, but that they might spend time speaking to her alone and that was something Ryan would not tolerate from any of them. To his annoyance, Devin had been watching him closely and was grinning in definite amusement obviously noting Ryan had counted the men present before he would sit down to eat.

Shooting a private glare at Devin, Ryan sat down and Aiden asked, "Is Bryn still asleep?"

"No, Nevan told me she ate earlier and went to the gym," said Ryan neutrally as he struggled to keep the irritation out of his voice though blasted Devin coughed a laugh so he suspected his thoughts about Bryn.

"Ah she must have noticed some of the new equipment she requested had arrived," said Aiden pensively.

"New equipment?" demanded Ryan again irritated Bryn never mentioned anything to him, but then he had to admit, his wife did not have to explain every single action she made, he just wanted to know what she was doing all the time and wondered if he ever would know half of it.

"Customized gymnastics equipment she requested to keep some of her skills sharp or so she said. She mentioned Fiona took her to private lessons ever since her earliest memories until the accident and one of her martial arts instructors taught her to continue the skills while blind. I suspect I don't want to know just how she has been using those skills or I might have heart failure," said Aiden dryly and all the men laughed knowingly.

Ryan did not join in any conversation though he listened carefully, he finished his breakfast quickly and excused himself, "I'm going to head to the gymnasium as well," he said ignoring Devin's humorous expression. Unfortunately three of the men, Foss, Stanton, and Tank chose to join him to his disgust noting that each one of them seemed dressed to workout which he knew must be entertaining Devin quite a bit.

Instead of inviting the men to follow him, Ryan stretched his legs, but that tactic did not work as the men did the same to keep up with him so that they all arrived in the gymnasium together. Soon as Ryan caught sight of Bryn, his attention instantly swiveled from the men as he gawked at the variety of equipment. Without any safety padding on the floors in case she fell, Bryn was doing an array of exercises on a modified balance beam that extended three times longer than an actual competition standard beam. She was performing tumbling exercises such as assorted flips back and front, aerial cartwheels as well as other riskier exercises as if she were on a floor not a two inch width surface so that now he understood how she managed to run around the ledge so easily when they caught her on that building.

"Sheesh, she moves like she was on a larger surface, no wonder we had so much trouble catching her," murmured Tank nearly mirroring Ryan's own thoughts.

Still frozen on the spot, Ryan and the other men watched as Bryn transitioned over to suspended rings that men used competitively and certainly not women, the two rings hung above her over twice again as high as she was tall. One of the men gasped behind him, though Ryan did not know who, when Bryn leapt up easily to seize both rings from a flat footed stance, no spring board as men might use in competition. Instead of hanging there as they might expect, Bryn began to perform actual exercises a competitive male gymnast would do in a routine, which required a great deal of upper body strength even for a man.

"Wow," said Foss admiringly, "I had no idea she had such upper body strength. I guess it explains how she tossed men around at the mountain installation."

They watched as she ran a gamut of exercises on a single high bar, uneven bars, parallel bars, and equipment obviously customized for unusual exercises and it explained a great deal about her abilities they never understood until that moment.

They finally broke their paralysis once Bryn began to use spar equipment like a long weighted bag or a punching bag and entered the gymnasium without commenting on their observations. The men began stretching though Ryan noted Bryn glanced over her shoulder once when she heard them enter the room other than that, she seemed to ignore all of them. He was not sure how he felt about that.

Unsurprisingly, the men gravitated to the weights or the weighted machines ignoring the gymnastic equipment and Ryan did the same initially keeping a sharp eye on each of the men in case they attempted to start a discussion with his wife.

Foss' voice distracted him, "You're wearing a wedding band..." his voice trailed off and his glance shot to Bryn, "I guess you really were serious about her. Good thing I kept my hands to myself then," he grinned at the sharp glance Ryan gave him.

"I kept my eye on you back at Drury," said Ryan irritably.

Tank laughed merrily, "You're lucky he didn't deck you last night after she hugged you then," he said humorously.

Ryan snorted, but did not comment, Foss said, "Hey, that wasn't my fault! I didn't even know who she was at first she looked so different!"

"I know. She did it to shock you. We had a discussion about that later," said Ryan sharply.

Shaking his head in amusement, Tank chuckled at Foss' discomfiture, "It could have been you Tank, so I wouldn't laugh too hard," said Foss irritably.

"He knows I'm married even if I keep my ring off during my duties," snorted Tank with grin.

"Why do you do that?" demanded Foss.

Tank turned serious suddenly, "In our work, family can be exploited as a weakness. My family lives under another name completely unassociated with my professional name on file," he said.

"Then how did you know he had a family?" said Foss swiveling on Ryan again.

"The way he interacted with Bryn told me he had family. I've spent a long time observing people Foss," said Ryan pointedly.

"And you?" demanded Foss turning to Stanton who remained uncharacteristically quiet.

"Whether I have a family or not is my own business," said Stanton in flat voice, "She didn't belong there for obvious reasons that had nothing to do with her skills. You remember how Crease acted around her."

Stanton missed the glances shared by the three other men at the mention of Crease, but they chose not to comment on the subject particularly since Bryn's sharp ears undoubtedly heard every single word they already uttered.

Their conversation had distracted them from Bryn's activities so when she approached and spoke, they all jumped in surprise, "Ok, time to spar," she was pointing at Stanton, "This time it will be a fair fight!"

Stanton sneered at her, "I don't think so or your husband just might flatten me if I looked at you wrong," he said condescendingly, "Ask him to spar with you."

"I already have. It's your turn or are you afraid of sparring with a girl?" sneered Bryn in turn goading Stanton.

Stanton stood up threateningly, "You're no girl," he spat out.

"Say it, I dare you," snarled Bryn completely ignoring the other men.

"Bryn…" said Ryan uncertainly, but she cut him off with a gesture to the other men's collective surprise, even Stanton who was now regarding her more warily.

"I'm padded this time and I made certain I can't hurt you, see?" she held up padded hands and flexed padded feet at Stanton, "So I won't bruise your tender skin," said Bryn condescending in her turn.

No one saw Aiden, Devin, and Kolski watching from the doorway, "Uh oh," said Kolski uneasily, "I was afraid of this."

Instead of looking grim, Aiden and Devin grinned at the Commander, "She's just taunting him. We've seen her act the same with her husband," said Aiden humorously.

"Are you certain about this? I can't vouch for Stanton's physical response. You recall what I told you last night," warned Kolski.

"I think he actually likes her and doesn't want anyone to know it. I was watching them last night and it was more like a game with them even if I did wonder at first. Ryan would have never let a real argument continue between them, he's the gage I watch to know if it's a serious matter and she has beat him silly several times in a fit of temper, without any padding," commented Devin with a smile.

Kolski let out a nervous breath, "If you're both certain about this...," he said with trepidation.

"If it turns serious there is no blame to you sir, but I think Devin is correct in this," said Aiden holding up a hand in reassurance.

"All right you b...," Stanton changed what he planned to say, "woman, you better watch it or I will thump you hard," he snapped.

"Pads please," interjected Ryan to Stanton pointedly.

"He doesn't need them," insisted Bryn beginning to square off ignoring the implied warning, "Come on or have you been too lazy recently to move those big feet?" she taunted.

Stanton glared at her furiously and moved away from the weight machines, he glanced at Ryan, but the man remained sitting even if he did look tense so it meant he was not going to interfere in any sparring match. Inwardly Stanton wished he would because he was not certain of the outcome of this little confrontation.

"Whew, I can smell you from here," said Stanton pinching his nose, "I'd say that is unfair advantage attacking me with your stink as well."

"Ha! Since when did you get so fastidious? Besides at least my stink is due to sweat not personality like yours is," Bryn sneered tauntingly.

"Why you little…" growled Stanton and the sparring session began, his main hope was that she was tired from all her earlier activity so that it would be an even match, if he was lucky.

To his surprise, Stanton was making headway though he kept glancing in Ryan's direction in case there was an indication he should stop before the man killed him for beating on his wife. Round and round they went for at least a good hour until Stanton managed to pin Bryn on the floor in apparent triumph.

Aiden began to laugh, "My granddaughter is a wicked terrible woman," he said humorously and even Devin was grinning.

Kolski glanced from the sparring to the two men, "I'm confused, what do you mean?" he demanded.

Devin said, "Watch!"

Stanton was surprised by his success until a sly expression crossed Bryn's face, "My turn," she said.

Next thing Stanton knew he was flying through the air and landed flat on his back gasping for air, completely winded from the unexpected launch that preceded Bryn springing to her feet.

"Come on, get up! Don't just lay there like an idiot," said Bryn in a bored tone.

Managing to get to a sitting position, Stanton glared at her still gasping for air and noticing her husband grinning humorously though Foss and Tank looked surprised.

Once he managed to get enough air back in his lungs, "I'm a dead man I think," said Stanton in disgust.

"Bah you're only a little bruised. Are you going to go back admitting a woman beat you up?" taunted Bryn.

"You're no woman! You're a tornado in disguise," growled Stanton irritably fully aware there were more men laughing behind him from the sound.

Though Stanton sounded serious Bryn knew that he was not and winked at him, but to her surprise, he winked back before he made a show of sighing for the observers benefit.

Kolski was grinning now, "She let him win? Oh that's going to knock him down a peg or two," he laughed.

"As I said earlier, Bryn is a terrible woman teasing him like that," grinned Aiden, "Bryn stop terrorizing that man," he called inciting more laughter.

She did not stop until she had a knee on Stanton's back, "Ok I give up! Are you happy now?" grumbled Stanton.

Bryn let Stanton up and noticed the other men grinning along with the newer arrivals, but Foss could not resist taunting Stanton, "So you'll have to admit a woman beat you now," he said wickedly.

Stanton grunted, "No I won't. I'll only admit a Shadow beat me, a Shadow of Ireland," he said with uncharacteristic grin.